Dear [illegible],
Hope you enjoy!
Fondly,
Doug R.

In a Grain of Sand

A Medical Mystery Novel

Douglas Ratner M. D.

; In a Grain of Sand

A Medical Mystery Novel

ISBN: 1481193066

ISBN 13: 9781481193061

Acknowledgements

Many thanks to Ms. Vicki Hessel Werkley for her creative and meticulous developmental editing and for her extensive original writing within this work.

I would also like to thank Susan Walsh, MD, whose abilities are only dwarfed by her modesty, and my esteemed assistants, Marisa Sugalski and Julie Zisa, who truly understand the meaning of deciphering a doctor's handwriting.

Lastly, to my wife and best friend, Linda, and to my beloved children, Jess and Dave.

Prologue

Dan Marchetti sat motionless in the bleakly lit courtroom, trying desperately to make it all seem real. He watched his portly attorney raise another point of order with the presiding judge, a bespectacled man with a gangly build, close-cropped hair, and a red bowtie jutting out above his robe, reminding Dan of Bill Nye, the Science Guy.

The unreality of the situation made it hard to keep focused on what was being said. His mind flashed briefly to the coding patient whose eye had popped out while he tried to bring her back with vigorous chest compressions…now he stood indicted for two murders.

Dan squeezed his eyes shut, the voices now only a buzzing in his ears. He recalled the thunder of applause in his proudest moment: accepting his diploma as part of the graduating Class of 2005 at Tufts Medical School. Hearing those words "Dr. Dante Michael Marchetti," he'd stood on the stage, clutching his parchment as the traditional academic hood, green for the field of Medicine, was draped across his chest and over his shoulders. All the years of study, hard work and sacrifice seemed finally worthwhile. Scanning the crowd on that day for his parents and his younger brother, he read on their exhilarated faces "Our Dante—a doctor!"

"The Commonwealth of Pennsylvania," a booming voice broke through the buzz of recalled applause, "versus Dante

Michael Marchetti." Dan's eyes snapped open, almost surprised to see a courtroom instead of that distant auditorium.

More voices: The judge's . . . his attorney's . . . the judge's. And then, breaking through the cacophony in Dan's head, the question directed at him: "Do you understand the charges against you?"

Another flash of memory reminded him of how all his panic had been replaced by a sense of eerie relief that day in the ER, once they realized it was only a prosthetic eye that'd leapt from the woman's eye socket. No relief from this moment was likely coming now.

A voice—could it really be his own?—replied quietly, "Yes, Your Honor."

"How do you plead?"

"Not guilty on all counts, Your Honor."

Because of the seriousness of the charges as capital crimes, Dan had already spent four appalling days and nights in jail, denied any chance of release on bond. Now, at his preliminary hearing, his lawyer would take the opportunity to petition for bail.

Biting his lip so the pain would bring him back to reality, Dante concentrated on the certainty that his future, especially any hope for short-term freedom, lay in the hands of that lone judge. Tasting the metallic trace of blood on his tongue, Dan forced himself to tune in to his attorney's words.

"Your Honor, Dr. Marchetti's parents and brother have driven over eight hours to attend this hearing today. Many of his colleagues from the hospital are present to show their support, as well as patients whom he treated there. My office has been swamped with telephone calls and emails from others who could not attend but wanted to offer character references and to ask how they could be of assistance to him.

"Dr. Marchetti's not a flight risk. Since his hospital privileges have been suspended at this time, he couldn't possibly be any danger to the public. . . ."

He was a doctor not a danger; it was his job to *save* people's lives, damn it. How could anyone think he'd willfully killed two patients?

CHAPTER ONE

"Almost midnight already," Dan stole a glance at his new watch as he made tracks for the on-call room to catch a little nap while he could. Admiring the bright yellow face, light blue trim and black Velcro wristband, he discovered he'd neglected to remove the $12.99 price tag from his Kmart special. Sheepishly, he peeled off the tiny sticker and tucked it into one pocket of the spanking-new white coat he wore over his scrubs.

At twenty-eight, he was three years older than many of his fellow interns. After college, he'd spent a few years traveling Europe, working as a waiter and an English teacher while experiencing the cultures of Italy, France and Switzerland. Then the years of medical school, and now he was ready to settle in and put it all into practice. Running, sports and close attention to his diet had kept his six-foot-one frame lean and toned enough for the rigors of internship but he'd never thought of the face he saw in a mirror as handsome. There was no mistaking his Italian heritage—when, at twelve, he'd lamented his Marchetti nose, his mom had suggested he "think of it as 'definitive'"—but those genetics also bestowed an easy tan, dark brown eyes and curly hair. And through the years, more than one girl had commented on his "endearing grin" and the kindness of his eyes.

After hanging his white coat on the rack above his cot in the on call room, Dan noticed for the first time the spaghetti stain on one pants leg of his light-blue scrubs. "Come on man, what kind of shit is this?", he muttered under his breath. He wondered how many people had seen it—patients, his superiors, other medical colleagues. Was it there when he met Dr. Hugh Ballard, revered Chairman of Medicine—and the director of the residency program? How could patients trust a doctor to manage life and death if he can't keep spaghetti sauce off his trousers?

Glancing around himself, he took in the pale-green walls, the pair of mismatched chairs, the dog-eared medical journals heaped in one corner, the empty Styrofoam containers crowding the phone on the battered nightstand. Anxiety slowly began to build, not helped by the vagaries of scheduling which had dropped him directly into the risk-fraught world of the Coronary Care Unit for his first rotation.

His thoughts touched on the epic poem of his namesake, Dante Alighieri. With a little chill he remembered the end of the lengthy cautionary inscription over Dante's Gates of Hell, *"Lactate ogne speranza, voi ch'intrate...*Abandon all hope, Ye who enter here." The Coronary Care would be intense where he needed to be ready for anything at any time. As his CCU attending, Dr. Glenn Covington, had said earlier today during orientation, "Chest pain can come at all hours and with every complication you've studied."

He punched the lumpy pillow and tried to get comfortable on the narrow hospital cot. He was already tired. Though he was only three and a half hours into his first official twelve-hour overnight shift, he'd clocked in an additional four hours at the beginning of the day. He had come in to walk through morning rounds thinking it would give him a heads start on figuring out how the unit worked for his eight p.m. to eight am When the intern assigned to the eight a.m. shift, Diane Werner, had a last-minute childcare emergency keeping her from reporting to duty before noon, Dan offered to stay. Usually some poor unsuspecting resident, who thought he or she had the day off would be abruptly assigned to show up; never a way to make friends among your peers.

At noon, a grateful Diane took over and arranged the four hour pay back for later in the month. Watching the exchange, Covington grinned at him "Okay, enough, Marchetti. Go home, eat lunch, enjoy the afternoon, and I'll see you when you start tonight."

Dan found himself too excited to leave the hospital. After bolting a burger and coffee in the cafeteria, he spent the rest of the day getting the lay of the land, as his pop would say, acquainting himself further not only with the facility, but also the people who kept it functioning and the technologies he'd be using.

He ate dinner, again in the cafeteria, with Diane, who was still on duty, and another new intern, Alexander Cole, who'd also come in early before his evening shift in the CCU.

Dan had met Diane months ago when they came to interview on the same day; they'd maintained friendly but a purely professional email contact since then. As a Deerwood "local" and former DCH employee, she'd been able to advise him on a number of decisions, including which apartment complex to choose. A decade and a half older than the other new interns, she'd been a nurse before deciding to attend med school and become a physician.

Married, with three young children on summer break, she spun Dan and Alex a humorous account of her morning: husband with a flight delay getting back from a business trip; one possible babysitter already gone for the July 4th weekend, the other on jury duty; an eleven-year-old son mad because she wouldn't let him get fireworks; a six-year-old with heat rash; and a new collie puppy puking crayons on the white carpet. Her fellow interns laughed till they ached. It was clear to Dan by the way the hospital staff had responded to Diane's tardiness with good-natured variants of 'didn't know interns get to sleep in!' that she was a well-respected member of the DCH community.

And she was well-attuned to the hospital's politics and sensibilities; she'd already warned them about what she called the "DCH Grapevine." Her husband played cards with some of the more respected attendings.

Lying back on the cot now with his eyes closed, Dan still couldn't seem to switch his mind into "rest mode." Instead, it offered a procession of new faces, and he tried to remember the names to go with them all. That'd be a challenge for a while, but ten of the other new interns, including Alex, would also be dealing with it. Only Diane was ahead of that game too.

Dan had liked most everyone he'd met so far, and was glad his first month was with Covington, who was not only a top heart man but also shared Dan's passion for baseball. Though now sixty-five, in his early years Covington had spent three seasons as a minor league utility infielder. His body might be thicker and slower moving, but his clear blue eyes missed no detail, and, Dan found, the man was quick to assess a newbie's knowledge and skills.

Theodore "call me Teddy" Nash, Dan's very first patient, was the 63-year-old owner of a legendary east coast dinner theater. He'd been admitted the previous day when he sustained a heart attack after completing only two minutes of a treadmill stress test designed to determine if his arteries were blocked.

Before entering Nash's room on rounds this morning, Covington had brought Dan up to speed on the case—how the patient's condition had proven resistant to all medications that could slow his heart rate. Dan could see, if Nash went south on them again, it might take some drastic action to save him.

Inside the room, Covington had scarcely had time to introduce Dr. Marchetti as his new intern when the expression changed on Nash's affable face, and he whispered, "Doc, my heart's racing again, an' I'm having a little trou . . . ble . . . breath . . . ing. . . ."

Dan glanced at the monitor: SVT at 180 a minute and blood pressure dropped to 78 systolic.

Covington's voice asked, "What do you think, Dr. Marchetti?"

Dan looked to the older man, searching for clues in the unreadable face. "Gotta get that heart rate down."

Covington nodded. "How?"

"Well, since none of the meds broke through . . . diving reflex?"

Dan saw approval as Covington nodded again and made a "go ahead" gesture. Dan turned to the nurse standing behind them, Cheryl Herrera. "Ice, please. Quickly." As she rushed out, Dan grabbed the empty basin on Nash's bedside table. "You hang in there, Teddy. We'll get you fixed up right away." He moved past Covington and hurried to the bathroom to half-fill the basin with cold water from the tap. Cheryl appeared at his side with a clean pitcher filled with ice, which she added to Dan's basin till he said, "Enough. Thanks."

When he returned to the patient Dan focused entirely upon Nash. "Okay, Teddy. I need you to sit up on the edge of the bed for me." Nash did so, staring at the basin with some trepidation as he struggled to breathe. "This won't be much fun, but I'll explain later." Dan set the sloshing basin carefully on Nash's lap, out on his knees. "Hold this." When his own hands were free, Dan placed one reassuringly on the man's upper back. "Now, I need you to trust me, okay? I want you to take a really deep breath, then put your face as far into the water as you can and hold it there until I tap you. Understand?"

After glancing at Covington, Nash nodded, his grey eyes wide and round. Clutching the sides of the basin, he drew as deep a breath as possible and thrust his head into the water, flinching as some splashed out on legs barely covered by the thin hospital gown.

Dan kept an eye on the yellow face of his watch and saw the seconds tick away. Only thirty of them, but it must've seemed like eternity to the patient. Dan tapped his shoulder, and Teddy emerged, gasping for air, his white hair plastered to his skull and dripping ice water down his neck. The ever-efficient Cheryl handed Nash a towel and took away the basin.

"Good God, Doc!" Teddy whooped as Dan took his wrist and confirmed what he saw on the monitor: the pulse had dropped from 180 to 82. "Now tell me why I had to do *that!*"

"We call it the diving reflex," Dan explained. "When you plunge into cold water—the colder the better—the body shuts down certain responses, and it'll lower your heart rate. How're you feeling?"

Still mopping his head and neck, Nash considered. "Hey, I guess it worked, didn't it? My heart feels back to normal, and I can breathe again. Some trick! Will it last?"

Covington spoke then, moving back to the bedside. "Maybe. It may just take care of things—like rebooting your computer." His eyes twinkled as he included Dan in his smiling gaze. "Better take care of yourself, Teddy . . . keep your heart quiet. Don't make me send Dr. Marchetti back with another bucket of ice water." Next stop for Teddy, the electro-physiology lab.

Remembering that now, lying in the on-call room hours later, Dan chuckled and basked again in the regard he'd sensed from Covington. He'd also acquitted himself well with the other patients they'd seen. Tricky as Coronary could be, they hadn't lost a one. Patient Raymond Lawlor had given them a scare for a while, but he, too, had come around. Not bad for his first day at work and only his sixth day in Pennsylvania.

He'd only arrived in Deerwood late the night before orientation, extending his Florida vacation to the last possible moment, He hadn't had time to see more of the town itself than when he'd first come to interview six months earlier.

The idea of a community hospital appealed to him more than some University program that'd probably be more impersonal. Yet, he didn't feel he was giving up much for the small-town atmosphere he sought. DCH, with the bottom four of its ten floors nestled into the hillside of a scenic river valley, had a sophisticated flair and a solid reputation. For a suburban facility with just three hundred beds, it boasted state-of-the-art medical technology, thanks to generous donations from the wealthy patron family's Candlebury Foundation and a renowned teaching faculty drawn to the family friendly community so close to Pittsburgh.

It seemed he had only closed his eyes for a minute when the phone rang shrilly from the nightstand by his head. He flailed an arm toward it, bashing against the brown Formica surface, much-abused by countless groggy interns over the years.

"Dr. Marchetti," he mumbled into the receiver.

"It's Cheryl."

"Oh, hi. Thought you went home."

"Split shift. Not sure whether I should bother Dr. Covington with this question. Dr. Clay and Alex are tied up with Millie Sorensen."

"The post-op surgical repair in Room 4?" Dan felt himself swimming back to the surface. "They need me?"

"No, it's Mr. Lawlor—the acute anterior-wall M.I. He seems to be throwing some couplets despite the lidocaine drip. But BP is good; he's pain-free; pulse is 80 and regular; and except for the extra beats, he's basically resting comfortably."

"Okay, right there. Give Covington a call just in case." Dan hung up the phone, making the old nightstand wobble, a perfect mirror of his own sudden level of confidence. Eager and anxious to answer the call, Dan decided not to bother with his coat for what was likely a brief foray. But, walking down the hall, he regretted the choice when he remembered that stain on his scrubs. Casually placing a hand where it could hide the spot, he contemplated his next move with Mr. Lawlor. Undoubtedly, if the couplets were as real and as frequent as described, he'd have to up the lidocaine to cut back on the abnormal heart rhythms. But what if that wasn't the best or only remedy?

He reminded himself he had back-up. The night shift's senior resident in charge, Dr. Clay Lebeau—a lanky, soft-spoken 30-year-old from Louisiana—radiated quiet confidence, which sealed the deal on his nickname: *Big-Easy*. At eleven-thirty, he'd urged Dan to "go get some rest. You've clocked seven and a half hours already today. It's all quiet for now; Alex and I can handle this." Alex Cole, the other new intern on nights, had appeared confident, perhaps even cocky, as he waved good night.

Pressing the metal wall-plate that opened the doors, Dan stepped into the spacious CCU. Individual patient rooms, arranged in a semicircular pattern, faced a central telemetry console with a monitor for each room. Below these, a spotless white writing surface formed the physician's desk. Matched chairs placed conveniently in the center gave the area the look of a TV studio's control room.

The place was quiet for now, between scenes, like a Broadway stage before the curtain rose. He approached the central telemetry station. Unlike a play, it wasn't starlets, but two middle-aged CCU nurses, their graying hair clipped short in near-identical, no-nonsense styles, who sat at the console desk, watching his entrance in silence. Dan knew most of these nurses had been working in the CCU for ten years or more and were quick to pass judgment on interns. He saw one of them give the other a look that clearly said, "This guy probably doesn't know his ass from his elbow."

Dan resisted the urge to glance down; hoping to God his hand was still obscuring the spaghetti stain. Nodding to them, he asked pleasantly, "How is everyone tonight? Mr. Lawlor still in Bed 2?"

Faint smirks appeared on their faces. "Yes, Doctor," they said in unison. Dan tried not to look like a deer caught in the headlights and turned toward Room 2. He saw that Room 4 was also lighted; the door open, but the curtain drawn. Apparently Clay and Alex were still dealing with their post-op patient.

Dan walked into Lawlor's room. Cheryl was already there, laughing with the patient as she adjusted the leads attached to his chest beneath his hospital gown. She looked up now and gave him a welcoming smile, then spoke to her charge: "You remember Dr. Marchetti from this morning, don't you? He's one of Dr. Covington's interns this month."

"Sure. How are ya tonight?" Lawlor appeared a lot better now than he had earlier in the day. The color in his face was no longer ashen but pink and healthy looking, and his hair had been neatly combed. "Don't you guys ever go to sleep?"

"Yeah, we get to sleep." wanting to keep things casual, not alarm his patient. "Just thought I'd check on you before turning in. Any chest pain?"

"Nah, I'm fine," he replied good-naturedly. "Don't know why I'm even here instead of home in my own bed."

"Well, Mr. Lawlor—"

"It's Ray, remember?"

"Okay, Ray." Dan started to feel more at ease; his patient seemed so improved, in such good spirits, somehow reassuring Dan that he had done well earlier in the day. No mistakes and no surprises with this one; Lawlor could just remain stable and recover. "As we discussed earlier, your EKG shows evidence of a possible heart attack," Dan told him, "and we're waiting on the blood chemistries to confirm it. We're looking for cardiac enzymes. If the heart muscle undergoes cell death, as occurs in a heart attack, then these enzymes are released into the bloodstream."

"But they took my blood a long time ago." "Chemistries usually take a few hours to run. In any event, everything is stable now, and you should do just fine."

"That's great news. When can I go home, my boys are worried?"

"We'll take you up to the telemetry floor in a bit, and eventually you'll go home. Then, you'll undergo cardiac rehabil—"

Dan never finished his sentence, interrupted by an alarm sounding on the telemetry unit above Lawlor's head. It showed the irregular, wavy pattern all-too-familiar from textbooks: ventricular tachycardia. Lawlor's eyes rolled back in his head, his color changing from the pink he'd shown sixty seconds before to a dusky blue.

"Oh, shit!" Dan cried. "Call a code!" But the CCU nurses, having seen the lethal rhythm on the monitor at the telemetry console, were already pushing a crash cart into the room. Someone had hit the code button, and Dan heard the hospital P.A. system blaring repeatedly: "Code 99, CCU-2; Code 99, CCU-2; Code 99—"

Be cool, Dan, he coached himself, *think clearly*. The odd analogy of football's two-minute drill popped into his head: no time to huddle, just do each thing as quickly as possible. First they had to restore blood pressure with a normal, efficient heart rhythm. The concept was standard medical practice; this patient, however, was real, Dan's first at-bat since he'd come up from the minors. And no Covington there at his elbow to bail him out if he made the wrong play.

"Paddles set at 200 joules, please!" As Dan waited the few seconds it took to charge the defibrillators, the code team came barreling in: senior resident Clay Lebeau and Alex, followed by an anesthesiologist and a respiratory therapist. With both disappointment and relief, Dan offered the paddles to his senior resident, but Clay shook his head. "You go on now. You know what to do."

The paddles were charged, and as Dan leaned against the side of the bed to apply them to the patient's sternum and left side, Cheryl warned—firmly but not loudly—"Clear!" Dan quickly broke contact with the bed, flushing in embarrassment. The charge hitting him would've created the season's first fireworks lighting him up like a Christmas-in-July tree. He saw a knowing smirk on one of the older nurses as she left to keep an eye on the central telemetry console. The other one, assisting Cheryl, was hiding her own smile.

"Clear!" Dan repeated. The paddles in place, he pushed the button and was momentarily awed by the sight of Lawlor's flaccid body springing to life—arms and legs jutting into the air as if they belonged to a marionette. The monitor showed a transient return to normal heart rhythm, but within a few moments, it was back to v-tach.

"Charge!" Dan's voice was lower, more determined, surprisingly strongl "Come on people." The anesthesiologist—Dan couldn't remember his name—pushed a tube into Lawlor's airway, and the respiratory therapist, Vinny something, attached an ambu-bag and started squeezing oxygen into the patient.

Twice more, Dan defibrillated Lawlor. "One amp sodium bicarb. . . one amp calcium chloride. . . . Also, let's get some pressors ready." Dan saw Clay nod approval, and, working quickly and efficiently, Cheryl and the other nurse administered the medicines.

"Code 99, CCU-4," the P.A. system blared suddenly, "Code 99, CCU-4—"

"Crap!" Clay said. "That's our Miz Millie. You've got this, Dan, Vinny. C'mon, Alex; I'll need you." The anesthesiologist didn't have to be told but quickly followed the other two from the room.

Good God, I'm on my own after all! Certainly he had great support staff anticipating his every need and order, but he was the one s'posed to save this guy! Long minutes dragged by as Dan alternated chest compressions with defibrillations. Fatigue crept into his body, settled, threatened to sap him.

Flexing arms that felt like jelly as he started yet another round of compressions, he glanced up at the clock: ten to one. "How long have we been working on him?"

"Forty-two minutes," Cheryl answered rather mechanically." Doc...."

If Lawlor could be resuscitated successfully, it would've occurred by now. Dan stopped pushing on the man's chest and said firmly, "Enough."

One simple word but with so much impact. If the patient could talk, how would *he* react to "enough"? Dan shook his head against the slide of his thoughts into confusion and absurdity. Looking at the other faces before him, he saw various reactions to the situation, some sadness and resignation but mostly detachment. Cheryl's eyes regarded him with sympathy, or was it pity? His own eyes suddenly glazed over with tears. It was only then Dan realized that his senior resident Clay Lebeau was standing close behind him. Clay reached over to give Dan's shoulder a comforting squeeze. "Go ahead," he said softly. "Call it."

"Time of death," Dan intoned, "twelve fifty-four a.m. Could someone please get me the patient's home phone number?" He'd met Mrs. Lawlor earlier in the day when her husband was admitted; she clearly adored him, as did their two teenage sons, one of whom had Down Syndrome. It was obvious the boy hadn't understood the significance of what was happening when he saw his father lying in the hospital bed. "Come home," he'd said. "and play baseball with me." Who would explain this to him . . . and how?

"Dan? Here's the number."

He thanked Cheryl and took the slip of paper.

Clay gave Dan's shoulder another supportive touch. "I gotta get back to my Miz Millie. I left Alex holding down the fort."

"How's she doing?" Cheryl asked.

"We got her back, and she's stabilized . . . for now. . . ." The nurse nodded at this implication, and Clay headed toward Room 4.

Dan was unable to avoid a tiny twinge of envy for Alex Cole's first-code experience as he made his way out to the physicians' desk.

The veteran nurse watching the monitors there avoided his eyes but was no longer smirking. No one wanted the interns to *fail.* Look foolish, sure, but not lose a patient, especially not his first time out.

Following the formality, Dan called the patient's local family doctor first and left word with her service of Lawlor's passing. He did the same for Covington's service who confirmed he was on the way. Then he punched in Mrs. Lawlor's number. As the phone rang, he found his mind escaping to the past few weeks of his vacation: the fun of letting go after graduation; his first surfing lesson; volleyball and running on the beach; making love in that little cabana with a woman he barely knew.

"Hello?" Mrs. Lawlor's tired and frightened voice sounded as if she'd been crying and was emotionally spent. "Is this about my husband?"

"Yes. This is Dr. Marchetti. I'm so sorry. . . ." He heard a long gasp and the sound of the phone dropping. Then there was silence. "Hello? Mrs. Lawlor . . . ?" No answer, though he could hear the line was still open.

He waited, uncertain what to do; a few moments later, someone picked up the receiver and spoke anxiously. "Hello?"

"Mrs. Lawlor?"

"This is her sister. The news is bad, isn't it?"

"Yes, I'm sorry," Dan told her. "Mr. Lawlor just passed away. I'm so sorry." Like a dark wave, despair overwhelmed him, roiled in the pit of his stomach. There were questions he'd been instructed to ask, but they seemed so brutal. "I need to find out what funeral parlor you prefer, and," he swallowed to keep the nausea at bay, "do you wish to view the body before we send it down to the morgue?" Thank God there was no need to ask her the other question about agreeing to an autopsy.

"Oh, I'm not sure. Let me talk to her; we'll call back in a few minutes. Thank you for all that you tried to do." A little sob escaped. "I can't believe this. He was smiling and laughing when we left him tonight. . . . Those poor dear boys. . . ." Her voice trailed off.

"Once again, I'm so sorry." Dan winced, hearing the same empty phrase come out of his mouth. "No, I'm so happy, he chided himself.

"Yes, thank you," she said in a barely audible voice, followed by a final click on the other end of the line.

It was done. Dan rushed to the nearest bathroom and lost his dinner, wondering how soon he'd feel like facing marinara sauce again. Shakily, he rinsed his mouth and splashed water on his face, remembering the thrill of sea spray on sunny beaches and the laughing eyes of that girl—Sonja, wasn't it?—as she drew him into the cabana. Leaning now against the edge of the sink, he stared at himself in the bathroom mirror. His brown eyes had never looked so lost. "I'm not cut out for this shit" he told himself.

Dan's eyes closed tiredly, and he rested them a minute longer, then ran one hand through his unruly dark hair, preparing for his return to the CCU.

Dr. Covington had just arrived; too bad he'd made the long drive back only to find they'd lost the patient. "Are you okay, Dan?"

Dan nodded without speaking, avoiding the attending's eyes, there was only so much compassion he could stand, and wrote the Code 99 note in Lawlor's chart before handing it to Covington for review.

Clay and Alex joined them, saying Millie Sorensen seemed out of danger now. With the unit quiet again, Clay suggested one of the two interns take advantage of the on-call room as he and Covington pulled both charts to review.

"Should be Alex's turn," Dan mumbled, though he wanted nothing more than to get out of there for a while.

"No way!" Alex exclaimed, his naturally pale face flushed, his tea-brown eyes alight. "This's the most exciting night of my life! I couldn't sleep a wink right now." "You got to be fuckin' kidding me." Dan thought to himself.

"Go on, then, Dan," Covington said, and Dan gratefully escaped.

Retreating toward the on-call room, he began to hyperventilate and made himself stop. He knew the images of the last sixty minutes would be impossible to erase from his memory as he obsessively went through each step of the code. A man had just died before his eyes despite Covington's assurance that he had done everything right. So much for his inordinately expensive education and all his efforts. Shaking his head, he reminded himself that sometimes, the disease wins.

He slipped into the on-call room and closed the door on the rest of the hospital . . . the rest of the world. Collapsing on the cot, he tried to close his eyes and sleep, but he couldn't bear the movie replaying in his mind. Dan's eyes snapped open, saw his white coat, emblem of all his medical achievement, mocking him from its hook. He tried to distract himself by studying every other detail of his claustrophobic surroundings: a stain shaped like New Jersey on one green wall; the scent of stale coffee from the Styrofoam containers on the nightstand, the almost-inaudible drip of the tap in the nearby bathroom. And over in the far corner where the medical journals were strewn, the unmistakable centerfold of a *Playboy* magazine was peeking out.

Dan stumbled over to where the magazine lay partially obscured and retrieved it from beneath the latest issues on bariatric surgery, then resumed his place on the cot. He scanned the fold-out of a voluptuous redhead, draped over a green velour loveseat. Dan could only feel self-disgust at the thought that he was seeing this while the Lawlor kids were getting used to never seeing their dad again.

He hurled the magazine back into the corner and pulled the pillow over his head, as if that could squash away the thoughts. Hot tears rushed into his eyes and throat.

"Beep, beep, beep. . . ." his pager sounded. Set for *Voice,* it continued "Dr. Marchetti, CCU—stat! Dr. Marchetti, CCU—stat!"

"Stat—from the Latin *statim* —without delay, immediately" some long-ago lecturer droned in memory. Sighing, Dan hauled himself to his feet, on the way to his next challenge or maybe just the next circle of Hell?

CHAPTER TWO

"*Girl-y!*" a sudden, hollow-nasal voice rolled through the aisles of the Deerwood Pet & Feed Center.

Linda Ferrante, dropping her selected items into her shopping basket, laughed and left the Aquarium Section, moving around the corner into the next aisle. She grinned up into the gigantic birdcage and greeted the store mascot, "Hey there, Mack!" Fluffing his almost-impossibly-brilliant plumage—red, green, blue, yellow—the big Scarlet Macaw hopped down to a tree branch perch closer to her and reached out one gnarled, taloned foot to grip the bars separating them.

How great to have a place where she could partake of a little "critter therapy", petting and playing with small animals of varied species, and still comfortably enjoying the environment. Darlene's pet shop provided only the scents of fresh grain, naturally clean animals and well-kept habitats. Imagine being lucky enough to work with animals all day. A far cry from the defense-attorney life she currently lived.

Not that law had been her first choice for a vocation! As if to remind her of this "imperfect fit," she suddenly found herself unable to ignore the way her shoes were pinching her toes at the end of a long day and a very long week. Those three-inch Audley heels were certainly flattering for her legs, but killer for her feet. Then, as if her body finally felt allowed to speak, it now had a lot to say. It seemed every article of clothing had its own complaint; especially the red Hugo Boss silk blouse, a gift from James that'd never fit quite right. But it was the best complement she'd found so far for this subtly pinstriped navy suit.

In that moment, Linda could think of nothing more important than getting home, slithering out of these torture-garments and into a soft, free-flowing sundress, then kicking back with a glass of red wine while she reheated the pasta-with-pine nut-pesto she'd just picked up from Luigi's.

At the store's front counter, Darlene was chatting amiably, perhaps even flirting a bit, with a customer who'd been standing there when Linda first came in. She could tell by his purchases, still waiting to be rung up, that he must be a serious freshwater fish-keeper. Usually she saw him dressed in a white lab coat with a hospital I.D. badge, but today he wore a cargo shirt tucked into matching crisp khakis.

Glancing toward Linda, Darlene acknowledged she had another customer waiting and reached for the fellow's items, saying brightly, "I better get these things rung up for you, Vinny."

Linda noted that he was attractive if you liked tall Nordic looking guys with buzz cuts. She preferred a more Mediterranean look, something that echoed her own dark hair, brown eyes and skin that always appeared perfectly tanned. He made a better match for Darlene, who was also blond and blue-eyed.

Vinny took his leave with a polite nod to Linda. When the women were sure he was gone, Linda grinned at the pet store owner. "*He's* cute. . . ." She let it trail off with the hint of a question in it.

Darlene dimpled and blushed. "He's sweet . . . and a good customer."

Linda gave her a "you're-not-fooling-me" look but didn't push it. Transferring the items from her basket to the counter, she asked instead, "So what're you planning for fun this week-end? In your spare time, of course."

Darlene laughed. It was one of their little jokes, the scarcity of leisure time either of them had over a weekend. With the store open on Saturdays, that only left Sundays for the top-to-bottom weekly scouring necessary to keep the place so spick-and-span, leaving little time for much else. But today, Darlene's face brightened. "Some girl-pals of mine are taking me to the play tomorrow night—you know, *Wait Until Dark* . . . ?"

A little stab of pain poked Linda's heart, but using skills she'd once learned as a fledgling actress, she managed to keep all traces of discomfort from her persona. Of course, she'd seen the posters all over town. Why did the local Candlelight Players have to choose *that* particular script for their big, mid-summer performances? Sure, it was a terrific little suspense drama . . . one close to Linda's heart. Not only had she illuminated its starring role in her senior class play, but some years later, she'd also chosen it for her own community theater directorial debut back in Boston. Facts that made it all the more dreadfully painful.

"How nice," she murmured. "Sounds like fun."

Outside, moving toward her car, Linda considered, how bad could it really be to watch a little theater performance of *Wait Until Dark?* But she could feel in her bones how bad it could be.

Linda paused a moment longer—key in hand, gazing up across the car's roof—lifting her face to the beaming late-afternoon sun. The rays caressed her skin. That's what she needed, sun and warmth...and to get out of these damn shoes!

CHAPTER THREE

Having switched to eight-to-eight day shifts for the last two weeks of his CCU rotation, Dan found his body clock still having trouble adjusting. He had to stifle a yawn, even as his stomach rumbled, ready for lunch. Tired eyes focused on the chart he held. Dan made notes as his newest patient Martin Siegel, a slightly built man in his seventies, described this morning's tennis match with his wife.

"Dolly and I hadn't been playing long". . . .the man's voice sounded frail and a little baffled, "when I got this awful chest pain. I thought it was indigestion,"

"I told you it wasn't my blintzes Marty,. . . that you should call the doctor." Dolly Siegel winked at Dan before turning her attention back to her husband. "But do you listen? No! You wait till you have to be brought in an ambulance."

Marty Siegel's hand lifted in a gesture of surrender, as if speaking was now too much of an effort.

Clay Lebeau's notes in the chart spelled it out clearly, anterior wall MI with pulmonary edema. A heart attack with fluid filling the lungs. In other words, Dan thought, this guy was one sick puppy. Assisted by nurse Cheryl Herrera, Dan examined Siegel, whose tanned body showed surprisingly little fat. Even clad in the flimsy Johnny coat, he looked distinguished: his full head of silver hair expensively cut, his nails perfectly manicured. A CEO, Dan surmised, or a senior partner in a TV legal series. Now with a blood pressure of 70 systolic, Siegel appeared ready to star in his own CCU drama, to exit the stage left.

Meanwhile, Dolly maintained her one-sided banter, oblivious to her husband's deterioration right before her. "I told you, Marty. It was too soon for tennis after such a bad flu"

"Flu?" Dan interrupted. "There was nothing about that in the chart."

Dolly shrugged. "We didn't think of it. That was almost two weeks ago, and he got well."

Dan shot a significant glance to Cheryl, and without a word needed she went to page Covington.

As Dan quickly finished up his exam and notes, Cheryl returned, escorting in the Siegels' son, Benjamin, a fiftysomething replica of his father. As soon as they were introduced he asked, "How bad is it, Doctor?"

"Your dad's condition is very serious," Dan told him, "but I believe we've intervened in time. We're fairly certain he's had a heart attack—his blood work will confirm that—but there's also a possibility he's contracted viral myocarditis, an inflammation of the heart muscle due to his recent flu." Ben Siegel's face showed he comprehended the gravity of that possibility, but before he could ask more, Dan continued, "The attending physician, Dr. Glenn Covington, is on his way; we'll need to work on your dad fast, without interruption. I'll make sure you're updated when there's any news."

Dolly still seemed more surprised than worried. "Well, okay, but I'm sure this will all blow over." She patted Marty's hand in farewell and didn't seem too perturbed by his feeble response, as if she couldn't believe anything bad would happen in her world.

Ben also said his good-bye and, looking worried enough for both of them, took his mother by the shoulders. “Come on, Mom. I’ll be here with you. Kathy should arrive any minute.” He nodded to Dan and let Cheryl show them toward the waiting room.

A moment after they were gone, Covington sailed in and clapped Dan on the shoulder. “Okay, what’ve we got?” “He’s going to need an aortic balloon pump and an inotrope.” Two hours in the cath lab and it was done. Exhausted and starving, Dan was eager to finish the pleasant task of updating the Siegels before he could take a break. But Covington put a hand on his shoulder and said quietly, “Let’s talk before we go see the family.” They moved to the physicians’ desk. Only one nurse was currently monitoring the consoles. She nodded knowingly at the older doctor and bustled away, leaving them some privacy.

Realizing that his fumbling and failure to answer more than the occasional easy cardiac question was about to be addressed, Dan tried to focus instead on the distraction he noticed on the counter: a plate and mug resting beneath a tented napkin with his name written in Cheryl’s fancy script. His mouth began to water, even though he knew that one of many intern chewing outs was about to begin. Steeling himself to apologize after hearing the list of his mistakes, he realized his attending wasn’t criticizing him but saying, “You did good work today, Dan. I know you felt clumsy, but you performed well your first time out. It’ll get easier as you gain experience. Some pointers: always get yourself in a comfortable position *before* starting a difficult procedure and take a moment to ‘think before you do.’ Correcting a mistake always takes much longer than avoiding it in the first place.”

Dan nodded, but Covington had more to say. “You’re off tomorrow, right?” Though his eyes remained kindly, his tone became more professorial. “Well, I expect you to read up on tachycardias and acute coronary syndrome. By next shift, be able to answer any question that I throw at you—from any source. No one leaves my rotation without becoming an expert in bedside interventions and diagnosis”

"Yes, thank you, sir," Dan managed to say in a voice barely louder than the sudden rumble of his stomach.

Covington chuckled then, his glance taking in Dan's waiting meal. "Missed lunch again? Tell you what: if you'll cede the privilege of giving the Siegels the good news, I can do that for you . . . not make them wait any longer."

While Covington left to speak with the family, Dan quickly attended to a ham-and-Swiss-on-rye, chasing it with green tea now room temperature, but still delicious. He was just wiping his mouth after the last sip when he saw Marty Siegel's son heading his way. Dan rose and moved around the counter. "What's up?"

"Dr. Covington told us how you assisted him, putting in a pump to keep Dad's heart from failing while he's being prepped for bypass surgery. Our whole family's so very grateful for what you've—" His voice cracked with emotion.

Dan gripped the older man's arm supportively. "You're very welcome. That's what we're here for."

When Ben found his voice again, he told Dan, "Y'know, I know your family... My kids were coached by your dad all the way through high school."

Ben grabbed Dan's hand in a forceful shake. Dan returned the warmth of the handshake, thinking how much he needed to feel something positive right now. Despite everyone's best efforts, in the past three weeks the CCU had lost several patients, though that first-night failure with Ray Lawlor still haunted him the most.

An hour later, as he finished the last of his paperwork, he saw fellow first-year Brian Callahan approaching and Dan lifted a hand in greeting. Brian had come in early, as promised, to repay Dan for three hours he'd taken for Brian at the beginning of the week. Though Callahan stood about the same height as Dan, he looked ganglier. Still he was handsome enough that the female nurses and house staff had voted him "Hottest New Intern." Aside from the guy's good looks and his almost non-stop joking, Dan considered him one of the brightest of the group.

"Hey, If you're lookin' for something to do, I heard a bunch of nurses and interns are meeting at Casey's for TGIF." He wore what Dan had come to think of as his "mock-mournful" expression.

"You sound really bummed, Bri."

Big sigh. "I'm Irish, remember. You wanna take this shift after all so *I* can go to Casey's?"

Dan chuckled. "Sure, sounds like a great swap—" He gave his friend a gentle punch to the shoulder. "Not!"

Already moving away to check in with Covington, Brian glanced back with a wink. "If you change your mind, you know where to find me."

Dan considered Brian's parting "prescription" for a pleasant Friday night: beer and burgers. It had been a long time since he took a real break. He figured he was presentable enough as he changed in the call room out of his scrubs and into his jeans and a wildly patterned red-and-yellow T-shirt with the word *Florida* worked into the design.

Brian was on call, but maybe one or two of the other new guys would be at Casey's. Dan had been hoping to talk to them about playing some ball together, baseball or basketball while the nights were still long and warm. And not just the guys. There were the female interns to get to know better. He thought of Diane Werner. In some ways, he'd already formed a closer bond with *her* than with the guys. But it was different with her: a woman, married with kids. A mentor rather than an equal.

He hadn't yet worked with the other two female first-year interns, but he sure respected what he'd seen at orientation and from rounding with them. Patty Yates had amazing focus and a warm smile but hadn't yet, as far as Dan knew, cracked a single joke. The exotic-looking Willow Blackstone, half Cherokee and half Chinese, had come from California, wielding plenty of wit but with a tendency to be acerbic and a bit militant. Maybe she'd chill out and relax more after she'd been at DCH a while longer.

The sun was thinking about setting as Dan nodded to the security guard and walked out the front doors of Deerwood Community Hospital. The sky, deep blue now, held a slice of rainbow low at the horizon. A typically gorgeous summer evening in Pennsylvania. Filling his lungs with the fresh-washed air, Dan felt suddenly invigorated and turned toward the pub. Nothing was very far away in Deerwood.

Recalling the first time he'd entered the community, he remembered driving past the big, forest-green sign with tan lettering that proclaimed: *Welcome to Deerwood, Pennsylvania.* Below the line of stated *Population,* he'd been surprised to see two lines from a favorite physician poet:

"The wild deer, wand'ring here and there,
Keeps the human soul from care."
—William Blake

Dan could still feel the sense of peace and promise he'd felt then as he passed 150 year old clapboard houses nestled in quiet cul-de-sacs. Near the hospital, several city blocks had been razed to build apartment complexes, state-of-the-art in 1990. A few of those, including his, were reserved at lower cost for hospital staff. Many of Deerwood's physicians and other professionals lived in Lake Harbor Homes, a gated community on the other side of Candlebury Lake, where posh new condos snuggled around its golf course and boat docks.

Now, passing the high school ball fields on the way to the bar, Dan reflected on his own family who still lived in the same upper New York farmhouse. Having a high school coach for a father hadn't been easy, even with all the extra training and mentoring. Throughout his childhood, Dan had frequently wrestled with both guilt and relief that he, at least, could please Pop with athletic prowess. Younger brother Jerry, though as capable in sports as most boys, seemed completely disinterested in excelling there. His gifts lay with numbers, at the piano and in debate, all areas where Dan, like their pop, felt beyond his depth. Of course, Pop had still tried to get Jerry motivated in the right direction—especially in baseball, which had always been the "family game" where generations of Marchetti men best found their bonding—but neither criticism nor pressure, bribery nor cajolery had ever lit the sports fire in Jerry.

Dan smiled, remembering that when anyone accused Sal of being too tough on his boys, he'd just say he didn't believe in giving kids a swelled head. His mom, Gloria Marchetti, was equally traditional in her warm, compassionate nature. The foundation of the Marchetti spirit, she was the rallying point for all their dreams and aspirations—as well as for their heartache.

Dan stared at the empty ball field, nostalgic for the passing of the days when all his younger self needed to think about was baseball and girls. He pulled his thoughts from the past and hurried past.

It was dark by the time he reached Casey's, but it was bright and noisy inside. Cheryl Herrera from the CCU stood at the bar picking up a beer and a dish of peanuts. She greeted him as he walked in. When he thanked her for the ham-and-Swiss, she dimpled. "Sure. Glad you got to actually eat it. Oh, been meaning to ask: that apartment at Woodside working out okay?"

"Yeah. You won't see it in *American Home,* but it's all I need. And only two blocks from the hospital."

Just at that moment Dan caught sight of Alex at a table off to the right with Diane Werner, Willow Blackstone and Dave Levine, all huddled around a huge pitcher of beer. Alex grinned at him, held up an empty mug and waggled it invitingly. Dan touched Cheryl's arm, almost apologetically. "I'm gonna go say hello. Catch you later?"

"Sure thing," the nurse answered, apparently not offended as she continued on her way to rejoin her friends.

As he headed toward his own group, Dan saw Willow rise and move toward him, hiking her shoulder bag to its customary position. "Leaving so soon?" Dan asked, hoping he didn't sound *too* disappointed.

She grimaced, and Dan liked to think he heard regret in her voice when she said, "'Fraid so. I'm on duty tonight." She displayed her nearly empty bottle of mineral water to show she hadn't been drinking alcohol. "Besides, I'm not used to this." Wrinkling her nose, she gestured at the smoky atmosphere. "In California, we outlawed smoking in bars *years* ago."

"Smart," Dan said, resisting a smile. He'd only known her three weeks, but he couldn't count the number of times she'd compared her new home in Pennsylvania to her life in

California—always unfavorably. He gestured toward the gang and the beer. "Maybe another time . . . ?"

The grimace gave way to a lovely smile, and she tossed her hair, waist-length and black-as-could-be, over her unencumbered shoulder. "Hope so!" It sounded quite genuine. "Bye!"

He watched her go, then turned back toward the table.

"Hey, what took ya, asshole?" Alex called, pouring a pint for Dan. Apparently he'd already had a couple. Dave, quiet as always, nodded a greeting.

Diane smiled warmly and said, "We were hoping you'd show up."

As Dan greeted her and folded himself into the chair across the big table from her, she introduced him to a man in a spiffy business suit as her husband Rick. Rick was just finishing a satiric tirade about a traffic jam caused by a disoriented doe and fawn that'd meandered onto Main Street. Diane laughed, "Ah, 'wand'ring here and there,' were they?"

"Yeah," Alex added in a voice just above loud-enough, "why do you think they call it *Deer*wood?" Sliding Dan's beer over in front of him, Alex winked, as if urging Dan to appreciate this witticism.

The younger intern lived down the hall from Dan, and the two had quickly struck up a friendship, hanging out together as often as schedules permitted, if only to share a few beers or watch late-night TV. Alex liked to talk about himself, especially about his meteoric school career. He had a right to be proud. He'd attended New York City schools as a child, skipping a couple of grades along the way, gone through medical school in a three-year program, arriving at his internship year at the advanced age of barely twenty-three. Did he really think that little wisp of a mustache, two shades lighter than his bristle-cut red hair, would make his pudgy face look older?

"Drink up, jerk-off!" Alex insisted and gestured toward the cluster of video game machines. "Then I'll whip your ass at Golden Tee." This was Alex's public face: a demeanor others viewed as arrogant. But Dan had come to know the insecure and rather sweet guy underneath it all.

At the moment no one else was paying attention. Rick and Dave had started discussing, with enthusiasm, rumors that District Attorney Bradden could become a candidate for the state Attorney General, and Diane was disagreeing with them both. Dan felt a world away from local politics. A video game would be a perfect escape.

"Damn," he said good-naturedly and drained his glass. "I better go practice."

"Fat lotta good it'll do ya. I hold the record on that machine." Alex refilled Dan's glass, and Dan took a big gulp before he carried it with him as he left the table.

It wasn't until he'd stationed himself at the golf-themed machine that he glanced over to the corner table where Cheryl had joined three other young women. He recognized another CCU nurse and raised his glass to them. They returned the gesture and the last two, whose backs were to him, turned to look in his direction.

One caught his attention. A stunner in a tight green T-shirt, body hugging dark jeans and a mane of wild copper hair. She raised her glass to him and pushed back her stool.

He nodded to her and grinned, hoping he appeared casual, as he turned back to the video game in progress, trying to focus and look cool at the same time. Suddenly, he detected a whiff of a spicy, mysterious fragrance just before he heard a low voice say, "Oh, too bad!"

Turning toward her, he caught from the corner of his eye the multicolored shapes on the screen blinking out. *Game over.* "Just not my day," he muttered.

She laughed softly. "The night is young."

She sat her tight jeans down on a chair she pulled from the closest table. In this light, he could see her hair was actually a rich auburn and the eyes, a smoky green. Dan took a deep breath. "I'm Dan Marchetti. I—"

"I know all about you," she interrupted, still smiling. "Real name Dante. First-year intern; graduate of Tufts; single; in the CCU this month, ICU next." She laughed, "I'm not a stalker, just the famous DCH Grapevine in action. I'm Nikki. Nikki Saxon. I'm an RN in pediatrics."

"Oh. Right. Have you worked long at DCH?" Dan felt himself blush at the lameness of his opening shot.

"Five years," she told him.

"So whatta y'think of the place?"

"It's a good one, with a great peds unit."

Dan fumbled for another subject. Certainly on their time off, they didn't need to be discussing work. A trio of guys in identical bowling shirts, their hands burdened by beer steins and smoldering cigarettes, sat themselves down at the table nearest Nikki, eyeing her with appreciation.

After an initial glance, she ignored the intrusion, keeping her back to the bowlers and her attention on Dan as she fanned the ever-increasing drifts of smoke away from her face. "Not the wisest place for healthcare workers to hang out, is it?" She had to raise her voice to be heard; someone had cranked the music decibels up another notch. "Wanna get some air?"

"Sounds good." Abandoning the video game console and his unfinished beer, he glanced over and caught Alex's eye, gesturing toward Nikki, who was already leading the way toward the door.

Dan enjoyed the view too as he followed her out into the night, longing to touch her reddish hair where it brushed her back, halfway down to that tiny waist.

Outside, they filled their lungs with the cooling summer air, but the smoke and raucous music trailed them out through the open door of the pub. "Let's walk," Nikki said and started off briskly, in the direction of the town's park. Dan followed and fell into step beside her, wondering how to start a conversation that might help him feel less foolish and inept.

When they could no longer hear Casey's, Nikki slowed the pace and studied him a long moment. "Maybe this'd a little presumptuous of me, but you look a little glum."

Dan regarded her with surprise. "Tough first rotation. I've lost a few patients, and I guess the three weeks have just given me a reality check."

"You'll get used to the work," she assured him. "It's natural to feel bewildered at first. But you find ways to make sense of things. And you have to remember: you can't save them all."

Dan gave a helpless shrug. "I get it."

"Some are going to die," she interrupted, "no matter what we do.

"You live close by?" Nikki asked suddenly. "We could go listen to some music. You have some mellow stuff, right? Not that loud garbage at Casey's."

Dan grinned. "Sure." God, what tunes *did* he have on hand? Mellow? Well, not Pearl Jam then. Would she think the Beatles were too unhip? What else might she like that could set the mood?

Smiling up at him, she took his arm. Her closeness, her fragrance, took away his breath and any powers of speech he might have left. She didn't hurry, but she didn't dawdle either; he pointed out his street, and they walked the long block to his apartment building in a silence that felt both comfortable enough to enjoy the fresh evening air and yet electric with anticipation.

The stairs up to his apartment were cluttered with bicycles and baby carriages. Avoiding them, Nikki brushed against him more than once, stirring both his senses and his imagination: her body would be firm, her skin milky white, and all indications pointed to a willing and passionate nature.

Could it really be he was about to get lucky? Or was she just a pretty colleague in search of relaxation and companionship?

His furnished apartment, provided by the hospital for a below market rent, gave the impression of having just been ransacked. The unfashionable avocado-green sofa sagged in the middle, and though at first glance the end tables appeared to be cherrywood, it was just contact paper over thick cardboard, the cheapest of all furnishings.

Mumbling an apology for the mess, Dan snatched a pungent set of exercise sweats off the couch, but Nikki was already headed toward the CD player on the bookcase.

He dropped his keys and I.D. badge into the caduceus-shaped ceramic dish on his coffee table. A whimsical graduation gift from brother Jerry, it provided a safe and memorable location for several items he couldn't afford to misplace, but now he wondered if it looked too sophomoric. Especially since, unlike the general public, a nurse would likely know the caduceus, with its twin snakes twined around a winged staff, was *not* actually a symbol for medicine but rather the Roman god, Mercury.

"Wine?" he offered.

"Please."

As she sorted through the heap of jewel cases, he tossed the sweats through the open door of his bedroom. Soiled laundry paved the floor, and he hadn't changed his sheets since he'd moved in nearly a month ago. Who knew it would matter? He hadn't spent much time in that bed, and he'd been too busy for bedroom guests. Dan pulled the door closed and headed for the kitchenette.

Thank God he'd dealt with the worst of the mess in there: vast cultures of microorganisms that'd been flourishing on unrecognizable fast food remnants. Though dirty dishes still overtopped the sink, he *had* washed two glasses in case Alex came over to share his bottle of merlot during the weekend.

Meanwhile, Nikki had chosen a disc and fed it to the player. Dan heard the distinctive piano intro for his Alicia Keys CD. By the time he'd poured the two glasses of wine, Nikki had clicked a few tracks ahead, and he recognized the song called "You Don't Know My Name." Handing her the glass, he wondered if she meant to be sending a message through the lyrics and searched her face for clues.

After giving him an enigmatic smile around her first sip of wine, Nikki lowered herself to the couch. "I think I have some crackers," Dan told her. "Maybe even some cheese."

She laughed softly, patted the cushion beside her. "Relax, Dante."

He sat where she'd indicated, but he didn't relax. He sipped his wine, watching her lean back comfortably to survey the room as if she might read him by his environment. She seemed to be trying to find something complimentary to say about his place and at last ventured, "Nice size balcony. It must be good for barbecue . . . having a few friends over."

He snorted in surprise at the thought. "Yeah, like I have any time for that kind of thing!"

She regarded him—still sitting bolt-upright on the edge of the couch—and said, "You really do have to learn to relax. You'll never make it otherwise."

"It's been a long day," he admitted, "a very tough three weeks." But that wasn't the only reason he felt wound tight as a clock. He took another long swallow of his wine.

"Think a neck massage would help, Dante?" Had the wine put that husky note in her voice? Was this the classic neck rub/ backrub gambit or was she just a new friend in nurse-mode? He managed to nod. "Dahn–te," she repeated, savoring the word, and he loved the way her mouth moved saying it. "That's a pretty intriguing name."

Dan wanted to quip something clever, but nothing squeezed out past the wine in his throat. With a languid smile, she set her glass on the faux-cherry end table and slid closer, still facing him on the edge of the sofa. Her hands, bare of any rings, pale and beautifully formed, yet surprisingly strong, reached first to grip his forearms, then his shoulders, then up around the back of his neck with her thumbs to either side of his Adam's apple.

At the first deep pressure of her fingertips in the muscles at the base of his neck, Dan's eyes squeezed shut, and a gasp escaped him.

"Too much?" her voice asked, but her fingers hadn't stopped their exploration.

"No." He opened his eyes, already feeling the relaxation… in his neck, at least. As her fingers worked upward on both sides of his spine, he stared down into her eyes, saw them darken with the beginnings of passion.

Dan couldn't remember the last time he'd had a massage from someone this accomplished, and he hated to do anything that would end the much-needed treatment, but he found he could not resist trying to kiss her. He bent to press his lips against hers, gently but not shyly. She didn't resist but didn't return the kiss either.

He pulled back to stare down at her, wondering if he should apologize. Though her fingers had ceased to massage his neck, they still held him firmly there, and she gazed up at him with an unreadable intensity. Then she smiled that languid, sexy smile he'd seen before, and her hands came around to cup his face and pull it down to hers.

Nikki's kiss was so hungry it startled him, but it pushed out all thoughts of a neck massage. Clumsily, he set aside his wineglass so he could wrap his arms around her. She pulled him down against her as she lay back on the sofa, allowing the length of their bodies to touch. The kiss deepened, and he heard her breath quicken, felt her hands caress his hair, his neck, his back, sliding lower to grip his buttocks.

Things were progressing much more quickly than Dan had expected and, even as they began to undress each other, it occurred to him that he should've been better prepared. Nothing would kill the mood faster than getting up to go rummage through his still-largely-unpacked moving boxes for condoms. Were they in the carton under the bathroom sink or with the stuff from his vacation?

Ah! he thought and reached for the pants he'd just dropped to the floor, fishing out his wallet and from that, one last Trojan still left over from his last tryst in Florida.

"What—" Nikki began, trying to see what he was up to.

Dan held up the slightly crumpled foil packet. "Safety first."

She laughed softly, a sound that made his pulse begin to race again. "Always." And she pulled him back into another long and fervent kiss, those strong hands of hers delighting across his now-bare flesh. He only hoped he could bring her as much pleasure.

Between kisses, she nuzzled his ear and whispered, "I sure hope you have more than one of those things!"

CHAPTER FOUR

Just inside the door of his studio apartment, respiratory therapist Vinny Orlander shrugged out of his white lab coat. Sighing, he tossed it over the back of the one comfortable chair, which also served as a catch-all, the only place in his life where he allowed clutter.

He straightened his new cargo shirt, a bit rumpled from a long shift inside the lab coat. Good to know this cotton-blend khaki would soon release any wrinkles; and each deep pocket had a satisfying button-down flap.

Tall and blond as his Norse ancestors, Derek Vincent Orlander preferred to wear his hair crew-cut, and he'd long ago given up trying to cultivate a convincing crop of facial hair.

His ice-blue eyes looked to the wall clock, a cheap model, generic except for the letters *L-E-V-A-Q-U-I-N* spelled out in the background; a gift from one of the many pharmaceutical reps that roamed the hallways of the hospital and cafeteria. Vinny had no problem accepting "freebies": calendars, keyrings, tote bags, you-name-it, and he'd never have to buy a notepad or a pen as long as he lived. Each of these trinkets required little more than five minutes attention to a drug rep, usually a sensational-looking saleslady. Vinny wasn't the real target; the doctors were. He was just being used to get to them. It was a game. He knew it, she knew it and everyone played.

He looked away from the clock to his compact efficiency kitchen thinking that he should be hungry for lunch, but food could wait. He had something far more interesting on his mind. He reached into the right inner pocket and pulled out an ampule filled with clear liquid. He couldn't help smiling. It'd been too easy to lift the vecuronium bromide from the intensive care unit's medication cabinet and stash it in that handy pocket. No one thought twice about seeing Vinny around the meds. He was an intrinsic part of DCH's interior landscape: fresh linens and intravenous tubing, bedpans and gurneys, Johnny coats and Vinny Orlander.

Lots of people might take comfort blending in so well, and he certainly used it to his advantage when it suited him, but mostly Vinny found it irritating and sometimes downright maddening. No one ever appeared to notice him, a familiar experience. Nothing he ever did his whole life had been good enough for his parents, or half as good as his big sister Astrid. He could feel his muscles begin to tighten, the anger burning a hole in his gut.

He took a deep breath, his attention going to the huge freshwater fish tank across from his couch. The mock-leather futon also unfolded to serve as a bed. He'd spent countless hours lying there, staring into that entrancing underwater world, just watching those colorful swordtails and tetras and barbs swim in and out of the environment he'd created for them. Each one had a name, and he had no trouble telling them apart.

"Hi, guys," he said, moving over to peer into the immaculate water. "I'm home." He'd swear they all got more animated seeing him; they raced through the hand-crafted tunnels and rock arches he'd constructed, painted and placed strategically.

He gazed with pride upon his most innovative feature: an up-sloping hill of adobe-colored boulders that rose well above the surface at one end of the fifty-gallon tank. The above-water area covered about a third of the tank's length; natural hollows formed containers for tiny terrarium plants.

Vinny's attention returned to the water as two Green Tiger Barbs, Chuckles and Phynn, played hide-and-seek in the honeycomb of pale-blue ceramic mesh. Vinny tapped the glass with the vecuronium vial. "Don't give me that. I fed you before I left last night. And don't worry . . . I won't forget to go out later and get some more supplies. Don't I always take good care of you?" A movement on the rocks and under a leafy plant caught Vinny's eye. "There you are," he said. The small bullfrog probably thought it couldn't be seen, hidden as it was. Vinny had brought it home several days ago but never given it a name.

Vinny set the vecuronium on the futon, reached quickly into the tank and managed to catch the frog without too much effort. "Gotcha." Gingerly petting the creature's head, he told it, "Bet you'd like to stretch your legs a little, wouldn't you?" and set it down on the spotless hardwood floor.

The tiny frog hopped several feet away, but finding it wasn't pursued, it stopped, looking back at its keeper.

"Stretch your legs," Vinny chuckled, unbuttoning the top pocket of his shirt. He drew out a plastic syringe and a needle, removed both from their packaging and assembled them. He picked up the ampule of vecuronium and deftly flicked its top with his right middle finger. With his left thumb, he snapped the tip of the vial; then he concentrated on the syringe in his right hand, priding himself on a new trick he'd learned: pulling out the plunger one-handed. This drew into the syringe a little air, which he could then inject into the ampoule before withdrawing its contents. He set aside the empty vial and regarded the loaded syringe with satisfaction.

With one long stride, Vinny stooped to pluck the frog up off the floor. Without hesitation, he plunged the needle into its belly and injected a tiny drop of the drug. Placing the startled amphibian back on the floor, he capped the syringe and placed it on the laminate counter before him.

At first, the frog hopped straight ahead as if to get as much distance as possible from its unpredictable keeper. But then it veered to the left and then to the right. Vinny waited, eyes narrowed for the effect he expected. It came. The frog's four limbs suddenly shot out straight from its body and froze there outstretched; the eyes, too, were frozen, wide open in terror but with no hint of movement. Mesmerized, Vinny repeated again, very softly, "Stretch your legs."

He'd seen the effects of this drug, a powerful paralytic, on humans, but it hadn't been so dramatic. After all, they were sedated and on a ventilator to breathe for them. The induced paralysis allowed the ventilator to do its thing without any interference from the patient's body responses. In time, a human patient would be "reversed" and allowed to breathe naturally. No such luck for the frog. Eventually, Vinny knew, it would cease to breathe, and then it would die. Vinny sat down next to it on the floor and stroked it gently with one finger. "I think I'll call you Stretch. You like that name?"

Riveting his gaze on the frog, he wondered if he'd be able to tell the exact moment that Death claimed it. A strange tingling thrill rippled through Vinny, arousing him in a way that brought another memory. Once, while engaging in rough sex, he'd lost control and nearly strangled a girl, until her well-placed kick brought him back to reality. That'd been close, and, though he'd apologized repeatedly and professed tremendous remorse, he wasn't sure he'd been completely sincere.

As the frog gave up its last gasp, Vinny moved to the syringe. He wrapped it in a piece of foil and placed it on the top shelf of his apartment sized refrigerator. "Come on Stretch, let's toss you back where you came from."

CHAPTER FIVE

Her pale face also turned to the warm rays of late-afternoon sunshine, Nikki Saxon sank even deeper into the comfy lounge chair on the deck of her Lake Harbor condo. Feeling utterly exhausted she thought back to the two grueling shifts she had completed back to back. What she really needed was a deep rejuvenating sleep which had been curiously unavailable to her these last few weeks. She tried to relax, absorbing every last ray of sun that her body could take, even though she'd never be able to tan. Not covered up the way she was and with SPF 60 sunblock on every bit of exposed skin.

She'd always loved the sun; its heat and light had frequently been the only brightness in her dreary, often dark, childhood. She'd lie for hours in the grass of any close park or on a tiny apartment balcony or even on the landing of a fire escape if that was the only option available. However, after a few blistering burns, she learned to stay covered with one sleeve over her face to protect her delicate too-white skin and became slavishly devoted to SP-45!

Nikki's thoughts were clearly on the more recent past, today. Reaching for the sunblock, she rubbed a fresh coating onto the backs of her hand. Stretching them out in front of her, she remembered how they'd looked like white stars against the sun-tanned shoulders of Dante Marchetti.

Was that only a week ago? It seemed like ages. She hadn't seen him since. They'd parted without awkwardness, but, thankfully, he hadn't asked for her number, and she certainly hadn't offered it. A phone call could be problematic. He knew where to find her, peds was only one floor above the CCU. Apparently he didn't want to find her. That was OK with her. Well, it wasn't okay, but it would have to do.

Nikki stretched, catlike, on the lounge, running her hands up through her loose wealth of auburn hair, remembering how Dante's fingers had felt tracking the same course. She had noticed him first when she spied him just inside the front doors of DCH. She was struck by his dark good looks and easy smile, the way he took a moment to greet the security guard, who called him "Dr. Marchetti." He hadn't changed into his scrubs yet, and she admired the way he filled those snug stonewashed jeans. Nikki had dawdled a bit, just within earshot but unnoticed by the men. As soon as she heard the guard ask, "How's the CCU treatin' you?" she moved on, knowing that she could ask Cheryl Herrera for information.

And she did, grilling Cheryl for the 4-1-1 on all the new docs to disguise her true interest. Nikki found reasons to be around the lobby when Dan might be arriving or leaving, and even a couple of excuses to appear in the CCU while he was on duty. But she hadn't called attention to herself and certainly hadn't asked Cheryl to introduce them. In her quiet moments, especially the many lonely ones, Nikki entertained herself with dreams of Dan Marchetti, of what he would be like as a doctor, a man, a friend, a lover. Especially as a lover. Who could guess the reality would almost live up to her wicked fantasies?

Nikki smiled up into the sunshine, watching yet again on the inside of her closed eyelids the movie of their time together. His tenderness, the thrill of his touch wherever his fingers strayed, his sensual mouth claiming hers.

She'd almost forgotten what it could be like. After all, in the past seven years she'd only had sex with Matt. And, for the last two years, it *was* just that: having sex. Not really making love anymore. Not the way it was with Dan. It'd been a perfect evening, except for that lumpy old sofa under her butt. And though now it didn't look like there would be a next time, it had been worth it.

Nikki focused on the warmth of the sunlight bathing her and told herself, t*ime for your Dreamplace. Take a little nap and go where everything is good and happy and safe.* But that is not where her dreams took her. Instead she was suddenly five again, listening to the heavy thudding and the sound of splintering wood that woke her.

She heard the sound of the front door bursting open in the living room, of it crashing back against the wall. As she cowered in her bed, Nikki heard the drunken bellow: "Frances!" and knew for sure who the intruder was.

Tony. . . . her father, Mommy said, though he'd left them before Nikki could remember them ever being a family. Sure, he came back. When he wanted something. And whenever they tried moving to a new place.

"Get out!" Nikki heard her mother's low voice from the front room. It had the trying-not-to-be-scared sound in it. "You'll wake Nikki."

"So what!?" the bad voice said. "What're you tryin' to hide from her? What a whore her mother is?" Slap! "What a pathetic piece a shit?" Slap!

Mommy was crying, saying something. . . .

"Oh, for God's sake, quit snivelin'! I'll take care of it," he said, his voice coming closer. Then Mommy's begging voice. Then "Dammit, Frances, go get in bed or I'll wake little Nikki up special-like."

Still barely breathing, Nikki saw the big, black shadow fill her doorway, stand there looking a long, long minute. Then he slammed the door shut—making the room completely black.

No-o-o!_*Nikki shot up in bed, gasping for air.* Never close the door! *Mommy knew that. There was no window, no light at all in the room except a tiny crack at the bottom of the door. They both knew it was really just a closet, big enough for her little mattress on the floor, but when* *they moved in, Mommy said, "See how great? We'll both have our own bedroom now! And I know you don't like the dark, so we'll always leave your door open at night and a lamp on in the living room, okay?"*

"That oughtta keep the little turd." Tony laughed. "Kids can sleep through anything. Now come on to bed."

Nikki flattened herself on the floor, her face pressed against the bottom of the door so she could breathe better. The voices were still close.

"Can't you just leave us alone, Tony?" Mommy sounded so tired. "We're finally divorced. You said you wanted your own life. Can't you let us have ours?"

"Yeah, this is some classy life you've carved out for yourself—"

Nikki heard a sound she recognized. Like punching your fist into a big pillow. But it wasn't a pillow. Mommy cried out. Again the sound.

"Shut up! You'll wake the kid, remember? I'll come here whenever I please. You're not much of a piece of tail anymore, but hey, any port in a storm. You belong to me, bitch—no matter what those divorce papers say—and you always will, because we made that brat together. That gives me rights."

"Oh, here you are!" Matt's voice jerked Nikki back into her present reality with a jolt. "I shoulda known you'd be out here tempting fate."

Nikki, eyes open now beneath the sunglasses, gazed up at her husband, a ruggedly handsome man reminiscent of a 1950s matinee idol. *Rock Johnnyface,* she used to call him in playful moments. And how perfect that he was, at that time, the manager of a movie theater. That's where they met and fell in love.

Seven years later, he had the same thick black hair and intense cobalt eyes; he hadn't put on a single pound. *Anchor Security,* read the embroidered patch on his forest-green uniform, which still managed to look pressed after a full day's shift. Nikki's eyes looked away from the holstered gun, not yet removed. She hated that thing. He'd made her learn how to use it for her own protection, but she'd refused to handle it since she got her certificate.

"Of course I'm out here." She made her voice sound light. "Such a lovely place to take a little nap. Just look how all the petunias are blooming!"

He didn't even glance toward the riot of color overflowing the redwood flowerboxes that edged the deck. "Seems like you sleep all the time now."

"I feel so tired, Matt. And I just can't seem to get good sleep at night. You've been pretty restless yourself; that doesn't help."

"Your sweating like a pig isn't so conducive either," he shot back. "And don't try to make this about me. I'm still doing *my* share of the household chores."

Nikki found the energy to spring up beside him, pressing her fingers to his lips. "Let's not fight." She wanted to be held. The way her mother once held her. Or better, the way Matt used to hold her. Better yet, the way Dan Marchetti had held her as he fell asleep beside her. She took Matt's hand. "Let's go in the bedroom and see if we can't find some way to relax each other so we both sleep better tonight."

"Not now, Nik." He dropped her hand and began to unbuckle the shoulder holster—almost as if he knew that would make her take an involuntary step backwards. "I gotta grab a shower." As she opened her mouth to coyly suggest she join him, he asked, "What's for dinner?"

Nikki hesitated, running one hand nervously through her tousled hair. "Hadn't thought about it yet."

Matt made an exasperated sound. "Well, too late now. I'll get something at Casey's. I'm meeting Chuck and Sully to watch the game and maybe play some cards after." He was heading for the sliding doors into the condo. "I'll be out late. Maybe you can get some sleep if I'm not bothering you so much."

The screen door whispered closed behind him. A moment later she heard his gun being deposited in the safe and then the *beep, beep, beep* of the locking code as it was activated. His steps sounded light and eager as he hurried upstairs to prepare for his evening out.

Nikki flopped back down on the lounge, fighting back tears.

CHAPTER SIX

Ducking out of the morning's drizzle and through DCH's main entrance vestibule, Dan paused as the inner doors whispered shut behind him. He brushed at his now-sodden scrubs, muttering, "Didn't look like it was comin' down that much."

The security guard on duty, Greg Vandenbosk, kept a straight face, but his blond eyebrows lifted as he observed, "There *are* some days you might actually consider driving to work."

Dan laughed, patted his trim belly. "Walking's good for the body—and the environment."

Vandenbosk, Dan's favorite among all the security staff, nodded, yawning. "I guess." He was only twenty-nine, but he looked older today.

"You getting enough sleep?" Dan asked.

"I wish."

"How *is* that brilliant baby?"

Now the smile came out, bursting like sunshine across the guard's face. "She's . . ." he paused, as if no words existed to describe the wonder of his first child, ". . . *great.* Just great, thanks."

Clapping Greg on the shoulder, Dan caught sight of his wristwatch. "I better scoot. Gotta get into some drier scrubs. Take care."

As soon as he'd changed, Dan joined the house staff, first-, second- and third-year residents, on duty for morning rounds with the ICU attending, Dr. Neal Driscoll. At barely thirty-five, Driscoll's youthfulness was refreshing. He seemed especially energetic this morning, and Dan caught Diane Werner's eye with a wink to show he was remembering her recent comment that Driscoll was the only one of the attendings to still have all his hair, all his teeth and all his enthusiasm.

The intensive care unit, much like the neighboring CCU, was set up with a central station of desk area beneath monitors, surrounded by the individual rooms. Here, though, they were arranged with surgical patients on one side and medical on the other. All were designated "reverse isolation" rooms: their filtration units prevented dangerous infections from contaminating other patient rooms through the air exchange system. Each could be sealed with a door in case of extreme susceptibility or contagion, but usually only the curtain was drawn for privacy, allowing patients to feel more connected and the nurses to better monitor those in their care.

Dan had found the ICU as daunting an assignment as CCU, but with more variety; any ICU must be prepared to treat a vast array of complex illnesses, always serious, frequently grave. Patients with these life-threatening conditions required additional nursing care, a higher staffing ratio than many other departments.

Medical interns faced enormous responsibilities in the ICU. In the weeks Dan had been at it, he'd decided the most important keys were to hone in on every detail and to reevaluate constantly since the patient's medical condition was likely to change from moment to moment.

Dan joined Diane at the consoles. Diane looked up and gave a tired smile. "Maybe today will be a light one. Only six beds right now, and look, everything's pretty calm."

He grinned. "Trying to jinx us?" He sat down in front of the computer and began checking for his patients' most recent lab values. "But I hope you're right. We could use an easy day for a change."

Working with her in ICU had only deepened the respect Dan felt for Diane.

"Diane?" Dan glanced over from his computer screen. "What made you leave nursing to go to med school? And with three kids, no less."

She chuckled. "You mean, what was I thinking? I'm not sure, except I'd gotten so bored." She shook her head, staring into the distance as if into the past. "Not with the work itself but more with the limitations of my role."

"Rick must be proud. And pretty understanding, I guess."

"Hmm...about that"she began, but before she could explain her rueful sigh, Dan's beeper sounded: *"Beep, beep, beep . . .* Dr. Marchetti, Radiology—stat!" He rose quickly as it repeated. Diane's nod showed she'd heard the message. He gave her an apologetic wave and hurried down three floors.

He found his emergency occurring at the CAT scan: an enormous, doughnut-shaped apparatus through which a table could move to align the scan for the appropriate body areas of a patient lying upon it.

An unconscious woman lay on the floor, not the table. Radiologist Dr. Paolo Lescani hovered over her, looking frantic. He was an older fellow, Italian-born, short and a little pudgy. Dan had had some fun practicing his Italian with him and talking baseball. A nice guy but now his wide eyes and beads of perspiration dotting his forehead's deep lines, showed just how long it had been since he had managed crashing patients.

"What happened?" Dan called, striding toward the tableau. He made sure his voice sounded much calmer and more confident than he felt inside. He could see the woman was breathing shallowly. Short and plump and in her mid-sixties, she had a face surprisingly similar to that of his mother, but much paler.

"I don't know!" Lescani answered. "She just collapsed as she was getting on the table." Dan bent over her, found a strong carotid pulse, caught a whiff of her perfume—the same one his mother wore, though he couldn't remember its name.

Motioning to a nearby life pack cart equipped with a defibrillator and other items for use in emergencies, Lescani asked in a panicky voice, "Whatta we do? Zap her? Start pumping?"

Dan shook his head. Even in English, Lescani's Italian accent was so pronounced and familiar that reflexively, before he was even aware of it, Dan slipped into the Italian he'd heard spoken so frequently at home and during his travels in Europe. *"Per che cosa bisogna quel CAT scan?"* he asked. Why did she need a CAT scan?

Lescani continued the conversation in Italian, which seemed to calm him, and Dan found it easy enough to translate: "For a neurological evaluation. She's had two fainting spells. Her physician's looking for evidence of a stroke . . . believes those episodes represent TIAs."

Dan nodded. *"Va bene."*

The patient, her wristband said *Damen, Sarah,* was now coming back to consciousness and breathing normally. Two orderlies arrived with a gurney at the same time the nursing code team, respiratory tech and one of the second year residents, Tom Slater, arrived. "She's got a good pulse. We should get her up to ICU," Dan directed. Tom nodded. Studying her more closely, Dan noted a bluish tint to her lips, almost obscured by her heavy makeup, a result of her blood's poor oxygen content. Her eyes now open and wide with alarm, she grabbed for the nearest hand—Dan's.

As she was being helped up from the floor and onto the gurney, he gave her a reassuring smile. "Ms. Damen? You've fainted, and as a precaution, we're going to take you to the ICU where we'll try to figure out why this happened. You're going to be fine."

Sarah Damen didn't let go of Dan's hand or take her eyes from his face as they moved into the waiting elevator. By now, Dan had seen a lot of scared people, but he found this woman's terrified face especially unsettling, as if she knew some deep, dark secret that he would soon uncover. When the elevator doors opened, Dan saw the senior resident, Jacqueline Norris, flanked by Wyndolyn Hibbert, the best charge nurse on the floor.

Jackie grabbed the chart and moved away to peruse it. The nurse, an ample-figured Jamaican woman who always wore bright pink, took the patient's other hand, patted it. "Me Nurse Wynnie, Miz Damen." Her voice, some fifteen years removed from its origins, was still melodiously accented and retained quite a bit of her homeland patois, something Dan had seen prove soothing and motherly for a number of her charges. "Gotta bed ah ready f'ya, now."

This patient, though, was clearly still anxious and refused to look away from his face or release his hand. "I'll be right there," Dan assured her, and, with a final squeeze of her hand, he freed his own and let the orderly guide the gurney where Wynnie indicated.

Dan went to the central area. where Jackie was studying Sarah Damen's chart. Peering over her shoulder, Dan asked, "What's it say?"

Jackie looked as crisp as usual, her waist-length walnut-brown hair pinned back from her face to fall like a shining curtain straight down her back. The only female third-year resident, Jackie was also keen-witted, wry-humored and one of only two members of the hospital staff who were openly gay. "Dr. Bruno thought she'd had TIAs."

"Which Dr. Bruno?" The Bruno sisters, Josephine and Melissa, were in practice together.

"Josephine." Jackie's eyes crinkled with amusement. "You know, the smart one."

As Dan nodded his agreement, Wynnie returned. "She ah tucked in."

They headed for Sarah Damen's room. As Jackie pulled the curtain to ensure privacy, Dan approached the patient smiling. "How're you doing?" He picked up her hand again and held it between his own.

"Much better now," she responded. Her face looked very tired. "It's been a strange two days. Nothing like this has ever happened to me."

"First time in the hospital?"

"Other than giving birth, yes." She paused, the worry deepening on her face. "Has anyone contacted my husband?"

Jackie introduced herself, "We've already called him. I told him you'd fainted again and were being brought to ICU. He said he'd be here as soon as he could. Don't worry, okay?" Jackie referred to the chart again. "I see here that you just returned from a trip to Virginia?"

"Yes, we were visiting my sister. Ten-hour drive. We got home late and went right to bed. The next day, my right leg was all swollen and very painful." Dan glanced at Jackie. Their eyes locked for a long moment, and he could tell she suspected the same problem: blood clots in the legs from being seated so long. Quickly going through their physical exam, they found the unwelcome evidence.

"I feel a cord," Jackie said quietly as she palpated Sarah Damen's right calf. Though Dan knew the cord, a large blood clot, was a very dangerous discovery, he reassured Mrs. Damen yet again, and the two physicians hastily left the room to confer.

"Those fainting episodes weren't TIAs," muttered Dan. "They were friggin' pulmonary emboli." Parts of the clot, an embolus, had broken loose, traveling in the bloodstream to the lungs, where they formed a blockage that severely limited oxygenated blood reaching the heart and, consequently, the rest of the body. There was precious little time to waste. For pulmonary emboli to have caused fainting episodes, either they were very large or there were many, many small ones. In either case, the next one could make Ed Damen a widower fast.

When Dan looked at Jackie to see what she wanted to do, she tilted her head in a *Go ahead* gesture. He signaled to Wynnie Hibbert, who came right over to listen for Dan's directions: "Heparin aggressive protocol, please, stat!"

He looked back at Jackie; she nodded assent. Heparin was the only possible therapy at that point. It wouldn't dissolve the clot that was already in the leg—undoubtedly the source of her pulmonary emboli, but it could help to organize it, clumping the cells more tightly, helping it stick to an artery wall so new clots were less likely to break free and travel to places where they'd be even more dangerous.

"Spiral CAT scan?" Dan suggested.

Jackie nodded again. "Call Lescani, and tell him Ms. D. is on the way back down." She moved away to give instructions for transport.

By the time he'd contacted Lescani, who didn't sound too thrilled with the news, Sarah Damen was back out of bed, back on the gurney, IV started, oxygen flowing through the nasal cannula from the tank tetherd to the gurney and on her way back down to Radiology. As Dan headed once more for the stairs, a ward clerk approached Dan with Sarah Damen's lab work.

"Thanks." Dan took the lab work and scanned the blood gas result. "Oh, crap." The percent of oxygen was in the 40s instead of the 90s. He didn't want to think about the family doctor's missed diagnosis. These things happened, even with someone as smart as Josephine Bruno. No point fixing blame. But now there was much work to be done, and quickly. He hurried down the stairs, knowing Dr. Lescani would welcome the company and he'd get a quick read of the scan.

Dan expected to see a more tranquil scene than the last time he entered Radiology, but the view was eerily similar. As the table came sliding out of the doughnut-shaped device at the completion of the scan, Sarah Damen was turning blue, her eyes bulging and her neck veins looked ready to explode. Dan rushed to her, and Dr. Lescani joined him, whispering "My God, my God" over and over in Italian.

"She's wiped out her entire left lung!" reported a technician monitoring the equipment.

Dan yelled, "Call a code—now!" To Lescani he said, "She must've thrown another damn embolus." He ripped away the woman's hospital gown to expose her blue-tinted life-less body. He began chest compressions while Lescani grabbed an ambubag from the life pack and started pumping air into her lungs at the appropriate times. Dan turned to the life pack monitor and got the wires attached to Mrs. Damen. The respiratory tech joined them, ready to help as needed.

"V-tach," Dan announced. "Paddles, please; charge 200 joules. Clear." *Zap!* Her arms and legs flew skyward, the eerie sight too familiar to Dan by now after his stint in the CCU. "Sinus rhythm; good pulse," he said. "All right, let's get her upstairs—stat."

As the three men got her transferred to the gurney and covered again, the tech, Vinny Orlander took the ambu-bag from Lescani, saying, "I'll get that now."

The radiologist relinquished it with obvious relief. At that moment, he felt Sarah Damen's fingernails clutch his right thigh, literally holding on for dear life. Her eyes registered pure terror, and with her other hand, she batted away the ambu-bag, to let out a piercing shriek that filled the small room.

A second of panic jolted into Dan's own soul like electricity down a lightning rod. With difficulty, he managed to free himself so he could get moving. The three of them, Dan, Vinny and the burly orderly, left Lescani in Radiology and hurried the gurney and life-pack equipment down the hall toward the elevators.

Reaching the elevators, Dan dismissed the orderly. "We can take it from here."

"No room anyway," Vinny noted as the two men squeezed in next to the gurney and the doors slid closed.

"Relax, now," Vinny soothed as he fitted the ambu-bag's little mask back over the patient's nose and mouth. "Let me help you breathe, okay?"

At that moment Sarah Damen's hand seized Dan's leg with the same intensity as before, her nails digging deep through the thin cloth of his scrubs. And then she lost consciousness; that viselike grip fell away, the hand completely limp.

"Shit. In the elevator, goddammit! V-tach." Dan maneuvered for position as best he could in the cramped space and charged the paddles, pulled away the hospital gown to reveal the blue chest with its burn-mark evidence of the earlier life-saving assault. "Clear!" He zapped her, but this time her signs did not bounce back. In fact, the wavering line of v-tach smoothed out to flatline.

"CPR!" Dan declared, climbing atop the gurney. There was simply no room to apply any firm-enough pressure otherwise.

"This is surreal," Vinny murmured, staring, mesmerized, at the woman, even as he automatically worked the ambu-bag in concert with the compressions.

The elevator doors finally opened, and there was Jackie with two nurses who grabbed the gurney and hauled it from the elevator car, through the ICU doors, and back into the room the patient had occupied earlier. Dan balanced himself for the ride, continuing to pump on Sarah Damen's chest. Vinny kept pace, still trying to fill the woman's lungs with oxygen. The entire ICU nursing staff, ward clerks and all physicians on hand gathered around Ms. Damen's room as Jackie moved to the head of the bed calling for and placing the endotracheal tube that would allow Vinny to keep pushing oxygen into her stiffening lungs. All around them, the others were a portrait of ironic helplessness. All that combined knowledge and training, resolve and caring, left powerless in the moment. There was not a thing anyone else could do beyond what Dan and Vinny worked feverishly to accomplish.

But it was becoming clear that Sarah Damen would not be getting another chance.

Dan looked up and shook his head. "She's gone." He sighed and pulled the hospital gown back into place as Vinny removed the ambu-bag. "Time of death—"

A sudden commotion at the main ICU doors interrupted him. A ward clerk called, "Mr. Damen, please wait here—"

"Where is she?!" another voice screamed. "Where *is* she?" A figure barreled toward them, wild-eyed and disheveled, oblivious to his misbuttoned sports shirt and to the arms trying to restrain him. He pushed past, shrieking, "Oh God!" as he hurled himself onto the gurney, knocking Dan aside, to lie next to his wife's motionless body. He began to kiss her face repeatedly as if this could suddenly revive her. "We had breakfast this morning," he wailed. "She was just fine." He fixed his anguished gaze on Dan. "What did you do to her?"

Dan straightened to stand beside the gurney. So many eyes! Were they wondering what it felt like to lose a patient and be blamed for it in the same moment? What about Jackie, standing there chewing her lip as she stared at him, had she ever endured such a thing? Only Vinny wasn't peering at him but stood, still clutching the now-useless ambu-bag, his pale blue eyes fixed with rapt attention on the lifeless body.

"Sarah! Sarah!" Ed kept keening. "Oh, God . . . bring her back—please!"

Dan closed his eyes to the scene. He motioned all the staff from the room, except for Wynnie, the charge nurse. Ed Damen deserved at least a moment with his wife. As he, himself, left the room, Dan saw the entire ICU staff standing there, watching him. Suddenly self-conscious, Dan realized tears were sliding down his cheeks.

Avoiding everyone's eyes, he went over to the writing desk and sat down with his back to them. On his closed eyelids he saw that vision of the Damens . . . of Sarah's face. But it blurred into that of his own mother. It was hard to imagine his father climbing up on a gurney to kiss her and plead with God to save her. But who knew what a man would do under such circumstances?

Dan became aware of voices behind him. Attending Neal Driscoll was discussing pulmonary emboli, streptokinase and the details of Sarah Damen's case with the house staff still present. "For God's sake! Would you please stop?" It was out of Dan's mouth before he could think to check it. Into the embarrassed silence, he added, "The woman just *died.* I just don't..." His throat closed on the words; he couldn't continue, couldn't bear the puzzled looks on the faces of his colleagues, his peers, his mentors. Ashamed of his outburst, Dan rose and left the unit, profoundly shaken and wishing desperately he had chosen another profession.

A few hours later, Dan and Diane were once again the only two people at the desk of a quiet ICU. Outwardly, he'd managed to compose himself within a few minutes of his meltdown and had gone on with his shift, as was expected. In this business, there was simply no time to fall apart. Dan was glad no one tried to talk to him about the experience. But now he turned to Diane and blurted, "Does it *really* ever get better?"

She paused, glancing away from the computer screen where she'd been checking labs, and regarded him while she thought it over. "Yes," she said quietly, ". . . and no." Dan could sense that what might seem on the surface to be a cop-out was the only truly honest answer. Diane tilted her head. "You thought Driscoll's discussion was . . . what—inappropriate? Premature? Insensitive?"

Try obscene, Dan thought, but he only nodded again.

"I know how you feel, but we are here to learn, and how better than from what we've just witnessed or experienced? Still, we don't check our humanity at the door. You should've seen Driscoll in the ER when he brought in his two-year-old in the middle of an asthma attack! You wouldn't even know he was the same guy, except he knew all the stuff that could go wrong, and that made him even more frantic."

"You'll learn how to deal, Dan. You'll do it because you took an oath that you would, and now you have to. You just cope.

"You'll get there," Diane told him with a compassionate smile. Dan thought of the husband comment interrupted by his call to Radiology. He wondered what the spouse of a woman like Diane would ever have to complain about.

Of course, some husbands had a right to complain. Unbidden, almost against his will, an image of Nikki Saxon invaded Dan's thoughts: that alabaster body draped across his old green sofa wearing nothing except the sparkle of that sexy ankle bracelet as he returned from his quest with the prize of more condoms . . . her radiant smile and the way her dark reddish hair fell back from her shoulders as she reached up for him. . . .

Dan squeezed his eyes shut, trying to banish that picture. Only a day later, he'd learned the truth. Back on duty in the CCU, he'd found himself alone with his best nurse-buddy, Cheryl, who had seemed to avoid his eyes all morning. She'd been at Casey's, seen him leave with Nikki. "I sure like your friend Nikki," he ventured.

"She's married," Cheryl said flatly, meeting his eyes at last, probably reading in them the shock he felt. "She didn't tell you? Well, I've been struggling with whether I should or not." She turned away, picking up some papers on the desk. "Do what you will. You're both adults. I just thought you should know."

To her credit, Nikki hadn't pursued him, hadn't even offered her number, though it was clear she was interested. She'd left it all up to him. And as much as it pained him, he knew what he had to do. Now, weeks later, he called upon that strategy again: Ray Lawlor, Nikki Saxon, Sarah Damen. They were part of the past. He needed to find a way to move on.

A few days later, the morning dawned bright and clear, and Dan woke feeling reborn. He didn't have to go to the hospital, a Sunday rarity so far in his internship. Instead, he had the luxury of sleeping late, then sauntering down to the corner bakery for two big bagels, just out of the oven.

Back at his own dinette table, he devoured them, slathered with cream cheese and washed down with his favorite strongly brewed coffee while he read the sports section of the *Deerwood Times*. Since the town was less than an hour from Pittsburgh, there was always news about the Pirates. He still followed his beloved Yankees, but he tried to keep current on the Pirates as well so he could talk ball with other DCH staff, where there was strong support for the team. Yesterday Diane had enthused about their Friday game, when they'd whipped the Phillies 11–2, and her hopes they could repeat the win on Saturday night.

"Ouch!" he said aloud, reading how, instead, Philadelphia had taken revenge there in its hometown, beating the Pirates by five.

Pouring a third cup of coffee, he reflected that he *could* be using the time to clean his apartment. He'd been promising himself he'd do that as soon as he had a free morning. But now, surveying his domain, he decided it wasn't so bad! Cluttered, yes. Dusty, yes. But after getting caught unprepared with Nikki, he'd made more of an effort—just in case. Not that Nikki would be coming back, but if lightning could strike once like that, who knows what else might happen? He was still keeping an eye out for Willow, but due to their schedules, he'd barely seen her in six weeks. Their encounters while rounding presented few opportunities to pursue a friendship, much less something more.

So he'd been making sure he kicked all his dirty clothes onto the floor of the closet and that he could get the door shut on that heap. All his unwashed dishes were at least rinsed and stacked in the sink, and no biology experiments were allowed to grow unchecked in either the kitchen or the bathroom. And now, time for some fun! For weeks now, everyone had been looking forward to a softball game between available members of the house staff and the attendings. It was scheduled for eleven at the park. Dan grabbed his mitt, his keys from the caduceus dish, and a fat, red apple to eat on the way. He stepped over the pile of throwaway medical journals strewn by his door, a reminder to gather them up and take them down to the recycling bin.

He didn't want to rush his walk on such a glorious morning. The recent drizzle had washed all the dust away beneath a brilliantly blue sky, and the sun's rays were already strong enough to bring beads of perspiration out on his forehead.

He hadn't anticipated how eager the others would be. He was the last to arrive, even though he was fifteen minutes early. Both teams were busy deciding their line-ups. He noted all the familiar faces, but . . . no Willow.

Not surprising. *Some* of the crew had to be on duty. In fact, at least half of the dozen first-years were missing, plus Clay Lebeau.

"Dan, get over here!" Diane yelled from right field. "Where ya been?"

Alex Cole, in left field, called, "We saved center for you."

Dan grinned at their excitement and took his position, tossing a few balls back and forth with Diane and then with Alex. Satisfied his arm was sufficiently loose, he called to nobody in particular, "Okay!"

The game began. Jackie Norris, her brown hair plaited into a long braid down her back, pitched the first ball, which sailed at least ten feet over Dr. Lescani's head, and catcher Frank Ryan had to scramble for it.

"Hey, some pitch there, Jackie!" yelled Mike Upton, an attending from the ER. "Get it down, like maybe two yards worth, huh?"

Unfazed, Jackie laughed with the others. Her next pitch was perfect, but Lescani was ready. The radiologist, his comb-over secured beneath a Pirates cap, swung compactly and sent a screeching line drive toward the gap in left center.

Dan, in motion as soon as he heard the sound of the bat hit the ball, raced toward that gap and easily managed to scoop the ball up into his glove.

Immediately checking his lateral momentum, he planted his feet. From the corner of his eye, he could see Lescani rounding first base and loping confidently toward second. With one fluid motion, Dan positioned his front foot, cocked his right arm, and threw a bona fide missile toward second base. The softball traveled so fast and the throw was so accurate that the middle-aged radiologist was at least fifteen feet short of the bag when second-baseman Dave Levine tagged him out.

For a brief moment, there was utter silence. It'd all happened so fast, players on both teams were still trying to take it in.

"Hey, Marchetti!" called Glenn Covington. "Y'never told me you had a goddam rifle on you!"

Dan grinned and saluted his CCU mentor with self-conscious pleasure. It really meant something to be noticed by Covington, who'd played three seasons for the Lansing Tigers, a minor-league affiliate of the Detroit Tigers by deferring his med school acceptance for those years. Renowned for his glove, still he'd never pushed his lifetime batting average above the low 220s, making med school an easy choice and setting himself up for a lifetime of ribbing, mostly about how the team had kept him on just to get some free on field suturing and splinting done.

When the ninth inning rolled around, the teams were tied 6–6 as the attendings came up to bat for their last licks. With one out, they managed to get Emily Bosnan, the cardiothoracic surgeon, on second and the ICU's Neal Driscoll on third; Covington came up to bat. The one-time Tiger took strikes on the first two pitches before lacing into the third, sending a long fly ball to deep right center field in a hit that must've carried at least three hundred feet. It was high enough to let Dan get underneath it, but it was also far enough to allow Driscoll on third time to tag up and score before Dan would be able to throw the ball back to the catcher. At least, that'd be the assumption of everybody . . . except Dan.

Watching the ball hurtling down toward his glove, Dan grinned. His throwing arm had always been a marvel; Pop called it a bazooka. Dan fired toward home plate. That ball whistled back the entire three hundred feet and smacked into the catcher's mitt, seconds ahead of Driscoll. Neal had actually slowed down, obviously incredulous that there was any play at all. Frank Ryan tagged him out, to enthusiastic cheering from the house staff.

After the game, Covington seemed to hang back and was the last to approach Dan.

"That's some arm you have, Marchetti!" Sincerity was written all over him.

"Thanks."

"Did you ever pitch for a semi-pro, or maybe a college, team?"

"Nah, never gave it much thought. By that time my focus was on medicine." He laughed. "I wasn't as smart as you—finding a way to have my cake and eat it too."

Covington nodded and smiled wistfully. "I still miss those days sometimes. Thanks for taking me back a bit." They slapped shoulders and went their separate ways.

Dan watched the others drifting away to their cars, heading to Casey's for the post game brewskies. Tossing his mitt in the air as he began to jog after them, he imagined a life as a professional athlete. No watching folks in pain and dying. Then again, saving lives just might beat out the perfect throw!

CHAPTER SEVEN

Eyes closed blissfully, Linda Ferrante turned her face up into the full force of the shower spray. Pushing her jet-black hair straight back with both hands, she let the water wash any lingering traces of shampoo down her back, her bottom and her legs and then swirl away into the tub drain. The fresh aroma of brewing coffee drifted to her nostrils, and she pictured her antique Joe DiMaggio coffeemaker on the kitchen counter noisily spurting and dripping as it once had done for her paternal grandparents. As she dried her body, a new song began on the radio: Celine Dion's haunting "My Heart Will Go On." This old favorite always brought tears to Linda's eyes, made her melt inside. Coupled with the sensual touch of the thick terrycloth as she rubbed the moisture from her skin, she drifted a moment in romantic memories of James. They'd been exclusive for some five years, lived together for two, breaking off the engagement just last year

There was nothing wrong with James R. Lowengaard III, if you were looking for an aggressive corporate lawyer on the rise, destined for a brilliant future as one of the youngest and most successful litigation attorneys in New York City. Certainly her parents had loved him. He was bright enough and pedigreed—and unquestionably white Anglo-Saxon Protestant.. Romantic and generous, he had impeccable manners, and damn! He was good in bed.

But their goals turned out to be quite different, and certainly she found nothing to love in the streak of professional ruthlessness she saw, his apparent inability to view anything from the perspective of the downtrodden or disadvantaged. He reminded her far too much of her parents, though *he* had no reason to legally change *his* name to lessen the embarrassment of an Italian heritage. Let them become Angela and Dominic Ferrin; she clung to Ferrante, one way of honoring her paternal grandparents, Rosealba and Giuseppe, who'd instilled in her, if not in their son, an enduring pride in their mutual heritage.

Life with James had been easy on many levels: an attentive companion with some shared interests and great sex as often as they could make their schedules mesh. She'd met him while attending Boston University Law School; though at the time her attention was much more focused on her first love, the theater. An active member of two amateur theater groups, she sandwiched her law studies between rehearsals and directing. While she received rave reviews for her performances and innovative directorial work, she barely finished in the top half of her graduating law class, much to the chagrin of her parents and obvious disappointment from James.

In the end, she let them wear her down. She dropped out of her theater groups, declined all offers to participate in creative projects and threw herself completely into law. Focusing the laser beam of her obsessive, compulsive tendencies onto her studies, she passed the bar exam on her first attempt. From there it'd been surprisingly easy to get hired at a good, middle of the road firm close by to the highly competitive New York legal institution where James was a rising star. She'd even been given some interesting cases and had proven herself on every occasion.

Linda had a good life. Yet it wasn't enough There'd always been a bit of an ideological rift between them, but in time newspapers, radio shows and cable TV shows became touch points of conflict until mornings became talk-free zones where nothing more controversial than bagels versus muffins was allowed. Linda knew she could no longer survive within the "locked box" where she'd allowed herself to be put. So she left. Quit her job; said goodbye to New York and to James; and moved to take a position at Glickman, Glickman & Berkowitz outside Pittsburgh.

Now, there was the irony. Finally free to live her life as she really wanted, what was she doing? Practicing law! And had she explored even the possibility of associating with the well-regarded local theater? No.

Linda touched the dark shadow beneath her right eye. At least the theater had taught her how to handle that problem.

Transferring toasted bread to a plate, she sat on one of the stools at her counter bar and spread the first piece of toast with egg salad. As she munched happily and sipped her coffee, Linda gazed around at her little domain. Of course it was tidy. Even before taking her shower, she'd tucked her bedding and swung the Murphy bed up into the wall, revealing the floor-to-ceiling mirror on its underside.

Considering all the big mirrors—out here and in the bathroom—Linda had decided shortly after moving in that this over-garage apartment hadn't been outfitted for anyone with body-image issues. Someone, undoubtedly her widowed, single-parent landlady, Beth Marshall, had done a fine job creating this homey rental space and making it a model of efficiency, comfort and aesthetics.

That underbed mirror made the room look larger by amplifying the natural light from a picture window across the southern exposure. On either side of this expanse, which offered a view across the grassy back yard to the woods in the distance, were two narrower windows with screens that opened to provide both an escape in case of fire and access to Linda's two bird feeders: one for seed-eaters on the left and another for hummingbirds on the right.

Finished with her meal, Linda poured a second cup of coffee and moved to the windows. Too early for her favorite birds, she noticed with satisfaction that both feeders were still well stocked. Down below in the meadow, a family of deer browsed near the salt lick Linda and Beth had set out.

Linda had never met an animal she didn't like. From the moment she could walk, she took every opportunity to get close to any non-human creature—even toddling right up to strange dogs and petting them on the nose. Her horrified parents admonished her about the danger, not to mention the germs, and made every effort to prevent such contacts; Linda, however, was frequently able to outfox them. Her first spoken word was *Dog*, and there was a question mark at the end, because it was clear she was asking for a dog of her own. Both her parents were beyond indifferent to animals. As her mother said, "I can't imagine why anyone would want some dirty, smelly, slobbering creature taking up space, peeing on things and costing the earth in special food and vet bills."

After a while, Linda gave up asking for a dog. But Dom and Angela Ferrin said *no* to every request, and Linda had no cat, no rabbit, no parakeet, no lizard—not even a single goldfish in a bowl.

Longing for the day when she'd be able to have a pet, she cultivated patience only to find all animals were banned in her college housing. Surely moving in with James would at last allow her to fulfill her dream. But no, he said, he was allergic to everything with fur or feathers (she wasn't convinced this was true, but he was careful to never have to prove it); all reptiles were "creepy" and fish as pets were "just plain silly." He'd even tried to talk her out of hanging one hummingbird feeder in an area where casual guests to his palace would never see it, but, on this matter, she put her foot down.

That feeder hung now outside her window, full of nectar and awaiting the first ruby-throats of the day. Again she was struck by the irony. When she moved here, finally free to choose a pet for herself in her new independence, she found it a larger dilemma than she'd imagined. Her work schedule would keep her away from home long hours, and that wasn't fair to a social creature like a dog—or a bird, for that matter. A cat needed less interaction, but she'd been reluctant to go that route because she couldn't forget James sneering, "Well, now you're leaving me, I guess you can get yourself a cat to keep you company like all the other single women living alone in their little apartments."

But then an avid interest of her landlady's son Tyler presented the perfect solution.

Linda turned now and walked across the small room to the north wall. She switched on the aquarium light in the big thirty-gallon tank and said, "Rise and shine, everyone."

Her fish were already active, flitting about their realm of sparkling, bubbled water and lush greenery swaying gently. Some of her many gouramis came to the surface to gulp air, and the little school of lemon tetras flashed about in unison. Linda sprinkled some Nutri-Flake on the surface and bent down to smile at her favorite who could always be found at the bottom of the tank: a red-tailed shark. It was her private lawyer-joke,this "bottom-feeder", and she'd named him Atticus Finch to remind herself there were good lawyers too.

Noting the time with surprise, she hurried to wash up her breakfast dishes, forcing herself to leave them in the drainer rather than drying and putting them away. "No time for dawdling," she admonished aloud.

From her desk just inside the door, near the aquarium, she grabbed up her purse and briefcase. As she turned out the lights at the wall switch, she told the fish, "Bye, now. Have a good day, everyone."

Two hours later, Linda shifted on the hard wooden chair. Beside her, her seventeen-year-old client was turned in his chair, talking in low tones with his parents, who sat just behind the courtroom railing. At least they were *trying* to keep the tones low, but the level was rising, and there were nasty undercurrents, insolence from young Cameron McClure, exasperation and desperation from his parents.

The only other people in the yawning courtroom were a bored-looking bailiff and a court recorder busily text-messaging someone and stifling giggles at the responses she received.

Linda suppressed her own yawn and groaned inwardly, picturing that morass of paperwork, neatly stacked but undisturbed for days now, waiting on her office desk. No doubt new files had been added in her absence. How would she ever advance in this career when her plate was constantly heaped with menial tasks barely worthy of a paralegal?

Noticing the bailiff moving to open the door to the judge's chambers, Linda turned to her client, signaling his immediate attention.

Cameron broke off mid-derisive-sentence, turned away from his parents to face forward. The transformation was striking. Not only clean-scrubbed and well-pressed in his thousand-dollar suit, he now managed to look as contrite and angelic as she'd instructed him to.

He'd been caught at a "huffing" party and in possession of alcohol and another controlled substance. He had a clean record otherwise, though Linda was convinced he'd only been lucky before now—or perhaps money had changed hands somewhere along the line.

At least he hadn't been behind the wheel of a car. With the current charges, Linda was confident she could get him off rather lightly. Another proud day in my career, she thought, looking away from her client.

"All rise," intoned the bailiff. "This proceeding is now in session. The honorable Andre LaCroix presiding."

As Linda and Cameron stood and straightened their clothing, Judge LaCroix swept into the room and took his place on the bench. An old-timer appointed a few decades earlier, he still showed class and breeding. Impeccably groomed and bright of eye, his handsome face appeared much younger than his sixty-plus years.

No shred of emotion showed on that face as he gave his complete attention to Linda's case for Cameron's spotless record, his remorse, the strong support of his parents—whose standing in the community was unimpugned.

"Sixty days' probation," Judge LaCroix said at last. "To be remanded to his parents' custody." He tapped his gavel to end the proceeding

Linda watched the judge leave the room. Turning to her clients, she saw Cameron's parents leaning over the railing trying to give him an awkward embrace; they were quite obviously relieved, and Ms. McClure was fighting tears. However, Cameron grabbed Linda and hugged her to him, saying, "Oh, thank you so much, Miss Ferrante" while his right hand, out of view to all in the courtroom, slid down her waist and hip to squeeze the outside of her thigh.

She pulled back sharply, but without drawing anyone's attention. Staring into those mocking grey eyes, she refused to say, "You're welcome" but, instead gave him a cool smile and pretended at humor: "Glickman, Glickman & Berkowitz—at your service."

His parents laughed nervously, no doubt feeling the aftermath of their stress, and added their fervent thanks, though they were respectful enough to call her *Ms.* Ferrante.

Standing at the top of the courthouse's impressive granite staircase, she took a deep breath. Linda started down the long series of steps. She smiled, thinking of her affable red-tailed shark. Did fish ever get tired of the life they lived, trading their freedom in the wild for a safe, clean environment where every need was met for them? Such an existence had never held much appeal for Linda. But here she was, haven't sent another little creep back to his entitled life and heading out to her mountain of paperwork that seemed to grow the more successful she was. Yes, it had been one of those days.

CHAPTER EIGHT

Returning from a long-delayed and much-needed meal break, Dan found the hall outside the ICU's doors crowded with three generations of what was clearly a single family: two sets of grandparents, the parents and a daughter in her early teens. Apparently no one was interested in the nearby lounge where they could sit comfortably; no one was talking, they all looked to him as if he had information they were seeking. He greeted them with a nod and moved on through the doors, which whispered closed behind him.

Jackie Norris looked up from the central physicians desk.

"Wow!" Dan tried for a light tone. "I go away for just a little while and . . . what's up?"

"Interesting new case for our team. Eleven-year-old, Steven, Steve Bailey, with what looks like meningococcal meningitis."

In the near-month he'd been assigned to ICU, this was the first time they'd had a child admitted. Dan felt himself frown.

"Who gave the clearance for a pediatric case? Whose service is he on?"

"Was Dr. Tischler, but switched to Haye's after the ER tap. Paul's down in the micro-lab now gram-staining the spinal fluid. Oh, guess he's done." She gestured, and Dan turned to see another physician out in the hall, talking to the family: Dr. Paul Haye, Chief of Infectious Diseases at DCH.

A strange, but not unfamiliar, nervousness rose in Dan. He just had to admit it to himself: seriously ill pediatric patients unnerved him. Losing them was the worst. He'd had some experiences early on, and now he did his best to avoid all things pediatric. Most of the seriously ill kids were transferred directly to the Children's Hospital but occasionally they ended up in the ICU for stabilization. This kid must be too ill to move yet. Of course, he'd never shy away from any patient assigned to him but maybe someone else could take Steven Bailey.

Dan watched Haye touch the father's arm out there in the hall, then gesture, encouraging them all toward the waiting room lounge. When they were reluctantly on their way, Haye turned to enter the ICU, approaching with the chart in his hand. He spoke to both Jackie and Dan: "Meningococci confirmed. When you get a chance, go to the lab to look at the gram stain." He turned to Jackie, "Any change while I've been gone?"

She checked the appropriate monitor and shook her head.

To Dan, Haye elaborated, "At last exam he was obtunded . . . completely out-of-it. I'm hoping the I.V. penicillin we started downstairs, two million units every two hours kicks in quick." He handed the chart to Dan. "He's all yours. Go introduce yourself to the family. Remind them they'll all have to take prophylactic rifampin, and I'll get the orders rolling."

Numbly, Dan took the chart, watching the older man rush away to find the appropriate nurses. Dan glanced at Jackie, who shrugged *I-don't-mind-it's-all-yours* kind of an expression before putting her attention on another one of the monitors.

Dan turned and made himself move toward the doors, out into the hall and around the corner into the floor's main waiting room: a spacious lounge shared, as needed, by the CCU and the ICU. It wasn't hard to find the Bailey family; they all sat in one corner as near as they could get to the doorway where news would arrive. Leaping up from the cushy teal-colored furniture as soon as they saw him approaching, they all gathered before him, avid as baby birds waiting for a parent to deliver a fat worm.

Dan introduced himself and nodded to each as they offered their names, but all he retained were the parents', Nora and Nate, and the daughter's, Jessica.

"Dr. Haye told you it is, indeed, meningitis and that you'll be getting a medication to help protect you from getting it too?" At their nods, he continued, hoping he sounded reassuring even while being completely honest. "As you know, this can be an extremely serious illness. But we've started Steven on some very heavy-duty medicine." Dan noticed the gazes slip past him for a moment toward the doorway, and he figured they must be thinking of Dr. Haye beginning the treatment in their absence. "This disease is especially contagious"—the eyes swung quickly back to him—"so we've isolated Steve to protect him and the other patients. Your visits with him will need to be limited, and it's probably best if it's just Mom and Dad." The four grandparents nodded their disappointed understanding. Dan looked at Jessica, who stood slumped and forlorn with both hands jammed in the pockets of her red windbreaker. "Young folks like you have to be particularly careful not to get exposed. Even after you get the preventive meds." She nodded, biting her lip against her tears.

When he figured Haye and the nurses had had time to get Steve settled, Dan said, "I'm going to go do my exam now. Mom, Dad, would you like to go too?" He rose, quickly followed by Nora and Nate. "The rest of you make yourselves comfortable. This won't be a quick fix."

Steve's parents, gripping each other's hands, followed Dan back around the corner and through the ICU doors; faces haggard with worry made them look older than the mid-thirties he judged them to be.

Just outside Steve Bailey's room, which was the closest to the entrance, stood a cabinet with drawers containing folded gowns and others holding masks and latex gloves.

Dan removed his stethoscope and put it in the top drawer, then demonstrated how to properly suit up as they all would have to do each time before entering Steve's room. First he cleaned his hands with sanitizing gel from a wall dispenser. He shook out one of the gowns, which, unlike a patient's Johnny coat, had loose-fitting long sleeves with elastic that gripped tightly at the wrists. He pushed his arms through and then tied the ties in back of his neck. He pulled on the gloves and donned a mask, but uncovered his mouth to tell the Baileys, "Just before you leave Steve's room, you'll remove these things. Gowns go in the laundry bag . . . masks and gloves in the medical waste bin. And hit the sanitizing gel out here. Okay?"

He left them under the watchful eye of Wyndolyn Hibbert, saying, "Nurse Wynnie will help you both. I'm gonna go on in and start my exam." He pulled his mask into place.

"Of course," Nora said. "Don't let us slow you down."

When the little room's door had swished shut behind him, Dan picked up the yellow plastic stethoscope on the bedside table and regarded his newest patient. Comatose, completely out-of-it, as Dr. Haye had said earlier. The boy was of average size for his eleven years, of very fair complexion beneath the heat of fever and the disease's characteristic rash. Wispy, pale blond hair stuck out in all directions, wildly rumpled after his encounters with various pillows.

As if to prove this point, as soon as Dan started his exam, the boy's head began to roll back-and-forth, further disarraying the hair. As his limbs thrashed briefly under his covers, Steve mumbled incoherently and then came to rest again without ever opening his eyes.

Dan pulled aside the bedding and Johnny coat so he could see the entire length of the boy. The rash covered most of the frail and hairless form. Dan had somehow forgotten just how innocent a prepubescent body could look. Steve's parents were both in the room by now, and Dan watched their eyes widen above their masks as they saw how the rash was progressing. He let the hospital gown fall back across the boy's torso, leaving the legs exposed, and fished a pen from his pocket underneath his own gown. The Baileys stared, mesmerized, as he drew a box around one area of lesions on Steve's right thigh.

"This will help me gauge the progression or regression of the illness," he explained gently. "Over the next hours, we'll be able to count whether we have more or fewer spots in the box." The parents obviously heard him but didn't look up. They fixed their stares on the patch of reddened blotches as if they would, at any moment, see them change before their eyes.

Dan checked the I.V. delivering high-dose penicillin into the boy's arm and felt pretty powerless. It didn't help to have Nora Bailey ask, "What now?" as if she could read his thoughts . . . and worries.

Dan stifled a sigh. "All we can do at the moment is support Steve's systems until the penicillin has time to wipe out the . . . uh . . .bugs." What he didn't say out loud was unfortunately, those organisms had a head start.

Again as if reading his mind, Nora said, "If only we'd brought him in as soon as he mentioned a headache and we noticed he was feverish. . . ." She was clearly the talker of the pair. Her husband stood just staring down at his son, who moved restlessly again, muttering unintelligible phrases. The man looked completely overwhelmed.

Dan reached to squeeze Nora's shoulder comfortingly. "Kids get fevers. Kids have headaches. Their parents can't run them to the ER for every little thing."

Nora's eyes welled as she whispered, "Thank you,. I just wish. . . ."

Dan nodded and completed his examination. "You two can stay in here with him a little while longer. Nurse Wynnie will let you know. And you can check back during the night, but remember to suit up each time." Dan removed the yellow plastic stethoscope, replacing it on the table, and began to shed his gown, gloves and mask, putting them in the proper receptacles by the door. "I'll be on-call all night, so feel free to ask me any questions you may have, okay?"

They nodded numbly and thanked him again as he slipped outside the isolation room. As he cleaned his hands with sanitizing gel, he saw Nurse Wynnie look his way, and he waved her over. He indicated the Bailey room with a nod of his head. "You'll keep a close eye on all of them, right?" As if he had to ask; this was Wyndolyn Hibbert.

She smiled sympathetically. "No-o-o problem, Dr. Dan. Mebbe you tek some rest now, eh?"

"Not yet. Haven't checked on my others for a bit. Ms. Walsh's fever come down? Good. Listen, the Bailey boy? Be sure to call me with any change whatsoever. No matter where I am, okay?"

This time she gave his shoulder a motherly pat. "All fruits ripe, Dr. Dan." He'd learned that meant *Everything's good.* "Me tink dat boy gwina be jus' fine."

"From your mouth to God's ear!" he said fervently and earned a radiant smile from her. He asked, "Did Dr. Haye write the family scripts for Rifampin?"

"'I'm did, but di gran'pa, 'im say, 'None us leavin' here t'go filla 'scription inna middle di night. Na while Steve so sick.' So Doct'r, 'im 'range fa meds be sent up from wi own hospit'l pharm'cy."

"Good."

She nodded. "Mi mek sure dey all tek it. Dey been askin' fa report. . . ."

"No-o-o problem," he echoed back her Jamaican motto, eliciting another smile. "I can take care of that." Dan headed for the lounge, where he found Steve's four grandparents quietly talking together—they looked up expectantly—and the sister, Jessica, sitting away from the others, trying to hide that she was crying. He gave a brief report on Steve's condition to the grandparents, making sure his voice was just loud enough for Jessica to hear, accepted thanks and handshakes, and then asked, "You're all clear on how important it is to take the Rifampin when it arrives? It's an oral medication, not a shot, and in case no one else mentioned this, don't be alarmed when your urine and tears turn orange. It's a normal—and a temporary—side effect. Anyone wear contact lenses?"

All those eyes looking at him were round as owls' now. "Nora does," someone said.

"Well, have her remove them or they'll be ruined by the orange stain. That's it for now; get what rest you can, and we'll keep you informed."

Some hours later, Dan's beeper dragged him from sleep: *"Beep, beep, beep . . .* Dr. Marchetti, ICU Medical—stat; ICU Medical—stat!" *So much for a quick catnap.* He'd spent most of the night tending to young Steve, looking in on him every half hour to monitor his urine output, listen to his heart and lungs, check his rhythm and vital signs. At times the boy was awake but still incoherent and babbling nonsense; his fever hovered around 102.

All the while, his family had maintained its vigil. Only the parents entered the room once an hour, sitting and holding his hand at bedside. When they weren't in the room, they came frequently to look in on Steve through his glass door.

Inside the ICU, Wynnie intercepted him before he got too near Steve's parents, who anxiously awaited him. "Blood pressuh tek a lit'le drop," she reported. "Sev'ty systolic. Urine ou'put drop ta 40 cc's last hour."

He gowned up quickly. Examining the unconscious boy and finding the blood pressure had dropped even more, Dan increased the normal saline running into the boy's vein. Mentally, Dan made a quick review of all the pediatric dosages for medicines he had looked up in the call room that might be needed should the boy's heart rhythm deteriorate . . . or stop.

Dan de-gowned and went out to reassure the parents.

At least he tried. They nodded that they understood, but as Dan massaged the sanitizing gel into his hands, he could see they were hovering near the edge. Dan knew there was a mental, maybe psychological, line most humans reach at some point in their lives. A place where reality becomes too painful, maybe unbearable, and they just "lose it."

"Go on in," he urged them. "If you check that box I drew on his leg, you'll see there aren't quite as many spots in it—a good sign." He saw the sudden hope in their eyes, almost as painful to see as the terror. Nora's eyes filled with tears as she thanked him yet again.

Off to the side, a bit away from the ICU's main traffic patterns, Dan lowered himself wearily onto a handy reclining chair, pushing all the way back into the soft tan leather until the angle was comfortable enough to catch a nap. He closed his eyes. "Hey, Dante," a voice said. "Need coffee?"

His eyes snapped open. *Nikki.* How could she look so good at this ungodly hour?

"I had to bring down some paperwork for Diane's new patient."

"From Peds?" Dan managed.

"Yeah. Twelve-year-old girl in with asthma. Her appendix perforated, so now she's a surgical case with some complications, and you guys get her."

"She's Diane's?" At least he was talking now.

Nikki nodded and brushed a wave of auburn hair back from her face. "So, do you want some?" When he began to stammer in surprise, she laughed and clarified, "Coffee. The machine on this floor's broken. My shift's over, so I volunteered to make a run to the cafeteria. Maybe pick up some snacks."

"Oh, coffee." The last thing he needed. "Sure. Thanks."

"Dash of cream and one sugar, if I remember correctly."

Dan felt his face flush at this reference to their one "morning after" breakfast nearly a month ago. "Yeah. Say, I'm sorry I never called you—"

She gestured dismissively. "S'okay. Cheryl told me she told you I was married. Sorry I didn't tell you myself, but I couldn't risk losing my chance to be with you. And I was right. If you'd known, nothing would've happened, right?"

When Dan nodded, Nikki smiled wistfully. "Well, sorry for the lack of honesty . . ." her smoky green eyes stared straight into his, unabashed, "but it was worth it." Then she turned away, calling back brightly, "I'll get that coffee now."

He watched her go. She was even trimmer than she'd been when he last saw her, and she really knew how to move. Amazing how sexy she could make a set of hospital-green scrubs look. Well, there'd be no sleeping now, Dan thought as he moved back towards Steve's room.

Completely suited up inside the room, Dan used the yellow stethoscope to listen to Steve's lungs. At the bedside, he gently raised the sleeping boy's upper torso, supporting Steve's weight as he applied the chest piece to the rash-mottled back. Steve's head dropped softly against Dan's chest, and the sensation of this living creature's face against him brought tears to Dan's eyes. The quietness of the ICU, broken only occasionally by the distant sounds of mechanical ventilators, lent a surreal quality to the moment.

Wynnie poked her head in to see if he needed anything and smiled at what she saw. "You gonna mek a gret daddy som'day, Dr. Dan."

Will I? At that moment the fragile frame Dan was cradling started to slip from his grasp. Looking down, he saw his patient's body stiffen; the eyes were open but rolled back, the pupils hidden beneath the lids. *Tonic clonic seizure.* "Wynnie!" he cried. "Dilantin, one gram load—now!"

She whirled and rushed away toward the med room. As his patient's muscles continued to violently contract and then relax to contract again, Dan held Steve's head to one side, ensuring any secretions from the boy's mouth would drain onto the pillow instead of into his lungs. Glancing up to check on Wynnie's progress, Dan saw the horrified faces of the Bailey family, all the adults, peering in through the glass. They hastily moved aside as Nurse Wynnie raced back, suited up and rushed into Steve's room with the bag of fluid medication. She moved past Dan to the I.V. stand and expertly connected the bag to the IVAC machine that would administer the drug at the proper speed. Dilantin could lower a patient's blood pressure to critical levels if given too quickly. After just a few minutes, Dan felt the seizure activity lessen in Steve's body and then cease altogether.

Though not unexpected, the seizure was worrisome. Convinced it was secondary to the meningitis itself, Dan still proceeded to order all the lab work needed to eliminate other causes, such as an electrolyte abnormality. He examined Steve thoroughly again, assuring himself that there was no reason to believe the boy had suffered a brain hemorrhage.

At last Dan emerged from the room, thankful that another potential disaster had been averted. "He's stopped seizing," Dan told the waiting Baileys. "Give me a minute . . . ?"

They nodded wordlessly, but their widened eyes fixed on him as if they'd never look away. Moving to the physicians desk, he dropped his weary body into the chair and scribbled quick notes in his patient's chart before returning to the family. Dan led them all back into the lounge where they could sit comfortably, though not a one of them was relaxing.

Feeling those seven pairs of eyes burrowing into him, he began, "We gave Steve a very effective seizure medication, Dilantin, which should prevent further episodes. If they do recur, we have other medicines at our disposal."

"What caused the seizure?" asked Nora Bailey.

"I'm pretty certain it was a result of the infection itself, though I've ordered some blood work to eliminate other causes. We still just have to wait out this disease. Everything that needs to be done is being done."

She blurted, "Is . . . is there any chance he's . . . suffered . . . brain damage?" She nervously ran her fingers through that wispy, pale-golden hair, unknowingly making it spike from her head almost like her son's; she was probably equally unaware her mascara was smeared behind the glasses she now wore so her contacts could avoid rifampin staining.

Dan found himself momentarily unnerved by her astute and appropriate question about a possibility he'd already considered. Still committed to reassuring the Baileys without downplaying the facts, he answered, "It's impossible to say for sure just yet. Let's hope not."

She bit her lip but nodded, and he placed his hand on her shoulder, facing the entire family. You have my word I won't keep anything from you." He hesitated, but then added, "I suppose it doesn't have to be said, but I want nothing more than to see that boy open his eyes and give each of you a big hug." He was surprised to hear his own voice. "Steve is always on my mind."

"Thank you." They all seemed to say it at once. Nora added, "The entire staff has been wonderful to us. The nurses are remarkable. Why Nurse Nikki even came to see him while you were gone earlier."

"Nikki?" Dan repeated.

Nora nodded. "She was Steve's nurse up in Pediatrics when he was in last year for an asthma attack. Steve adored her. She came down about another transferred patient, but she said she was off-duty and offered to keep him company while we were getting our medication. It was comforting to come back and see her sitting in there, all gowned up and holding his hand, humming a little song."

Dan murmured something about DCH having the best nurses in the state and then retreated to that tucked-away recliner to gather his thoughts and feelings. Pushing Nikki from his mind to focus on Steve, he lay back with one arm thrown across his eyes to hide the moisture there. How he wanted to see this boy come around, laugh and act like any other child, live a full and normal life. He felt ill prepared to witness the death of a person so young.

"Sorry it took so long," someone said. *Nikki.* He struggled to bring the recliner to a more upright position and reached to take the Styrofoam cup she held in one hand. "Had to wait for a new pot so I could bring fresh." He noticed a cafeteria cart across the room, surrounded by eager staff, and some Baileys, pouring cups from a restaurant-style pot and adding the cream or sugar she'd also provided. There seemed to be something else they were divvying up. . . . "I waited a little longer cuz I thought you guys might like some fresh pizza too."

The scent hit his nostrils then, and he was salivating before he even focused on the huge slice of pepperoni-mushroom on the paper plate she held out to him.

He set aside the coffee on the wide arm of the recliner. "Wow, thanks." Suddenly ravenous, he took a huge bite.

"Careful," she warned.

Too late. The cheese was still so hot it burned his tongue, but he really didn't care; it was the best pizza he'd ever tasted from the hospital cafeteria. When he'd munched enough to be able to speak without breaking all the rules of etiquette, he told her,

"That was really great of you. Especially to hang around after you were done for the day."

"Well," Nikki said quietly, "there's not much for me to go home to these days."

Dan stopped chewing, almost choked on the bit he was swallowing.

Nikki picked up Dan's coffee and held it as she sat herself down on the recliner arm. She was very close to him, but gone was all the flirtation and coyness. "Look, Dante. I'm sorry I didn't tell you the truth. And I totally get that you don't want to be involved with someone married." She smiled, but it looked sad. "In fact, I *like* that about you. And am I right you might be interested if I were divorced?"

"Definitely."

"Well, okay then. I don't really know where my marriage is going, so who knows about the future. . .? But in the meantime, I'm hoping we can be friends. The way you're friends with Cheryl and Diane, y'know? I promise not to involve you in anything about Matt, but most of us can use friends to talk to about the stuff we have to deal with in this job."

"Definitely," he said again.

"In fact, you look like you could use a listener tonight. I hear Steve seized while I was gone. . .?"

"Yeah, but he's resting okay now." Dan set aside the empty paper plate and accepted the coffee from her, took a long, satisfying drink. "I just don't know how you do it. All those sick kids, and they don't all make it."

"Not nearly enough of them. . . . You're thinking about this, and you haven't been up to peds yet."

"Don't plan to! I had my fill already. Senior elective in pediatrics in medical school."

"Tell me."

Dan closed his eyes for a long moment, staring back into the past. Then he looked right into her eyes. "Worst night of my life. I lost two teenagers in a matter of hours. One from cystic fibrosis and the other from leukemia." She didn't speak, but her eyes never left his as she reached to squeeze his upper arm, not the touch or gaze of a lover, but of a friend.

He continued. "Of course, I remember the kids, but it's their parents' faces I can't get out of my mind. I seem to have this image etched indelibly: those haunted expressions as they listened to me answer questions about their sons' deaths. I remember standing in an otherwise-empty waiting room. Behind them I can still see the wall clock marking midnight and rain sliding down the dark windowpane."

"Some of those images never do leave you," Nikki murmured. "Believe me, I know. . . ."

As he hesitated, she signaled him to go on.

"Well, Adam had cystic fibrosis. More kids are surviving longer, and into adulthood these days. But Adam would never have made it as long as he did without the efforts of his mother. Everything fell on her, since his dad was an officer in a Navy submarine and away from home extended periods of time—though he got leave to be there for Adam's last days. Anyway, I saw his mom each day, working with the nurses, taking on much of the treatment herself. And every single day, I watched her have to pummel her son's body .... "he paused," to clear secretions." He sighed. "There's a way mothers touch their children, embrace them." My own mom's like that, pure love, but Adam's mom ..."his voice raspy, trailed off.

Nikki nodded. "Most people love their kids and will do what they can to help them when they're ill, but some parents are even more special that way."

Fleetingly, Dan registered surprise at her view that *most* parents loved their kids. But he went on with his story. "Dylan's parents were special the same way. He had leukemia, and he was hospitalized the whole time I was in peds. Sometimes I'd see him running around the halls or the nurse's station like any other thirteen-year-old. And then he'd quickly succumb to infection, spiking fevers suddenly to 105 and barely surviving to the next day. "Nikki motioned him to continue. "Before he got sick he'd been a very active kid, especially interested in the outdoors and scouting; even little overnight campouts at a nearby state park.

They made the most of every second they had when he wasn't in the hospital."

Nikki prompted, "So both Dylan and Adam died on the same night?"

"Yeah." Dan sighed again. "That was enough for me. Guess I thought I could spare myself that headache by not going into pediatrics." He studied her a moment as if her face could reveal a secret. "How *do* you do it? You're peds all the time."

"Nurses like helping people get well. Me, I like helping the most helpless to feel better."

"But I can't imagine how many you have to watch who never get better. All those young lives cut short."

"It's hard," she conceded and gave a self-deprecating laugh. "I want to save them all. But I can't. And sooner or later, no matter what part of medicine you're in, everyone has to face the death of a person too young. It's inevitable. So you're actually ahead of the curve."

He grimaced at this distinction. "I guess. I just wish. . . ."

Nikki covered his hand with her own. "Me too. We just have to do what we can for those we *can* help. And every person, child or adult, is important . . . like every single grain of sand." "Oh, like in that poem?"

"Poem?"

"Never mind. I think I'm starting to lose it."

"Uh-huh, you're looking pretty tired. Coffee only works so long." She stood, reading the wall clock. "God, can it really be three a.m.? I better go. Let you get some sleep." Nikki pointed out, "Less noise in the on-call room."

"Maybe later. I wanna be right here if something else changes with Steve." He yawned, then blushed with embarrassment. "Sorry!"

Nikki smiled. "I rest my case." She looked even wearier now than she had earlier. Or maybe it was just thinking about going home. "Take care, Dante. See you around sometime."

He watched her cross to the ICU doors. *Just friends, now,* he reminded himself. Didn't mean he couldn't appreciate having another good listener in his life. It was an hour later but it seemed like seconds when he heard "Dr. Dan . . . hey, Dr. Dan. . . ." Wynnie Hibbert's sweet intonations called him back to consciousness.

He mumbled something, and she said, "Is'a Steve Bailey."

Blinking, Dan gazed up at Wynnie standing over him. He pushed himself to a sitting position on the recliner and steeled himself for the answer to his next question: "What's up?"

"'Im awek, talkin' bout breakfas'."

"No shit?" Dan was off in a flash toward the isolation room and gowned up in record time. Steve was sitting up in bed, rather glassy-eyed and gloriously disheveled but alive and awake and able to speak. "Nurse Wynnie said . . . are you Dr. Dan?"

"Yes, I am," he answered, sitting down on the edge of the bed. Dan placed his hands on the boy's shoulders. "Hey, buddy," Dan whispered around the sudden knot in his throat. "How *are* you?"

"I'm hungry," the raspy voice began. Then another thought, "Is Mom here?"

"Yeah, champ, your whole family's here. I'll go get them, but first I need to check you out a little. Okay?"

Dan examined him thoroughly, as he had so many times through the night. Convinced that his young patient was vastly improved and had turned the corner, Dan said, "You're doing great, Steve. I'm gonna go get your parents."

Outside the room, after giving Wynnie orders for the boy's meal, Dan eagerly headed to the lounge where he found all the Baileys. A few were asleep, in chairs or slumped against each other on the couches. Nora, of course, was awake, sitting sandwiched between her sleeping husband and daughter, both leaning heavily on her, and she spoke as soon as she saw Dan enter the room. "There's news?" Though her voice was low, everyone else was immediately awake, rising to approach him.

"Steve's awake and looking very good. Asking for Rice Krispies, though I think that'll have to wait a day or two."

They erupted with laughter and joyful tears, hugging each other as they released the tension that had mounted over long hours of fear, hope, despair and faith. Wet-eyed Jessica came and touched his sleeve, smiled up at him shyly. "Thank you for saving my brother."

Then everyone was thanking him, shaking his hand, slapping his back; he felt himself choking up and asked quickly, "Mom and Dad, want to go in and see Steve?"

This time it was Dad who spoke first, "Absolutely!" His wife had already hurried out to be with her boy.

Still laughing and talking excitedly, they all followed Dan out into the hallway. "Only Mom and Dad in the room for now," he told them. "Grandparents can look in the door the way you have before."

"What about me?" Jessica, hands back in her jacket pockets, stood looking lost and lonely as the rest of her family surged through the ICU doors.

Dan leaned down closer to her height. "I'm sorry, but I think it's safer for you if you wait a few days."

She nodded her understanding, but tears came again to her eyes, and she chewed her lip. Casting a glance toward her elders, all busy inside trying to help Nora and Nate gown up but getting in each other's way, Jessica drew something from her left-hand pocket and held it out to Dan. "Could you give this to Steve, please? Tell him I'm, like, really, really sorry I hid it?"

"Sure." Dan took the little stuffed bulldog and slipped it into his own pocket until he could find the proper moment alone with Steve. Dan winked at Jessica and grinned. "I'd be mortified to tell you how I tormented *my* little brother!"

She smiled with gratitude and headed resolutely back toward the lounge.

Dan turned and entered the ICU, watching the Baileys with pleasure. Stevie would be around for a long time. Dan looked through the glass and began to tell the nearest grandparent, "I'll be back to check on him again soon" when Nora Bailey signaled for his attention. She came quickly to the door and signaled to her mom, who suddenly grabbed Dan and gave him a big hug. "That's from all of us, Thank you, Doctor, so very much. From the bottom of all our hearts."

Tears began to run down Dan's cheeks causing Nurse Winnie to say 'Dere he go agin!" He quickly excused himself, hurrying from the ICU and into the nearest elevator. Once inside with the doors closed, he didn't push any buttons. He just let himself cry. He'd broken down the night Adam and Dylan died, but this was like no crying he'd ever done before. His weary body surged with pride and exhilaration and feelings he could never describe in words. He'd saved lives before, but this was different, this was a kid.

When he'd pulled himself together, Dan left the elevator and managed to slip unnoticed back to the consoles where he noted Steve's progress before slipping back down the hall to the on-call room where he hoped to catch some z's before the next crisis.

CHAPTER NINE

Alex Cole tried not to sound annoyed. "What time did Ballard's secretary say he'd be rounding this week?" He and Dave Levine were just two of the interns milling around the hallway outside the ICU, waiting for the Chairman of Medicine to arrive. Alex watched Dan Marchetti rush in. Dan made eye contact, waved and started toward them. But then Diane Werner distracted Dan, and he stopped to talk to her, apparently forgetting all about his other friends. Oblivious to it all, Dave still stared off into space with that look people get when they're reviewing details they've memorized.

Alex scowled. Was *everyone* going to ignore him today? "What time?" he repeated, more sharply.

Dave blinked at him as if coming back to the planet, though he seemed to've absorbed the question by osmosis. "Rounding? Secretary said ten a.m. sharp."

Alex's watch read 10:10. He snorted. "Ballard's never been on time yet."

Dave shrugged, at the same time stifling a yawn and drumming his fingers on the chart he held, a classic sign of too little sleep and too much coffee. "It'll be worth the wait, no matter what time he shows."

Alex had to agree. The Chief dropped pearls all the time. He can be a little long-winded sometimes, but he seems to know everything.

As if on cue, the elevator doors opened, and Dr. Hugh Ballard stepped out. It was hard to imagine a chairman looking any more distinguished. A tall, solidly built man, Ballard's thick hair was as snowy white as his impeccably pressed coat. Just above the Chairman of Medicine name badge, his lapel pin, commemorating his designation as a Master in the American College of Physicians, gleamed like a little golden sun. From his left-hand coat pocket protruded the earpieces of his prized Littman stethoscope, and his hand went there often in an unconsciously protective gesture.

Bright blue eyes peered at them all from behind wire-rimmed glasses, and he beamed as if nothing could please him more than to see these fine interns before him.

"Good morning! We'll be a little short today." Ballard winked. "Important meeting, I'm afraid." He made it sound as if he'd much rather be there with them. Alex saw some of those gathered relax a little as if relieved. Well, Ballard *did* have a penchant for delving quite deeply into the history of medicine while exploring cases. Personally, Alex enjoyed that, but it prolonged rounds that'd already started late, and more than once, Alex had heard senior residents mutter under their breath in frustration. But if Ballard heard it, he never let on, and it certainly didn't dissuade him. "Where shall we begin?"

Alex made sure he spoke first. "Right here in ICU: Arthur Kresky." He got a little thrill when Ballard looked directly at him and nodded. The group assembled attentively around their chairman; he was The Man and everyone knew it.

Alex had pretty much memorized the chart and began with confidence. "Sixty-two-year-old white male presented twenty-four hours ago with chest pressure with an acute inferior wall myocardial infarction. He's Q-ed out in two, three and AVF, received thrombolytics, beta blockers." Though he stared at some invisible point above Alex's head, Ballard listened carefully, nodding and scratching the side of his right cheek, a gesture familiar to all who had ever watched him concentrate. "Did well until this morning," Alex continued. "Became tachypneic, cyanotic; PO_2 in the forties on 100 percent rebreather, intubated; lungs clear; chest x-ray essentially normal; no left-ventricular failure."

Ballard dropped his gaze, and Alex found those clear, blue eyes riveted directly on himself, but the Chief said nothing. Alex soldiered on, trying desperately to read Ballard's face for a sign of approval. "VQ scan was low probability for a pulmonary embolus." Alex stopped talking and shrugged his shoulders. The case remained a mystery.

"What's his blood pressure doing, Alex?"

"Sir, BP dropped to eighty systolic during the night. They presumed it was a right ventricular infarct with right-sided failure. Neck veins were distended. They gave normal saline, and the pressure came up."

Ballard just shook his head. "Let's go examine the patient." He turned abruptly and led the way into Arthur Kresky's room. A thin, balding man lay unconscious, his breathing supported by a ventilator. Alex remembered from the social history that Kresky was a carpenter with a decades-long smoking habit. The only sounds in the room were those of shuffling feet as the house staff crowded in and of the rhythmic compression of the machine breathing for the patient.

Ballard pulled that stethoscope from his pocket and engaged it while placing his right hand on Kresky's chest wall. The residents studied their chief's every move, from how he listened to the patient's lungs to his examination of nail beds, for any clue, any key that would unlock the diagnostic box of unknowns. Why was this patient finding it impossible to oxygenate his blood? All the obvious causes had been ruled out.

Ballard removed his stethoscope and returned it to his left coat pocket, signaling he'd made his diagnosis.

Ballard walked thoughtfully back out to the central area and leaned a bit against the physicians desk, arms folded across his chest as he waited for everyone else to catch up with him. "Can only be one thing, ladies and gentlemen."

He looked again to Alex, eyebrows slightly raised in question. Alex glanced away from that blue stare. At least all the other faces around him were as blank as his own.

"Any other thoughts to help Alex out?" Ballard slowly surveyed the group. "Dan?"

Dan stood at attention. "A shunt, sir?" Dan whispered in a barely audible voice.

"Speak up, son, some of my senses are fading rapidly."

"A shunt."

Ballard listened, expressionless. "What kind?"

"Right to left, sir."

"Why?"

"Reverse flow through . . . some kind of septal defect." Dan paused a split second, and Alex could see something flicker across his friend's face as the last piece fell into place. "Patent foramen ovale, to be sure."

Ballard was smiling now, pleased as any teacher with a quick pupil. "What test will we need to confirm the diagnosis, group?"

"A 2-D echo, sir," Alex blurted, anxious to regain lost ground.

"Plain 2-D?"

"I suppose."

Dan offered, "We can do an agitated saline test right before we shoot the echo. The bubbles will be seen crossing the foramen."

Alex squeezed his hands till he felt the nails bite into his palms, struggling to keep his face blank as the Chief's eyes scanned the group. "Good...."

Ballard's beeper signaled, and he checked out the message. "That's my meeting, ladies and gentlemen. We'll pick up again next week. Alex, go ahead and schedule the procedures Dan suggested for Mr. Kresky."

As he exited, Ballard gave Marchetti a playful pat on the shoulder, in clear view of the entire group. If that bothered anyone else, Alex couldn't tell; nobody let it show, but certainly he couldn't be the only one feeling envious. "He's always showing us up," Alex muttered to Dave. "Always scoring points at our expense."

Again that baffled look on Dave's face. "Who?"

"Marchetti, who else?"

Dave returned to his charting. "He's smart; can he help that?"

"Smart, my ass," Alex bristled. "Lucky, that's what he is, with the cunning of a fox. Wait till he screws up."

Dave gazed at him as if he'd said blood was green. "Isn't he your friend . . . your neighbor? Don't you guys hang out?"

Snorting, Alex gestured. "Sure. He's always up for some free wine or beer. Acts so nice with everyone. "Trying to get ahad, trying to get ahead, trying to get ahead."

Dave just stared at him, and then Alex realized Diane Werner was also within earshot. He saw the two of them exchange a glance. "You'll see," Alex predicted. "Everyone's got a dark side. Marchetti's no different." He slapped the counter with the file he was holding and began to move. He marched off, aware they were still staring after him with looks of wonderment on their faces—but all the while insisting to himself that he really didn't care what they thought.

Down the hall, Vinny Orlander watched as one of the ICU nurses handed a laryngoscope to anesthesiologist Bodhi Malhotra, then moved away to adjust the I.V. meds for the patient lying supine before them.

Vinny reached out impulsively. "Dr. Malhotra? Please can I intubate her? I've watched it done a million times."

The attending looked down at their patient, a Korean woman in her seventies with pneumonia and some emphysema. Ms. Yoon drifted in and out of consciousness as her body struggled to oxygenate itself. "I'm sorry, Vinny. You're not even an intern. I can't. . . ." He hadn't been in the States all that many years, but already his accent was barely noticeable. His large, dark eyes were mournful as a disappointed hound's.

"Aw, come on, Doc," Vinny protested. "Didn't you ever wanna learn new stuff . . . maybe something a little above what others thought you could do?"

Malhotra grinned then, an impish light banishing that hound-dog expression, likely remembering some of the breaks, even shortcuts, he'd been given when he was knocking at the doors of opportunity. "Okay. One time only; that's it."

Vinny beamed, quickly grabbing the laryngoscope before Malhotra could change his mind, and moved into place at the patient's head, looking down toward her feet. There were two more ICU nurses in the room now, and though they all busied themselves checking on Ms. Yoon's lines, meds and urine output, he knew they were well aware of what he was doing. They wouldn't protest; it was Dr. Malhotra's responsibility. But they were sure paying attention.

How many times had he fantasized this . . . practiced it in his mind? Now it was coming true! With his heart galloping, Vinny positioned the woman's head, extending her neck to the proper angle. Gently, he slid the blade of the L-shaped instrument into her throat and let it pin the tongue back to expose the larynx. "I see the vocal cords!" His voice was low but excited.

"Good, good. . . ."

Though Malhotra's voice sounded distracted and bored, Vinny didn't let that faze him. Peering through the scope, he guided the endotracheal tube through the opening between the cords and into the trachea. *Perfect!* "I'm in! I'm in!" he shouted, unable to control his exhilaration.

Malhotra grinned indulgently, like a parent amused by a child's enthusiasm at stacking his blocks. "Very good . . . very good job."

He could try to sound more sincere! How many interns had he seen struggle with that task? Sometimes they actually failed and had to pass it off to an attending to avoid losing the patient.

Vinny got Ms. Yoon hooked up to the ventilator and watched as her coloring improved with the increased level of oxygen in her blood. Vinny's eyes searched for the faces of the nurses, looking for those reviews, but all three continued their work as if nothing special had transpired. Nothing special at all. By no one special at all.

A few hours later, Vinny followed Alex Cole from the room of a 53-year-old female patient newly admitted with pulmonary complications of recent surgery. Anticipating there would be orders, Vinny took out one of the small cards he carried in his lab coat pocket and poised his pen over it.

"She'll need an IMV of 12 and total volume of 700," Dr. Cole told him.

"Got it," Vinny answered, noting the numbers. The cards were a big help in recalling salient points from patients' charts. He kept hoping Dr. Cole, or *anyone*, would notice how efficient he was . . . how meticulous. But no luck so far. And it certainly wasn't going to happen right now.

He might as well be invisible, Vinny thought, pen still poised ready for any further notes. They'd reached the physicians desk, and Dr. Cole had already scribbled a quick progress note and order into the patient's chart. But then the chart underneath seemed to grab his attention, and he flipped it open. Vinny craned his neck to read the name: *Kresky, Arthur.* No one he knew about.

"Damnedest thing I ever saw," Cole muttered under his breath, as if he'd forgotten Vinny was even there.

"What was?"

"Huh?" Cole said distantly, still staring at Kresky's chart.

"What was the damnedest thing?" Vinny's jaw clenched as he did his best to keep a pleasant tone.

"Oh." Alex Cole blinked as if breaking free of a trance. "The agitated saline test."

"Come again?"

"My patient Kresky has a patent foramen ovale—a hole between his right atrium and his left atrium. It would've been there since birth but never closed on its own like it should have."

Vinny nodded, encouraging the intern to keep talking, including him in this discussion of a case.

"Up till now," Cole continued, "it'd posed no problem. But his heart attack led to failure on the right side of his heart; the pressure increased; and the blood flowed then from the right atrium to the left, bypassing the lungs." He looked again at the chart, studying the numbers.

"The test agitated something?"

"Oh, yeah! We put some air bubbles into his I.V. line and, with help from the echocardiogram, we watched them cross the atrium through the hole. Neat trick; diagnosis made." Cole's face broke into a huge smile.

"That was your idea—to do that test?" Vinny asked, wanting to congratulate him.

Immediately, though, Alex Cole's smile vanished behind a dark scowl.

Vinny was quick to say, "Sorry if I. . . ." It wasn't good to offend a doctor, even a first-year intern.

"No, it wasn't me. It was Dan. He seems to figure out everything."

Vinny watched the man catch himself, perhaps remembering, as Vinny did, one of the first bits of hospital lore you learn: *If someone passes gas on the tenth floor, within an instant, everyone on the first floor will know about it.*

"I would give anything to know as much as you do," Vinny offered, quite sincerely.

Still staring at Kresky's chart, Cole murmured, "Sometimes no matter how much you know, it just isn't enough."

"But you got to keep trying. I intubated my first patient today."

"Umm?" It was barely a response, much less any show of interest; he just kept scowling at the Kresky chart.

"Yeah, Malhotra let me." No reaction at all. "I got it first time. Perfect!"

Dr. Cole grunted some kind of a reply, but never even glanced at him. Vinny watched the intern toss down the Kresky chart and stalk away without one word of farewell. Vinny watched him go, fantasizing a time when the great Dr. Cole lay on a table in front of him as Vinny slowly shut down the oxygen flowing into his paralyzed lungs.

That evening, back home in his apartment at Woodside, Alex Cole focused on the tasks he needed to take care of before finally turning in for the night: *Brush teeth, rinse and store contact lenses, synch palm pilot.*

He sank down on his couch across from the big-screen TV and Bose sound system, but he ignored all that fancy equipment. In fact, he rarely used any of it except when he had visitors, which almost always meant his hall neighbor Dan Marchetti. He had bought it from a friend-of-a-friend back home in New York, at far below market value. Alex was pretty sure it was hot, but he tried not to think about that. It served his purpose: elevating the status of his humble digs, furnished very similarly to Dan's. Made it look like he had a little money and *could* get a nicer apartment if he chose to. After all, he was going to be a successful doctor in a few years. Might as well start acting the part.

That's why he leased the BMW. It was a coupla years old but in great shape and impressed the hell out of everyone who saw it, thinking he owned it. Well, Dan knew the truth. Alex had spilled the beans one night they were drinking together, actually blubbered about how much it was costing and how little he got to drive it, living so close to the hospital.

"You could get something cheaper," Dan had pointed out in that annoying know-it-all way of his. Everything was always so easy for Marchetti

Just one more thing to check before sleep, the latest test results for all the patients he was following. Though pretty certain he was up-to-date on them all, he knew he wouldn't sleep unless he reviewed them one more time. After all, he could be responsible for seventeen patients on his next shift: his six, plus Marchetti's and five from Werner. All these patients and their entire stories were in his BlackBerry's database. Alex shook his head in bewilderment as he set his things aside wondering how in the world did the old-timers like Ballard keep track of all this stuff back in their day?

When he fell exhausted into bed, sleep still eluded him, and he couldn't keep from reflecting on the day's events. Foremost in his mind was Ballard's face when Marchetti came up with that diagnosis. Just thinking about it made his chest feel heavy with frustration. Alex punched his pillow and forced his eyes closed, pledging to himself that the next brilliant diagnosis would be his!

CHAPTER TEN

"It hurts real bad. . . ." moaned seven-year-old Hannah. The quiver in her voice pinched at Nikki Saxon's heart; how well she remembered being confined to a hospital bed, young and scared and in pain. Hannah, who'd been hit by a car while riding her bike, was a few days past surgery to rebuild her shattered right leg and was now casted from ankle to hip.

"I know, sweetie," Nikki soothed, her voice low to avoid disturbing the two other patients, both sleeping, in the four-bed room. It was nearly midnight, and Nikki knew the child hadn't had any meds for several hours. Initially on a morphine drip, Hannah had been switched only today to oral pain meds.

Nikki picked up the girl's chart. "Let me see how much pain medicine the doctor ordered." Well accustomed to reading by the ambient light of the night shift, only a moment later Nikki smiled at her young patient and whispered, "Good news! I'll be right back." She went quickly to the med room and didn't even need to take time to use her key, because Julia Cleary was in there already, getting more antibiotics for her dog-bite boy. They greeted each other but didn't pause on their separate missions.

"This should help," Nikki said, returning to Hannah's room with a single tablet in a tiny, paper medicine cup. She handed it to the girl. "Got it? Hang on a minute. I'll get you some water." First she raised the head of the bed to make swallowing easier. Then she turned to the plastic pitcher and glass on the bedside table and poured half a glass of water, adding a straw to make the process as easy as possible. Hannah was already becoming used to the tablets and had no problem getting it down.

"Good job. You should feel better soon." Nikki took the empty glass and med cup and lowered the bed to a more comfortable sleeping level. "If the pain comes back, you just let me know. Or one of the other nurses if I'm not here. We'll make sure you don't have to hurt too much, okay?" The little girl nodded, but Nikki saw *something* in her eyes. . . . "Anything else I can do, honey? Something you want?"

"I want my mom," Hannah blurted, tears gathering in her eyes. Deerwood's pediatric unit had a very open visitation policy, one parent could stay with a child at all times, and additional visitors were allowed, within reason, for most of the day and evening. Hannah's mother had been in to see her for at least two hours each day, but from the social history on the chart, Nikki knew that she was a working single parent with two other children at home to care for and very little help nearby.

"I know," Nikki said, stroking the girl's hair, then carefully adjusting an extra pillow that kept the injured leg in the correct position. "She'll be back as soon as she can—tomorrow afternoon." The welling tears spilled over onto Hannah's cheeks. Nikki pulled the bedside chair closer and sat down. "I'm sure she'd be here right now if she could, but…."

"She has to stay with my little brother and sister."

"That's right."

"Cuz they can't stay home alone," Hannah continued as if reassuring herself with what she'd been told several times during her hospital stay.

"Right. But you're here with us to take care of you."

"And she can't come till the afternoon, cuz she has her job." Hannah was relaxing now, beginning to look drowsy. "So we can pay the rent and have food."

Hannah gave a mighty yawn, and Nikki yawned in response. The girl's eyes had closed, but when Nikki started to rise from the chair, they opened back up, the face suddenly anxious again. "Can you please stay with me . . . just till I fall asleep?"

"Of course." Nikki sat back down and took her young patient's hand. She began to hum a little tune she had hummed to other patients over the years, a lullaby a favorite nurse had once hummed for her.

Nikki sat watching Hannah's face as the meds and resulting sleep smoothed away every trace of discomfort and fear and loneliness. This was why she became a nurse. Thinking back on all those nurses who helped her through her own long recovery. Women so dear she'd memorized their names and still could recite them, in alphabetical order, like a litany, or a magic charm to protect herself from any present or future harm.

The lullaby was ended now, and Nikki could tell from the relaxation of the hand she held that Hannah was deeply asleep. But still Nikki sat holding that hand and comparing her own experience with Hannah's. True, she had been older, fifteen, and quite self-sufficient before she was so gravely injured, but she, too, had needed the solace and assistance of near-strangers to help her deal with the pain and the uncertainty of her future after hospitalization.

Cold fear curled all around 15-year-old Nikki, and she chewed the inside of her cheek to keep it at bay. "Let's not fight, Mom. Please just let me drive."

Frances—swaying slightly, car keys dangling from her fingers—tried to focus her vision on Nikki. "N't legal. Le's go; we're late."

<u>What to do</u>? Nikki wondered desperately. They simply couldn't miss this twice-postponed renewal interview with social services. Mr. Murphy, their caseworker, had bent over backwards to accommodate them, but there were rules, and he couldn't break them. If we lose our benefits, how will Mom get her medicines? Frances depended on those now; there was no going back without serious rehabilitation.

Though appointments frequently had to be canceled or postponed, when-push-came-to-shove, Frances had always before managed to drive where they needed to go, but was unaware her daughter had been teaching herself to drive, taking the car to a nearby supermarket parking lot at dawn every Sunday morning. Mom never even knew I was gone. She sleeps like the dead and really late every day. It'd been a little scary at first, getting from home to the relative safety of the parking lot, but Nikki 'd studied books about the mechanics of driving—thank goodness the Chevy was an automatic—and now, with practice, felt confident she could get them to their appointment more safely than her drug-muzzy mother.

Nikki had only just now confessed to her mom, who was so out-of-it she hadn't even gotten mad. "Did you have more than one pill this morning, Mom?"

Frances blinked. "Maybe." If so, it was accidental. Nikki knew, for all her faults, Mom didn't intentionally take too much. "I can drive, Nikki. Last thing we need's a ticket and you getting caught by the police."

I can think of worse things than that happening. She sighed. "Okay, Mom, but we gotta go now."

Mr. Murphy, he had everyone call him Mr. M., had warned them, "My hands are tied. If you want to keep your benefits, Nikki, you simply must get your mom to this meeting—and on time. My schedule's packed."

Looking away now from the car keys in Mom's hand, Nikki checked her watch. We'll probably be a few minutes late; let's hope he can still take us once we get there.

Normally Frances didn't drive too fast—and she was still only five miles above the speed limit—but when the light turned green ahead of them as they came to the corner of Pine and Wilson, Frances accelerated without paying attention to the cars that should be stopping for them. The red-light-running SUV slammed into the Chevy's passenger side and spun it across the intersection so the driver's side got T-boned by an oncoming bus.

It was weird, Nikki always thought, to remember so little about the crash itself. I'm sure there were horrible metal sounds, screaming, sirens, flashing lights. But those memories were no more vivid than some once-watched TV drama.

What she did remember was the hospital. She woke up—terrified and with both legs in casts—in the ICU at County Hospital. She tried not to cry, but she was so scared she couldn't even ask questions and find out what had happened. It helped some when the nurses arranged the curtain so she could see her comatose mother through the glass of the adjoining room.

Those nurses were like angels. Back then they still wore all white as they hovered around her with reassuring smiles and words. Not just the ICU nurses but those in the peds ward where she was moved before too long. The doctors were another story. Brusque, patronizing when they told her anything at all. "You're a lucky girl," one remarked. "Broken legs and a bunch of cuts and scrapes? Could've been a lot worse."

Like Mom. Frances, crushed by the bus, had massive internal injuries and trauma to the brain. It was a very long time before she ever woke up. By that time, Nikki had been on the ward a whole week. At least once a day, a nurse brought her back down to ICU in a wheelchair. Nikki would sit awhile, holding Frances's hand. The nurses encouraged Nikki to talk to her mom. Nurse Alice, Nikki's favorite, told her, "The comatose often hear what we say to them" and "She still has a good chance, and you can help her come back."

But when Nikki went to her mom's bedside and took up her hand, she experienced for the first time in her life that certainty of knowing a patient would not survive . . . perhaps did not want to go on living. Nikki fought it and tried to get Frances to fight too. When left alone with her, Nikki would whisper, "Come on, Mom. You can do it, and we can get through all this together. I need you, Mom."

CHAPTER ELEVEN

"Sorry," Dan apologized, even before his yawn was finished. "Uh . . . you saw Dr. Freibolt a month ago for some problem?" He blinked three or four times, struggling to wake himself up. It was two a.m., and still the Emergency Room was getting new patients. He thought of the in-house term *gomer* : Get Out of My Emergency Room, though it was now widely used as a more general pejorative for anyone taking up valuable time, space or energy anywhere in the hospital.

"Yeah, Doc. He said I had a balloon or something that needed fixin' in my belly."

Cold water in the face couldn't have brought Dan more awake or more quickly. This was no gomer. Sixty-seven-year-old Roscoe Delmar, unshaven and half-dressed in red sweatpants and what appeared to be his black-and-red plaid pajama top, was twisting and repositioning himself on the gurney, as if unable to find a comfortable position.

"What's bothering you right now?" Dan asked.

"Couldn't sleep tonight. Kept tossin' and turnin' in bed but the pain was too much."

"Where *is* the pain?" The man pointed to both the midline of his abdomen and to his mid-back. "I'm going to put my hand on your belly. Tell me if it hurts, okay?"

Delmar nodded, his eyes darting back and forth between Dan's hand and his face. "Yes-s! Right there!" His own face contorted in agony.

Dan immediately removed his hand, having recognized the pulsatile mass of a dissecting aortic aneurysm. Blood was now leaking into a previously weakened section of the body's main artery, filling and swelling it like water into a balloon. And everyone knows what happens if you keep pouring water into a latex balloon. "Sir, when you last saw Dr. Freibolt, what did he say he wanted to do about this balloon?"

Delmar flushed with embarrassment. "Oh, he wanted to operate, but I asked him if we could wait until after Labor Day. I have a big community barbecue planned." He managed a weak but proud grin. "I'm the main cook and organizer."

"I see." Labor Day was still a couple of days away. He'll be lucky if he sees sunrise, Dan thought as he checked the monitor. Blood pressure was 180/80. "I'll be right back." To the night nurse Sylvia Jenks he said, "Keep an eye on him. Especially BP."

Dan headed directly to the main desk in the middle of the Emergency Room and, grabbing the phone off the cradle, dialed the operator. "Hi, Dr. Marchetti here. Please get me Dr. Freibolt."

It took only seconds to reach the vascular surgeon, who answered groggily from his bed. "Yeah?"

"Dan Marchetti, the medical intern. Sorry to bother you, but I have one of your patients here in the ER—Roscoe Delmar. He appears to be dissecting."

"Shit, the stupid bastard . . . what's his BP?"

"It's 180 over 80."

"What time is it?" Freibolt asked, yawning.

"Just after two a.m."

"Okay. I'll come right in. Make sure you keep his blood pressure up."

Dan had barely hung up the receiver when he heard Sylvia call him from Delmar's room. He rushed back to find her in the process of increasing the saline fluid running into the patient's vein. Delmar had crumpled back on the gurney, eyes closed, moaning softly. "BP 60 systolic." Sylvia announced calmly despite the crashing patient.

"Let's start a pressor, and get out the mass trousers." Dan didn't have to tell her to hurry. Sylvia had the dark-brown rubberized device that might be able to save Delmar's life already at hand with its attached compressor within easy reach.

Dan helped her slide the rubber piece underneath their semi-lucid patient and wrap it snugly up around Delmar's legs and lower torso like a pair of pants. It took a few minutes to work out the kinks in all the velcro straps and to get the compressor insufflating air into the suit's inner lining. Delmar slipped closer to unconsciousness, mumbling incoherently, his blood pressure precariously low.

"Mr. Delmar," Sylvia called, enunciating slowly and clearly. "If you can hear me, we need to raise your blood pressure, and these inflatable pants will help us." No response. She met Dan's gaze with a grim look of her own; when she rechecked the patient's blood pressure a few moments later, "Seventy palp."

He's toast, Dan thought to himself. But aloud he said, "Let's up the dopamine.". Either Delmar would get on top of it and stabilize enough for surgery—or he wouldn't.

Another night nurse, Gail Sanduski, appeared in the doorway. "Hate to break this to ya, but I've got a woman crowning in room nine, and the OB-Gyn resident is tied up in Labor and Delivery. At least another fifteen minutes."

Sylvia asked, "You spoke to Dr. Pedersen yourself?"

"Well, Nikki Saxon called for me. She came down on a break to ask about my sister's wedding. Saw how tied up we all are and offered to help. She's trying to reach the attending now, I believe. She's already called in their obstetrician Dr. Majors."

Nikki! Now Dan noticed her sitting at the central station, talking into a phone.

Realizing he was the only physician present, he turned to his nurses. Gail Sanduski, a tall stringbean of a woman in perfect contrast to Sylvia Jenks's two hundred fifty pounds stood staring. Panic crowded in on him. "Geez! Alex finally got a dinner break, both the attending and the OB resident are unavailable, I've got an aneurysm crumping, and now a woman's giving birth!" Dan gulped air into his lungs.

Gail moved closer, touching his arm gently. "You're not alone here." Her brown eyes were so comfortingly calm, Dan could feel his anxiety begin to recede, barely.

Sylvia looked up from the man in the inflated trousers and assured Dan, "I've got this, Doctor.. I'll beep Dr. Cole back down here. . And that baby won't wait."

"Too right," Gail said cheerfully, leading the way toward room nine. "It's her third, and it's coming pretty fast."

Just outside the room, Dan paused and confided to Gail, "I only delivered one baby as a med student! And the attending was right there."

She smiled and repeated an old med-school adage: "See one, do one, teach one."

Dan had to laugh, and that, too, helped relax him more as he entered the room and saw a good-looking African American couple who appeared to be in their late thirties. The patient lay motionless for the moment, resting between contractions, and seeming very relaxed and unworried. Her husband stood at her shoulder, clumsily patting her hand and appearing far more nervous. Dan made his voice sound easy and confident. "I'm Dr. Marchetti." He glanced at the chart Gail showed him. "Mr. and Mrs. Hamilton? Keesha and Louis? How ya guys doing tonight?"

She spoke right up. "Well, third time around for us, but this baby seems impatient. And he's got a big head like his daddy's."

Lou Hamilton smiled weakly at the joke and kept patting his wife's hand as he asked, "Where's Dr. Majors?"

"She's on her way in, and the OB resident will be down shortly. He's delivering another baby upstairs."

By now Dan was seated on a stool at the foot of the gurney, staring at the sheet draped over the woman's upbent knees and down past her feet in the stirrups. He could tell by her change in breathing and the sudden tensing of her body that the next contractions were beginning.

Dan placed his hands on her bent knees, hesitating a moment as if hoping for further instructions—or for that resident to arrive and take over. Lifting back the drape, he saw the top of the infant's head crowding the opening of the birth canal—a full head of damp, dark hair. At his side, Gail nudged him and he slid his hands into the gloves she held for him.

"Ahhh, the baby. . . ." Keesha panted, sounding remarkably calm.

"Push!" Dan urged, and Lou's and Gail's voices joined in, "Push, push, push. . . ."

Dan watched the crown of that head strain to push free, like a shoulder against a door not quite open enough.. He opened his mouth to ask Gail for the Mayo scissors in case an episiotomy became necessary but there was no need.

The head popped suddenly through, followed by a *whoosh* of hot amniotic fluid, soaking Dan's scrubs all the way to his skin.

Lou Hamilton was still telling his wife to "Push, push, push. . . ." but those directions were no longer needed!When Dan gently rotated the head so the shoulder could present, the whole baby came shooting out like a wet and slippery seal pup and Dan almost failed to catch it. For one harrowing heartbeat, he bobbled the child before gaining purchase. Staring down at the precious cargo he held, he watched the dark, wizened face screw up against the bright lights and erupt with a bellow.

Gail's voice murmured in his ear, "Nice catch, Dan." Then, to the parents, she announced, "It's a boy!"

"Lou Junior!" the dad said proudly. He and Keesha were gazing at each other with adoration, blissfully unaware of Dan's near-fumble and that it was Gail who guided Dan through the next steps. When he had the umbilical cord securely clamped, he asked if Lou wanted the honor of cutting it, but the man shook his head with a little shudder. Dan still gave him credit for being there at all. Not every husband could face the ordeal of labor and delivery, even one as relatively easy as this.

Gail took the baby, who was still crying, from him and started cleaning the infant prior to routine tests to make sure everything was okay.

"Good lungs," Lou said with a huge grin.

"Lord!" Keesha winked at Dan. "His daddy's big head *and* his big mouth!"

Dan laughed, but before he could respond, Sylvia Jenks's huge frame suddenly filled the doorway. "Room two's crashing, Doctor!" She was gone as quickly, back to Delmar's side.

"I'll handle this, Dan." Gail told him. Dan raced to Delmar's bed but he could see it was already too late. The monitors were flat-lined, and Sylvia looked up at him, shaking her head.

Delmar's face made a hideous sight, bluish and blotchy with the tongue half-severed. Dan had heard of that happening: a patient's teeth clamping involuntarily during cardiac arrest. Delmar's mouth was a bloody mess, and Dan was relieved to have an excuse to look away when Sylvia spoke: "You should go get cleaned up."

Dan looked down at his drenched and stained clothing, now cold where it clung to his skin. He shivered. "Yeah, in a minute." He made himself look back at Delmar, wondering just how important that barbeque would seem to his family now. Aloud, he said, "Well, there wasn't much hope for him, even if the rubber pants *had* worked."

Sylvia frowned. "Yeah, about that. . . . Weirdest thing. Those mass trousers failed . . . deflated."

Dan stared at the nurse. "Come again?"

"I thought maybe the valve was broken or something, so I inflated it again, but I guess it was too late for Mr. Delmar."

Sudden exhaustion swamped Dan, and he found it hard to grasp this simple conversation. "It deflated?"

Sylvia nodded. "So far it's stayed re-inflated."

"But how could that happen?"

"I dunno. Slow leak, maybe? Valve malfunction?"

"Maybe. Better get it checked out by engineering. Were you in the room the whole time?"

"I was gone a few minutes. Went to get another saline bag to hang, and when I got back, I had to catch the phone. By the way,

Freibolt's stuck on the turnpike. All lanes closed for a jackknifed 18-wheeler." She gazed regretfully at Delmar in the now-useless pants. "Soon as I got back, I saw they were deflated. I went to get you, but you were *really* busy. So I came right back and pumped them up again."

"How long ago was that?"

"About fifteen minutes. And see? Still working."

"Doesn't make sense," he said, and Sylvia just shook her head in agreement.

But Dan couldn't let it go. Could the valve not have been closed correctly the first time? That could happen. Though it seemed unlikely with someone as capable and meticulous as Sylvia Jenks. Best not to mention *that* possibility; he could see she already was feeling bad enough about losing a patient in her care. No need to add extra guilt, or risk offending her by questioning her conscientiousness, especially as the guy really was a dead man walking as soon as his aneurysm had blown.

While they were entering a time of death in the records, a voice called from the doorway, "Hey, where's the mom-to-be?" Glancing over his shoulder, Dan saw the OB-Gyn resident Gary Pedersen.

"Room nine, but you're too late. What took ya?"

Gary shrugged, looking as tired as Dan felt, but managed a philosophical grin. "Babies arrive when they're ready."

Dan turned to fully face the resident, indicating his wet scrubs. "Tell me about it."

Gary laughed. "Oh, man! I see you got baptized." He waved and moved off toward room nine.

When Dan turned back to Delmar, Sylvia was removing the mass trousers from the lifeless legs. "You losing your magic touch, Marchetti?" someone said behind him.

Alex, Dan's exhausted brain processed. He turned and stared at his friend, who was looking past him at the corpse of Roscoe Delmar. Strangely, a half-smile crooked the corner of Alex's mouth. "What?" Dan managed.

"Never mind." Alex Cole turned his attention to Sylvia. "Nurse, we need you for a new admit in pulmonary crisis. Room seven." She immediately left Delmar and bustled out.

Alex followed her, calling back over his shoulder, "Can't win 'em all, can we, Marchetti?"

What's with Alex these days? Much of the time he seemed his old self: knowledgeable and focused at work, friendly and talkative off-the-clock. They still found time to watch sports together and tip a few brews, though Dan had noticed that, unlike their early days, Alex was much slower offering to buy, so Dan ended up paying more than half the checks, still it was worth it to have a buddy to hang out with.

But *that* wasn't the same as it used to be either. Talking sports and women, music and movies was fine, but if the conversation turned to work or anything about medicine, Alex seemed to start tensing up, getting testy and argumentative and needlessly competitive. Sure, he'd always been that way if anyone else was around, but he used to let that fall away when they were alone.

What did Alex have to be so uptight about anyway? They were all in the same boat, trying to learn to be good docs, trying not to lose too many patients along the way, and Alex seemed to be doing at least as well as the rest of them. Better than most, in fact. But he definitely seemed off lately. Still, Dan was too tired to ponder it much longer.

Gail Sanduski poked her head in the door. "Thought you'd like to know. Little Lou Junior checked out just fine. They're all on their way up to Maternity. They said to thank you very much." She studied him. "You really should get cleaned up, Dr. Marchetti." Gail winked. "Before yet another emergency rolls in."

Dan groaned, then yawned, the exhaustion returning in a rush. "Haven't tied up the Delmar case yet. Gotta make some calls."

"It can wait. I checked his file. Next of kin's a brother in California; *he* would probably appreciate your waiting a few hours before you phone him, three-hour time difference there, y'know. Dr. Freibolt called to say traffic was moving, and I gave him the news. He should be here within ten minutes. Drs. Cole and Upton are back on the floor; they've got the new admit. So. . . ."

Dan yawned again, letting her nudge him from Delmar's room. "So I can grab a shower and change of clothes. Thanks."

Through the open door of room seven, he could see Alex and their attending, Mike Upton, working on the newest patient, a very-pale young man with an apparent gunshot wound in his side. Vinny Orlander was in there too with his life-saving equipment.

With lead weights on his eyelids, Dan headed for the central station to leave Delmar's chart. The chairs were empty. *Nikki!* he remembered suddenly. He hadn't gotten a chance to talk to her. She just helped out where needed and then was gone; back to her own work in peds.

Heading for the on-call room, Dan couldn't pry Nikki out of his thoughts. So lovely and graceful. So capable and caring. Smart, funny, sexy, thoughtful. Dedicated to medicine and healing. Of course, he reminded himself, she wasn't available. Whatever problems she was having at home, he bet her husband was an idiot!

Four weeks later, on the last shift of his ER rotation, Dan was ready to congratulate himself on making it through another high-energy, high-risk assignment. Walking back with a belly full of pot roast and all the trimmings from the cafeteria, he checked his watch: 9:59 p.m. Ten hours and then a whole day to sleep before facing the trials and tribulations of Nine West. He had to smile. After the units and ER, the medical floors should be a piece of cake. Maybe after awhile, he'd miss the drama of those intense rotations. After all, he'd learned so much in three months. Reflecting back, he recognized there'd been no other time during his ER stint quite as fraught as the Delmar–Hamilton Night, as he called it. Like a famous prizefight: Birth vs. Death. And calling it a draw. There'd been plenty of other interesting and challenging cases, the majority involving alcohol, drugs, violence or motor vehicles, or all of the above.

Tonight it seemed eerily quiet. Until a familiar raucous laugh caught his attention, and he spotted Dr. Mike Upton, standing across the room, talking animatedly to one of the male nurses. Hank Currie was a good guy who usually tried to avoid Upton's incessant crude stories as much as the long-suffering female nurses, and he looked now toward Dan with a deer-in-the-headlights gaze, pleading for rescue. A hulking and powerful fellow,

Hank reminded Dan of a bear, especially with his bushy eyebrows and wild mop of brown hair, but he was surprisingly lean and agile and his huge hands proved exceedingly gentle and reassuring to ER patients.

This in contrast to Upton, who had the bedside manner of an annoying frat boy who thought he was hotter, funnier and smarter than his buds. Aspiring, it seemed, to offend everyone, he'd reached the age of forty-three without losing his taste for scatological and sexual humor, rude practical jokes, and a ready leer that couldn't hide, even in the tiny cave formed by a thick black mustache-goatee. And his cue-ball head, shaved and waxed till it shone, was undoubtedly an attempt to hide a receding hairline and any grey beyond it. If he hadn't the uncanny ability to choose the quickest path to the right diagnosis in the midst of chaos, the staff would have long ago figured out a way to send him on his inappropriate way. In fact, the more chaotic the better, as if his neural pathways required disorder to fire.

Dan tried to avoid hearing exactly what Upton was saying as he gestured to Hank with some x-rays he was holding, but the tone was unmistakable. Across the room, Dan saw Gail Sanduski filing charts with a thoroughly disgusted expression. As soon as she noticed Dan, she smiled with relief and held up a chart. "New patient for you, Dan."

"Yeah, got a live one for ya, Marchetti," Upton called loudly, waggling those x-rays at *him* now. With a grateful look, Hank Currie took the opportunity to escape, hurrying off toward the elevator with the single word, "Dinner" cast over his shoulder.

"Chest mass," Upton continued, almost as loudly as before, though Dan had nearly reached him. "Big one."

Dan cringed wondering if the patient was close enough to hear. "I heard you." Keeping a respectful tone with this clown was never easy, but he was the attending.

Laughing as if Dan were joking, Upton assured him, "No worries there. No-speak-a-de-English, y'know?" He held the chest x-rays up toward the light, ignoring the lit reading boxes. "Yep. Really big chest mass." He smirked as if enjoying a private joke at Dan's expense. "Came in with severe pleuritic chest pain."

Dan took the films from him and went to hang them on the reading box where he could see them better. "Could be mediastinal." The bright white area appeared to be in the center of the chest, between the lungs instead of inside either of them. "She a smoker?" Dan knew the patient was female because of the ample breast shadows on the films.

"Don't know," Mike answered with a shrug. "Probably."

Dan looked his way. "Don't know? Did you get a history?"

"Not that easy with the language barrier. Besides, I prefer to leave all the detail work to you young geniuses."

"Sure." Dan found it impossible to hide his annoyance. Upton was as lazy as they come. "I see the ER's just teeming with patients."

The attending grinned and answered, "Gotta go see a man about a horse." As Gail joined them, he gave her a broad wink. "A very *large* horse, if you know what I mean." Then he laughed heartily at his own joke and headed for the restrooms.

Dan shared a grimace with Gail. "God, I'm not gonna miss *him* next rotation. My condolences on being stuck with that guy."

Gail's eyes twinkled as she handed him the new patient's chart and led the way toward the appropriate room. "Well, this time, he would've *loved* to keep the patient. But *she* very clearly asked for a 'new doctor.'"

Mystified, Dan entered the room, reading from the chart. "Hello, Ms. . . Elena Guillermo? I'm Dr. Marchetti and—" He glanced up, and the words tangled in his throat so nothing more could get out.

Sitting on the edge of the gurney glowered an absolutely gorgeous young woman of perhaps twenty-five. Above the very-snug spandex pants in fire-engine red, even the unflattering lines of the incongruous blue Johnny coat couldn't hide the abundance of bosom hinted at on the x-rays. She looked anything but sick. Dan noted the shining black hair parted on the side and falling to her shoulders, the perfectly applied makeup and red nail polish, the matching red-satin stiletto heels with a sexy ankle-strap.

And her eyes! Huge and, in this light, so dark they appeared blacker than her hair, they smoldered now and greeted Dan with challenge, even as she winced in sudden pain. "No Upton?" she demanded, breathing in short, shallow breaths.

"No Upton," Dan confirmed, smiling. Upton must have set a record pissing this looker off. Pointing to his name badge, he said, "New doctor. Dan Marchetti."

She nodded, seemed to relax a bit, but her eyes locked with his as if to say *We'll see how it goes with you,* and Dan could tell the jury was still out on him.

"Ah!" The involuntary cry wrenched from her as she leaned farther forward, clutching the edges of the gurney with white-knuckled hands.

"Are you in a great deal of pain?" Dan asked, still making no move to touch her.

She tilted her head ever so slightly, as if to indicate that she didn't understand. "I no speak" she managed to whisper between obviously painful breaths, "very well Eenglish."

"We need an interpreter," Gail commented. "But I think everyone's gone home. Even Alma Ramirez. She's a nurse on the ninth floor. She's from Argentina."

"Ah, *si! Argentina!"* exclaimed Elena, pointing excitedly to her chest and then holding her hand there, pressed against the pain.

Dan and Gail both nodded their understanding, but Gail told Dan, "I'm pretty sure Alma's on days right now. I'll make a call after you've done your exam."

Dan nodded, reading her loud-and-clear. He certainly didn't want to be left alone while examining an offended woman who didn't speak the language and had already had to demand a "new doctor."

Dan held up his stethoscope, "I need to listen to your heart and lungs, Ms. Guillermo." She stared at him with suspicion. He put the earpieces in place and pressed the disk of the chest piece to his own upper body to demonstrate. Then he faced it toward her and asked, "Okay?"

He started first on the outside of her Johnny coat, though he knew that wouldn't be enough. He modeled for her when to breathe in and out, and she followed his example, even though it was obviously painful to breathe as deeply as he indicated. When she relaxed a bit more, he pulled gently at the edge of the blue cloth and placed the chest piece just beneath it, saying, "I need to listen *under* here." Elena looked uncertain.

Her reluctance was clear, but she said, "Okay."

"Debajo," Gail said suddenly and shrugged at Dan's surprised look. "Funny what words you pick up here and there."

"Debajo?" Elena repeated, looking from one of them to the other. "No Upton?"

"No Upton," Dan promised solemnly. He held his gaze steady on hers for the long moment those dark eyes probed his, hoping she could read his intent there.

Finally, with another wince of pain, she nodded assent. *"Debajo."*

With the greatest of care, Dan slowly and respectfully moved his hand and stethoscope chest piece beneath her clothing, first around her upper chest, then, very cautiously, beneath her left breast. She kept her eyes locked on his, and he sensed she was watching for the slightest hint his intentions were not entirely medical. Apparently Dan was passing the test, because, still watching him closely and continuing the deep inhalations and exhalations, Elena pushed herself completely upright, battling the increased discomfort. This lifted her heavy breasts and made it easier for Dan to hear her lungs and heart from below. When he removed the stethoscope's disk and applied it to her back, she slumped a little forward again with obvious relief.

Dan moved back a step. He had heard a clear "rub," a sound most likely of that mass coming in contact with the pleura that lined the chest cavity and covered the lungs. Such pressing together of tissues with every breath certainly explained the chest pain.

Her eyes sought his verdict.

"Do you smoke?" Dan asked, pretending to take a cigarette in and out of his mouth. She nodded *yes*, seeming somewhat embarrassed to admit it. He wasn't surprised, as he'd detected a faint odor of cigarette smoke, even though her hair was very clean and her fingers showed no nicotine stains.

Chances were good that mass was a cancer, yet she appeared so healthy. Slender without that too-thin look of so many girls today; clear, bright eyes; tawny skin that glowed with well-being. The chart revealed vital signs taken when she first came in. Pulse rate, BP and temp were all slightly elevated, but easily explained by stress, anxiety and anger over her first encounter with Upton. The pulse-ox reading showed the saturation of oxygen in her blood to be a little low, but she'd been breathing shallowly to lessen the pain. Dan was surprised that except for the pain, she seemed relatively healthy, something not well explained with a large cancerous mass.

He patted her shoulder gently. "Okay. I will be back soon." With two fingers pointed downward, he mimicked legs walking out to the main area and then back into the room. Understanding dawned in her eyes, and she actually laughed, though that broke off quickly with the pain it caused. She nodded.

As Dan and Gail left the room, he told her, "See if you can find that interpreter, okay?"

"Sure." Gail's mouth quirked with a teasing smile; she kept her voice low. "You seem to be doing okay on your own, Dr. 'No Upton.'" She moved away toward the phones and, with luck, an interpreter.

Mike Upton himself was back at the light box, staring at Elena's chest x-rays. He looked up with great curiosity and a little smirk as Dan joined him. "Get that history you wanted?"

"Not too much; need an interpreter. But she *does* smoke. Exam didn't reveal anything except the rub you'd expect from that mass where it is." He pointed to it on the x-ray in front of him. "She seems completely healthy otherwise."

"Healthy? I'll say. Quite athletic, in fact." When Dan looked at him in complete bafflement, he asked, "You didn't find out? She's a stripper at the Kit Kat Lounge."

"A stripper. How do you know?"

"I never forget a . . . you know . . . *face.*" His open palms were coming up to describe those breasts.

Dan looked away, back at the x-rays that revealed the truth within that ample bosom. "Think it's CA?"

Mercifully distracted, Upton glanced to the films again. "Possibly. Lung or maybe lymphoma."

Dan kept staring at one of the images . . . he couldn't seem to look away. No longer was it about avoiding Upton's raunchy comments but almost as if something were calling to him. . . . Dan pulled the film free and took it around to the side of the unit, stepped on the foot pedal to activate the hot light, and held the film up to it. "What're you looking at, Dan?" Mike Upton came around to peer over his shoulder.

"Calcification, maybe. Or something. . . . Geez, it looks like a *tooth.*"

"A tooth?!" Upton squinted at the image then clapped Dan on the shoulder. "Well, I'll give you it's an irregular calcification, not surprising for a large mass. But I don't see a tooth. Then again, you're the intern so you run it down to Radiology and see who's down there to check it out. I think you're hallucinating. Good thing you're almost finished with ER. You need a rest."

Dan rubbed his eyes and ran a hand through his rumpled hair. He *was* tired. But it *did* look like a tooth.

"First, let's get some labs, blood gas, a bed upstairs, some pain meds going. . . ." He sounded as if he were reading from a cookbook. "Write the orders, okay?" Upton yawned and stretched. "I'm heading for the on-call room before the universe realizes we got a practically empty ER here."

Dan offered, "How 'bout I get a CAT of her chest in the a.m.?"

"Yeah, good idea. Wouldn't mind having some pictures of that chest myself." He winked and snickered. "Such a *tooth*some lass!" That really cracked him up, and once again, he made his exit on gales of his own laughter.

Dan looked around, saw Hank Currie and Gail Sanduski, both of whom just rolled their eyes to show they'd heard the exchange. Those two long-suffering nurses made an interesting pair standing side by side. Dan smiled at them and opened his arms in a gesture that said of the now-absent Upton, *Whatcha gonna do with someone like that?*

Quickly, Dan wrote the orders, the first for Elena's pain meds, and both Gail and Hank came to take care of them. Gail confirmed she was still waiting for a call-back from any of three people who might serve as an interpreter. Finished with his tasks for now, Dan buzzed Radiology.

"Dr. Schneiweiss," a voice answered.

"Oh, good. Working late again, Pete? It's Dan Marchetti. Can I bring down some films to review with you?"

"Sure. Nothing to do but go home and be with the family."

"Oh, I'm sorry. It can wait—"

Pete's guffaw cut him off. "My joke. Y'see, we're on the thirteenth day of my sister-in-law's visit, and I swear I'm about to fake a coronary and get admitted here so I don't have to go home till she's gone. Sure, bring those babies on down."

As Dan was hanging up the phone, Brian Callahan, the other intern on duty for the shift, came strolling in, yawning and blinking. "Upton said I should come on back. Anything new?"

Dan filled him in on what was known of Elena's case and said, "I'm gonna take her films down to Pete and get an official reading. Shouldn't be long."

Dan took the stairs down to Radiology and greeted the amiable tow-headed Pete, who'd recently earned the honor of DCH Employee with the Largest Nose.

"Patient came in with pleuritic chest pain; smoker; everything normal otherwise. In fact, the very picture of health." Dan handed Pete the films, and Pete—all business now—hung them and scrutinized each silently. Dan fidgeted. "Sorta looks like a lymphoma, but I thought I saw *something*. . . . Probably just n artifact in the imaging. . . ?"

"Oh, you mean this tooth? You've got good eyes, Dan. Good instincts. So what do you think that means?"

Dan searched his memory banks, remembering how certain crude tumors formed from rudimentary embryonic cell layers and sometimes included bits of hair, bone, fat, teeth. "It's a . . . teratoma?"

Pete smiled his approval. "Think so. *Could* still be a lymphoma—or even a malignant teratoma—but with her health so good, I bet it's benign."

"Great."

"Either way, it'll have to come out. Better call Bosnan." Pete Schneiweiss checked his watch. "You can use my phone. I'm gonna head home." He sighed and gave Dan an ironic smile.

"Thanks for staying, Pete."

Schneiweiss shrugged into his windbreaker. "Thank *you* for bringing me something interesting to look at."

"You should see the real thing," Dan murmured. Then, off Pete's cocked eyebrow, he elaborated. "She's *gorgeous*. Mike Upton says she's a stripper at the Kit Kat."

"Mike would know." Pete smirked."Well, no more dancing for her . . . not with the scar she's going to have."

Dan hadn't thought that far ahead. He waved good-bye to the radiologist and sat down by the phone. *What a shame!* Not that she'd have to give up dancing with her chest exposed, but that her cure would involve what she'd probably view as disfigurement. Well, Emily Bosnan, a top-notch cardiothoracic surgeon, had at an early age undergone a double mastectomy. It was hard to imagine anyone more sympathetic or capable for Elena's predicament. Dan dialed Bosnan's service and left a message. He took a few minutes to prepare: using the department computer to refresh what he'd learned about teratomas, planning what he'd say to Elena Guillermo, and hoping to God Gail had found an interpreter. Then he made his way back upstairs to his patient's room in the ER.

He found Elena sitting back comfortably on the bed, smiling and eating some lime jello. The pain meds had obviously kicked in. She'd slipped out of her stilettos—which lay nearby on the floor—and now sat like some teenager with her bare feet up on the bed, knees bent, and those lovely red-clad legs unconcealed by the hospital gown. She'd been talking in Spanish to another young woman sitting at her bedside, but as he entered, Elena gave him a huge smile, then pointed toward the other woman with her spoon. *"Mi prima, Doctor Marchetti."*

He looked to the other woman and held out his hand. "You're the interpreter? Nurse Alma Ramirez?"

She shook his hand, laughing. "Interpreter . . . yes. Nurse . . . no. I'm Elena's cousin Yolanda." She looked a few years older but was pretty and fit enough that Dan wondered if she practiced the same profession.

"Thanks for coming in, Yolanda. We can really use some help with translation."

"So I hear." Her dark eyes teased him, but gently.

"Please tell Elena that we've found what looks like a growth in her chest." Dan pointed to the area between Elena's breasts. "When she breathes, it rubs against her lungs and causes the pain." He waited for Yolanda to catch up with him.

He watched Elena's eyes get very serious, and she set aside her jello. Neither of the women was smiling now. "What kind of growth?" Yolanda asked, even before Elena—her eyes suddenly fearful—could prompt her. "A cancer?"

"It may be, but we think it's *not* cancer." Yolanda quickly conveyed this, and the fear eased a bit in Elena's eyes, which she kept riveted on his while she listened to the conversation. "We think it's a kind of benign tumor called a teratoma. This one's pretty unusual and seems to have a tooth in it."

"A tooth? She swallowed a tooth?"

"No, no, nothing like that. This type of tumor is very . . . rudimentary." He paused, wondering just how much English Yolanda knew. When she nodded she understood him, he went on. "They have pieces of tissue from different parts of the body inside. Not all would show up on an x-ray, but the tooth did."

Yolanda turned back to her cousin and translated this, then the words Elena spoke in response: "What now?"

"Surgery—"

Yolanda interrupted. "But if it's not cancer . . . ?"

"It has to come out," Dan told her. "It's already causing her terrible pain. It'll continue to grow . . . interfere with her breathing." While Yolanda conveyed all this, Dan decided against telling them that, if the mass broke into the trachea, Elena could even cough up hair and fat and other tissues.

"Will there be a scar?" Yolanda asked.

Dan looked away from Elena's piercing gaze, at Yolanda. "Oh, yes. The surgeon needs to make an incision through her breastbone." He traced the line down his own chest.

"No, no!" Elena wailed. "Dancer. No cut, no cut!"

"We have no choice," he told her, meeting her gaze steadily now. "I'm sorry." This she didn't seem to understand.

"She's a . . . dancer," Yolanda repeated, giving her shoulders an unambiguous little shimmy.

"Yes, I know."

"She will not be able to make a living anymore." Yolanda's eyes implored him to amend this course of action. Tears gathered in Yolanda's eyes. "Her family in Argentina depends on her."

"I'm sorry." Dan looked first at Yolanda, then at Elena, addressing her directly. "You must have the surgery to stop the pain. The growth will keep getting bigger" When Yolanda had translated this and Elena's expression remained unpersuaded, he continued, "You won't be able to dance if you can't breathe." Now, as Yolanda's voice explained his words, tears filled Elena's eyes as well.

Dan reached out to comfort his patient by holding her hand. "I'm so very sorry." Elena immediately brought his hand to her lips and kissed it, holding his gaze with what he read as gratitude and high regard.

And just like that, Dan felt the stirrings of arousal. Funny, all the time he was examining her magnificent breasts, he'd felt completely professional. Yet now it was undone by this woman's appreciation. Feeling the rush of color to his face, he gently freed his hand and used it to pat her shoulder awkwardly, answered her soft, *"Muchas gracias!"* with "You're welcome, Elena."

Gail came in to say, "They've got a room ready for her upstairs, Dr. Marchetti."

At the end of a rapid exchange in Spanish, Yolanda turned to Dan and said, "Elena wants to know if this is really weird . . . if she's a . . . how you say . . . freak or something?"

"It's very unusual," Dan said to them, "but not in a bad way.." As Yolanda conveyed this, a thought came to Dan, and he couldn't resist. "Tell her she's an exotic dancer with an exotic tumor!"

It was good to see Elena laugh again.

CHAPTER TWELVE

Nikki just looked at it. Sitting on the edge of her bed, slumped forward onto her lap, she stared down at the silver chain with the broken clasp, lying half-hidden in the thick carpet—seeing the name "Pam" spelled out in diamond-studded cursive. Nikki knew it was an ankle-bracelet. She wore one just like it but bearing her own name—a gift from Matt back when he cared about *her* ankles.

She couldn't look away. Couldn't pretend it wasn't there. Her numb fingers reached for the anklet, but they refused to touch it, stopping short as if it were a poisonous snake lying there, just under the edge of her bed.

This was what she'd suspected. He'd been sleeping with Pamela McDermott, a fellow officer at Anchor Security; a fellow resident of this Lake Harbor Homes complex. Late twenties, athletic and tanned with very-short blond hair and deceptively innocent blue eyes. A body-builder, she looked healthy as a police horse.

Nikki flopped back on the rumpled green bedspread, arms outstretched, eyes squeezed shut, feeling the utter exhaustion of her last shift, especially the loss of little Ryan after months of chemotherapy. Despite the cheerful hot-pink of her scrubs, Nikki felt a million years old.

The world seemed to spin slowly around her, but she didn't open her eyes to make it stop. Instead she watched the parade of memories on the movie screen inside her head: how much Matt talked about Pamela when she was first hired, openly admiring her fitness and strength, her intelligence and knowledge of law enforcement, her prowess with a handgun. Nikki hadn't worried; she and Matt had always talked candidly about people they found attractive. She never felt threatened as she felt she understood Matt and had no trouble with lavishing him with the attention and admiration he craved as a result of the rejection he felt winding through New York's foster care system. This despite having her own dark thoughts and memories to battle knowing that she could never share her memories with anyone, not even Matt. Still, something had changed over the last year. She'd found herself pulling back into her own thoughts more and more, simply not responding to his needs as she always had before. Whether fatigue or depression, she knew she had changed.

Even the sex, which had always been terrific, became humdrum and wearisome. As he initiated it less and less frequently, she did not step up to motivate more. By the time she realized there was a real problem, it was already too late. Matt no longer seemed interested at all.

About then Pamela was hired, and it gave them something new to discuss at least: how her shooting scores topped everyone else's at Anchor; how she beat Chuck at arm-wrestling; how Sully asked her out and she turned him down flat, so he was saying she had to be a lesbian. But after awhile, Matt stopped talking about Pam. At first Nikki assumed the novelty had finally worn off or that maybe he'd found out she really *was* a lesbian and felt embarrassed for his attraction. A little voice at the back of Nikki's mind kept trying to warn her to pay more attention, but she ignored it.

The next thought galvanized Nikki like an electric shock... *but the anklet is here, on* my *carpet . . . in* my *bedroom.* She shot up to stand staring at it, quivering and faint, with bile rising in her throat. *Omigod, omigod. How* could *he?*

Strip the bed and burn everything! a voice screamed inside her head, but she didn't move. She knew she could never touch those sheets again. She just stood staring at the bed, trying to keep breathing, trying not to collapse, fighting tears and the almost overwhelming urge to vomit.

Nikki heard the sound of the front door opening, then closing. Matt's voice called, "Nikki?" but she didn't answer. There was the sound of his gun going into the safe and the *beep, beep, beep* .. Then the *swish* of the patio door as he looked for her out there. At last, the soft sound of his boots on the carpeted stairs, coming up to the bedroom.

In the doorway, he blinked at her with surprise and said, "There you are. Why didn't you answer?" When she still didn't speak but stood hyperventilating and chewing her lip, he asked, "You okay?"

"How *could* you, Matt?" she managed to say.

"Wha—whatta y'mean?" But he knew. His eyes flicked involuntarily toward the bed, then back to her face. "What're you talking about?"

She swooped down and captured the ankle bracelet, held it up with two fingers as if it were that snake or some kind of toxic medical waste. "How could you bring her here to *my* bed?"

For a long moment they both stared, mesmerized by the swaying anklet chain she held up between them, at the word "Pam" written in diamonds. Then their eyes locked, and she watched him try to decide what to say. At last he said, "It was just this once." Then he shrugged and answered the question. "Her roommate's parents are in town. . . ."

Nikki's eyes went back to that dangling proof of her marriage's end, still held aloft, burning her fingers. She tossed it over onto the bed. She didn't plan to sleep there ever again. The anklet landed a few feet from Matt, almost sliding off the edge of the green satin bedspread. Nikki saw him look at it, but he was too smart to pick it up right then.

"Nikki, I'm sorry. I didn't mean for it to happen." He ran a hand through his matinee-idol hair, but for once he seemed completely oblivious to his appearance. "It's just sometimes when you see someone at work. . . ."

A vivid memory of Dan Marchetti flooded her senses. "Too true," she murmured. The impulse to wound him was there. To let him know she'd also found pleasure outside their marriage. That someone young and virile had found her attractive too. But it wouldn't be fair to bring Dan into any of this. His participation had been completely innocent. She took a different tack. "Being attracted doesn't mean you have to act on it." She winced at her hypocrisy.

"I know, but it's sorta hard to resist when someone really pays attention to you. Makes you feel special." All traces of guilt were now gone from his eyes. "You've been shutting me out for months now."

That's it. Blame it all on me.. She sucked in her breath. *Not this time.* "Get out."

"What?" His eyes widened. She could see he was surprised she wasn't falling into the game as she'd always done before.

"It's over. I'm filing for divorce."

"But, Nikki, *I* can't just get out . . . can't leave here. The contract, remember . . . ?"

In the depth of her pain, she *had* forgotten. Since Lake Harbor's gated community was protected by its sister company, Anchor Security, employees were privileged to buy in at a much-reduced price, but their own mortgage was only viable at that rate as long as Matt lived on the premises.

He moved toward her, reaching for her arm. "C'mon, Nikki. Let's talk."

"Don't you touch me!" He jerked to a halt as if she'd struck him. She knew he'd never heard that tone from her before: cold, unrelenting, perhaps even menacing. A voice she'd only ever once used with her father on the last day she saw him long ago. An old but too-familiar feeling engulfed her. *Trapped . . . can't breathe! Can't be in the same room with this man. If he can't go, then I just* have *to.*

She whirled and rushed to the closet, pulling out two big duffel bags, which she opened on the window seat instead of the bed. With great efficiency she began to fill them with jeans, tees, sweaters, underwear, socks, sleepwear, matched sets of scrubs. She pushed an extra pair of shoes into an outside pocket.

"Divorce?" Matt was saying. "Don't be silly. You're just upset . . . overreacting." He was trying to sound paternal and in-charge, but she could hear the note of panic in his voice.

She didn't bother to answer, just went into the master bath and pulled out her travel kit. Those early years with her mom, trying to keep one step ahead of her father, had taught her to be prepared to pick up and leave at a moment's notice. She'd never gotten past having a bag of toiletries ready-to-hand. Mom had called it a *travel kit*, but they both knew its secret name: *escape kit.*

She didn't even have to look inside. She knew it was already stocked with her favorite soap, shampoo and grooming items, a duplicate set of makeup, and trial sizes of everything else she'd need. Nikki took the bag back out to the bedroom and tucked it into one duffel. She zipped everything shut and hefted both bags to her hot-pink shoulders.

Matt stood blocking the doorway. She realized he was still talking, but she hadn't heard a word. Amazing what you can tune out once you know how, and she'd learned very well. He was asking her questions, and she did register a few words: "bank accounts . . . credit cards . . . mortgage . . . taxes . . . paying bills . . . ?"

She pushed past him, using one bag as a buffer so she didn't have to touch him. "We'll decide all that later. I'm through talking today." She hurried for the stairs.

He called after her, "Wait, Nikki. *Please. . . .*" Such a heart-wrenching sound. *Too late. Too late.* "Where will you go? How will I know you're somewhere safe?"

"You can reach me on my cell." She ducked into the living room, leaned over the back of the couch to grab her purse and tote bag where she'd left them when she returned home from work. Adding these to her shoulders, she moved toward the front door. She looked back at him; he was halfway down the stairs from the bedroom. "And do *not* try to contact me for at least twenty-four hours. I won't answer your calls until I'm ready to talk to you."

At last he stood speechless. She watched him a moment longer—that too-handsome face looking a little angry but mostly forlorn. Shifting the weight of her burdens, Nikki reached for the doorknob, her eyes still holding his gaze. "Good-bye, Matt."

She turned and left what had been their home, closing the door gently behind her. In the garage, she quickly dumped everything into the back seat of her Camry and slid behind the wheel. But then all motion ceased. She stared out through the windshield and whispered, "Okay, what now?"

She rested her clasped arms across the top of the steering wheel. Where could she go? Who might help her . . . take her in? Julia Cleary was the only friend close enough to share this, and she, living in her elderly mother's spacious home, would have room for her; both Clearys would welcome her. But they'd just left for a month's stay at their ancestral home in Ireland and she had no way to contact them.

She slumped forward, let her head fall against her arms on the steering wheel. *God, what am I going to do?* Eyes closed, she sat motionless and silent, too exhausted, too numb even to cry.

Three hours later, eyes closed, arms outstretched, Nikki lay back across the narrow bed in Cabin 22 at the Six Bucks Motel.

Built back in the heyday of motor courts and when Motel 6 provided decent rooms for six dollars a night, the place had only three years ago been renovated and completely refurbished. The old sign remained: carved wood with the motel's name outlined in green neon and flanked by silhouettes of identical five-point bucks, three on each side. Owner Donna Simmons, a former nurse, had given Nikki a break and included tonight for free.

She'd found Number 22 surprisingly clean and well maintained. Its basic furnishings were like most hotel rooms'. There were end tables with lamps; a writing desk and chair; a surprisingly roomy dresser supporting a good-size TV complete with cable and a CD/DVD player on a base that swiveled to accommodate viewing from the bed or the inviting brown-velveteen recliner. But there was also an efficiency-kitchen unit, almost identical to one she and Matt had as a wet-bar in their den, combining a sink and single-burner hotplate on the top and a compact refrigerator below. Above a postage stamp of Formica counter, a microwave oven had been installed beneath two wooden cabinets meant to hold a minimum of cookware and foodstuffs.

The bathroom, sparkling white except for the green shower curtain, held no surprises, unless you counted the plushness of the towels and that the rent included complete linen service. That would be a godsend.

Nikki sighed. *My new domain.* It was worlds apart from the spacious condo with all the fine furniture, fabrics and ornamentation she'd so carefully chosen with Matt, but now this was the place that felt safe. And she had most of what she needed for a week or more, thanks not only to her toiletries travel bag, but also to what she considered her other escape kit, a tapestry tote she took with her everywhere. Cleverly constructed, its hard sides were double-walled, concealing pockets where she stashed photocopies of her most important personal records, so she was never without access to her vital information. But to further protect herself from identity theft, she filled the bag with items that would appear useful—a small first aid kit, tool set, her address book, packets of antibacterial wipes and the like, that shouldn't tempt a thief. When she was out of the house, she kept it securely locked in the trunk of her car.

But she'd have to go get some of the original records from the condo, items she should have in her possession: birth certificate, passport, documents for her car and insurance policies. She needed some warmer clothing and footwear now the season was turning. And she could pick up the vitamins and herbal supplements Matt always teased her about taking; the CDs and DVDs he'd never listen to; those few mementos she'd managed to hang onto from her childhood, including one precious photo of her with her mother, both of them smiling.

Her head began to spin, churning with thoughts of their joint checking, shared credit cards, the way they'd commingled their funds . . . trusting that they'd always be together. Such a leap of faith for both of them, and now. . . .

Why does everyone always leave me? Tony, her father, or her sperm donor, as she called him, had never even been there for her. Then her mother was gone when Nikki needed her most. And the other people in her life had always fallen short. Some were even very good to her . . . sincerely cared about her . . . but when-push-came-to-shove, their needs or priorities always got put before hers. And all the apologies and good intentions in the world couldn't change that.

Eyes still squeezed shut, head still wheeling, Nikki grasped handfuls of bedspread on either side of her, as if that could help her hold on to this life of hers, careening out of control. The thought came unbidden: *Maybe I should just go back.* Certainly Matt would want her back . . . welcome her . . . beg forgiveness . . . promise the affair was ended . . . *mean* it. There was no question Matt still loved her, as she did him. They'd just lost sight of each other for a while. They could put their marriage back together, maybe get some counseling and they could go on without the pain and embarrassment, disruption and financial hardship of divorce.

No. Her eyes popped open, and she waited for the world to stop reeling around her. She knew she could never trust him again and that once again, the past would have to be forgotten and only the future counted.

Nikki rose quickly and went to her tote bag, leaned against the two duffels she'd left just inside the door. She took it back to the bed and got comfortable, letting the richness of the ivy-patterned tapestry soothe her through her fingertips and her eyes. Then she rummaged inside and brought out the suede address book with special plastic windows to display business cards. It took her awhile to find the one she sought; it'd been in there nearly five years, the numbers never called.

Glickman, Glickman & Berkowitz/Attorneys at Law, it read and below that *Samuel Glickman, Junior Partner.* There were both an address and phone number for the office, but Sam himself had scrawled his home number between the blocks of text. When he pressed the card into her hand, his eyes brimming, he'd insisted, "If you *ever* need a lawyer for *any*thing, you call me. If it's not something we handle, I'll find you the person you need. I promise." His wife Adah nodded, mopping her tears of joy and relief but too overcome to speak.

All because Nikki had helped save little Abby's life—had believed the daughter they so cherished would survive when everyone else had given up hope.

Four-year-old Abby was admitted to Nikki's peds ward suffering from carbon monoxide poisoning. She and her seven-year-old brother Jed had been playing "fort" in a backyard playhouse on a blustery November day when Jed decided he had the perfect solution to keep them warm: charcoal briquettes in the family's small hibachi, which he hauled from the garage. Having many times watched his father use lighter fluid to get the charcoal started, Jed had no problem creating their "fireplace" of smoldering coals. Later, when he opted to return to the house, complaining of a bad headache, Abby was too drowsy to get up from the floor where she'd curled up for a nap. So Jed left her, carefully closing up the playhouse so she'd stay safe and warm. At the house, when asked, he'd answered simply that his sister was still "in the playhouse" before going to lie down till his headache was better. By the time Adah went to check on Abby, the child was unconscious and completely unresponsive.

Oxygen revived her in the ambulance on the way to DCH, but Abby didn't recover as quickly as hoped even with sessions in the hyperbaric chamber. Nikki gave her as much attention as she could: checking on her frequently while caring for her other patients and spending any break time sitting beside her bed, holding her hand and talking to her whether she appeared conscious or not. But when Abby's condition hadn't improved after more than sixty hours, even Dr. Tischler had to admit to the Glickmans that the prognosis appeared grim. Nikki recognized a certain look in all their eyes. She called it the Letting-Go Look, and there were times when she was glad to see it in the eyes of patients and relatives, because it meant they were ready to accept an unhappy but inevitable outcome. At the sixty-five hour mark, on her way into Abby's room, Nikki passed the Glickmans in the hall, tearfully discussing alternative care arrangements. But she knew they, and the doctors, were all wrong and she told the parents that Abby would recover. She promised that she would make sure that Abby was not left alone until she could smile at them again. And they believed her Over the years, many people had commented on Nikki's uncanny knack for knowing that certain children could survive against the longest of odds. She had a way of sensing some indefinable fortitude of spirit that could carry a person past the usual limitations of mortal flesh. And she was seldom fooled.

And Abby Glickman had proven the doctors wrong. Beyond surviving, she was now a thriving, happy fourth grader. The only after effect seemed to be a slight dragging of her right foot, but she didn't let it hold her back physically or socially. Every year she sent Nikki a birthday card, at first assisted by her mother but now on her own, with a note to bring Nikki up to date. Sometimes they'd see each other at the park or in a store, and Nikki always got the biggest hug from the girl and any accompanying parent.

Nikki stared at the business card she held. She'd call tomorrow about filing for divorce.

Despite her absolute certainty she was doing the right thing, her stomach felt suddenly hollow and fluttery. Wild thoughts, questions, doubts, regrets, tried to invade her mind. To settle herself, she reached again into her tote, this time into the double-walled pocket that balanced the one concealing her important papers, and pulled out her journal. This one was saddle-brown, but over the years she'd filled books of black, grey, tan, red, maroon and various shades of blue and green. She opened it and unclipped her favorite pen from a pocket inside the front cover, a compartment that also held a 2004–2006 calendar and a number of lists where she recorded birthdays and anniversaries of co-workers; auto service and gas mileage; medical, dental and beauty appointments; bill payments and other important events in her life.

Nikki flopped down on her belly like any teenage girl preparing to pour her heart out into her diary within the sanctity of her own bedroom. Turning to the next blank page and writing the date, she noticed she wasn't even halfway through the book. Long ago she'd given up trying to keep a one-book-for-one-year rule. There were years she'd filled three and times when at least two years composed a single volume.

Nikki sighed, smiling, and began to write.

CHAPTER THIRTEEN

Linda Ferrante grimaced and took another sip of coffee, trying to fill her nostrils with its pungent aroma. She'd managed to limit her time at the courthouse defending punks to only a few quick cases. Instead, today she was hunkered down with extra paperwork and research for Glickman, Glickman & Berkowitz using her considerable writing skills to move along several important cases and putting her in charge of the paralegals and office interns. While she enjoyed the enthusiasm of her staff, much of the tasks were mind-numbingly boring, and they also kept her cooped up all day with the malodorous Kip Carpenter.

An exemplary employee at G, G & B, he was a nice enough man, a shy and skinny forty-year-old with a touch of grey at his temples. From the beginning, Linda's acute sense of smell had been affronted by his habitual bad breath, but for the last few weeks, he'd been suffering from some terrible allergy that clogged his sinuses so that he not only was constantly sniffling but also forced to breathe through his mouth.

Linda set aside her now-empty mug and reshuffled the papers she'd been perusing, then clipped them together and put them in her *Out* box. Behind her, Kip sniffled, then released a long, gusty sigh, no doubt expelling yet another tide of fetid breath. At least their desks were against opposite walls instead of facing. She leaned closer to the shelf that held her caddy for organizing office supplies. Behind the forest of upright scissors, rulers and writing implements, she'd secreted a small plug-in air freshener. But she couldn't seem to keep her face close enough to it.

She was just wondering if the new Evergreen Spice scent she'd seen in the store might be more effective than this Heavenly Gardenia, when her phone rang. Startled, she grabbed for it as guiltily as if she'd been caught in some underhanded plot against a colleague. "Hullo?" She winced; too late to answer properly: "Ms. Ferrante. How may I help you?"

A crisp female voice commanded, "Please hold for District Attorney Bradden" and was gone before Linda could make any reply.

A long moment of dead air followed, then a *click* and his resonant voice, sounding very cordial: "Ms. Ferrante . . . Linda? I hope you'll remember our meeting at that Bar Association mixer recently."

"Of course. How are you?" not able to keep the curiosity out of her reply.

"Fine, fine." He chuckled. "I must say you made quite an impression on me."

Linda swallowed nervously. That hadn't been the first time they'd met, but he probably didn't remember those earlier encounters, because she'd maintained such a low profile. But the last time, he'd interrupted a conversation she was having with a small group of other defense lawyers and had inaccurately cited case law to them. Already annoyed at his interruption, she didn't stop to think whether it might be "politic" to correct the D.A. She just did: courteously but in such succinct detail that it was clearly irrefutable. He'd laughed and saluted her with his wineglass, asked her name and what firm she worked for.

Before Linda could think of anything to say, Bradden went on, still sounding amused. "You really piqued my interest, so I've been checking you out. Besides all the good folks at G, G & B, I talked to the law firm you worked for in New York. Quite impressive work there. Everyone spoke very highly of you. And, as it happens, I'm well acquainted with James Lowengaard."

It didn't seem to matter that she remained silent; he just kept talking while she wondered desperately what this was about and what did James have to do with this?

"I didn't realize you'd done so much prosecutorial work—and with such commendable results. It seems one of Deerwood's brightest lights is hiding under a bushel basket."

She had to say *something*. "Uh, well, thanks. . . ."

"So I think it's time you came out to shine. May I take you to lunch next week?" But as she tried to find an appropriately polite way to decline a date, he added, "I'd like to offer you a job."

Shocked into silence, Linda's first thought was *No Thanks.* The idea of working in the D.A.'s office held very little charm, especially under the authority of an arrogant political carnivore like Scott Bradden, but behind her, Linda could hear Kip Carpenter begin one of his unrestrained sneezing fits. "What kind of a job?" she managed in a low voice.

"As an Assistant, naturally. I can guarantee a sizable bump over your current salary. Let's meet so I can give you more details, answer all your questions. Shall we say, next Wednesday, noon at the Arms?"

The hotel offered fine dining with a superb lunch menu from the grill. She pictured herself savoring a delectable meal in one of those sumptuous booths, sitting across from the District Attorney, a man any woman would admit was easy-on-the-eyes as Nonna used to say of her favorite movie actors. Realizing lunch didn't mean she had to accept the job, she agreed, "Okay, Mr. Bradden."

"It's Scott to you, Linda, whether you come to work here or not. Now, I just realized I'm about to be late for a meeting, so I'll let you go. See you at noon on Wednesday; bring your appetite."

He clicked off even as she was saying, "Bye." Linda set down the receiver and stared at it. She wondered why he had reached out to her. Was he looking to improve his gender balance? Maybe he wanted a New York touch? But why did he mention James? Ah, that was it! Knowing what she knew about Bradden, this had to be related to his next career move. There'd been a lot of speculation around the G, G & B water cooler lately, especially when they heard the state's Republican Party had endorsed Bradden as their candidate for Attorney General. He had the brilliant mind he needed, the courtroom savvy and the lust for power. All he needed now was the money.

Linda bit back a sudden chuckle. *Of course!* He'd found out from James that Dom and Angela Ferrin were her parents. That explained everything. Not only were they well-respected attorneys but also real estate barons, famous for filling the war chests of favorite political candidates. All Republican, naturally. Linda started smiling. James must not have mentioned how far to the left she was from her parents and him. And wouldn't it be a good thing to have a bleeding-heart liberal in the middle of the District Attorney's office?

Yes, she should think this over very carefully. Go have a nice lunch and listen to what Scott Bradden had to offer. Especially now she was pretty sure his interest in her wasn't romantic. Behind her, Kip blew his nose loudly and productively, following up with several vigorous coughs. The kind that make co-workers duck for cover. She respected her bosses, she thought but maybe it was time for a change.

Linda had just returned to her paperwork when one of her bosses, the younger Glickman, appeared in the doorway. Both she and Kip greeted Sam; he nodded to Kip, then turned his attention to her, handing her a sheet of paper with some notes.

"I know it's not your usual thing, Linda, but I'd like you to handle this for me. Nikki Saxon is the nurse who saved our daughter's life, and now she needs to file divorce papers. I want someone who'll treat her with the utmost compassion and attention. She'll be coming in today at ten a.m., and I'd like you to do at least this initial meeting."

Linda blushed, not only at the pleasure of receiving a rare compliment, but also at the guilty knowledge she hadn't mentioned her planned lunch with Scott Bradden the day after tomorrow to talk about the new job opportunity. "Of course. I'll treat her as if she were my own sister."

Glickman nodded, and Linda knew the strange stiffness of his features meant he was trying not to make a face at the ambient odor of the cubicle. "Uh, Müeller's in court all day today. You can use his office." He paused, then as Kip looked up, added quickly, "More room in there. And I'm sure she'll appreciate the privacy."

Linda felt a smile quirk her lips, and she let her eyes thank Glickman for the small upcoming reprieve from KipLand. "Yes, very much appreciated, I'm sure."

CHAPTER FOURTEEN

Dan entered room 915 and introduced himself to the couple awaiting him. Joseph Bonfiglio, the patient, looked to be in his mid-thirties, and, though he gave Dan a ready smile, seemed too pale for his Italian heritage and embarrassed by the sagging on the left side of his face.

Bell's palsy, Dan thought. "So, Mr. Bonfiglio—" He broke off abruptly and laughed at the grimace he saw. "Ah, Joseph . . . ?"

The grin was back; this was the kind of guy Dan liked right away. "I'm Joe. Not even my mother calls me Joseph anymore. And this is my wife Sue."

Having already shaken the hand Joe offered, Dan turned to do the same with a cute brunette showing worried eyes and a slight bulge in her yellow maternity T-shirt proclaiming *Yes, I am!* over a downward-pointing arrow.

"Hey, Doc, okay if I call you . . . " he was reading the nametag as if making sure he'd heard right, "Dante?"

"Make that Dan, and we're in business."

Both Joe and Sue laughed. The way their heads tilted unconsciously toward each other hinted they'd been laughing together for many years despite their youth, but Dan could hear the underlying nervousness.

"So, Joe, how have you been feeling?"

The man gave a little nod, as if making up his mind about something. "I like you . . . feel I can trust you. Good, firm handshake; not afraid to laugh or be called by your first name—and a fellow *paisan* to boot."

Dan found it a little disconcerting to learn he'd been under such scrutiny—and from the person *he* was supposed to be evaluating!

"I'm gonna level with you, Dan. Not so good lately. Always been healthy as a horse; I eat right, keep fit. Painting houses is strenuous work, y'know. My little business has really taken off with all the renovation in this area. But now I'm feelin' tired all the time. Had to hire extra college kids to help out this summer." He paused to swallow, the effort clearly uncomfortable. "My throat's been sore for more than a week. And now this." He pointed to the left side of his face with a sheepish, lopsided grin. "Damnedest thing."

"Well, let me check you out, okay?" Dan proceeded to get Joe's history and complete the physical exam. Joe, indeed, had a facial nerve paralysis, extreme pallor and yellow-pinpoint Roth spots in his eye grounds—ominous signs. Dan saw something else in those eyes, a certain look he'd seen before in patients who suspected they were seriously ill.

"Beep, beep, beep . . . Dr. Marchetti, call hematology lab 3455 . . . 3455."

"One minute, Joe." He gestured toward the bedside table. "Mind if I use your phone?" He winked. "Local call."

"No problem. But leave a quarter." Joe turned his attention to his wife, patting her hand reassuringly as they started talking about visiting hours and when the rest of the family might arrive.

Dan dialed, and the phone rang once before the tech down in the lab got on, sounding urgent: "Dan, your man's got leukemia or something. Better treat him in a hurry."

Dan recognized the voice. With a name like Isaak Zoller and the initials I.Z., it was easy to see why everyone called him Izzy. And the private joke among the house staff, who referred to him as the "extra resident" because he so enjoyed participating in the diagnostic process, was asking, "Izzy a doctor yet?"

Dan didn't want to give Izzy the wrong idea about the weight of his contributions, so he ignored Izzy's opening comments and asked simply, "What do you have for me?"

"Bonfiglio's hematocrit is 22 and WBC 150,000 with 45% blast forms—looks like myeloblasts. Platelets are 22,000."

Shit! Dan could feel his entire body stiffen as he tried not to look at Joe. Fortunately, Joe didn't know the call concerned his tests, and in case he suspected, Dan wasn't ready for him to know the gravity of the news. He managed a light tone. "Thanks, Izzy. You're the greatest. A true member of the hall of fame of lab techs."

Izzy laughed out loud. "Fuck you, Marchetti. You with him now?"

Forcing a chuckle, Dan answered, "Yeah."

"G'luck with that."

They both hung up, and Dan turned to his patient. "Joe, I'll be back later to see you after we have some more of the lab results. Okay?"

"Sure." Joe pushed back his covers. "I'll just take this opportunity to hit the john." He struggled awkwardly to his feet, wrestling to keep the flimsy hospital gown protecting his dignity. "Damn. Hate these things." Joe started for the bathroom, clutching the gown behind him to hide his bare buttocks but still exposing far too much of his well-muscled legs. Add to that those little, DCH-issued terrycloth slipper socks with non-skid soles and Joe offered a poignant glimpse of "patienthood."

"Oh, by the way," Mandy said to Joe, "You have visitors, your mother and your kids." She glanced at Dan to include him in her next question. "Should I send them in?"

Dan gestured that it was fine with him; he'd finished his exam. Joe's face lit up with the mention of his family, but he said, "Give me five minutes to do my thing and get back in bed, okay? No need to subject *everyone* to a floorshow."

"I'll catch up with you a little later," Dan told him, and Joe nodded as he slipped into the bathroom and closed the door.

Mandy shared a look with Dan. He could tell she'd guessed the seriousness of Joe's illness. She went to straighten Joe's bedclothes and check the level of ice water in the pitcher. Dan followed Sue out into the hall and waved as she left him, on her way toward a cluster of figures not far down the corridor. Dan had a quick view of a woman in her fifties shepherding three little girls, one perhaps six and the others, clearly identical twins, probably three years younger, all with round faces amid mops of wildly tousled black hair.

Would Joe live to see them grown? The labs were consistent with acute myelogenous leukemia and the Bell's palsy meant central nervous system involvement. He could be gone before his fourth child even arrived.

The pain of that made Dan's whole body ache as he moved to the nurse's desk and flopped down into the chair, feeling ninety. After a long moment, he placed a phone call to Joe's primary physician, Barney Jackson.

"Damn!" Jackson said wearily. "Been seeing Joe his whole life—well, haven't seen him often; he's always been one of my healthiest, God, that poor family." His voice cracked ever so slightly. "Okay, I'll come by late this afternoon after my office hours, say sixish, to give him the diagnosis myself." "Could you contact Cyrus later for me? See if he can be there?"

"Of course." Dan had first met the oncology attending while on his ICU rotation. Though smart as hell, Klonter was harder to read as a person: his wispy blond hair and mustache seemed perfectly matched to his reticent and self-effacing manner.

"If you're available," Jackson continued, "would you like to be there too?"

After Jackson hung up and Dan left a message with Klonter's service, he sat wondering how Joe would respond to such news. Worry started to surge up in him, fueled partly by how much he identified with the laid back *paisan*, but someone else's emergency interrupted.

"*Beep, beep, beep* . . . Dr. Marchetti, Room 902, stat . . . 902, stat!"

Dan leaped up and rushed down the long hall. He hadn't seen any patient yet in that room and hoped it was a super elderly gomer just waiting to move on. He clenched his jaws hard, pushing the thought of Joe and his family to the back of his mind.

The new patient just required some oxygen and reassurance and Dan next looked in on Elena Guillermo who was two days post-op. He found her doing very well, and Dr. Bosnan expressed both great pleasure at how smoothly the surgery had gone as well as the news that the tumor was benign. "We sent it down to pathology for a frozen section," she told Dan. "No malignancy. You might want to go down there and take a look at it. Not every day you see a teratoma—much less one with both a tooth and hair in it."

By the time he returned to Joe's bedside, he had become militantly optimistic about the young family man's chances. Barney Jackson and Cyrus Klonter told Joe he had leukemia . . . cancer. The two of them said the usual things about grave illness and unknown outcomes; they talked about the treatment that was needed to bring him into remission and how they wanted him to stay in the hospital awhile—in addition to the intravenous chemotherapeutics—they injected another powerful drug into the fluid bathing his spinal cord and brain in order to clear out the leukemic cells there.

Joe, and Sue sitting beside him, listened without interruption. When prompted, they nodded that they understood, but Dan was sure they weren't taking it all in just yet. He saw the blankness of their faces, eyes that seemed focused inward on the turmoil of their own thoughts, and the way they grasped each other's hands so tightly the fingers started turning blue from lack of circulation. When asked if they had any questions, they both shook their heads.

Neither Jackson nor Klonter offered answers for some pretty important unasked questions like causal factors, life expectancy, hope for a cure. Certainly no one mentioned the strong possibility that Joe had less than nine months to live.

Dan wasn't sure what to think of this "Don't ask; don't tell" approach. He couldn't tell if the family physician was simply deferring to the oncologist as the better person to broach such grim subjects. Further, he couldn't tell whether Klonter refrained because of reluctance born of his own shy nature or if his years of experience had proven it was more beneficial to let the patient ask for these details when really ready to hear the answers. Dan, of course, kept his mouth shut. It wasn't his place to jump in and open up momentous topics; he was here to learn from the experts.

Still, he thought when Jackson and Klonter had left, the Bonfiglios would start to ask some of the questions—especially after the news had sunk in a little. But Joe and Sue just stared at each other—still gripping hands—then both started reassuring the other. Sue looked to Dan, reached out one hand to him, drew him closer. "We're glad you're here with us."

Yeah? Just wait'll I start jabbing needles into your back! Thank God, Joe's mom arrived with his three little daughters, and the conversation got lively. Dan stepped back as Joe and Sue cuddled the girls close and started explaining how their papa had to stay in the hospital awhile so he could get better but not to worry. All soothing tones and cheerful smiles.

That evening, Dan headed home by walking out of his way through the park, needing some time to process how closely he had identified with the Bonfiglio family. He headed for a favorite spot, a lakeside bench in a little stand of weeping willows. Since it was hidden from view till he was nearly upon it, he didn't see till the last moment that it was already occupied. Starting to walk past, he recognized the long auburn hair and the slender figure dressed in jeans and a dark green shirt. She looked up as his sneakers crunched toward her over the scattered leaves. *Nikki Saxon!*

Her face brightened. "Hi, Dante!" She'd been sitting in the middle of the bench, not inviting a casual passer-by to join her, but now, she scooted over, leaving him plenty of room if he wanted to sit. He did, lowering himself with a little groan at the way his body felt after too many nights on the creaking on-call cots.

Nikki laughed. "Sounding old, Dr. Marchetti!"

He laughed and stretched. And turned to face her, for the first time that her eyes were a little red and puffy, as if she'd been crying. Her whole face looked tired. He'd gotten a bit used to that look. Not just overstressed young interns but everyone who pulled long hours and worked variable shifts and, especially, those who dealt daily with misery.

Nikki looked thin. He realized she was wearing the same outfit as when he first met her: black jeans and that long-sleeve polo shirt in Deerwood High green. Those garments had been deliciously snug three months ago, but now they fit her more loosely. Not at all unattractive, just different. Maybe more was going on in her life than just the stresses of work. Dan remembered what Cheryl told him about the marriage being unhappy. Had it gotten worse?

The sudden honking of a wedge of Canada geese winging southward pulled Nikki's gaze to the sunset sky above them. Furtively, Dan took the opportunity to glance down at her left hand where it rested on the bench between them. No wedding band, but did she ever wear one? Certainly not that first night they met, and since then on other occasions at DCH, he hadn't noticed because, by that time, it didn't matter; he knew she was married whether she wore a ring or not.

"I love this spot," Nikki murmured, still gazing at the view.

Dan turned his face to the beauty of the dying day, the way red and gold light rippled across the water toward them just before the sun sank out of view beyond the trees on the lake's opposite shore. "Yeah," he said, "me too." She looked at him with those sad eyes, a shade darker green in the dimming light, and he felt suddenly as awkward and stirred as the first moment he met her. Remembering their pledge to stay friends, he put on another voice, imitating a lounge lizard with a worn-out pickup line: "You come here often?"

She didn't laugh, but she *did* smile, taking most of the sadness from her eyes. "Mainly when I need to think about serious stuff."

Ah! Was she going to open up . . . tell him what was going on . . . let him be a friend . . . show her he could be a good listener? "Oh . . . ?"

But the suddenly stiffening breeze ruffled her reddish hair, pushed long strands across her face. She shivered and rubbed her sleeves to warm her arms inside. "Ooooh! Time to go, I guess."

He hopped up. "Yeah. It'll be dark soon. Thanks for sharing the spot."

She rose and began to move in the opposite direction. "Any time."

He gave her a little wave and started to turn away, but her voice called after him…"Dante!"—and he spun around at the intensity in it.

But she didn't say more. After a moment, she just sighed and shook her head, gave a little hollow laugh. "Nothing, really. It was nice seeing you again."

Keeping it light, he doffed and flourished an invisible hat, bowing over it. "The pleasure was all mine."

They both laughed and waved and went on their way as if this had only been a chance meeting of two friendly colleagues—as it should be. Dan wanted desperately to look back, watch her go, but he didn't.

CHAPTER FIFTEEN

"Dr. Dan!" Elena Guillermo beamed as soon as she saw him enter her room.

"Hi, Elena . . . Yolanda." Dan nodded, smiling, to his patient and then to her cousin. The two of them were gathering Elena's belongings, including items supplied by the hospital, basin, pitcher and the like, so she could be discharged from DCH.

"Ready to go home?" Dan asked, unable to think of anything more inspired.

"Yes!" Elena said before Yolanda could try to translate. "Home!"

Only at that moment did he realize this might be a sensitive question. After all, where was Elena to go? Certainly she could still share Yolanda's little apartment for a while as she healed. But Dan had once overheard Yolanda telling Alma they needed two incomes to pay all their bills and still send money back home to the relatives who depended on them. How was Elena to find work now . . . and doing what? He didn't want to think about the work many strippers fell into when they couldn't dance for money anymore.

As if she could read his thoughts, Elena pointed toward her chest and said excitedly, "I . . . got . . . job!"

"Hey, cool!" Dan felt himself flush with surprise, embarrassment, confusion. He was afraid to try to ask what, but she was eager to tell him and turned to Yolanda with a gesture for her to take over.

"Yes," Yolanda confirmed. "Alma's uncle Jorge Ciervo manages a dancing school. You know . . . ballroom . . . dancing. As soon as 'Lena's all healed, she goes to work as an assistant instructor. That was the work we both did at home in Argentina," Yolanda told him with a gently chiding tone. "We know how to do all those 'real' dances, you know. 'Lena is a hometown champion in tango. In Argentina, we know how to do the *real* tango."

Dan could feel himself blushing. How unfair of him not to see these women as more than the role they were forced to play here. He tried to dig himself out. "Will you be working there too?"

Yolanda laughed and tossed her head in a mockingly flirtatious way. "Oh, no. I can still make much more money at the Kit Kat."

Dan laughed with her, hoping his color would soon be back to normal. "Dr. Bosnan gave you Elena's discharge orders?" Still smiling, Yolanda pulled the folded pink sheets from her pocket and waggled them. "And she explained everything, so you're both clear on how to care for the incision and when to come for follow-up and everything?" At her nod, he said regretfully, "Then I guess it's time to say good-bye."

Elena understood enough of that, gave Dan another little hug slipping a small piece of paper into his hand as she turned, and sat down in the wheelchair. Yolanda put one bag of Elena's belongings on her lap and carried the other two herself.

Dan was left alone in the room studying the paper, a small business card. *Ciervo School of Dance,* it read with an address on Main Street, a phone number and a little silhouette of tango dancers. He turned it over and found a cell phone number written with beautiful precision in blue ink.

He carefully placed the card in his pocket where it couldn't get lost. Hard to mistake the meaning, the invitation, of the card. Should he accept? Certainly leave her to the healing process . . . but perhaps a call or two to check on her? See how her English was coming along. Let her get started in her new job . . . on her feet and feeling less dependent again. Then a dinner date with the beautiful Argentinean who after all was not his patient and required no follow up from him? What if it got serious? Would he ever *have* to tell his parents she used to be a stripper? Could his brother, Jerry keep a secret like that?

It was easy to imagine holding her, making love to her, but could he imagine falling in love with her . . . making a life together? Was she looking to settle down . . . and with an American man? Maybe a rich American doctor as a fast-track to citizenship? *No, not Elena.* His folks might think that, but Dan found it hard to believe the Elena he'd encountered would marry for any reasons other than love and true commitment. She probably wouldn't *mind* marrying a prosperous American physician any more than he would *mind* becoming a wealthy doctor, while being a *good* doc was his first goal and priority.

"What now?" he murmured, seeing again Elena's beautiful face just before they parted earlier today . . . those smoldering eyes. "What's my next move?"

No tango lessons, that's for sure, but maybe an easier, gentler form of dancing. On the insides of his eyelids, he pictured her in his arms, slow-dancing in an otherwise-empty room, their bodies in full contact. Heavenly image, heavenly warmth cuddled in that blue cloud of a shirt. Dan drifted off into a dream that did not end with dancing, where she was healthy and athletic, and the scar on her bare chest was hardly noticeable at all.

Shaking his head to clear it of all thoughts that seemed wildly inappropriate in a sterile hospital room, Dan walked down to the cafeteria. Appetite soon ruined by another too-dry, too-salty cafeteria-tuna-casserole congealing on his plate, his paperwork miraculously all finished, and all the rest of the house staff busy with their own duties, meals or naps, Dan opted to pay a surprise visit to one of his favorite patients: Joe Bonfiglio.

Dan knocked lightly on the closed door of the private room where Joe had been moved before beginning his seven days of intensive chemotherapy. "Room service?" Joe's voice came faintly through the door.

"Yeah," Dan said as he entered. "You ordered the pineapple-anchovy pizza?" Joe tried to give him a big grin, but he looked a little green-around-the-gills. "Sorry, Joe. That was dumb."

Joe, as usual, was all forgiving. "Well, kinda hoped you'd be delivering beer. Not much appetite for food these days. In fact," he swept a hand toward the Luigi's box on his bedside table, "I have more pizza than I can face. Help yourself; no sense it going to waste."

Just seeing a Luigi's box could make Dan salivate. He opened the lid and stared down at a whole pie missing only one piece. "Wow, thanks," Dan said, "My favorite: The Works!" His eyes devoured it first—the rich red sauce, thick melted cheeses, mountains of veggies and sausage—even before he could get a slice to his mouth. *Still warm. And perfect.*

Joe smiled like a proud father who'd "brought home the bacon" for a ravenous son. "For a minute there, I thought you were here to stick more needles into my back."

"Nah," Dan told him between bites. "I'm as good as my word. This morning was the last injection of Methotrexate. The Idarubicin was only the first three days, and I see you're off the infusion of Cytarabine."

Joe chuckled at the litany of pharmaceutical names. "That's easy for you to say, Doc. Yeah, no more chemo for a while, but Klonter says I still have to stick around another coupla-three weeks 'cuz I'll probably get really sick till I start getting better."

"Yep. We want to make sure your counts stay in the right ranges, keep you from getting dehydrated, try to prevent or control any infections."

Joe watched as Dan finished a second piece of pizza. "I'm always glad to see you, Dan, but I can't relax till you tell me if there's some reason for this visit. Maybe my bone marrow results came back?"

"No!" Dan spoke with such surprise, he actually launched a small piece of mushroom with the word. He picked it off his sleeve and grabbed a napkin from the handy stack by the box. Wiping his mouth, he thought how paranoid a patient could get. House staff rarely showed up unless they were trying to get you to take something or do something you probably would rather avoid. "Probably tomorrow for those bone marrow labs. No ulterior motive, Joe. Just thought I'd come see how you were doing."

Joe relaxed with a little sigh of relief. "I'm okay . . . I guess. Considering, y'know. . . ."

While Dan packed away a third fat slice of Luigi's best, they talked some football, some local news, some family—including the costumes Sue was making for their girls to wear on Halloween: a fairy princess, a cheerleader and a doctor. "That one's for you," Joe told him. "My Josie, she's the oldest, she's really focused on medical stuff right now. Says she 'wants to be like Dr. Dan and help sick people get better except be a girl doctor!.'"

Dan felt a blush rising. "I'm flattered."

"I just hope I'll be outta here so I can see them . . . help give out the candy."

Smiling confidently in the face of Joe's wistful expression, Dan assured him, "You will be. Even if you have to stay the full three weeks."

"Promise?"

"You know I can't promise . . . but I'll bet you."

"What?"

"How 'bout that beer you've been wanting?"

Joe brightened. "You're on."

Dan made as if to leave then, but before he could say goodbye, Joe interrupted him with, "Hey, in the meantime, a game of hearts?" his raspy voice seemed to plead.

"Sure." Dan closed the pizza box and set it on the foot of the bed. He moved the bedside table to a more convenient alignment, cleared away everything except the old deck of Bicycle playing cards he'd come to know over the last week, and sat in the visitor's chair.

"Deal!" Joe commanded, "and prepare to lose big-time," desperately trying to sound upbeat.

They played for half an hour paying little attention to who had accumulated the most points. Dan thought maybe finally Joe was ready to ask those big questions everyone had been avoiding, but he didn't. He just yacked and joshed and laughed, slapping his cards down as if he had nothing more important to care about. But then he began to wilt visibly.

"I've worn you out," Dan said at the end of the last hand, rising to clear everything away.

"Only way you can win," Joe mumbled, sinking back into his bed and closing his eyes. "Thanks for the company."

"Sure." Dan pulled up the covers and dimmed the light.

Without opening his eyes, Joe whispered, "Hey, take the rest of that pizza with you . . . finish it or share it . . . ." before sliding into sleep.

Dan left quietly, the Luigi's box in hand. For a moment—remembering how delicious the pizza was—he thought he might be ready for another slice. But then he realized he'd completely lost his appetite once again.

CHAPTER SIXTEEN

"You can't say no," Willow Blackstone had told him, gazing up into his face. Her eyes were very large and dark and, yes, slightly almond shaped. "I'm cooking dinner for you tonight. At my place."

Now, eight hours later, Dan stood on the landing a moment before knocking on her apartment door. He stared at the whimsical jack o'lantern in her window: it was smiling and toothy but with a decidedly Asian slant to the eyes and warpaint on the cheeks. He been trying for nearly four months to hook up with the intriguing first-year intern. Now, finally the stars, and their schedules, had aligned, putting them both coming off-duty on a Friday morning.

Meeting in the cafeteria, Willow hadn't just rushed away as she often did; in fact, her entire focus seemed to be on engaging him. Dan wasn't sure how they got to talking food, but the next thing he knew, she was extolling the tastes she'd left behind in California, as well as delicacies of her combined ethnic heritages.

"Have you ever tasted buffalo?" she asked. "Well, you should try it. It's much leaner than beef, and I like the flavor even better."

Feeling out of his depth, Dan said something about not realizing buffalo were part of Californian Indian culture. "Oh, they're not really. My father's people were from the Plains tribes; it's my Cantonese side that's based in California."

"But you can get buffalo to eat in California?"

"Sure. There're several ranches in the state raising buffalo for market." She laughed. "Believe it or not, I recently found a store in the next county here that carries it, though they import it from Canada." She studied him a moment. "Y'know, I have some avocados that're gonna be perfect tonight. Why don't you come over, and I'll treat you to a real California Buffalo Burger with all the trimmings."

"Sounds like a lot of work. . . ."

She laughed, "Not nearly as much as the water dumplings and steam buns I had to make when my brother visited last week!" So here he was, feeling exhausted because he'd been unable to sleep in his hours off, about to knock on her door, wondering what would happen that night . . . what he wanted to happen. Willow was still a bit intimidating. Always so quick to take offense at any perceived slight to her bloodlines, her gender or her home state.

Dan wondered what he hoped might happen. That ideal connection with a person who'd truly understand his life and its current limitations? Or just a quick roll-in-the-hay with a California free spirit, avoiding a relationship that was bound to be high-maintenance during a period in his life when he just didn't *have* the time or energy?

Certainly there was nothing to hold him back from either. Nikki was out of reach, and who could guess what might happen with Elena—if anything ever did. There were no ties between them, only a future possibility. And certainly it'd be easier to take Willow, with all her complexities and complexes, "home to Mama" than Elena, the former stripper from Argentina. Besides, dating a patient..... didn't seem right.

Dan lifted his hand to knock, and the door pulled open. "There you are!" Willow exclaimed with a huge grin. "The coals are perfect; come on in."

He followed her inside. She looked so different tonight, clad in a long, flowing silk thing—not a dress or robe exactly—barefoot and obviously braless. Her long black hair was loose and gleaming against the turquoise silk.

He had a moment to notice her spotless apartment, rich in details from her dichotomous ancestry: painted fans and embroidered Chinese wall hangings, some kind of intricately beaded leather pouch and, on the coffee table, what could only be buffalo horns. There was also a huge map of California with about a hundred colorful pushpins stuck in various locations. Before he could ask the significance, Willow had put a glass of white wine in his hand. "Napa Valley White Zin," she told him. "Come on out on the balcony."

Again he followed her, tasting the wine. "Oh! That's good!"

She flashed a smile back over her shoulder, took a sip from her own glass before setting it aside. She gestured toward one of those collapsible canvas chairs. "Relax. You're the guest."

Dan sat focusing his eyes on the small hibachi with glowing coals and a foursome of TV tables, two laden with all the dishes, implements, napkins and condiments they'd need. On another were the open wine bottle, some covered containers and a large wooden bowl full of fresh-spinach salad with many colorful and intriguing ingredients. From the fourth table, on which he also saw a plate of whole-wheat buns, already buttered and browned on the grill, Willow took up a platter with four gigantic ground-meat patties and transferred them to the grate over the coals. Within moments the juices were dripping down to spit on the charcoal, and the steam and smoke rose with such an exquisite odor that his stomach rumbled audibly.

She glanced back over her shoulder, eyes dancing, and interrupted his embarrassed apology, "No sweat. You sound hungry!"

They talked a little as she attended to the burgers, but it was all so easy and unchallenging that Dan paid little attention. He felt himself unwinding, relaxing—going with the flow, as they say. Very California.

She had him refill their glasses and rearrange things so they both had a TV table to use, and he pulled over the other canvas chair for her.

Just before the burgers were ready, Willow topped them with thick slices of Jack cheese that melted down their sides. She placed them on the garlic-butter-toasted buns and offered not only steak sauce, ketchup, mayo and brown mustard, but also a homemade guacamole. He took her lead and declined the more familiar condiments to slather his buffalo cheeseburger with the pale green avocado sauce, expertly seasoned and with just a touch of chili-heat on the tongue.

"God, this is delicious!" he managed between bites, and she grinned at him, licking a trail of squeezed-out guacamole from the side of her hand.

When they'd wolfed down those first burgers, with a minimum of conversation, she served them bowls of salad, topped by a dressing she'd made based on a sweet salsa—flavors he'd never sampled before in a salad.

"Forget the spinach," she told him. "You can call the rest of this 'Native American' . . . all ingredients Europeans got from us: tomatoes, peppers, black beans, red beans, corn kernels, pumpkin seeds. Ready for your other burger,?" She uncovered the container where she'd kept the last two warm.

He couldn't believe he was nodding *yes*. He'd had more than enough food, but just thinking of the flavors of that mild cheese and velvety-cool avocado against the novel taste of buffalo meat was simply irresistible.

They ate the second burgers more slowly, savoring each nuance of flavor as they finished the wine. Like sex, sometimes the first time is a little too fast to get the most enjoyment out of it, Dan thought.. He sneaked a sideways glance at Willow.

"I didn't make dessert," she told him, holding his gaze as if to judge his reaction.

He wondered if he should say something witty, but he chickened out and patted his belly instead. "Don't know where I'd put it. I made a pig of myself." Realizing she had matched him bite for bite, never mind her trim figure, he blushed his embarrassment. "That was the best meal I've had in Pennsylvania," he told her, quite sincerely. "Thank you, Willow."

She smiled. "Coffee?" She rubbed her bare arms. "Let's go inside; it's getting cool out here." Those braless nipples gave proof to her words.

She let him help her clean up and carry in everything that couldn't wait until the next day, but she was very efficient and had the kitchen under control by the time the coffee had brewed.

He sat on the well-pillowed couch where she pointed, and she soon sat down beside him to serve their coffee. In Dan's world, ceramic mugs were a classy upgrade from those ubiquitous Styrofoam cups, so he was surprised to see her set out fine bone china with lavender spirals deftly sketched around the delicate cups. They talked more about food as they sipped. He admitted he wouldn't be giving up beef for buffalo, but he'd really enjoyed it. She got him to talk about favorite Italian dishes his mother made until he was actually feeling a little nostalgic. Or was that just the wine? Certainly the coffee was making no dent in the wine, the huge meal or his fatigue.

She drained the last sip from her cup and clinked it down into its saucer on the coffee table, turned to him and took his empty cup to saucer it as well.

Willow Blackstone leaned toward him, her knee against his leg. "Now," she said. "Let's just see about this." She lifted her face, and Dan stared at the glowing, dusky skin, the wide, black eyes looking now more mysterious and exotic than ever before. The red lips parted, and he could see the pink invitation of her tongue tip.

Of course he kissed her. With all he felt about her seductive beauty and his gratitude for a wonderful shared meal; his deep respect for her abilities as a doctor and the beacon of spirit that always radiated from her. And she returned it with energy and sweetness and a message of willingness in the way her body pressed against him with only thin fabric between them.

Panic surged in Dan. He should be only moments away from condom-ready, but nothing was happening. Nothing! Frantically, Dan considered what he might do, might lead her to do, to get his engines started. How could he avoid missing out on what would surely be a delightful experience? This was a novel experience for him and he felt his heart rate speed up and his muscles clench.

But the kiss ended, and Willow pulled back in his arms, regarding him solemnly . . . perhaps curiously.

"This just isn't happening, is it?" she asked with some bit of wonder in her voice. "Or is it just me?"

"No," he assured her. "I'm sorry, but it just doesn't seem to be—

"I get it!" she said cheerfully. "Sometimes it's just like that with two people. The chemistry on some level isn't right." She gave him a mischievous grin. "Who knows—maybe we were brother and sister in another life." She leaned up to plant an almost sisterly kiss on his mouth, then moved out of his arms. "Darn. I was hoping this would work out. I've had my eye on you from day-one, Marchetti."

"Yeah, me too."

"Well, at least we know now. We can stop wondering . . . trying to make something happen. We can still be friends, right? This isn't gonna make some big awkward thing between us?"

"Not for me."

"Good. Me neither."

"Guess I should go now." He started to rise. "Thanks again—"

"Y'know, I was really looking forward to company tonight. Gets pretty lonely in this business with our crazy schedules. Wanta just hang out for a while? I'm not really in the mood to talk," Willow apologized. "How 'bout some TV? There's a *Monk* marathon going on right now. . . ."

"I *love* that show!"

She scrambled up and pulled aside a Chinese screen to reveal a small TV set. She returned to the couch armed with the remote. "Get comfy." He leaned back against the big pillows. She sat down, pulling her bare feet up under the folds of her turquoise skirt. "Think we could snuggle a little?"

"Sure." He opened his arms, and she sank back against him with a grateful sigh. He brought his arms around her gently, enfolding her like a father or a brother.

And as they watched the hilarious obsessive-compulsive TV detective, Dan was struck by how good it felt to hold someone this way. It feels good, you think?" She nodded in agreement.

CHAPTER SEVENTEEN

Joe Bonfiglio didn't look good, but he definitely looked better than he had over the past three weeks. Though dressed in his street clothes, he lay back on his bed. Propped up against the pillows with his eyes closed, he seemed frail compared to the day he was admitted nearly a month ago. Dan could see loose wisps of hair on the pillow that was new.

"Hey, bud," Dan said quietly, and those brown eyes opened.

"Hey. . . ." The face managed a smile, but it almost seemed too great an effort.

Motioning to the pink discharge orders folded on the bedside table, Dan said, "Hear you're busting outta this fine hotel."

"Yeah. Just waiting for Sue to come get me. Can't wait to get home."

"So I win the bet! You'll be home tonight to pass out candy to the trick-or-treaters."

"Ah! So I owe you a beer."

"I think that was a six pack. But that's okay. Can't have it while I'm on the grounds anyway. Tell y'what: you drink one for me, okay?"

"Gladly." Joe's was a brave attempt at their old camaraderie, but it didn't fool Dan. He knew Joe was reeling from this morning's news.

As at other points during Joe's treatment, Dan had made sure to be present when oncologist Cyrus Klonter gave the Bonfiglios important news or updates. Dan was there when the labs came back identifying certain chromosomal abnormalities in Joe's bone marrow, not a good sign, and when they told him he'd have to be put on I.V. antibiotics because of a gram-negative infection he'd picked up. In between, Dan had visited at least once every day he was on duty and had often dropped by on his days off, just because he knew.

And Joe was lonely. His wife was the only family who came to see him; limiting visitors decreased opportunities for contagion, and of course, no kids. Not that Joe would want his girls to see him sick as he was, lying there with all the tubes into the multi-port in his chest. Tubes keeping him hydrated, fighting his bacterial infection, delivering other drugs to prevent viral and fungal infections.

And, of course, the cancer had fought back. As the first week's chemotherapy killed cancer cells, and many newly forming healthy cells, those dying cells had poured toxins into Joe's blood and laid him low. Sure, he was some better now, well enough to go home, but the post-treatment news, delivered by Klonter this morning, was devastating.

"The latest tests on your bone marrow," Klonter had said, his eyes on the papers he was consulting, "show no appreciable clearing of the cancer cells."

Dan saw Sue, sitting beside Joe's bed, clutch her husband's hand so tightly that he winced and clenched his jaws. Sue bit her lip and teared up, but neither of them spoke.

Klonter gave a little cough, still not making eye contact. "We'll go ahead and discharge you today, as planned. I'd like you to go home and think things over . . . discuss the options. Then come back next week and tell me how you'd like to proceed."

"Options?" Joe managed.

"You can continue to fight with chemotherapy. We have a couple of different drug protocols you could try. Basically, cycles of five days of treatment followed by three weeks off.

"For how long?" Sue asked, unconsciously stroking her rounded belly with her free hand.

Klonter shrugged. "Until remission . . . or a clear indication the body is non-responsive."

Joe stared at Klonter, who still avoided his gaze. "Or . . . ?"

"Or you can remain at home on palliative care . . . or hospice."

Sue gave a little gasp and began to cry, but quietly.

"I'm sorry it's not better news," Klonter told them, his sincerity almost painful to see. When he'd gone, Dan could only stay a few minutes longer. As he expressed his regrets, Joe and Sue barely acknowledged him, so wrapped were they in their own dazed thoughts.

Now, hours later, Joe sat dressed for discharge, looking twice his age after his harrowing illness, treatment and prognosis. But he pulled himself together a bit and asked, "So, Dan, what do you think? Sue and I will talk more after we've had time for it all to sink in, but I think I'm gonna fight it."

Dan just shook his head, a lump in his throat.

"God knows I'm not eager for more chemo! I've heard people say it's worse than dying and now I know what they mean. And if I don't have much time, I hate to use it all up puking and lying around too weak to enjoy my family." Dan nodded his understanding, and Joe continued. "But I'm young, and I've always been strong, so maybe I can still beat this." His eyes misted. "And I'd sure like to be here to see my son get born, his voice trailed off."

Knowing the stress of these last weeks had led to some worries in Sue's pregnancy; she'd opted to have an amniocentesis, which, thankfully, had come back normal, and had revealed the fourth Bonfiglio child would be their first son.

"No good Italian boy," Joe murmured, "should grow up without ever seeing his father." Dan offered a sympathetic grin, having no alternative to offer. But Joe had an idea and ventured hesitantly, "What about, you know . . . weed?" Apparently seeing no censure in the surprise Dan was sure must be on his face, Joe continued, "I hear it's good for chemo side effects. Gives you the munchies back and all. I could use some of that now."

"Well, there *is* a synthetic version of the active ingredient available by prescription. . . ." Dan began in a low voice since he'd left the room door open. "But. . . ."

"Doesn't work too well, does it?" Joe finished his thought with a knowing nod. "That's what I hear. What about the real deal? The smokable stuff, I mean. Never thought I'd end up a dope-head, but I'm kinda in a jam here, so—"

Dan was silent for a moment, pondering Joe's question. In general, he was in favor of anything that would benefit the patient, but there was no getting around the fact that even for medical use, marijuana was still illegal in most of the United States, including Pennsylvania.

Dan had a sudden urge to get in his car and drive to that strip mall where the local dealers hung out. He'd bring some back as readily and cheerfully as filling a request from Joe for an Italian combo from the deli. But while Dan, like any former student, was acquainted with the stuff but not since beginning his intership...

"I think I'd better get Joe outta here," Sue's voice said suddenly with forced levity from behind them. "Better get outta bed, Joe. I saw the nurse coming down the hall with your wheelchair."

With effort, Joe slid off the bed and stood gingerly, steadied by Dan's firm support on his arm. "It's about time. I've got a big night ahead of me. Hope you bought lotsa candy; I'm gonna give every kid a double handful."

Fighting his own emotions again, Dan embraced the sick man, warmly but gently in his awareness of the frailty of Joe's once-robust body. "You take care now." Dan managed to make it sound light. "You guys keep in touch; let me know when you'll be here in the building, okay?"

Amid the good-byes and the arrival of Nurse Gallagher with the wheelchair, Dan slipped out of the room and down the hall in the opposite direction the Bonfiglios would take.

Out of sight, he took a moment to pause and collect himself at one of the huge glass windows along the corridor.

Leaning his hands on the sill and staring out, he realized he was looking down at the lovely green peace of Woodlawn Cemetery, not the best town planning board move, he thought. Bowed forward till his forehead rested against the cool comfort of the glass, he noticed the long strands of dark hair on his sleeve. *Joe's hair.* He closed his eyes so he didn't have to see it, but he didn't brush it away either.

CHAPTER EIGHTEEN

Staring vacantly, Nikki Saxon pushed her half-empty shopping cart down the cereal aisle of the Deerwood SuperMart. She paused, gazing at the array of brightly exuberant boxes before choosing spoon-size shredded wheat. Without enthusiasm, she tossed the box into the cart where it joined bread; fruit; packaged cheese and cold cuts; cans of tuna, beans and ready-to-heat soup. Nikki consulted her mental list: *Milk, yogurt, tea bags, paper towels.* Not much room in her tiny kitchen for more. And after a month on her own at the Six Bucks Motel, she was bored-to-tears with the same limited choices. Mostly she ate in the hospital cafeteria: not great food, but there were some things she actually liked. It was hot, and she didn't have to cook it herself on a tiny burner . . . or clean up afterwards. Besides, there was often company: other nurses and hospital staff, sometimes even relatives of her young patients. Occasionally, she saw Dan Marchetti. He always smiled and waved, but seemed too much in a rush to stop and chat.

Lost in thought, Nikki wheeled her cart around a corner and halted before the organic peanut butter. Trying to decide if the extra cents were worth it, she found herself eavesdropping on a pre-teen who was dramatically flouncing her hair as she stomped down the aisle ahead of a beleaguered appearing mom-type. "You're so mean! If I was with Dad tonight, *he'd* get them for me!"

Giving Nikki a sardonic grin and shake of the head, the mom quickly followed her wayward child and Nikki missed the follow up to what appeared to be a common challenge.

How was she able to keep her cool? Single moms sure had it hard, something she regretted not realizing till it was too late.

Fourteen-year-old Nikki, her insides a roiling sea of pain and anxiety, despair and disgust, felt the waves of anger rise up through it all. Hands on hips, she surveyed the wreckage of the room—a tiny combined kitchen-dining-living area—surrounding her. Smashed coffee table, two brokeOn lamps, ripped-down curtains, a litter of mismatched silverware and crockery, papers scattered everywhere—most crumpled or torn. And that spaghetti stain on the wall? Most of the pasta had slid down onto the shattered plate on the floor below, but all that red sauce . . . . Nikki sighed. I'll never get it outta that old wallpaper.

Just thinking of the tasks ahead exhausted her. I have homework, *she lamented.* And a test tomorrow in geometry. *But the mess had to be cleaned up. Like all the others her Sperm Donor had left behind him. Over the years, Mom had tried, even with their limited resources, to get away, moving them to one place after another, but Tony always found them, and brought them back if they'd gotten too far from his sphere of influence. So much for the "Order of No-Protection," as Nikki called it. The farther away they got or the longer it took him to find them, the harsher were Tony's punishments: the verbal abuses, the threats, the beatings, the rapes. Nikki knew what to call things now, even though she was as powerless as she'd ever been.*

Once, only once, she'd tried to intervene, pull Tony off her mom, pounding him with her small twelve-year-old fists and yelling for him to stop. He'd turned on her, punched her so hard in the face that she actually bounced off the wall before hitting the floor. Tony turned to Mom and growled, "That better never happen again, Frances. You hear me? I gave that little bitch life, and I can take it away. Don't think I won't."

He swung back to glower down at Nikki again and repeat, "Don't think I won't."

Late, her mom was adamant, "Promise me, Nikki. Promise me you won't ever do that again. Don't get in his way; don't try to stop him; don't try to protect me—though that was wonderfully brave of you, sweetheart. Bad as things may seem, he can make them worse. Believe me, nothing could hurt me more than if he really harms you. Promise me."

Nikki had promised and had kept her promise, sometimes having to physically remove herself to keep from interfering, cloistering herself in another room and trying to plug her ears against the sounds of what she could not prevent. Of all those emotions, all those terrible, terrible feelings, the helplessness was the hardest to bear.

And two years later, it was much the same, only worse, because now Nikki felt so alone. She stared at her mother, who sat slumped in a splintered chair, gazing out the window as if there were something to see out there besides the stains on the stucco wall of the next apartment building. Frances had pulled a thin cotton robe—ripped at the shoulder—over her nakedness but seemed to have no thought beyond that. Surely she felt the bruise coming up on her cheekbone . . . or the splinter of glass Nikki could see embedded in an ooze of blood on one bare foot. Yet she appeared oblivious to it all.

How *can* she be? *Nikki wondered.* How can she just give up? *Hands on her hips there in the wreckage, Nikki addressed her mother. "Don't guess you're gonna help me at all?" Perhaps Frances didn't even hear her, maybe her ears were still ringing from the Tony's fists, as she made no attempt to answer. With a grunt of disgust, Nikki began putting the room in order.*

If only a life could be put in order this way. Pick up the broken pieces; throw out what can't be repaired; scrub away the stains; make it look like nothing ever happened. But even that wasn't enough. Nikki stared at the wallpaper with its now-indelible—no matter how much she rubbed—spaghetti smear among the faded daisies. Some marks could not be hidden . . . or forgotten.

Over the years, as Frances had lost her early bravado and any will to stand up to Tony, he'd found it harder to invent excuses to beat her up. No matter what he said to her, demanded of her, she would simply say, "Okay, Tony" But having his way was rarely enough for him. He regularly smashed their belongings and tore Frances's clothes, sneering at their cheapness. He began to make a habit of arriving at mealtime so he could peer into pots and mock their meager contents. And always the line, "Well, food stamps just don't buy what they used to, do they?"

Makeup only covers so much, and broken ribs take time to heal. Hard to keep a job like that. Got so it was hard to get her out of bed, and now she slept most of the day away while Nikki was at school. I can barely get her up to eat dinner when I have it ready. *Because, of course, all the cooking and cleaning fell to her. They had to eat, and everything had to look okay if a social worker dropped by.*

How Nikki hated that. Depending on a welfare check every month and making do with it. Much as she knew about everything, Nikki never did really understand how Tony could get out from under child support, but with his position in the legal system, it seemed he could pretty much do whatever he wanted. He certainly kept getting them dragged back to his home county, and, once they were part of the social services system, it was much harder to try to relocate—even if Frances still had the will to keep trying.

"God damn it!" Nikki muttered as the soapy water made the stain even larger on the worn wooden flooring.

"Don't cuss, sweetheart," Frances said wanly, without taking her eyes from the window. Furious, Nikki stood and hurled the wire sponge clear across the room into their kitchen sink. Biting back even worse swear words, Nikki glared at her mother and declared, "You're pathetic!" But Frances seemed not to hear.

I am not going to live like this the rest of my life! Nikki promised herself in that moment.

Grown-up Nikki leaned heavily against her shopping cart, biting her lip to hold back the tears. Who would've guessed how that would all turn out? *I should've treated her better . . . been more understanding.* Though grown-up Nikki, now trained and experienced in the health care field, well understood the complexities of domestic violence, psychological abuse and clinical depression, still a tiny part of her clung to the unforgiven emotions of that damaged child: pain, fear, helplessness, disappointment, despair, resentment.

How could she not *stand up for herself? What good was protecting me if she didn't protect her own life—and that left me vulnerable after all?* With the pain of that convoluted truth, Nikki shoved her cart forward, despite her tear-blurred vision, and crashed it into another cart. "Oh!" she cried, blinking furiously. "I'm *so* sorry" Her eyes came clear, and her voice froze in her throat.

"No biggie," said Dan Marchetti, grinning apologetically as he maneuvered his cart out of her path. "Wasn't watching where I was going." He glanced away, perhaps to ignore her wet eyes, and waved a hand at the array of laundry detergents. "So many! All claiming to be the best. Any recommendations?"

Quickly dabbing away the rest of her tears with one sleeve, Nikki mumbled. "Sorry. Allergies." Then she leaned to pick a box from the shelf. "I like this kind." She handed it to him for review. "Works fine; smells good; softens in the wash. And it's economical."

Barely glancing at it, he plopped it into his cart. "Good enough for me. Thanks." He looked directly into her eyes. "Great to see you. I see we're on the same wavelength today."

Then she noticed he, too, had chosen apples, bananas, seven-grain bread, salami, provolone and very similar canned goods but had opted for Koko Krisps instead of shredded wheat. "Not very inspiring, huh?"

"Well," he laughed, "when you're cooking for one, it's hard to get too inspired."

"Yeah, same here." She watched that thought sink in, saw the spark of curiosity in his gorgeous brown eyes as he tilted his head in polite inquiry. She took a deep breath. "I left Matt last month. I've filed for divorce."

"Oh. I had heard something about that on the floors but wasn't sure if it was just the usual DCH gossip." He shifted his weight, and she liked the expression in his eyes as he said, "I guess I should say I'm sorry."

She shrugged. "No need. It's just over. Neither of us is blameless, of course, but I found out he'd been having an affair for even longer than I'd suspected."

Dante nodded uncomfortably, probably remembering his part in her own infidelity. Nikki decided to let him off the hook for an appropriate comment. "So what's for dinner at *your* house tonight? None of that stuff, I hope. Now, I *know* you have a real kitchen."

Sheepishly, he confessed, "I've gotten pretty fond of a particular frozen meatloaf . . . it's good hot, and leftovers make great sandwiches. Just haven't picked that up yet."

"I could use a real home-cooked meal for a change," she told him. "I'm renting at the Six Bucks, and it's just burners and a microwave."

"Don't tell me he's got your house, Dan asked quizzically - not that it's my business, of course."

She gestured. "It's complicated. Legal. Boring. Besides, I really like the Six Bucks—except for the food situation. I love to cook." She paused then hurriedly continued, "How 'bout I cook for us both at your place tonight?"

Another promising expression in those eyes as he answered, "Don't often get a chance for a home-cooked meal." Something flickered in his eyes, and he glanced away toward the laundry soaps, then quickly back again. "Sounds great. Whatta y'have in mind?"

"Well, what would you most want tonight that I could make at your place, with your equipment?" Ah, there it was: the blush she remembered.

"Steak!" he managed. "A good ribeye. But I've already put away my grill for the season."

"That's okay. You've got a broiler, right? I make a killer marinade. How 'bout baked potatoes with sour cream and some fresh, steamed broccoli?"

"Perfect. I'm buying, of course. You just tell me everything you'll need. Want some wine?"

"Sure." She gazed down at the meat and cheese in her cart. "I need a few more things for myself too. Guess I better go by my place first, put away the refrigerated stuff."

He turned his cart so it was facing the same direction as hers and spoke quickly—: "S'okay. You can bring your cold stuff up and put it in my fridge."

She nodded. "Oh. Okay. I need milk and yogurt." She pushed her cart forward, and he let her move by him to take the lead. In the narrow aisle, her arm brushed his, raising every hair on her skin with the energy of that touch, and she could tell he felt it too.

CHAPTER NINETEEN

Not bad for a government office, thought Assistant District Attorney Linda Ferrante as she surveyed her new domain with satisfaction. The huge oak desk dominated an acre of thick, burgundy carpet, despite the rich detail of the other furniture in the room, a comfortable sitting arrangement with a loveseat, as well as the two chairs facing her desk, all in a reassuring shade of grey.

Towering bookcases covered three of her walls—filled near capacity by leather volumes, many gleaming with their gold embossments. But it was the fourth wall, at ninety degrees to her desk, that Linda loved best about the room: its huge plate glass window looked out on an idyllic scene, a wooded cove on the edge of Lake Candlebury. Weeping willows brushed the manicured lawn; deer sometimes came to drink at the edge of the pond where there was, at all times, some gathering of ducks swimming, feeding, playing in the placid waters.

Worlds away from that cramped cubbyhole shared with Kip Carpenter. Linda grimaced. It hadn't been as easy as she thought to leave Glickman, Glickman & Berkowitz.

Certainly making up her mind to accept Scott Bradden's offer had come easily. Even before she'd finished her meal with him there at the Deerwood Arms, she knew she was going to say *yes.* She wasn't fooled by his impeccable manners and solicitous behavior, she knew he was still the same ruthless jerk beneath it all, and to make sure she kept a clear head, she stuck with mineral water while he nursed a scotch-on-the-rocks with his steak sandwich. Her Lasagna Florentine was exquisite, and she savored each forkful, speaking little and letting Bradden lay out all the perks of his proposal: fat salary, great benefits, her own spacious office with a view, and work that would be stimulating and meaningful by putting the bad guys away.

But, as her father always said, "Never appear too eager. Whoever it is, whatever it is, make 'em sweat!" This was one time she was willing to follow his advice. Dom Ferrin, after all, was an ultra-successful attorney and businessman, and though Linda didn't admire most of his tactics, he knew how to "swim with the sharks" and remain the eater, not the eaten.

So she'd left Bradden with a cool "Let me think on it awhile, Scott," and he didn't even urge her not to wait too long, as she'd thought he would. But, when she finally did accept and went to give her boss notice, it wasn't easy to see the depth of disappointment in Sam Glickman's eyes. "I understand," he'd told her. "Your talents are being wasted at our firm. We just can't offer you anything more right now." He'd been so good about not asking for a full thirty days, Bradden wanted her to begin by the first week in November, and assured her, "If you ever want to come back, there'll be a place for you as if you never left."

On her last day, the office staff had thrown a party to say goodbye, wish her well . . . even though many of them would probably now be opposing her in court since G, G & B was a defense firm. Nice party, Linda remembered. No costumes, but plenty of black-and-orange decorations—which extended to the huge cake reading "We'll Miss You, Linda!" Apple cider was lifted in many toasts, and Kip Carpenter himself had carved five stunning jack-o'-lanterns, all with individual sad expressions.

Now, four days later on the Friday of her first week in the new job, Linda felt glad the transition had been as easy as it had. In fact, the only case she regretted leaving behind was the Saxon divorce.

Linda stared out her big window, down at a pair of ducks, swimming a bit away from the little flock on the pond, nibbling affectionately at each other's necks.

Thinking back to the first time she met Nikki Saxon a month ago, Linda recalled how the woman had never once cried during the meeting—though her remarkable green eyes had misted up more than once. And in a moment of clarity, Linda had tuned in to something more—a person oft-wounded in life, someone who had on many occasions been disappointed, betrayed, disillusioned by those she counted on. Easy to be sympathetic and to admire this pediatric nurse who was saying she didn't want to take her husband to the cleaners.

"I don't think Matt will be difficult to deal with," Nikki'd said. "We had a long phone call. He's so sorry and wanting to get back together and trying to be reasonable. Hoping I'll change my mind—though I won't. Anyway, Matt shouldn't be too much trouble."

But Nikki had been wrong. In Linda's first meeting with Matt, he *was* contrite, cooperative, offering to be generous, a likable guy trying to correct an error. But later, when it became clear Nikki wasn't coming back to him, he changed, hired that shark Warren Wilcox and started fighting every move Nikki made, no matter how equitable.

Linda made sure the best available lawyer at G, G, & B, Jenna Hudson, would take over the case. But there was still that twinge of guilt at abandoning Nikki. And a bit of nostalgia, missing her old colleagues. Shaking her head in self-reproach, Linda moved back to sit behind her desk in that oh-so-comfy, ergonomically correct chair, filling her nostrils with the fragrance of eucalyptus instead of Kip Carpenter's breath. "Time to move on," she whispered, as if saying it aloud could make it so. "Time to be the grown-up." After all, it'd been a good first week, a warm and respectful welcome from the resident staff, this dream office, a pile of work folders in her inbox, but low stress . . . nothing too pressing, nothing too boring and certainly nothing she couldn't handle.

Linda, reaching for the next file on the top of the stack, realized she was actually looking forward to this new life and the challenges ahead of her.

CHAPTER TWENTY

Arriving early for his day shift on Eight East, Dan lifted a hand in greeting to Dave Levine, who acknowledged it with a yawn before quickly resuming his paperwork, preparing to turn over his cases.

Now, three weeks into his November rotation, Dan was never sure who'd be in his care when he returned after a day off. The east wing of the eighth floor, classified as the Step-down Unit, was populated by patients who no longer needed to be in ICU but required more assiduous care and monitoring than in a regular room. Many were only on the ward briefly before moving into a bed on one of the medicine floors, perhaps even across to Eight West. "Did the fall-from-tree come around?" Dan asked.

"Mr. Odom?" Dave yawned again. "Yeah, regained consciousness yesterday. Already moved upstairs to . . . uh, let's see . . . Nine East. Seems just fine."

"Glad to hear it. So who're you leaving me?"

Dave brought him up-to-date. But on the last chart, Dave frowned and tapped it with his fingernails, seeming annoyed.

"What?" Dan asked, craning his neck to better see the name: *Salter, Jane.* Without reading the notes, he remembered a 42-year-old white female with a pancreatitis that'd resulted in Acute Respiratory Distress Syndrome when her sepsis-damaged capillaries allowed fluids to seep into her lung tissues. Dan nodded. "Pancreatitis and ARDS. She getting worse?"

"Not really. Not getting any better either, but that's not the problem." Dan waited, eyebrows lifted, and Dave continued, "It's her damn husband—he's just flipping out. Got to calling me every hour to get an update on her condition."

"Every hour? That's a little much."

"No kidding. And now he's started appearing out of nowhere whenever I go out in the hall, all angst-ridden with his inane, 'How's she doin', Doc?' Hell, yesterday he practically followed me to the crapper."

Dan laughed with him as they shook their heads. "People get crazy. . . ."

Dave nodded. "I had another fight with Suzanne last night."

Dan blinked. One subject of conversation often flowed directly into another with Dave. Dave and girlfriend Suzanne lived at the mercy of what Dan considered the "Grapevine Double Whammy" She was also a DCH employee, a clerk in the accounting office, there were always two separate, and sometimes contradictory, pools of gossip swirling around them. Dave called her "hot-hot-hot." A good description: drop-dead beautiful, passionate about a plethora of social causes, and volatile as any redhead had a right to be. At a mere nineteen, she was an independent working woman, and Dave sometimes had trouble keeping up.

Their stormy relationship was DCH legend: their continual heated fights, their equally ardent make-ups in between, and their seemingly unquenchable will to forgive each other and try again. One night, while Dan and Dave were both on duty, Dan had overheard Dave threatening to call the police to come after her if she failed to return his car before his shift ended. Turned out later she'd borrowed it, then lent it to her crazy-ass brother, but *he* had been involved in a fender-bender and didn't actually have a valid driver's license, much less a way to prove he hadn't stolen the car. It was a real mess . . . like the Dave–Suzanne relationship itself. "You guys still fighting about the car?"

Dave shook his head. "Not exactly. She *did* ask to borrow it again for a similar favor! Then called me a selfish elitist when I said 'No.' She's fuckin' crazy, but she does the craziest things sometimes . . . says the craziest things."

"A real 'doorknobs' kinda night, huh?"

Dave laughed at the reference to a shared observation: old-fashioned doorknobs make everything look distorted. "Worse than that! It was a 'kontiki birds' kind of night."

Dan chuckled. "Now *that* sounds serious—if I knew what it meant!"

"Ever been to Disney World?"

"Yeah. In fact, just before I started here at DCH."

"I was pretty young the first time I saw the Tiki show, and it really creeped me out!"

"'In the Tiki-Tiki-Tiki-Tiki Tiki Room,'" chanted Dan, "'All the birds sing words and the flowers croon—'"

"Enough!" Dave, laughing, actually covered his ears. "God! Did you fuckin' *memorize* the thing? I used to *dream* that song. My older brothers, of course, thought my misery was great fun and took every opportunity to chant the song, try to weird me out. Eventually.'kontiki birds' became our kid-code for anything weird."

"Got it! Yeah, I have kid-code with my brother too. So it was a kontiki encounter with Suzanne?"

"Yeah, but it's been the whole night here for some reason! Mrs. Bilenko, the 300-pounder in 842, just suddenly woke up after three days comatose . . . right when Nurse Earl was doing a blood draw. The woman sat straight up, hauled off and slugged him with her other arm. Poor Earl smacked back against the bedside table, sent everything clattering to the floor. She yelled, 'Stop doing that!' and then just lost consciousness and fell back in the bed."

Dan couldn't help chuckling as he pictured the scene with the wiry little male nurse reeling from the attack. But then he asked quickly, "She okay? Earl okay?"

Dave nodded. "She's awake again now, resting quietly and *very* apologetic. Earl's fine. Sporting a black eye and embellishing the tale no-end every time he tells it. You'll get your turn, I'm sure."

Dave checked his watch. "Time to go. But I wanta look in on Jane Salter one more time before I leave her to you."

"I'll go with you." Dan took the patient's chart and scanned it as they headed for Room 850.

Just as they passed the Eighth Floor waiting room, Jane Salter's husband popped out, calling, "Hey, Dave—hang on a minute!" Dan felt Dave bracing beside him. Salter, a thin, ruddy-complected man of maybe forty-five, wore tight jeans, cowboy boots and a western shirt with the top four buttons left open to reveal curly grey chest hair and a large medallion. Considering the demeanor Dave had described earlier, Dan expected to see an expression of anguished worry.

But Salter seemed quite relaxed, sauntering up to clasp Dave's arm as if they'd been friends for years. "So, Doc; how is she?"

Dave hesitated a moment, obviously just as surprised by the man's jovial attitude—so incongruous considering his wife's grim medical condition. "Well, Mr. Salter—"

"Now, you're s'posed to call me Terry, remember?"

"Well, uh . . . Terry," Dave continued, "she's holding her own.". As I told you earlier, it'll be a day-to-day thing, and—"

"Yeah, that's what I expected," Salter interrupted, clearly not listening, "so I'm prepared for the long haul." And motioned behind him. Looking past Salter, Dan could see back into the waiting room, which had undergone a transformation. A cot was set up in one corner, its covers rumpled and strewn with magazines. On the windowsill, a portable television flashed a series of channels at the touch of a woman wearing a snug sweater and one-size-too-small jeans above high heels. Her head of platinum-blond curls looked familiar. Having located *Wheel of Fortune*, she turned around, and Dan recognized the attractive, fortyish face of Eleanor Gordon, wife of patient Rodney Gordon, who currently lay comatose after suffering a large bleed within his malignant brain tumor. She gave Dan a wan smile as their eyes met.

About half the seats in the waiting room were occupied by family members of other patients, all registering varying degrees of annoyance, probably as a reaction to the cheering and cheerful music pouring out of the game show.

Dan tuned back in to what Dave was saying to Salter: "I'm going off duty now, and your wife will be under the care of my colleague, Dr. Marchetti, here."

Salter turned his attention, and a cheerful grin, toward Dan. "Hey, glad to meet you . . ." he leaned to read the I.D. badge, "Dante!" He winked. "You don't mind me calling you by your first name, do you?"

"Not at all," Dan replied, still marveling at the unusual scene in the waiting room . "We're about to go look in on your wife. We'll let you know right away if there's any change, okay?"

Salter's curly head had swiveled back toward the waiting room. "Sure, sure." He gestured toward the cot and TV. "I'm sure I'll be seeing you two a good deal more before this is all over. S'long for now."

Giving a jaunty wave of his hand, he pivoted on one boot heel and returned to the group in the waiting room.

Dan and Dave just stared at each other for a long moment before turning to continue down the hall toward Jane Salter's room.

In a low voice, Dan began to complain, "I find that guy really irritating, man."

"No shit." Dave moaned, punching Dan in the arm before they went their separate ways.

Late in the afternoon, as Dan started to walk briskly past the waiting room lounge, hoping he could avoid being accosted yet again by Terry Salter, he paused mid-stride, struck by a very different scene. The TV was turned off, and the room was almost empty. Only Salter and Eleanor Gordon remained, laughing as they played cards on one of the end tables . . . and flirting with each other! Hurrying on, Dan grimaced.

Dan flopped dejectedly into a chair at the empty physicians desk. Admittedly, it was natural that healthy people, possibly on the brink of losing a spouse, might find comfort, and perhaps more, in the company of someone in the same rocky boat. But in the waiting room of the ICU?

Sometimes, Dan had found, it was hard to keep perspective on the whole issue of "relationship." It was pretty depressing to see how many of the older docs were divorced, separated or just unfaithful. Even the ones who managed to fall in love, marry, start families seemed to have an awfully hard time holding it all together.

As always at these moments, his thoughts turned to his touchstone in such matters, DCH's chief of peds, Norman Tischler. The quintessential children's doctor, firm but gentle, endlessly patient with both kids and their often-demanding parents, he was also a devoted family man. The way his face lit up when he talked about his wife and four daughters! The incredible warmth in his voice.

Yet, despite his sixty years, he still managed to keep in good shape, playing tennis at least twice a week, most often doubling with his wife. Winking, he'd once confided, "I want to dance at all my *grandchildren's* weddings!"

He was certainly a model for how to do it all, and well. Too bad he seemed the exception, not the rule. Dan sometimes felt it was more honest just to keep relationships on the light side and admit that medicine was a stern taskmaster.

Speaking of relationships. That'd been hot, running into Nikki at the store; her volunteering to cook for him; the succulent ribeye and terrific wine; being able to invite her into his bed, freshly changed that afternoon. They'd already made love once before the first doorbell, and Nikki had found irresistible ways to convince him it was better to stay in bed with her than go to the door. Thank goodness they'd bought candy they both liked, peanut butter cups, because they'd been eating their way through the four bags during the weeks since.

Why not simply relax and enjoy it? Wasn't this exactly what he'd been hoping for: great sex and companionship with someone who understood the stresses of his life? Nikki provided all that and more. Beautiful, smart, funny and a great cook to boot. Though sometimes he wondered if she wasn't trying too hard to be casual, making sure that he didn't dump her like her soon to be ex-husband.

And there were signs that all was not as sunny as she seemed determined to portray. Despite her smiles and obvious enjoyment during their frequent intimate moments, she never seemed to sleep very well at his place, often getting up in the middle of the night to shower, saying she was sweaty. It'd been a bit of a surprise that Halloween night, the first time he'd seen her naked in four months, how much her body had changed. When once he gently expressed concern, she only laughed and said, "It's just the job . . . the damn divorce . . . Matt being an ass. Just stress and you know how to help me with that," laughing she wiggled her eyebrows. "Don't worry."

But he *had* and finally wore her down. She agreed to see her own primary care provider, Josephine Bruno.

Josie hadn't found anything in her initial exam that couldn't be chalked up to the stresses in Nikki's life, but, thorough as always, Josie had ordered a batch of tests, and they were all awaiting the results...

"Beep, beep, beep . . . Dr. Marchetti, Room 833, stat . . . 833, stat!"

Recognizing the room number of a 'bad lunger', Dan leaped up and hurried down the hall. By the bed he found the pulmonary medicine fellow, George Anastos, listening to the lungs of a middle-aged, cyanotic-looking man.

"Get Respiratory Therapy, stat!" George barked and, to Nurse Coral Parker, "Sixty milligrams I.V. solu-medrol, stat!"

Dan quickly placed the call, then went to his newest patient, who was gasping for air. Using his own stethoscope to listen to the fellow's lungs, Dan commented, "He's not moving any air."

Nurse Coral got an I.V. running, and within minutes, the respiratory therapist, not the ubiquitous Vinny but some other blond guy, had arrived and was setting up to give an aerosol breathing treatment.

George leaned over his patient. "Mr. Monroe, how're you doing?"

"Not so good." The voice was barely audible, and he was looking bluer by the minute. "Please help me . . . I—" He fell back on the bed, unconscious, and his electrocardiographic monitor revealed a dangerous slowing of heart rate. Dan could tell he was about to stop breathing.

"Need to intubate," George said. "Want the practice?"

"Yes!" Dan stepped close and eagerly took the laryngoscope Coral placed in his right hand.

"I'll push the atropine," George told him.

Dan took a deep breath and willed his hands to steady. He carefully positioned Monroe's head and slid the scope into the patient's mouth, applying pressure down and forward to expose the larynx. He smoothly pushed the tube between the two bands of tissue making up the vocal chords.

"Lifetime of heavy cigarette smoking," George commented as the respiratory therapist reached to take over, attaching an ambu-bag to the tube and getting the alternate inflation/deflation going.

After a few breaths, the RT asked, "Should I go get a ventilator?"

George nodded, and Dan took over with the ambu-bag. George gave a listen through his stethoscope, then declared, "Good sounds bilaterally." In only moments, Monroe's color improved, and his heart rhythm stabilized, though he remained unconscious. "Good intubation, Marchetti."

A ward clerk came in, handed George a copy of the patient's arterial blood gas numbers. "Shit," the resident muttered. "Big-league acidosis." He looked at Dan. "You recognize this guy?"

"Not really. Should I?"

"Charlie Monroe. Used to manage the Pittsburgh Pirates. Retired five years ago; does some scouting now."

Dan nodded. "Yeah! Didn't recognize him."

As he turned away to write orders that would return Monroe to an unconscious state. George shook his head. "People just don't look themselves when they're blue."

CHAPTER TWENTY-ONE

Nikki, pretending to relax against the pillows on the sofa, watched Dan walk toward her from the kitchen. The light of Thanksgiving sunset, illuminating the room through the balcony's glass doors, fell softly on the folds of his spice-brown velour shirt. As he rolled down the sleeves, he was looking toward her, but she could tell he wasn't really seeing her. His brows were knit together, and he seemed to be chewing the inside of his lip in deep thought.

"Finished?" she asked to bring him back.

"Yeah," he said, still distracted. "All done."

"Thank you so much for doing all those dishes."

"Least I could do." He sat down where she made room for him. "Thank *you* for all the terrific cooking. Everyone seemed to have a great time."

He meant the guests, of course. The two of them had managed to keep Nikki's news from surfacing. In fact, the others seemed to be enjoying themselves too much to notice they weren't as light-hearted as usual.

Alex Cole behaved himself more than usual, leaving most of his pomposity, and all his profanity, at home. He clearly was trying to attract Julia's attention without making a bad impression on her mom. Julia, who'd never looked cuter, seemed receptive to his interest and positively sparkled, especially after her third glass of wine. Sure, there was the age difference: not only was Julia older than all the interns, but Alex was the youngest of the bunch.

Julia Cleary and her mother Myra had been back from their Ireland trip for some six weeks now, but, thrilled to have "new ears" in Alex and Dan, were eager to yet again recount their detour to their ancestral village on Kenmare Bay in County Kerry. Nikki had heard it all several times before, but she didn't mind hearing it again. Not only did it keep the focus off her, but it was wonderful to see her friends lit up with such joy.

"Trail rides on the beaches!" Julia said, and Myra chimed in, "Trail rides in the mountains!" And they both said together, "It was just Heaven!" and laughed as they regarded each other with true affection.

In her more-reserved-than-usual role today, Nikki was also more observant, noticing how much Myra ate, how she had seconds of all the sweet and high-carb dishes—including two full pieces of pie instead of the halvesies the rest of them shared in order to taste both apple and pumpkin.

When Julia very gently tried to say something to Myra, that perennially jolly mom countered, "I know, I know, honey. But everything Nikki's made is *so* delicious, and it's a special day. It's not like I do this *all the time!"* And though Julia dropped the matter, Nikki saw the little face she made about it.

Hours later, when Nikki and Dan shooed everyone out without allowing them to help with the cleanup, Nikki took care of the leftovers while Dan started the dishes. Again, they'd worked with few words needed, and with the TV, after a day dedicated to football, now silent, a kind of peace had settled over the apartment.

Nikki finished first and moved to start drying dishes, but Dan told her. "Let them drain. You go get a little rest."

She'd nodded. At eight p.m. they both had to be back at DCH for their shifts. They just counted themselves fortunate they'd had the day shift off.

She'd relaxed as best she could, wondering what he was thinking about and he seemed to still be pondering, as he joined her on the couch."

"That cranberry stuff was fantastic," he sighed. "And those pies!" He gave her a little smile. "Glad you didn't listen to me about only having to feed five mouths so only needing one pie. We'll be pigging out on homemade pie with our other leftovers through the whole weekend."

"Gotta be thinking ahead. . . ."

He shifted his position slightly. "Speaking of which. . . ." He paused, as if gathering his courage; he took her hand. "I've been thinking. . . ."

Here it comes! Nikki found she was holding her breath. Steeling herself, she gave him her full attention and waited for that big shoe to drop.

"You've got a rough road ahead of you for a while," he began. "You're really going to have to conserve your energy and focus on your own health exclusively."

She was just formulating the words that would let him off the hook, ease his guilt at dumping her. But he kept talking.

"So I think you should move in here with me."

"Wha . . . what . . . ?"

"Been thinking about what you told me: you won't be working; you'll have co-pays on the medical bills; you'll have to get back and forth to the outpatient clinic; there'll be days it'll be hard to take care of yourself. I know finances are all screwed up because of the divorce. If you move in here, at least you can pocket the money you'd be paying the Six Bucks."

Still disbelieving, Nikki searched his eyes but saw nothing except openness. "Are you *sure?*"

"Yeah. And I don't mean you moving in here to keep doing all the housework. Let me take care of you for a change . . . at least as I'm able. She was laughing now but with wet eyes. "So I guess we're roommates now?"

She burrowed against him, trying to set aside all the medical, marital and financial challenges awaiting her. Clinging to him as the tears poured from her eyes, she whispered fiercely, "I'm thankful for *you.*"

CHAPTER TWENTY-TWO

Nikki had awakened him for a full breakfast at ten, just before she left to keep an appointment with her divorce attorney. Dan had dawdled over the eggs and sausage and applesauce-topped pancakes, actually finding time to read the paper and savor a third cup of excellent coffee. Then a long, hot shower and into the freshly laundered scrubs Nikki had left for him.

She, too, seemed increasingly happy with the way things had worked out. She was the one who drove back and forth to her place when they weren't spending time together. But she'd been spending more and more time at his apartment, so he'd insisted she bring some things there for convenience. She barely filled one drawer of his dresser with folded scrubs and sweats, underwear, socks and several of those long cotton nightshirts she liked to sleep in. Neither of them had much that needed hanging in the closet, but she hung two pairs of jeans and three sweaters instead of putting them in a drawer. He found it oddly comfortable to have a few of her toiletries tucked among his in the bathroom. Sometimes when he was in the shower alone, he'd open the bottle of her shampoo just to inhale the scent of her hair.

As for the housework she insisted on doing, Nikki assured him, "I *love* to cook, remember? It's really the only creative thing I've ever done." And at his guilty protests over the other housekeeping, she'd just shrugged. "No big deal. Nurses clean up after people. It becomes second nature. Relax, Dante. Cooking and cleaning make me feel human again."

Dan noticed Nurse Coral approaching. "Hi, Dan." Pursing her lips, she shook her head. "Have ya seen 'Salter's Saloon' yet?"

"Salter's Saloon?" he repeated blankly.

She didn't stop, obviously on her way to administer some meds. "That's what the staff's calling the waiting room lounge now."

Bewildered but only slightly curious, Dan started down the hall to check on the baseball coach Charlie Monroe, but couldn't help pausing at the waiting room door.

There was Terry Salter, animatedly recounting what appeared to be war stories, Dan caught the phrases "Persian Gulf" and "wounded twice" and "Purple Heart", to a small group of rapt listeners. A few had been there the other day, including Eleanor Gordon, but they all seemed much more appreciative of Salter today. The place sure looked "lived-in": newspapers and magazines scattered about, some discarded clothing, stray soda cans and numerous tall paper cups, some set aside, but most clutched enthusiastically. The TV was on in the background with the sound turned off, and Dan noticed yet another cot set up on the far side of the room.

Apparently it was a *humorous* war story, because as Salter brought it to a dramatic close with wildly rolling eyes and gesticulation, his audience burst into guffaws and knee-slapping. And at that moment Salter glanced toward the doorway. "Hey, Dante! Wait up!" he called, because Dan was already trying to make his escape. Reluctantly, he paused, hoping he looked as if he needed to be somewhere else—stat.

"Anything new on my wife?" Salter asked, his face slipping into a more serious expression.

"I haven't seen her yet." Dan tried to keep moving on down the hall; Salter fell into step. Dan halted. "Nothing new in Dr. Levine's notes, though."

Salter nodded gravely. "Well, you know where to find me. And by the way," he actually puffed up a little, looking proud. "I've taken a leave from my job . . . for as long as it takes for her to get better."

In the long moment of silence, during which he failed to congratulate Salter on such a selfless act, Dan saw the man's eyes flick back toward the lounge. Clearly a break from work made this into a kind of sick holiday. He had a new set of friends who'd offer comfort unconditionally, all drawn together by serious illness while he played the grieving spouse.

As if afraid he might be missing something back in the waiting room, Salter clapped Dan on the shoulder, saying, "Well, gotta get back." His ruddy face lit up. "Say, I hear you'll be here till late. When you get a free minute tonight, come by. We'll have a drink together."

"I couldn't possibly do that", Dan told him, a little stiffly. "Though I'm sure you mean a soda or something like that, because it's against DCH rules to have alcohol on the premises."

Salter laughed. "Oh, sure, sure!" He gave Dan a broad wink and pressed a finger against his lips, as if they were sharing a secret. "Anything you say, Doc!" And he clapped Dan's shoulder again before heading back to Salter's Saloon with a jaunty wave.

Dan gave himself a little shake, as if to dispel the "creep" he felt on his skin. Down the hall in Room 833, he found Charlie Monroe sleeping peacefully, leaving the efforts of respiration to the ventilator. Monroe had a half-century of smoking making it less likely that he'd ever get off the machine." Come on, guy," Dan whispered to the sleeping coach." He felt the squeezing of his arm hard. "I bet you've still got some good innings in you."

Leaving the Coach, Dan turned right to start his walking rounds for his other patients. He never quite understood the self-destructive habits of so many people.

Hours later, he returned to Jane Salter's room. . Her urine output was dropping, and Dan needed to find out why. Not that anything else about her condition was improving.

"Hey, you eat dinner?"

Dan turned at the sound of Nikki's voice and saw her at the doorway, lovely in leaf-green scrubs. It was almost time for her own shift down on peds.

"Not yet."

She held aloft a brown paper bag. "Turkey,Swiss and tomato on rye?"

Nikki grinned, hanging on to the brown bag till he could wash up, and came all the way into the room to give him a quick but hearty kiss on the mouth. Her smile faded as she regarded the comatose patient. "That's your pancreatitis and ARDS, right?"

"Yep. Meet Jane Salter."

With a little shock, Dan realized he'd never once seen Salter at his wife's bedside. Always the lounge. If Terry Salter was so committed that he was setting aside his job and sleeping at the hospital, surely he could *visit* her occasionally! Strange.

They left Jane's room and went to the nurses' station so he could write down his changes in the fluid orders for Jane Salter. He started to tell Coral, but she reminded, "It's eight. I'm off. Here comes Earl."

Nikki set the lunch bag on the desk. "I'll come down on break just before you leave at midnight." She was already heading for the elevator.

"Great," he called after her. "And thanks again for the sandwich."

Dan watched her greet Nurse Earl and Alex Cole, who were both coming on duty but had stopped to argue about last night's football game. Alex glanced up. "Hi, Dan. Heard you were half-shifting with Dave."

"How ya been, Alex? Haven't seen you too much lately."

"Yeah, the nature of the beast. Catch ya later tonight, okay?" He hurried off toward his patients. No evil twin Skippy today.

Dan turned to Earl and brought him up to date on Jane Salter's fluids. "I'll take care of that right now," Earl said.

When the nurse was gone, Dan washed up and sank into a desk chair to enjoy his turkey sandwich, washing it down with a long-cold cup of coffee he'd poured hours ago and forgotten. He ate slowly, marveling at the perfection of the thing: just the right balance of meat and cheese; enough tomato to get good flavor but not enough to make it soggy; there was even fresh lettuce and his favorite spicy brown mustard. How'd he get lucky enough to have Nikki in his life?

"Great sandwich!" he greeted her some four hours later.

Smiling at the compliment, Nikki asked, "You ready to take off?"

"Just about. I wanna have one more look at Jane Salter . . . check that urine output."

Nikki nodded. "I'll go with you."

"Listen, we'll sorta have to sneak past the waiting lounge or we may get tied up for a while. Most of Mr. Salter's audience has gone home; he gets especially clingy then, according to Dave."

He quickly filled her in on the man's holding court in Salter's Saloon and about the fellow's flirtation with Eleanor Gordon, whose own husband had had to be resuscitated earlier that very day. Nikki grimaced and followed him quietly down the hall.

As they neared the lounge, Dan noted that it appeared empty. The lights and TV were off, and there were no sounds of voices or laughter. But there were other sounds, soft and furtive, and Dan realized that the lights were always left on. That room was always open for the relatives of the seriously ill.

It took a moment for Dan's eyes to adjust to the dimness, but the big window on the far wall let in a lot of light from the nearly full moon beyond. There was a sharp intake of breath beside him, and Dan knew Nikki was seeing what he was seeing.

The two cots had been shoved together; on them and beneath a thin hospital blanket, two entwined figures moved in an unmistakable rhythm. Nor was it difficult to recognize those two curly heads, one graying, one platinum, Terry Salter and Eleanor Gordon, getting it on right here in the waiting room. Both their spouses lay just doors away, barely clinging to their lives—and losing ground.

Dan felt Nikki's hand grip his arm so hard he almost yelped, but that brought him back to the moment, and he let her push him away from the door and on down the hall.

"The *bastards!*" Nikki ground out between clenched teeth. He'd never before heard such vehemence, or such venom, in her voice. "The bastards!" Her eyes brimmed with tears. "How'd you like to be fighting for your life just to go back to a partner like that?!"

Sure, Dan was shocked by the event, and thoroughly disgusted, but nothing as intense as Nikki seemed to be feeling. He saw that it must have pushed all her buttons about her own husband cheating on her.

Pleased to see Jane's urine output was stabilizing, Dan checked his watch and saw it was nearly midnight. Time to go home and look forward to tomorrow when both he and Nikki had the full 24 hours off.

"*Beep, beep, beep* . . . Dr. Marchetti, Room 833, stat . . . 833, stat!"

Dan said, "Shit! That's Monroe."

Nikki looked up with glistening eyes. "I'll see you at home."

He gave her a quick wave and hurried toward Room 833, thinking, *"See you at home."* Nice ring to that. When he arrived at Charlie Monroe's bedside, Nurse Earl was already there, and only moments later, Vinny Orlander rushed in with more respiratory equipment.

Earl began, "Oximetry readings show he's desatting and—"

"Mucous plugging, maybe," Vinny interrupted, then mumbled on as if hoping the physician-in-charge wouldn't take offense. "That could be why his blood isn't getting saturated with enough oxygen. Right, Dan?"

"Could be," Dan answered. "Let's suction him and see."

Looking annoyed, Earl finished his intended sentences, "Sorry I had to call you, Dan. Dave's not here yet. Alex is tied up . . . Mr. Gordon's crumping over in 825."

Nodding, Dan temporarily disconnected Monroe from the ventilator so he had access to the breathing tube he'd placed yesterday. Vinny quickly moved to the wall-mounted suction device, fetching the attached tube with its loose, retractable plastic covering. Dan took it from Vinny, inserted it into Monroe's breathing tube and began suctioning. As the suction did its job, Vinny grinned at Dan looking for confirmation that he had made the right diagnosis but Dan was looking past him as Alex Cole trudged in, looking even wearier than usual.

"Gordon?" Dan asked.

"He's gone," Alex answered with a heavy shrug.

Dan wondered if Eleanor Gordon will spend the rest of her life remembering what she was doing while her husband breathed his last. Would she even care? Maybe there was a history to their life together that explained her bizarre attraction to Salter. Still, you would think there were limits to decent human behavior.

Alex gestured toward Monroe. "I'll get this. You were s'posed to be off twenty minutes ago."

"Okay, thanks." Dan handed the suctioning tube to Alex and, wondering where Dave was, headed toward the physicians desk to make his last notes.

"Sorry!" Dave Levine arrived, rumpled and groggy. "Suzanne *said* she set the alarm. . . ."

Dan grinned and started to fill Dave in on the changes in the last twelve hours.

Rubbing his face, Dave said, "Go on, get outta here; I've kept you long enough. Alex can bring me up to speed. Thanks for staying."

Dan didn't protest, glad he wouldn't have to recount the loss of Rodney Gordon or the affair in Salter's Saloon. A few minutes later, he left the building and walked briskly toward his apartment. Thank God he didn't have to be back to DCH for a day and a half.

Upon returning to the hospital, Dan learned Jane Salter had died the same night as Rodney Gordon. In fact, only about an hour after he went off-duty. In a way, it was a relief. It'd gotten so unlikely Jane could recover, and now she wasn't suffering anymore. But, unexpectedly, there was a bit of an uproar about the case.

Somehow Jane Salter's PEEP had gotten dialed up to twenty, when he knew he'd made sure it was no more than five. With her Positive End Expiratory Pressure set so high, her BP had dropped to a dangerously low, and ultimately fatal, level.

Naturally, Nurse Earl was blamed at first, but he'd just about come unglued with outrage to be accused of such carelessness. And while anyone could make a mistake with even good employees sometimes dropping the ball, it *was* hard to believe of Earl, especially seeing his righteous indignation and his well earned reputation for being meticulous. But who else? Alex . . . or Dave? Everyone was tired and stressed and it is every doc's nightmare: causing someone's death—especially through carelessness.

And then a new rumor, based on the fact that Rodney Gordon had died less than two hours earlier . . . and Earl's gossip about what he'd seen in Salter's Saloon. Maybe one, or both, of the spouses had just hurried things along? Maybe they'd conspired together? Hard to believe, but stranger things have happened in Kontiki-land, Dan thought.

Blessedly, the two passings meant Dan didn't have to see either of the spouses again; they'd cleared out the day before, and the waiting room was returned to its normal configuration and dignity. As for Terry Salter and Eleanor Gordon, who knew where they were now? Calling relatives . . . making funeral arrangements . . . weeping inconsolably in guilt-stricken grief? Or were they in each other's arms, each comforting the other, perhaps even rejoicing. Dan had to let the image go....people do what people have to do.

CHAPTER TWENTY-THREE

Nikki Saxon gripped the sides of her chair even more tightly and managed to whisper, "Wha . . . what . . .?"

Dr. Josephine Bruno, her brown eyes full of reflected pain, leaned closer across her desk and spoke gently: "I said, It looks like Hodgkin's Lymphoma.'"

"Cancer." That absurd word stuck in her mouth and refused to come out as a question.

"Yes." Josie waited, let it sink in.

So much for denial, Nikki thought. All those months of chalking the night sweats and weight loss up to stress; the last few weeks brushing off Dante's worries. Most recently, ignoring the concern in Josie Bruno's manner as they discussed Nikki's rather inauspicious lab results from her blood work.

And now, because Josie had insisted they explore further and had directed Nikki to have a chest x-ray that revealed a "fullness in the mediastinum" followed by a needle biopsy from the tissue within it, Nikki was being forced to face the truth. "You're sure?"

Josie nodded. "Needle biopsy revealed Reed-Sternberg cells."

"Shit."

"I know, Nikki. I'm sorry." Josie was more than her general practitioner; she was a colleague and a friend.

Nikki sighed. "So what now?"

Picking up her pen, Josie started writing on the papers in the folder open on her desk. "I'm referring you to Cyrus Klonter for further staging and treatment."

"Klonter?"

Josie looked up and said frankly, "I know. Not 'Mr. Personality,' but he's the very best around here when it comes to oncology itself . . . to treatment."

Again that word. "Yeah, treatment. Not surgery. . . ."

"Not surgery," Josie agreed. "Maybe not radiation, but chemotherapy for sure."

"God." Nikki's hands ached from gripping her chair. She couldn't think. Maybe she couldn't even breathe! She thought of all her chemo patients...hair loss, puking, exhaustion, death!

"Do you have any more questions?" Josie Bruno, a small woman two years older than Nikki, had wispy brown hair, cut short around her high cheek-boned face and was looking at Nikki with compassion and concern.

Her kindness and caring just poured out, knowing how to support the spirit, and soothe, if not completely dispel, one's fears. And those eyes would stay on you till you asked your question or finished a thought. Maybe that's the best thing about her as a doctor; she gives you the time you need, and she always really listens.

"Not right now, thanks. A lot to think about."

Josie nodded. "Well, here's the referral to Dr. Klonter and a coupla sheets I printed for you with a lot of information about Hodgkin's. Don't think that just because you are a nurse that you should know all the answers. Ask questions, get opinions, reach out whenever you need to talk. And remember, there's a good cure rate for this disease. You're young and otherwise healthy, and I think we caught it early."

"From your mouth to God's ear," Nikki murmured, rising to take the papers Josie extended toward her.

Outside Dr. Bruno's office located in the large medical complex just east of Deerwood Community Hospital, Nikki stood blinking back tears, trying to decide what to do next . . . where to go.

Definitely not DCH. She needed to be alone to think, plan and cry. She'd walked from Dante's apartment at Woodside, leaving her car there beside his rarely used Honda.

Knowing suddenly where she needed to go, she started walking east toward the municipal park. She didn't slow or stop until she reached her favorite bench overlooking the lake. She sank down on it gratefully, and felt its peace enfold her, even though its leafless late-November trees didn't screen her from view as they had in the summer. Not to worry. The park was deserted, except for an expectant band of ducks, who immediately quacked toward her, hoping for handouts. There was no one else to watch her break down sobbing. The ducks fell silent and made a quick U-turn, paddling away toward a cheerier atmosphere.

Long minutes later, when the tears were done, Nikki blotted her wet cheeks on her sweater sleeves and tried to recall everything she knew about Hodgkin's and chemotherapy. She didn't bother to pull out the pages she'd tucked into her purse. Time enough later to really educate herself. She just wanted to deal with what she already knew and feared. Putting aside thoughts of odds and percentages, of survival vs. death, she just let her thoughts run about the daily reality of her future months. She pictured herself lying in bed sick-as-a-dog after an infusion.

She could avoid the big question no longer. What about Dante? Nikki gripped the edge of the park bench as she had the chair in Dr. Bruno's office. Marchetti was a great guy: promising young doc, attractive, fun to be with, treated her like a queen. And he was clearly delighted to have her in his life. But what first-year intern needed a girlfriend with cancer? It wasn't like they were married or engaged or even officially committed to each other. They'd never even discussed becoming exclusive.

But now? Why would he want to deal with her being ill? Why should he even try? Sure, he's a doc, but what sane person would *choose* to treat illness all work day and then come home to serious illness in a loved one?

Beyond that, what if he was one of those people, she'd seen plenty of them through the years, who just can't get past the fact that someone was branded by cancer. She'd seen more than a few relationships come apart over cancer: friends, colleagues, parents of children she'd taken care of. After all, there're no guarantees with that disease; it could always come back. You had to live with that ax hanging over your head for the rest of your life, and so do the people who love you.

And just how much did he really care? She knew he liked her but like wasn't love and she had to admit, he wasn't in love with her. Of course, she was in love with him. She thought she had time to wait for him to feel that way, too. But now time was what she didn't have.

Nikki scuffed her feet in the dry leaves and watched the band of ducks returning, still half-hopeful as they approached the shore. She needed courage. Not only to battle her cancer but to face Dante and tell him the news. To prepare herself for however he reacted.

She stood up, deciding, *I'll take what I can get.* Showing empty hands to the disappointed ducks, she turned resolutely to walk back to the apartment and wait for Dante to come home. What was it they'd planned to do tonight . . . something for tomorrow?

Tomorrow! The reality—pushed from thought by today's shocking news—now crashed in on her. *Oh, God!* Tomorrow was Thanksgiving Day, and she was cooking dinner for Dante, Alex and the Clearys. *God!* she thought again, walking more briskly. *Just kill me now.*

By the time Dante dragged in from his shift, Nikki had taken an hour to write in her journal before starting to work on tomorrow's dinner and was now pulling a Dutch apple pie from the oven.

"Mmmm!" he said appreciatively. "That smells like Heaven."

"Thanks." Nikki managed to avoid his eyes as she bent to retrieve the second pie: pumpkin custard in a graham cracker crust. She adjusted the oven's heat and slid in the pan filled by four whole garnet yams, their purple skins glistening with a fine film of vegetable oil to keep them moist. "Hungry?"

"I could eat," he admitted. Looking down at the various spatters on his scrubs, he added, "Shower first though" and headed for the other room.

Nikki dished out a bowl of last night's beef stew and placed it in the microwave, ready to zap when he returned. Picking up her kitchen knife again, she went back to cubing dried bread for the stuffing.

After much thought, soul-searching and writing seven pages in her journal, she'd decided not to tell Dante about the cancer until the following night. She just had to act like nothing was wrong until they got through tomorrow It might work if she kept her mind on the food. She'd made her cranberry–orange relish that morning, hours before going to the doctor. How happy she'd felt! Singing to herself as she food-milled together two entire bags of fresh cranberries and a pair of whole, seeded oranges. Sweetened and refrigerated to steep together, by the time it was served, the juices would've married the flavors perfectly. She remembered thinking how great it was making so much. Plenty extra to freeze in meal-size portions to enjoy in the months to come. But now it seemed unlikely she'd be sharing those meals with Dante.

What else? The fourteen-pound bird would fill the small apartment oven, so she'd bake her pan of dressing tonight. Then tomorrow, when the turkey was done and out "resting," she could drizzle the top of the stuffing with butter and let it brown while she made the gravy and Dante mashed the potatoes. Quick heating of peas, yams and rolls. Get everything on the table. A great meal to share with friends but would it be her last?

Dan returned looking completely refreshed in his favorite old jeans and a blue fleece pullover. Setting the finished bread cubes aside, she started chopping celery. He came up behind her, took her around the waist and kissed the back of her neck. "I must be the luckiest guy in all of Deerwood. Maybe all of Pennsylvania."

Tears stung in her eyes; she was glad he couldn't see them. She got her voice to work. "Busy day?"

He sighed. "Monroe almost crumped out on us again. Thank God, he's a fighter." Letting go of her, he grabbed a celery stalk and started munching.

She leaned to start the microwave. "Anything else going on?"

"New patient. Small bowel resection . . . fighting an infection. Oh, and Suzanne locked Dave out of their place... not sure why."

Nikki managed a smile. "Interesting duo?" When the timer buzzed, she pulled out the stew, waited while Dan rummaged in the dish drainer for a big-enough spoon. "So, pretty quiet on Eight East, then?"

He leaned against the counter and tucked into the stew, savoring a hefty spoonful before answering. "Well, there's still a lot of hoopla about the Salter/Gordon deaths."

"Oh?" She'd gone back to her chopping so she wouldn't have to keep looking at him..

"Yeah, there were so many of us around, and they can't pinpoint when Jane Salter's PEEP got changed. All of us saying, 'I know it was right when I last saw it.' Remember, I checked to make sure it wasn't above five?"

"I remember," Nikki said, looking at him now with concern. "Do you need me to tell anyone that for you? You're not in trouble, are you?"

He shrugged and swallowed another bite of stew. "Don't think so. Most people seem to want to blame Earl, but I believe him. He's Mr. Obsessive. Anyway, lots of us on Eight East that night: Earl and Coral; Dave and Alex and me; Vinny Orlander. Not to mention the straying spouses."

"Think they did it?"

Shrugging again, Dan opened the refrigerator and refilled his bowl with more stew. "Sorta doubt it. They were pretty tied up in the lounge. Earl saw them snuggling before we did, and they were found lying asleep together when Jane was discovered dead. Doesn't seem like they'd have time to pull that off." Turning back to lean against the counter, he arched his eyebrows at her in a comical expression. "Unless, of course, they hired a hitman."

Nikki tried to laugh, to put herself in the easy joshing mood they'd been sharing the last few weeks. But she couldn't.

Dan's eyes narrowed, and he regarded her closely now. "Hey! You okay? You seem kinda down."

During her silence, realization dawned; she saw it in his eyes. "Wait minute! You were s'posed to get your results from Josie Bruno today!"

"It can wait—" Nikki started to say.

But that wasn't going to work. He stood bolt upright, entirely focused on studying her. Every doctor cell in his body was quivering at attention, seeking the truth . . . the diagnosis. "Tell me, Nikki."

Her hand made a little involuntary movement, like throwing something away, her voice barely above a whisper. "She says it's Hodgkin's."

"Oh, my God!" He was across the little kitchen in a heartbeat, gathering her in a wonder of an embrace, holding her against him tightly yet gently, one hand cradling the back of her head. "I'm so sorry, baby. You shoulda told me right away."

Nikki was crying now and clinging to him.

Two hours later they were back in the kitchen, finishing up the dishes. They'd spent a long time in each other's arms on the sofa, talking together, crying together. She'd left once to rescue the yams from the oven. They discussed the *knowns* about Hodgkin's, referring to the sheets Josie Bruno provided. They talked about chemo and various drugs; they talked about her finances and health insurance; they even talked about how this would affect her divorce and when exactly she should tell Matt, who'd begun to drag his heels in the divorce proceedings. But, in the end, Nikki realized, Dan had said nothing really concrete about how he viewed their future together.

Talked out, they'd returned to the kitchen. He chopped the onions for her and she finished the dressing, put it in the oven to bake.

He washed the last item, the stew bowl he'd used just before she unhinged his day, rinsed it, and handed it to her to dry. "That's it, I think." He glanced around to make sure, then let out the water and cleaned the sink.

The oven timer dinged, and Nikki grabbed the hot pads to pull out the pan of dressing when Dan opened the door for her.

She set the pan on top of the stove and then covered it loosely with aluminum foil. “This should be fine out here overnight,” she told him. It was already nearing midnight. “I have to get up at five to put the turkey in the oven. Then there’ll be some room in the fridge.”

He nodded. “So what will you need me to do tomorrow?”

“Set the table. Mash the potatoes. Help me get stuff heated and ready for the table. Carve the turkey.”

He nodded again. “And you’re sure you don’t want to tell anyone tomorrow?”

“God, no! No sense ruining *every*one’s Thanksgiving. Sorry you found out.”

“Not the kind of thing people should deal with alone,” he told her, He dried his hands and rolled his sleeves back down, asking, “Time for bed?” She saw the immediate misgiving in his expression. He mumbled, “I mean—“

“S’okay. I’m too tired for anything but sleep anyway.” Before now Nikki couldn’t remember a bit of awkwardness between them when it came to sex.

He reached out, pulled her into his arms, held her as tenderly and sincerely as ever, then murmured, “You’ve had a hard day, and we’ve got a big one ahead of us tomorrow. Let’s get some rest, Nikki.”

Minutes later, they spooned comfortably together, and after kissing her ear and whispering, “I love you, Nikki” he promptly fell asleep. She, utterly exhausted in body, mind and spirit, slipped from beneath the burden of all her worries and drifted off, safe and comforted, for now, at least, in Dante’s arms.

CHAPTER TWENTY-FOUR

The floor team, including Dan, formed a rapt semicircle before Dr. Felton Garfield, the seventy-year-old Professor of Medicine and Chief of Neurology. But he, too, was listening as the medical attending, Dr. Selma Braunstein, presented an especially mysterious new admission from the previous evening. Garfield peered through his half-moon reading glasses, focusing on the patient chart opened to the lab results. His hair, what remained of it, was combed straight back like a symphony conductor's; he seemed to cultivate that sense of drama in every movement. His lower face lay beneath an immaculately groomed beard more grey than white, and, though his fingers showed the unkind touch of arthritis, Garfield loved to twirl bits of that facial hair while he listened intently to presented cases. Today he was wearing another of his "December ties", this one diagonally striped red and green, and tacked with a tiny golden Christmas tree.

Dan could see, like the venerated Chairman of Medicine, Hugh Ballard, this man clearly enjoyed his exalted status, the doctor other physicians sought out.

"Thirty-six-year-old white male," Selma had begun a little nervously. The housestaff looked at each other. They weren't used to seeing nerves among the attending staff but clearly Braunstein was baffled. "Presented with right arm and leg weakness, hours after complaining of a migraine headache." Selma paused, ran a hand through her short, reddish brown hair and chewed her lip.

Garfield looked up from the chart, now removing his glasses and taking the end of one earpiece in his teeth. He waited.

Selma shifted uncomfortably and continued. "Physical exam essentially unremarkable except for a dense hemiparesis of his right upper and lower extremity Some conflicting sensory changes that appear to come and go with downgoing plantars and equivocal position sense on the right. Labs are within normal limits, as were the cranial CT Scan, which was negative for a bleed. He's on narcotics for pain but getting only moderate relief and no change in his paresis since admission."

"Interesting. Any previous history of this?"

Selma nodded. "Three or four times this year, he says but no primary care physician we could call."

"Really." Garfield said it without any inflection at all. "Let's go pay Mr. . . . ah—" he quickly squinted at the name on the chart, "Mr. Jeffrey Winters a visit, shall we?"

Garfield's entourage divided like the Red Sea, allowing him to enter the room first and amble toward the bed while the rest of them crowded in after him with Selma in the lead.

The patient, clean-shaven but tousle-headed, looked up suddenly, blinking. "Wha—?" He struggled to sit more upright.

"It's okay, Jeff," Selma assured him. "This is our Chairman of Neurology, Dr. Garfield."

Winters's gaze swept over all their faces . . . twice . . . his nervousness apparent to all, and increasing.

Garfield, too, apparently sensed the man's anxiety and sat in the bedside chair so he wouldn't be looming. "Hey, Jeff, how *are* you today?"

Winters squirmed, his whole right arm hanging limp, his eyes riveted on the elderly physician's hands as if he feared his wallet would be lifted. In a comforting gesture, Garfield leaned to take that limp hand in his own and patted it encouragingly.

"All right, I guess," Winters ventured at last. Then, gaining confidence, he continued, "That is, considering I can't move my right side and this migraine's about to blow open my head."

"Yes, yes, I understand." Garfield rose and bent to speak to Winters in a low voice still audible to the group. "Can you indulge an old doctor for one moment while I examine you?" He winked. "These youngsters think I can still teach them a thing or two."

Jeff smiled, clearly put at ease by the older physician's disarming style. He nodded.

"Mr. Winters, please lie flat on your back, if you will." The patient obliged, and Garfield moved the bedding out of his way. "Now, please try to lift your right leg an inch off the bed."

"I can't, Doc. It's paralyzed from the migraine."

"Humor me, please."

The patient tried to comply. The residents watched their mentor slide one arthritic hand under both Winters's limbs until it rested beneath the good left leg while Winters struggled mightily to raise the paralyzed one—but to no avail.

"Damn. Migraines do this all the time to me," Winters complained, relaxing his body totally, his face registering complete disgust at his futile effort.

Pulling his hand from beneath Winters's legs, Garfield stood up to his full height and spoke with unexpected briskness. "Well, then!" His voice had lost all the softness. "Whenever you're ready, Mr. Winters, you are free to walk out."

With that, the Professor of Neurology turned toward the residents, signaling an end to the bedside visit.

"Wha—at?" Jeff Winters was the only person to say it aloud, but Dan could see everyone in the house staff looked as completely baffled as he, himself, felt.

The residents again opened a path as the Chief of Neurology strode out, leaving the patient with his mouth agape. Glancing between the two, the young docs quickly moved to follow their mentor from the room.

Out in the open area, Garfield turned to face them and declared in a voice that meant to be heard by the patient, "He is a fake, doctors. How do I know this?"

They all glanced at one another, still disconcerted by the abrupt about-face, much less the challenging question. No one seemed brave enough to venture a guess.

"A good neuro exam, that's how." He paused for effect and lowered his voice ."Jeff's good leg never tensed while he tried to lift the one that was purportedly paralyzed—the complete opposite of what you should find. With a truly paralyzed limb, the patient always struggles to lift that limb by desperately contracting the muscles on the good side."

Still no one spoke; they let their nods and eyebrows express their sudden understanding and chagrin that they'd not foreseen the answer. Selma Braunstein looked especially embarrassed that she hadn't performed a thorough-enough physical exam.

"Furthermore," Garfield continued, "his bad hand was anything *but* paralyzed while I held it and he was distracted by my exam."

Dan glanced back into Winters's room, saw their patient scurrying around, gathering his belongings while his Johnny coat flapped open around his bare buttocks.

"He's on the move," Dan offered to anyone within earshot. "Completely recovered and not even trying to hide it."

Alex Cole chuckled. "Not even gonna wait to see if we call the police."

"Dirtball!" said Selma Braunstein with disgust. "As if we don't have enough on our plates..." she lamented to no one in particular.

"We must have compassion for the addicted," Garfield told them. "But that doesn't mean we can afford to let them scam us while stealing our time, treatment and resources from those who legitimately need them." He twirled some beard hairs in anticipation. "Now! Next patient?"

Trailing the others to Mrs. Jameson's room, one ear cocked to the status review Alex was giving the professor, Dan wondered if he'd ever be that capable, knowledgeable, insightful as Garfield? Ever?

"Maybe," he decided under his breath. "In about fifty years or so!"

Later, in the cafeteria, Dan sat down next to Willow. "So," she said after munching a hefty bite of her pastrami sandwich. "How's the neuro elective treating you?"

Dan considered, staring down into his bowl of clam chowder; he stirred it, as if that could help him locate more pieces of clam than potato. "It's been good. Interesting." For the moment it was fairly quiet in the DCH cafeteria, and Dan could feel himself relaxing in the now-easy company of a good friend. "I'm learning a lot."

"Heard you were right about our Vanessa Hemphill."

Dan nodded. "Just lucky."

"No, I've watched you." Willow pointed at him with her spear of dill pickle. "You have a gift for putting all the pieces together and seeing the whole puzzle." With a nod to emphasize her words, she bit the pickle in two and savored its crunching as she waited for his response.

"Thanks."

It *had* been a sweet insight. Vanessa Hemphill, a twenty-two-year-old white female in her first trimester of a first pregnancy, had complained to Willow, at present on an OB/GYN rotation, of great fatigue and muscle weakness, trouble swallowing and, increasingly, shortness of breath.

"MG just never crossed my mind," Willow admitted. "Not even when she went into crisis and couldn't breathe."

Dan shrugged. "Concentrating on neuro, I'd been reading up on lesser-seen diseases. I'd just studied an article on MG presenting in the first trimester and then disappearing for the rest of the pregnancy—but maybe being passed on to the baby."

Myasthenia gravis—an autoimmune disorder causing great muscle weakness, most dangerous for the respiratory muscles—could be hard to diagnose in anyone, especially before a dramatic crisis. In Vanessa's case, fatigue and muscle weakness could be chalked up to trying to stay active during pregnancy, and the problems with swallowing and breathing, to anxiety.

"It was the drooping eyelid that made the pieces fall into place," Dan explained. The disease sent antibodies that interfered with how nerves connect to properly signal the muscle causing the droop. Thankfully, MG didn't affect heart muscles, but it could easily shut down respiration. His quick preliminary diagnosis and call to neuro got Vanessa fast-tracked to plasmapheresis, where the harmful antibodies could be washed from her blood, for the present at least.

Now that Vanessa's condition, which had been present but very mild and transitory before the pregnancy, was identified, immunosuppressant medication would be prescribed going forward. There were hopes the child wouldn't suffer from the ailment, despite the possibilities for a genetic link.

"Good thing you were on our floor when I went to look for help." Willow popped the last bite of her sandwich into her mouth.

Maternity and related services were housed on Six East, while peds filled Six West. "Coincidence," Dan insisted. "I was just on my way to see Nikki at break."

Chewing, Willow considered this new topic and swallowed. "So how's that going, Dan? The Nikki thing?"

He looked away from Willow's exotic eyes, unable to avoid a quick memory of kissing this lovely young woman, so willing in his arms.

As if reading his thoughts, she reached to touch his right hand, which couldn't seem to stop stirring his chowder. "Hey, I'm happy you found someone. I'm just sorry about *her* news; that was a shock."

Relaxing again, he murmured, "You can say *that* again."

Willow dabbed her mouth with a holly-sprigged paper napkin. "I'm glad you hooked up with Nikki. I loved working with her on my peds rotation. You can learn so much watching the nurses, and she's just great with the kids. Nikki's a good person, and I hope—"

Willow's cell phone buzzed her, and she checked the text message. "Oh, good. Got three women in labor, and it looks like the one with twins is ready to deliver." Sometimes I wish I had done straight medicine like you so that I wouldn't always be the newbie on these rotations!" Dan grinned. He knew Willow was very proud, almost to the point of conceited ass sometimes, that she had matched into her highly competitive anesthesiology residency that required a year of rotating through all the clinical services. Rising and picking up her tray, she regarded Dan with a compassionate gaze. "I'm so sorry this cancer thing is happening to you and Nikki. Let me know if I can help. And I really mean that; it's not just words. You're my friend . . . and so is Nikki."

"Thanks," Dan managed and then watched as she bussed her tray and hurried away toward a world of new lives ready to begin.

This cancer thing. Sudden and shattering as an earthquake. Aftershock followed aftershock as they identified and faced various ramifications of her illness and its treatment. Since getting the news from Josie Bruno three weeks ago, Nikki'd seen Cyrus Klonter several times. Dan accompanied her to every appointment he could manage with their work schedules, but he couldn't get to them all. After a PET scan to view the extent of the mass in Nikki's chest, a CT of her pelvis and a bone marrow biopsy from her hipbone, the oncologist set the staging at IIB: symptomatic, but with no sign of the disease below the diaphragm. Apparently, the only lymph nodes affected were those in her chest, snugged against the sternum. As predicted, Klonter felt it safe to forgo both surgery and radiation, treating with chemo alone. One small relief.

Dan crumbled saltines into his now-cold chowder thinking about the future. Having her so sick and weak and needing his help . . . losing all that beautiful red hair? What would it be like for him to leave a long day caring for sick people at DCH and go home to care for a sick person in his own bed? And though the guilt of thinking about himself weighed on him like chainmail scrubs, he couldn't help wondering how all this would impinge on his daily life, his career and future, his own stress levels and peace of mind.

He knew there'd been no obligation, no expectation on Nikki's part. But she really had no one. In fact, when her ex heard she had lymphoma and was moving in with a young doctor, he hadn't taken it well at all. Dan wasn't there, and Nikki didn't give many details, but it was clear to Dan that Matt had said some very hurtful things, beyond a complete disregard for the fact the woman he'd married had cancer.

Dan gazed toward the distant wall of the cafeteria, where swags of seasonal greenery tied with big red bows did little to inspire a festive spirit in him.

"Well, you really missed out, Dan." Alex Cole slid into the seat Willow had vacated, setting his tray on the tabletop and grabbing up his fork to attack a huge plate of macaroni and cheese. Dan waited as the first bite was dispatched and Alex could continue. "I got to see that service dog of Jilly Hoyt's alert to an oncoming epileptic seizure. Uncanny. Made the hairs stand up on my arms." He took a quick drink of his coke and grinned. "I *love* neuro. Glad I'm staying all month. Where're you off to next week?"

"Urology," Dan answered. He'd decided to split the month of December with two electives: two weeks neurology; two weeks urology. When Alex snorted with laughter, Dan warned, "Don't start with the jokes. I've heard 'em all."

As Alex stuffed forkfuls of mac 'n cheese into his grinning mouth, Dan reflected how good it was good to see him happy again.

Alex picked up his napkin and regarded the holly-printed border with the cheery prediction, "This is gonna be my best Christmas ever!"

As Dan finished the rest of his lunch—a soggy paste of cold cracker-and-chowder accompanied by an anemic iceberg salad with some grated carrot and a single piece of tomato—he looked ahead to his own holidays. "Thanks again, Alex, for helping us out."

"No problem." With a smug wink, he added, "After all, *I* won't be using my apartment that weekend."

Dan lifted his water glass in salute. Though Julia's mom Myra approved her daughter "dating" Alex, she would be too old-fashioned, and too Catholic, to accept their sleeping together "out-of-wedlock." And she was too well acquainted with her daughter's work schedule for fudging on that excuse. So they'd been left with only furtive trysts at Alex's and never any overnights. Now the upcoming Christmas holidays were providing a perfect opportunity. Myra would be spending Friday through Sunday at a family reunion in Cleveland; fortunately, Julia had to work Christmas Eve Day and December 26, so couldn't attend the whole event in Ohio. She'd be staying home until Christmas Day, when Alex would drive her to the main celebration and then back home that same night. Myra planned to return late Monday. She'd expressed her relief that Julia would have company on Christmas Eve, attending the traditional party at DCH. But she remained blissfully unaware her daughter would have Alex as a weekend guest in her home.

Dan couldn't believe it had been six months since he'd seen Mom and Pop and Jerry! Fortunately, Dan's schedule, too, released him from eight a.m. December 23 through to eight a.m. the twenty-sixth. His parents and brother planned to drive the six hours from their hometown in New York to spend the night of the twenty-third with Aunt Carmella in Altoona; they'd leave there to arrive in Deerwood about eleven a.m. on Christmas Eve Day.

How great, getting to spend Christmas weekend with his family. And how ironic, like Julia, he was choosing to "protect" his parents' Catholic sensibilities from the fact he was sexually involved with a co-worker. Nikki was the one who first saw the wisdom of this, at least for now, and it was she who pointed out, "If Alex is going to be staying at Julia's, maybe he'd let me stay at *his* place . . . move my stuff in there for the weekend."

They wouldn't be hiding their relationship completely. Before Thanksgiving he'd broken the news to his ecstatic mom that he was "seeing someone." Not only would Nikki be sharing the holiday weekend, still some ten days away, but she'd already been working with Mom via phone to plan the special "Seven Fishes" dinner for Christmas Eve and the next day's feast as well.

Dan's place was too small for his whole family to stay there though Jerry would use an airbed in the living room; Mom and Pop had booked a room at a local Best Western.

Dan stood up, feeling the weight of those chainmail scrubs again, and lifted his tray.

Alex quickly followed suit and made a wild stab at changing the subject to lighten the mood. "This intern stuff is pretty easy, don't you think?"

Dan smiled slightly. "How so?"

Alex eagerly kept the ball moving. "It's coming easy, bro, real easy."

They both laughed as they left the cafeteria, but it sounded forced, even in Dan's ears.

CHAPTER TWENTY-FIVE

"It's the Marchetti family tradition," Mom was telling Nikki in the kitchen, her tone almost apologetic. "The only way another person can learn our family's lasagna recipe is if you become part of the family through marriage or adoption."

"And," Pop said, "you have to make one improvement before you can use it. My mama was very strict about that."

Dan, who'd come, unnoticed, upon the tableau after his morning shower, saw Nikki laughing and blushing as if she didn't quite know what to say. Pop regarded her affably. "You're a little too old to adopt. . . ."

"So," Mom continued, "the only alternative is. . . ."

"Ah, a conspiracy in my own kitchen!" Dan interrupted, reaching to take Nikki's hand and draw her close with one arm around her.

Gloria sniffed. "Just explaining why Nikki has to go sit in the living room while I put the lasagna together."

Nikki took up the play with a little pout. "Here I thought I was gonna get a blockbuster recipe for lasagna, but I find out I'm not qualified."

Mom arched an eyebrow. "Not *yet*. . . ."

The four of them laughed but with an undercurrent of embarrassment. "Quit fishing, Mom," Dan told her. "Come on, Nikki. Take a break. I'm sure Mom'll need your help again when she's finished with the 'secret stuff.'"

"Oh, I will!" Gloria assured them. "You can help me with the eggplant parmesan. Sal will help me with this." She turned to him. "You go get the white plastic bag in the Coleman."

Nikki was still laughing. "So, after all that shopping I did, I still won't even know all the *ingredients* that're involved?"

Dan shook his head. "We're a devious clan, I'm afraid. But I'll tell you, not counting the sauce with sausage and meatballs, there're three kinds of chopped meats and four cheeses in it."

By then they were getting snuggled together on the couch. Dan could tell Nikki was a little disappointed, but not hurt. And probably a little titillated by the heady subject of marriage into the Marchetti family—something Dan had certainly never mentioned to Nikki.

Soon enough, Sal came over and tapped Nikki's shoulder. "Your turn again," he said and took her place on the sofa when she hopped up and rejoined Gloria.

With the sauce finally simmering on the stove, Nikki and Gloria served hot mulled cider and everyone settled in the living room to open gifts. Dan was glad Nikki'd made Mom see the wisdom of agreeing the visitors wouldn't be exchanging gifts with her. Nikki's efforts shopping, prepping and assisting in the kitchen were well-balanced by her inclusion in the family holiday feasts. And since Dan's finances were limited, and the Marchettis had already spent so much for the meals and travel, all the Marchettis had settled on a twenty-dollar "stocking-stuffer" limit for family gifts.

Sal gave each of his sons a new baseball cap: for Jerry, a replacement for the Yankees cap he'd worn so long it practically disintegrated; for Dan, a Pittsburgh Pirates cap, black with the yellow-gold *P* in buccaneer-style lettering. "So you can fit in around here," Pop teased him.

From Jerry, Pop received an I.O.U. for "Five hours hard labor around the Marchetti Homestead. Your Choice—even windows, gutter-cleaning or shoveling snow."

Dan presented his dad with a framed bio of Charlie Monroe, downloaded from the Internet, complete with a photo from back in his heyday, and autographed by Charlie himself during one of his earlier periods of recovery. Having told Pop about his connection with Charlie at DCH, Dan was pleased, and relieved, to be able to say, "As of a coupla days ago, Charlie's off the ventilator, breathing on his own again and looking much better."

Gloria had knitted long, tasseled neckscarves for her boys, using super-soft variegated yarns: shades of blue for Dan and dark grape-purples for Jerry.

The Marchetti boys were on the same page for their mom. Dan had found a new figurine for Gloria's giraffe collection: a single crystal shape of a momma bending her long neck down to touch her baby. Jerry's gift proved to be a gold-tone giraffe brooch with little pretend topazes for spots.

Dan and Jerry traded gifts that were almost identical in size and shape. *For* his brother, a hot-off-the-presses DVD of sports bloopers. *From* his brother, a CD of his band's original music. *MoonMist* was the title, and, Dan could see now, the name of the group itself. There in the dynamic cover photo, Dan could see Jerry at the keyboard, frozen in the moment but as animated as any of the other musicians, and in front, Miss Misty Moon herself: close on the microphone, blond hair flying, tiny leather skirt, crop top and all.

Dan managed a quick but significant glance at his brother as he said, "Thanks, bro. I'm really looking forward to listening to this!"

Jerry gave a dismissive gesture, but his expression was smug. "Yeah, no hurry. Not exactly Christmas music."

"Yes," Mom said. "It's a little *loud* for our taste. Of course, it's very *good*—if you like that kind of music."

Because of the Nikki-Gloria pact, Dan was the only one to exchange gifts with Nikki. He'd wanted to get her something she could use in the long weeks ahead of chemotherapy. Something both useful and comforting or distracting. Still, it couldn't raise suspicions or seem inappropriate, like a set of cozy pajamas. He settled on three books by Robert Zubrin, a favorite author of Nikki's.

She was obviously delighted and apparently on the same wavelength. Her gift to him was a pair of DVDs: the first two seasons of the TV show *Monk*. A favorite for both of them, something they currently taped to watch together, Dan had missed the early seasons while in med school. As he gave her a *Thank You* kiss on the cheek, he knew she'd been thinking this'd be something they could share during the times she wouldn't feel like going out to a movie or some community event.

Soon only one present was left, chosen by Dan and wrapped by Nikki, this DVD set of European travel programs would be carried back to Aunt Carmella when the Marchettis returned. Now that all the other gifts had been opened and shown and appreciated, Nikki and Gloria went back to the kitchen to finish preparing the feast. It turned out there wasn't any football of interest on the tube, but the Marchetti men found plenty to talk about until dinner was served.

Like yesterday, after the blessing and toasts—today with a hearty Chianti—there wasn't much conversation for a while, just complete attention to savoring the food. They passed around the huge serving bowl of sauce, crowded with meatballs and sausages, and ladled it over the baked lasagna, followed by a liberal sprinkling of freshly grated parmesan. Dan had wolfed down his first serving before he even touched his *insalata verde* with its cold greens, artichoke hearts and big pieces of tomato.

Nikki was the first to speak as the sauce was passed around for second helpings. "Not only is the Marchetti Secret Lasagna simply exquisite," she proclaimed, raising her garlic bread to salute Gloria, "but this eggplant is *divine.*"

"Well, that recipe's no secret," Mom reminded, glowing with the praise—and probably the relief of having this meal be just as big a success.

"You better believe I'll be making *this!*" Nikki vowed.

"Add veal or chicken, you got a whole meal. And it's only fair that you invite Dante over to share it."

Nikki laughed, sending a sidelong glance at him. "I think that can be arranged."

When it was time for dessert, Nikki went back to the other apartment and retrieved the big, pink *Luigi's* box still waiting in that refrigerator. As directed by Gloria, Nikki had selected an assortment of Italian pastries, including *cannulicchi,* finger-sized cannoli, some flavored with vanilla or orange, some with cranberries or candied citron.

Jerry helped his dad with the dessert liqueurs. When Sal had poured four little glasses of crystal clear sambuca, Jerry dropped three coffee beans into each so they floated on top. As he was setting a glass in front of each of the Marchettis, his father told Nikki, "Dan says you're not too fond of anise flavoring?"

Nikki wrinkled her nose. "Right. In fact, I *detest* licorice."

"Ah!" Sal intoned. "For *you* we have Amaretto di Saronno!"

"Oh, I *love* amaretto! Thank you."

"Don't put that amaretto bottle away too soon, old man," Dan chided. "I think I'll have to have some of that too."

As they tucked into the heavenly pastries, Mom admonished, "Save room! Save room!"

"For what?" Dan asked around a bite of a snowflake-shaped *pizzelle* cookie, but his mom only smiled enigmatically. She waited till they'd done justice to the Luigi's array; then she bustled into the other room where the Coleman apparently still held treasure. She returned beaming with a huge New York cheesecake.

"It's the real thing," she told Dan. "From your favorite place back home."

"Oh," he moaned in ecstasy. "I've really been missing *that.*"

"We can all have a little piece," Mom said, "then leave the rest for you to finish over the next few days. Maybe Nikki could come over and help you."

"Count on it!" Nikki declared, rising. "Espresso for everyone, right?"

The rest of the day, wet and rainy outside the apartment but warm and cozy within, slid past them as the Christmas music played. The women insisted on doing all the cleanup this time while the men played some cards—their traditional game of casino. When Nikki and Gloria joined them, Jerry, as self-appointed Entertainment Chairman, had thought of everything, and he brought out the family's well-used copy of the murder-mystery board game *Clue*. "I remember playing this!" Nikki said. "It's been a long time since I've uttered the words, 'Col. Mustard in the Library with a Candlestick!'"

For the whole day, as far as Dan could tell, there was never an awkward silence. Either people were thinking of new topics to share or were, for a time, comfortable without the need for conversation. Late in the day, they snacked on leftovers and drank more eggnog.

Around seven pm, Pop said, "Well, I think your mom and I should get back to the motel. We know you have to be at work by eight in the morning, and we all want to get an early start for Carmella's."

Jerry hopped up, intending to drop his parents at the Best Western and return here with the car. That'd make it easier in the morning to leave when Dan did and pick up his parents at the motel.

The farewells were a little emotional for Dan, tugging at him in a way that made it difficult not to tear up. Mom, of course, was blubbering, and then Nikki joined in. Nikki and Mom kept hugging each other, thanking each other, vowing to talk soon on the phone. "Holy cow, ladies!" Sal protested. "This isn't the departure of the *Titanic!*" But Dan could see his old man was having trouble too, blinking rapidly, his voice tight in his throat.

Sal slapped Dan on the shoulder and shook his hand, and that turned into a manly, back-slapping sort of embrace. "Good to see you, son. You look good, despite all the stress you must be under. You let us know if you need anything, okay?"

Gloria's attention swung from Nikki to her son, and when she hugged him, Dan was surprised at her fervency. He wasn't sure she'd ever let him loose.

"You seem a little thin, Dante," she said tearfully. "You have to eat well to stay healthy with an important job like yours. People are depending on you."

"Okay," Jerry broke in, laughing. "Enough tears and guilt." He jingled the car keys. "The stagecoach is leaving the barn."

Of course, there were more tears and hugs, but finally Dan was alone in the apartment with Nikki. Each stared at the other, and they both sighed a great gust of relief. Wordlessly, they fell into each others' arms and sank to the sofa where they sat, holding each other. In the blinking tree lights and the soft background music, pleasant instrumentals of seasonal favorites, they sat enjoying the peace of a successful holiday and the bit of solitude they would have before Jerry returned. After a time, Nikki whispered, "Thank you, Dante," and he gave her a little squeeze, but that was all. Nothing else needed saying.

Only a half hour later, the old "shave-and-a-haircut" knocking on the door signaled Jerry's return. As Nikki rose to answer it, Dan let her know, "I told Jerry *everything*, so you don't have to worry about spilling any beans."

She smiled back over her shoulder. "That's a relief!" Letting Jerry in with a welcoming smile, she told him, "Well, I'll be on my way. It was so nice meeting you, Jerry."

"Hey, don't leave. I've been hoping the three of us would have some time together."

Clearly pleased, Nikki said, "Likewise, but I can't stay up too late. Gotta be at work at six tomorrow."

"Y'know," Jerry said, including Dan in his gaze, "the two of you could stay together here tonight. The folks can't come back and surprise us; I've got the car. Heck, I could even go down and sleep in the other apartment if you guys wanta get noisy."

Nikki and Dan laughed, and she said, "Thanks, but I do have to make it an early night, and I need to start packing up over there to move back here."

"Stay for a little while," Dan urged. "Let's finish that last bottle of Chianti."

As they sat in his living room, sipping the wine and talking, he could feel that sense of relief flowing through them all, now the parents were gone and they could truly relax. Nikki got Jerry to talk about his business and tell her about his girlfriend, and Dan, observing more than participating, found himself again surprised and impressed by his little brother's maturity and insights.

Finally, though, Nikki sighed and left her place beside Dan on the sofa. "It's time," she said and carried their empty glasses to the kitchen. She returned to lean down and kiss Dan goodnight, saying, "Don't get up."

But Jerry uncurled himself from the beanbag to embrace her. They both said how glad they were to meet each other and how they were looking forward to seeing each other again sometime soon. At the door, she pointed to Dan. "You! I'll see you here tomorrow night . . . about eight thirty?" Dan nodded. "Don't eat too much. We have *tons* of scrumptious leftovers." Then, to Jerry, "You! Have a safe trip home and give my love to your parents."

A moment later she was gone, and Jerry dropped back down into the beanbag, grinning. "Well, bro, she's a keeper."

Dan heard the echo of Alex's words not long ago, and in the same way, he saw the awkward realization in Jer's eyes as he remembered the Hodgkin's. He started to apologize, but Dan waved it off.

"Well, but she's got a really good shot at a cure, right?"

"Docs don't talk about 'cure' when it comes to cancer, but yeah, you're right about the odds being very good for survival and recovery."

"But. . . ?"

Dan shifted uncomfortably and looked away from his brother's suddenly piercing gaze. "It's just . . . though I feel pretty confident in Nikki's recovery . . . I'm not really sure if the *relationship* will survive . . . endure."

"But you love her?"

Dan looked back to meet Jerry's eyes. "I think so. But I'm not certain she's . . . you know . . . The One."

Jer nodded with an expression of sad understanding. "Well, seems like you've got time to let it all play out. Bridges to cross before you have to make any final decisions."

"Yeah . . . bridges."

"You'll be dealing with a lot over the next many months, as if a freakin' medical *internship* isn't enough!—and just remember

I'll be there for you. Whatever you need that I can help with." Maybe he could see Dan's eyes getting wet. "Well, no birthin' no babies the way you did!"

Dan laughed. "No, but we can sure run interference for each other with the folks as we break the news about our personal lives."

"Yeah, thanks. I can use that."

"Jer, you're closer to them than I am these days. Lemme ask you something. How much do you think it'll matter if we choose women who aren't Catholic?"

"It'll matter," Jerry answered. "They want things to go on a certain way, to continue the dreams of their forefathers. But that won't be a deal-breaker. After all, they know we're both not really practicing anymore, and they just ignore it. I think they'll be disappointed, but how they feel about the girl will be much more important."

"I sure hope you're right."

"Yeah, Dan, me too!" He laughed, and Dan remembered the "flashy" lead singer on the *MoonMist* cover. "I've got a steeper hill to climb!"

After they'd changed into their sweats and set up Jerry's bed, they talked for a while longer about their parents and Jerry's impressions of how well they were really doing—especially Mom.

She always downplayed her chronic heart condition and was careful, while leading a very active life, not to overexert herself physically.

"It's hard to tell about her," Jerry admitted. "*I* think she gets tired-er a little sooner. . . but she denies it or has some excuse."

Dan frowned. "What does Pop say about it?"

"Oh, he goes along with *her,* and I can't really tell if he agrees with her or is secretly concerned but not wanting to worry *me.*"

Dan sighed. "Guess we'll just have to keep a careful eye on her. Well, it'll have to be *your* eye, but keep me posted if you see anything that worries you at all."

Jerry nodded, "Will do." Dan yawned, getting ready to call it a night and excused himself to the bedroom. But Jerry cocked his head and said, "Okay, bro. I know you're holding out on me."

"Wha-at?"

"I know there's at least *one* urology case you couldn't share. Come on, I need a bedtime story."

Dan chuckled. "Okay. You asked for it. It's called Peyronie's disease and something you should know about if you're thinking about having kids. This fellow came in—nearly forty and good health. But some years ago, when he was teaching his little son how to play baseball, the kid accidentally whacked him a good one across the crotch with his bat."

Jer grunted and made that face men make when genital injury is mentioned. "The kind of thing you see all the time on funniest video shows. Like that's really funny."

"Uh-huh. So this guy got a terrific smack across the top of his penis, and he didn't know it, but sometimes when that happens, there's a lot of bleeding inside and the layers of tissue separate."

The expression on Jer's face showed increasing horror.

"When that heals, it can form a dense patch of scarring, we call it a plaque, and that keeps contracting and starts to bend the penis. Which is most noticeable, of course, during erection."

"So the guy could still *have* an erection?"

"Yeah, but the thing is, his plaque got so bad, it was like his penis was bent around looking back at him, and he couldn't, you know . . . successfully . . . have intercourse."

"Whoa. And he didn't go to the doctor?"

"Not until his wife threatened to divorce him. At first, he thought it'd go away, and as it got worse and worse, he was too embarrassed. It's been five years since he's been able to properly make love to his wife."

"So what did y'do for him?" Jerry demanded. "Is he gonna be okay?"

"Yeah, probably. He'll have to have surgery to remove the plaque and that should solve it. Only thing is, that usually leads to a little shortening of the penis."

"Ouch! Not a *good* thing."

"No, but I gotta tell you, with this guy, it probably won't matter that much. Let's just say he had plenty to spare."

As they dissolved in whoops of laughter, Dan was glad this end of the apartment didn't share walls with any other.

CHAPTER TWENTY-SIX

"You're late, Marchetti," barked Max Koehler, Chief of Urology.

Not an auspicious start to this rather intimidating elective. Dan stared at the hulking figure before him, glowering eyebrows met like bushy black caterpillars above a splotchy-red nose, and considered whether to offer his excuses. Nikki had cautioned him: "Remember, Koehler's a little Old School. Prefers his interns in lab coat, pressed shirt and tie." So Dan had hurriedly replaced his comfy scrubs with a crisp shirt and his one good tie placed on his dresser. Then, already running a minute late, he'd been the only doc in sight when a nearly comatose drug overdose got dragged by her almost equally stoned boyfriend into the DCH main lobby instead of Emergency. Dan'd made sure they both got safely to the ER and then ran for his clinic duty.

Simply apologize and let it go at that? The man's temper was legendary, best epitomized in the oft-told tale of how he'd hoisted two bungling medical students off the floor by their neckties while their eyes bulged with pure terror. Of course, Koehler was severely reprimanded, but no one ever forgot the story—or failed to pass it along to the next crop of newbies. And the two students, upon completing their rotation, received gifts of clip-on ties from the house staff.

"I'm sorry, Dr. Koehler." Dan made sure his voice sounded as sincere as he felt. The Chair of Urology glared at him a moment longer, as if to see whether he could still elicit groveling. Then he *harrumph!*ed, handed Dan a chart and said, "Been saving Curtain Six for you."

Dan glanced down at the name: *John Penny*. Giving Koehler a respectful nod, Dan went off to see what awaited him. His patient sat, fully clothed, on the edge of the exam table with his legs spread wide apart, his hands resting across his lap. His wife stood next to him, touching his shoulder and looking scared.

"Good morning, Mr. and Mrs. Penny. I'm Dr. Dan Marchetti." They forced smiles and nodded to him. "How can I help you today?"

They exchanged glances. John Penny, a huge man with tufts of grey hair surrounding a bald pate, wore oversized horn-rimmed glasses that were still too small for his face. His wife, Edna, according to the chart, nearly matched him in height but was much slimmer, and she had an abundant head of fluffy grey hair.

After a few awkward seconds, avoiding Dan's eyes, John spoke up sheepishly. "Doc, I got this problem." He sighed. "No easy way to say this, so I'll show you."

John slid gingerly from the exam table to a standing position, unbuckled his baggy trousers and let them, along with his huge boxer shorts, fall to the ground, revealing "the problem."

"Mother of God!" Dan blurted. "How long have you—" Words failed him.

John helped him out. "Had a ball-sack the size of a watermelon?" Dan nodded, still speechless and staring. "Six months, I guess."

Edna piped up. "He has an awful time in the bathroom. In fact, I have to help him with his penis or else he pees all over himself."

Dan tried to imagine his pop and mom having this conversation with a young doctor. Dan pulled his eyes away from Mr. Penny's problem and focused them on Edna's face. "May I ask why it took so long to seek help?"

She shrugged, looking embarrassed and regretful. "We thought—hoped—it would go away." She looked to her husband, reached to smooth an errant curl of hair. "But now he gets so short of breath, we're just plain scared."

Dan regained his composure. He quickly began a complete exam, using his stethoscope to listen to John's lungs and heart, then asking a long list of medical questions and carefully noting the responses on the chart. At one point, Dan made a noble, but futile, attempt to thoroughly examine John's scrotum. Holding the monstrosity in both hands, Dan found it had the consistency, fluidity and unpredictability of a water balloon.

But through his exam, it became clear that Dan's patient was actually suffering from, at the very least, severe congestive heart failure. Well, the CHF they could deal with and sort the rest out later. "Okay! You can get dressed now," he said crisply. Seeing the desperation in their frightened faces, he smiled comfortingly. "I'm sure we can help you. I'll be right back." Dan quickly exited as Edna helped her husband get his scrotum back into his boxers. Just beyond the curtain, Dan found himself trying to gather in all he had just seen.

"Madonna Mia!" he whispered.

Shaking his head, Dan moved off, seeking Dr. Koehler for consultation. When he found him, the big man's caterpillar eyebrows headed for his hairline, and his face split into a huge grin. With a chortle that came from deep in the belly, he clapped Dan on the shoulder and exclaimed, "Welcome to Urology, Marchetti!"

CHAPTER TWENTY-SEVEN

Eyes closed, Nikki Saxon pretended she was lying back on her patio chaise instead of an infusion lounge in the DCH chemo clinic.

Round Two, she thought grimly. Her first session had been two weeks earlier on the third of January, but in the prior week, last week of 2005, her last week working at DCH before going on medical leave—she'd had plenty to attend to preparing for her chemotherapy.

First, of course, there'd been a lot of "moving back in" from Alex's. Though she'd packed most of her things before she departed for work, so Alex would have room to move his own belongings back in whenever he returned, she'd left it all inside his apartment, because Jerry was still at Dan's. When she arrived home from work about three, she went to retrieve her things. She knocked and heard him call distantly, "Come in!" As she opened the unlocked door and entered, his voice continued, "Been expecting you, Nikki. At least I *hope* that's Nikki and not some wayward ax murderer." He appeared in the doorway of his bedroom, hands still full of the items he was unpacking.

She grinned at him. "No ax murderers here."

"Oh, good, cuz I'd hate to have a mess in here." With the hand holding his toiletries kit, he gestured to the white-and-metallics Christmas decorations around the living room. "This place looks sensational. I'm gonna leave everything just the way it is, at least through New Year's. Julia will love it."

"You and Julia have a good time?"

Alex positively beamed, lighting his tea-brown eyes even more. "It was *wonderful.* Even the whole Meeting-the-Family thing. You?"

"Yes, for us too. Amazing, but everything worked out." That seemed so little to say about how included and appreciated and *loved* she'd felt with Dan's family.

Nikki and Alex shared wide smiles of mutual relief; then he hefted his burdens and tilted his head back the way he'd come, inviting her to follow. She left her duffel and other possessions where they waited by the front door and went to lean in the bedroom doorway, watching him finish his unpacking.

"Thanks for leaving everything so spotless," he said, "stripping the bed and towels and all."

"Least I could do after you had the place all ready for me." She folded her arms across her chest. "So dish! What's Julia's family really like?"

Alex laughed and launched into a series of wryly told stories about Clan Cleary and its rollicking Christmas celebration. Judging from Alex's tales of how tough the family banter got, even though very loving, it seemed Myra, as baby of the generation, had always gotten the worst of it from her older siblings while proving to be the most sensitive to any teasing. It also shed some light on her food issues.

Alex reflected. "There was always someone urging us all to eat and drink more. *Lots* of rich food and plenty of 'spirits,' if you know what I mean." He shook his head. "I couldn't believe how much Myra consumed in just the hours we were there. Y'know, the more they picked on her, the more she laughed it off, but the more she ate." Nikki could hear the genuine concern in his tone.

"So Julia tried to help her?"

"Yeah, she deflected a lot of the comments, she can give as good as she gets with that crew, and then discreetly tried to convince her mom to ease up on the food, but we know how that usually ends up."

Nikki ventured, "Myra getting defensive and treating Julia like *she's* being a bully?"

He nodded and shrugged. "Really frustrating. For *me* as well as Julia." Everything now unpacked and properly located, he wrestled his emptied roller duffel into the closet, then turned back to Nikki and grinned. "But the time alone with Julia at *her* place was just heaven. Actually *sleeping* together instead of just having sex. Y'know?"

Nikki nodded, surprised at his openness. She didn't interrupt.

"We could feel like grown-ups instead of two high school kids having to lie about, and hurry through, our time together." His face looked wistful at first, then very serious as he told her, "I don't want to go back to that—stealing moments here and there. I've gotta find a way to get Julia to stand on her own more . . . not have to be at her mother's beck-and-call." He ran a hand through his reddish hair and sighed. "I really *like* Myra, but. . . ."

Eyes closed, looking back into the past instead of at the I.V. line inserted into the central port an inch below her right collarbone. But before moving the boxes in, they shared a long, frank discussion about their individual and mutual needs, then formulated a plan.

They moved Dan's desk and its chair out into the living room, trading it for the TV and all the audio equipment so she could watch TV or listen to music and books-on-tape while resting in bed. Moving one of the tan company chairs into the bedroom freed up some space in the front room and made it possible for a guest to sit while visiting Nikki, even if she needed to be in bed.

They'd tried to think of everything in that week, laying in an ample supply of high-nutrition shakes for times she might not feel like eating. She replenished her favorite supplements, those not contraindicated by the chemo, and added ginger tablets for combating nausea. She'd finally shown him the four Christmas-gift-to-herself headscarves and watched the tears well in his eyes. She told him about wig-shopping in Pittsburgh with Julia and showed him a picture of what she planned to order when it could be properly fitted.

They packed the time they had with as much physical intimacy as they possibly could, banking against the long weeks ahead when merely touching or being touched might be unwelcome contact.

Her last week at work was harder than she thought it'd be. Smiling through the regretful farewells and little gifts from her young patients and their parents, knowing they were unlikely to be there, one way or the other, by the time she could return. Then there was trying not to see the shadows in her co-workers' eyes. Especially during the agony of that little "Good Luck! Good Health!" party Julia arranged at the end of Nikki's last shift. No doubt of all the sincerity, but difficult to be the focus of so much attention—and fear.

After spending a suitable time forcing smiles to express her genuine gratitude for her colleagues' outpouring of good-will, after sipping some punch and finishing a slice of the sheet cake that wished her well in excruciatingly green icing, she'd gone down four floors to Nuclear Medicine for her MUGA scan.

Some time later, as she lay on the table hooked up to the EKG equipment and beneath the gamma camera recording the movement of radioactively tagged red blood cells through her heart, she knew it was only the first in a series of MUGAs over the next few months. Multi-Gated Acquisition scans measured the amount of blood the left ventricle pumped out to the body with each heartbeat. She expected her initial Ejection Fraction to be normal—somewhere between 50-75%— and it could then be compared to future scans to make sure her heart wasn't being damaged by adriamycin, one of the four chemotherapy drugs she'd be receiving in a regimen abbreviated ABVD.

On New Year's Eve, she and Dan curled together on the bed and watched the ball drop in Times Square. Dan had insisted on champagne so they could toast the New Year: 2006. "Here's to all the good things it'll bring us both!" he declared, as if the strength of his voice could make it so. She'd managed to smile at him and mirror the toast, but she felt a chill along her spine, and dread fell heavily across her like a shawl on the shoulders of a very old woman.

Though Dan had duty all New Year's Day, those hours stretched empty before her; she had few preparation tasks left to accomplish. So she started out walking him to work, hand-in-hand, wanting to share her every possible healthy moment with him.

But as she neared the imposing ten-story face of DCH, she felt herself pulling back. In a sudden flash of memory, she felt again the pain of those last moments before officially beginning her medical leave of absence. At the nursing office, she turned in her keys and badge but her face must've given her away, because dear Mrs. Tillman, who'd worked there ages before Nikki was hired, gave her a motherly look and said, "That's okay, honey. You can hold on to those. You'll be back 'fore too long."

Now, as then, Nikki thought, *I hope so!* But even still possessing those precious symbols of her DCH "identity", tucked out of sight in her bedside drawer, didn't ease Nikki's sense of disconnection as she neared the building.

She stopped at the corner, huddling down in her coat. "I'm gonna head back. I'm starting to get a chill."

He squeezed her hand and kissed the top of her head. "Sure. You stay warm and dry. I'll see you tonight."

She turned toward the apartment but glanced back to watch him hustle across the street and greet security guard Greg Vanderbosk just inside the main doors. She could tell they were wishing each other "Happy New Year!"

Tears blurred her vision as she hurried home. After languishing in a long, luxurious bubble bath, she spent most of the day writing in her journal, looking back on the monumental changes during the last year of her life and speculating about what the next year would hold for her.

On Monday she kept an appointment with her divorce attorney, returned her library books and made sure all the bills were paid. Several people, including Julia, called to wish her well on the following day, but she let them all go to message. She took the call about her MUGA scan, getting the news that, as hoped, it showed a good, strong EF of 72%, giving her the final green light for her first chemo treatment on the next day. A relief on one hand, that this part of her ordeal was finally in motion, she wasn't looking forward to being admitted to the hospital for that initial infusion. That way, the central port could be implanted in her upper chest, plus her blood and vitals could be carefully monitored to make sure there were no unforeseen reactions to the chemo drugs.

Such as *Tumor Lysis Syndrome,* she thought weeks later.

The first day wasn't too bad. But then it was like her body had suddenly realized it was under attack and began to fight back. Nausea and vomiting made it hard to keep anything down. The meds prescribed for that helped some but not enough. Dan was so good: comforting her, bringing her whatever she needed—often before she could ask. He fielded her phone calls and, at her request, asked everyone but Alex and Julia to hold off visiting for the time being. It was *not* a pleasant week-and-a-half, and then she started to feel a little better. A couple of days when she managed not to lose her scrambled eggs and fruit smoothies and she'd felt almost human.

Too soon, and here she was back for her second treatment. But something inside her reminded, *Attitude, Nikki!* Everything she'd read and witnessed, experienced and believed told her that attitude could be as important as medicines . . . prayer . . . the support of loved ones. She worked to summon up memories of how people used their thoughts to heal their bodies. Heck, she herself had led kids to envision such therapy, which served to focus and calm them at the very least.

Different images worked for different people. What would work for her in battling this cancer? She decided to imagine her body taking in the chemo as a series of futuristic weapons vanquishing the enemy invaders. There may be collateral damage to some healthy cells, but they were sacrificing themselves to a good cause. A bit of peace *did* follow those thoughts, and she opened her eyes, saw the clock on the wall with its disappointing news. Another hour and a half to go.

Eyes closed again, she settled herself, breathing deeply and slowly, trying to relax herself to another place and time. Soon she could almost feel the leaf-patterned sunlight on her face and smell the scent of woodland flowers, feel gentle nipping on her limbs. Opening her eyes there in the dream, Nikki saw four white fawns, dappled with gold, nuzzling her arms and legs. She smiled at them, at the deep compassion in their eyes. She trusted them completely. *They're here to make me better,* Nikki realized and suddenly noticed that each fawn had spots that formed a letter: *A, B, V, D.*

And then she knew their names: *Adriamycin, Bleomycin, Vinblastine, Dacarbazine.* Four powerful drugs nibbling away at the cancer in her body. Closing her dream-eyes, she gave herself to them.

CHAPTER TWENTY-EIGHT

Eyes riveted on the monitor screen before him, Vinny Orlander absorbed the information offered by, lighted symbols, illuminated dials and, most significant of all, the numbers. Blessed numbers . . . so pure and factual and unrelenting.

Filled with a great sense of peace and purpose, Vinny copied the appropriate numbers onto his clipboard. Beautiful numbers. So perfectly formed and exquisitely legible. The only time he ever got even second-hand praise from his mother was when she chastised his almost-perfect sister over the fact that Vincent's letters were proper and right. "She never could match my precise figures," Vinny whispered with a tiny smile of satisfaction. He quickly looked around to see if anyone had heard, but he was still alone, except for the sleeping patient attached to the ventilator, Charlie Monroe. The numbers told Vinny that the Coach should be able to come off the machine soon; not that anyone ever asked his opinion. As he continued his careful notations, he couldn't help reflecting for the thousandth time on the injustice of it all:

he could furnish information meticulous in both form and accuracy, but was he allowed to inscribe those numbers directly on a patient's chart? Oh, no, he had to write them on some silly sheet of paper and let a *doctor* enter those same numbers into the real chart. So of course, that meant he had to check after every doctor, make sure they'd gotten the numbers right and that they were legible. No one wanted a patient to be adversely affected. After all, who was sure to get blamed first? The ignorant tech, of course!

Glancing up from his clipboard, Vinny saw Dan Marchetti enter the room and nod in greeting. Only once had Vinny caught an error, and Dan had immediately thanked him and not with the grudging attitude that often "rewarded" his diligence and discretion..

At Charlie Monroe's bedside, Dan looked down at the patient, then glanced to the ventilator's monitor, but Vinny spoke up, keeping his voice low to avoid waking the patient: "His numbers are looking good, Dr. Dan. He can probably come off the machine today, don't you think?"

Marchetti took the clipboard Vinny handed him and the patient chart with the last set of numbers, comparing them. "You may be right. These stats do seem promising. But, of course, it's not my call. He's George Anastos's patient, not mine anymore."

"I know. You're doing Urology right now. But I noticed you still come see him every day you're working . . . keep up with the case."

Very quietly, and turning so his lips couldn't be seen from the bed, Vinny asked, "You surprised he made it through this last time?"

Just as covertly, Dan admitted, "I've been surprised *every* time. But he's a tough old bird. . . . Hey, what's the sour look for?"

Vinny raised his eyebrows in surprise and to change his expression. Vinny laughed off-handedly and shrugged. "This time of year, 'tough old bird' reminds me of my *Bestemor*—my grandmother." Dan laughed. "Yeah, the old 'pretending-for-the-relatives' thing! You going home for the holidays, Vinny?"

Chuckling, Dan nodded. "*Bestemor?* Is that . . . Norwegian?"

"*Ja! Snakker du norsk?*"

"No. I spent some years traveling in Europe and picked up a few words here and there. You called your mother Mamma. Isn't that Swedish?"

Vinny's laugh came out like a little bark of surprise. "Yeah. My mother insisted we call her that instead of the Norwegian—"

"Mor?"

"That's right! Not the usual words to pick up. . . ."

Dan shrugged. "I like languages. Is your Mom Swedish?"

"Part. Using Mamma instead of *mor* was really because the word *mord* means homicide or maybe murderess, and she just didn't like to be called anything that sounded so similar." Vinny, who'd avoided learning any more of his ancestral tongue than absolutely forced to, reflected that if there was a word for "murderess of the spirit," that would really fit her!

"Well, have a good one!" Dan said, looking ready to take his leave.

Vinny, still searching for topics to prolong this encounter, decided against asking about Nikki Saxon. Thanks to the DCH grapevine, most of the hospital staff knew she was in the process of a messy divorce and had moved in with Dan right after Thanksgiving. Not everyone knew yet she'd been diagnosed with Hodgkin's and would be going on leave to begin chemo right after the holidays. Vinny made sure he knew as much about everyone as he could, and that was easily accomplished, since people often conversed as if he weren't in the room. Maddening as anonymity could be, it had its perks..

During the lull in their conversation, Dan had turned to scan Charlie Monroe's monitor one more time. He patted the old man's hand and whispered, "Keep on swingin', guy." Then, to Vinny, "Gotta get back to uro clinic.

"See ya next week." Vinny watched Dan go. He returned his attention to the clipboard and Charlie Monroe's numbers, but he was barely back in the flow of his work when a harsh voice interrupted.

"God! Are you *still* doing Monroe? I need you in ICU." Vinny didn't look up at his supervisor Jason Spiro who was sure to give him orders whether he answered or not. "Muñoz needs suctioning again and an albuterol treatment—stat."

Vinny clenched his teeth. Twelve damn years at this job, and he still got pulled away from the important stuff to suck phlegm

"Vinny!" Spiro actually pulled the clipboard from Vinny's hands and tossed it on the bedside chair. "Muñoz. ICU. *Stat!*"

Not trusting himself to respond in any way, Vinny swept out of the room after grabbing the clipboard and stalked toward ICU. *Respect!* That was the thing most lacking in his life.

Vinny was really fuming by the time he got to the Muñoz bedside.

Vinny took a moment to calm himself, force his hands to stop trembling with rage. What he needed tonight was a girl. He thought immediately of Trudy, a member of the DCH housekeeping staff. She'd come in handy more than once. She was sweet but homely and shy, and it was clear she comforted her loneliness with food. Still, she kept a tidy house and was always clean, always willing. And she liked rough sex. Or, at least, she tolerated it without complaint, so what was the difference?

Vinny felt himself becoming aroused. Yes, just the thing he needed tonight!

CHAPTER TWENTY-NINE

When Dan arrived at DCH early the next morning, Greg Vanderbosk seemed to be watching for him. The security guard's blue eyes were uncharacteristically serious.

"Yeah," Dan answered, stifling a yawn, "it was a long night." Even with the staff alerted and a relatively short wait, it seemed to take forever for the examinations, x-rays labs and other tests. Diane and the attending, Mike Upton, surprisingly unobnoxious for a change, were very thorough. Diane, who'd been a nurse, and the nurses on duty—Hank Currie and Gail Sanduski—treated Nikki like gold.

Not all Nikki's test results had been available right away, but the CAP was confirmed, and her blood count showed not only the low white cell count of neutropenia, but also the low red cell counts and platelets.

Dan stayed until they had Nikki settled in a single-bed room in the Oncology unit on the fourth floor. They had her I.V. delivering piperacillin and ready for a first daily dose of gentamicin.

As she got relaxed and drowsy, she insisted, "You go on home and get some sleep. You have to be back to work at eight a.m." She wouldn't hear of it when he suggested he just catch some *z*'s in the on-call room. Finally, he gave in and went home to the apartment, which seemed eerily empty without her. But feeling the great relief of having, for the moment, no responsibility to or for anyone but himself, he fell immediately and deeply asleep.

Now, rested and eager to check on Nikki, Dan still took another few moments with Greg. "What's new with that future president Ivy Vanderbosk?"

Greg beamed. "Nine months old! And she is already says dada!"

"Wow! That's one smart kid."

Greg laughed and waved him farewell as Dan hustled on to shed his outerwear and visit Nikki before his shift. He found her awake and resting comfortably. She still wore the DCH gown she was admitted in and the jaunty, multi-colored cap on her bare head.

"Hi, honey." He kissed her forehead, *much cooler,* and then her lips.

"Better," she assured him. "Think I can get out of here fairly soon?"

He checked her chart and saw, with approval, they'd started her on Neulasta to augment her white cells and Procrit for the red. "Not *too* soon," he said. "Your numbers were dreadful, and it'll take awhile to get everything back in balance, and to make sure the infection's licked."

She made a little face at him, a strange sight without brows, lashes or lipstick. She looked like a little kid. But her concern was very adult in nature: "Well, if I'm in here past Tuesday, you'll have to bring me some things—the bills as they come in and my checkbook."

"It's only the twenty-fifth," he pointed out.

"February. Short month."

"Right. I forgot"

Nikki continued, "I got a message...Dr. Klonter will be in to see me this morning."

"That's good. He'll be able to tell you a lot more about where everything goes from here."

As Nikki nodded, saying, "I don't s'pose I'll like it much. Especially when he tells me I won't be starting my next chemo on time." Looking resigned, she nodded past him to the wall clock. "Almost time for your shift."

"Yeah, I better go. You need anything?" She shook her head.

Two minutes later, Dan walked out of the elevator on the seventh floor and headed for the physicians desk. Theo looked up. "What's new here?"

Theo grimaced. "You're not gonna like it." He handed the chart he'd been holding to Dan. "Leo Ackerlynn threw a clot, and it went to his brainstem."

Clots weren't unexpected when a patient had to lie in bed so long, but normally, blood flow would carry one into the right side of the heart and then upward through the pulmonary valve and artery into the lungs where it could be dealt with as a pulmonary embolism. But not with Leo's uncorrected TOF. The narrowed valve and restricted right ventricle had slowed the pulse of blood and pushed the clot through the septal defect between the two ventricles. Once in the left side, the clot was pumped out through the aorta with the oxygenated blood. Out into the body and, in Leo's case, up to the base of the brain, causing a massive stroke.

"God," Dan said quietly. "No improvement over these findings, huh?"

"'Fraid not. Looking more and more like Locked-in Syndrome."

Awake, aware, but completely unable to move or communicate And *unlikely to change.* The term "brain dead" came to mind, but it wasn't right. When people were truly brain dead, in a persistent vegetative state, the lower part of the brain still operated, keeping them alive, allowing them to move, except the upper brain was so damaged that it could no longer function or have any hope of recovery. That mind was simply gone.

But in the case of Locked-In, all indications were that the upper brain remained quite functional, but the damaged brainstem prevented practically all voluntary muscle movements.

"What about his eyes?" Dan asked, knowing that Locked-Ins can usually blink at least one eye voluntarily.

Theo sighed. "He blinks, but we can't tell yet if it's purposeful."

Theo nodded again. "And, of course, his wife is convinced he's communicating clearly, that he'll be coming back from the stroke, and that we're just giving up on him."

"I guess that wasn't too hard to predict." Dan looked back to the chart, wondering about Leo's treatment to prevent more clots, since there was no thought of trying to close the septal defect. But the CT scan had detected a small bleed at the stroke site, so anticoagulants were out.

"Yeah, he's on the surgery schedule for an IVC filter later today and, if he hasn't started to recover, still can't swallow, they'll do a PEG at the same time."

Dan nodded. With one of those nifty umbrella-like filters inserted and deployed within his inferior vena cava, Leo could be protected from further clots traveling upward toward his heart from the lower half of his body.

Meanwhile, unable to swallow, the patient needed to have nutrition delivered into his stomach if he had a hope of surviving.

"You've told the patient and his wife what's planned?"

Theo glanced away. "Uh . . . no. Sorry. Driscoll and I consulted and decided to give it some time to see if both the procedures would be necessary."

"You mean you guys left it to Covington and me to not only inform the patient, but also his ooh-so-affable wife?"

"Uh . . . 'fraid so. Sorry."

Dan punched his friend's arm gently. "Thanks."

"Besides," Covington's voice said from behind them, "Dan's really good at that kind of thing." He chuckled. "In fact, I feel confident you can handle this one on your own."

Covington wasn't the kind to pass the buck. Dan knew he must think he could navigate a tricky learning situation. Dan nodded, and Covington turned back to Theo. "Fill us in on the other cases on the floor."

Theo expertly provided what details the dayshift needed and took his leave.

After a few more moments exchanging ideas with Covington, Dan went first to check on Leo, and was relieved to find the patient, at least for the moment, alone.

"Hi, Leo. It's Dr. Dan Marchetti. He took the man's limp hand and squeezed it gently not knowing whether those half-opened eyes were seeing him. "We're still hoping the stroke can resolve to some degree, so you try your best to communicate, okay?" Dan paused. "Did they set up a blink code with you, Leo? Once for yes; twice for no?" No eyelid movement at all. Was he trying to convey something but can't quite manage . . . or is there just no one at home?

Dan patted the hand. "You keep trying. Once for yes; twice for no. I'm going to give you a little look over, okay?"

Still no blink. But, as he did his physical exam, Dan saw blinking resume, though very randomly and not in response to a question, even "Are you in any pain?"

Finished with the exam, Dan ended his notes with "no definitive response via blinking" and moved to stand where he could look into those staring brown eyes and would be within the range of their vision.

"Leo, placing an IVC filter—by way of the femoral vein in your thigh—would help catch other clots from below the heart, where they were more likely to form.

For the feeding tube, first a scope will go through your mouth to confirm the anatomy of your stomach and choose the site for the placement of the feeding tube. Then a small incision would be made on your belly and the feeding tube placed where it could deliver nutrition."

Dan saw no change of expression in Leo's eyes as he talked, though the eyelids closed and opened more than once to refresh the still surfaces of the eyeballs "Do you understand what I've been telling you, Leo?" He blinked. "Hey! Were you answering me?" Leo's eyes closed once, then again. What did that mean? Dan wondered in frustration. He wasn't intentionally answering? Or that he *had* managed to do that but had now lost the control? "Can you answer me again?" No response from Leo.

"You're just confusing him!" Gwen's sharp tone startled Dan as she pushed past him and went to stand on the other side of the bed, taking up Leo's other hand. "It's okay, sweetheart; you just take your time, and don't worry about making mistakes. Do you want to try again now?" Leo's eyes closed and remained so. "That's it; just rest." Gwen looked up accusingly at Dan. "What were you telling him?"

"I was outlining the two procedures that're planned for later today: one to prevent more clots from reaching the heart and one to make it possible to feed Leo if he remains unable to swallow."

"Now tell *me.*" When he'd described the Inferior Vena Cava Filter and its placement, Gwen questioned why they had to cut into his leg vein and then push something all the way up to a place just below his heart, but perhaps she realized this might bother Leo, so she interrupted herself. "He'll be sedated, right?" Even as Dan nodded, she went on to the second procedure. "I assume you'll want to install a feeding tube if he can't swallow?" Again, he barely had time to nod before she pushed on: "If it's a PEG tube, you don't have to explain. We've been feeding Esther that way all her life."

Of course. Pharyngeal atresia. Esther's constricted throat could probably swallow small amounts of liquid, but real nutrition in volume would need to be delivered a different way. "Yes," Dan said. "A PEG."

Gwen leveled a challenging look at Dan, motioning him to follow her out the door. "I've been on the Internet this morning researching Locked-In Syndrome. Those doctors Driscoll and Epplewhite said a lot about how short the survival rate is and other negative stuff. But I found other information. Are you acquainted with a book called *The Diving Bell and the Butterfly?*"

Before he could bring it to mind, she forged on. "It was published in France in 1997, written by Jean-Dominique Bauby, the editor of a famous French magazine. He ended up with Locked-In Syndrome, and he wrote the whole book, dictated it, by blinking his left eye for each letter of each word."

Now Dan remembered. He had read it in college. It took Bauby two years to write it and then he died of pneumonia two days after it was published. "Yes, communication *can* be possible with purposeful blinking and a clear code—"

"And scientists are working on new technologies that interface the brain directly with a computer. Even if it's not immediate, Leo *will* get better and be able to communicate. You'll see." With that, she put her focus on her husband.

With the sounds of the ventilator working behind him, Dan walked back down the hall, thinking about Esther. How much would she, *could* she, comprehend? The girl would certainly understand the feeding tube that would soon protrude from her dad's tummy; she wouldn't be able to remember a time when she hadn't had her own. But what'll it be like for her when her father can't hug her . . . touch her hand . . . speak to her . . . move?

Dan sat down at the physician's desk, reaching for another chart. Dan gazed, unseeing, at the new chart, unable to set aside the Ackerlynn family.

Dan had read a review of Bauby's book that'd described it as a vivid combination of a lifetime's re-lived memories blended with observations and descriptions of life all within that very narrow isolation of his present existence plus exuberant flights of imagination and whimsy.

What of Leo Ackerlynn? Dan wondered. How will he cope with perhaps years trapped within his own diving bell of isolation? And does he have it in him to find the beauty and liberation of thought—the butterfly of imagination—to help him survive it all without madness? And if not being able to communicate drove someone mad, how would we ever know?

CHAPTER THIRTY

For a short time, at least, Nikki had thought of it as "the Good Christmas," that year she was ten. Tony had found them in their newest place back in early November, after their longest-ever time in hiding, and actually seemed like a different person. At first, she'd been even more skeptical than her mom of his "I'm-so-sorry"s and his "I'm-a-changed-man". But all through November, he visited in a respectful way . . . always sober, never angry or sarcastic. Any worries about his ruining Thanksgiving were avoided because he apologized that he had to be elsewhere; Nikki and her mom were thankful for that, just in case. It could've been a good holiday for the two of them, if Mom hadn't been so very sick. Nikki never was quite sure what was wrong with her, but it was clear she was in a lot of pain. When Tony returned after Thanksgiving, he surprised them both by paying for Frances to see a doctor—and for her expensive prescriptions.

Then into and through December, the peace continued, and Nikki felt herself begin to relax just a little. Her mother did *get better, though the medicines seemed to make her tired, and she had to nap a lot. Pretty soon, she couldn't go to work anymore, but Tony said, "That's okay. I paid your rent and utilities for a coupla months." He handed Nikki an envelope of twenty-dollar bills. "I know you're responsible enough to do the food shopping, right?" She was, and no matter how she tried to fight it, she couldn't help a thrill of pride that someone, even Tony, had noticed. She was already doing most of the cooking and cleaning. Easy enough to add the shopping. There was a surprisingly well-stocked corner market only a block away from the third-floor apartment they'd lucked into last spring; small but allowing her to have her own little bedroom. There was even a window that opened onto a fire-escape platform, where she fantasized she might be able to escape to read outdoors in good weather. Sometimes she could, but far too often, the ground-floor tenant's big black dog was out in the narrow strip of concrete "yard" between the buildings. Though she'd tried to make friends with Wolf—she'd heard the owner yell this name often amidst terrible cursing—the dog would not warm up to her. If she tried to sit outside when he was out, Wolf would never stop barking at her until she went back inside.*

As Christmas drew near, Nikki kept watching for signs it would be another bad one, but Tony kept good to his word. He actually bought a fresh tree, a pretty one that smelled like Heaven, and everything needed to trim it. He put two gifts beneath it, one for each of them, saying, "No, don't worry about getting something for me. I have everything I need, and I know your budget. I just want to give you two a good Christmas for a change."

On the day before, he brought all the groceries for an easy Christmas dinner, a small turkey, canned cranberry sauce and gravy, boxed stuffing, frozen peas, heat-and-serve rolls, and the ingredients for that famous holiday casserole: cans of green beans, mushroom soup and french-fried onions. Nikki, who'd already begun creating more imaginative fare in the meals she cooked, knew she'd have no trouble putting it all together with little help from her mom.

On that Christmas Eve, having said, "I can't stay over tonight," he encouraged them to open their gifts before he had to leave. "In my family, we always open the presents on Christmas Eve." He winked at Nikki. "That way they don't get mixed up with what Santa brings They're not a big deal," he told them as Mom stripped away the paper and held up a pretty pink nightgown—the kind that was soft and warm instead of sexy.

"Thank you, Tony," Frances said, smiling at him. "It's lovely."

Under Tony's expectant gaze, Nikki opened her box, breath held and teeth clenched, wondering what it would be and whether she'd be able to pretend she liked it. "Oh!" she sighed. From the nest of green tissue, she lifted the white ceramic cat. A good seven inches tall, it had green jewel eyes and wore a red velvet collar and Santa's cap with white-fur trim. "Thank you," she said quite sincerely, but still without having to call him Dad; he didn't like for her to call him Tony, said it wasn't respectful. "He's just beautiful. I'll name him Yulie . . . you know, for Yule." It was a word she'd only learned that year, and her parents laughed but with affection.

Nikki loved that cat. It sat beside her plate while she ate dinner. She took it to bed with her that Christmas Eve night, told it some secrets and fell asleep no longer caring that Santa wouldn't be visiting her home. The next morning, Yulie accompanied her to the bathroom for her shower and sat on the kitchen counter watching as she started the feast.

Tony arrived a few hours later with a cakebox from the bakery and two bottles of sparkling cider. Again, the winking. "Nikki, this will be our champagne. You're too young for the real thing; your mom doesn't drink, and now I don't either." Nikki wasn't sure this was entirely true—sometimes she thought she still smelled alcohol from his skin, if not his breath—but she smiled and nodded.

When everyone had eaten more than enough of everything, Tony let Nikki do all the clearing, the packaging up of leftovers, the washing of every single pot and glass and plate and utensil. Again, Nikki preferred that to having to sit and talk with him while Mom cleaned up. Of course, Tony didn't offer to help, but why should he? Hadn't he provided every element of the feast and celebration?

When finished, Nikki grabbed up Yulie and started for her room, hoping to leave her parents to their nuzzling on the sofa. But Tony called to her as she passed. "Wait, honey. Come here and sit down for a minute." Reluctantly, she went to sit where he indicated, on the other side of him. She made sure there was some distance between them so her leg wouldn't have to touch his.

He didn't seem to notice. "Thank you, Nikki, for doing all that work. It was a perfect meal, and I can see you're very good at keeping a kitchen. You're really growing up, and I'm proud of you." He sounded so sincere. "Y'know, I'm not the only one who noticed. Santa left a present for you at my house last night. Said your door was locked; no chimney, of course." Laughing at his own joke, he rose. "I'll just go get it from the car."

Nikki waited nervously, eyeing her mother inquiringly, but Mom just shook her head and shrugged.

Tony returned with a huge giftbag, adorned by a smiling, waving Santa and cascades of curling ribbon, and set it with a flourish at her feet. Kneeling down beside it, Tony gazed at her so intently she couldn't look away. "I haven't been much of a father to you, Nikki. . . . I'm truly sorry about that, and I want to show you just how much." He gestured to the bag.

Suddenly, fear lay cold in her belly. But there was nothing she could do except look into the giftbag. Surrounded by red tissue paper, a very large basket was crowned by a big red bow.

"Go ahead, sweetheart," Mom urged and Nikki reached in and opened the lid of the basket.

A snow-white kitten peered up at her, blinked green eyes bright as jewels, and leaped up onto her lap with a pleasant jingling of the tiny green bells on its red velvet collar. "Mrrr-ow!" it said.

"Oh!" was all Nikki could manage before she enfolded it in her arms and buried her face against the fur. The kitten began to purr, and Nikki could feel the rumble throughout her body.

In the next moment it became obvious Mom was as surprised as she was. "But, Tony! We can't have a pet. We can't afford to feed and take care of another body."

"Now, Fran," Tony was saying. "Don't worry about that. He's had all his shots; he's already neutered. Down in the car I have the biggest sack of cat food I could find, bags of litter and a pan. Nikki's showing herself to be so responsible. I'm sure she'll do all the work herself. Right, Nikki?"

"Oh, yes!" she kept her face buried, unable to look at either of them, but made sure her voice was heard.

Still, her mom resisted. "I don't want some smelly litter pan around in view, and the bathroom's too small."

Mom had never wanted her to have a pet.

"Give the girl a chance, Fran. Nikki, you'll keep the litter box in your room, won't you? And change it whenever it needs—even if that's every day?"

Again: "Oh, yes!" into the white, purring fur.

"Well, Fran?" Tony asked.

Long, excruciating moment. . . . "Oh, all right. She can give it a try."

"Thank you!" Nikki cried, so relieved and excited, she actually reached over and hugged her father around his neck . . . until she realized what she was doing and released him. She grabbed the kitten on her lap and bounced up off the sofa, away from both her father and her mother, on the way to her own room.

"What'll you name him?" Tony asked, beaming happily at her.

"Yulie!" She paused, considering the conflict, seeing the ceramic cat she'd abandoned on the sofa. She didn't want to go back for him.. "Christmas Eve Yulie can be Yulie the First. This one will be 'Real Yulie.'" At a safe distance now, she said, "Thank you . . . Father . . . for a very nice Christmas . . . especially for my Yulies."

His grin got even wider. "You just take good care of them, hear?"

Except for meals or other times it would be impossible, Nikki tried to spend most of her time in her own room when her father was at the apartment. There she could curl up on her bed and read with Yulie lounging across her lap while the ceramic Yulie seemed to watch over them from his home atop her bookcase. She wasn't eager to spend more time than that with Tony, but the atmosphere seemed easier and hopeful. She was beginning to get used to it.

Then it was time to go back to school. The first few days, she left Yulie alone in her room with the litter pan and an untippable bowl each of kibble and water. Mom complained the cat cried for her, so after that, they let him have run of the apartment. While Nikki was away, Mom reported, he spent a lot of time searching for her but usually ended up sleeping on top of the refrigerator, where he could survey his kingdom like a white leopard in a towering tree.

Nikki came home the Monday of the second week and found her mother sitting with her sewing things spread out on the table, mending one of Tony's shirts; she'd been doing a lot of these tasks recently. Mom put a shushing finger to her lips and nodded toward her nearly closed bedroom door. Tony had stayed the night, and neither of them had been up when she left for school. It was then she noticed the window to the fire escape was lifted several inches. "Who opened that?"

"I did. Tony said it was stuffy in here."

Realizing she hadn't yet been greeted, and the perch atop the fridge was empty, dread struck Nikki. "Where's Yulie?"

"In your room."

That door was closed, so it could be true. "How come you put him in there?"

"I didn't. You *did. Don't look at me that way. Tony said you'd put him in there before you left for school. Cat must be getting used to it. He's been quiet all day."*

Nikki rushed into her room, calling the kitten's name, but he was not there. The food and water she'd left looked untouched. Sick fear twisting in her guts, she hurried back to the window, pushed it fully open and crawled out, calling for Yulie. Down below, Wolf started barking ferociously. She didn't want to look down, but she knew she had to.

There on the concrete were bloody lumps and rags of flesh, some with white tufts of hair that could not be snow. From Wolf's fangs dangled the red velvet collar, and when he shook his head as if savaging a toy, the little green bells jingled.

Nikki hardly recognized the sound that ripped from her. That couldn't be <u>*her*</u> *voice. She'd never heard anything that piercing, that anguished. Wolf even stopped barking, though some other neighborhood dogs were startled into taking it up. Nikki was vaguely aware of several people coming to their windows to peer out; a couple yelled at her.*

She was still screaming when her mother grabbed her from behind and dragged her back into the apartment and slammed the window. Tony came busting through the bedroom doorway, dressed only in his boxers and a T-shirt, his hair awry on his head. "Good God, girl! Shut up!"

"Yulie's dead—" Nikki shrieked, "and you killed him!" Her clueless mom was trying to calm her down, asking what had happened, and since Tony stood there as if truly bewildered, giving him the benefit of a doubt.

"He knows what happened—what he did!" Nikki growled, her eyes never leaving Tony as she spoke to her mother. "He closed the door to my room while Yulie was out here. Then he got you *to open the window." Beyond the fury she felt toward him was the fury she felt toward herself. That she could be fooled. That she could be taken in by his elaborate plan to conquer her, waiting until she'd thanked him . . . hugged him . . . called him Father! "Yulie went out, and Wolf tore him to pieces."*

"I told you the cat was your responsibility," Tony said in a "reasonable parent" voice, not even attempting to deny her intuitions. "I thought you were mature enough to take care of it. If something happened to it, that's your fault."

A sound came from Nikki's throat. Tony might have mistaken it for grief instead of rage, for he pressed on: "In fact, if the cat got out, it was probably trying to find you *after you spoiled it with so much attention."*

Perhaps he thought she'd just dissolve into a pool of sobbing despair and heartbroken remorse. "Bastard!" she spat. "You cruel bastard! I hate you!"

Frances gasped and began to cry. Whatever plans Tony might've had to preserve his pretended innocence, his whole man-of-change disguise, crumbled now. "Never speak to me like that again!"

Feeling her power, Nikki tossed her head in a way she knew made her hair flounce defiantly over her shoulder. "You're not the boss of me! You never will be!"

Murder flashed in his eyes, and he bellowed some retort, grabbed her by a clump of that insolent hair and dragged her toward the table. Fear jolted through her but she didn't panic, even in her moment of complete helplessness. Her mother was yelling now and trying to stop him, but he shoved her aside. Mom fell to her knees as he grabbed up the sewing scissors and sawed through the hair he held, cutting it as short as he could. Nikki struck upward at him and broke free, but it was too late. Her precious red hair spilled from his opened hand. He clutched at her, trying to cut more, but she fled to her room and slammed the door. Perhaps he remembered she had a good, stout deadbolt in there; he didn't try to follow her. Instead, she could hear him taking it out on Mom.

That was how the one-and-only "Good Christmas" ended, and it was only the beginning of a long and terrible time.

CHAPTER THIRTY-ONE

Baby rats are just so cute, Linda thought, grinning in delight! Their bright black eyes and tiny pink noses with those twitchery whiskers . . . the delicate pink paws that were more like little hands, meticulously grooming their gleaming fur: some dark grey, some black-and-white, some light brown.

She made squeaky kissing sounds near the screened top of their glass habitat; immediately, the little ones responded with great interest and curiosity, bounding nearer across their fragrant, shaved-wood bedding. Standing on their hind legs, they stretched up toward her inquisitively.

Smiling, Linda pressed her fingers to the screen so her scent could drift down to those wriggling noses. She loved rats! Even those tails, which she knew from handling pets of a childhood buddy, were neither hairless nor slimy but ingenious tools for a rat's balance. A perfect pet, except they only have a lifespan of one thousand days, and you get too attached to go through losing such a friend every two, three years.

She halted in front of the large cages of birds, at first hardly noticed by the doves cooing, canaries trilling, finches *peep*ing and a flock of colorful parakeets all conversing at once. Linda offered the same squeaky kissing noises that had intrigued the rats; all avian sounds ceased at once. But this feathered audience proved tougher than the furred. The young birds, as yet untamed, eyed her from the safety of their perches with varying levels of suspicion. A few others, perhaps more accustomed to interaction with shop patrons, sidled closer or began to show off by wrestling with their toys. Careful to obey the posted sign: *"Please! Do not whistle to the birds! Thank You!"* Linda continued trying to engage their trust and interest with sounds and reassuring words, finally rewarded as she saw several more relaxing in her presence. Three even started up a twittering dialogue as if she'd moved on.

She checked the watch on her arm holding her shopping basket and then glanced to the front counter of the store again where Darlene was engaged.

That customer had been chatting with Darlene when Linda first arrived; not wanting to interrupt what seemed a companionable exchange, Linda had smiled and nodded to Darlene and gone to the Wild Bird section to choose the suet cakes she preferred. Heading back to the counter, she could hear the fellow was describing some YouTube videos of goldfish being trained to do tricks, so she'd wandered away again, but now, she might be late back to work if she hung out longer.

She approached the counter slowly, and looking at some items along the way as if still shopping, to give them the chance to finish their conversation. Darlene had just said, "You never answered my question about your holidays, Vinny. How *were* they?"

Recognizing the fellow fish-keeper she'd seen there before, Linda remembered he worked at the hospital. She watched him screw up his face in exaggerated anguish.

"Excruciating." He laughed. "Just what I expected. Just like always. The down-side of 'family traditions,' I guess."

Darlene gave him a sympathetic smile. "But you survived."

"Yeah," he said dryly. As he finally noticed Linda's approach, he hefted his bag of purchases. "Bloodied but unbowed."

When the two had said their good-byes and Vinny was on his way to the door, Linda set her suet blocks on the counter and put away her basket while Darlene greeted her, "Hey, Linda. Hope *you* had good holidays . . . ?" She began ringing up the sale.

"Better than that guy's, I guess, but that's not saying much." She changed the subject. "Unfortunately, I have to scoot right now, but I wanted to tell you, my fish *loved* that little Christmas tree. I'd like to get other things for them to experience, but I didn't see much on the shelves."

Darlene beamed. "I ordered some brand-new figurines. Check back in a week or so."

"I will." Linda paid, thanked Darlene and hurried out. Heading for her car, she reassessed her own Christmas weekend at her parent's home, now a few weeks had passed. She was learning how to better prepare herself: preempt the food-related hassles, batten down the hatches for the shots across the bow, and smile till her cheeks hurt. Expect her parents to be distant and disapproving, their colleagues to be unbearable politically and far too aggressively inquisitive about her professional and personal lives. Plan a quick and easy getaway that would allow her enough time back home to "decompress" before returning to work.

Her expectations of parents and their cronies were right on, but the worst was seeing James again even after her mother had told her that of course he would be there. He was an old family friend and she should get used to seeing him. After all, she had left him so why should it be awkward. But Linda hadn't anticipated his looking so good or to be so charming. Or for herself to feel so physically attracted to him. He'd kept it all very platonic at first: affable, talkative, attentive to her as to any old friend. But then, late Christmas Eve, she found herself alone in the kitchen, making sure she had everything ready to create her quinoa casserole the next morning. All the other guests and the staff had gone to bed. Mother had stayed with her, fussing to make sure Linda didn't mess up any of Estelle's hard work on the "real meal." But then, Angela Ferrin abruptly bade her daughter "Good night" and left her, mercifully, alone.

When satisfied with her preparations, Linda turned off the kitchen lights and moved toward the stairway up to her room. The grandfather clock at the base of the stairs had struck one when James emerged suddenly from the shadows. He caught her in his arms and murmured, "Merry Christmas!"

Heart pounding, she squeaked with surprise, but the sound was covered by his heavy mouth on hers in an oh-so-familiar kiss: passionate yet tender. He tasted so good, smelled so good, felt so good against her. It was hard to fight their history. And did she really have to? If she wasn't going back to him was there anything wrong with a no-strings attached romp? A night of passion with no strings? After all, sex had never been the problem between them. But in the end, just as his warm hands were sliding up under her sweater, she broke off the kiss, stepped back and brought her hands up to block his advance. She made her decision unambiguous, speaking clearly and calmly, and refused to listen to his entreaties, even when he said with his little-boy-lost voice, "But, Linda . . . I still *love* you."

"I'm sorry, but nothing's changed." She brushed past him and went quickly, but with dignity, up the stairs. "Good night."

Thankfully, the lock installed during her Privacy Phase of adolescence was still intact on her bedroom door. She shot the bolt but felt a little silly. She hadn't slept well at all, tossing and turning in that chaste bed of her childhood.

That was the worst part of the whole weekend, Linda decided now, turning her Prius into the parking lot behind her office building. Suddenly swamped by a wave of the emotions she'd felt that night, disappointment, frustration, annoyance, anxiety, and that soul-numbing loneliness she'd been ignoring, she commanded her brain to change the subject and think about the part of the weekend that had gone very well. She grinned.

The quinoa-based Christmas-Revenge Casserole that was her mother's gritted teeth concession to Linda's vegetarian sensibilities. First of all, it was perfectly cooked, the best she'd ever made. Second, everyone loved it, even Father, and the guests raved about the subtle nutty crunch of the quinoa in the rich white-cheese sauce, the bright green broccoli florets and pieces of red bell pepper. Several complimented the use of Christmas colors. Linda had kept her part of the bargain, letting everyone believe the quinoa casserole had been Angela's cutting-edge menu choice, and that made it unnecessary for her to say what *she* thought of it, though Linda's peripheral vision had revealed Angela consuming hers as appreciatively as the guests.

Only James was likely to catch the undercurrent of tension, for he certainly knew the Ferrins' abhorrence of the Italian red, green and white. But he'd taken her lead and kept mum, though he did send her a veiled glance with his quirking smile.

In fact, to his credit, he was especially well behaved all Christmas Day. True, he'd been a little quieter than usual, but especially courteous and amiable, as if trying to prove her rebuff hadn't hurt his feelings, perhaps even that he didn't really care. And fortunately, she wasn't spending another night but, instead, starting the drive home in the late afternoon.

And, bless his heart, James was one of the guests who pressed Angela for her wonderful recipe to give to their own cooks. When her mother stammered and looked blank, Linda took pity on her and swooped in. "I have Mom's recipe on my home computer," she announced. "I'll email it to her, and she can send it to all of you, okay?"

Now back in the parking lot, Linda locked her car and buttoned her coat. Hurrying toward her office, she smirked. That old proverb about Revenge being a dish best served cold is true, but sometimes Revenge can be just as sweet served piping hot and vegetarian in Italy's favorite colors!

CHAPTER THIRTY-TWO

Alex Cole thought, as he rapped a familiar tattoo on Dan Marchetti's apartment door, the worst month of his entire life was finally over.

Dan opened the door almost immediately, and Alex greeted him with a grim, "Am I that predictable nowadays?" as he entered the room.

Dan shrugged, closing the door. "We're both off today. You probably saw Nikki's car leaving."

Dan tilted his head in assent. "Hey, how 'bout a Yogurt Sunrise smoothie? I was just gonna make a batch."

Alex flopped dejectedly on the old green sofa. "Oh, I don't know. . . ."

Undissuaded, Dan moved to the kitchen and started pulling ingredients from the refrigerator. "Come on, you look like you need some protein and some antioxidants. This weather gets me down too. You been eating at all? You're looking kinda thin and pasty, man."

"Are you getting any sleep?" There were other sounds now of liquids being poured.

"Bad dreams."

"I hear *that.* A month in the ICU, or ER or CCU, can be rough. I don't know how the nurses survive."

"They don't have the same responsibility as docs if things go wrong."

The blender whirred, making conversation impossible for several long moments. Then Dan countered, "Yeah, but we come in and handle the crises, and then we're gone except to check on people. But the nurses deal with the moment-to-moment care . . . the having to *watch* patients suffer, *listen* to them moaning and crying in fear and pain."

The voice had gotten closer toward the end, and when Alex looked up, Dan was standing in front of him, holding out the pinky-orange drink. "Strawberry-O.J.," Dan said, "with protein powder and extra Vitamin D."

Thanking him, Alex took the tall, frosty glass. "Are you trying to make a point about nurses and stress?"

Dan's eyebrows lifted, as if inviting comment. He sank into the beanbag chair across from Alex, lifted his glass in salute and drank deeply.

Alex frowned. "I *know* Julia's under a huge amount of stress, but that's no excuse for what she's done . . . how she's treating me." Alex drank now, and the fresh, sweet tang of the first nutrition he'd had in probably twenty hours squeezed his taste buds and brought tears to his eyes. Or maybe that was just feeling how lucky he was to have a friend like Dan Marchetti.

They nursed the smoothies in a long, companionable silence, then set the empty glasses aside.

Dan studied him. "So, Alex, what else is going on?"

He couldn't answer at first.. Finally, he managed to say, "It's been one shithill of a month."

Dan gave a lopsided grin and touched the side of his head where the Irishman had clobbered him. "I'm with you there."

"*B*ad enough all that with Myra and Julia, but since then, I'm having trouble concentrating. I've made some stupid mistakes

. . . not big ones . . . and, thank God, someone's always had my back. So in addition to my personal life sucking, I'm not even a good doctor anymore."

Dan nodded. "Hey, we all feel like that and you've had some rough cases. I heard about that ruptured triple A you guys lost. Tough one."

Yeah, having an abdominal aortic aneurysm take out a 29-year-old was hard to deal with. "It wasn't just him. You hear about the NF patient?"

Dan's eyes narrowed with interest. "No! I have yet to see one in the fle—oh, wrong phrase!" He grimaced, then waited to hear more details.

"Barely more than a teen; twenty last month. Jimmy Kittle. He did look a lot like the classic 'Elephant Man.'"

Neurofibromatosis . . . von Recklinghausen's. Disease. This genetic mutation made neural crest cells develop abnormally as they grew into nerves and their coverings, skin, and bones, especially of the head and neck, forming tumors almost anywhere nerves were present, both internally and externally. Where most visible, these presented as large lumps and bulges primarily just under the skin, which had to stretch to cover them. And while it was true that Joseph Merrick, the original Elephant Man, likely had Proteus Syndrome and not neurofibromatosis, both diseases were often horribly disfiguring.

"How typical?" Dan asked.

Alex drew a deep breath through clenched teeth. Dan could afford to sit there and take a clinical interest since he didn't have to watch the kid die, Alex reflected, but maybe talking about it would help to exorcise its memories. "Extensive tumors covering his whole head and neck . . . one eye completely obscured; some of the *café-au-lait* spotting on the skin; the bowed legs, much of the bones of his scalp tumorous"

"Why was he in ICU?"

"He wasn't. I was just taking my break, and a code was called in Radiology, so I went to help. They were trying to do a CT scan to assess damage from a fall he'd taken, but he lost consciousness, and it was obvious he had an intracerebral bleed."

Alex swallowed. "God, Dan, I could *see* his head growing while we stood there."

"Who was on duty?"

"No neurosurgeon in the house. They put in a call to Dr. Choi, but he was hung up. Selma Braunstein was the attending, but she was giving me a chance to step in and learn something." Alex looked past Dan, back into memory. "I stared down into that one fixed and dilated pupil; a nurse called a 60-systolic BP, and I remember saying, 'We've gotta drain that.' When Selma nodded, I asked for normal saline, wide open and a 14-gauge Gelco. Trying to find the best spot, I palpated that mass of tumors on his temple. It felt like an old tire covered with huge, rubbery bubbles. My whole index finger sank all the way into the tissues." He looked down at his hands, clenching each other now, and shivered. "I just froze—just stood there, watching the bleed swell his head like a gigantic water balloon."

Alex found he couldn't go on. After a minute, Dan prompted gently, "His skull was that soft?"

Alex looked directly into Dan's compassionate eyes. "Turned out he didn't have any bone at all on that part of his cranium. That's why a fairly minor fall resulted in such severe bleeding."

Dan nodded. "So what'd you do?"

"Courageous me said, 'Dr. Choi should be here any second.' But Selma said, 'No time.' Took the needle from me and inserted it right into the side of Jimmy's head. Blood just geysered out . . . sprayed all over her: white coat, sleeves, skirt, nylons . . . some splashed on me, but not as much."

"Mother of God. He didn't have a chance, did he?"

Alex shook his head. "It was clear by that time, but there was no DNR; his mom had brought him in and asked for us to do whatever we could for him. Selma looked at me and said, 'Someone has to go talk to his mother.' Clearly, it wouldn't be good for *her* to go, splattered all over with the kid's blood. I said I'd go, and Selma reminded me to clean up. I slipped out of my lab coat, and a nurse dabbed me off."

Dan gave a sympathetic wince. "And how was that—talking to the mom?"

"Not as bad as I thought it'd be. She was ready, I think, for the worst news. She was obviously praying when I found her. I introduced myself and brought her up-to-speed, making sure I was very clear that draining the bleed was only a temporary measure, and there was quite likely permanent brain damage. She just nodded and said, 'He's always been such a good son. We knew his life was precarious,—especially with no protection for his brain on that one side, but we wanted him to have a normal life, so we protected him—and taught him to protect himself—as best we could and gave the rest to God, you know?'

"I had to nod, Dan, even though I couldn't *imagine* what that life would be like."

Alex rubbed his face, and Dan nodded but didn't interrupt him. "Meanwhile, I saw Jin Choi arrive, but I didn't follow him in. Frankly, I couldn't face going back in there, Dan. It was easier to just sit and listen to Mrs. Kittle talk about her son. Turns out his fall was because he was standing on a chair, reaching up into a cabinet to get something for his mom. The amazing thing is, she could talk about that without any guilt. 'He knew he wasn't s'posed to climb like that; he knew the risks. I have to believe it's God's plan. And Father O'Malley says it's the quality of a life that matters, not the quantity. I have to believe that too.' About then, Choi came out, and I introduced him as a staff neurologist, and he told Mrs. Kittle, 'I'm afraid your son is going downhill again.' And she just looked at us with quiet tears starting to roll down her cheeks and said, 'Let's let him go. His dad is out of town on business, but may I be with Jimmy, hold his hand?'"

Alex's voice choked off a moment, and he swallowed hard. "Choi said of course and took her in to her son. Courageous me? I went to the bathroom and bawled my eyes out. Then went straight back to the ICU."

Dan gestured. "It's not like I've never cried after a tough case. Bad diseases kill good people. Kids too. I keep hearing how we have to get used to it if we're gonna be docs."

"That's the thing, Dan. I don't know anymore if I *can* be a doc. And after my parents sweated and slaved, breathing years of perchloroethylene in that damn dry cleaning store, to put me through med school . . . give me this opportunity. . . .

Dan sat up straight on the beanbag, leaned earnestly forward. "Hey, man, I mean it. We all feel that way some days . . . lotsa days!"

"I just feel lost, Dan. Every second, I feel sure I'm gonna wimp out or screw up."

Dan regarded him with concern. "Hell, Alex, your confidence is shot right now. All that's happened with Myra and Julia . . . these really horrible cases. It's April now and new rotations for both of us. Leaving ICU and ER behind! Where'll you be?"

"Geriatrics. Ha. More chances to lose patients."

"We're gonna lose some no matter where we are. Give yourself a break, buddy."

"I just don't think I'm cut out for this, Dan. I don't think I have the guts."

"Look, Alex. I'm not the best resource here. I'm in the trenches with you. You need someone to talk to with even more perspective than me. Someone who's been through it all and survived and is living the life. Why not go talk to Bob Weyland?"

Alex shot up from the sofa as if yanked. "I don't need any damn shrink! I thought I could just talk to a friend and keep that in confidence." He was moving toward the door, but he'd have to get past Dan first, who'd also come to his feet.

"Hey. No worries. You can always talk to me, but I don't feel like I can give you enough. Weyland's a good guy. I've even talked to him a coupla times."

"Yeah, well, I better go. Thanks for the smoothie."

Dan's brown eyes looked both worried and helpless. He took a step closer so he could reach out and grip the top of Alex's shoulder as he tried to squeeze past. Alex knew he tensed up and could see Dan's concern deepen as he said, "Well, okay. But I *am* here whenever you need to talk. I don't mean to crowd you, but—"

"Yeah, thanks!" Alex slipped away, grabbed the doorknob and made his escape. But as he hurried down the hall, Dan must've been watching him go, because he called, "Hey, tomorrow's the first day of Major League Ball. We'll have to catch some games together when our schedules mesh."

Without looking back or speaking, Alex waved an acknowledgment before rushing to open his apartment door and finally letting the tears flow.

CHAPTER THIRTY-THREE

Sliding from a dream into wakefulness, and trying to return, Nikki Saxon burrowed her head against her pillow, but the sensation stopped her cold. Though instantly and fully awake, she did not open her eyes but still pretended sleep.

She heard the door click quietly behind Dan as he left for work, but still she didn't stir. Everything seemed harder to face these days, and now this.

"Quit your whining!" she whispered, gathering her mettle to open her eyes, roll up on one elbow and make herself look down at the pillow. Several clumps of long, auburn hair lay on the pale green case, and she could feel the uncustomary touch of air against as many patches of bared scalp.

So there it was. The beginning of this phase. In truth, she'd seen the first signs a couple of days ago, on Sunday. Feeling for the first time in five days that it actually mattered to tidy herself beyond the perfunctory, she'd brushed her hair with her usual long strokes, then noticed her hairbrush completely clogged with a mat of shed hair. Like someone'd been grooming an Irish setter! She'd finished the task as gently as possible and hidden it all from Dan . She knew he would just try to sympathize and comfort her with reminders it was inevitable and it would all grow back. And pity was not going to help either one of them get through these long months.

Nikki forced herself upright now, sat on the side of the bed, gripping the edge of the mattress. After a long moment, she took a deep breath and then combed both hands up through her hair, allowing her fingers to glean what they might. She could feel tiny clusters of hairs giving way . . . letting go . . . giving up; she saw them there, defeated, lying across her palms. As strongly as she had once wished she could retain her treasured mane despite the chemo, she now as vehemently wished for it all to be gone. Every single hair seemed suddenly an individual, a separate loss to be grieved. Too painful, she needed this pain to be in the past, not her future

A little sob escaped her. She gathered the hairs from her pillow and rose, then dragged herself into the bathroom, still clutching all the lost tresses; these she laid on the counter. Pulling out the bottom drawer of the faux-marble vanity, she rummaged at the back for the items she'd stashed there: her good, no-cutting-paper scissors and the electric clippers she'd bought during the pre-Christmas sales.

Nikki studied herself in the large, well-lighted mirror. Holding her head at just this angle, she couldn't see any of the bare patches; her auburn wealth appeared intact. She gave herself another long, savoring look at what would soon be gone. Unbidden, the chilling thought struck through her: You'll never see this view again. Struggling with the sense of foreboding, she reminded herself that it would grow back, all chemo hair did. To break the spell of the mirror, she grabbed up the scissors and began to cut off her hair, letting it fall across the sink and counter. Just the tearing sound of the blades against the strands twisted a knot in her stomach and quickened her breath as she tried to push away the old memories. *Tony's dead! He has no power over me. This time it's my decision!*

She cut quickly, before she could change her mind, and when it was short enough, she dropped the shears, feeling a little faint, and gripped the vanity's edge again. Vanity! That's a good name for it, she told herself as she gritted her teeth and refused to cry.

After a few moments, she plugged in the electric clippers and started at the very center of her forehead, "buzzing" away the rest of her hair in long, determined strokes, clenching her teeth to counteract the reverberation of the little machine against her scalp and skull beneath. When she'd finished she turned off the unit. She ran her hands over the reddish stubble that was left. What an odd sensation—like rubbing a living brush. The whole situation felt peculiar, like a dream she knew was real.

She couldn't take her eyes from the mirror. She'd never before seen or felt this head; as she turned it in different directions, she saw the bare patches were even more noticeable now, spoiling even the possibility of any "modern-young-woman-in-search-of-avant-garde" fantasy. She shivered and rubbed her pajama sleeves. It was amazing how much her dense head of hair had served to warm her. Now she felt deep in the bones cold.

Focusing on the areas that looked splotchy, thinking how this haphazard patchwork would soon be more widespread, she moved decisively to gather her razor and shaving gel from the back corner of the bathtub. She shook the pressurized can, then began spreading the pale green foam all over her head, covering every bit of hair stubble. Now *there* was a bizarre image in the mirror! Hands rinsed, she turned on the little wet-dry razor and began pulling it back across her scalp as she had pushed the clippers. Strange sound, strange sensation amidst the familiar "Spring Rain" scent of her shaving cream.

It took a while to shave her head completely, and, even then, there were probably places that needed more attention but were impossible for her to see. With a damp washcloth, she wiped away all residue of hair and foam, another strange sensation, and patted her head as dry as she could, stared at it gleaming harshly under the lights. She shivered again. Nikki gripped the edge of the vanity once again, her knees suddenly jelly. *I've got to lie down.* But she took a moment first to sweep all the hair into the wastebasket, deciding what was on the floor could wait. She tidied the other things to one side and out of the way in case she didn't get back to it before Dan returned.

She clicked off the lights and rushed back toward the bed. But she stopped first at her bedside table to pull from the drawer a little crocheted cap—inexpertly formed but obviously made with love from heavenly-soft yarn in her favorite colors, a gift from Abby Glickman who had been told by her dad that Nikki was sick but would be better soon.

Nikki pulled the silky cloud over her naked head and dove beneath the covers, still shivering. She lay, warming slowly thinking that she should've taken a shower while she was up and shoulda had some breakfast. And should've called Julia to tell her they were on for the wig shop this Thursday. And should've returned Jenna Hudson's call about the divorce. How could she feel so exhausted? This was supposed to be the good week between the bad week and her next ABVD. She should be taking advantage of it. But exhaustion pressed down on her, and every trace of energy drained out.

Nikki huddled under her covers, burrowed her face into the pillow and slipped away.

CHAPTER THIRTY-FOUR

Heart Month, Dan reflected, noting the lace-trimmed, red-foil hearts taped to the wall around the February calendar. Valentine's Day was a factor, of course, but all month his focus would be The Heart, since his February rotation was, appropriately, in Cardiology.

Of all the human body's intricate systems and organs, the heart had always most fascinated Dan: that amazing four-chambered pump autonomously delivering oxygen to every cell of the body and whisking away a hefty share of its waste products. In fact, it was probably the main catalyst for his becoming a doctor.

Gloria Russo Marchetti's heart, weakened by rheumatic fever in childhood, had nearly taken her life when Dan was only twelve. Remembering how scared he was while trying to be the brave big brother. A terrible day.

It was doctors who saved her with a quick operation to open up her dangerously narrowed heart valve. He knew now they'd performed an *aortic commissurotomy,* that her ongoing condition was called *moderate aortic stenosis,* and that down the line, she'd need surgery to replace the failing valve completely. But back then, what he really remembered most was seeing her lying so pale and eyes-closed in her hospital bed and the fear in *his* heart that she'd never wake up. Then her eyes opened, and she gave him her special smile. The doctor, standing at the bedside in his white coat and stethoscope was beaming, and Dan felt engulfed by a tide of gratitude and admiration for the man. That was the moment Dan stopped dreaming about being a ball-player or a coach like his pop and started thinking about becoming a doctor.

"Dan?"

He turned with a smile, recognizing the voice of Dr. Glenn Covington, the attending on Dan's very first rotation, in the CCU, back in July. He had recently been promoted to Chief of Cardiology. Dan was part of the unanimous sentiment that it couldn't be more deserved and couldn't happen to a nicer guy.

The Chief nodded toward the calendar Dan had been staring at while lost in thought. "Only a few weeks to go, eh?"

It took Dan a moment. "Oh! Start of spring training?" The big grin he got in response reminded him how the cardiologist had managed to live both dreams—becoming a doc and playing ball professionally once upon a time. "You still following your Tigers?"

Covington laughed. "Sure. And the Pirates. Can't live around here and not have hopes for the Pirates."

"And the Steelers", Dan added. In four days *they'd* be playing Super Bowl XL against the Seattle Seahawks. "Well, *hope* is certainly the apt word for both teams, Steelers now and the Pirates soon ."

Blue eyes twinkling, Covington pointed out, "Well, the Pirates signed that new hotshot pitcher Trey Hartmann. Maybe *he*'ll be that magic 20 game winner we keep praying for!"

"Yeah. Charlie Monroe seems really enthused about the guy. Boy, it was great seeing Charlie well enough to go home."

"Well, Charlie won't be *staying* home," Covington was reminding Dan now. "He'll soon be off to spring training with the rest of the Pirates. Florida weather will do him good but I hope he has really figured out a way to give his lungs a rest and to stay off the smokes."

"Wouldn't mind some of that sun myself," Dan said, thinking of the freezing temperature and sleet outside as he'd walked to work.

Theo Epplewhite joined them, handing several charts to Covington, who checked the names before passing them on to Dan. "Please fill Dan in on the cases so far."

Theo nodded a greeting to Dan, but he was all business as he began to rattle off names, diagnosis, results and pending studies. Dan worked efficiently, jotting down the jargon and abbreviations that would let him get oriented until he got a chance to go through the charts and examine the patients themselves.

Covington broke in. "Good summary, Theo. I can bring Dan up to speed on the details. Go ahead and take off."

"Oh, thanks." Already moving away, he tossed another shy smile over his shoulder. "See ya."

Dan thought Epplewhite was less uptight then when he first started, a good change which didn't impact his professionalism around patients. They hadn't shared any rotations for several months and hadn't seen each other socially. Dan noted the departing colleague's footwear. Gone were the white leather mocs, the ones that'd earned him the "Shoes" moniker, replaced by something equally comfortable, no doubt, but dark in color, far less expensive and less likely to show body fluids.

Covington reviewed with Dan the cases that were most worrisome, the elderly CHF, the pericarditis, the difficult tachycardia, the three MIs or *myocardial infarctions,* heart attacks, before Dan went off to meet the patients and introduce himself as one of their new doctors.

Several hours later, Dan was more tired than expected. It was hard not to see himself in some of the patients. Ones who gave typical histories of working too hard to climb the professional ladder with too much stress and now were reaping the fruits of an unhealthy lifestyle at age 50 or 60. Just thinking about it made him feel worn out, and his shift had hours still to go. And he should have felt rested beginning this rotation.

He'd just *had* a full week off, his first actual vacation time since beginning at DCH. He'd been scheduled for one back in early November, but he'd traded with another of his first-year cronies when Lee Jang's great-grandmother died and he needed to travel to Korea for her funeral. Back then, though tired, he still had a lot of early fire-in-the-belly energy. Where had all that gone?

Trudging down the hall to the desk area, Dan grimaced. After Thanksgiving, everything changed. Nikki moving in was a *good* thing, but their life together, everything in their world, was now under the pall of her cancer. That first month of chemo had been rough on them both. Much more on Nikki, of course, but he hadn't predicted how wearing his own helplessness would be.

Reactions and responses to chemotherapy could be quite diverse, but Dan had to admit he'd thought Nikki would do better than she had. For all her preparation, all her medical training and experience, all her prior healthful eating and supplementation, all her positive attitude, she'd been completely flattened by the nausea and vomiting, the muscle pain and weakness. She told him the meds for these symptoms helped some, but, he could tell, not nearly enough. It was hard to even get her to drink the nutrition shakes. Dan often felt like a nag, or a storied Jewish mother, telling her she should eat, she should rest, she should move around a little! Neither he nor Julia Cleary had managed to get her out of the apartment beyond what was absolutely necessary.

Other aspects of their life were also proving unexpected. Certainly he didn't mind that she couldn't cook and clean for him the way she'd hoped to, but he sure wished she'd quit apologizing about it. He had to admit, he wanted the old Nikki back.

Unbidden, the image flashed in his memory: that first view of her naked, lying on his avocado-green sofa: pale-skinned and willowy thin, yet rounded, vibrant, alluring; the glory of auburn hair curling around her heart-shaped face; the smoky-green eyes lit with desire. Different now. So thin and languid, sometimes dull-eyed. And the hair.

Of course he'd known that would go, but he'd also thought it would be more gradual, with time to adjust to it as it thinned. But no. He'd come home from his last dayshift before his vacation started, ready to kick back and concentrate on spending supportive time with Nikki. He found her where he'd left her twelve hours earlier: huddled in bed. But in the meanwhile, she'd cut off all her hair, shaved her head completely.

It'd been difficult not to react, show how he truly felt when she pulled off the little knit cap. He kept telling himself, *It's her hair . . . her chemo . . . her process. She has to find a way to take charge of what she can.* There seemed so little within her power these days.

Two mornings later, she and Julia went off for a day in Pittsburgh, the first time Nikki dressed up at all for weeks. She'd come home from Pittsburgh with a wig stand and various things she'd need to care for her new hairpiece when it was ready. Laughing, she'd taken those items into the bathroom while pointing out, "Plenty of room on the counter after I put away all the stuff I won't need for another six-seven months." In the front room, Dan and Julia stood, eyes locked, hearing the muffled sound of various shampoos, creme rinses, styling gels and sprays and implements being moved around, tucked away in cabinets.

Julia's teeth caught her lower lip, her eyes moistening. "Hey, Nikki," she called, obviously attempting to keep her voice light, "I'm gonna run along now."

Nikki came back out of the bathroom, looking tired but smiling. "Thanks so much for today. Your company meant a lot."

Julia embraced her. "Sure thing, sweetie. Anytime." Then she hurried off before, Dan suspected, her tears could get away from her.

When the door shut behind Julia, Nikki seemed to wilt all-at-once. Dan stepped close and took her in his arms to support her. "Long day?" Nikki nodded wordlessly against his chest. It was, after all, the longest she'd been out of the house since she started chemo twenty-three days ago. "Need to rest?" Again the nod.

He helped her undress and get back into her pajamas before rolling into the bed. When he asked if she wanted him to bring her some food, she shook her head and swore she'd had an actual meal at an IHOP with Julia. Probably true. She had likely put up a brave front all day for the benefit of her best friend.

The following day, January 27, happened to be Dan's twenty-ninth birthday, and he found out the girls' shopping trip had netted more than a meal, new scrubs for Julia and Nikki's wig purchases. He hadn't expected any kind of celebration, but Julia and her mom Myra showed up with a big, candle-encrusted devil's food cake, a couple of Mylar balloons and humorous birthday cards. They also brought a gift Nikki had bought for him in Pittsburgh: a deluxe box of See's chocolates.

Now, almost a week later, as Dan reached the physicians desk in cardiology and sat to make some notes about his new heart patients, he was still thinking about the wig. The girls had gone back to Pittsburgh today to pick it up after a final fitting. They'd arrived back at the apartment shortly before Dan left for this eight p.m. shift. Nikki was wearing the wig, and it looked good on her . . . not exactly her own color but close, not as long or thick, but most people wouldn't even recognize it as a wig. Wouldn't know she was having chemo, except for the no eyelashes, no eyebrows thing.

People usually didn't think about, talk about, that. 'Cause "losing your hair with chemo" meant not only what was on your head, but every bit of body hair as well. Dan had somehow focused on a bald Nikki but not the rest.

Wearing a wig or scarf, the lack of body hair was concealed by clothing, especially during a winter that'd suddenly grown even chillier without her mammalian protection. But Dan saw the difference in her attitude when her brows and lashes were all gone.

Again unbidden, an image of her naked body. But as it was now: frail and white, completely hairless, like a large, bald child with breasts. Dan remembered holding her the first time after seeing her this way. She nestled against him like any child seeking comfort, and he was actually glad he didn't feel aroused. He felt . . . what? Not repulsed. Certainly not stimulated. Unnerved. That's the word.

Forcing his attention to the patients' charts and his work at hand, Dan allowed a last errant thought from one of Nikki's favorite science fiction writer, he felt like a stranger in a strange land.

What seemed days later but was actually mere hours, Dan signed out—making sure Theo Epplewhite had no questions—and headed for the exit. As soon as he stepped outside into a bitter-cold morning, Dan shivered down into his coat and wished he'd taken time to change into warmer pants for the walk home.

It wasn't snowing yet, but a few little ice pellets flicked his face as he began the barely two-block trek. And despite the discomfort, he found himself dawdling. Taking a deep lungful of the cold, damp air, he admitted he wasn't so eager to get back home these days. Weary in this month of nightshifts and topped up, for the moment, with attending to the needs of others, especially the very ill and needy, he longed to retreat to his apartment, crawl into his bed alone and just sleep until it was time to get ready for his next shift.

But, he knew, that wouldn't be possible. He had to find out how Nikki's night was and make sure she had dinner and breakfast. If not he'd somehow get her to eat. And then there was laundry and going through the mail, paying bills. Maybe then he could sleep. At least he didn't have to walk her to chemo today since it was her week off. Not that he minded. He was glad, even, to fire up one of their cars and *drive* her there. But she was the one who pointed out how little exercise she was getting, what a short distance it was to DCH, and that she *could* walk there on her own.

Slow as his steps were, Dan soon found himself entering the Woodside Apartment complex. Climbing the stairs, he remembered her next infusions began Tuesday, the fourteenth. Valentine's Day.

Though Nikki had assured him the holiday didn't really matter that much to her, he found that hard to believe. He'd told her, "We'll just celebrate the night before; that's my night off." At least, this late in her third two-week cycle, just before her next treatment, she'd probably feel better than at any other point. He promised to rent, and watch with her, the chick-flick of her choice and planned a nice dinner, but easy to digest, with lots of chocolate. That was one of the things that still tasted right.

As with her skin's increased sensitivity to the sun, another reason she stayed holed-up in the apartment, it was dacarbazine's other side effect that gave her that metallic taste in her mouth and made almost everything she ate taste "off." When he'd commiserated with her on this, she'd laughed and pointed out, "At least it's *chocolate* and not *liver* or something that still tastes the same."

Dan let himself into the apartment with barely a sound and was glad, for he found her sleeping. He thought of waking her but what if she'd just fallen to sleep after a rough night. He crept back to hang up his coat. Then he collapsed on the couch and closed his eyes knowing he'd get up soon and try to entice her to eat just a little. The weather would keep them inside which was a shame since she hadn't been out of the bedroom in the week since the last infusion session.

Except for the Super Bowl party. Alex had insisted on throwing it assisted by a very willing Julia. Dave and Suzanne attended, though they left, bickering, shortly after the end of the game. Three other interns, Frank Ryan, Patty Yates and Reuben Powell, were able to make it. Most of the other first-years were on duty or trying to catch up on sleep between shifts. Diane Werner had laughed when Alex announced his group invitation. "I'd *love* to come just be a guest," she told him. "Shoot, I'd bring my kick-ass five-layer guacamole dip. But my husband very considerately invited everyone in his office to a party at *our* house."

"Let me guess," Patty had correctly deduced. "*Without* consulting you first and probably telling them all, 'Sure, bring the kids!'"

It was a good group, Dan recalled now. Even Suzanne had behaved herself till near the end. And Nikki had done surprisingly well, considering how little social contact she's had in six weeks. But for Super Bowl Sunday, she'd dressed in some new sweats, what she liked to call "fleece", that didn't look too baggy on her, and she wore the wig. While Dan was assisting Alex in setting up the keg, Julia even slipped over and helped Nikki put on a little makeup to give her face some color and pencil on a hint of eyebrows.

Everyone was nice to Nikki. They all knew her from DCH, of course, even Reuben, who'd started out on his peds rotation and would probably do another soon, since he was completing a med-ped residency that would allow him to sit for his specialty boards in both after only four years. They all knew about Nikki's situation and treated her with caring; but he didn't hear a single note of pity in anyone's voice.

A good group, good food and a good game. After having a touchdown pass overturned, the Seahawks still scored first with a 47-yard field goal, and they kept that lead into the last two minutes of the first half. That's when Steelers quarterback Ben Roethlisberger ran a 1-yard sneak, and the touchdown held up under review.

During the half-time festivities, Nikki slipped out, saying she just wasn't up to the Rolling Stones today and that she'd be back later in the game. Dan knew she probably needed a little nap and maybe a chocolate protein shake. She hadn't eaten much of the feast potlucked together by the attendees. He saw her nibble baked potato chips with the mildest of the dips, but she avoided the salsa, the chili and the buffalo wings.

Nikki wasn't back in time to see Pittsburgh push their lead to 14–3 on their first drive in the second half, thanks to running back Willie Parker's thrilling 75-yard touchdown run—a Super Bowl record. Then the Seahawks scored, and Dan went into the bedroom and gave Nikki a call. When she answered sleepily, he said, "Oh, sorry to wake you. Just wondering if you were coming back over?"

"Oh, yeah. Didn't mean to stay so long. I'll be over in a few."

Nikki was back on Alex's couch, cheering with the rest of the gang, when, on a fake reverse, Antwaan Randle El hurled a 43-yard touchdown pass to wide receiver Hines Ward. That game-winning TD, and four other receptions for a total of 123 yards plus 18 yards rushing, earned Ward the Super Bowl XL's MVP award.

The gathering broke up shortly after the game ended.

As the door thumped closed behind them, those remaining looked at each other. "I think the *real* controversy is about which of this year's commercials was the best."

"The Bud Light Magic Refrigerator," Reuben declared without hesitation. "No question."

"I don't know," Patty responded. "I always like what they do with the horses."

Frank laughed. "Shall we go hoist a couple at Casey's and hash this out?" A few moments later, after goodbyes and thanks to the hosts, they were gone and only the four remained: Alex and Julia, Nikki and Dan. He watched Nikki push herself to her feet and start reaching for the near-empty pretzel bowl.

Julia took it away from her, chiding, "Let me get this, Nik. You're our guest. I think you could use a little nap."

When Nikki started to protest, Dan said, "I'll help them clean up. You go on and rest a little." She made a little more protest but seemed relieved when they shooed her out the door.

"She actually did pretty well," Alex said quietly. "Better than I expected."

Julia nodded. "It's just so hard to see her like this. She's not the Nikki I know."

Easy to see how much happier Alex was, but Julia, too, was blossoming. Her mom was more accepting of Julia having extended time away from home for "dating" Alex. And Julia was spending less time with her mom on the interests they'd always shared: traveling, the symphony, antique shopping. Not just because of Alex but because Myra was not up to as much as she used to be. Her increasing weight and slow-to-heal sores on her feet made walking more difficult—as was her breathing. Dan had seen that himself on two occasions when Myra came with Julia to visit Nikki at the apartment. She was puffing just from the walk from the elevator, never mind being unable to use the stairs as she used to. She couldn't drive anymore because the diabetes was affecting her vision. That meant if Julia didn't drive her and she couldn't find anyone else, she often used this as an excuse to miss appointments or simply pass up opportunities for outings.

A subtle guilt thing for Julia. On one hand, Myra says, "That's okay, honey. You go ahead with your own plans. I can get a ride. Don't worry." But when Julia did, she often was faced with the guilt of having her mother miss a social event or—worse—a doctor appointment.

Such clever and covert entrapment, holding Julia close while pretending to let her take some distance. Probably all unconscious as Myra was not an evil person. Like for most people, as she loses the ability to do for herself, she clings tightest to what she holds most dear. But Julia deserved to have a life of her own.

Are all parents torn by this paradox? The responsibility to love, nurture and protect a child, while teaching that child to be independent in thought and deed. And how do parents really let go of grown children, especially as their own needs grow?

So many terrifying things in this life, Dan thought as he lay on his couch while Nikki slept in the next room. Finances; failure; heartbreak; loneliness; parents with life-threatening health problems; surgeries; cancer; chemotherapy. But parenthood itself? Probably the most terrifying of all.

CHAPTER THIRTY-FIVE

"Sometimes parents have to make tough choices," Reuben Powell told Dan.

Dan studied his fellow first-year intern knowing he did more peds rotations than any of them. "So, because of the child, my patient, Leo Ackerlynn, chose not to have his *own* heart repaired?"

Reuben shrugged. "Said they had enough on their plate at the time."

Born twelve years ago, young Esther Ackerlynn, daughter of Leo and Gwen, displayed numerous birth anomalies, including hydrocephalus, horseshoe kidney, and pharyngeal atresia so acute, hospital staff found it impossible to get a feeding tube down her occluded throat and into her stomach. Considering this, and their certainty the infant was severely retarded, the doctors had strongly advised the Ackerlynns to let the child expire without painful interventions or false hope. But the couple, especially Gwen, wouldn't even consider the notion. Gwen herself found a way to get the necessary tube into the baby and deliver life-sustaining nutrition. Esther beat the odds, stayed alive and was able to leave the hospital. Her parents said it made no difference that she needed constant care; that was what parents *did.* Gwen quit her job as a nurse and stayed home to provide for Esther's every need, keep her company, find ways to stimulate her mind. Leo had taken on extra cases at the insurance company where he worked, hanging on for to the healthcare coverage, while he started an online consulting service at home. And Esther thrived within the limitations of her condition, which proved to be every bit as serious as the doctors warned.

But, Dan thought, Esther Ackerlynn was not his patient. It was her doting father, Leo. He had entered the world some forty-two years ago with a life-threatening congenital condition: Tetralogy of Fallot.

"His TOF went uncorrected as a child?" Dan recalled from the history.

Reuben nodded. "Apparently he was born in rural South Dakota. Small hospital, limited staff. Symptoms showed up early, though he wasn't cyanotic at birth. They sent him to the nearest medical center that could even consider opening him up to see if they could correct at least one of the defects, but they found, additionally, coronary arteries that were misplaced, making it impossible for their facility to fix anything."

"They just sewed him up?"

"Uh-huh. Told his parents to take him to Sioux Falls and find some heart specialists. But the family was poor, and not very educated, and they decided to put it off till they had more money. Surprisingly, Leo did pretty well by just taking it easy physically, and no one ever got around to following up."

Mentally, Dan had thoroughly reviewed what he'd learned about Tetralogy of Fallot in med school; he'd certainly never seen an uncorrected case before now. A *tetralogy* refers to an occurrence of *four,* and in TOF—named for the French physician who drew attention to the syndrome, four anomalies of the heart usually proved fatal before the age of fifty if uncorrected.

First, a narrowed pulmonary valve decreased the amount of blood that could pass into the lungs to receive oxygen when the right ventricle compressed to empty itself. Some of that blood was squeezed sideways through the second defect—a hole in the wall between the ventricles—forcing oxygen-poor blood to mix with the newly oxygen-rich blood that the left ventricle then pumped out of the heart through the aorta. But the third problem lay with the aorta itself, which could be mislocated or misaligned in various ways. The last anomaly was a result of the others: those problems left the body's cells starving for oxygen. So the right ventricle pumped harder and harder, trying to deliver adequate oxygen, but that only built up the muscular wall of the ventricle, further decreasing the capacity of the chamber.

Besides the significant four, numerous other abnormalities could accompany TOF, including unusual coronary arteries such as those Leo's early surgeons found or a right-sided aortic arch or a septal defect between the atria as well.

"Amazing he did so well," Dan said of Ackerlynn.

"Yeah. All the way till he was thirty. That's when a scare with shortness of breath got so severe he called a doctor buddy of his in the middle of the night and ended up hospitalized with pneumonia." Reuben chewed his lip, looking thoughtful, as if recalling what the patient had told him. "Didn't really have anything to do with the TOF, but when the docs saw his scars and found out he was uncorrected, they all wanted him to get surgery right then. He was in Pittsburgh, so there was no lack of medical expertise, not to mention thirty years' advancements. They urged him to get the valve and the septal defect repaired at the very least."

"But that's when Esther was born," Dan supplied, "and they decided to concentrate on *her* medical treatment instead."

Dan couldn't help wondering if there might not be more to it than that. Beyond the financial and the logistical, what about the emotional aspects? What about denial? Leo came from a family where a certain level of denial had worked: the *"Maybe if we ignore it, it'll all go away"* approach. They never followed up on the TOF, and nothing bad happened. Then he married a woman who defied the common wisdom of physicians to have her child both live and function. Reuben seemed to completely accept the Ackerlynns' view of the situation. He was already learning to treat the family as a whole. Still, it's a thin line between denial and all the reasonable reasons not to act. Dan sighed. "Well, he got another twelve years out of the status quo. But then came here a year ago with endocarditis?"

Again, Reuben's response was "Yep. How did he respond to treatment?"

"According to the chart, seems to have done pretty well on naf and genta."

Ten minutes later, Dan was back in Room 712, introducing himself once again to Leo Ackerlynn and his wife Gwen, who sat vigilantly at his bedside. "And you must be Esther," Dan said to the girl leaning against her mother, though there was an empty chair only another foot away.

Dan was aware the girl, who appeared to have complete concentration on some kind of electronic game she was holding, had actually been checking him out. Now that he'd included her, she looked directly at him with a shy smile and a nod. "I'm Dan."

"Dr. Marchetti," Gwen corrected, and there was a flavor to the word *doctor*—as if it left a bad taste in her mouth.

Esther studied him openly: wide, guileless face framed by blond braids with pink bows that matched her demure pink dress and tights and "comfortable" shoes. Her body carried about twenty extra pounds and her enlarged cranium showed the consequence of her hydrocephalus, despite her corrective surgery.

Gwen caressed her child's arm. "Take your game and go sit over there, sweetheart. You've almost got that puzzle figured out." Obediently, Esther moved to the far end of the room and sat in the chair next to 712's other, currently empty, bed.

Gwen's expression changed as she shifted her gaze to Dan, and her mouth compressed into a hard line. He put his attention on the patient, whose eyes couldn't follow as much as he would have loved to.

As he bared Leo's chest for the stethoscope, Dan saw the criss-crossing of old scars across the bony ribcage, remnants of the surgery in his infancy. The murmurs in Leo's heart valves were clearly audible. Dan had never heard sounds like that before.

Everything about Leo seemed quiet and pinched and brittle, even his thin mustache, though that was obviously genuine.

Gwen, on the other hand, was rounded and supple, settling gently into her forties. But her opinion of hospitals—and doctors—couldn't be more obvious. It was doctors who'd given up on her daughter, told her to let her baby die, told Leo he must have dangerous heart surgery all those years ago. Yet her child was alive and happily absorbed with a puzzle game across the room. And, in Gwen's mind, at least, Leo himself had been doing just fine. Well, till now anyway.

His examination finished, Dan studied the two I.V. bags hung on the pole; they were timed to dispense their medications separately via a PICC line that entered a vein in Leo's arm. Mulling over the numbers again, he wrote a new directive for one of the meds.

"Are you changing his medications?" Gwen demanded.

Dan faced her. "Not the meds themselves. Just a dosage."

"Your husband seems to be responding well."

Turning once again to Dan, Gwen tried to sound more cheerful. "You been following the Olypmics?"

Dan nodded. "I've caught some of it." The Winter Games had opened in Turin, Italy. "Love to watch the skiing though I'm really more of a Summer Games guy."

"Did you happen to see the snowboarding? Well, the kid who took home the Gold in Halfpipe, Shaun White, was born with TOF."

"Hadn't heard that." Dan decided not to say the obvious out loud, that Shawn must have had his defects corrected, since Gwen had begun to relax a little.

Just then, Dan saw Julia Cleary appear at the door to the room, dressed in scrubs with the top brightly patterned in red, blue and yellow. She gave him a little wave to let him know she *did* want to speak to him.

Including both Leo and Gwen in his gaze Dan said, "But I have to go now. Let me know if you need anything, okay?" Gwen only gave him a grim nod.

Out in the hall, he found Julia waiting for him. He could see now her flashy blouse was printed with cartoon dogs and cats, denoting her peds status. "Didn't want to disturb you," Julia apologized.

"No problem. I was finished there. What's up?"

"I'm worried about Nikki." Little lines knitted Julia's brows closer together. *She looks so healthy.* Perfect weight and body tone, light-brown curls shining around her face, blue eyes wide and clear and focused. But serious. "I just now stopped by to see her on my way to work. She's not looking good."

"She told me she was fine when I said good-bye." Dan felt almost apologetic. "I hate to hover over her, y'know?"

"I know! She *acts* like she's fine, but I think she may have pneumonia again. She won't let me take her temp or listen to her lungs, but her cough is dreadful. And she shivered like she might be starting chills."

Surprised, Dan reflected, "Hmh! I haven't heard her cough much at all."

"I think she's loading up on cough syrup when you're around. She's got the stuff with codeine, right?"

"Geez. I hadn't a clue."

"I know. It's so hard to hang back, respect her independence. I have to force myself not to treat her like one of my own young patients. "Yeah. Wishful thinking."

"You may have to step in—*make* her come to the hospital. She's stubborn."

Dan saw Julia check her watch. "Thanks so much for alerting me."

Dan went to the phone at the physicians desk. On dayshift this week, he didn't have to worry as much about waking her: interrupting a nap was different from disturbing a hard-won night's sleep.

Nikki answered the phone coughing.

"Hey," Dan said, as if surprised, "that doesn't sound good."

"I'm okay," she responded. "Let me get a drink of water." He could hear her swallowing, and afterward, the coughing subsided. Her voice sounded weak and thick, despite her effort to be cheerful as she asked, "What's up?"

"Oh, I just called to say *Hi.* I was thinking of bringing some DCH chicken soup so we could have lunch together. But I'm worried about that cough. Now I think I'd better come listen to your lungs."

"I know, but we can't do that right now. Jenna Hudson's on her way over here to take care of that paperwork we talked about. Remember?"

Dan grimaced. "Yeah. But—"

"Listen, I'll call you when we're done. Next break you have, you can come check me. If you think it's pneumonia, I promise I'll go back to DCH with you. Okay?"

Just that much talking made her sound worn out. Not wanting to strain her more, about all he could say was, "Okay, but—"

"There's the doorbell!" she interrupted. "That'll be Jenna. I'll call you—" and she was gone.

Dan frowned at the phone handset as he replaced it. *That paperwork.* How could he forget? Two nights ago, Nikki has suddenly stated "No hospital." between sips of a smoothie.

He actually laughed, thinking she was joking. He had heard that declarative statement so often from patients. Or from relatives explaining why they'd waited so long to bring someone in. Sometimes it was even too late by then.

"I know hospitals," Nikki pointed out. "You can get way sicker there . . . pick up something new."

Truth to that but absurd. Like those who say, "People *die* in hospitals." People die everywhere. Most people get well in hospitals—and some that do die there, it's cuz they waited too long to come in. He went to sit beside her on the couch, put an arm around her. "What's really going on, Nik?"

She looked away. "It's not hospitals I hate. It's the thought of being *in* one again . . . being a patient. My mom *died* in a hospital. I almost did too."

"But you didn't. The doctors and the nurses saved your life."

"I know. It's not rational. I just can't let go of the feeling that if I go in, I won't come out."

Do a really big favor for me?"

A cold finger of dread touched Dan between the shoulder blades. He tried to keep his voice light. "What kind of a favor?"

"Would you agree to hold my Power of Attorney? Be my designee in my living will?" He couldn't speak right away, and she slid out from under his arm, sat up and set her half-full glass on the coffee table. "I know it's a lot to ask, but I really don't have anyone else." As if she could read his thoughts, she added, "I certainly don't want *Matt* to be in charge of such a decision for me. Heck, he'd be likely, out of guilt or uncertainty, to keep me alive too long. And with all the shit he's been pulling with this divorce, I just don't want him to have that final power over me."

"I understand," Dan managed. "But are you sure—"

"Listen, I trust you more than anyone else on earth, even Julia, and who's better qualified than a physician to determine if and when to pull the plug?"

She sensed his reticence. "I already have a living will drawn up that very carefully lays out my wishes regarding various conditions and procedures. But it designates Matt. I don't want to force you to agree to anything you're not comfortable with, but I don't intend to be admitted to a hospital until I have someone else's fingers on the plug. If you don't want to do it, I need to find someone else. I already planned to meet with Jenna sometime this week to tie up some other paperwork."

Still reluctant to assume such a momentous responsibility, Dan had to force himself to "walk the walk" as well as "talk the talk." Okay," he said at last.

Her smoky green eyes bored into him. "And you promise you won't keep my body alive on any of those machines if you know for sure that *I'm* gone?"

Knowing what she meant, he nodded. "I promise."

He watched her relax, smile with tired satisfaction as she snuggled against him again, murmuring, "Thank you, Dante."

He had hugged her frail body gently. "But I'm sure you won't even need it. You're gonna be just fine."

Dan started now as the phone on the physicians desk rang, ripping him from the memory. He answered. "Oh, hi Patty. No, Reuben's not here right now. Haven't seen him for, oh, forty-five minutes or so. Did you try his cell? Well, if you don't reach him on that, call back and let me know. Meanwhile, I'll leave a note here on the desk. Sure. You're welcome."

Writing the note, Dan was happy that they'd been seeing a lot of each other since the Super Bowl party at Alex's three weeks ago. Somehow, it was comforting to remember that life goes on, the world keeps turning.

His own cell rang, and Dan answered. *Nikki.*

"Jenna says there're a few things for you to sign too. Can she come by in about an hour?"

"Sure. Tell her to have me paged from the lobby, and I'll come down to meet her."

It was almost exactly an hour later that he got the page. He was just finishing up a check on his angina patient and said he'd be down to meet her in the main lobby. He found her there—folder and pen in hands, about ten minutes later, sitting on one of the comfortable sofas, her expensive coat draped beside her. The beautifully cut charcoal pantsuit could be a twin for the navy one she'd worn the only other time they'd met. He remembered the early-forties face with impeccable makeup, the casually tousled short blond hair, the piercing grey eyes. The frown was new, and he assumed it was because he'd kept her waiting.

But as he sat and began to apologize, her face lightened and she assured him the little delay was fine. "Actually, I just wanted to tell you I'm concerned about Nikki. I was surprised, and distressed, to see how different she appears from only last week."

Chagrined, Dan admitted, "I heard that earlier from her friend Julia. It appears she's been hiding a lot from me because she didn't want to be hospitalized before she had her . . . paperwork . . . in order. I feel terrible it's slipped past me."

Jenna touched his arm. "Don't be hard on yourself. I know you'd do anything to help her." She smiled. "Don't look so surprised. People confide a lot in their divorce attorneys.

Dan reached out for the pen and folder she held. It had a sturdy back cover to facilitate signatures. "I'm sure you're right. Let me get these things signed and then maybe I can get that ball rolling."

When he'd quickly read through and signed the pages, Jenna slipped them into a leather portfolio she pulled from beneath her coat and stood up. "As soon as I've processed these, they'll be in effect, and you'll have Nikki Saxon's Power of Attorney. If I go now, everything will be in effect by the close of business today." Dan helped her into her coat. "So you can tell her she has no more excuses. It's up to you now, Doctor."

He nodded and thanked Jenna. "I'll do my part. If she's as sick as I'm hearing, I'll have her admitted to DCH tonight."

Six hours later, Dan was finally on his way to check out Nikki. He had called twice and she said she was fine but a feeling of dread was building around his heart. Jogging for home as snowflakes swirled around him, he felt grateful for the extra movement. When Patty Yates had dropped by to see Reuben, she reported the temperature hadn't been above freezing all day.

Dan heard the coughing as soon as he opened the apartment door. In the bedroom, Nikki looked awful. Feverish, trembling with chills even as the skin of her forehead burned beneath his hand. Under the bedclothes, her flannel p.j.s were drenched.

"Hey, honey. How y'feeling?" as if he had to ask.

"I've been better," she managed through chattering teeth. She tried a smile, but her lips were parched and she was obviously in pain.

He reached for the half-empty bottle on the nightstand, noticing the thermometer lying there. Given how hot she was to the touch, he was not surprised to see it's last recording was 102 degrees. When she finished the bottle of water and handed the empty back, he said, "Sit up and let me listen to those lungs."

Dutifully, but not without difficulty, she complied. Dan lifted the sodden pajama shirt and placed the bell of the stethoscope on her back. He didn't have to direct her how to breathe; she'd observed the ritual often enough.

There it is. The short, high-pitched fine crackling and popping sound he'd expected to hear at the end of each indrawn breath. He didn't have to ask her to cough for him; that happened naturally, and didn't clear the crackling.

Dan pulled her shirt back down. "Guess where you're going."

"Probably not the Bahamas. Did Jenna get to you?"

"Yes, and by now all that paperwork should be filed and in effect. No more excuses."

Nikki shook her head weakly. "I'm ready. Can you help me shower and dress?"

He wanted to say, "Geez, don't worry about that!" but stopped realizing that Nikki knew it would be unlikely that she'd have another chance to shower and pretend to feel normal once she became a patient. When he helped her out of bed and into the bathroom, Dan saw she'd hung some clothing on the back of the door: that new fleece set, underwear, warm socks.

After she'd slipped out of her sweaty pajamas and hung them on a wall hook to dry, he assisted her as she stepped into the tub. He took down the handy personal shower and found a water temperature suitable for her fevered body. He didn't peel off his own clothes and join her as he used to, but he removed his sweater, leaving the T-shirt. If he was careful enough about back-splash, he hoped to minimize getting too wet.

As Nikki leaned against his supportive arm and applied the liquid bath gel she preferred, Dan was surprised to find he hardly noticed the pale hairlessness of her body. The shock was gone at least.

Gently, he rubbed a washcloth over Nikki's bare head and shoulders, then across her upper back where it was hard for her to reach. His mind flashed suddenly to Joe and Sue Bonfiglio, whom he'd seen recently at DCH. Actually, he'd run into them earlier, back at the end of December when Joe was in getting some tests. He hadn't looked good, and it was clear his chemo wasn't winning the battle with his leukemia. Dan hadn't said anything to Nikki about it, because he didn't want to be telling her about someone so near her age who was, in reality, not *living with* but *dying of* cancer. Nor did he mention seeing the Bonfiglio family last week. Joe's mom was herding the three little girls; Sue was now gigantically pregnant, and walked with a heaviness born of more than her belly's weight. Inside the hospital, Joe had removed his warm hat, and his bald head gleamed beneath the lights. Easier for men. Even the absence of eyebrows and eyelashes looked less shocking than on Nikki.

Dan had taken Joe's lead at each encounter, not probing past a "How're you doing, Joe?" answered by a "Been better, doc."

Dan steadied Nikki on the bathmat while she dried herself feeling luckier than Sue, knowing Nikki would get well and beat her disease.

Dried, Nikki sat on the closed toilet seat and donned the pieces of clothing as Dan handed them to her. "Wanta wear Cammi?" he asked.

She'd named her wig shortly after wearing it the second time, announcing, "That's short for Camouflage." It waited now where it spent most of its days: adorning the wigstand on the counter.

Nikki shook her head. "It'll come off as soon as I'm admitted. I've got a couple of caps in my bag."

In fact, Dan found when they returned to the bedroom, she'd already packed a little duffel for herself to take to the hospital. "Hey," he said. "While you put on your shoes and coat, I'll go down and warm up the car."

"I hoped you'd say that." Sitting on the edge of the bed near the sneakers she'd set out, she stretched a fluffy-yarn cap over her scalp. That one always made him smile. Created by another of her former patients, it made her look like a spiky-haired rocker with a coif of bright purple, orange and lime green. She returned his smile.

He leaned down and kissed her forehead. "You wait here. I'll come back up for you."

Dan hurried back into his own coat and gloves, stethoscope in pocket, and downstairs to the covered parking. He knew it might take awhile to start up his Accord. He'd used their cars more frequently since Nikki started treatment, trading off to keep them both running well, but he still preferred to walk to DCH when weather permitted, and she rarely went anywhere except to chemo-related appointments.

As he waited, he pulled out his cell phone and dialed the ER. Diane Werner picked up. Surprised, Dan said, "Thought you had the night shift."

"I'm in early, so they put me to work."

"Busy?"

"A little. Car vs. motorcycle with multiple injuries. A guy with hydronephrosis and a case of food poisoning. Quieting down now. Why?"

"Got another bed, I hope? I'm bringing Nikki in. Sure sounds like a community acquired pneumonia."

"Oh, so sorry. Of course, we've got room. Bring her on in."

By now, the Accord's engine was purring, and the interior was heated enough. He turned off the motor and hustled upstairs to get Nikki.

She was waiting on the sofa, shoes on, gloves on, duffel at her feet. He saw she'd chosen her hooded parka that would keep her head and neck warmer. Taking her bag, he gave her a hand to her feet, and she zipped up the jacket, gazing around the living room as if memorizing this haven he'd given her. Dan took her in his arms and hugged her as close as their bulky outerwear would allow. "It's gonna be okay, honey. Come on, let's go get you well."

Monday came with the first truly Spring-like weather of the season. Taking his coffee cup to a cafeteria table that held a discarded *Deerwood Times,* Dan sat and managed, one-handed, to uncover the Sports section's headline: PIRATES LOSE BUT PHENOM IS BORN.

The article was about Trey Hartmann, the Pirates' new hotshot from the Midwest. Yesterday, apparently, he'd pitched a total of seven scoreless innings. The Brewers scored the two winning runs in the last inning off a Pirate reliever. Trey'd been sensational, however, allowing only four hits and striking out seven.

Dan wondered how Charlie must be feeling. During his confinement at DCH, the old coach had spoken so highly of the new call-up. Apparently this Trey Hartmann wasn't one of those overpaid-but-lazy professional athletes that Dan'd always despised. Time would tell if he'd live up to the hype.

Speaking of time, Dan checked his watch, then rose, gulping the rest of his coffee. He was hoping to stop in to see Joe, who'd been admitted to oncology last night. He wanted to get in the visit before he was due to see patients at the eye clinic. Nikki had heard of what was likely to be Joe's final admission from one of her friends who had stopped by during her chemo infusion.

Dan grimaced now as he arrived at the hospital and headed down to Four West. Even knowing this day was coming made it no less hard to say good bye to a friend. He greeted the nurses at their station and told them he wanted to check on his former patient. Charissa herself nodded and pulled out Joe's chart for him, silent but with a sympathetic expression that clearly said HIPAA be damned. That federal privacy law was meant to keep everyone who wasn't providing direct care for a patient away from charts, but she knew that Dan could provide answers to questions Joe and Sue that they didn't always feel easy about asking Klonter.

Dan studied Cyrus Klonter's notes. *Pneumonia.* The lab values showed Joe's white count was off the wall—his leukemia running completely unchecked now, uncheckable. Joe'd had some time on the outside with his family, but precious little of it. Barely more than five months.

Walking into the room, Dan was immediately struck by the change in Joe's appearance just since last month when he had greeted the arrival of Joey Jr.

The whole family was there with him. His mom was keeping an eye on the three solemn-faced girls as they colored pictures on individual clipboards while Sue sat close to the bed, holding little Joey where Joe could have him rest next to him in the crook of his arm.

Mustering what cheer he could, Dan greeted his former patient. "Hey, Joe . . . how's it going?"

"Fine, fine," Joe managed, but unconvincingly. Dan greeted Joe's mom and wife, then found a grin for the kids, all of whom wore jeans and black baseball caps turned backwards. "Hi, guys," he said and playfully righted the hat of the oldest child, JoAnn, so that the gold-colored Pirates logo faced forward. "No wonder they haven't won a game yet!"

He could tell by JoAnn's eyes that she knew he was kidding, but, unsmiling, she countered, "Not my cap's fault. They pulled Trey Hartmann too soon."

The adults laughed at the refreshing spirit of this bright 7-year-old.

Baby Joey began to fuss and squirm, and Sue observed, "I think someone needs a change."

"And this time it's not me," Joe managed to quip.

Taking Joey into her arms, Sue wrinkled her nose. "Nope. This one's all Joey." Her gaze bore into Dan's across the space between them, and she asked, "Would you like a minute with Joe? I think he'd enjoy a chat with a grown-up male. I know he was hoping you'd come by."

Dan could see the strain on her face. "Sure," Dan said, reassured now his intrusion was welcome.

Sue rose with her cargo and glanced at her mother-in-law. "I'll take Joey to the changing station in the ladies room."

Joe's mom rose, too, and said to the girls. "I'm ready for a little break. Anybody else want a donut with sprinkles?"

All three girls popped up with shining eyes, tossing aside their coloring to cry, "Me! Me!" Each in turn went to kiss Daddy's cheek and tell him "Bye" and "See you soon." He wondered exactly how Joe and Sue were handling this. What and how much they'd told the girls. A few moments later, they were all out the door, Marie and the girls toward the elevator, Sue carrying the baby and the diaper bag toward the ladies room. She called after the others, "I'll meet you in the cafeteria."

Alone now with the patient, Dan went to sit beside the bed and put his hand on Joe's. He looked so pale, so gaunt. At the corner of his mouth, active herpes lesions added further insult to illness.

"That's one beautiful family you've got there, Joe."

"I know. I'm a lucky guy. . . ." His voice broke on the last word, and he looked away, blinking hard. "It's just so hard to believe, Dan. Six months ago, I was the picture of health, on top of the world, and now. . . ." He swallowed. "I just hate leaving Sue with all this ."

"It's good she's got your mom."

"Thank God for that. She's been really helpful with the girls . . . maintaining some sense of normalcy and peace." He looked at Dan now. "You see, we've been honest with the girls. They know I won't be coming home from here because I got a bad disease that doctors can't fix, even though they've done everything they can. And that they don't need to fear getting such a thing 'cause it isn't contagious.

"I know I don't have much time now, Dan, and I want you to know I hope to go out as easy as possible, for everybody's sake. Sue and I thought about it and talked it over . . . told Doc Klonter. The DNR is on my chart. When the time comes, I just want to go. Last thing my family needs is having people pounding on my chest, stabbing me with needles, hooking me up to machines, y'know?"

"I absolutely do." Dan cleared his throat. "Listen, man. I'm so glad to know you and your wonderful family."

Joe nodded, his eyes filling again. "I'm ready to go, Dan, but I just can't seem to get past how goddam *unfair* this is to *them.* To Sue . . . my little girls . . . my son." With that, he began to sob.

Dan rose from the chair and sat beside him on the bed, embracing that frail body in the thin hospital gown, feeling every bone of his ribcage. Dan held Joe in his arms, rocking a little, hoping the wordless sounds that were coming from his clogged throat would be heard as supportive and comforting.

Dan's own eyes filled and overflowed as he wept for this man. For the whole family who loved him and would miss him terribly.

When Sue returned with the family, Dan made his way out quietly, wondering if Joe would be there when next he had a moment to visit with him. Wiping his eyes, he took a minute on the stairwell to prepare himself for moving out of the world of visitor and back into the role of doctor.

At clinic, he straightened his white coat and looped his stethoscope around his neck as he stepped into the first room. A 90-year-old great-great-grandma who'd recently had cataract and lens replacement surgery, sat waiting in the big chair flanked by a variety of instrumentation that could be swung in front of her to evaluate a her eyes and vision.

Sharp-as-a-tack, impeccably dressed and coiffed, she'd taken to heart the current wisdom that people need to be their own advocates. She had no problem voicing concern that her vision in that eye wasn't "as good as it should be by now."

After thorough examination following what he'd already learned from Ivans, Dan was soon able to reassure her the eye was healing normally and well. "People recover at different rates," he told her, "for a variety of reasons—"

"Well, sonny," she interrupted with a quirking smile. "I hope you're not about to tell me it has anything to do with *age?*"

Dan laughed, adopting a light and teasing tone. "Not at all. In fact, recent studies seem to suggest that the mentally gifted may heal more slowly."

That earned a delighted response, and Dan was soon on his way to the next patient, a young man who needed a complete eye exam in order to apply for a job in a small factory where he'd be assembling tiny components.

Finishing with the laborer, Ivans met him in the hallway and invited Dan to join him; handing over a chart so he could peruse the thorough medical history already taken.

Rita Rice, a 41-year-old schoolteacher, had presented with complaints of blurred vision, headache and trouble driving at night. A clinic nurse had noted her vital signs—all normal—and administered a routine visual acuity test that showed the right eye as normal. The blurring and diminished acuity affected the left eye only.

Inside the examination room, Ivans introduced himself and Dan to the nervous-looking brunette. "So how are you, Ms. Rice?"

"Oh, you can call me Rita." She dimpled. "All my parents call me that." She lost the smile. "Actually, I'm a little more worried than when I first came in. I didn't realize my left was so much worse or that there's a blind spot. I have noticed a big difference in my color vision." She pointed to a decorative poster on the wall. "Those roses look perfectly red from my right eye but very faded with just my left."

Dan caught the significant glance from the attending before the man sat on the stool and took up his ophthalmoscope, saying, "Well, let's take a look, shall we?"

Dan watched Dr. Ivans work, peering into each eye through the lighted, handheld instrument and then performing other elements of a physical exam for clues about pupillary function, peripheral vision and ocular mobility. As the patient complied with the directions to "Look up . . . look down . . . look right . . . look left. . . . " it was clear this wasn't completely comfortable, though she didn't complain.

"Is that painful?" the ophthalmologist asked.

"Yes. When I move my eyes, the left one hurts."

"Let's check the pressure." He signaled to Dan, who plucked a tissue from the box and handed it to Rita. As instructed, she tilted her head back, and Dan administered the anesthetic eyedrops that would allow the tonometry device to touch and lightly compress the surface of her eye without being felt.

Dabbing away the excess liquid on her cheek, Rita said, "I *do* have some glaucoma in my family, but so far my checkups have been okay."

"Good," Ivans said, swinging the slit lamp table around in front of her. "Chin in the rest, please; forehead against the bar."

Pretty sure it's not glaucoma that Ivans is worried about, Dan thought. Several of the presenting complaints were symptoms of optic neuritis, an inflammation of the optic nerve. It was a problem he knew well from his Aunt Carmella who'd been dealing with it off and on for thirty years. In fact, optic neuritis was frequently associated with multiple sclerosis and could be a precursor to the ailment; often the first indication.

As his attending conducted an exam of the external eyes—lids, lashes, conjunctiva, corneas, irises, anterior chambers, lenses—through the magnification of the slit lamp, Dan carefully entered the findings as Ivans reported them in his calm medical-speak. "Okay, Rita. I'm going to check the pressures now." Ivans switched on the cobalt blue light. "You've had this done before, right? So you know to look straight ahead and hold your eye as wide open as possible."

The little tonometer advanced and touched the surface of first one and then, after repositioning, the other eye. Dan wrote down the numbers for both eyes when Ivans told Rita, "Yes, good pressure. Fifteen in both eyes."

"That's a relief," Rita said.

"A few more things I want to check. I need to dilate your pupils first." On that cue, Dan set aside the chart and again handed her a tissue. This time he chose the dropper bottle with the red cap, then stepped close to instill the mydriatic, dilating, drops. As she blotted the excess, Ivans said, "It'll take a few minutes for your eyes to dilate, so we'll be back shortly."

Dan retrieved the chart and as he followed Ivans from the room dimmed the lights at the wall switch. They didn't talk until they reached the nurses station, where they learned there were no new patients waiting at the moment. Ivans took the chart in order to enter more notes in his own hand. Then he looked at Dan. "What do you think?"

"Symptoms point to optic neuritis in the left eye.

"You know the implications?"

"My godmother's been battling MS since before I can remember, so I know quite a bit about the disease and early signs."

Nodding, Ivans offered, "The eyes aren't just the windows of the soul, as they say, but can also be windows to the brain and circulation as well."

Optic nerves are, in truth, an extension of the brain and central nervous system, the only place where damage to the myelin sheath covering parts of the CNS can be seen without surgery. Likewise, the blood vessels of the eye are the only place to view microcirculation in an "unopened" body.

The eye was fascinating and intriguing in its complexity. Not everyone agreed. Some people he knew, like Theo Epplewhite, were actually squeamish about them. He'd once admitted to Dan, "I just want to learn the very basics I'll need to know to make a referral and leave the rest to the Eye Guys. Eyeballs're just too fragile and *personal* somehow."

Dan accompanied Ivans back into the exam room, leaving the lights low. Dan admired his mentor's easy patter with the patient even as he lowered her chair into a semi-reclining position, donned the lighted headband and picked up the large lens that would allow him to peer down bifocally into each of Rita's eyes. As was customary, he began with the right eye, and Dan wasn't surprised that all his findings, which he spoke for Dan to write down, were normal.

But when Ivans switched to the left eye, his findings included, "Mild edema of the nerve, involving the whole nerve" but "no hemorrhages" and "no macular star." When he finished, he cheerfully told Rita, "If you'll spare us another moment, I'll let young Dr. Marchetti take a gander. He hasn't seen this before, and he can learn something from you."

"I'm perfectly comfortable," she answered with a chuckle. "And you can take the schoolteacher out of the classroom—"

"But they can never stop teaching!" Ivans finished with a chuckle. He traded Dan his equipment for the clipboard and wrote some more notes while Dan fitted the headlamp and bent to look into Rita Rice's left eye with the indirect ophthalmoscopic lens.

The fundus, or inside surface of the eye, was a pretty peachy-golden color, and Dan noted for himself the details Ivans had reported: the clarity of the vitreous humour that filled the back space of the eye ball; the diameters and condition of the blood vessels; the lack of scars, leaky vessels or tearing in the retina. And there, at the farthest point from him, at the back of the eye, he could see the rosy-pink optic disc or cup, the head of the optic nerve. That cup should be only one-third the diameter of the nerve itself, but here it was swollen and puffy.

"Thank you," Dan said as he pulled back, shut off his headlamp and put away the lens. He grinned at her, cranking the chair upright again. "Teachers are a national treasure."

Smiling, but looking nervous again, she asked, "So what did you fellows learn from me?"

Ivans raised the level of the room's lighting a bit, but not enough to bother her dilated pupils, and handed the chart back to Dan, who could see he'd written "Probable optic neuritis OS" meaning in the left eye only. Ivans sat on the stool and told Rita, "This looks like an inflammation of the optic nerve called optic neuritis."

She nodded. "What causes it?"

"A variety of things, like viruses . . . Lyme Disease, herpes zoster—"

"That's the chickenpox and shingles virus, right?"

"Yes. Also some toxins, such as methanol and lead, can cause it; fungal infections, autoimmune diseases, pressure on the nerve from various sources. So our next step is to do some testing and find out what our culprit is. Then we'll know how best to treat it." He began writing on a referral pad. "Take this to the nurses' station and they'll schedule you for an MRI of your eyes and optic nerves. Then we'll know more."

Dan noticed Ivans hadn't said anything about multiple sclerosis yet. No sense terrifying her until they could rule out other causes. There're other bad things it could be—like a tumor. The good news was, she'd come in right away and would soon have an idea of how to proceed. There were even medications that could delay, perhaps deflect, the development of MS. Dan made a note to himself to read up on MS at home this evening so he'd be prepared both for Ivan's inevitable questions in the morning, but also so that he'd sink the knowledge into his head, ready to retrieve when he was the attending and not a resident.

Just after nine-thirty that evening, Dan left the Clinic area feeling tired but satisfied The last patient of the day had come in complaining of irritation in the same eye as her new corneal transplant. Tissue rejection was always a risk, though that turned out not to be the problem.

A nervous sort and a little flaky, she nattered on at every moment she wasn't needing to be completely still for her exam.

At Ivans's invitation, Dan sat on the stool to take a look through the slit lamp, admiring the precision of both a running stitch around the perimeter and individual stitches—called interrupted suturing—at key points around the edge of the new corneal "button." Amazing what can be done with transplants. But as a patient who also had retinal problems once said, "I'm looking forward to the day whole eyes can be transplanted, like in the movie *Minority Report.*"

In the end, after careful questioning, they learned the patient had mixed up several of the instructions on her post-surgical medications. They got everything straightened out—including how she had to shake the bottle of anti-rejection steroid drops *every* time she used it—and Dan wrote it all down for her, since she'd misplaced the original orders. An easy fix and a good case to end on.

Now, headed upstairs, Dan turned his attention to what lay ahead and began to feel, amidst the tired satisfaction, a bit of anticipation. In less than forty-eight hours, he would be at PNC Park watching a Pirates batting practice, maybe even participating; a guest of Charlie Monroe who had not forgotten his promise to Dan when he finally was well enough to return to the world he loved. And right now he was on his way to tell Joe Bonfiglio about it, give him a little ray of sunshine maybe.

But as he entered Joe's room on Four West, he could tell it was too late. Dr. Klonter was in the room, conferring with Nurse Charissa, who saw Dan first and nodded a somber greeting. Beyond them, in the bed, Joe lay still except for his labored breathing, his nose packed with bloody gauze. Sue sat beside him, holding his left hand in both her own and speaking quietly to him.

"Nasal hemorrhage?" Dan asked Klonter as Charissa departed. Chemo would've dropped Joe's platelet count dangerously low, preventing proper clotting.

The oncologist nodded. "We've hung another ten units." His expression didn't look optimistic. "We'll see." He handed Dan the chart for a quick perusal and said, "I'm glad you're here."

After Klonter reclaimed the chart, he led the way to the bedside, sitting across from Sue, who glanced up and smiled wanly, eyes brimming, at Dan. He turned his attention to Joe, breathing softly, "Joe" as he took the near-lifeless right hand.

The patient attempted to smile. Far beyond their customary banter, he managed to whisper, "Dan. . . ."

So fast. So unfair, Dan thought as his throat constricted and his eyes got wet. It had been only hours since he'd held Joe as he let go of being the brave dad and husband if only for a moment.

As if reading his mind, Sue said, "We're glad you're here, Dan. A little while ago, Joe said good-bye to his mom and the kids. Marie took them home so I could stay. But he was hoping to see you one more time."

Dan looked into Joe's tired brown eyes. "This is good-bye then?" The man nodded almost imperceptibly but didn't speak. Sue did it for him. "Joe told me the two of you had talked and said what you needed to say to each other. But I want to thank you too."

Dan reached over to squeeze her shoulder, but before he could manage any words, Cyrus Klonter's beeper went off, calling him to a "Code 99 . . . Room 440—stat. Room 440—stat!"

Uncertainty shadowed Klonter's face. He'd obviously intended to be here to see Joe out, but now he had another patient possibly dying down the hall.

"I can stay with Joe and Sue, if you like," Dan offered. There was a quick exchange of eye contact and nods all around as the Bonfiglios showed they were content with Dan's being there instead of their oncologist. He nodded solemnly, patted Joe's arm with a meaningful gaze and then was gone. Dan slid into the vacated chair, still holding Joe's right hand while Sue clung to the left. Joe looked from one to the other of them, but then his eyes widened as blood began to pour past the styptic-impregnated packings in his nostrils. Dan was quick to help him sit forward so he wouldn't suffocate on his own blood. Obviously, the ten units of platelets he'd been getting intravenously couldn't stem the tide.

Choking back his feelings, Dan hoped to keep his own distress from upsetting Sue even more. Just then, Joe Bonfiglio closed his eyes and stopped breathing, sagging in Dan's arms. Gently, he laid the body back against the pillows and, using a corner of the bedsheet, wiped away the blood on his friend's still face.

Dan felt for a carotid pulse and checked his watch but not because he found anything to count. He met Sue's gaze and shook his head. She, weeping softly, claimed Joe's left hand and lifted it to lay her cheek against it.

Dan felt an unexpected sense of calm wash through him: Joe's torture was ended, the long battle, over. Tragic as this was, perhaps the Bonfiglios had truly found the acceptance they needed at the end of those stages of grief.

Meanwhile, monitors had alerted staff to the change in Joe's vital signs, but with a DNR in place, there was no need for blaring codes or heroic, brutal attempts to bring Joe's body back to life. People came in . . . nurses and techs, intern Patty Yates. Charissa helped Sue to her feet and guided her away to do what she needed to do next while the body was prepared for family viewing in a few hours.

"Time of Death: 8:31 p.m." Dan said quietly and Patty wrote it on the chart. Klonter would fill out the death certificate later.

Cyrus Klonter came in, and his expression showed he'd been successful with his other crisis. The oncologist regarded him solemnly, then put an arm around Dan's shoulders. "Go on home, Marchetti. Thanks for standing in." Wordless, Dan nodded and left the Oncology ward. Thankfully, at this late hour, he didn't run into anyone else he knew as he made his way to the locker room and pulled on his coat. He hurried past Greg Vanderbosk at his security station, merely raising a hand in greeting instead of stopping for their usual chat.

Dan strode out into a crisp spring night and hurried his steps toward the apartment. Breaking into a sprint, he let the sobs take him.

CHAPTER THIRTY-SIX

Nikki drifted upward toward consciousness. She'd been in her *Dreamplace*, swimming underwater in the crystal-clear pond. Like the fishes, she had no need to breathe in those comforting waters . . . no fears . . . no thoughts needed at all.

Now she lay, eyes still closed but with the sense of bliss slipping away. Beyond the buzzing in her ears, the sounds were familiar . . . and the smells, not entirely pleasant. Her eyes opened. Still the hospital. How long now? At least a week: four days plus on antibiotics, but when the continued high fever and more tests identified her "bug" as fungal, she was switched to another drug; now three days on that.

Still feet like crap—not even close to them letting her go home. She had never wanted to be in a hospital again as a patient. Squeezing her eyes shut, Nikki did everything she knew how to force herself out of the real world . . . to escape. But she couldn't get back to her Dreamplace.

"Hey, Nik," a soft voice ventured. "You awake?"

Nikki opened her eyes, trying to smile at Charissa Carmichael, senior RN for Oncology.

"Ooh, you look dry. Let me get some water for you." Charissa quickly poured the gold-plastic glass full and then helped Nikki skooch up enough to use the straw. "Yes, I can see you needed that. Don't worry, that's not the last glassful on the planet."

Nikki had always loved her sense of humor and the fact that she was a fellow science fiction buff. Charissa was often referred to as "The Chickenwoman" because she kept a variety of pet chickens that were treated like royalty; thanks to her nursing skills, they all lived half a decade beyond a normal lifespan. "Another?"

With her mouth now hydrated enough, Nikki was able to lick her lips to moisten them. "No, thanks." She found she could even smile comfortably. "But could you pour another one for me before you leave?"

"Sure." First, though, Charissa checked Nikki's vitals while she told a funny story about her rooster Pip, who could stare down cats.

"So how *am* I?" Nikki asked when Charissa was finished checking her.

"Well, you know your fever's still up. Doesn't look like the fluconazole is working, and you know what that means."

Nikki grimaced. "Amphoterrible?"

The antifungal drug amphotericin had gotten its best-known nickname in large part for the kidney damage it could do, but also for the severe side effects that often developed shortly after the first dose: fever spiking higher and ghastly chills.

Charissa patted her hand. "I'm sure Dr. Klonter will order you some dilaudid first. You know, before that was common practice, we used to call amphotericin 'Shake 'n Bake.'""I remember seeing it," Nikki said with another grimace. "Patients cooked with fever, and the whole bed would quake with their shivering."

"Those were the days!" Charissa began to pour another glass of water. Before she finished, Dr. Klonter came into the room and nodded to them both in greeting. Charissa's beeper went off and she gave Nikki a little wave on her way to the door.

Cyrus Klonter studied Nikki's chart, pursing his lips with—*what?*—disappointment? Dissatisfaction?

Nikki asked the question she'd asked Charissa, "So how *am* I?"

"I don't like the numbers on that fever. The fluconazole isn't knocking it down the way it should." He looked directly at her, hesitating as if reluctant to voice the next step.

"Amphotericin?"

He actually smiled. "Nurses make great patients. They know the score."

"But I can get dilaudid first time out, right?"

The smile widened. "Nurses also make tough patients, 'cause they keep docs on their toes. You're way ahead of me, aren't you?"

"I just want to get well and back home."

"Let's see what we can do about that." He ran through his physical exam, finding nothing to dispute his earlier opinion. When Charissa, passing in the hall, glanced in, Klonter gestured for her and wrote orders for the course of amphotericin—with dilaudid.

"Right away, Doctor." Charissa winked at Nikki as if to say, *we nailed that, didn't we?*, and bustled away to set up the treatment.

"We got a timeline?" Nikki asked him now.

"If you respond to the amphotericin over the next five days—and all other signs are good—we'll switch you to oral meds and discharge you."

"Great!"

"Well, the news you *won't* want to hear is this means we'll have to delay your chemo another week. So instead of just missing one and adding it to the end, you'll have three weeks in between, and you'll have to re-mark your calendar."

She nodded. "But we keep on with ABVD . . . not change to something else?"

"Right. We'll check your echo before the next dose, but I don't expect there to be a problem with your heart. All things considered, the ABVD seems to still be the right course."

Before he left, Klonter moved the over-bed table closer so the plastic glass of water was near enough for her to reach it.

"Don't worry, Nikki. We'll get you back home soon. After all, I've gotta get you back on track with the chemo." His eyes twinkled above the a small smile. "Everyone up in pediatrics is giving me a hard time because I haven't cured you and gotten you back to work there yet. Norm Tischler even threatened to make me come read three stories a day to the kids until I get you back to his department."

Nikki smiled. What a picture that was: stuffy Cyrus Klonter reading *Where the Wild Things Are* to kids who could be sneezing and hacking and mopping their noses on their forearms. "I'll do my best," she told him.

When Klonter departed, Nikki reached for her water and sipped. Five days. That should be by March tenth. When she was admitted, it was still February. Now it was days into the new month. For something to do, to stretch her mind a little, she tried to remember some of the new intern assignments. Patty Yates replaced Spence Austin as the intern here in oncology; Alex and Theo were in ICU; Diane had moved to cardio; Dave and Brian to general med. Couldn't remember the others, or no one's mentioned Lee, Frank and Reuben.

Of most interest to Nikki, Dan had left cardiology for a second stint in the ER, this time alongside Willow. She wondered if they'd get closer. Time working together under the stress of the ER could do that, and Nikki hadn't forgotten Dan telling her he'd once been attracted to that exotic beauty. Even when she kept reminding herself she could trust Dan, still a little voice would insist, *you were wrong about Matt.*

During the week she'd been an in-patient, Dan had visited her at least twice a day, even on his days off when he was trying to deal with all the regular chores of daily life, including those she usually handled, and get a little rest. But when he was on 24 hour duty, he made it a point to drop by whenever he got a meal or break, often bringing her special treats to get her to eat more, since her appetite was worse than ever. That's when he'd sit and talk, sharing about his patients. She didn't have to say much to encourage him.

"I said good-bye to Leo Ackerlynn today," Dan had told her on the last day of February, after his last shift in cardio.

She'd touched his hand, had even managed to whisper, "That must've been hard." You can't help getting a little attached to some of them.

"Yeah. We'd sure hoped he would improve, but he really is locked in, and none of us can perceive any intentional eyeblink communication—though, of course, Gwen's convinced of the opposite."

"All the docs on this case, agree the kindest thing might be to stop working so aggressively to keep Leo alive. His lungs were a mess before the stroke, and now they're worse." Dan sat beside Nikki's bed, considering the case. "Much as his wife and child love him, depend on him, now he's totally dependent on Gwen, and there's little hope that will ever change." "What?!"

"Sort of anyway. At the end of my shift today, I went to say goodbye and found him alone, which doesn't happen very often."

Nikki nodded to encourage him to continue, but Dan was staring straight ahead, as if seeing back into those moments.

"I took his hand the way I usually do and told him I'd be moving to my new rotation but how glad I was to've met him . . . how courageous I thought he was . . . how sorry I was for the way things had turned out. I was straight with him about the condition of his various organs and what kind of care he was going to need long-term and the possible time frame for brain-interface technology in our area. I talked about his wife and his charming daughter, how much they love him. I didn't have to say what was really in my heart: Gwen's going to have a hard enough time continuing to rear Esther on her own. The last thing Gwen needs is to also have a completely helpless invalid at home. I know if Leo has his mental faculties, he's well aware of the burden he is and will increasingly be on his family."

"So I told him," Dan was saying, "I said, 'I've come to believe people can have a profound effect on whether or not they survive. Many people can make the decision for themselves to just let go and let nature take its course.'"

Nikki, though she'd long found this true, was so surprised, she rolled up on one elbow, staring at Dan. "You did?! You told him that?"

He nodded. "And I told him not to worry about anyone else. He wouldn't be letting anyone down. Told him, now was the time for him to do whatever was right for *him*."

Now, a couple of days later, Diane Werner, who was now on cardio and assigned to Ackerlynn, had let Dan know that Leo was still hanging on, and nothing had changed.

Nikki sighed, trying to shake off her feeling of melancholy, and to avoid thinking about her upcoming Amphoterrible treatment. She hoped Dan would bring with him some good ER stories today.

Standing, she gingerly found her slippers and took a small walk up then down the hallway. Returning, she sat again, pillow-propped in her hospital bed catching her breath. She smoothed her pale-green pajama top, which had gotten a little wrinkled while she was wearing the matching robe. Days ago she'd gladly traded a DCH Johnny coat for the sleep set she'd packed. She adjusted her shamrocked headscarf donned in acknowledgement that it was March. Using a little hand mirror, she applied some lipstick in a subtle shade that wouldn't look garish against her very-pale skin.

Certainly many staff members of DCH had dropped by: other nurses; Norm Tischler and everyone else working in peds; Dan's fellow interns who'd become her friends as well; techs, security guards and office staffers; even Hugh Ballard, the Chairman of Medicine came by. Vinny Orlander, that handsome Norseman tech, didn't exactly *visit*, but he'd given her several breathing treatments during her early days and was particularly sweet and accommodating. He even tried to entertain her with some personal anecdotes about his family.

Often, especially during that time she was so sick and could barely register visitors' presence, these were brief visits. But since the Amphoterrible started working its magic, the appearances were longer and included people from the community: her primary physician Josie Bruno, her former landlady at the Six Bucks, Donna Simmons and several people related to Glickman, Glickman and Berkowitz. Nikki'd expected to see Jenna Hudson, who knew all about her pneumonia and hospitalization, but apparently she'd told her boss Sam, so the whole Glickman family dropped in, the kids still ecstatic about going to the Olympics and traveling in Italy. Jed mangled a few phrases in Italian, and young Abby had crocheted yet another cozy cap for Nikki; this one showing increased skill and bedecked with lovely glass beads from Venice. "This one's for dress-up," Abby directed. "So you have to get better so you can wear it out on a date or something." And before she left, she hugged Nikki's neck and whispered, "Maybe *you're* in the hospital now, but you'll always be *my* favorite nurse!" bringing tears to her eyes.

The most surprising visitor—and bearer of the best fruit-and-chocolates gift basket, had to be that nice Linda Ferrante, who'd passed the Saxon vs. Saxon divorce case to Jenna before going to work for the D.A.

Least surprising? Matt Saxon neither came in person nor called—as Dan's parents and brother had done.

Determined to not think about Matt, she continued her mental listing of visitors. Myra Clearly. Julia had brought her mom by the very first day Nikki was feeling better and promised to visit often but she had called to apologize for not coming, saying she didn't feel well herself.

No surprise there. She looked dreadful, more weight than ever, bad color and puffing like a train after the short walk from the elevator. But it was great to see her and the others who had dropped by. Her room was crowded with flower arrangements, get-well cards and cheery little gifts. What a profound sense of being valued by people she cared about. And Dan had remained at the top of that list.

She had much to write in her journal when she got back home. Not just what she'd experienced as a patient this time around, but also new insights in looking back into her past. With the book in the hidden pocket of her tapestry totebag in the back of Dan's closet behind her boxes of extra shoes, she knew she had been overly cautious and paranoid before her trip to the ER and hospitalization. Dan would never stoop to reading her journals. He wasn't that kind of guy. And if she somehow died in the hospital, by the time he found the journals, it wouldn't matter that Dan learned all her secrets.

"But none of that matters anymore," she whispered now, alone in Room 410 and two days away from discharge. "I'm almost well, and I'm going home."

Charissa Carmichael bustled in with a big glass of orange juice graced by a purple bendy straw. "Dan asked me to bring this to you. Apologizes he can't get away on a break right now."

Nikki's perceptions were sharpening again. She could tell something was up by the tension in the senior nurse's whole body and the way she didn't quite make eye contact. "Bad case in the ER?" Nikki asked. Charissa only nodded. "But Dante's all right?"

"Oh, sure." Charissa was already to the doorway. "I've got a full house too. See you later."

Nikki knew something was up and recognized Charissa's 'don't upset the patient chatter. For Dan's sake, she hoped it wasn't a kid.

It was another hour before she got the news, and it was not delivered by Dan..and it was as bad as she feared.

Engrossed in one of the Christmas books from Dan, she slipped away from the reality of the hospital room until a sudden cry snatched her back from the Red Planet: "Oh, Nikki!"

She looked up as Julia Cleary rushed into her room, pale-brown curls quivering around the stricken face, blue eyes terrified and brimming with tears. Nikki thrust the book aside and reached for her friend. "My God, Julia—what's wrong?"

"It's Mom. She had a terrible fall and hasn't regained consciousness yet. I was at home and got the EMTs out there really quick but it is so horrible! Dan's working on her right now in the ER, but I'm just so scared. . . ."

Nikki made room on the edge of the bed and pulled her friend down where she could enfold her in an embrace. Julia collapsed against her, fighting back the tears, for some reason. "I shouldn't be bothering *you,* Nik. You've got enough on your own plate."

At that very moment, Alex Cole, was hurrying down the hallway toward Room 410, chewing his lip till he could taste blood. Beside him, Dan Marchetti matched his stride, equally grim-faced. Such compassion in those brown eyes! When Dan reached over and put one hand on his shoulder, Alex had to look away to keep his own eyes from welling up.

Dan's voice said gently but firmly, "You can do this."

Just outside 410, Alex drew a deep, shaky breath and followed Dan into the room. He saw Nikki first, then Julia, sitting on the other side of the bed, clutching her friend's hand till Nikki winced.

Alex saw Julia's blue eyes look first to his face, then to Dan's, where they stayed while she asked, "Is Mom dead?"

"No," Dan answered. "But she's still comatose." Julia's face relaxed a tiny bit before Dan continued, "I'm afraid she broke her neck at C-2, and there's been considerable damage to her brain tissue and localized bleeding."

"From hitting all those stairs and the basement floor?" Julia's voice began to inch up towards hysteria. Nikki began to rub her back in slow circles to calm her.

"Yes. We did numerous x-rays and called in Dr. Garfield, who administered extensive neurological testing. I'm afraid the prognosis for recovery isn't good. We have no way of knowing yet if there's a hope of her ever regaining consciousness."

Julia, while nodding to show she was hearing and understanding, was biting her lip hard and got a glazed look in her eyes, as if peering inward to call on her inner resources as a nurse; she'd need that as she struggled to push herself beyond the shock and dread of the patient being her own parent. Julia sucked in a breath before speaking. "So, we'll just have to wait . . . give her some time to come around."

"Well," Dan said with reluctance. "There's another factor." Julia's expression froze as she waited. "The damage to the brainstem is permanent. I'm afraid we may have a case of Ondine's Curse. . . ." His voice trailed off almost as a question.

Julia nodded. "Yes, I know what that is. CCHS."

As a peds nurse, she was acquainted with the birth defect of Congenital Central Hypoventilation Syndrome.

"Well, in this case, think of it as central sleep apnea, because the respiratory centers in the medulla are depressed so that breathing stops during sleep."

Alex felt a moment of bizarre detachment, like leaving his body so he wouldn't have to feel its growing distress. Instead, he mused, *how elegant Medicine can be.* To name this condition Ondine's Curse after the German folktale where the water nymph Ondine traded her immortality for the love of a handsome knight who pledged his every waking breath would be a proof of his devotion to her. When she later caught him being unfaithful, she cursed him, saying that he would have his waking breaths, but if he ever fell asleep, his breath would be taken, and he would die.

Julia had asked some question about treatment, and Dan was answering: "Well, she's no longer my patient. We've moved her from the ER to ICU where she could be better ventilated and monitored. Neal Driscoll is in charge, and she's Alex's patient now."

Julia's blue gaze came back to him, and he was pleased to see a touch of relief cross her face. She trusted him as a doctor. Then the daunting thought, does she expect me to magically make her well? Alex swallowed hard and managed to speak for the first time since entering the room. "That's why we both came to talk to you . . . to lay out your options."

That pretty face squinched up in bafflement. "Options? We'll just wait and see how long it takes for her to come out of it, right?"

Even as a nurse, denial was often the first response to tragedy. After all, this was her mother, and she's never lived away from her in all her twenty-nine years.

"There seems little chance of that," Alex told her gently. "Remember, this is the same kind of neck injury Christopher Reeve suffered, plus the Ondine's and—"

"But what're you going to *do* for her?" Julia interrupted.

"If she's to survive at all, she'll be on a ventilator for the rest of her life, so she won't be able to speak or eat properly. Beyond that, she's certainly paralyzed from the neck down."

"But she's still my mom, Alex! She's still inside there."

This was worse than he thought it would be. He could handle her grief, but not this scary statement of fact, said coldly with little outward emotion. As if by saying it, it became the truth. "I'm sorry honey, we don't even know that for sure. In fact, it's doubtful."

Thankfully, Dan spoke up. "I'm afraid the fractured skull has resulted in an acute bilateral subdural hematoma."

"But you're draining it?"

Dan nodded. Alex had seen the burr holes drilled in Myra's skull to allow the escape of the huge pool of blood collecting under the membrane covering the brain, but this part of the case had been under Dan's care, and he continued. "We don't believe the bleeding has stopped yet. If that's the case, or if the swelling continues even after it stops, we'll need to talk about the possibility of surgery to relieve the pressure."

"Of course we'll do the surgery if she needs it. Why wouldn't we?" For a moment no one answered Julia. "You don't mean we shouldn't do anything . . . just let her *die?*" Her eyes were wet, but she still hadn't cried.

Nikki spoke up very quietly, "Myra loved her life, her antiquing and travel, good food and riding horseback. Do you think she'd want to live out that life lying in bed, unable to move or talk or breathe on her own? Hooked up to a machine forever"

Julia broke then, wailing uncontrollably."

Though the two interns remained helplessly silent in the face of Julia's anguish, Nikki continued to stroke the back of her sobbing friend and murmured, "You have to think of what's best for Myra now."

"But how can I let her down? She's done everything for me all my life, she gave up her own opportunities for me."

Nikki handed her the box of tissues. "I know you don't want her to suffer."

Dabbing her eyes, Julia admitted, "No, no, of course not, but I don't know *what* to do for her."

Alex couldn't quite bring himself to say what needed to be said outright, but thank God, Dan could: "If you remove her from the ventilator now, she'll just pass in her sleep."

"I can't do that! What if she's still in there?"

Dan reminded, "It's a bad bleed, and the brain wave readings are pretty conclusive otherwise."

Nikki repeated her earlier question: "And even if there *is* some brain activity, would she want to keep *living* like that?"

Before Julia could answer, Dan spoke again. "I know you said Myra doesn't have a living will, but did you two ever discuss what she might want in this situation?"

"She wants to live!" Julia declared. "We're Catholics. We believe in Life, not murder."

Alex blinked. He and Julia had shared a comfortably ecumenical relationship. Neither openly practiced a childhood faith, except with the family, and no spiritual differences they might hold had ever come into conflict.

"That's not *murder,*" Nikki was protesting.

"It's killing her. That can't be God's will."

Before he could gauge the wisdom of his comment, Alex had blurted out, "But if we don't intervene and she just passes, isn't that truly God's will?"

Julia's complete focus snapped to him, and he'd never seen such an expression of fury and dislike on that sweet face, especially not aimed at him. "How dare you say that! How can you be so cold after Mom's always been so good to you?"

He should have remembered, Anger follows Denial. Half aware of the other voices in the room, Dan talking medical and Nikki reassuring Julia that the three of them supported her and were only trying to help her decide what was best for her and for Myra, Alex found he couldn't speak at all. Tongue frozen, he stood watching the others wondering why he felt like the enemy when all he wanted to do was wipe the pain from her eyes and get her to face reality, the truth.

Having listened to her friends and medical colleagues, Julia told them, "I just can't decide on that right now. And I'm sure not ready to just let my mother leave my life yet. No matter how easy some of you think that should be.." Throwing the last statement towards Alex, she mopped her eyes and blew her nose. "I need to call the family . . . let them know what's happened and hear what they have to say . . . whether they want to come see her."

Alex thought back to those nice-enough people he met in Cleveland at Christmas; siblings who taunted Myra into obesity. More Catholic than Julia it would be easy for them to say 'do everything' but they wouldn't be the ones to take on the burden and expense of caring for a person in Myra's condition. If she didn't place her mom in a care facility or hire someone to take care of Myra at home, she'd have to quit working to do it herself; and if she quit working, it would probably take all of her resources before Myra passed on. She might even lose her house.

"I do want to give her a chance to wake up," Julia was saying. "I owe her that. And some of the family may want to come see her and help me decide." Julia seemed to have reached the third phase, Bargaining to buy time.

Perhaps Julia was struggling now with Catholic guilt over her mom's accident and what she might have to do, but Alex found himself racked with Jewish guilt. How often had he thought back to those magical Christmas days, loving the fact that Myra wasn't there and they had the space and time to really love each other without sneaking around. But he had never wanted this, just hoped that somehow she'd move back to Cleveland. Maybe he was horrible, encouraging her to pull the plug to ease his responsibility as a doctor and to free Julia to live the comfortable life with him that filled his dreams.

Julia was hugging Nikki, wrapped in her arms and crying again, completely ignoring him. He wondered if he was a fool to think they would ever have a life together. Now that he could be the physician who couldn't save her mom…maybe even the one to turn off the machine. One thing he did know for sure. This was the worst day of his life.

CHAPTER THIRTY-SEVEN

Too restless to sleep, even at three am, Nikki Saxon got out of Bed 410-A and pulled the robe on over her pajamas. As her Amphoterrible treatments took hold though the port placed under her skin near her right collarbone, she was free to move around without the encumbrance of dragging an I.V. pole. Decked in the jammies set and matching slippers Dan had brought from home, she'd been eager to travel around DCH and get some exercise.

It was not easy. Already laid-low and out-of-shape from the weeks of chemo, she found the time spent battling pneumonia while lying in a hospital bed had taken a surprising toll on her strength and stamina. She quickly learned she had to pace herself and not go too far afield, thus limiting where she might wander.

Nikki had made a point not to go visit Dan while he was on duty in the ER, even if she knew it wasn't busy at the time. So she, like many other DCH in-patients, took short walks along the hallways, in her case on just those two floors: the fourth and fifth. The third floor below her held little interest: Orthopedics, Rehab, Physical Therapy, Psych. Patients on view there probably appreciated their privacy.

Just one time Nikki went to the staff lounge, completely empty at the moment, and watched a couple of programs on the bigger TV they had there. But toward the end, Dr. Mike Upton came in. When he saw her, he gave her an enthusiastic greeting and sat right down with her for a long conversation, full of mostly his voice. When she was finally able to plead fatigue and a need to get back to her room, Upton had walked her to the elevator, never ceasing his string of self-aggrandizing tales. She hadn't returned to the staff lounge since.

She'd considered visiting patients, but until recently, she hadn't known any patients on those two floors. Of course, all that changed yesterday when Myra Cleary had her catastrophic fall.

On one of her hall-walks, she ran into Vinny Orlander, who knew all the patients in DCH who had respiratory problems, and she asked if Ackerlynn was still in Cardio. "Oh, no," Vinny answered. "His wife had him discharged a coupla days ago."

Incredulous, Nikki blurted, "Don't tell me she's taken him *home* to care for?"

Vinny shook his head. "Even *she* knows she can't handle that. Not with her daughter to care for too. She transferred him to RespirCare over in Oakdale. A vent-farm, y'know?"

Nikki kept from wincing at his reference to a facility where comatose patients were more-or-less warehoused on ventilators. "That's too bad."

"Yeah. Sometimes you just gotta let people go. He couldn't communicate at all—no one except his wife even believed he was trying. That's not life in my book. There comes a point where it seems it stops being care and just becomes torture, know what I mean ?"

"Preachin' to the choir," Nikki told him, as he checked his watch. With a sad nod, they parted and went their separate ways.

Reaching the elevators on the fourth floor, Nikki pushed the *Up* arrow and waited, reflecting on Myra and Julia. She had never heard Julia pull the Catholic card before. Maybe facing the imminent loss of her mother had sucked her back into the solace and structure of childhood convictions.

In front of Nikki, the elevator doors hushed open; she entered and pushed the *5* button. Even the elevator seemed sleepy, taking a long time to respond letting Nikki return to thoughts of that horrible night of Myra's fall. When Julia'd decided for sure she wanted to wait on the relatives, the men left; they were both still on duty upstairs. Julia stayed awhile longer to be comforted by Nikki but when she left, Nikki allowed herself to grieve a bit for the friend she too had lost when Myra fell. Myra had always included Julia in special events and was always kind and nurturing. It was hard to think of the days and weeks ahead, maybe even years, when she would just be a form lying still on a bed with the sound of the ventilator filling the space.

The elevator doors finally closed, and soon the machinery hummed Nikki upward.

Returning to her thoughts, Nikki remembered that it was just after Dr. Klonter had left her bedside today and she was smiling at the news she would soon be going home when she looked up to see Julia in the doorway. Nikki simply held her arms open, and Julia collapsed into that refuge, lamenting but with no tears left. Nikki listened wordlessly to Julia: she hadn't slept; she hadn't eaten; she'd done nothing but fight with Alex, both in the ICU and when he came to her house after his shift. She'd refused to let him spend the night, even though he volunteered to sleep on the couch. She didn't know him anymore, he wasn't who she thought he was!

Nikki wanted to balance her friend's perceptions, say the truths that came to mind: Alex *was* trying to support her and help her to not feel alone; rather than just trying to seize an opportunity to move in with her and keep her from spending all her money! But instead, Nikki stuck to the "There, there" approach, soothing Julia and only softening the edges with phrases like: "Oh, I think Alex wants what's best for Myra . . . and for you."

"Keeping my mother alive is what's best for us both!" Julia flared, and Nikki backed off knowing that if she came on too strong, Julia would push her away, too. And Julia needed her friendship now more than ever. Still, Alex was not the villain here. It was just a tragic accident and Nikki's heart broke for all of them, Myra, Julia and Alex.

When Nikki asked what the relatives had said and when they were coming, Julia admitted no one was able to travel from Cleveland. All of them were either too frail to begin with or down with the flu. Would any come after they were well again? Julia seemed to skate around the question, except to say, "It doesn't look like anyone will be able to come later either." And, apparently, they weren't going to make it easier for Julia, holding fast to their Catholic line about preserving her life at all costs. Funny, Nikki's Catholic parents and visiting priests often talked about not needing to use extraordinary means when trying to make that awful final decision for their critically ill children, but she knew that she wouldn't win that argument against the adamant voices from Ohio.

Julia slowly shook her head; even the usually bouncy curls seemed bedraggled, the blue eyes dull and hopeless. "I just don't know what to do?"

"Who *do* you trust? Dante? Me?"

"Of course. Both of you."

"We're telling you the same things about Myra's quality of life and chances for getting any better."

Julia's tired eyes closed. "I know. And maybe you, all three of you, are right. But I can't think about just . . . stopping treatment . . . letting her be gone. I can't."

So Nikki just hugged Julia and said, "I'm here for you."

Julia sighed in what sounded like relief or gratitude and squeezed Nikki's arm. "I know you are, and I appreciate it so much." A moment later, she sat fully upright, smoothing her clothes and trying to fluff her dispirited curls. "I should pull myself together and go back to Mom. They shooed me out while they gave her some breathing treatments." Julia left Nikki's bed and went into 410's little bathroom to splash water on her face and eyes. By the time she returned, Nikki was on her feet, robed and slippered. Julia halted in surprise. "What's up, Nikki?"

"I didn't get to tell you, but I'm being released tomorrow. Now I'm officially cleared of contagion, I can go visit the ICU with you."

So Nikki had gone, accompanied by her best friend, to see that friend's mom lying in Bed 12 of ICU. Alex wasn't around, and that probably eased the situation a bit. Julia made Nikki take the bedside chair to rest, and Nikki was glad for that.

Myra's bulk filled the bed, and beneath the covers, her chest rose and fell gently according to the will of the ventilator.

Nikki reached out for the swollen hand lying so still. She'd never forgotten Nurse Alice's words, "The comatose often hear what we say to them", and she always treated such patients accordingly, even when there seemed no hope at all. "Hey, Myra," she'd said. "It's Nikki here. Thought I'd return the favor of all your visits to wish me well." Behind her, Nikki had heard Julia begin to cry.

That was hard, Nikki thought now, emerging from the elevator on the fifth floor, which was as low-lighted as the floor she'd just left. The wall clock read 3:16, and all looked quiet in the ICU as she peered through the doors.

She was going to have one last visit with Myra. No matter how long Julia might choose to keep her mom alive, Nikki wouldn't be visiting any medical floors on DCH until long after her chemotherapy was finished and her immune system was healthy again. She couldn't afford to have another bout of infection like this one

At Nikki's touch on the access panel, the doors opened and closed as soundlessly as her fluffy slippers scuffing her inside the unit. She saw Wynnie Hibbert and Tiffany Layne, their backs turned to her, discussing a chart in Room 2.

She slipped past the other rooms and paused outside Number 12. Inside, she could see Vinny Orlander looking at a chart and adjusting the dials for Myra's ventilator. As he turned to leave, Nikki stepped aside, squeezing beside the door so he never even saw her as he exited the room and, waving to the nurses, left the ICU.

Nikki scooted into Myra's room and sat in the bedside chair. She took up the dear woman's hand and whispered, "Hi, Myra.

It's me again . . . Nikki. Didn't have much chance to talk earlier." Nikki wanted to try of her perceptual gifts to see what she could intuit about Myra's condition and prognosis.

She sat and talked softly for a while, following Nurse Alice's perpetually relevant advice, telling Myra how glad she was to've known her, how much she appreciated all the kindnesses, how she'd often fantasized Myra as her own mother. But through all of this, Nikki sensed nothing of Myra there in the room. And certainly no inkling of the will to survive.

Then, remembering Dan's story about his counsel to Leo Ackerlynn . . . that letting go could be the kindest thing a patient could do for those left behind, Nikki decided, not for the first time in her life, to do the same.

"I know you love Julia and your life together, but I hope you'll consider how chained she is by this situation, she's in agony trying to do what's right for you, and how her indecision chains you to these machines. I know you worry about her . . . don't want to leave her alone and unprotected. But I want to tell you, you've raised a strong woman in Julia, and she's more independent than you know. She can have a happy life if she's free. She has Alex right now, maybe permanently, but she needs the chance to find out." Nikki squeezed the limp and puffy hand. "It's okay to let go, Myra. Trust Julia and let her have her life."

CHAPTER THIRTY-EIGHT

He was just drifting asleep when an intense buzzing sound jerked him back. Cell phone! He'd left it on vibrate-only next to his wristwatch on the nightstand. He managed to grab it with his functioning left hand, thumb the appropriate button and whisper, "H'lo?"

"Dan? Sorry to bother you, man. . . ." *Alex.* "But I need a big favor." His tone held a flat-affect quality that'd become increasingly familiar over the past week . . . ever since the Myra Disaster. Alex didn't wait for Dan to respond before elaborating: "I really hate to ask you, but no one else who's off-duty can sub for me today. I've called everyone else. I . . . I just can't go in there today. . . ."

It's been a helluvva week for Alex—no question. First, Myra's fall and emergency hospitalization with the devastating Ondine's diagnosis. Next it was Julia's meltdown in response, her anger focused on Alex, even though Dan and Nikki were also gently suggesting the kindest thing was to just let her mother go. Then, there was the puzzle of Myra's death in the ICU, while Alex was officially on duty, though he was asleep in the on-call room when they notified him. Unfortunately, there was a lot of mystery around the circumstances. The ventilator had been found on the wrong settings, though everyone, Alex, respiratory therapist Vinny Orlander and the nurses on duty, swore fervently they hadn't changed it from what was ordered. Julia, the determination of her mother's fate suddenly wrested from her control, broke down completely. And when Alex tried to comfort her, she turned on him and yelled, in front of house staff and within earshot of patients and their relatives, "You hypocrite! You *wanted* her to die!"

Dan could feel the sick horror of that dreadful scene in his gut even now, a week later.

"Hey, Dan . . ." Alex's voice prompted, "Are you there?"

"Yeah." He kept his own voice low. "Nikki's still asleep."

"Oh. Sorry." Alex drew a shaky breath. "Like I said, I hate to ask. But can you help me out?"

Remembering Alex's stricken face as Julia spat her painful words at him, Dan murmured, "Sure." Glancing at the clock—*7:10*—he added, "You call Driscoll and let him know I'll be in for you. I'll grab a shower and get right on over there."

"Thanks a million, Dan!" He sounded about to cry as he started to say more, but Dan gently cut him off and pressed the *End call* button on his cell.

With great care, he eased his arm from under Nikki. She stirred, reaching for him, and he whispered, "Sorry, Hon. I've gotta go in to work for Alex. You go back to sleep. I'll see you tonight." She made a sound of disappointed acceptance and snuggled deeper into the covers.

He found clean scrubs to put on after a quick shower. Then he bundled up, including not only his heavy coat, gloves and cap, but also fleece sweatpants pulled on over the scrubs trousers, plus the multi-blue neckscarf Mom had knitted for Christmas.

After scrawling a hurried note to Nikki in case she woke without remembering what he'd told her, he hustled downstairs and out into the cold. Immediately, he tucked his nose and mouth down into the scarf's super-soft warmth.

To distract himself as he jogged in the frigid air toward DCH, Dan let his thoughts return to his friends Alex and Julia. How someone in ICU had called the ER and asked if Dan could be sent over because Julia was flipping out, refusing to speak to Alex, and there was no other physician available. Screaming that she never wanted to see Alex again, Julia almost had to be pulled away from Alex as he stood like a statue with a look of despair before he turned and fled the ICU. Dan shook off that memory now. So much for hospital staff being used to death and loss. He shuddered and pushed away the certainty that *someday* he'd have to deal with the deaths of loved ones too. Surely he'd do better than Julia Cleary. *Please God.*

Once Alex had left, Julia dissolved into wrenching sobs. At first, no one seemed sure what to do or say to comfort her.

Tiffany Lange, looking blown away by the drama she'd been witnessing, whispered, "Isn't Nikki Saxon Julia's best friend? Isn't she here at DCH?"

"Just discharged this morning," Dan had told her. "She's home sleeping." Tiffany nodded her understanding that they couldn't call on Julia's best friend. Predictably, it was Wynnie Hibbert who stepped up to enfold Julia in motherly arms and rock her with soothing tones. Got her calmed down enough to deal with the necessities related to her mother's death.

But it wasn't long before Nikki took up the slack. As soon as she'd heard about the meltdown, she'd phoned Julia and become her major support system. Dan had overheard the conversation, how clear Nikki was that Alex was still her friend and that she didn't believe he'd done anything wrong, but that in all other aspects of the situation, she was "there for" Julia 100 percent. Just home from a dangerous illness and hospitalization, still battling cancer and gearing up to resume the rigors of chemotherapy, still Nikki had found an inner strength to help her.

For the first few days, Julia was frequently on the phone with Nikki. Soon she started coming over, after making certain she wasn't likely to run into Alex in the hallway, mostly while Dan was at work.

Rather than depleting Nikki, these contacts seemed to strengthen her. Dan, who couldn't help being concerned, had asked Nikki if it might not be too much stress for her, but she told him, "Don't worry. I'm taking care of myself, and it's the least I can do after all the care Julia and Myra gave *me*. Helps me not feel so sorry for myself, y'know?"

Dan had to admit that so far so good as the inner set of front doors swished open for him. He hurried into the warmth, lifting a hand in greeting to the two security guards conversing there in the lobby, though Greg, his favorite, appeared to be off today. After quickly shedding and stowing his outerwear in his locker, Dan zipped to the cafeteria to pick up a bowl of watery oatmeal with a scoop of granola and some fresh blueberries floating on top. He wolfed it down on his way to the ICU.

As he reached the area outside the doors to the unit, Dan found a crowd of people spilled out from the designated waiting lounge. Normally those waiting because of a patient in the ER or ICU seemed reserved, concerned, perhaps terrified; they tended to speak in low, serious tones. These were young, looking to be in their twenties, and they were swapping tales, in animated voices and with raucous laughter, about someone named Rory. A miasma of cigarette smoke and alcohol fumes hung all about them as if every pore were outgassing last night's partying. Everyone he could see was wearing at least one piece of green clothing. The most solemn, a mini-skirted, willowy girl of perhaps twenty-one, nervously chewing her lip while she tried to laugh at the conversation, even had her hair dyed green. The majority of the other heads were varying shades of red-brown.

One of those heads, this one with disheveled shoulder-length fiery red hair, turned to reveal a puffy male face flushed around the bloodshot eyes. Focused now on Dan, the fellow moved unsteadily toward him, calling, "Hey! You my brutha's new docta?"

Embarrassed to be caught off-guard emptying his oatmeal bowl, Dan answered quite honestly, "I don't know yet. I just got called in. If you'd all like to take a seat in the lounge, I'll find out and come tell you what's going on. Patient's name?"

"Rory Maguire!" said another voice, softer but firm, as a woman in her forties pushed past the threatening figure to smile anxiously at Dan. "I'm Erin Maguire, Rory's mother . . . and Shane's." The resemblance in hair and eye color was unmistakable.

Dan quickly introduced himself, repeated his pledge to return with information, and exited into the sanctuary of the ICU. Brian Callahan appeared from Room Four and gave Dan a sad smile. "Looks like you caught my 3.17 Bullet after all."

Dan followed Brian back into the room, surprised to see Cheryl Herrera, the nurse from his first rotation in CCU. They nodded to each other, but his attention went immediately to Neal Driscoll, the attending, who greeted him with, "Oh, good, you're here. Thanks for coming in for Alex. I'll leave Mr. Maguire to you. I'm needed for a bleeding ulcer in Room Eleven. I'll let Brian fill you in on the case if he doesn't mind hanging around a little longer. . . ?"

Even before Driscoll was gone, Brian began: "Rory Maguire, 25-year-old white male, arrived in the ER at three a.m."

Dan stared down at the unconscious patient, whose breathing was currently supported by a ventilator. His extreme pallor made his freckles stand out even more on his fair skin. His hair, the same flaming red of his mom and brother, was unruly and long, though cut shorter than Shane's

Brian's voice held a note of sad vindication. "Not too hard to guess this all started as a St. Patrick's Day party at Casey's Pub. Anyway, after a drinking contest, Rory and his brother Shane got in a fight over a girl named Bridget. Maybe you saw her out there...green hair and a really short skirt?" Dan nodded. "Brother Shane tried to leave the party with Bridget. This genius here ran after them to the parking lot and decided to stop them by leaping up onto the windshield of Shane's car." Shane slammed on the brakes, and Rory was thrown off, ending up under the wheels." *God!* "Kicker is, Dan, Shane panicked, thought the wheels were still *on* Rory, threw it into reverse and backed up *over* him at a different angle."

As Cheryl prepared to replace the patient's urinary catheter, Dan picked up the chart and scanned the list of injuries as Brian told him, "It was touch-and-go in the ER, but we got him stabilized enough for surgery." *Lung damage, kidney damage, broken ribs, pelvic fracture, shattered ankles, early ARDS. The worst damage to the spleen and liver.*

"You'll see they did the best they could under the circumstances," Brian was saying. "Removed the spleen, but the liver was just torn and soaked in blood."

As Cheryl pulled back the patient's hospital gown and began to thread the catheter into Rory's penis, Dan stepped over and peeled back the huge, white bandage pad taped on the man's abdomen. Startled, he found the wound still open, giving full visibility to dusky-looking liver tissue, tourniqueted with big rubber bands—like toy airplanes when he was a kid—wrapped several times around a clamp. *Gruesome!*

"Lacerated *and* macerated," Brian said. "Miracle they got that bleeding stopped. They didn't suture him up so they could keep that gizmo in place, and so they'd have instant access if the bleeding starts again. You guys'll need to keep an eye on it."

Both Cheryl and Dan nodded. Amazed at the ingenious contraption, he remarked, "MacGyver lives. Anything else?"

Brian shook his head. "Dismal lab values, but you've got the chart. I don't envy you dealing with his family. That brother was sharp with me. Gotta feel guilty as hell, y'know. And *you* don't have the buffer of being Irish."

Dan gave him a grim nod. "You go on. Thanks for staying to fill me in. Better take the back elevator and avoid that crew out there. They're my responsibility now."

As Brian departed, Cheryl threw Dan a dimpled smile. "Good to see you again, Dr. Dan."

"Likewise. I was surprised to see you here."

"I've worked ICU a lot when we're short-handed. With Nikki and now Julia on leave from peds, we've been having to shift around a lot of the nursing staff . . . bring in some new people." Her attention was focused, frowning now, on the catheter she'd inserted. "Did you meet Sondra Kirby, the new hire, out there?"

"No but I'm sure I'll—"

"Damn," Cheryl interrupted—but quietly and not in response to his answer.

Dan could see that though the catheter was properly placed no urine had yet moved into the tubing.

"That's not good," Cheryl muttered. "Not good at all. Guess his kidneys are shot."

No wonder his creatinine level's sky-high, Dan thought as he quickly perused the "dismal" lab values Brian had mentioned. Muscle enzymes also high. Low blood volume. Clotting parameters askew. Not to mention shock, the shredded liver and lungs so bad he has to be ventilated. The guy was a train wreck, and younger than Dan. Clearly he wasn't going to make it.

Pulling his stethoscope from his neck, Dan listened to Rory's lungs. "No breath sounds on the right side," Dan told the attentive Cheryl. "Let's get some chest films, stat." She nodded and went off to make the call. Dan suspected the right lung had collapsed under the onslaught of his conditions and treatment including the ventilator which kept him breathing. His ARDS, acute respiratory distress syndrome, required high machine pressures to force oxygen into his ravaged lung tissues as body fluids seeped into the air spaces. But shock and the very use of those high pressures could cause a lung to collapse, a medical Catch 22.

By the time Dan had finished the rest of his exam, with nothing pointing to a good prognosis, Cheryl was back, and he asked her to put a clean bandage over the open abdominal incision while he went out to update the Maguire family.

Nodding, Cheryl told him, "I think Sondra finally convinced them to wait in the lounge."

It was Erin Maguire who saw Dan first and moved toward him. "Let's sit down over here." He directed her to the two chairs a little way down the hallway outside the sliding doors. They sat and Shane came to stand next to his mom, towering over her but with one huge hand reassuringly on her shoulder. Bridget didn't join them but had edged within earshot. Shane cleared his throat to speak, but Erin Maguire signaled for him to wait, and she asked, "How's my boy doing, doctor?" She managed a tremulous smile. "He's better now, right?"

Dan took a deep breath and looked directly into her green eyes. "I'm sorry, but Rory's condition could not be more serious." Somehow she kept that smile pasted on her mouth, but she seemed to stare right through him as if she hadn't heard or couldn't really comprehend. When Shane made a sound of exasperation, or maybe skepticism, Dan continued before the brother could speak. "All of his systems are shutting down: kidneys, liver, lungs. He has broken bones and undoubtedly some nerve damage. His injuries are quite extensive and life-threatening."

Shane growled something profane, but Dan avoided eye contact, thinking what he would never say aloud, you killed your brother, man—and for what? Winning the favors of a girl with a short skirt and green hair? Behind him, he heard the girl sob and then continue to cry more softly.

Erin's demeanor couldn't mask her fear and worry, but her voice came firmer now. "Rory's in God's hands. He'll pull through!"

"Hell, yes!" Shane blustered. "He's a tough Irish finn. Takes more'n that to kill a Maguire."

Erin patted Shane's hand on her shoulder but kept her gaze on Dan, who tried again to prepare them for what had to be the inevitable.

"Mrs. Maguire, Rory is gravely ill. Though we're doing everything that can possibly be done for him, you need to understand that his kidneys aren't functioning; his liver may not even be salvageable, and he might have a collapsed—"

"Code 99! Code 99—ICU!" echoed suddenly throughout the hospital corridors, just as his own beeper went off: *"Beep, beep, beep* . . . Dr. Marchetti, ICU Medical—stat; ICU Medical—stat!"

Dan leapt up, excusing himself, and hurried back to the unit. Brushing through the doors, he saw a radiology tech with some portable equipment, looking lost. The fellow motioned Dan toward Rory Maguire's room. Just ahead of him, Sondra wheeled the crash cart in next to the bed. Cheryl was already there, checking vitals, and Vinny Orlander stood beside the ventilator, ready to help. Dan's eyes caught the monitor, which indicated a marked bradycardia, a perilously slow heart rhythm.

"BP 60; pulse 35," Cheryl called.

Dan slipped in on the other side of the bed, pulling down his stethoscope. "I take it Darren hasn't done the x-rays yet?"

"No," Cheryl told him. "Just as he arrived, the patient bradyed down, and his BP fell."

Vinny's beeper went off, and he glanced at the message. "Dr. Driscoll needs me . . . ?"

"Sure, go ahead," Dan said and turned his complete attention to his exam, listening carefully to Rory's chest. Still no breath sounds on the right. That lung's gotta be collapsed, and now we must have a tension pneumothorax. Apparently air had escaped the lung itself, pushed out through a tear in its tissues, maybe from a broken rib, and into the pleural cavity surrounding the lung. Trapped there, it forced backward, compressing the lung from the outside while the ventilator kept pumping in more air. And now it's crashing his heart and BP—life-threatening. That pressure had to be released, but there wasn't time for a traditional chest tube. Rory Maguire would be dead before a surgeon could get the proper device installed.

"Tension pneumo?" Cheryl asked.

"Think so." Remembering the lab session on emergency procedures, he called, "Get me a 14-gauge Gelco, and a vacutainer, a hemostat and some saline." Cheryl and Sondra, who'd joined them, were quick to gather the items. Cheryl handed him the Gelco syringe as his fingers marked off the second intercostal space on the right side of Maguire's ribcage. With one firm thrust, the Gelco needle penetrated the chest wall into the lung cavity, followed instantly by an audible rush of air, allowing the collapsed lung to expand immediately. Crisis averted. For the moment at least.

"BP 120 over 60," Cheryl announced with satisfaction. "Pulse 76 regular."

"Cool," Sondra said quietly from just behind Dan. In her left hand she held some of what he'd called for—a hemostat and a one-liter bottle of saline—and in the other, a vacutainer. He took that plastic cylinder from her right hand and quickly attached it to the Gelco, then poured in some of the saline. Air bubbled into the fluid, and the makeshift chest tube was complete. "Never seen that done before," breathed the new hire.

Dan and Cheryl shared a quick smile. Old ER trick. Let's get a surgeon on the honker for the real thing," Dan told the nurses. "And please get this contraption secured with the hemostat and some tape."

As they hurried to fulfill these orders, Sondra handed the hemostat to Cheryl and went off to call Surgery, Dan mused on the ethical issues of saving a life. Maguire hasn't got a hope of survival. But he is so young! Only a matter of time before he succumbs; in fact, his body was already trying to die.

It was one kind of irony for Dan to snatch a man back from sudden, certain death only to preserve him for a lingering certain death. Even more ironic that Rory would've died not from his medical condition, that multitude of grave internal injuries, but because of the treatment itself: mechanical ventilators, without which the patient wouldn't survive.

Did it really make any sense to save him? Not acting had been unthinkable without a Do Not Resuscitate order on the chart. Watching Cheryl carefully tape in place the improvised chest tube, Dan said, "We should probably get a DNR from the family before we have another crisis."

Cheryl looked up at him with her mouth in a grim line. "Yeah? Good luck with that."

As if this discussion had somehow penetrated to the patient, Rory began to stir. His eyes opened then widened in confusion? Fear? No wonder: waking up with a big tube down your throat and some contraption stabbed into your chest. Cheryl had already moved to the pole with its hanging bag of medications, including a sedative that was clearly no longer sufficient. Her eyes turned to Dan for direction.

"Two more milligrams Ativan, I.V." Putting his attention on the patient, he picked up the nearest hand as it began to wave around. "Take it easy, Rory," Dan told him. "You've had an accident, and you're in the hospital." Maguire was trying to speak, grunting nasally with rising panic. "You won't be able to talk right now, because of the equipment helping you breathe." Hard to believe someone so badly injured could still fight for life.

The vocalization stopped, but the body started to thrash on the bed. Dan held onto the hand reassuringly as Cheryl soothed in her best voice, tones of both nurse and mother, "Just try to relax, honey. We're taking care of you." Rory's eyes focused on her. Right about then, the Ativan took hold, and he slid back into blissful unconsciousness.

The makeshift chest tube still looked secure and Dan peeled back the new white bandage to see that the tourniquet was still holding back any bleeding from the liver.

"What the *fuck* ya doin' t'm'brutha!?"

Dan glanced over his shoulder, startled to see the reincarnation of a wild Irish warrior. Looking past the bulk of Shane Maguire, he saw Sondra on the intercom as she called for Security: "Code Blue to ICU! Code Blue to ICU!"

Oblivious to that, Shane continued, "An' what the *fuck* is that in his belly an' sticking outta his chest!?"

Dan moved nearer him. "We had to correct a complication caused by the ventilator, a collapsed lung." Though aware Cheryl was now more sheltered behind him, mostly Dan's changing position was to mask from Shane's view the gruesome condition of his brother's body and the various contraptions piercing it. "He's stable right now, but—"

Shane's face contorted with surging terror, guilt, despair. His huge fists balled threateningly, and his still-whiskeyed breath swept over Dan as Shane bellowed, "You butchers're killin' 'im!" Swinging his arm wildly and unexpectedly, his fist smashed into Dan's left cheekbone with a sickening *thwup!*

Flashes of light amidst the pain. Shoulda ducked was Dan's last thought as he toppled over backwards, unable to stop his fall. Despite his flailing arms, he hit the floor flat out. He actually felt his head hit the linoleum, and bounce, but then he was aware of nothing at all.

CHAPTER THIRTY-NINE

Dan studied his reflection in the bathroom mirror. His rather spectacular shiner, once angry purple and red, now, a week later, had faded to a queasy yellow-green, as had the point-of-impact bruise on his left jaw. He touched that gently. At least x-rays had shown the hairline fracture of his jawbone would heal on its own without surgery and he'd gotten lucky on the concussion, too.

"Good thing you've got that head of thick, curly hair," Nikki'd teased. "Great way to cushion a fall."

Though he remembered his head hitting the floor, Dan had to admit that not much else was clear. His vague memories included lying on a gurney in the ICU with Neal Driscoll and the nurses hovering over him to check his vitals. Beyond them, that Viking Vinny Orlander was sitting atop a prone-but-still-bellowing Shane Maguire while the Mack-truck security guard, Burt Pollard, snapped handcuffs onto Shane's wrists. As Burt and Vinny pulled Shane to his feet and hustled him toward the exit, his mother Erin followed, wringing her hands and crying, "Calm down, boyo; you're in enough trouble!"

After tests, x-rays, and a brain scan to diagnose the severity of the head trauma, there was no question that he was going home. "You've still got a week's vacation coming," Ballard had said. "Take it and make sure you report back to the ER if you have any worrisome symptoms. I wouldn't even let you go home if you didn't have one of our best nurses promising to watch you like a hawk."

Since Dan had walked to work and someone was needed to transport him safely home, Vinny volunteered. Living so close to DCH, Dan was glad the favor didn't take Vinny away from work for very long.

The RT drove very carefully to avoid jostling Dan and then helped him from the car and steadied him all the way up the stairs and to the apartment door. Dizzy, aching, nauseated, Dan was glad for the assistance. Cheryl Herrera had called from the hospital to forewarn Nikki. Thanking Vinny profusely, Nikki allowed him to help get Dan all the way into the bedroom before she insisted, "You can get on back now. I've got him."

She already had the bed turned down for him and some sleep sweats laid out ready. She helped him trade clothing and tumble into that cozy refuge.

Nothing like having a nurse to take care of you, Dan remembered thinking before collapsing into sleep. Buoyed by her new feeling of well-being, and, she said, her delight in having him home with her, Nikki'd cooked delicious soups and soft stews, fruit puddings and other delights delicious and easy on his healing jaw. It'd been a week of nurturing and cuddling that moved their bond into new territory, but Dan found he wasn't quite up for sex yet. Snuggling had to do.

And the sleep. All those wonderful extra hours. Sometimes Nikki would nap with him, but she wasn't needing all that sleep she used to require.

It wasn't like she was focused entirely on him was all the time. Frequent long phone calls from Julia absorbed a huge amount of Nikki's time, and on several occasions, her friend came by to pick her up and take her out for the day, even if it was only just to Julia's own home where she felt terribly lonely, bereft of her mother's company.

When, concerned for Nikki's health and stamina, Dan commented on the "energy suck" Julia had become and how it was too bad Alex couldn't be there to help her through it instead.

Nikki made an exasperated sound. "Yeah, you're preaching to the choir! Julia's convinced herself Alex actually pulled the plug on Myra. I told her I was positive that wasn't true, and she should give him a chance to set things right with her. She says she just can never trust him now."

"Ridiculous."

"I know. But she's not completely rational. If I try to talk her back to reality, she'll cut me out too, and then she'll be all alone, and I'm not convinced she wouldn't try to harm herself."

"Wow. You really think she'd do that?"

"Nurses, like docs, know lotsa ways to take themselves out, and she gets in some pretty dark places. I haven't quite had the nerve to tell her I think she's rejecting life with Alex because, on some level, she doesn't feel she deserves happiness anymore. You know, because of all the guilt *she* feels over her mom's fall and death."

"You mean she's blaming Alex because she thinks *someone* has to be blamed, and she doesn't want to . . . what? process? . . . her own guilt?"

"Something like that."

Dan didn't like seeing Nikki so down-hearted. He took her into his arms and nuzzled her neck. "What made you so smart . . . and wise?"

"Experience," she murmured sadly.

"First day of Spring tomorrow," he'd said, changing the subject and not wanting to press her on what that experience might be. He still felt that she would tell him more of her past life when she was ready. "What shall we do to celebrate?"

Undoubtedly considering how her taste buds would soon be altering back to "chemo askew," Nikki had offered, "I guess it better involve chocolate in some way."

Now, leaving the bathroom to dress for work, Dan noted that the weather didn't seem to know it was now Spring. Deep cold; snow and ice pellets in the wind, but no accumulation to make the bleakness pretty. Tomorrow, March 26 already, rain and drizzle were predicted with the snow and ice.

He ducked into the bedroom to kiss Nikki's ear where it peeked out of the covers. Dan went to the kitchen and downed a dose of ibuprofen with a peach-mango protein shake. When he'd bundled up and had his car keys handy, he slipped out of the apartment and hurried downstairs. It took awhile to warm up the engine of the Accord, but he was soon on his way. It felt strange driving such a short distance but he figured he needed to be careful for a few more days till he was one hundred percent.

Dan's thoughts turned to Alex as he pulled out. His friend seemed still completely demoralized by the Myra Cleary case: treating someone he cared about with such a terrible prognosis; actually *losing* the patient under suspicious circumstances; being questioned at the hospital; being accused of murder, then utterly and unfairly rejected, by the woman he loved, and wanted to care for, with, apparently, no hope of reconciliation.

At least he'd started taking his shifts again. With Dan on vacation from the ER, they'd needed all the interns pulling their weight, so Alex was back in the ICU.

Turning off his motor in the DCH parking structure, Dan shivered slightly. The trauma of being assaulted had faded, but he really didn't want to be anywhere he'd have to overhear any details about how the Rory Maguire case wound down.

Early in his imposed "vacation," Dan had made it clear to his co-workers he just wanted to forget the whole Maguire clan. No, he wasn't suing them; they had enough hardship.

Now, as he arrived in the ER, he was warmly greeted by nurse Gail Sanduski, who handed him a chart. "Hope you're ready to hit the ground running. We're swamped."

Dan headed for Bed One. "Arlen Novotny?" he asked as he noted the fellow waiting for him, seated on the edge of the examination table. *Forty-year-old white male; computer programmer; looks fit but not athletic.* "I'm Dr. Dan Marchetti. What can I do for you?"

They shook hands, agreeing on first names, and Arlen looked a little sheepish. "Sorta feel dumb coming in about this—I'm fine now—but it's happened several times, and it's getting worse . . . scary."

"What exactly is it that happens?"

Arlen pushed his glasses farther up the bridge of his nose. "Out of the clear blue, with no warning, a really loud noise goes off in my head . . . like an explosion . . . *inside* my head."

Dan nodded and began his physical exam. "When does this happen?"

"Usually when I'm just falling asleep; it jerks me awake with a shot of adrenaline . . . sometimes there's a brief flash of lights. This time was the loudest it's ever been."

Dan nodded again. "You were just falling asleep this time?" That would've been around seven-thirty . . . early to be going to bed.

"Yeah. I'd pulled an all-nighter finishing a work project, then worked my regular hours."

"Sounds like stress and fatigue were both factors."

"I'll say!"

"It's happened before, you say. Is it mostly the same?"

"Pretty much the same noise. But this time it was scarier 'cuz my heart was really racing, and I had trouble breathing." Nervously, Arlen asked, "So what's wrong with me, doc? Something serious? Some brain tumor? Just plain going crazy?" and Dan heard the real fear in his voice.

Dan stifled a smile. "Well, it appears that you have what we call Exploding Head Syndrome."

"What!?"

"It's not as bad as it sounds. It's also called 'auditory sleep starts.' You know how you can startle awake suddenly when you're falling asleep?"

"Yea-h-h. So this happens to other people?"

"Oh, sure. Some hear explosions coming from inside their heads the way you do. Some experience screams, loud voices, buzzing, ringing . . . even waves crashing on rocks. The good news is: so far as we can tell, it isn't dangerous."

Huge relief washed over the patient's face. "Whew! What causes it?"

"Again, we really don't know yet. There're theories, but that's all they are at this point. It doesn't appear to be related to epilepsy. However, it *does* seem associated with fatigue and stress, so being watchful of those factors should help you treat it."

"Just finding out it's not dangerous and I'm not crazy will bring my stress way down! But can I make it stop?"

"Some people only experience it once or a few times. Others will have periods where they have several episodes, then it'll remit for stretches of time. Perhaps just tuning back your anxiety and staying well rested will help."

"What if it gets worse?"

"Well, a few people have been treated with clomipramine . . . an anti-anxiety medication."

Arlen shook his head. "That sounds like what my aunt uses for obsessive-compulsive disorder, right? She's had some nasty side effects. I'm not real keen on getting started with antidepressants. I try to keep my medications to a minimum."

"Good man. So your doctor's orders are: Don't worry about your head exploding. Get more rested sleep. Lower your stress . . . try some relaxation exercises, yoga, bio-feedback—even just deep-breathing."

Arlen pumped Dan's hand gratefully. "Thanks so much, doc. That's a real load off my mind." They both laughed at the intended pun.

CHAPTER FORTY

Dan wolfed down a ham sandwich as he drove to PNC Park—the Pirates' home field on the bank of the Allegheny River. Upon arrival, he had no trouble finding the gates of the players' parking lot. He pulled up next to the kiosk and fished out his driver's license, then handed it to the attendant.

"Member of the press, sir?" the young man asked pleasantly as he scanned his list of people who could be admitted.

"No, just a friend of Charlie Monroe."

"Oh, Mr. Monroe!" The grin was quick and obviously genuine. "He's quite a character. Place wouldn't be the same without him. Ah, here it is: Dr. Dante Marchetti." He looked up from the sheet of paper. "You a real doctor?"

Dan smiled and nodded. He was used to the question but always wondered if they thought he was too young or maybe looked more like he taught history than he spent much of his time pounding on chests and palpating bellies.

Perhaps the fellow sensed this. "I mean, are you the doc who pulled Coach through?"

"One of many."

"Well, we're all grateful. Thanks." He leaned inside his kiosk to find the right gate pass, then handed it to Dan. "Park anywhere, and show this to the heavyset guy at the players' entrance. Enjoy yourself."

Dan took the pass with his name hand-written on the front. Dan recognized Charlie's scrawl from the gift he had autographed for Pop's Christmas present. For the first time in a long time—especially the last few days—Dan felt a real surge of excitement and anticipation. Charlie had mentioned the possibility of Dan pitching a few balls on last night's call to set up the logistics.

Dan drove his blue Accord into the smaller parking area and moved in among all the Porsches and BMWs, Hummers and flashy sports cars: players' toys.

Ever since courts ruled in favor of free agency back in the mid-70s, players' salaries had risen astronomically, with multi-million-dollar contracts now commonplace. Even scrubs who warmed the benches were making seven-figures. Many fans resented this especially as tickets started to make a night out with the kids unaffordable to the average Joe. But, as Nikki had once pointed out, PNC was more fan-friendly than most parks. Its general admission tickets still started at nine dollars and it was one of the few venues left that allowed spectators to bring in their own food and beverages.

Dan parked and grabbed his duffel on the passenger seat. He was already dressed comfortably in grey sweatpants and a light blue hospital shirt, but he expected he'd get pretty sweaty and wanted to have dry clothes to change into afterward.. He nervously tweaked the brim of the black Pirates cap Pop had given him.

The guy at the entrance checked Dan's pass and gave him brief, clear, easy directions to the locker room, then told Dan, "I'll call Charlie and let him know you're headed there."

Dan made his way through the quiet corridors of the 5-year-old stadium that'd been built on the footprint of the imploded Three Rivers Stadium.

Soon, up ahead, he could see Charlie Monroe peering around the partially open locker room door. He still looked frail, leaning against the door for support. Dan noted the coach's dusky color. Little gasps accompanied his words: "Hey, Doc! Been waitin'. What kep' ya?"

"A really bad case of conjunctivitis," Dan answered, matching the coach's grin.

Charlie blinked, startled. "Pinkeye?"

"A patient—not me."

"Oh! Good." The old man reached to embrace him then. "Great to see you, Dan!" Despite the body's frailty, Charlie's grip was surprisingly strong . . . for a moment at least.

Purposely keeping the conversation away from medicine or breathing, Dan grinned widely. "Gotta tell you, I'm thrilled to be here."

"Glad," Charlie puffed. "You . . . deserve . . . some fun."

Dan's resolve crumbled. "You feeling okay, Charlie? Breathing okay?"

Monroe jerked a thumb over his shoulder. "My O_2's in here. Come meet the guys. Told 'em all aboutcha." sending a ripple of nerves through Dan. as he wondered just what the old coach had said to the players. Inside the door was parked a gleaming, red-and-silver power chair—boldly emblazoned "Scalawag." In a basket between two saddlebags, Dan saw a compact portable oxygen tank in its cylindrical carry-bag with a padded shoulder strap. Charlie went to his scooter but didn't sit down or even drape the tubing of the nasal cannula around his face. He just held the tiny twin nozzles against his nostrils and, eyes closed in relief, breathed in the flow.

As Dan waited for Charlie to breathe more easily, he could hear a cheerful rumble of voices, punctuated by metallic locker-door noises, from around a nearby corner. He knew the guys were setting up but he didn't hurry Charlie.

When the coach's color was a little better, he sighed and opened his eyes, then deftly slipped on the shoulderbag, bandoleer-style, and fitted the cannula properly around his face. He gave Dan a resigned and wistful smile but saved his breath, merely slapping Dan on the back as he guided him toward the team.

Around that corner, Dan got a quick impression of a rather crowded space with some thirty strapping lads pulling clothes off and on. Some sat on cloth-backed, fold-up wooden bench seats to put on their heavy socks and cleated shoes. Others were still slipping into the plain, white home-team uniforms. Even more home jerseys, plain and pinstriped, hung with grey road uniforms and street clothes. The uniforms were spanking clean, and many of the players seemed fresh from the showers; still the place smelled like a locker room. No mistaking that.

The men were ribbing each other and predicting how the practice—and later game—would go. They'd lost their first home game against the Dodgers but squeaked by them 7-6 last night; they sounded pretty confident about winning tonight's game.

This wasn't his Yankees, but Dan recognized many of the faces from news coverage and the local paper and he'd been following more closely since Charlie's hospital stay.

But all the activity and boastful, competitive banter ceased as soon as Charlie and Dan came into view. Every player focused complete attention on the intruders.

"Gen'lemen," Charlie said, "meet my doc, Dan Marchetti. He's to blame for keepin' me alive so I can give y'all hell an' keep kickin' your butts when I feel like it."

The players laughed in an easy way that helped loosen the muscles in Dan's neck. Some nodded or spoke or lifted a hand in greeting. Dan nodded back and lifted his own hand in group acknowledgment. Monroe continued, still conserving his breath. "Dan's jus' gonna hang out, shag some flies . . . maybe strike summa you out in batting practice."

Dan could see the spark of interest, perhaps amusement, at this challenge. "Welcome, Dan." A player off to his right, already fully dressed and ready for the field, stepped up to offer his handshake. Dan recognized the close-cropped red hair above a smiling face full of freckles. *Trey Hartmann!*

"Hey, thanks. It's an honor to meet you, Mr. Hartmann."

The kid was young enough and still new enough to it all that he blushed. "Gosh, call me Trey! I don't have to call you Dr. Marchetti, do I?"

"No, no. Dan will do just fine." Liking him right away, Dan was surprised at the young rookie's physical presence. He looked more like he belonged in the NFL than the major league. His shoulders and chest were so heavily muscled that Dan had no problem guessing he must spend countless hours in the weight room.

Charlie stepped over and clapped Trey on the shoulder. "It's easier to ride my scooter the long way around. Take care of my doc here, okay?"

"Sure!" Trey actually seemed enthused.

Charlie surveyed Dan's outfit. "He's got a cap. Rustle up some shoes for him. I'll meet you guys on the field."

A moment after the old coach left, Dan could hear the motor of the mobility chair around the corner.

"What shoe size, Dan?" Trey asked, walking to his locker.

"Ten."

"Well, I'm a $10^1/2$. Close enough." He held out a pair of shoes. "Here. Use these spares."

Dan thanked him, took the footwear and sat down on a bench, setting his duffel on the next seat. By now, the last of the players were leaving, headed for the field. Quickly, Dan exchanged his shoes for Trey's, thankful that he was wearing thick socks.

When Dan stood up, ready to go but unsure what to do about his duffel, Trey pointed to it and said, "You can leave that anywhere. It'll be safe."

Trey opened a pack of chewing gum and hurriedly shucked three sticks and stuffed them into his mouth. He offered the pack to Dan, who gratefully settled for just one piece.

Jaws too busy to speak at the moment, Trey motioned for Dan to follow him through a door leading to the dugout and from there onto the PNC playing field. The almost-forgotten sound and sensation of walking in spikes washed Dan with a sense of unreality.

Dan felt he had been dropped into a fantasy world where somehow he was actually walking out onto a major league field wearing the shoes of the league's hottest rising star. Anxiety rippled through him all over again. What if he screwed up? Really bad? Then again humiliation would be a small price to pay for an experience he'd be telling his grandkids about!

Emerging from the dugout, Dan felt momentarily disoriented, finding home plate to his right instead of his left, where he'd expect to see it. Nikki had told him it was a purposeful move by the owners to sit the home dugout along the third-base line instead of the first, assuring that the Pirates, instead of the competition, would be inspired by the view of Pittsburgh's impressive skyline.

Trey grabbed some equipment, flipped a glove to Dan, and back-pedaled some distance away before he tossed a ball to him. By the time a space of seventy feet had opened between them, Dan had caught the ball and smacked it back to Trey.

The new hope of the Pirates grinned, but cautioned, "Take it easy, Dan. Otherwise, your arm'll be super sore tonight—and worse tomorrow!"

Dan easily caught the soft tosses and returned them, still incredulous that he was there at all; much less working with Trey Hartmann. Watching Trey watching *him*, Dan couldn't help wondering what Trey was thinking of him and how dorky he must look with his face lit up like a kid's at Christmas.

"You've played ball before?" Trey called.

"Some. My dad's a high school coach." Dan was hoping that the question came because he didn't look completely awkward returning the throws.

Tossing another soft one back, he marveled again at the fluid motions of this professional athlete born to the role and destined for greatness. The rookie sensation, brought up from the minors after only two years, during which he'd led Triple A in wins and earned-run average, was now being touted as another Nolan Ryan. His fastball, clocked at ninety-eight miles an hour, had so much movement that TV cameramen reveled in following struck-out batters as they returned to their dugouts, most seen still shaking their heads in disbelief. According to Nikki, the Pirates were hoping Trey could be the base of their rebuilding program, but he couldn't do it alone, or overnight. After last night's win, the team was still only standing at 2-7.

And he was sure management was delighted to have a good-hearted, good-natured, down-to-earth Nebraska farmboy; a perfect antidote for all the ills of baseball: salary wars and temper tantrums, drunk-driving and sexual misconduct, scandals over gambling and the use of steroids and recreational drugs.

"Let me see you come over the top more, Dan."

He nodded at Trey's instructions and began throwing with more of an overhand motion. This seemed to cause less strain on his arm, while adding more control. Too cool!

After a few more throws that allowed Dan's muscle memory to embed this new lesson, Trey tossed the ball and glove to one of the eager-to-serve batboys. "Let's do some running," he called, waving for Dan to follow.

Taking laps on the 18-foot-wide warning track along the outfield fence, Dan saw Charlie Monroe zipping around the field in his Scalawag, monitoring other players engaged in various forms of exercise. Another coach was working the fielders by hitting "fungos" to them with a longer and thinner fungo bat.

Dan put his attention back on his laps: running side-by-side with Trey, not competing, just taut muscles propelling them with efficiency and grace. The joy of it flooded Dan, even as the sweat began to bead and trickle and flow. The hospital shirt clung to his chest and back, but the breeze cooled the dampness. He revelled in the mindless moving of his muscles, so different than the way his body moved between the drama and tedium of his hospital work. God, he had forgotten how much he loved sports and running.

As they closed the next lap, Charlie drove over to meet them. Trey and Dan halted together, as if synchronized, faces flushed, chests heaving, adrenaline surging.

Charlie tried to look stern, but there was no mistaking the affection in his tone: "Well, ladies, hope you're not all tuckered out from that little stroll?" Since he still wore his oxygen side-pack, his breathing was better, his speech more fluid. "Time for you to pitch, Hartmann."

Grinning, Trey tugged the bill of his cap to them and loped off to the mound. There he positioned himself behind the L-shaped mesh screen that would allow his pitching arm a clear field but protect him from any balls batters might be lucky enough to hit back.

As Dan accompanied the scooter back toward home plate, he saw another of the kids who helped with equipment, a towheaded lad of perhaps thirteen, dash out to hand Trey a mitt, then hurry back to help wherever he could. Trey donned and flexed the southpaw glove, then chose a ball from the tall bin on his side of the screen. "Batter up!" someone yelled.

"You go on to the batting cage," Charlie told Dan. "I gotta go sort something out." He whipped the Scalawag around and zoomed off toward two players who'd been practicing together but now appeared to be growing increasingly argumentative.

When he reached home plate, Dan went to stand behind it, outside the steel-mesh batting cage that'd been rolled in to capture all unhit baseballs until they could be collected at the end of practice.

As Dan watched, Trey's first batter, outfielder Ricky Mossberg, stepped up and took his stance for the first pitch.

Unhurried, Trey began his windup. His physique reminded Dan of the great Jim Palmer, the Baltimore Oriole's ace for many years. Same pitching motion and great assortment of pitches: hard fastballs, sliders and change-ups. Maybe Trey would end up doing underwear ads, too, Dan chuckled to himself as he breathed in the heady air of a professional ball team.

Trey's tosses were straight and understated with no grandstanding, so the batters, Mossberg and those following him, were able to get their swings in. After all, it was *batting* practice.

But in the meantime, Trey's arm was also getting the warm-up and stretching it needed. Winning teams are built around a solid pitching staff. Good, lively young arms—that's what scouts like Charlie were always seeking out. In fact, the average major league team employed 15–20 such headhunters to scour leagues across the States, the Dominican Republic and Mexico seeking bona fide major league talent. And it was every scout's dream to find a Tom Seaver, a Sandy Koufax, or a Trey Hartmann.

Dan recognized the Pirates' pitching coach, William—"call me Dex, not Willie"—Dexter studying Trey from the sidelines. "Two more batters," Dex called to Trey. "Then we'll give someone else a shot." With his thick white mane and deeply tanned face, Dex typified the image of the ex-major leaguer, addicted to the game of baseball, using his teaching skills in order to stay connected to the game.

Now the team's third baseman, Kieran Poole, took a bat from the tow-headed kid and assumed his stance in the batter's box. He had the confident, almost cocky, manner Dan remembered seeing him display on television. Understandable given his ninth year in the majors and vying for the batting title most years. Each pitch Trey threw him was neatly deposited over the leftfield fence or lined in the gaps in the outfield, sure doubles or triples. His last hit was a wicked line drive that caromed off the leftfield wall with a sound like a cannon-shot when it left the bat. All motion stopped on the field; every head turned.

Poole dropped his bat matter-of-factly and headed for the warning track to begin his compulsory wind sprints.

Shortstop Randy Percado stepped up next and struck on two pitches and singled on most of the others.

Dan saw Charlie putt up to Dex . Dex nodded and called to Trey, "One more pitch, Hartmann."

"Yeah!" Percado yelled. "No more meatballs. Show me your best stuff!"

Trey grinned delightedly and sent a blistering fastball, which the would-be hitter swung on and missed by a mile.

As Dex called, "Careful what you wish for, Percado," the vanquished batter just shook his head wryly and grabbed his mitt to go shag fly balls. But first, he visited Trey on the mound. "Nice heater, rook. I'm sure glad you're on *our* side!" They high-fived each other and went their own ways: the shortstop to the outfield, and Trey dropped to the grass behind the mound to do his customary hundred sit-ups.

Still leaning comfortably with his arms resting on the metal crossbar of the batting cage, Dan wondered with interest, who would be next up feeling he could watch this for hours.

"Hey, Marchetti!" Dex shouted. "You're up!"

Holy shit! Dan snapped upright, suddenly sweating again.

And there was Charlie, grinning like a kid behind his O_2 cannula. "Yeah, hustle it! An' try t'keep from throwin' into the stands—those balls aren't cheap, y'know."

Heart pounding, Dan reached out to take the mitt the tow-headed batboy had run up to offer thinking what the hell had he gotten himself into! This was real baseball and these were pros who didn't have time for amateur hour! What would Pop be thinking if he was watching him now. Proud or just waiting to throw an arm around his shoulder and tell him that failing at this level was OK, too, as they walked out together.

He'd forced his legs into motion so they'd take him, despite his hesitation, out to the mound. Ahead of him, two more bat-boys were wheeling the L-screen around to accommodate his right-arm pitching instead of Trey's left. Beyond them, Trey paused at the top of one of his sit-ups to grin encouragingly. "Hey, just relax. You'll do fine."

"Oh shit!," Dan mumbled, turning to position himself on the rubber. He still couldn't bear to look up at the batting cage yet. He heard Dex call for Odell Shaw to bat.

"Do your thing, Dan!" Charlie urged. "But no spitters or knuckles, now—hear?"

Dan stood holding the ball, head down, trying desperately to control the trembling in his hands. The blob of gum in his mouth had lost every vestige of spearmint and seemed to only be making his mouth drier; all he could think to do was swallow it. Still he couldn't seem to make himself move.

All of PNC Park seemed to ripple with tension. No wonder. Two-and-seven wasn't an illustrious showing for the season so far. This team had a lot of work to do, and he was holding up the train.

Steeling himself to begin his windup, he lifted his eyes, ready to confront his opponent, the pitcher-now-batter Odell Shaw, and had to blink at the unexpected sight. The player was garbed from mask to shins in a catcher's protective gear.

Dan felt his mouth fall open, and Charlie guffawed, slapping the handlebars of his Scalawag. Other players laughed too, but good-naturedly, inviting Dan into the joke. He managed a smile and tweaked the brim of his Pirates cap to salute Monroe. Dan could feel that tension ease, across the ballpark and throughout his own body. Maybe he could best serve the team as comic relief if it turned out being a high school phenom was too many years ago!

Dan drew a deep breath, squared his shoulders with home plate and began his windup.. Even as the ball left his fingers, he winced, fearing the worst. The ball smacked the dirt at least two feet in front of home plate, and the batter had to jump to avoid being struck by the bounce.

Humiliation swept through Dan like a tide and, unfortunately, made him try to correct the situation by immediately throwing another pitch. This one sailed over Shaw's head by almost a yard. Could he make a bigger ass of himself? He expected catcalls and laughter, but the players remained silent, probably as embarrassed for him as he was for himself, he thought.

"Settle down, Doc," Dex yelled, but not unkindly. "Don't aim. Just throw it!"

If only it were that simple. But then again, what kind of fool wouldn't listen to a professional pitching coach? Dan released a great sigh and followed Dex's advice.

That next pitch was perfect: over the middle of the plate with good velocity. The batter swung and fouled it off. Again and again now, Dan delivered the balls, each successive one crossing the plate with significant zip and movement. The batter soon shed the once-humorous protective gear, acknowledging the legitimacy of Dan's throwing arm, and was now earnestly dug in at the plate, awaiting each pitch with a face that showed deep concentration.

By the time Dex called for the next batter to succeed Shaw, many other players had gathered around the batting cage, and Dan liked to think those were admiring expressions they wore.

"Hey, Doc!" Trey's voice called from behind him. "Those're *some* 'aspirins' you're handing out."

Dan turned to see that ever-ready grin with the perfect teeth destined for a Wheaties box as well as those underwear ads. "They're a little choppy—"

Finished with his sit-ups, Trey rose from the turf and came to stand nearer Dan. "Yeah, but your pitches're powerfully thrown, and your control is really impressive. Just try to find your rhythm. I'll catch ya later." He moved on to go do some more pre-game stretches.

Dan resumed pitching with a new batter and soon settled into that rhythm he sought. Sweat drenched his hospital shirt, making it plaster itself to his torso. His arm began to tired but the thrill was there again making him wonder what would have happened after high school if he had tried to do this professionally. Could he have figured out a way like Covington to have both medicine and baseball? Was that even possible in today's game? Catching himself with a rueful shake of his head, he cut short the fantasy of warming up for his start that day and tried to just be in the moment. And he it wouldn't surprise him to find out Charlie, bless his heart, had arranged this bit of pitching success, told the hitters to go easy on him, just to give him a once in a lifetime thrill…and it was!

But it was also time to get out of the way of these professionals getting ready to do their jobs. Dex was changing batters again, and Dan caught his eye, tapped his wristwatch—which also reminded him he had to get back to DCH in time for Clinic. Back to his day job!

Dex nodded and called Odell Shaw to pitch next. Dan shook hands with this former opponent as they passed. Odell gave him a big grin and a smack on the arm. "You got a real gun there, Doc." Dan thanked him and moved on. Hoping to slip out without disturbing or delaying the practice further, Dan raised a hand to all the nearby players and said, "Thanks, guys!" To Dex, he said, "Please pass along my gratitude to all the other guys too, okay?"

"Sure." Dex started to say something else, but his cellphone rang, and he apologized, "Been waiting for this call. Take care." As Dex moved away for more privacy, Charlie drove up on his scooter. His lips were a little blue again, though he was wearing his O_2, and his face was completely solemn. He was staring at Dan as if he had never seen him before. Or were his lungs suddenly worse? "You okay, Charlie?"

"Jeez-Louise, Danny. How come you never told me about that howitzer arm of yours?"

Was he serious?. "I told you I'd played ball in school. I was always best at pitching." Dan shrugged. "I just never thought of continuing with it in any serious way."

"Why the hell not?"

Dan shrugged again. "When it came to choosing a career, I couldn't see baseball as more than a great game, a diversion. I sure didn't want to coach teens like my pop, and my parents always wanted me to be a doctor. Heck, *I* always wanted to be a doctor. I got recruited to a couple of mid-major schools but not on full scholarship and I knew I couldn't both play ball and get the grades I needed for med school. Turned out to be an easy decision.

Dan lifted the bottom of his shirt and mopped the perspiration from his face to hide the sudden embarrassing flush as, just for a moment, he considered what it would mean to be in front of a crowd, Mom and Pop sitting close to the field, Jerry shouting his name and roaring with the fans *Marchetti, Marchetti* as he held the runner on first before turning to face the opposing team's slugger. Just for a moment. "Thanks, but—"

"I know." Charlie waved a dismissive hand. "You've *got* a job. A damn important one. I should know."

Removing his cap to let the wet hair cool his head, Dan felt his world shift back from what ifs to here I am. "Speaking of which. . . . I better grab a shower and get on my way."

"Another minute? Got something for you." Charlie turned to pull a black cap from one of the cart's saddlebags and hand it to Dan. "You earned that today."

Dan took it and saw it was much like the one he'd returned to his damp head, except it had a red underbill. Charlie flicked that with his fingernail. "Pirates were the first team ever to have that. We only wear these with the home team alternate uniform. This cap's special, from 2001 when we opened PNC Park looking forward to our 'New Era in Baseball.' It's historic."

Dan actually felt tears in his eyes. "Hey, thank you so much. Won't put it on till I shower. But I can't thank you enough for all of this, Charlie." He leaned down to embrace the old man noting how frail he was beneath his Pirate windbreaker.

The coach seemed choked up too, and started rummaging in his saddlebag again. "Here're your tickets. Two for Tuesday night, May 9th, right?"

"Oh, yeah."

"And there are a coupla passes so you can come see us before the game."

"Wow. Thanks a million. Being here has made my week, my year—. My dad's not gonna believe it!"

"Good, good," Charlie interrupted, blinking rapidly and seeming eager to end the long goodbye. "You better get on now." With that, he zoomed off to chastise some player he'd seen not giving a full effort.

"Take care of yourself!" Dan called after him, and the coach waved back over his shoulder.

Dan glancing quickly around the field, wanting to thank Trey and wish him well for tonight's game but spotted him deep in discussion with Dex. Not wanting to interrupt, he headed to the dugout and locker room for a much needed shower.

When freshly showered and dressed in the warm-up suit he'd brought in his duffel, Dan sat in the otherwise-empty PNC locker room, pulling on clean socks and then his Nikes. Lacing up his own shoes he marveled again that he had been pitching to real honest to goodness professional ballplayers while wearing Trey Hartmann's spikes.

Speaking of which, he leaned down to lift the loaner pair, wondering what exactly to do with them. Didn't seem considerate to just leave them there on the floor like cast-offs. He noticed the door of Trey's locker was slightly ajar. He'd stick them in there and leave a thank you note for the young southpaw.

He found a pen in the outer pocket of his duffel but no paper—except the holder for the tickets Charlie'd given him and no way was he using that. Glancing around, he saw a clean paper towel on another bench and quickly dashed his message: *"Dear Trey— Thanks so much for the loan of your shoes and showing me such a good time. Great meeting you. Best of luck for a terrific season! Dan*

After tucking the note into the laces on one shoe, Dan opened the locker door even wider to place the pair inside. Dan had to chuckle. Below the shelf jammed with books, toiletries and such, the main part of the locker sprouted a tall tangle of unkempt papers, unwashed clothes and many unidentifiable items. No wonder the door didn't latch.

Maybe it was best to just close the door and leave the shoes as originally planned, he was thinking but already in those moments of deciding, the mass had begun to shift, leaning against the hinges so the door now couldn't close more than half way.

Dan tried to reshuffle the mess, which only made it accelerate its slow-motion avalanche toward the floor. Embarrassed, Dan dropped into a squat, his hands trying to thwart the tide . . . failing. What if someone came in and caught him rooting around in Trey Hartmann's locker like some kind of stalker?

Dan scrambled to make things right, but getting that stuff back into the locker wasn't easy. Especially since a number of slick magazines increased sliding capability, and odd-shaped items—another mitt and an extra jockstrap—made stacking anything precarious. Attempting to preserve Trey's privacy, even while desperately collecting and realigning the scattered papers, Dan tried not to read anything written. But a word suddenly seemed to leap out at him.

Ophthalmology. Dan couldn't help it; his attention snapped to the pale blue business card paperclipped to a yellow physician's referral form. *Huskers Ophthalmology Partners,* announced the blue card, *Catherine G. Becerra, MD, eye physician and surgeon.* The address noted a town in Nebraska Dan had never heard of before. The referral was to a neurologist in that same town, recommending an MRI of the optic nerves.

Dan froze, unable to look away and, for a long moment, unable to even think. Then he felt that eerie ripple of déjà vu. In the clinic, it had been Rita Rice getting this referral. Could Trey be headed for MS!?

"Dan?" a voice called as someone approached from the dugout. Trey's voice. "Y'still here? Wanted to run in an' say goodbye."

Dan didn't move. No sense trying to hide what'd happened. Trey came into view with that signature grin of his, though his expression fell into almost-comical bafflement. Dan started apologizing, trying to explain about the shoes and the locker hinges.

But Trey's eyes were riveted on what Dan held: the blue card clipped to the yellow paper. The grin vanished, and his fair complexion blanched, accentuating every freckle.

"I wasn't trying to pry," Dan insisted, lifting the paper he held. "It just caught my eye."

Trey glanced around as if making sure they were still alone. "You're a doctor," he said, coming to sit across from Dan. "Can I speak in confidence?"

"Absolutely."

Trey took it, set it aside on the bench seat, but still didn't speak. Instead, he began to help Dan try to get his mess layered back into the locker. Dan worked in silence, grinding his jaws together to keep from asking questions. Together they managed to get the locker contents stabilized and the door completely closed. Like an old man, devoid of the boundless energy that had seemed to radiate from him, Trey removed the referral sheet from the seat before lowering himself to sit again.

As Dan took the seat beside him, Trey stared down at the referral. "Wondered where this got to." He tried, unsuccessfully, to chuckle. "I'm not the tidiest person in the world." He sighed. "Guess I'm glad it was you who found it instead of someone else." He still looked pale, and his hands trembled.

"Are you okay?" Dan asked.

Trey nodded, still looking at the paper instead of Dan. "While I was home off-season, I started having trouble with my right eye. Things got blurry all of a sudden, and it hurt something awful. Scared the shit outta me, so I went to my hometown doc—the one who delivered me. He sent me to this ophthalmologist, and *she* said it was optic something—inflammation of the nerve."

"Neuritis," Dan supplied quietly.

"Yeah, something like that." Trey went on, "Said I should see this neurologist, get an MRI, because in healthy people my age, this's often an early sign of multiple . . . scle—" He couldn't seem to get the word out and settled for, "MS."

Off-season was months ago, yet Trey still had the referral, Dan thought but said, "What'd the nerve doc say?"

Trey really avoided eye contact now as he admitted, "I never made an appointment."

"You still having symptoms? Blurred vision . . . eye pain?" Dan kept his voice calm and low while wondering how in the world was he managing to play ball—and so well?

"Not really. Seems to've cleared up." He looked at Dan with hopeful, but anxious, eyes. "So I guess it's not serious after all. Right?"

"Maybe," Dan answered. "I hope so. Glad to hear the eye's better, but I gotta tell you, I think you should still follow up."

"Why, if everything's fine? Why risk the media finding out about it now I'm on their radar for the season?"

"The ophthalmologist's right. Optic neuritis can be caused by lots of things—some more serious than others and some not so serious. The MRI and neuro consult could rule out MS. Then your docs can look for some other cause so *that* can be treated. What if you have Lyme disease? You'll sure wanta get *that* treated before it causes too much damage." Trey nodded, looked more hopeful again. Dan almost hated to continue. "But if it *does* show a possibility of MS, a physician should be monitoring the situation."

Trey gazed dejectedly at the floor. "If it *is* MS, I don't want to know."

Dan had already run into many people who delayed a visit to the doctor because they believed a truth unknown couldn't hurt you. Which often meant they delayed treatment way past the 'easy stage' or had spent needless time worrying when a benign problem turned out not to be the cancer they feared. Still Dan asked, "Why's that?"

"If I can't see . . . can't run . . . my career is over before it really gets started."

Picking up on this, Dan asked, "You having difficulty running? Or any other symptoms with your arms or legs?"

"No, but that's what'll happen to me eventually, right?"

"Trey, you're putting the cart before the horse. First thing is to rule out everything else. And even if the eye symptoms *are* related to MS, it could be years before there're any other readily observable signs. Besides, there're several different types—all quite variable. MS wouldn't necessarily stop your career, especially not right away. The important thing is to find out what's going on so you can take care of yourself." Trey made a face like a little kid tired of being lectured but Dan went on. "Bottom line: ignoring it, whatever it is, won't make it just go away."

Trey sighed. "I know."

"Have you talked to the team doctor yet?"

"God, no. He's best buds with one of the owners, and I just don't trust him not to out me. Y'know, if the guys upstairs find out, they might not want to take a chance on me."

Dan well understood the sensitivity of the situation and why Trey wanted to keep it quiet. But he was a doctor as well as a fan and he needed Trey to see him as a help not a hindrance. "Look, Trey, I understand you don't want to deal with more doctors and tests right now, but if you need to talk, off the record, just man-to-man, don't hesitate to contact me."

He looked directly into Dan's eyes for the first time. "I'd like that. Thanks." He glanced up at the wall clock. "But right now I better get back out there before someone comes looking for me."

"Yeah, I gotta get going too." Dan grabbed the paper towel note from the shoe laces and scribbled his home and cell numbers. "Call me anytime."

They both rose. "Charlie says you have tickets for the May 9th game. Maybe we could get together for a coupla brews around then."

"I'd like that." They shook hands, and the gesture turned into a back-slapping hug. Dan hefted the duffel strap to his shoulder and snugged his new, red-underbilled Pirates cap onto his still-damp hair. Maybe the talk had helped, maybe not but Dan felt he had taken it as far as he could for today.

They parted, and Dan hurried out. It was a hard drive home. At first, he couldn't stop thinking about Trex. Was it his imagination or did everyone around him seem ill? Helpless and frustrated, Dan forced himself to focus on something else.

What better than the early part of his PNC experience: the sheer joy of physical exercise among professional athletes treating him with great respect.

Soon the vivid memories spiked Dan's adrenaline all over again. *What* a rush that was! Unforgettable. He couldn't wait to tell Pop and Jerry.

Hands quivering on the steering wheel, he recalled how effortless and easy the pitching had felt. Sure tomorrow his arm and shoulders would be screaming but worth every throb. And it couldn't've come at a better time. Losing Joe Bonfiglio two days ago; Nikki still in chemo and completely distracted by Julia Cleary's downward spiral and best friend Alex seeming on the verge of his own meltdown. And now this situation facing Trey.

Dan jerked his thoughts back to the joy of playing ball, of the life of those men with whom he'd just shared the day and imagined again what it would feel like making a living playing a game! How different that was from the working lives of his peers toiling in the day-to-day anguish that existed inside any hospital. He wondered, not for the first time, if he was really up to it all.

CHAPTER FORTY-ONE

At Scott Bradden's wide gesture toward the settee across from his desk, Linda Ferrante sat down, crossed her long legs comfortably and smoothed her cerise wool skirt. She watched him study her shapely legs, his mild interest an amused blessing rather than an offense, as he lowered his well-tailored self into a leather receptacle that was more a throne than any mere chair: a standout piece of furniture; even in this room, richly upholstered in deep chocolate brown with tons of gold and brass accents.

His eyes came up to meet hers. He skipped any greetings, asked if she was finding her position as an Assistant District Attorney interesting and noted, "I'm sure it's an adjustment from what's primarily a defense firm."

She nodded and saw the subtle change in his body language as he switched to the real business-at-hand. Clearly small talk, or any discussions not centered on him was superfluous. Tapping manicured fingertips on the lone olive-green folder lying atop his desk, he let his gaze pin her in place. "I have a special case I'd like to entrust to you. It's rather delicate," he continued. "May be nothing at all. But then again. . . ."

She waited with more curiosity than she would've predicted. She made sure nothing in her demeanor betrayed her impatience or eagerness for something more interesting than the long-winded depositions waiting on her desk. She waited with all the cool aplomb she could muster.

Suddenly he grinned. "Yes, I think you're just the person for this little project." Still he didn't open the folder, though his fingers caressed it. "I believe we may have a serial killer at Deerwood Community Hospital."

That made her blink. "At DCH?"

He seemed pleased he'd startled her. "Yes. A series of suspicious deaths going back some nine months or more."

"What do you mean *suspicious?* People *die* in hospitals all the time."

"Granted. And, admittedly, they were all people in dire circumstances, seemingly hopeless. That's what makes it look like a mercy killer may be at work."

"One of the staff, then? Any particular floor or department?"

"No, spread out. ER, ICU, Coronary Care, mostly ventilator cases. Statistically speaking, it just looks . . . fishy."

"Anyone look like a suspect?"

"Well, the hospital's Care Review Committee found no negligence on the part of any healthcare professional. But who knows how much of that's just corporate CYA? Some of the press has been nosing around based on several complaints from concerned relatives of deceased patients. That's how it came to my attention."

Linda was well aware of Bradden's connections with several staff members of the *Deerwood Times,* both editors and reporters. It allowed tips to flow freely in both directions: he'd get early warning of intriguing possible cases, and also, by leaking details of ongoing cases, could "massage" publicity and public opinion for the department's benefit—and his own.

"I decided to look into it," Bradden continued. "But under-the-radar for now. I've put a private detective on it, Stacey

Conover, a guy I've used on several other matters of discretion, and he's compiled some kind of database to see which people overlap on the suspicious deaths." Bradden glanced away from her eyes. "I'd like for you to go meet with him at his office and see if you can put a solid case together on someone."

So he wants the meetings away from his office. Linda wondered if he had chosen her as the most expendable if this case blew up in the wrong way. Bradden handed the chart to her but motioned to her to read it later, elsewhere.

"Are the police looking into this?" she asked, slipping the file into her brimming brief case.

"Not yet. So far it's just those complaints filed by loved ones, plus some deaths without complaints but with questionable details. These may just be matters of malpractice in which case, of course, we'll let the families deal with it. But there's just a chance we can stop a killer."

A coup for his political resume came immediately to mind, but Linda quickly chided herself. Her assessment of his motive might be spot-on, but it was always good to stop a killer. But a mercy killer? As an animal lover, she'd often been struck by the reality that one of the most caring and humane things a pet-keeper could do was end the terminal suffering of a beloved companion. Human beings, of course, were another matter but in many cases, the dilemmas might parallel quite closely.

"How do you want me to proceed?" she asked.

His gaze swung back to her. "Go meet with Conover; find out what he's learned, what's still to be dug into. Keep me informed and keep it low-profile. I don't want to stir up a hornet's nest over at DCH unless and until we have a clearer picture of what's actually happening—and who's culpable." She rose, clutching her briefcase. "It's Friday, Linda. Do this errand for me after lunch; then take the rest of the day off." He handed her a business card from Conover Investigations. His eyes held hers. "Just remember, you've got my back on this."

"Of course."

Outside Bradden's office, she glanced at the business card, and realized she knew the name Stacey Conover. She remembered how, shortly after she moved to town, a series of news stories hit big in the *Deerwood Times.* The case ended with a terrific coup for D.A. Bradden: the conviction of a local school superintendent as an Internet stalker. But before the man finally confessed, there'd been a firestorm of controversy and public hysteria. And though it turned out the only young woman involved was a twentysomething instructional aide he'd dated in secret, the early investigation and speculation in the media had parents nearly rioting at a school board meeting, in terror for the safety of their children.

Stacey Conover had been the investigator cited in the news. Recalling the few times she'd seen Conover actually interviewed on TV newscasts, Linda pictured a rumpled Columbo look-alike, disheveled hair, five o'clock shadow, stained lapels and all, perpetually chewing a toothpick as he answered questions in a gravelly tone often punctuated with the type of throat clearing grunts that bespoke years of tobacco misuse.

Linda shivered in the center of her perhaps-too-fastidious soul. She was a little less than thrilled at the thought of meeting the great man in person!

CHAPTER FORTY-TWO

Growling under his breath, Vinny Orlander slammed his arms through first one sleeve, then the other of his down parka and headed for the hospital exit that would take him to the parking structure. Climbing into his maroon Taurus, he grabbed the steering wheel with such force that for a second it seemed he would crush the faux leather wrapping into the plastic itself. Slamming into drive, he steered out onto Deerwood Blvd., seething about the most recent exchange regarding the Myra Cleary case. Julia had gone postal after her mother's death and had everyone on edge but as always, any 'mistake' with a vent patient always was the fault of the respiratory tech till proven otherwise but this was ridiculous. He'd already been to the Care Review Committee twice and all staff, including him, had been cleared. So why did he just spend another hour and half with the Chief of ICU and that twit Jacobs having to answer inane questions like "And can you explain again how you set the ventilator based on the last written orders?" If Jacobs wasn't his immediate supervisor and therefore the guy who did his evaluations, he'd of knocked him down right there and shot him up with a bit of nasty paralyzing drugs! Then what fun watching him gasp his last waiting for Vinny to turn his vent setting to the right numbers.

Turning on the street that would take him to his apartment much quicker than his usual more sedate drive, Vinny realized he didn't want to go home. Not even the prospect of his usual de-stresser, lying on the futon and watching his fish in their huge tank, would be enough to soothe him today.

He drove past his apartment building and on, not paying much attention to his route or any of the views. Instead, his mind was back on the Cleary Controversy. Three weeks gone by, and still the DCH grapevine was abuzz with conjecture and gossip. Everyone was talking and speculating. Was there a vent-killer loose at DCH? Had Julia and/or Alex killed Myra for money and all this angst was for show?

Beyond the DCH staff, other people were asking questions about the case—and some earlier ones. Relatives of patients, two plain-clothes police detectives, some local reporters, and that scruffy guy hanging out in the cafeteria. Vinny had seen him several times at different tables, different times on different days. Always minding his own business it seemed, writing in a notebook as if oblivious to all around him. But Vinny knew better. Clearly the guy was an observer, and spent much of his time wisely just listening. A lot of grapevine news got disseminated in the cafeteria. And though the man looked familiar, Vinny didn't place him till something about the ever present toothpick clicked. He was that private dick guy from the school case.

Vinny took his presence to mean that it was more than Myra's case being looked at by the cops; making sense out of the other big topic for Ye Olde Rumour Mill: all the suspicious deaths recently. Everyone wondering if someone was killing people at DCH? Vinny recalled Sheila saying, "Maybe Julia knows something about Alex that we don't. He was odd when he came here, and lately he's been *really* weirded-out. Maybe he's the vent-killer."

Alone in the car, Vinny's lips quirked in a tiny smile wondering what secrets might be revealed...even about the good guys like Dan Marchetti. Thinking of Marchetti, Vinny felt some of his anger returning. Not even a thank you after he'd driven him home after his clocking by that Irish guy. And his hot girl friend all but pushed him out of the apartment lest he get any of his germs in their little love nest.

Vinny suddenly realized he was headed directly for the Pet Center and took a deep breath. Why not? It was a place he always felt safe, happy, relaxed. And if there weren't a lot of customers, maybe Darlene would feel like talking to him.

He parked in front of the store, pleased to see the other parking spaces were empty.

Inside, he found Darlene alone—or at least with no other customers. The place was alive with the gentle sounds of happy birds, and on her shoulder perched Mack, the Scarlet Macaw.

At the tinkle of the bell above the door, Darlene glanced his way and gave him a radiant smile. Fit and supple in her snug jeans and red-plaid flannel shirt, she wore her golden hair swept back into a ponytail with a fringe of bangs across her forehead. "Hey, Vinny!" she exclaimed. Her eyes were smiling too, a color he always thought of as "sunshine blue."

"Hi, Darlene." On her shoulder, Mack raised and opened his wings and croaked, "Com-pany!" Vinny reached over to chuff the parrot's neck feathers. "Good afternoon, Mr. Mack, how's it goin'?"

"So!" Darlene twinkled. "What can I do you for?"

His thoughts quickly went from Mack to Darlene. Knowing that she was not likely to be interested in a guy like him, he had to think fast. He had already brought supplies just a few days ago. "Uh, I decided I might want to get a Siamese fighting fish after all. You were going to tell me what you thought last time I was here but we got interrupted."

"Ah! What is it about these fish and good looking men?" Her eyes sparkled. "Beautiful but dangerous. What I always say is that Siamese fighting fish can't play well in the sandbox. They are always looking to attack before they are attacked. To kill or be killed. That's why it's best they have their own tank, especially for the males. Putting two together means only one survives...

the bravest and strongest I'm sure. There are some smaller fish species that seem to be able to co-exist with the fighters, but I always wonder if the little fish end up living in fear. Always being afraid doesn't sound like a great life to me. Anyway, come look at the new shipment I told you about" She led the way to the back of the store, Mack clinging to her shoulder, waving his wings and bobbing his head to show off as he passed the cages of his feathered kindred, chortling, "Walkin' here!"

Vinny was stunned. He had never heard her talk so long and that line about good-looking had to be a come-on. He hurried down the aisle, practicing his 'beautiful woman and dangerous men" line in his head. But before he got the words out, Vinny was struck still at a fairy world of color and movement in front of him. Dozens of small bowls, each containing a single fish, shone with colors that ranged from flame orange to metallic blue. Flowing tails seemed to fill the tanks, some single, some double, some arranged like violent halos as they circled back around the heads. They were magnificent.

Darlene laughed. "I knew you'd love them. I've been waiting for a chance to sell you a beauty."

Twenty minutes later, Vinny had chosen two males; a magenta wonder that despite its small size seemed to own the space in it's transport bag and a sleeker blue green mix with strangely hypnotic bulging eyes and red tinged lips.

As he followed her back toward the front counter, where she had quickly added two individual aquarium bowls specially designed with small filtration units, Vinny snapped out of his fish reverie. He quickly ran through options for getting back to the 'good-looking men' space but as always, the smarter half of his brain told him again that good women were not for the likes of him. A sudden image flashed in memory: the bullfrog stretched frozen and breathing his last after Vinny paralyzed him. Explaining that little part of his life to someone like Darlene was so unlikely that Vinny snorted. Darlene looked up quizzically.

"Just thinking of something funny," Vinny explained. "Really, it was nothing."

For a moment, he thought she looked disappointed. Maybe there was a chance that she'd understand. But before he could gather his thoughts, *Ta-twingle!* The bell over the door sounded as two preteen boys rushed in, shaking drizzle from their hoodies followed by the harried mother of one of them.

Mack squawked and flapped up from Darlene's shoulder to perch on the highest shelf behind her, then warned, "Look out!"

"Hey, did the new snakes come in?" one boy asked excitedly.

Darlene nodded, her attention momentarily on the intruders. "Yes, Kyle. They're back in the Reptile Nook." The boys were already on their noisy way up the aisle ignoring the "Be careful and don't run" injunction from the mom, clearly mere background noise to the pair. Darlene's blue eyes swung back to Vinny with a child-tolerant smile.

But in that moment when her focus had wavered, so had his courage. He was already hefting his unexpected purchase and turning for the door. "Thanks, Darlene. Gotta go! Have a nice weekend."

"Yeah . . ." her voice said behind him, and he could swear it sounded wistful. "You too. . . ."

CHAPTER FORTY-THREE

It wasn't easy to ignore her surroundings. The windowless office, small when the building was constructed back in the '50s, was now almost claustrophobic, overwhelmed by its floor-to-ceiling shelves stuffed with thick books, folders and storage boxes, all sprouting untidy tufts of paper documents. Linda sensed decades' worth of tobacco smoke permeating every surface, despite the fact that no single item related to smoking was in evidence.

Stacey Conover, still standing though she was now seated, offered, "Coffee? There's a machine at the end of the hall. I'd be glad to get some for you." That toothpick seemed to cling magically to one corner of his mouth as he spoke.

She slipped out of her coat sleeves and smiled. "No, but thank you."

She studied him. He was younger than she expected him to be from the remembered TV appearances; closer to her age than to Bradden's. He wore no wedding band; Linda knew from the quick internet research she'd done that he was divorced and had a teenaged son in New Jersey. His business was modest but solvent, his work considered reliable and thorough among the lawyers at the office.

Conover shuffled through the sliding heaps of folders on his desk and pulled out an olive green one that matched the one she'd brought with her. Pursing his mouth in a way that made the toothpick dance, he launched into the topic at hand. "Bradden tells me you'll be my contact and conduit to his office."

She nodded.

"And he explained the premise about a mercy killer at the hospital? Good!" From his opened folder he pulled a packet of stapled-together pages and handed it across to her. "Your copies." As Linda perused the spreadsheet, surprisingly comprehensive and well-labeled, Conover explained, "I've been compiling facts about the house staff and other medical personnel, you know, med techs, respiratory therapists, phlebotomists, physical therapists and so forth, who HR said were signed in on the days of the questionable deaths. As you can see, I've also included other patients assigned to the doctors, room numbers . . . that sort of thing."

Linda skimmed the sheets, impressed despite herself with the complexity and organized forethought of the work. She wondered how he had been able to get information so quickly given the laws regarding confidentiality at a hospital but decided don't ask, don't tell might work now in the earliest stages of the investigation. It did help explain why Bradden wanted to be an arms-length away until there was solid evidence. "And?"

When she looked up, he was watching her, worrying that damn toothpick with his teeth. "I ran a macro to see which employee names came up matched with any patient deaths at DCH over the last ten months. Those considered in any way suspicious are designated in red ink." Some were also marked with asterisks, but she didn't interrupt his monologue. "As you can imagine, nurses' names came up frequently—especially in the special care units. But when you compute the actual suspicious deaths, those tended to be attached to the same people who rotated in their assignments or worked throughout the hospital. I came up with three names linked in some way, even if only possible proximity, to *each* of several suspicious deaths."

As she listened, Linda continued to study his spreadsheet. When he stopped talking, she repeated, "And?" before looking up.

Conover handed her another sheet of paper: pale green and with only three columns: Patients; House Staff; Ancillary Personnel.

"Respiratory Therapist, Derek Vincent Orlander," Conover said as he slid another sheet to her. This one an employee profile from the DCH internal website, including a color photo. Darlene recognized him right away as the fish-guy, Vinny.

"Alexander James Cole, M.D.," Conover continued passing the next sheet. "First year intern. And finally, Dante Michael Marchetti, M.D. Also a first year intern."

As the last profile passed into her hands, Linda stared at the photo of that charismatic guy she'd admired in the DCH emergency room, Nikki Saxon's significant other. Linda would bet a month's pay that he couldn't be involved but then scolded herself for thinking like a woman rather than a lawyer. "What do we know about these gentlemen beyond what I can read here?"

"I listened quite diligently round DCH. Orlander's been there a long time. He's considered good at what he does but doesn't seem to have any real friends there. People tend to overlook him, though God knows, that'd be difficult to do—he's built like a fuckin' Viking! Oh, sorry for the language."

She looked up at him then, saw him watching *her*,_as if to gauge her response and sensitivities. She gave him the tiniest of nods. "And professionally?"

He grinned, deftly moving his toothpick to the opposite side of his lip. "Pretty excellent evaluations though with a coupla reprimands for overstepping occasionally. Times when he changed ventilator settings because a doctor couldn't be located quickly enough; each of those citations also included a note that his action had been exactly what the doctor would've ordered, and, in one case, was life-saving. Yet, most of these suspicious cases have involved improper ventilator settings, though there's nothing close to concrete evidence that Orlander was responsible, even by accident. On duty, yes. Present in the vicinity, perhaps. More than that, nope. And by the way, he makes no bones about believing in the right to die, the ability to choose not to resuscitate."

Linda pulled up the second sheet. "Cole?"

"Also excellent evaluations and apparently a very good new doctor. Youngest of the 2005-2006 interns, it sounds like he came in pretty cocky and obnoxious, but seemed to grow on folks. Fell very hard and publicly in love with a favorite nurse, Julia Cleary, who returned the favor." The toothpick twirled as Conover ground it between his teeth. "Now here's the interesting thing: about two weeks ago, the nurse's mother had a bad fall and ended up in a terrible condition where, *if* she survived her other injuries, she'd have to be on a ventilator for the rest of her life. Most of the staff, I surmise, felt the kindest solution was to let Mrs. Cleary go rather than forcing her to stay alive with a machine breathing for her while the family finances were sucked down the drain."

"She had a DNR?"

"No. For religious reasons, it seems, the daughter refused that option. Then when her mom died on her own, and there were questions about the ventilator setting, Julia accused Cole of 'pulling the plug.' I hear the mom had sort of been in the way of a full *adult* relationship, if you catch my drift. Also, the skinny is that Cole's overextended financially and was loath to see his intended's fortune slipping away, or alternatively a Kavorkian wanna be. So, though pulling that plug might've been the best thing for the patient, there were some significant motives for Cole to have her out of the way."

"How do things stand now?"

"Officially, Cole is cleared at DCH, but Julia dumped him rather viciously in front of their colleagues and she is still out on a long-term leave of absence. Cole's taking the whole thing very hard."

"Was Cole Mrs. Cleary's doctor?"

"Not at the time of her death, though he looked in on her often in the ICU . . . she was supposed to be his future mother-in-law, after all. He'd admitted and treated her in the ER, but her resident at the time of her death in the ICU was actually this other fellow, Dante Marchetti."

Linda thumbed to the last profile and studied the photo. Those beautiful brown eyes, full of intelligence and a touch of humor, seemed to stare back directly into her own with such openness, she again found it hard to believe he could commit even the crime of jaywalking.

"Marchetti's the oldest of the intern crop," Conover had been saying, "because he spent some time traveling and living in Europe, primarily in Italy. He's gotten glowing evaluations, seems the star of the class but also a favorite on a personal level. Kind, understanding, good-natured, fun. Male staff admire him. Female staff all seem to have a crush on him, even the married ones, but know he's committed to a live-in relationship with a DCH nurse, Nikki Saxon, who's, as it happens, battling cancer."

Linda nodded, not feeling the need to reveal that she knew Nikki. Conover forged on. "Again, here's where it gets interesting. The two of *them* live in the same apartment building as Cole, who seems to be one of Marchetti's closest male friend. And the two nurses, Saxon and Cleary, are also best friends."

Linda gave him a little smile. "Here, I thought TV medical dramas were complicated!"

The detective leaned back in his chair, clasped his hands behind his head and stared up at the ceiling pensively. "Yeah. Just imagine what a pressure-cooker life it must be working in a hospital. All these personalities and crises and life-or-death responsibilities, interrelated and often conflicting. Everybody stressed out, exhausted. What a stew! Gotta love the possibilities!"

She kept her tone very neutral. "So what're the suspicions related to this Marchetti?"

He looked at her again, but continued to lounge, rocking a bit. "Complaints were lodged by relatives of the patients whose names are marked with asterisks: Damen, Delmar, Salter, Cleary, *all* Marchetti's patients, though, of course, that last one was pointed toward Cole. All cleared by the hospital m and m board."

"Eminem?"

"Mortality and morbidity...death and disease. They call it a Clinical Review Committee at DCH but it's the same. It's where cases that die unexpectedly or have some unexplained complication get reviewed by the hospital head honchos."

Linda sighed. "I have to tell you: this doesn't look like much."

Defensiveness edged his tone. "My database includes several more suspicious deaths, both with and without complaints. But I thought it made sense to narrow the investigation to patterns of repeated coincidence before investigating anyone further." He sat forward, leaned his arms on the desk, teeth grinding the toothpick. "If nothing turns up with them, we can cast a wider net, look at more cases. We also have to note the possibility that these aren't the work of a single person. Heck, Cole and Marchetti are buds."

"What if there's nothing there at all? I'm afraid the whole thing still sounds rather tenuous to me."

Conover actually reached up and removed the toothpick from his mouth and pointed the chewed end not exactly *at* her but *toward* her. "Look, your *boss* seems to think there's something to find. I don't make the evidence. I just find what I find and report it back to my *client.* That's it."

Conover took the toothpick and waved it a bit. "Two years ago I quit with the cigars," he told her affably. "Got damn tired of the Columbo jokes, but I had a little health scare too. These have gotten me through."

She smiled briefly at him. "Whatever it takes, eh?" She tucked all the new material into the pockets of the folder in her lap then into her briefcase. "I'll relay all this information to Scott Bradden, and I'll get back to you if he has any comment at this point." She slipped back into her coat, then rose. "And I'm sure you'll let me know as soon as you have anything to add."

The toothpick was back in place as he stood up. "Yes, I'll keep you informed."

She offered her hand, returning his firm grip and hurried towards the exit remembering her last task before heading home on this Friday afternoon. She had been doing some research and wanted to ask Darlene's opinion about a commercial bird blend that was supposed to draw more songbirds to her feeder. Also, she needed her opinion on whether she thought a nesting box might be an interesting addition to her backyard this Spring. Linda had no need to think about her route as her red Prius seemed to know the way to the pet center. Instead, her thoughts remained tangled in the conversation of the last half hour. She kept seeing the face of that Dante Marchetti. Remarkable that he was on the list but she knew that he deserved as much honest scrutiny as the other two. What a cruel twist of fate, she thought, if Nikki Saxon had won the triple whammy of a jackpot: divorce, cancer and loving a murderer.

Shaking thoughts of killers and victims from her head, Linda parked in front of the center and approached the shop's doorway, looking forward to seeing Darlene and grabbing a little of the stress relief she could always depend on when interacting with Mack the Macaw and the other animals.

Just then, the door opened with its familiar jingling bells, and a departing customer exited toward her. She found herself looking directly at the name badge of the man she now knew as Derek Vincent Orlander, another suspect in the DCH mystery. She glanced up toward his face, but he barely seemed to notice her, gazing forward and hurrying as if eager to get his purchase home . . . or perhaps, to flee an uncomfortable situation.

She avoided the temptation to look after him and caught the door before it closed. Inside, Mack joyfully screeched, "Hel-lo!" Darlene, a little sad-faced, glanced Linda's way and then brightened visibly.

"Hey, Linda," Darlene called. "What's new?"

CHAPTER FORTY-FOUR

Nikki Saxon frowned. Behind her as she finished up at the sink, Trey Hartmann continued to oppose everything Dan said about the possibilities for treating MS if that's what the test results showed.

Knowing Trey would be joining them again for breakfast before Dan accompanied him to the follow-up appointment with Dr. Choi, Nikki had taken time to make a substantial meal, even though she had her own plans for the day.

Poached eggs and whole-grain French toast with raspberry syrup had brought raves from Trey, but sandwiched between a variety of querulous comments. Granted, he, the whole team, was still smarting from last night's 4-7 loss to the Diamondbacks and Trey was taking a lot of the blame onto his own young shoulders. He querrously blamed his missed batting practice because of time *wasted* on all the neurological tests yesterday and the stress of having to worry about the results. Nikki would have thought he'd be a little tougher given how much discipline it takes to become a world class athlete. Still, she had to admit, she hadn't taken her own early 'cancer' days so well!

She continued to listen carefully to all the levels and layers of the dialogue. Dan was doing a pretty good job not getting distracted by Trey's attitude . . . staying patiently on the subject and a hopeful note. But after almost three months close contact with the intern, she could clearly detect the underlying strain, especially when Trey used words like pointless and hopeless . . . when he dismissed thoughts about a positive future. She wondered how Dan was keeping so calm especially having just had his soul sorely tried by Alex. Hearing Trey talk about giving up must bring him back to that terrible night.

Her frown deepening, Nikki squeezed the last of the water from the sponge and tossed it in its basket behind the faucet. She wished this Trey affair would hurry and resolve. The stress and worry was not good for any of them.

"Hey, Nikki, thanks for another terrific breakfast."

She turned to Trey, who'd come up behind her. On his youthful, freckled face, sincerity glowed through the shadows.

She gave him a sisterly hug. "Any time." And buck up, she thought to herself.

Dan, dressed in a lab coat over scrubs so he could go directly from the appointment to his noon shift in the ER, seemed to have a sudden thought. "Say, Nik. The landlord's s'posed to be here in the building this afternoon. Could you ask him about that leak under the bathroom sink?"

"Sorry. Can't. I'm at DCH today, remember?"

She saw memory dawn. "Oh, yeah." And then the grin, because he was as pleased as she was for her to be attending the nursing seminar that she needed to stack up some of her continuing education credits needed for her recertify. Trying to keep up through the free credits that came through her nursing journals or on-line had been harder than she thought. She was hoping a classroom type course would shake some of the cobwebs from her brain and she'd start feeling like a competent nurse again. With only four more chemo sessions, she expected to return to work soon.

Nikki shot a glance at Trey, whose back was turned as he slipped into his windbreaker. Unseen by Trey, she waggled one fist beside her face, signaling Dan: *Call me?*

He nodded, and a few moments later, the men took their leave. Nikki stood alone in the quiet apartment. Today's session of the seminar was scheduled for 1:30 to 5:30 p.m., but Nikki found herself eager to be back at DCH. By leaving early, she hoped to visit some old friends, knowing it would feel strange without Julia to welcome her back. She had begun to feel that Julia might never return to DCH or Deerfield and for a moment she let herself mourn the passing of Myra and the many unintended consequences from that tragedy.

After an invigorating shower, she dressed in her favorite dark green scrubs uniform and applied careful makeup, including the addition of penciled-on eyebrows, and decided to wear Cammi without the extra cover of a scarf. The wig had proven to be a good, secure fit and flattering to her face.

She dug her DCH ID badge out of the drawer and picked up the keyring languishing beside it. While not needed today, something about handling the proof she'd once been entrusted with access to specialized areas of the hospital, to drug cabinets and confidential files, made her feel like a valuable nurse again. She carried both badge and keyring to the dining room table, setting them beside her purse with the notepad already tucked in the back pocket.

The clock read a quarter to eleven. Having had a late breakfast after Trey arrived, Nikki wasn't really hungry for lunch yet, but she knew she'd need some good protein before the seminar. Remembering she'd boiled a dozen eggs only yesterday, Nikki quickly transformed half of them into a savory cilantro egg salad and was just spreading some on toast when the phone rang.

"I'll have to be quick," Dan's voice told her. "We're still at Choi's office. Trey's gone to the restroom, but he'll be back soon." He didn't wait for her to ask questions; nor did he talk down to her medical knowledge. "The MRI shows a large lesion in the area of the optic nerve and a few very small-but-diffuse lesions on some of the nerves controlling the lower extremities."

Dan paused. "Choi says only time will tell how progressive it will be."

"Treatment?"

"Choi wants to start him immediately, as in today, on I.V. Solu-medrol for a three-day course. Then taper down with oral meds. That should have a quick anti-inflammatory effect . . . alleviate his current symptoms some—for the short term at least."

"What'd he say about long-term?" Nikki asked.

"Well, he didn't really broach that yet since Trey seemed like he wasn't taking much in. But I read Choi's notes. He seems to think, after we've seen how Trey tolerates this treatment and adjusts psychologically, he'd be a good candidate for beta-interferon injections."

"He can be taught to administer those to himself."

"Right."

"That's long term," Nikki said. "What about now? Today, you said for a first treatment? At DCH?" How well acquainted she was with the Outpatient Infusion Pavilion overlooking the Terrace. There were even private rooms where Trey's identity could be better protected.

Dan sighed. "Yeah. Choi said that'd be best. Just in case there're any adverse reactions—"

I think he'll jump at any excuse to postpone while the team's still in town. They've got, what? Six more home games, eight nights before they're off to Atlanta?"

"Yes. Plenty of time to finish that three-day course away from Pittsburgh proper. No game tonight. Tell him he's welcome to stay over with us again so he doesn't have to make that round trip to his place."

"Thanks, Nik."

She glanced at her watch: 11:20. "What about right now?"

"They squeezed him in for an appointment at noon. I plan to ride herd on him so he doesn't cut and run. Figured we could sit on the Terrace to wait for his appointment, rather than inside the hospital."

"What about your shift?"

"Already called in. Dave's subbing till I get there. Oh! Here he comes. Catch ya later."

The connection clicked off before she could say more. Quickly she finished the sandwich she'd been making for herself, then made and wrapped two more. These went into a large insulated tote along with paper napkins, a trio of apples and three bottles of water.

Nikki pocketed her keyring, clipped on the ID badge and left the apartment with her purse on one shoulder and the tote on the other…off to DCH to surprise her favorite fellows with lunch before her seminar.

CHAPTER FORTY-FIVE

Nikki Saxon was only five minutes away from Julia's house when the cellphone in her purse began to ring. Keeping her eyes riveted on the rain-slick road ahead, Nikki fumbled in her purse on the passenger seat. So who would it be . . . Julia? Dante?

She was completely unprepared for the voice that answered her nervous "Hullo?"

"Hey, Nik . . . ?"

"Matt?"

"Long time, eh?"

Matt had made their divorce proceedings so complicated and contentious, that Jenna Hudson had advised they have no communication without her participation to protect Nikki's interests. Off guard now, Nikki could think of nothing to say, but this was Matt. They had loved each other once. The least she could do was not hang up.

As she pulled the Camry off onto the muddy road shoulder and parked, his voice hurried on to fill the void. "I've been doing a lot of thinking, Nik . . . about what a fool I've been. To betray you like that and throw away all our years together . . . all the good times we had and the life we shared."

Staring out through the windshield where raindrops slid down like tears, Nikki still remained silent, not trusting herself to speak.

"I don't have any excuses, Nik. I was wrong, and I feel just awful about hurting you. I never really meant to do *that.* I don't know if you can ever forgive me, but I'm hoping you can, because I'm truly, truly sorry."

Gripping the steering wheel with the hand not holding the cell, Nikki closed her eyes and found her voice. "That's good to hear, Matt, and I appreciate you saying so."

"So, can you forgive me?"

Nikki didn't hesitate this time. "Pain and anger can poison our lives." Nikki knew she wasn't entirely blameless in the events that took them to this point. "So yes, I forgive you."

"Oh, Nikki!" The strangled sound of Matt's voice as it caught in his throat brought tears to *her* eyes. She could easily picture his handsome features, her Rock Johnnyface of old, twisted with pain. "Oh, honey, come back home and let me make it up to you."

Her eyes snapped open. Her tone had cooled considerably by the time she was able to answer: "Wouldn't it be a little crowded in that bed? What does Pam say about it?"

He actually sobbed. "She left me, Nik! Cheated on me and left me. That's when I knew for sure I'd made a terrible mistake letting you go."

He was crying audibly now. "Let's stop this divorce and start over together, okay?"

"Stop the divorce?"

"It's just a financial nightmare. I don't want to have to sell the condo and split everything up. And our lawyers are costing us both a fortune. . . ."

How typical, dragged his heels forever while Pam was likely egging him on, and now that he was alone again, he thought he could just wave a wand and have the past be forgotten. "I can't do that, Matt. You're sorry. I forgive you. Now it's time for you to move on."

"Like you have?" Matt's voice carried new undertones now. When she didn't answer, he pressed on. "Yeah, I know all about your hot young doctor—"

"Are you drunk, Matt?"

"I've had a few. So what?"

"It's nine in the morning is *so what!* Look, this isn't getting us anywhere. We need to hang up now and continue to communicate through our lawyers while we finish the divorce."

"No, honey! Don't say that . . . we can work this out if you'll just try—"

"I'm hanging up now. Good-bye, Matt."

She heard the plaintive, "Please don't shut me out—" before she could press the button to end the call. Almost immediately, her phone began to ring again. Quickly she turned it off. Shaking, she tossed the cell into her open purse. She leaned her forehead against the wheel and let the tears come. She found genuine tears for Matt, who had been a very good husband for most of the marriage, and she knew his turning away from her had been partially the result of her own distance from him. Two broken people with not enough strength to heal each other. There were tears for what they'd had together and what she'd lost. But they couldn't wash away what she'd found with Dan . . . what she desperately hoped to hold on to as long as she could, as long as he let her.

She didn't need this on top of everything else that was crashing around her. Here she was, three days away from her next ABVD treatment and on her way to spend time supporting a best friend devastated by the loss of a parent. Knowing she would be listening to yet more repetitions of Julia's anguished laments as she processed her loss—all the while resisting the urge to grab her friend by the shoulders and shake her hard, "Wake up! Alex didn't kill your mother, and her passing after that horrible accident was the best outcome for everyone! Even you!"

And after Julia, Nikki knew she'd be needed back at the apartment where a disconsolate Alex often moped about and where she had a full schedule providing comfort for an overworked, overly responsible first-year intern, whose life was continuously fractured and stressful—even when he wasn't being attacked and concussed by his patients.

Bottom line, there was no way she'd consider trying to save that marriage with Matt. There's no going back. It may be April first, but she was no fool.

CHAPTER FORTY-SIX

Dan poured Nikki's Quick Mesquite-Lime marinade over the pair of T-bone steaks, turning them to coat both sides. He covered the square, glass dish and slid it into the refrigerator next to the 2-pound tub of extra-veggies potato salad he'd picked up at the market with the steaks and two bottles of wine.

Sighing, he pulled out the first bottle of *pinot grigio,* uncorked it and poured a glassful. What a day it had been, not at all what he'd planned or even imagined when he got up this morning.

Dan took his glass to the sofa, kicked off his Nikes and got comfortable, hoping the Dylan CD he'd put on earlier would help him relax.

Saturday, April 15—all taxes, thankfully, in the mail—was supposed to be his day off. Coupled with the Sunday, this made a nice cap for his two weeks in ophthalmology, providing a mini-break before his second 2-week elective began in the ENT Clinic. Without Nikki's company for most of the weekend, Dan decided to put a little time into kicking back and maybe getting Alex to relax a bit, too. Alex was a complete wreck and, despite Ballard's understanding and switching him with another intern from the intensity of another ICU rotation to a less intense ward month, he still seemed to be more out of it then in...a dangerous condition for any doctor but especially for an intern who needed every case to 'stick' and move him further along the knowledge curve. He'd been slinking around like someone who didn't even care about medicine, barely doing his job and not seeming to notice when others took up the slack for him. Finding out Julia was leaving seemed the last straw. "Now I'll never even get a chance to *try* to win her back," Alex had lamented to Dan a few days ago.

Realizing today—Julia's actual departure date—would be especially hard for his friend, Dan had proposed he meet Alex for lunch in the middle of Alex's eight-to-four shift. The DCH cafeteria didn't merit his changing from the comfortable scrubs he was already wearing at home. He merely clipped on his ID badge and was on his way.

Just as Dan exited the elevator on Ten East, glancing around for Alex, the P.A. system blared: "Code 99, Room 1003; Code 99, Room 1003; Code 99, Room 1003—" He forgot about Alex. Like Pavlov's dog, he thought, hustling toward Room 1003, ready to be a doctor.

In the room he found a surprising sight: an unconscious patient lay, gown askew, on the floor. Above him knelt Alex Cole, seemingly frozen and as if trying to remember how to administer basic CPR.

"What happened?" Dan demanded. When Alex didn't move or speak, Dan shook his arm. "What happened!?"

Alex just stared at the patient . . . mumbled, "Don' know . . . he jus' arrested. . . ."

Dan dropped to his knees and reached across the patient to grab the stethoscope draped around Alex's neck.

A moment later when the crash cart arrived, Dan had ascertained there was no heartbeat and voiced this. Vaguely, he was aware of other staff gathering around him: Diane Werner, some nurses and an RT—not Vinny this time. Though Dan wasn't technically on duty, he took charge, smoothly directing the efforts. No one seemed to mind, including Diane, who offered an encouraging smile and handed him the laryngoscope. Certainly Alex made no objection; he'd shrunk back to sit in the corner formed by the bed and the wall, staring blankly at his coding patient.

Dan quickly had the fellow intubated and hooked up to the flow of O_2 from a wall unit, but the "One amp epi!" Dan called for failed to kickstart the flatlined heart. It took a few additional precious minutes—and more than one zap from the defibrillator—before he and Diane managed to restore the patient's sinus rhythm and pulse. Whether there would be irreversible brain or cardiac damage, he was alive; they'd done their job.

Just as a nurse announced, "BP 110 over 70," the attending, George Anastos, arrived accompanied by an orderly with a gurney.

"Good!" George said, taking a quick look at the monitors. "Let's get him on a stretcher and down to ICU—stat. Good work, guys."

In a matter of minutes, the room was nearly empty: George and Diane had rushed away the gurney bearing the still-unresponsive patient; other staff had scattered to where they were now needed most.

Having never risen from kneeling on the floor, Dan moved off his aching knees to sit beside Alex, leaning back against the bed. Dan didn't speak for several minutes, making sure everyone else was gone, giving Alex a chance to say something first.

Finally, in a low and gentle tone, Dan asked, "Alex?"

Alex didn't open his mouth. He just stared at Dan with those weak-tea brown eyes, which were now devoid of even the pain Dan had become used to seeing there.

"Tell y'what. I'm here. I'll take the rest of your shift for you. Go home. Eat something; get some sleep. Let's talk tonight. Shift ends at four, right?"

Alex nodded, still unspeaking, but it was, at least, a response.

"Okay. Well, I'm 'baching' it tonight, so how 'bout I go get us some steaks and *vino?* T-bones and *classico* your favorites, right? Been a long time since we've had a guys' night." Hoping he didn't remember the reason they'd be alone was because Nikki was away helping Julia disappear from his life, he added, "Come over about seven-thirty. Okay?"

Alex nodded again, looked as if he might be trying to thank Dan but couldn't get out even one word.

Dan rose, reached down and helped Alex to his feet, gave him a quick embrace before his still-silent friend headed for the door.

Maybe he'll finally open up tonight, Dan thought now, sipping his wine on the sofa. He checked his watch, 6:17 pm and figured he had some time to chill before starting the briquettes. He leaned back against the cushions, put his feet up, closing his eyes as the music flowed around him. He let his mind drift. The Yanks off to a slow start but seeming to get ready to pound their division again. Wonder how the Pirates will do tonight . . . second game against the Cubs. They'd beaten the Dodgers the day he'd gone for batting practice, but then lost the next and then the following night to Chicago, putting them now at a dismal ten games below five-hundred.

He smiled sleepily. He'd never forget his day with Charlie. Draining his glass, Dan set it aside without even opening his eyes. Memories of that most pleasurable afternoon drifted slowly into an image of himself in a Yankees uniform, no, make that the Pirates, pinstriped for a home game, striding to the mound at PNC Park, picking up the resin bag, juggling it with his ungloved hand, then looking back toward home plate. He'd pitch when he was good and ready! Squinting into the batter's eyes, he beamed the thought: *"Hit this baby, if you can!"* His windup and pitch embodied the grace and power of the very greatest fastballers. Flawless! The ball a mere blur to the naked eye. The batter—and those who followed him—would swing hard, only to eventually return to the dugout cursing the name of Dan Marchetti . . . but with grudging respect. Lightning fast and deadly accurate! His ears filled with the roar of the screaming fans.

Dan came awake slowly, blinking in the changed light, half expecting to see outfield grass and the crowd-packed stands beyond. He had really gone out!. Yawning, he sat up, checked his watch: *7:50!* In a muddle of thoughts he both realized, he should have started the coals long ago and wondered, where the hell is Alex?

Perhaps Alex, too, had fallen victim to some well-needed Intern Sleep. Dan yawned again. Given the time, the smart thing was to go wake him up and ask whether he wanted to eat broiler steak right away or wait for the grill.

Shoeless, he padded down the hall, knocked on the door and waited, listening for a call from inside. None came. He knocked again, a little louder. "Alex?" Still no response. He tried the door in case Alex had left it unlocked for him as he often did. Locked. Maybe he'd rested, then gone out? Maybe went to get some ice cream or something to go along with dinner?

Dan went down to the far end of the hall where he could peer down into the parking lot. Alex's beamer was in his space.

Frowning, Dan headed back to Alex's door. Both his knock and voice were louder this time: "Alex!" Nothing. Unease curled in Dan's belly. "You awake? Come on, buddy—open up!"

Could he be sick or something? Dan's brain flooded with flashes from the past weeks of Alex's life: the pain of losing Myra and then Julia; the suspicions against him; the distractedness and slippage of work ethic; the inability to concentrate on everyday life, even with a job as important as being a doctor.

And the most recent image from this morning: Alex slumped against the hospital bed, completely immobilized, as his patient slipped away. This was a guy who was always aiming for success, striving to do the most . . . be the best. How might such abject failures impact a person like Alex?

Cold sweat popped out on Dan's brow; dread ran through him like sickness. "Al-lex!" he bellowed, pounding on the door. "Open up!" He kept pounding and yelling, but no answer. Several doors opened along the hall, but when his neighbors realized they knew him, most of them quickly retreated, apparently glad to let someone else deal with whatever-it-was. Only the nearest neighbor, Mitch Smolinski, asked, "Sure he's in there?" He sounded slightly annoyed. By the look of him—Pirates T-shirt and gym shorts, frosty beer bottle in hand—he must be trying to kick back after a hard day wrestling refrigerators.

"He may be sick," was all Dan could think to say.

"Don't you have a key?"

"Dammit! Yeah. Thanks!" Dan sprinted for his apartment and the key resting in the caduceus candy dish.

Alex's door opened easily, and Dan entered, finding only silence. He grimaced, nose twitching at the garbage-scented stuffiness. Leaving the door open, he called out but heard nothing. The place was a mess, as if inhabited by a person who'd ceased to care. Dan found the bathroom empty and, glancing into the bedroom, saw only the rumpled covers of a bed that needed changing weeks ago. The whole room smelled worse than the others—like a rank laundry hamper. Dan grimaced again and backed away.

Where can Alex be? Dan looked around the living room for some clue, perhaps a note, but found nothing of that sort. Just overdue bills and scattered IRS forms littering the table. Then in the kitchenette, beyond the sinkful of decay-encrusted dishes, on the counter amidst all the clutter, he saw the uncapped sample pill bottles—all for Ativan, all empty.

Shit! Panic clutched Dan. "Al-lex!" Dan rushed back to the bedroom and around the bed to the other side. And there lay Alex Cole, face down.

Omigod! Omigod! Omigod! Instinct taking over, Dan dropped to the carpet beside the prone figure, turned him over. Pale though bluish, sweaty, but breathing . . . barely. Pulse thready. If he loses it, he's going to need CPR—and quick! Turning and shouting HELP, Dan felt again for a pulse. None.

Breaths first. At the hospital there was always a handy Ambu bag or at least a mask for protection. As Dan tilted Alex's head to the proper position, pinched the nostrils shut and sealed his mouth over Alex's, he was thinking, that he'd been taught not to do it this way these days, too many bugs you can get, but his mask was in his antique doctor bag, in the trunk of his car. By then he'd seen the first breath inflate Alex's chest and now heard it whisper out of the mouth against his listening ear. No obstruction to his lungs.. He quickly added a second breath, then began chest compressions.

Working his way through the first set of thirty, his mind sought a way to phone 911 without leaving his patient—who could die if he stopped CPR. Working in the hospital where help was always just a step away, he had forgotten the first step in an emergency...calling 911. Having left the apartment without his cell phone, he frantically glanced around and patted Alex's pockets.

"Hel-l-lp!" he yelled, drawing the word out, hoping it would carry better. "Somebody! Please help me!" Time for two more breaths, then back to compressions and yelling.

"Dan?" a voice called tentatively though the still open apartment door. "Dan? You in here?"

"Yes! Bedroom! Hurry!"

Mitch Smolinski sauntered in with that beer bottle in his hand. "What's happen—" As soon as he moved close enough to see Alex collapsed beneath Dan's hands pressing the chest, Mitch's mouth fell open. "What the fuck—?"

Dan's doctor voice—calm, firm, confident—came from his body, which felt none of those things. "Listen carefully. Overdose. Call 911 for an ambulance.

His neighbor, who undoubtedly thought of himself as macho and unflappable in an emergency, continued to just stare mutely, looking a little wobbly on his feet.

"*Now,* Mitch!"

The man blinked, then slapped his pocketless shorts. "Cell's in my place."

"Bring it here, but don't wait to dial. Tell 'em Ativan overdose."

Mitch, finally galvanized, spun on his heel and rushed away. Dan kept up his 24-second sets of two breaths, thirty compressions, but Alex's skin remained blue-tinged. Moments later, the longest moments Dan could ever remember, Mitch was back, sans beer and speaking into his cell phone.

He was finishing their address and then said, "Yes, there's a doctor giving him CPR." He came close, squatted down and held the phone to Dan's ear so he could say, "Marchetti here," before he offered his clinical findings and answered a couple of questions.

Time for more breaths. Mitch put the phone to his own ear so he could be available to the dispatcher while they waited for the ambulance.

His arms blazing in pain thanks to the prolonged CPR, Dan realized Mitch was hovering woodenly without an offer to assist, Dan snapped, "For God's sake, man, help me out. Kneel down and do these compressions."

Wordlessly, Mitch took Dan's place as he moved over. Mitch relinquished the phone, then placed his interlocked hands as Dan directed and began imitating what he'd been watching.

"Remember the John Travolta song 'Staying Alive'?" Dan asked. "You know: 'Ah, ah, ah, ah—stayin' alive'? That's exactly the rhythm you want."

Hesitant and clumsy at first, by the time they could hear sirens, Mitch had it down, allowing Dan to report to the dispatcher on the cell as he alternated shaking more circulation into his arms.

Less than a minute later, two paramedics swept into the apartment with their gear and a gurney. Dan recognized the older man and young woman but couldn't remember their names.

"Hang on, buddy," Dan whispered into his unconscious friend's ear before moving aside so the rescue squad could place an airway for Alex and attach EKG leads on his body.

"I got a good pulse," Sheila announced. "We'll take it from here." The ambulance guy grabbed Dan by the arm and helped him rise stiffly to his feet. Mitch lumbered up on his own.

When the EMTs had made certain Alex's blood pressure, heart rate and rhythm were acceptable, they quickly got him strapped to the stretcher, ready to transport. "Thanks for all your input," the woman said. "Sure helps to have a good doc on-scene."

Her partner offered, "Wanta ride along?"

"Yes!" Dan exclaimed. "Meet you at the bus." Moving toward the door, he thanked Mitch, made sure he returned his cell and asked, "Will you get Alex's door locked after us? I have his key." Dan caught a flash of his neighbor's face as he agreed: still looking dazed but pretty relieved. He said something, but Dan was already halfway down the hall.

Inside his apartment, he grabbed his own cell phone and keys and let the door slam locked behind him; at which point he realized he was still shoeless as he headed towards the stairwell. By the time he got downstairs, the paramedics had wheeled Alex to the ambulance and loaded the gurney. Dan hopped, sock-footed, in and pulled the door closed behind him. The crew had just finished the communication to DCH: ". . . Vital signs stable; airway in place." The ambulance headed the two long blocks to DCH.

No one spoke; the only sounds beneath the wailing siren were the cardiac monitor's bleeping and the *shush* as the airbag inflated and deflated.

Dan stared at Alex's face—now grossly distorted beneath the oxygen mask—and tried to calm the shaking of his hands. He began to feel sick to his stomach now he had time to start thinking about what'd happened . . . and nearly happened. His friend had nearly died.

Later Dan decided that ride was the longest two blocks he had ever traveled.

CHAPTER FORTY-SEVEN

Climbing the stairs to the apartment, Nikki Saxon tried to shake the sense of sadness that'd followed her from the Cleary property where she had already developed a system for quickly checking that no emergencies had happened in the two days since her last check. The home, once filled with love and laughter was now just a house. If it weren't romantic nonsense, she'd say it was almost as if it *missed* Julia . . . and Myra. Well it wasn't romantic nonsense to admit that she missed her friend, more every day and with no sense that she would ever come back to Deerwood or DCH.

Even in those few hours she spent at Julia's uncle's house on the Easter weekend, Nikki could see how the family enfolded the grieving young woman. Other members of the clan were there for the holiday, and they all exuded love and support and compassion. But there was something more . . . something a little creepy. The words *velvet entrapment* came to mind. All done with love but she couldn't help remembering some things Alex had said, after returning from Christmas, about how Myra's family manipulated *her,* eroded her self-esteem and independence.

Reaching the apartment, Nikki hefted her keyring, even heavier these days with the keys from the Cleary property, and opened the door. Without hesitation she'd agreed to serve as a sort of property manager while Julia was away. Julia'd insisted on paying her a monthly stipend to monitor the people who maintained the gardening and general upkeep. Beyond that, Nikki was free to use the home as a getaway, with or without Dan, to appreciate all the perks . . . like that big-screen TV that'd so delighted Alex. So far, they hadn't managed to find time together and Julia didn't enjoy being alone for any extended time in the cold, cavernous space. Not even to write in her journal undisturbed.

As she closed the door behind her, Nikki saw Dan had picked up the mail before leaving for work and had left it on the table. It was the greeting card that caught her attention, left standing open atop its envelope as if on display.

She crossed to the table and lifted the card, admiring the soft watercolor tones of a peaceful woodland scene with deer in a sunlit meadow. The envelope's return address proved her intuition about its origin: Alex Cole's parents, Gabe and Shelly. Nikki left it with the rest of the mail until she'd fetched a cold bottle of mineral water from the fridge and settled herself back at the table.

After a long, thirsty pull on the bottle, she took up the card again. Above the soft-eyed deer, a flowing script font read: "Thank You for all your kindness. . . ." The inside was filled in a beautiful hand that must be Shelly's, though both of them had signed at the bottom.

It was pretty much what Nikki expected: heartfelt gratitude for Dan's friendship with their son, for everything he'd tried to do for Alex since they'd both become interns, but most especially two weeks ago.

God, that was hard on Dante. Nikki remembered arriving home on Sunday afternoon to find their apartment empty and two T-bones over-marinating in the refrigerator beside a pair of wine bottles, one opened. No note. No sign of Dan. She first figured he had been called in to sub for someone as his cell went to voicemail, as it would if he had it turned off within DCH. She tried ringing Alex, but that went to voicemail too. She hoped that rather than working, the two of them were out together; something Alex, who was coming apart like a worn-out quilt, could really use.

Perhaps an hour passed, she had unpacked and put away all her travel stuff and even grabbed a shower, before Dan finally called. His voice sounded flat, exhausted: "I'm at DCH with Alex."

Her breath caught at the pain in his voice. "Are you alright? What happened?"

"Alex overdosed on Ativan."

"My God! How is —"

"He's okay. Still in ICU. So far, no indication of permanent damage. But emotionally, he's been a basket-case."

"I'll be right there."

She'd rushed over to show her support for Alex, how truly surreal to see *him* looking so wan in a DCH bed fussed over by the staff, and for Dan, exhausted. Much later that evening, when she and Dan were back at the apartment, she got him to tell her all about it while she broiled the steaks and heated a can of baked beans. Turned out he hadn't eaten much of anything over the last thirty hours . . . just some mac'n cheese Wynnie Hibbert had ordered from the cafeteria and stood over him until he'd eaten it all.

Dan had recounted Alex's meltdown at the hospital, his failure to appear for the dinner invitation, finding him unresponsive and, with the help of Mitch Smolinski and the paramedics, getting him to the hospital in time to save his life. Then there were the hours of waiting to see if Alex would regain consciousness. Apparently, Dan hadn't left Alex's side, not even after the patient finally awoke, six hours after being admitted.

"Sitting by his bed all that time," Dan had told her as he dried the just-washed plate she'd handed him, "I had too much time to think . . . not just to worry about the outcome, but to wonder about a lot of things." She'd nodded in encouragement, handing him the other plate to dry as he continued, "Of course, I couldn't help wondering about whether I should've seen it coming . . .

Finished with the dishes, Dante hung the towel to dry and ran a shaky hand through his still-uncombed hair. "I've tried, but I just can't imagine the despair he must've been feeling to take such a drastic action. Ending your life is one helluvva statement!"

Nikki took his hand, leading him to the comfort of the sofa. "First year interning? That's a trial-by-fire. I've watched it year after year. Some hopefuls just don't make it ."

Nikki, her arms already encircling him, brushed the curly hair at his temple and murmured soothingly, "You're okay, Dante . . . you'll *be* okay. You aren't Alex."

"But he's as good a doc as I am —"

"Tell you what *I* think. He came here *over*estimating himself; you always *under*estimate yourself. The truth caught up to Alex, and I guess he couldn't face it. Its very hard when you've always been the best at everything you try. Intern year is a lousy time to learn you are not perfect or necessarily the superstar... but I've seen it happen before. I just hope someday you can appreciate the truth about *your*self."

He mumbled words that sounded neutral but might've included something like, "You don't know the real me." As if *anything* this man could think or do or say could be *that* bad, Nikki thought not for the first time. It was time to nudge him out of his melancholy before he spiraled downward too.

"Oh, I *know* you're a man of many talents," she'd purred beside his ear, touching the lobe with the tip of her tongue. Then they were kissing, and Nikki gave him the comfort of her body there on the old green sofa where they'd first made love. Intercourse still lacked the ecstasy and passion of the days before her illness and the chemotherapy, but it was painless enough, and it gave her great joy to ease Dan's needs. She could only hope the rest would come back when she was finally well.

Can't wait for chemo, only five more treatments, to be over, *Nikki* thought, reaching for her water bottle again. She had to set aside the Coles' card in order to open the bottle cap. She drank, thinking of them. Such nice people. Completely blind-sided by Alex's actions. Of course, they didn't know how much he'd lied to them about his relationship with Julia, not telling them she'd left him and his finances . . . his state of mind. How many times she had dreamed about the 'right parents' when she was cleaning that last tiny apartment and fearing that Tony could still show up at any moment. Even the right parents can't protect you from pain and tragedy. That was a lesson she had already learned watching the final breaths of terminal children but somehow this little thank you from Alex's parents brought it all home again. She remembered their faces when she'd met them at DCH, the day they came to take Alex home to New York when he was released. They looked like baffled children forced to be grownups.

The last lines of their Thank You card drifted back to Nikki's mind: *And thank you so much, Dan, for taking care of everything in Alex's apartment. He improves every day, and he sends his best to you and Nikki.*

Of course, because Dan had his ENT elective, *she* had been the one to do most of the work: packing up all of Alex's belongings and shipping them to his parents' address. Well, she hadn't shipped *everything*. The stash of porn she'd found wrapped in a tattered blanket at the top of the closet had gone in the trash. She didn't think his mom or dad would appreciate it and she doubted Alex would miss it.

There were some other papers with the magazines; when she glimpsed the outrageous rental contracts for his BMW and entertainment system, she'd quit reading and sealed those items in an envelope marked with his name and the word *Documents*, surmising his parents weren't the type to open it without invitation.

It was funny he hid *that* stuff, Nikki had reflected, as if anyone would be interested in them? Maybe he only hid them once he started seeing Julia; not wanting her to discover his early spendthrift habits.

Julia. Nikki had waited several days—making sure Alex was, indeed, recovering—and thinking well about what she'd say before she called. Planning to start with only the bare facts, she'd dialed and after the briefest greeting, Nikki had said, "I have something to tell you that will probably be a shock, but everything's okay now." How often she had said those words on the peds floor: "*You're okay*"; "*Your loved one will be okay*"; "*I'm okay*"; "*Everything's okay*"—even when it wasn't quite true. It usually meant, "*nothing else can really be done about it right now. Waiting might help. All you can do is get through it.*" During Nikki's long pause, Julia hadn't said a word, so Nikki forged on. "Alex took an overdose of Ativan on Saturday, but Dan did CPR and got him to the hospital in time to revive him." Still no response except, perhaps, Julia could be crying softly. "His parents will take him back to New York as soon as he's released." A little muffled sound. A sob? "Doesn't appear there's any permanent damage."

Nikki waited. Finally Julia said, "Okay." Then after another long moment, "Thanks for calling. I've gotta go now . . ." and the phone clicked off.

They had talked at least three times since then, but she never mentioned Alex once. In fact, she doesn't ask about Deerwood at all, Nikki realized. Not even her property. All she wants to talk about is her family there and all the things they're doing. Didn't even skip a beat when Nikki told her about having tickets to watch the Pirates at PNC. Nikki shivered. It was hard to shake the feeling she was losing her—and not in a good way, not to a life that will really benefit her. Nikki rubbed her forehead where an aching had begun. Myra, Julia, Alex. How could everything have gone so wrong?

CHAPTER FORTY-EIGHT

Linda Ferrante took an eager bite of her cheese sandwich. Pepper jack on sprouted whole wheat with fresh cilantro and just the right balance of Tex-Mex tomato sauce. She felt herself relax against the wooden slats of the park bench as she closed her eyes and chewed with unhurried pleasure. Such a treat to leave the office and a cup of microwave noodles behind. She stretched her legs out; happy to remember there was more to life than work. Like warm sunlight on one's face and the earthy scents of late spring. Savoring another bite, Linda followed it with a long swallow from her container of citrus-infused tea. Squirrels called in the leafing trees above her, perhaps reporting on the prospect of sharing her lunch.

Whump! Something heavy landed on the park bench that backed against hers. Linda's eyes snapped open, but she made no indication that she'd noticed the interruption as Conover settled himself. Amid grunting and snuffling suitable for a bear came the rattling of a brown-paper bag and then the lighter-weight wrapping of a sandwich. A moment later, the aroma of a well-spiced meatball sub wafted to her nostrils. *Mmmm.* Being a committed vegetarian didn't mean she couldn't appreciate the savoriness of her old favorites from her Nonna's kitchen.

As the detective snarfed away in obvious appreciation for a minute or two, Linda nibbled at the other half of the cheese sandwich she'd cut neatly on the diagonal to form two triangles.

Finally, the voice behind her—even before the mouth was completely cleared—said quietly, "Sorry. Just *had* to get some food in me first. No breakfast, y'know."

Back to back, any casual passer-by would judge them as strangers merely sharing a location without interaction. As on their two prior meetings, neither would speak if anyone else was in view. It was silly, Linda conceded to herself, so cloak-and-dagger but far preferable to revisiting his cascade of an office or other indoor space Conover might have suggested. Especially after Bradden went out of his way to say, "Your meetings and conversations with Conover. . . ? Keep them as brief and private as possible."

Linda heard soft swearing behind her and a sound that could be paper napkin scrubbing spilled sauce from trenchcoat fabric. Her lunch finished and patience worn thin, she checked her watch. "Did you have something to report?"

The scrubbing sound continued for a bit, perhaps a good cover, as Conover replied, "My New York contacts turned up nothin' usable on Alex Cole, though apparently the family has stayed in touch with Marchetti."

Linda frowned as she chewed her last bite of sandwich. It was still hard to imagine Marchetti involved in killings.

Perhaps reading her thoughts—or just well acquainted with her opinions—the detective's voice continued, "I know you don't like either of them for those hospital deaths, but we can't just ignore them."

"But you got to admit suicide doesn't fit the profile for Cole to be a mercy killer."

By the sounds coming from down-bench, Conover was back at his sandwich, but he managed a muffled response:

"True, unless he was trying to cover his tracks and it went too far?"

"The way the medical report read, Marchetti barely saved his life. You'd think a doc would allow himself some wiggle room if this was just an attempt to deflect suspicion," she countered. "And besides, why now? Why would he have thought he needed to cover his tracks? Have you been letting it slip that there's an official investigation or that you are looking at DCH staff?"

Conover snorted. "Hey, nobody knows anything or will know anything till I get the OK from your boss to surface. And yes, I'm that good! I'm just saying that you can't cross either of the docs off the list. Cole could have been in it alone and got overwhelmed by guilt but his pal got there too soon. Or maybe they're in it together, some kind of sick partnership, and Marchetti decided he couldn't trust Cole now that his little heart had been broken so he waited just long enough for his 'partner' to tragically succumb. That nosy neighbor showing up might have screwed up Marchetti's plan. You gotta think of everything in this business no matter where it leads... and remember, bottom line, they're docs with knowledge and access. "

Eyes focused on the lakeshore, Linda noticed something must have startled the ducks, the parents were quickly escorting their babies to safety. She pulled an apple from her insulated lunch bag. "OK, but where's the logic in all of this. Have you found anything in their backgrounds that makes you think they're killers, mercy or otherwise? Partners or not?" She bit into the apple and chewed thoughtfully

"It's like I been telling you. Finding the threads that connect these deaths to these guys just starts the process. Now I gotta understand them, get into their heads. And I certainly haven't eliminated Marchetti as a suspect in his own right. Even though his superiors and colleagues have a better opinion of him than of Cole. 'Nice guys' sometimes turn out to be murderers too.

"And how about this one, what if Cole decided to take an extra step to expedite a future mother-in-law's demise but asked his buddy to look the other way—or even participate just this one time? Heck, you read those reports, too. Julia Cleary was the only one who wanted to keep her mom alive hooked up to the tubes. And if not the first time, if Cole and Marchetti were already a 'mercy team', the Cleary death would have been the easiest with the most benefits."

Linda sighed and swallowed bits of suddenly tasteless apple. She knew she had to work harder to keep an open mind. Conover might be crude, but if something funny was going on at DCH, it had to be stopped. "Where does this leave us?"

"I'll have my New York contacts keep an eye on Cole and do a little more background snooping. I'm planning to take a harder look at Marchetti. Especially after such a heroic 'save.' Wouldn't be the first time hospital personnel brought people to the brink of death before rescuing them for all the attention."

"And that profile would mesh with that of a repeat killer, I guess."

"Yep. It's time we officially checked that out, too." He belched, but quietly, as if behind his hand, before saying, "By *we* I guess I mean *you,* because you have the profiling shrinks at your disposal, right?" Noisily, he crumpled his paper refuse. "So I'll double-down on Marchetti—and that other guy with access, Orlander. He's definitely an odd duck. Other than that . . . I guess we'll just have to wait and see if the really suspicious deaths have stopped now Cole's gone . . ." He hoisted himself from the bench with another belch. "Or if they continue without him."

No need to answer. No need to say they'd email each other when the next meeting was needed. She couldn't actually hear his footfalls recede any more than she'd heard him arrive, the word *gumshoe* came to mind, but Linda knew he was gone.

Gone, too, was her appetite. She tossed away the rest of her apple, delighting two squirrels that must've been watching her hopefully.

Despite this warm and sunny May first afternoon, Linda felt the shiver all the way down her spine.

CHAPTER FORTY-NINE

As Nikki set the table for three, she couldn't help feeling excited. A true celebrity, Trey Hartmann, would be sitting right here in their own apartment, enjoying her leg of lamb roasted with rosemary potatoes.

Dan had wanted to grill something out on the balcony, but the weather was too cool for comfort late that afternoon and early evening. "We can take a coupla brews out there before dinner," Dan'd decided. They could use whatever privacy the balcony provided. After all, the visit wasn't primarily social; Trey was coming to discuss in more detail the possibility of MS. She'd only learned about this a few days ago.

Certainly, there'd been no hint from Dante when he returned from batting practice months ago. Instead, he'd chosen to highlight for her the thrills of cavorting with the pros, running laps with Trey, pitching the batting practice, joking around with the players. True, she'd sensed *something*, but had chalked it up to his ongoing sadness over Joe Bonfiglio.

Then, a few weeks later, she'd fielded a surprising phone call. It rang four times before she remembered that, though home from his shift in the ER, Dan was still in the shower. She leapt up from the computer where she'd been reviewing information for an upcoming nursing seminar, and dived for the phone before it could go to voicemail. She gave a breathless, half-laughing "H'lo?"

There was a pause, as if the caller wasn't expecting her voice. "Um, is Dan at home?"

"Yes, he is. Hang on a minute." She saw Dan emerging from the bathroom still toweling his hair and held out the cordless handset to him. "It's Trey Hartmann!"

The expectant look that'd been on his face shifted as a shadow passed over it, but his voice stayed friendly as he took the call. "Hey, man! How're you doing?" He took the phone with him into the bedroom, surprising Nikki. But he didn't close the door, something she would be willing to accept as a true call for privacy.

Nikki took herself back in to the computer and immersed herself in the on line workshops she'd need to keep her license current. Harder than she expected, she worried that even her brief time away from pediatrics had put her behind. Anger at the unfairness of cancer and all it indignities, pulled her into a dark place so that she actually startled when Dan appeared beside her and replaced the handset in its cradle. "I invited Trey Hartmann for dinner."

"No problem. One guest isn't hard and how cool...Trey Hartmann!"

"Look, there's something I have to tell you. In strictest confidence."

She listened attentively, and with appropriate surprise, as he told her all about the locker room encounter at PNC and Trey's resistance to taking charge of his own health. No question why Trey wanted to keep this under wraps for now.

"I know I should have asked first but I told him about *your* illness," Dan said.

"You thought that might put him more at ease. I get it. I just hope you can reach him . . . talk sense into him about getting a complete and accurate diagnosis. And I guess I am the closest we've got to an expert on hearing bad news at the worst possible time. You know I'll help. I just wish you could catch a break when it comes to friends in trouble! Sometimes I think you take on so much that you lose *you*. Know what I mean?"

"Yeah but hey, isn't that what we all said to get into med school…we just want to 'help people'. Not make a ton of money and get the MD license plates!" Dan tried to grin.

Now, placing the last folded napkin on the placemat Trey Hartmann would use, Nikki pictured the vibrant young athlete she'd watched with awe on her TV screen, thinking how scared he had to be…terrified for the ramifications to his baseball career and his life. Living scared, what kind of life is that for a young person. Sighing, but satisfied with the table setting and fresh-flower centerpiece of cheerful oxeye daisies, she moved toward the bedroom.

And she knew that Dante was scared, too, of not hitting the right note. Telling too much or too little. According to Dan, the pitcher was teetering on that fine line between worrying enough to get checked out or worrying so much he shut down in complete denial and did nothing until it was too late.

Staring at herself in the full-length mirror, she adjusted the ends of her multi-colored headscarf thinking she wouldn't mind impressing their guest. Absent-mindedly, she smoothed the lines of her brightly patterned knee-length tunic. The prints weren't identical, definitely more "flowers" on the tunic than the scarf. But the colors were the same and Nikki knew that on her slim body, they 'worked'. Deciding the snug leggings still made her calves look too thin, she quickly changed to white silky-knit pull-ons.

Just as she walked back into the living room, redolent of roast lamb and rosemary, she heard voices out in the hall. The door opened and Dan, carrying the six-pack he'd gone to the store for, ushered in a tall, grinning, freckle-faced fellow dressed casually in jeans and a T-shirt under a black windbreaker. "Hey, Nik! Look what I found wandering around downstairs. Trey Hartmann."

As soon as he was inside the room, Trey exclaimed, "Wow—what a smell! Roast lamb, right?" He inhaled deeply, and a beatific expression washed his face. "Takes me right back to my mama's kitchen."

Must be hard for a country boy to be so far from home even if that meant he was the envy of every Pittsburgh fan within shouting distance, Nikki thought. "Well, I hope mine's half as good as hers must be. Why don't we take the beer and some snacks out on the patio and enjoy the sunshine while it's still warm enough?"

A short time later the men were drinking their Bud from the cans and munching blue-corn tortilla chips heavy with onion dip as they talked baseball and laughed together. Nikki could sense Trey relaxing.

When she'd finished her seltzer, Nikki excused herself, pretending she had more work to do preparing dinner but making it clear she needed no help. "It's piddly little stuff," she assured them lightly, "to get everything ready at the same moment. You guys just relax and have another beer. I'll give you a shout when everything's ready."

She went back in, closing only the screen door behind her. That allowed the kitchen aromas to roll out past the drapes, closed more than halfway to protect the furniture from the afternoon sun, and wreathe tantalizingly around the hungry men.

In truth, she had the meal completely under control, and nothing needed doing just now. When the timer went off, she'd remove the roast and leave it to set while she made the gravy. Till then, she was free to eavesdrop.

Nikki didn't like thinking about it that way, more a chance to gather facts that might help Dan help Trey was how she convinced herself to quietly stand just behind the flowing drapes. She could hear every word said on the balcony. It didn't take the guys long to get down to it. Dan had held back, leaving the ball in Trey's court, as it were.

Big sigh. "Can't thank you enough, Dan, for offering to talk to me—and in confidence."

"Glad to do it, man. Knowledge is power. Whatta you want t'know?"

"There's no cure for MS, is there?"

"No . . . but there're treatments that can help, new research every year, and all sorts of adaptations and resources."

For a moment only the sound of tortilla chips being crunched. Then Trey's apologetic tone: "Uh . . . I haven't made that appointment with a nerve doctor yet. I know I should've . . . should . . . but I just can't seem to bring myself to do it."

Nikki could almost *hear* a lazy shrug in Dan's voice. "Well, you know my stance. Same as your eye doc. The important thing is finding out *what* caused the eye problem and going on from there."

"It's just . . . hard to face the *possibility* of MS. I've seen it up close. My favorite teacher ever, Mrs. Carver, who showed me in third grade just how patient and funny and creative a teacher could be. . . she got MS the year after I was in her class. Over the next few years, she seemed to go downhill quicker and quicker. I kept in touch with her after I left elementary school. Right around that time she had to quit working, so I had to visit her at home. My folks and I got to be good friends with all her family." Big sigh. "By the time I graduated high school, she couldn't move, couldn't see well, couldn't speak clearly, had problems with her memory and her breathing. Then she couldn't use the bathroom by herself. No surprise, she got so depressed, she just kind of gave up. The stress on her family was horrible—not to mention the medical bills. Finally, they couldn't care for her themselves and had to put her in a nursing home . . . where she died." The last words came out choked and Dan heard the fear within the sadness.

"Dan, I just can't tell you how awful it was watching such a dynamic, happy person lose all her abilities, her zest for life, her dignity . . . and eventually, all hope. I can't have that happen to me—not before I'm ninety, anyway."

Dan gave a token chuckle for this attempt to lighten the heavy mood. "I'm sorry about your friend," he said. "That was a particularly bad case. MS does progress quickly like that sometimes, but not always . . . in fact, not usually. Each patient is a distinct individual, so no two will have the same experience, symptoms, progression or outcome."

Trey grumbled, "What's the difference?"

Dan responded as if Trey'd asked the literal question: "The relapsing-remitting forms of MS tend to be more common. There'll be periodic exacerbations, as they're called, of symptoms, but also periods of remission . . . perhaps feeling completely free of the illness. Many people can be relatively stable and not significantly impaired for months, years or even decades at a time."

"I couldn't live like that!" Trey burst out. "I mean, never knowing what's coming next, being dependent on doctors and medications and other people!" He stopped short with an embarrassed laugh. "Boy, did that sound selfish, or what?"

"S'okay, Trey. Understandable. But I hope you'll remember that many people do well with MS. So much so that *West Wing* featured a successful, two-term U.S. president with MS."

"Yeah, but that was TV."

"Well, I do have a coupla people close to *me* with MS. One's my godmother, Aunt Carmella. She's in her fifties and only recently has MS kept her from doing everything she always wanted to do. And by everything, I'm talking about a pretty spirited life as the family world traveler and sage. Now she sticks closer to home but she's got a great doctor who works with her when it comes to meds and following up on new treatment options.

Not giving Trey a chance to interrupt, Dan forged on with his second story. "The other's my college roommate Jake. He's late twenties like me, diagnosed a few years ago. When he's having a flare-up, he uses a cane, but other times it's really not very noticeable to the average person. He's the head graphic designer for a New York ad agency. He travels, and he still swims and skis. Hell, his life is busier than mine! We barely have time to keep up with email."

Trey's patio chair creaked, as if he were shifting his weight impatiently, but he still didn't speak, so Dan finished his point. "Now, neither of them asked for MS. They don't pretend that it's easy or that they're perfect, heroic people. Believe me, I know they're not; I've seen them both have dark days. But they both adjusted to it."

"Yeah, well," Trey said at last, his tone sardonic, "neither of them pitches professional ball, do they?"

"No," Dan admitted. "But I think you should cross that bridge only if and when you come to it." Listening carefully to the exchange, Nikki wondered if Dan was losing patience and worrying that he wasn't getting through. "And, Trey, I don't have to remind you, there're no guarantees in any sport. One injury can end a career a hell of a lot quicker than MS."

"Baseball's my life!" Trey's voice shook with an emotion that tore at Nikki's heart. "It's all I ever dreamed of, what my parents sacrificed for, what I've worked for 24/7 since I was ten. If I can't play, I might as well kill myself!"

Nikki felt the jolt in her very core, stifled a gasp and could only imagine what Dan must be feeling so soon after Alex's attempt.

Dan's voice came quiet and calming. "I don't like to hear you say that. A close friend of mine at DCH almost took himself out last month. Traumatic for everyone, especially his folks. He's just lucky there's no brain damage from what he took." Trey tried to say something, but Dan finished his thought: "And he's a medical person. Lay people can really screw up . . . end up vegetables."

Trey's tone was flat and matter-of-fact. "I've got a gun." Nikki, jaws clamped, shivered. "Licensed, permit and all. I've had a gun since I was nine. Nebraska farm-boy, y'know."

Dan's voice made it clear he wasn't charmed by this attempt at levity. "Take it from an ER doc, you don't wanta shoot yourself. Those botched jobs tend to be far worse than overdoses."

Trey dismissed this with, "I grew up with guns. I know what I'm doing and how to do it right."

Dan thought fast, remembering from his psych rotation that suicide as an abstract was a different animal then suicide with a plan. He had to be careful here not to lose Trey with platitudes or false cheer. Dan let his voice get hard "Okay. Different thought here. Remember, *somebody's* got to *find* the body, and someone's gotta clean it all up. You can maybe check out and think that's the solution, but know that the pain you leave behind will be worse than anything you are imagining now. If you get to that place, you owe it to yourself and everyone around you to reach out for help."

Nikki bolted upright as the kitchen timer went off; nearly falling against the drapes and giving herself away. She rushed to still the timer and pull the roast from the oven with shaking hands.

Steadying herself against the counter, Nikki looked towards the balcony, not quite daring to return till she got her self under control. She contemplated the depth of Trey's apparent refusal to live with MS and the bad karma that had brought another wounded soul to Dan's doorstep. Nikki felt her eyes well as she thought of Alex, Julia, even the tragedy of Joe that had made his internship too personal when it came to life and death.

Nikki breathed deeply and pushed herself upright. Chastising herself for her maudlin thoughts, she moved to warm the asparagus and taste the gravy, adding just a pinch more of salt. But the thoughts returned…what if he wasn't successful in persuading Trey—even after all his good counsel? What if he wasn't able to stop someone else's attempt? What would it do to him to go through it all again?

Afraid of hearing more till she had time to process, she called loudly, "Dinner in five, guys!" and hurried to move the roast, potatoes and asparagus into an artful arrangement on the serving platter.

CHAPTER FIFTY

Nikki's teeth sank through the hotdog bun and into the plump frank inside it. Her mouth flooded with the well-loved flavors of favorite condiments. And it all tasted so good, her eyes actually brimmed with tears. It seemed months since she had truly enjoyed food. It must be the magic of baseball. A week out from her most recent ABVD treatment, she was feeling pretty good, and thrilled with the prospect of watching a pro game sitting next to her guy. They'd both opted for jeans and lightweight long-sleeve pullovers, his red, hers black-and-gold striped. Since he was wearing the special red-underbill Pirates cap Charlie'd given him, Dan had insisted she take his other cap. He even tugged it into place atop the shoulder-length auburn fall of the Cammi wig, then kissed her.

The weather was just right, partly cloudy but almost 70 degrees with a light breeze in from center field. Charlie had come through on the tickets too. Right behind the hometeam dugout. Seated there at ground level, they were close enough to touch the players as they'd come onto the field for their pre-game warm-up. Only a win could make this night more perfect, she marveled, as she looked around and saw PNC was only half full; not surprising since the Pirates' current standing was 40-54. The team had lost all but one of their last five games battling the Mets and then the Cardinals.

Savoring the last of her hotdog and chasing it with a small sip of soda, Nikki thought back to the night before when Trey had shared that roast lamb dinner in the apartment. The guys had come from the balcony, leaving behind, thankfully, the discussion of MS . . . and suicide.

Over the meal, about which Trey raved, they quite naturally spent most of the time talking baseball. Though she hadn't been trying to impress Trey, and was actually trying hard to not treat him as an another unwelcome complication for Dan, she soon found herself charmed by his country ways and his compliments on her knowledge and understanding of the game, her recall of stats, and her loyalty to the hometown team, despite their record.

Before long, Trey turned from the specifics of Pirate performance to a happier topic: bugging Dan about his own skill as a pitcher.

"Y'know, Dan, Coach Monroe and Dex *still* haven't stopped raving about what an arm they saw on you during that batting practice." As Dan laughed in surprise and shook his head, Trey paused with a forkful of rosemary-flecked potato, gave Nikki a broad wink and turned back to Dan. "Quite frankly, those of us on the Pirates pitching roster are thinking we'd better watch our backs."

"Anyways, saving lives is important business. After all, what *we* do is just a game."

Now Dan leaned forward earnestly. "To be perfectly honest, sometimes I wish I *could* be in your shoes."

"Hey, at this point, it looks like I'd be better off with the smarts to be doing what you're doing . . . making a real contribution." Trey's tone held a derisive note, and Nikki knew he was thinking about how his physical body was letting him down.

"And what about *your* contribution?" she asked with a lighter tone. "How do you think medical people could cope with what they see every day if they didn't have athletes to watch and envy and trash-talk . . . complain about their perks and salaries?"

Trey grinned at her. "Hadn't looked at it that way." He turned to Dan. "You're one lucky man. Not only a meaningful career ahead but a woman like this beside you: wise as she is beautiful . . . a great cook, and she knows her baseball."

Dan grinned and winked at her while answering Trey. "Yep. She's a keeper."

Nikki laughed, tilting her head to acknowledge the compliments, but then turned the tables. "So, Trey . . . are you seeing anyone?"

He blushed vividly and squirmed, also laughing. "Nah, no time. Too much traveling."

"Don't kid me now. I know you players get followed like rock stars."

He seemed even more embarrassed than before. "Sure, lotsa women hang out by our hotels, but I'm not interested. Besides, they're there looking for the big shots. Not rookies like me. . . ."

Now, an evening later, watching Trey finish his warmup wind sprints on the PNC playing field, Nikki again thought that what he meant was he was not interested in those type of women. He wanted someone to match his midwest values, who would love the shy farmboy for his heart and not his wallet and fame. She saw him look her way, wave, then head toward where she sat beside Dan.

Removing his cap to wipe his sweaty forehead, he seemed to be having a little trouble catching his breath. Even with his hands on his knees, though, Nikki was struck again by his stature. Some girl was going to be very lucky when he gave that big heart to her. Finally standing straight, he looked up.

"Hey, Nikki . . . Dan. How y'doing?"

As the men shook hands, Dan exclaimed, "Great! Just great. Charlie couldn't've given us better seats."

A couple of kids came over, tentatively holding out Sharpie pens and game programs for Trey to sign. He graciously spent a few moments with each, asking about them personally, but soon they all scampered away to show their Pirates treasure to their parents. Trey turned back to Dan with his own self-conscious smile. "That never gets old! Say, I want to thank you both again for your hospitality last night and that wonderful meal. Could I return the favor by taking you guys out for a bite after the game?" To their protests, he answered, "I *know* it's not necessary, but I'd *like* to." He beamed at their agreement, then said, "I know you have passes to come back after the game, but I'd kinda like to get outta here before it gets *too* late."

"Sure," Dan said. "I've had my time in the Pirates' locker room."

Nikki laughed. "And I wasn't really planning to go in there."

Trey nodded. "The other thing is, even though there's a slew of great eateries here at PNC, I'd rather get away from the park entirely, have a little more privacy, y'know?"

As she and Dan nodded their understanding, he continued, "There's a really fine little mom-and-pop trattoria not too far away. A best-kept-secret kind of place. If that sounds okay?"

Dan laughed delightedly. "I never pass up good Italian food!"

"Terrific. I'll meet you in the players' parking lot as soon as I'm free."

Just then Charlie Monroe buzzed over on his Scalawag scooter. "Hey, Trey. Enough schmoozing with the riffraff. Almost game time." She'd only just met him that evening, shortly after they'd arrived as he seemed so eager to make sure they had a good time, stopping just short of promising them a win in case he jinxed the team.

Play started at 7:05 p.m. with Trey pitching and the Arizona team up first. He handled them in short order: the batters, in turn, grounded out to second, flied out to deep left, and struck out looking.

The Pirates were up. Their first batter also struck out, but then, after Randy Percado singled to second on the second baseman's error, Rick Mossberg doubled to deep center field, pushing Percado in to score the game's first run.

Nikki and Dan cheered and whistled, hoping Mossberg would make it in, too. But a fly ball and then a foul out ended the first inning, 1-0 Pittsburgh.

Back at the pitchers mound for the top of the second, Trey dispatched the first two Arizona batters before the third doubled to deep right field, putting him halfway to a Diamondback score. But Trey took out the following batter, retiring the team and preventing a score.

After a pop-fly out, the second Pirate hitter, Kieran Poole, homered to deep left, bringing Dan and Nikki to their feet cheering—and raising hopes of more runs in the second inning. But it wasn't to be, and Nikki consoled herself by telling Dan, "We're still up 2-0."

And that's the way it stayed for four more innings; though both teams managed singles and doubles, none of those hitters made it to home plate.

By the top of the seventh, Odell Shaw had relieved Trey at the pitcher's mound, and foiled all three Diamondbacks with his grounders.

First up for the Pirates, Kieran Poole doubled to deep center field, and, while next-up Percado grounded out, Poole was able to get safely to third. Cruz Guzman came in as a pinch hitter with a stance that meant business and Nikki joined the fans as they stood and began to chant.

Beside her, Dan was also focused on the batter. He whispered, "Wonder if Guzman's hamstring is good enough to run. It was really bothering him at our batting practice. Could be why he's not catching today."

Sure enough, when Guzman doubled to deep center, he stopped at first; not trusting his legs to carry him quickly enough to second and the speedy Niles Walton was sent in to replace him after the play stopped. But all the attention was on Kieran Poole, who made it to home plate, scoring the Pirates' third run.

"Three-zero Pittsburgh! Maybe we'll have that win . Maybe even more runs to come." Nikki punched Dan's arm then began to cheer with the crowd as Percado—who'd scored the first run, was coming up to bat. But as it turned out, Walton never got a chance; the next Pirate hit into a double play, ending the seventh inning.

Though they got another hit in the bottom of the eighth and the D-backs managed one in the top of the ninth, the game ended at 9:25 p.m. with that same score, 3-0 Pittsburgh.

Nikki and Dan didn't hurry to leave their seats, knowing it would take Trey awhile to shower, dress and meet them. They sat, instead, in the afterglow of an infrequent win in PNC Park, talking and laughing, enjoying each other's company.

When they did leave for their car, they made it a leisurely stroll, holding hands like high school kids, then sat talking in the blue Accord. A few players came out, alone or with companions, moving briskly toward their vehicles. Nikki took a deep breath, filling her lungs with life and youth and the satisfaction of a true fan in the afterglow of a win.

A while later, Charlie Monroe scootered out and stopped to chat. He looked tired but ecstatic with the game's outcome.

Nikki and Dan sat another long time, watching other players leave, but soon they were checking their watches every few minutes.

"Trey couldn't have forgotten us. . . ?" Nikki said.

Dan frowned, staring toward the players' entrance. "Not Trey." He gripped the steering wheel, looking worried.

Nikki took another look at her watch. "Hope everything's okay."

"Yeah, me too." Then he thumped the heels of his hands on the wheel. "I'm gonna go check. Just in case."

"I'll stay here," Nikki told him. "In case Trey leaves from a different door or something. Besides, I'm still not hankering to see the Pirates' locker room."

He gave her a quick smile even as he opened his car door. Patting his pocket for the pass he hadn't thought he'd need, he assured her, "I won't be long."

Dan showed his pass to the security guard at the door answering that yes, he did know the way and was waved through. As he made his way along the remembered corridors, he tried to tell himself not to fret. Any number of things can tie up a player's departure. Post-game revelry or media attention—particularly after a hometown win!—or visiting VIPs or even just more fans wanting autographs. But Dan couldn't shake the nagging sense that something could be wrong, especially with Trey. Certainly, he'd pitched well enough, allowing only five hits and no runs in six innings, but he'd struck out swinging in the fifth. Was Trey having trouble with his vision? His strength?

He could hear loud, excited voices as he rounded the corner leading to the lockers and benches. Under the bright lighting, he saw a gathering of players, most fully dressed. They were crowded around another man, who sat splay-legged on the floor, leaning against the bank of lockers and looking dazed. Trey. He, too, was fully dressed, crisp khakis, a red polo shirt open at the throat, moccasin-style shoes with soft, smooth soles, which Dan could see until Trey drew up his knees, looking defensive amidst the agitation around him. Trey's teammates were asking him questions, and he was shaking his head, gesturing dismissively.

Ricky Mossberg was the first to see Dan. "Say, Doc! Glad to see you. The team's doctor already left."

Dan moved over quickly. "What happened?"

"He fell," Cruz Guzman answered.

"I'm okay," Trey insisted, sounding exasperated, as if he'd already said this a number of times. "I just slipped—"

"I spilled some shampoo," Niles Walton was saying most contritely. "I'm so sorry, man. I thought I got it all cleaned up."

"No worries," Trey assured him. "Just caught me by surprise. Got the wind knocked outta me. That's all."

But Dan didn't see him pop up to prove that. "Did you hit your head . . . lose consciousness?"

"Nah, nothing so dramatic." Trey was starting to look very self-conscious. "Thanks, everybody, for your concern, but it's not a big deal…really!"

But Dan could also sense some of the other players were as unconvinced as he was. A few looked to him openly, others from the corners of worried eyes.

"Hey, guys," Dan said. "I can take this from here. I'm sure you all have places you'd like to be right now . . . people waiting for you. I'll give Trey a quick once-over, and we'll be on our way."

"Trey's leaving with you?" asked Odell Shaw.

"Yeah. We've got my girlfriend and some Italian food waiting for us."

That seemed to put minds at ease. The other players began clearing out with grateful farewells to Dan, to which he responded with congratulations on their win. Their parting shots to Trey included some ribbing, but seemed much gentler than one would expect if everyone felt completely satisfied.

At one point, Trey started to get up, but Dan signaled him to just wait and relax. When his teammates finally had retreated, Trey said quietly, "Thanks, Dan. It's pretty embarrassing to be the post-game entertainment."

"Nothing to be embarrassed about. It's great to have teammates who care." Dan got comfortable down on the floor facing his patient. "You're sure you didn't hit your head?"

"I'm sure."

"Have any pain? Muscle cramps or anything?"

Trey shook his head.

"Good. Squeeze my hand, please, as tightly as you can."

"Dan—"

"Just humor me, okay?" Dan continued working his way through a cursory neurological exam. "The other hand, please. . . . Now follow my finger with your eyes. . . . Thank you."

Whenever possible during the brief exchange, Trey had maintained focused eye contact, as if trying to read Dan's findings from his expression. Now Dan returned that direct stare and asked meaningfully, "Is there anything else I should know?"

Trey's gaze suddenly slid away. "Nah. What you see is what you get."

Dan shrugged thinking that was probably not the whole truth but knowing there was little he could do now to challenge Trey. "Okay then."

Trey started to get to his feet, and Dan rose too, steadying his friend with one hand at the elbow. Trey sat on the benchseat opposite his locker and stripped off his moccasins. "Think I'll put on some shoes with a little tread." While he replaced his footwear, he continued, "Sorry this's taken up so much of your time. You and Nikki must be starving."

Dan chuckled. "There's no rush on our account. We managed to pack away two-and-a-half hotdogs apiece during the game."

Trey grinned, looking relieved the topic of conversation had shifted from his health. "Just give me a coupla more minutes to get the rest of my stuff together."

"Sure." Dan sat to wait, watching Trey closely, trying not to be obvious as he looked for any problems with balance or movement. Finding none, he hoped that a little food and better shoes might actually be the best prescription after all.

Forty minutes later—leaning his arms on the red-and-white-checked tablecloth—Dan felt even more relaxed about Trey's condition. As Dan sampled his first bite of linguini alfredo, *delicioso,* he watched his two table companions laughing together. Trey looked like himself again, and God, was it good to see Nikki with that much life in her eyes and smile. Already preparing to return to work in July, including a new training seminar coming up this Friday, she'd begun taking more time with her appearance and spending more time away from the apartment. "Out in the world again," she'd joked. "Out among the living." And only yesterday, studying her bald head in the bathroom mirror, she'd said, "By Christmas, maybe I'll have enough of my hair back, I won't feel I even have to wear a wig!"

Where would they all by Christmas, Dan wondered. Would Trey have been able to help the Pirates crawl out of the crapper? Would he even be able to finish this season with the team? Did he have MS or something else? Could it be treated without keeping him from pitching? If all went against him, what "other life" might he start creating for himself? And would he be around to find it?

And as for himself, his first year of internship would finish at the end of June, right after Nikki's last treatment. Then what? A second year of residency at DCH? Somewhere else? Or would he be out of medicine entirely?

Where had that thought come from? It was true that he was having a particularly hard month in the ER as the schedule got shifted to account for Alex's absence. He hadn't intended to have a third month this year but Hugh Ballard had assured him it would be good, sharpen his skills. Though after just seven days of car crash victims, bullet and knife wounds, domestic battery, a child-drowning, as well as a couple of missed diagnosis that he thought he should have caught before the attendings, he was yearning to return to the relative peace and rational cases of the eye or ENT Clinics. And with increasing frequency, he began to daydream about baseball. The trajectory of his throws from the outfield, the smell of the freshly cut grass. These flights of fancy they had a way of creeping back in while he was trying unsuccessfully to staunch the arterial flow of yet another teenage boy acting out some *Jackass* movie stunt . . . or covering the face of yet another patient who didn't make it despite his skill and efforts.

"Earth to Dan!" Nikki and Trey had said it in unison and now laughed at his flustered response.

"How long was I away?" he asked.

Nikki pointed to his empty plate. "Well, you sucked down your pasta in nothing flat."

Sheepishly defensive, Dan laughed too. "Well, it *was* superb."

Trey nodded. "Told ya."

They finished their meal as a threesome, all fully engaged in an enjoyable conversation that stretched beyond baseball to comparisons of Dan and Trey's childhoods. Nikki declined to join, insisting, "Oh, I'll just listen to you boys. Your stories are much more interesting than mine would be."

Eventually, Dan realized all other diners had departed, and the couple who ran the place had discreetly begun preparing to close by lowering blinds, upending chairs onto distant tables and sweeping the floor. Dan's watch said almost midnight, and when he glanced across at Trey, the young pitcher looked suddenly exhausted. Nikki too.

"Hey, guys. Let's fold our tents. Good thing none of us have to work in the morning." He reached for the check on the little black tray where their waiter had left it an hour ago, but, yawning, Trey brushed Dan's hand aside. "My treat, remember? I'm making the big bucks."

Clutching the bill, he rose and led the way toward the cashier at the front of the restaurant. Walking behind him, Dan immediately noticed that the ballplayer's steps were more tentative than before—despite the floor-hugging tread of his shoes—and at one point, Trey brushed the wall on one side. Too subtle for a casual observer, but Dan the physician found it striking, as if Trey was having trouble judging distance or coordinating his movements.

Outside the trattoria, Nikki slipped her hand into Dan's as the three of them walked in silence to the little parking area where they'd left their cars. Only two other vehicles remained, both in the spaces marked "Reserved" near the back door of the eatery.

Dan squeezed Nikki's hand before releasing it, then smoothly angled himself between Trey and the door of his car.

Dan saw surprise register in his friend's eyes, and, though the three of them were obviously alone, still he kept his voice low as he asked Trey, "So how long has your vision been blurry again?" It was the old trick of doctors, lawyers and detectives: state the suspicion as fact, making it harder for the "suspect" to evade the question with a simple *yes* or *no* answer. Better still, more information often got disclosed in the process.

"I—uh—" Trey stammered; his look of astonishment began to tighten, as if he would deny everything. But then he released his breath in a huge, gusting sigh and shrugged in surrender. "A coupla days."

"How're your legs?" Dan asked.

"Guess I overdid with my wind sprints tonight—" He'd blurted this out before realizing how much he was revealing.

Dan pressed on. "It's been, what?—three months or so since your appointment with the eye doctor?"

After a long moment, Trey nodded.

Dan kept his voice warm and friendly, but there could be no mistaking the determination in it. "That's it, Trey. You really *have* to get that neuro consult now. Two acute attacks in such a short time, plus new symptoms, that's serious."

Nikki grasped Trey's arm and wouldn't let him look away from her gaze as she told him, "Listen to Dante. He knows what he's talking about. You can't fool around with this."

To answer them both, he started to make excuses and name obstacles: fear of revelation in the media and among his teammates or his bosses . . . trying to fit in an appointment on such short notice before the team left for its next away-games.

But Dan waved all that aside. "I'll call in a favor with a top neurologist in the DCH network. Bet you a dollar he can fit you in tomorrow morning and that we can even get your testing done before game-time and without publicity. Doing that in Deerwood instead of Pittsburgh should keep it low-profile for you."

"But I have practice tomorrow afternoon."

"Bet you another dollar if I call Charlie and tell him we're having a really good time together, he'll let you off the hook just this once. He told me you never ask for favors."

"Deerwood? I live all the way over in Tollton. I just made that long drive last night for dinner at your place."

"That's another point. I don't think it's a good idea for you to drive any more than absolutely necessary—especially at night—until the visual symptoms resolve."

Dan got an idea but should really consult Nikki first. Perhaps she could read his mind, because, catching Dan's eye, she insisted, "You just come stay with us tonight. We've got an air bed and a sleeping bag. Done deal." Trey started trying to decline, but she wouldn't hear of it. Maybe she could also sense Dan's fear their friend wouldn't keep, or even make, an appointment without Dan getting him there personally.

"Come on, man," Dan said gently, "you're outnumbered. And Nikki makes a helluvva breakfast omelet."

Trey flapped his arms helplessly and tried to grin, but in the lights from the buildings, Dan could see tears in his eyes. "Two against one. No fair." He gestured to his car. "What about—"

Nikki spoke right up. "I'll drive Dante's car, and he can drive for you."

"Or," Dan offered, sensing Trey's need for some shred of independence in the situation—and perhaps a need to be alone with his own thoughts for a bit. "Or you can drive right behind us all the way there."

That's what Trey chose to do.

CHAPTER FIFTY-ONE

Having spent the last several hours snatching two teenagers back from the jaws of death, as Diane Werner had put it, Dan thought, sometimes prayers get answered even in the ER.

Dan found satisfaction, too, in the symmetry of it: one boy, one girl; one situation completely accidental, the other self-inflicted though not intentional. The 16-year-old boy, despite his allergy awareness, hadn't thought to ask if the homemade apple pie at an after-school party contained anything peanut. Unfortunately, the crumble-crust did, and, delicious as it was, it'd nearly ended the boy's life.

On the other hand, the 12-year-old girl had been huffing: inhaling toxic fumes to get high. In this case, correction fluid from her father's desk drawer. So many ways for kids to get stoned. Thinking back to his teen years, Dan was suddenly grateful for the strict Italian coach of a dad who expected and got obedience.

The ER was quiet for now, empty of patients. Mike Upton was off enjoying a break, and the four on-duty nurses were attending to all the responsibilities they caught up on when not dealing with patients. Dan finished the last of his notes about the two cases and stretched as he checked the wall clock.

Dan had won both his bets from last night. First, he'd managed to obtain an initial appointment for Trey with Dr. Jin Choi, an attending on the DCH Neurology staff. It'd been easier than he expected.

Though his watch showed well past one a.m. when Dan, Nikki and Trey arrived at the apartment, Dan had called Choi's service to leave a message. Dan was frank in his message, conveying the urgent need for an appointment before the ballplayer had to go on the road again, or before he could chicken out. Dan expressed, too, his hope that any testing could also be done ASAP, while still allowing Trey to arrive at PNC Park for the pregame warmup that same evening. As a final note, Dan emphasized the need for confidentiality above the norm to protect Trey's identity.

All this paid off. The following morning, even before the three had finished their breakfast omelets, Choi's office called with an appointment for ten a.m. The receptionist said there'd been a cancellation, but Dan couldn't help wondering if his colleague hadn't actually "shoe-horned" Trey into the schedule out of his own curiosity about the ballplayer in question.

Second, as soon as the appointment was booked, a quick call to Charlie Monroe excused Trey from practice, freeing him up for the day.

"So, Dan . . . ruminating on how lucky you are?"

Glancing up into Vinny Orlander's cool eyes, Dan dismissed the little chill he felt touch the back of his neck. "Lucky? I don't follow. . . ."

"You managed to save both those kids this afternoon." He gestured to the equipment he'd apparently just removed now it was no longer needed. "I lost *mine* night before last."

Not exactly *his* patient, since he's only the respiratory therapist, Dan noted, but Vinny, like almost all the medical staff at

DCH, probably felt deeply responsible for those under his care. "Heard about that. Another huffer, right?"

Vinny looked away, but his voice was low and tight. "Stupid kids. Think they're invincible. Don't realize even just once can cause heart failure. Much less making it a real habit."

"Diane said this guy had quite a history."

"Apparently. His folks said they'd tried everything . . . locked up all the solvents and spray cans, glues and paints, everything they thought could be used for its gas—all the way down to cooking-oil spray and permanent markers. Grounded him so he couldn't go out and score anything."

"What'd he use?"

"Turns out one of his buddies is the son of a dentist, and the brain trust he called friends swiped the office key, broke in and stole a tank of nitrous oxide. They thought it was a great joke to take it to this kid's house while his parents were out at a Nar-Anon meeting. His pals survived, but he didn't. Some party!"

Dan nodded at Vinny. "You huff too much at once, or too many smaller amounts at too-short intervals, your BP tanks, you lose consciousness, and your heart stops. That kid, and his parents, never saw it coming."

Vinny grimaced, thinking for the hundredth time that he was not an idiot and of course he knew how nitrous oxide killed. His life was all about chemicals and lungs. "Diane did her best," Vinny declared, "but I could see right from the start, that kid was toast." And with that, without another glance at Dan or a good-bye, Vinny grabbed hold of the equipment and wrestled it ahead of him, out of the room.

Weird guy, he thought again, but Dan had little time to consider further. The ER doors swept open, and in rushed an agitated young couple. Both white-blond and fair-skinned, their pale-blue eyes screamed terror through their jaw-clenched silence. It took Dan half a heartbeat to recognize Greg Vandenbosk, whom he'd never before seen out of uniform. The woman clinging to his arm must be his wife Anika and within the bundle Greg clutched to his chest in a Disney-princess patterned sheet was their baby, Ivy.

"Help her!" Anika pleaded. "She can't breathe."

Sure enough, as Greg pulled away the sheet, Dan could see that the infant's skin, exposed around a bright-pink swimsuit, displayed a horrifyingly blue-grey shade. The tiny face, mirroring her parents' fearful blue eyes, looked even duskier around the eyes and gasping mouth.

For a few minutes, everything seemed to happen at once. Dan guided the family into an examination bay and, helping Greg place Ivy on the table, called for oxygen. Even as Nurse Gail Sanduski handed him an infant-size soft-plastic mask with the flow already calibrated, Dan was making soothing noises to his tiny patient, "Hi, Ivy. I'm Dr. Dan. Let's put this band around your head so the cup part fits over your nose and mouth to help you breathe, okay?"

Greg's voice attempted a cheery calm. "It's OK sweetie. You'll be OK soon. Daddy's right here"

Meanwhile, that affable bear of a nurse, Hank Currie, joined them and asked for someone to come fill out the paperwork. Apparently, in their panic, and since Greg was used to going pretty much wherever he wanted in DCH, the Vandenbosks had bypassed the admitting-desk process and come directly to find a physician. They both stared at Hank. As was often the way, neither parent seemed able to take their reassuring hands from Ivy.

"You go," Anika told Greg, her touch still soothing the child. "I'll stay with her."

Reluctantly, Greg let his hands slide away, saying, "I'll be right back, honey." Hank put a friendly arm around the young guard's shoulders and led him from the room.

As Gail quickly took Ivy's vitals and weighed and measured her carefully since most medication, if needed, would be very dependent on the baby's size, Dan began asking Anika a series of questions. First he confirmed that the nine month-old had no history of heart concerns—the most likely culprit for insufficient oxygenation. Such cyanosis would've been seen with Tetralogy of Fallot and some other congenital cardiac problems.

"Hey, Ivy," Dan kept up a soft patter to calm the child. "You don't remember me but I remember you when you came to visit your daddy. He introduced us and said you were the best baby in the whole world?" She seemed to follow his lips as he continued to talk to her in the gentle sing song. "You tried to grab my stethoscope. Now let's use it to listen to your heart. Okay?" Talking to babies, another language.

She reached out one chubby hand as he pulled the instrument from his neck as if to grab it again. The stethoscope detected nothing unusual, not even a murmur, as he listened to her chest; and clear lungs ruled out pneumonia. The numbers Gail reported proved the blood pressure normal for her age and weight according to the chart Gail showed him while giving the results. And the pulse was not higher than one would expect in such an anxious situation. The pulse oximeter, however, showed her blood with only 92 percent oxygen saturation, too low.

As he helped Ivy lie back down, Dan tried not to show how stumped he felt. Greg had now returned, and Dan could *feel* both parents' eyes boring into him, displaying their uneasiness.

If not the heart or lungs, the other main post-natal, after birth, association for a "blue baby" was, he felt the little thrill of déjà vu, methemoglobinemia resulting from nitrate poisoning! This time, not part of a huffer case, but one where the chemical was ingested. A lesser-seen form of anemia, it resulted when hemoglobin in red blood cells lost electrons—and, thereby, the ability to carry oxygen to the body's tissues. The useless cells built up in the blood, displacing healthy, oxygen-transporting cells; a concentration of 70 percent methemoglobin could be fatal. Fortunately, the body's stomach acid usually dealt with nitrates in the diet. But some people were genetically deficient in the most-essential enzyme and the gravest danger falls to infants, as all babies are born lacking the enzyme, which develops naturally during the first three months of life, a time before they'd be eating foods that contain nitrates.

But Ivy's well past that three-month threshold, he thought, so it can't be that. He called for a blood draw, including CBC, chem 7, and blood gas. Concerned there might be an as-yet-undiagnosed heart defect, he also called for a portable chest X-ray and an echocardiogram and directed Gail to get Ivy hooked up to a heart monitor. "We'll need a pediatric cardiologist. Who's on call?"

All around the anxious family, the nurses, including two more who'd just joined them, moved calmly and efficiently to fulfill Dan's orders and requests. Hank hurried away to call for the X-ray unit as Gail applied the cardiac leads to Ivy's ashen skin. Mary Dahl started the I.V after drawing blood samples from the port so that she wouldn't have to stick the tiny patient more than absolutely necessary. Dan called for fluids to keep the vein open with glucose 5% in water.

All the while, Ivy'd remained a model patient, barely whimpering even when the needle stuck her to start the IV. Not a good sign as it was likely she was conserving her strength just to breathe. Dan studied the child as he asked more questions, primarily about what Ivy might've been exposed to, and listened carefully to the answers Anika and Greg provided: all potentially harmful substances secured out of sight and reach; a diet of breast milk, formula, a little apple juice; and some beginner solid foods, meticulously prepared at home.

Ivy's wide eyes never seemed to leave Dan's face as if she knew this stranger was there to help her. Even with the extra oxygen, Dan saw that she hadn't yet 'pinked up' and his worry increased. He quietly asked the nurses to call for the on-call peds resident to come down to the ER stat.

"What's wrong with her?" Anika blurted.

Hoping he sounded unperturbed and confident, Dan answered, "We're still trying to figure that out, aren't we, Ivy?" Then glancing to her parents, he asked, "Has she, or anyone in your families, ever gotten blue like this before?"

"No," Anika answered. "She's been perfectly healthy. All of us are super-healthy."

"When did she start having problems?"

Anika frowned, thoughtful. "Well, over the last few weeks, she's seemed to tire more easily. Had a little trouble catching her breath sometimes. But she kept snapping back. I thought it was normal."

"What about her color? You've said she was never blue before, but has she been pale? Grayish?"

"Hell, Dan" Greg's bark of laughter strangled through his nervous tension. "We're Dutch. We're *all* pale!"

A chuckle rippled among those gathered around the child, easing the intensity of the moment, but Anika continued the thought: "You know, maybe she *has* been a little gray the last few days."

Guilt settled on the young mother's face. "I should've noticed that more. I've just recently gone back to work part time, and I'm afraid I come home exhausted."

Several voices, the most adamant Greg's, assured her there was no need to blame herself for not noticing.

As soon as Hank rolled in the equipment, Dan oversaw the speedy chest X-ray, and then studied the films with the ER senior resident, Dr. Tracey George, who was working with Dan for the first time. Neither of them saw any clear signs of heart defect or pulmonary problems. "I'll take these down for a reading as infant films can be tough," Tracey said. "You stay here since you know the family and they trust you. Page me right away if there is any change."

Nodding as she left, Dan turned to catch Mary hanging up the house phone. "Those labs back yet?" Mary looked a bit bewildered. She reported the numbers for the complete blood count and chem 7 panel. All perfectly normal. "What about the blood gas, Mary?"

"Not sent yet, Dr. Marchetti. You have to draw that."

In the rush of the moment, Dan had forgotten that in a child so young, only a physician was permitted to draw a gas and assume the liability of injuring a tiny artery. Chagrinned and wondering again if he was meant to do this doctor thing, Dan called to Mary, "Let's do it quick. We need answers." Then turning to speak to her quietly so that he would not be overheard by the anxious family, he said "And call respiratory . Tell them we may need them to prepare for an infant resuscitation. I'm worried she may tire and crash."

Dan took the blood gas kit and quickly reviewed infant sticks from his peds and newborn rotations. As Dan turned again towards Ivy, he saw she wasn't quite as stoic this time, beginning to whimper and squirm. It reminded him of how much he hated peds and the thought of hurting such a tiny being. Still, Tracey was in radiology, the peds resident hadn't yet arrived and Ivy was not getting better.

Successfully entering the artery, the plunger moved up as the blood entered the vial. He heard gasps and soft expletives above his bent head and no wonder: the blood filling the tube was the color of chocolate.

Greg's voice broke through, "What the *hell,* Dan?" Anika's eyes got wider than ever, and her teeth clenched her lower lip with such force Dan knew she must be tasting blood.

"It's okay," he told the Vandenbosks. "I'm pretty certain I know what this is now." He handed the vial to Mary. "Hurry this down to the lab. Tell them to test specifically for the methemoglobin level."

But Mary didn't move, staring at the tube of brown blood as if it were radioactive.

"I'll take it!" Hank offered and sprinted away.

"Tell us, Dan!" Greg pleaded.

Even as he turned to focus on Ivy's parents, he was aware of the stricken Mary whispering, "I didn't know . . . I shoulda seen that!" Sylvia put an arm around the younger nurse and led her out to the central area, murmuring what sounded to Dan like reassurances.

Dan reached out, touched Greg's arm in a gesture meant to convey patience. Looking to Gail, the only nurse remaining at the moment, he asked, "Did Tischler say he was staying late today?"

Gail nodded. "Think so."

"Give the peds resident another call and ask him to find Tischler. Tell them I have a nine month-old methemoglobinemic." As she moved quickly to the house phone, Dan gave his complete attention to the Vandenbosks, but before he could speak, Anika ventured, "Methemoglobinemic. . . ?"

"Those brown blood cells you saw have lost their ability to carry oxygen, so she keeps getting less and less. This is a very serious condition, but now that we know what the problem is, we're moving quickly to correct it. The next minutes to hours are crucial to getting this turned around."

"What will you do?" Anika asked apprehensively.

"I've called for the head of pediatrics, and he'll know precisely what treatment will be best for Ivy. But right now, in the time we have before Dr. T. can get here, we need to track down exactly what's caused it all so we can fix *that* problem and prevent this from happening again."

Aware Ivy was still riveted on him, he told her, "You're a little bit of a mystery, you know. Usually this happens to tinier babies, not big girls like you. But you've got us all fooled so far."

"What *could*'ve caused it?" Greg asked.

Dan explained how by the age of four months, infants could produce the digestive enzyme that allowed their bodies to process nitrates so they don't keep the hemoglobin from doing its job. He nodded to Gail as she returned to report, "Tischler's on his way down."

"Nitrate?" Anika repeated. "Where would she get that? I've heard of those in hotdogs and bologna, but we don't eat that stuff. We're vegetarians."

"Well, there *are* nitrates in some good-for-you veggies—carrots, beets, spinach, string beans."

"Omigod! I've started giving her strained carrots. I make them myself!"

"Wait, now," Dan insisted. "I really don't think that could be it. Even if you gave her a lot of those things I mentioned, the levels just shouldn't be high enough. In fact, under normal circumstances, and in moderation, even processed meats don't pose a risk for methemoglobinemia. It's gotta be something else. Remind me what other things besides mother's milk you feed her."

"A little baby cereal . . . apple juice . . . that's all."

"You mentioned formula. . . ?"

Anika looked embarrassed. "Just the mornings when I'm at work. She likes to have a bottle to hold on to, carry around."

"Do you mix it with anything?"

"Sure. Just water."

"Bottled water?"

Greg spoke up now. "We've been trying to economize. We gave up bottled water. Better for the environment, too, all those plastic containers, y'know?"

Dan nodded. "So tap water?" Now *they* nodded. "City water? You use filters?"

"We live way out in the country," Greg said. "We have our own well."

Dan knew he was on the right track; he could *feel* it. "Where do you live?"

"Out in Brookfields."

"Oh!" Gail exclaimed, straightening with a snap. Relatively new to the county, Dan had never heard of that community so looked to her for enlightenment. "Long-time agricultural region," she explained. "Lots of fertilizers, pesticides, animal waste washing into the water table."

Dan turned back to the Vandenbosks. "You have a sewer system or a septic tank?"

"Septic," Greg and Anika said in unison.

Dan nodded. "There could be leakage from that too. All those contaminants accumulate, concentrating nitrates. You'll have to stop ingesting your well water. It may be clean enough to drink, but it's not safe enough."

No doubt considering what they'd been drinking, the pair grimaced. Anika said, "Omigosh, I've been giving Ivy *bottles* of it! I wanted to limit the amount of fruit juice she drank because of the sugar content. So I've been filling her bottles with *water!* "She paused. Feeling good about how healthy that would be for her!"

Dan could see the young woman was close to tears, and as he —and Gail and Greg—tried to reassure her again, Dan considered again the high-wire act of parenthood. Perhaps trying to shift the focus elsewhere, Greg pointed out, "All of us have been drinking that water. *We're* just fine."

"Sure," Dan said. "But the amount of water adults consume in relation to their body weight is very different from an infant's.".

At that moment, Norm Tischler, the venerated head of pediatrics, swept into the room, greeting Greg and Anika even before acknowledging Dan and the nurses with a nod. Then he bent down to grin at Ivy. "So you must be the young lady who's given us such a puzzle: our Mystery Blue Girl." She looked up gravely but focused on the new face. He stood upright then and turned to Dan. "Good call, Marchetti. I talked to the lab. Her methemoglobin level is at 47. This is only the fourth time in my career I've seen methemoglobinemia, and never before in someone over three months." He turned to Ivy's parents. "We need to get Ivy admitted and on up to the pediatrics floor. We'll treat her with a drug called methylene blue, put it right in her I.V. That will help her inactive red blood cells regain their electrons and start doing their job again."

"How long?" Anika asked.

"Could be hours or a day or two." He looked to Ivy. "You're gonna get some really special medicine. It's blue! Imagine that: the Blue Girl gets blue medicine to make her all rosy pink again!"

In a matter of minutes, Tischler had whisked the Vandenbosk family away to his own realm on Six West, but not before Greg and Anika had pumped Dan's hand and thanked him profusely for saving their daughter. In the relative quiet that followed—while the nurses tidied up and sanitized everything in anticipation of their next emergency, Dan slumped down on a stool next to Tracey who had returned in time to hear the plan and to report that the chest X-ray had looked fine to the radiologist. Dan stared at the paperwork, completely exhausted. She grinned and said "OK, now for the truly important stuff…documenting! Dan nodded and closed his eyes as he felt the usual post-crisis adrenaline wash-out taking him away.

"Hey, Dan," a voice said. "You look like you been rode hard and put away wet."

He looked up into Gail's twinkling eyes. "Sorry, Dan. Farm-girl expression. You look wrung out. And you missed dinner."

"Upton back yet?"

Gail shook her head. Then, as if on cue, Mike Upton sauntered in, stretching luxuriously after a long stint napping in the on-call room. "I miss anything?"

Just at that moment, Sylvia Jenks returned, ushering their next patient toward the nearest exam bay. The man, burlier even than Hank Currie, clutched his belly, moaning about five-day-old chili just before he suddenly vomited, spattering Upton's shoes.

"You go," Gail told Dan under her breath.

"He's all yours, Mike," Dan called cheerfully. "I've gotta go grab some dinner."

He was barely out in the hall before he heard his name called.. He turned, saw Nurse Mary Dahl, her face still showing the ravages of tears. "I just wanted to apologize, Dr. Marchetti. I'm so sorry I didn't mention the dark blood when I drew the first sample."

"Hey, s'okay, Mary," he told her gently. "You probably never saw that before. In truth, neither have I. I just heard about it in med school."

"But I should've *said* something. It looked weird to me, but I've seen a lot of weird things in nursing."

Thinking of weird things *he'd* encountered in the few years he'd been involved in medicine, Dan smiled. "Yeah, well, it seems a lesson learned. If you see something you don't understand, speak up."

A shadow passed across her face, and she murmured, "Not all doctors are as open to comment."

"Well, if the doc won't listen, tell a nurse with more seniority. If Dr. Werner's around, tell *her*. Don't forget, she *was* a nurse; she knows the score from both sides."

Dan gazed after her, considering how difficult it must be sometimes for nurses. They had a lot of training and in-the-trenches experience with patients; they observed symptoms, behaviors, attitudes and reactions physicians often missed because of their limited "face time" with patients. Yet, doctors have all the power. Stomach growling, Dan turned again toward the cafeteria.

As soon as he had his food, thankfully no chili on the menu today, and had found a quiet corner where he could sit alone, Dan turned on his personal cell phone and checked for messages.

He found a cheery "Hi, honey. Hope you're having a good day in the ER!" from Nikki, and a voicemail left by Trey Hartmann:

"Hey, Dan. I know you're workin'. Just wanted to let you know I finished all the testing, it wasn't too bad, and I've just now parked at PNC in time for warm-up. I have another ten o'clock appointment tomorrow with Dr. Choi to get my results. I wonder if you can be there with me for that? Just leave me a message; I'm headed in for the game now. What a relief we're off tomorrow: no game, no practice. Well, see you tomorrow . . . I hope."

Without hesitation, Dan hit the button to dial back Trey's number and left the message that, of course, he'd be there for the appointment. "I have the same shift as today—noon to midnight—so come by our place first, and I'll go over with you."

Ending the call, Dan turned to his bowl of soup, silently praying that Trey wouldn't chicken out tomorrow. The first mouthful of the Cajun-spicy chicken gumbo brought tears to Dan's eyes, it was that hot. He savored four more bites, trying to still his thoughts and just be in the moment.

But foreboding curled in Dan's belly, and he pushed away the bowl of soup he suddenly found himself unable to eat.

CHAPTER FIFTY-TWO

Nikki'd hoped to see Greg Vandenbosk at the front-entrance security desk so she could hear how Ivy's methylene blue treatment was progressing, but she found the post manned by a young fellow she'd never seen before. Worried he wouldn't recognize her, she was glad she had clipped on her ID. As if it mattered; the guy barely glanced at her before nodding her through and returning his gaze to the fascinating papers on his desk.

Though she knew the seminar would be held in one of the conference rooms on this main floor, Nikki went, instead, to the elevator down to the floor below and headed for the Pavilion, a wing only added six years ago. At the juncture of the two corridors, a glassed-in foyer opened onto the Terrace.

That courtyard was especially well-named, for beyond its inviting grass-and-flagstone expanse with shade canopies supported by elegant concrete columns, the area *was* a terrace carved into the slope of the hill one floor below street-level. And like the fourth floor itself, in fact the whole north side of the hospital, the Terrace overlooked the valley below. There were four picnic tables and a number of benches, all angled to maximize their patrons' view.

She'd expected to find a number of people enjoying the area at this time of day, but there were only four figures in view. A pair of young women Nikki recognized from the Physical Therapy department had just picked up their lunch trash and were chatting as they headed to the far end where a stairway would take them back down to the third floor.

One bench was occupied, and she recognized the two men at once, even coming up from behind. Smiling as she thought of the surprise lunch she toted, Nikki moved toward them. Her soft-soled shoes made no sound, but still she couldn't quite catch their words…at first.

"Dammit, Dan! What don't you unnerstan'!" Trey exploded, suddenly leaping to his feet. "Back off!" Nikki froze mid-step—and saw the departing therapists turn to glance back before hurrying on out of view. Heart pounding, Nikki slid behind the cover of the nearest pillar and strained her ears, not wanting to intrude but needing to know.

Dan said something in a calm and quiet tone. Trey plopped back down on the bench, his voice still louder than normal. "I can't be taking *steroids!* Not after all the scandals."

Nikki could barely hear Dan's counter: "Solu-medrol is a *corticosteroid*, not an anabolic one. Since it's medically necessary, it's gotta be completely permissible for you to use it."

Dan followed suit, and Nikki missed what he said next. Surreptitiously, she moved nearer, till she was sheltered by the pillar closest behind the men and screened from other views by the lush plantings. From here she could watch the guys, but they wouldn't see her without turning. She could discern now that Trey was still trying to postpone the process. "It can't cure me," he challenged. "*Can* it?"

"No," Dan admitted. "Steroids can't repair the nerve damage that's already there." Nikki saw Trey shrug before he asked, "Then what's the point? I'm done."

Somehow Dan kept holding on to his patience despite having to bite is tongue to keep from pointing out how much better the prognosis might have been if Trey'd acted sooner. "Many people have significant relief with solu-medrol. It's worth trying." Then, as Trey started to protest again, Dan interrupted, "Look, you're here. Minutes away from a treatment that *could* relieve all your current symptoms. You have no game this evening; you can stay over with us tonight. Get your second treatment tomorrow. I bet if we clue Charlie in, he can get you excused for tomorrow night's game. Stay over again; get your last treatment on Saturday. Who knows? You might even be able to play that night. Then you're on oral meds and—"

"Doesn't matter." The utter dejection in Trey's voice tore at Nikki's heart. "They're not gonna let me play ball anymore. You know it, I know it. And all I am is a pitcher. There's nothing else for me"

"We don't know that."

"Yeah, we do." Nikki could sense the heroic effort it took for Dan to keep his exasperation and his own anguish beneath the surface.

Trey, at least, seemed oblivious. "There's no way I can continue performing at a major-league level. Before long I probably won't even be able to pitch at a *Double A* level, much less something in between. I bet I played my last game last night," he said with tears thickening his voice. "And it was crappy at that."

"Look, Trey. It's almost noon—"

But the young pitcher ignored him. "I've been reading on the internet, and beyond what I need for baseball, my eyes, my arms and legs and balance and all that, I have a lot more to lose. Who knows how long before I might not even be able to . . . you know . . . do it in bed! What woman is going to want me like that? No career, no wife, no kids even to teach to play the game I love. What kind of life is that? And how am I gonna support myself, or my folks who need help to keep their land going. This can't be real" Nikki heard his muffled sobs.

Dan sighed but he kept his voice calm. "I won't lie to you. Some of those things *might* happen, but it's far more likely you can have a long, functional and happy life, with someone who digs you. Let's cross those other bridges when you come to them, *if* you come to them."

Trey shook his head. "I don't think I can face this whole MS thing, Dan." His voice, eerily lifeless, raised the hairs on Nikki's arms, twisted her stomach with foreboding. "I can't."

Nikki stilled a gasp and saw Dan flinch as if he, himself, had been struck by a bullet. Suddenly she couldn't breathe. All she could think of was escaping that place, that moment.

She fled back toward the building, clutching, as if to a life jacket, the straps on her shoulders: her purse, the forgotten lunch tote. Slipping, undetected, back inside the foyer, she found new determination.

CHAPTER FIFTY-THREE

The whole thing had started a few minutes ago, when Cindy'd rushed back from her break to whisper excitedly, "There's a celebrity down in the Pavilion!"

Russ looked up from his paperwork with only mild interest. "Oh, yeah? Who?"

Russ is a good guy, Vinny had thought, standing, unnoticed, nearby. Vinny's opinion of Cindy fell far short of that; he found her lazy and careless—a bad match for this post-surgical ward. He'd learned the hard way she was also a tease sexually and a mean gossiper.

That essence animated her now as she leaned in and revealed in a low voice, "Trey Hartmann!"

Russ's face showed his surprise and, now, genuine interest. "The hot new Pirates southpaw?"

A third nurse moved closer. "Oooh! I'll say he's hot!" Joyce was older than Cindy but always eager to talk about what she called "eye candy" among the patients, visitors and staff. "I don't know . . . red hair and freckles really do it for me." It was at that moment she'd noticed Vinny standing there in his "wallpaper mode," hoping to remain undetected.

Perhaps embarrassed by what she realized he'd overheard, Joyce put on her best "supervisor" face and said coolly, "Thanks, Vinny, but we don't need you anymore right now. Take a break—I'll page you when 816's treatment is finished."

Dismissed, he'd shuffled off as if it didn't matter, but now, stooped behind the cart, he listened for more details.

Still keeping her voice low and conspiratorial, Cindy was just saying, "Yeah, I saw him at the outpatient desk, with that, you know, stunned look?" Russ and Joyce nodded; all hospital personnel knew that stunned look of the newly diagnosed. "He was with Dan Marchetti, who was asking for admission paperwork to be filled out."

"For what kind of treatment?" Russ asked.

"Dunno," Cindy admitted.

"God," Joyce said. "Y'don't think he has *cancer,* do you?"

The three just looked at each other in consternation. Vinny massaged his back where it was protesting his position and decided to move on. He slipped silently away. Knowing he had time before he'd be paged to pack up the equipment, he headed towards the fourth floor curious to see how the star pitcher and star intern had crossed paths and whether there was any role for a star respiratory tech.

CHAPTER FIFTY-FOUR

Light-headed from her sudden flight, Nikki slipped silently into private infusion room 3B and took a position where she could peer into 3A. A&B were designed as single rooms, where for a little extra, patients could be guaranteed some privacy.

The young pitcher was already sitting slumped on the edge of the recliner, looking at the floor instead of at either Dan or the nurse who was taking and recording Trey's vitals. Nikki recognized Nancy Eaton, a veteran nurse who'd on several occasions infused Nikki herself. Always kind and respectful, today Nancy looked tired and more than a little harried.

"Just relax," Dan was telling Trey. "Lie back and put your arm here on the rest."

Woodenly, the patient obeyed, as if all protest had been drained from him. Dan continued a light, distracting bit of conversation while Nancy expertly prepped Trey's arm and inserted the intravenous port that could be left in place until the I.V. treatments were completed two days from now. Trey didn't watch the insertion and gave no indication that he'd felt it, nor that he was listening to Dan's words.

Nancy told Dan, "I'll go get the solu-medrol Dr. Choi ordered." When he nodded, she patted Trey's shoulder. "I'll be right back, Mr. Hartmann."

He might'nt've heard for all the notice he gave, staring into space. In the nurse's absence, Dan, too, fell silent.

Behind the dark blue curtain, Nikki, still feeling light-headed and weak, scolded herself. Her own chemo treatments required that she carefully keep up her calorie and fluid intake but the sandwiches were stashed untouched in the conference room. She checked her watch, still forty minutes before the seminar would begin.

Nancy returned with the I.V. bag in one hand and a clipboard with an attached pen, in the other. "Looks like we somehow missed one of the forms during registration. If you'll just initial this paragraph and sign at the bottom, Mr. Hartmann. . . ."

Trey took the clipboard and began to read the sheet pinned to it. From what she'd covertly witnessed earlier, Nikki knew he'd barely glanced at all the other papers he'd been given to read or sign. But now he focused on the task as Nancy hung the I.V. bag on its stand and connected the tubing to the port in his arm. She didn't, however, start the drip while she watched Trey peruse the form.

As Trey continued to read, looking more-and-more attentive, Nancy glanced at her wristwatch and shot a glance at Dan, who shrugged.

They squeezed Trey in, Nikki remembered. Nancy might be pressed for time with her other duties, but as an experienced nurse, she didn't rush him.

"Shit!" Trey blurted. "No way I'm signin' *that!*" He tossed the clipboard onto the recliner. It slid to the floor with a clatter; the pen went rolling. Now glaring at Dan, he accused, "You never told me this stuff has all these side effects. Neither did Choi."

"That wasn't intentional," Dan answered quietly. "Guess I was so concentrated on all the *benefits* of treatment."

"Well, I don't want it."

The nurse, who'd bent to retrieve the clipboard and pen, checked her watch again and glanced toward the door as if she expected any minute someone would come to see what was keeping her.

Dan lifted his hands imploringly. "Look, that's a standard informed-consent. We have to tell you every possible side effect or complication. You ever read the list of side effects for *aspirin?* The majority for solu-medrol are pretty minor. The chances of you, or any one person, having most of them is statistically very remote."

"'Statistically very remote,'" Trey repeated the doctor-speak in mocking tones. "Like getting fuckin' MS, right? But it's my right to refuse, isn't it?"

"Yes, of course, it is," Dan conceded. "But I hope you'll reconsider. Trey, I feel really sure this is your best shot for right now . . . that the benefits will outweigh the risk of your having, even temporarily, a couple of the more common side effects on that list."

When Trey didn't respond, Nancy placed the clipboard, with reattached pen, beside his legs on the recliner and offered, "Would you like a few minutes alone to think about it, Mr. Hartmann?"

Not looking at either the nurse or his friend, Trey nodded wordlessly, and the other two moved from the room and into the hallway

Nikki, her shoes as silent on the polished floor as on the flagstones, slipped over to the doorway where she could hear Nancy and Dan speaking in low voices in the corridor.

"That works sometimes," the nurse was telling the young doctor. "Just backing off and letting them wrestle to their own conclusion. They usually choose what's best for them; they just like to feel it's *their* decision."

"I'll remember that. I'm sorry for the delay. I know you guys're jammed today."

"Yeah, and I said I'd cover for Maureen so she could attend the seminar."

"No reason to hang you up. Why don't you go on. I can start a drip. I was planning to sit with him a little while anyway."

"The way you do sometimes with Nikki," Nancy added. Still Nancy hesitated. "Are you sure, Dr. Marchetti?"

"Yeah. He's a friend. He'll be staying over with us the next coupla nights. I plan to drive him home whenever he's finished."

"You and Nikki have Trey Hartmann as a houseguest? Wow."

"He's really a nice guy. Too bad you had to meet him in full denial-resistance mode."

In the next pause, Nikki knew Nancy was weighing her options. Her workload versus the fact Hartmann was the clinic's patient, and her responsibility—not Dan's. But in Medicine's political hierarchy, even a first-year MD trumped an experienced RN. And anyone who knew Dan knew he could be trusted to take responsibility. "Okay," Nancy said. "Thank you."

Nikki hurried back across 3B to take her post at the edge of the blue curtain.

Dan was just reentering 3A. Trey lay back on the recliner, once again looking worn down and apathetic. He still held the clipboard.

"Hey, guy," Dan said with forced lightness. "You make up your mind?"

Without glancing up, Trey held out the clipboard.

Dan took it, scanned it and smiled. "Good! Wise choice." Trey made no response. Setting aside the signed consent where staff would find it, Dan started the drip and made a minor adjustment. "It may sting a little just at the beginning." Then he pulled a chair over where he could sit beside the recliner.

Nikki couldn't tell if Dan was really relieved at Trey's compliance or whether he was wondering if what he was seeing was surrender and maybe a way for Trey to get everyone off his back. . . biding his time till he was able to take his fate into his own hands?

Nikki shivered. She hated guns and someone had to find the body, and someone always had to clean up.

Ignoring Trey's mood and behavior, Dan stood beside the chair and said, "Thought I'd sit and talk a while, if that's okay with you. . . ?"

"Whatever . . ."

"I know you are feeling like nothing will get better, right now," Dan said as he watched the solu-medrol slowly flow into Trey's vein. "But don't give up. You're strong and you can fight this."

Nikki checked her watch again. She would need to head down to the seminar soon but didn't want to miss anything important.

Before Trey could answer, Dan's beeper went off. He checked it for the extension trying to contact him. "Scuse me a second," he told Trey and went over to the house phone to be connected. After he'd said, "Marchetti here," he listened, then promised, "I'll be right there."

Hanging up, he went back to Trey but didn't sit. "Sorry, guy. They need me in the ER. Pile-up on the Interstate, and we're getting a bunch of 'incoming.'"

Trey nodded, actually looking more relaxed. "Sure. Go be a doctor. I'm fine here now."

"Good. I'll be back as soon as I can. And don't forget you're coming home with me after this."

"Sure," Trey repeated. "Don't worry about me."

"Can't help it," Dan said, failing to mask the emotion in his voice. He reached to squeeze the other man's shoulder.

Trey covered that hand with his and managed to say, "Thanks."

That moment, that exchange, brought sudden tears stinging into Nikki's eyes. Then Dan was gone, his white lab coat flapping as he dashed toward what awaited in the ER.

Nikki took a moment to wipe the tears from her eyes. She straightened herself and went to the other end of the blue curtain and around it, into 3A. Trey glanced up, obviously startled to see someone entering his space from there and even more surprised to see her. "Hey, Nikki! Didn't expect to see you."

She gave him her brightest smile and began to take his vitals and readjust the IV bag.

He surveyed her crisp scrubs and ID badge, perhaps remembering he'd last seen her in sweats this morning as she washed up after breakfast. "I didn't know you worked in this department."

"I'm a nurse. We always show up where we are needed. You doing okay?"

"I guess. Considering. . . ."

"I know this must be hard for you" Reaching up she checked the flow rate again then sat down close to him and began to hum.

"What's that you're humming?"

She smiled. "Just something to make you feel better. It works with my pediatric patients when they're scared and feel alone. I learned it from a nurse who took care of me when I was younger and in a hospital for a while."

A moment later, he murmured, "Hey. You should bottle that tune. Right now I just want to rest till this is all over. Today has just wiped me out, you know?"

"I know. Just relax. There's plenty of time to talk when you come back to the apartment tonight."

"You two have been very good to me. I've been giving Dan a bit of a hard time but I think it's time I grew up. Don't you think?" Trey yawned, closed his eyes and seemed to drift away.

She took his hand and gave it a gentle squeeze, allowing, as she had with so many others, a wave of her most heartfelt compassion to flood into him. "You take care, Trey. I'll tell Dante you are feeling better. He'll be so glad."

Nikki gave one last squeeze to his hand as she moved quickly to the door, on her way to the seminar. As she passed Vinny Orlander she ducked her head so that he wouldn't see the tears she felt ready to fall for Trey and all the patients who got dealt a bad hand.

CHAPTER FIFTY-FIVE

Linda Ferrante had just kicked off her pumps and settled into her chair for her favorite evening entertainment: watching the deer family materialize, like ghosts, from the dusk shadows across the meadow below. As she raised her wineglass to her lips, anticipating that first glorious sip of Lambrusco, her cell phone rang. She groaned, realizing it was still in her purse, over by the door.

Defiantly, she sat and let the damn thing ring, savoring the light sparkle of the red wine's progress across her tongue and then the after-hints of fruit and flowers before she rose and went to pull the phone from its handy purse pocket. She checked the display as it rang for the fifth or sixth time. *Bradden.* She flipped open the case, ready to complain that she was barely home from the office, but the D.A.'s voice cut her off: "Local news. Right now. My office tomorrow—six a.m. sharp!" He hung up before she could say a word.

She padded back across the room in her stockinged feet, dropped into the chair. Trading her cell for the TV remote next to her wineglass on the end table, she clicked on the set.

"And now for that breaking news report we promised." The local sportscaster, mic in hand, stood in front of Deerwood Community Hospital. Across the bottom of the screen scrolled: *SUDDEN DEATH OF PITCHER SHOCKS PIRATES.*

"An official spokesperson for Deerwood Community Hospital has just confirmed rumors that Pirates rookie phenom, Trey Hartmann, died suddenly this afternoon, apparently of cardiac arrest, while undergoing treatment at one of DCH's outpatient clinics. Citing privacy laws, our source declined to disclose the condition for which Hartmann was being treated, but stated that the death was unexpected and that full resuscitation efforts were initiated immediately, but to no avail. Further, the spokesperson revealed that the cause of Hartmann's cardiac arrest is still unclear, pending the results of an autopsy, but assured us that the hospital will investigate the circumstances fully."

No wonder Bradden's wetting his pants, Linda thought as she continued to listen in disbelief. Another suspicious death at DCH—this time linked with a sports celebrity.

The scene on the tube had changed: The station's other sportscaster was speaking now, live from the field at PNC Park. "Shock waves have rolled quickly through the Pirates organization where players, coaches and trainers alike denied knowledge of any illness." Stepping to the side, he included another young man in a two-shot. "This is Hartmann's fellow pitcher, Odell Shaw. What can you tell us, Odell?" He tilted the mic toward the stunned-looking African American face.

"I still can't believe it. Trey was younger'n me . . . strong . . . fast. He took care of himself. He was a great guy," Shaw's voice broke on the last word. "Everybody loved him."

With a compassionate "Thank you," the reporter stepped away to a one-shot. "Most of the team is away from PNC today, since there's no game tonight, but a few people gave us statements. Batting coach William Dexter seemed mystified by the events of the day, saying, 'Hartmann was the picture of health . . . at the top of his form. It's a devastating loss, not only for our team but for all of baseball and everyone who knew him.'"

The Pirates had never been Linda's team. She'd grown up a loyal Yankees fan, like her grandpa, but, since moving so close to Pittsburgh and needing to function among her mostly-male colleagues, she'd made it a point to stay informed about baseball in general and the Pirates in particular.

The newscaster continued his coverage by reporting how Hartmann's parents were being flown in at the club owner's expense on his private jet.

"Retired manager, Charlie Monroe, now the team's senior scout, discovered Hartmann and had become a mentor, said on behalf of the club, 'The Pirates will assist Trey's family with whatever arrangements they desire, whatever they need. It's the least we can do, as Trey is—was—also part of the Pirates family. For right now, we ask that the media give the Hartmanns some space and privacy during this difficult time.'

"Monroe also told us the team had considered canceling its home game here tomorrow against the Florida Marlins, but decided to play in Hartmann's honor with Odell Shaw pitching."

Linda's cell rang again, and she wasn't at all surprised to read the display: *Conover.*

"Ferrante," she answered.

"I'm sure you've heard the news. Just wanted you to know things're heating up. I moved a few rocks at the hospital, and all kinds of things crawled out. For one thing, I found out that, though Hartmann was pronounced dead in the ER when they couldn't get his heart started, he actually *died* in the infusion clinic, where people get drugs for stuff like chemotherapy. Patients don't usually *die* there. So that's suspicious."

"Oh?"

Conover seemed not to notice her less than enthusiastic response. "Our young Dr. Marchetti's fingerprints are all over this. Maybe quite literally. For one thing, apparently he was the one who administered whatever drug was being infused, and are you ready for this? *Hartmann wasn't even his patient!*"

Still hard to see the guy as a serial killer but there did seem to be a facts stacking up against him. She just wished Conover didn't sound like he relished this so much.

Unfazed by her silence, the detective finished the conversation all by himself. "I know what you're thinking, no solid evidence yet, but there *will* be. And knowing Bradden, he'll probably want to see you early tomorrow. Now you have something to tell him. Don't worry, I'll have plenty more to share. I'll be in touch as soon as I do." For the second time in an hour, a caller hung up without waiting for a reply from her.

She slowly set aside the phone and turned back to the TV screen. The news report had become a biographical sketch of Trey Hartmann's short life, snapshots and home movies of him growing up in rural Nebraska, followed by still photos and news footage of his rise to fame.

Linda felt a tightness in her throat, realizing just how young he had been and how unfair life could be. She clicked off the set, picked up her wineglass and settled back in her chair. Looking out the big window, she turned for the solace of her deer. But they were gone.

CHAPTER FIFTY-SIX

Dan's watch read two a.m. as he slipped, exhausted, into his apartment. Impossible to believe just thirty-six hours ago Brian Callahan was pronouncing Trey dead in the ER. Dan rubbed a hand across his eyes, as if he could wipe away the memories. Blinking in the dimness, he had to concede that it was all real, every bit of it.

All the apartment lights were out except the little bulb over the stove. Just enough light to see the note Nikki'd left on the table when she went to bed, *Turkey sandwich in fridge,* signed with her usual *N* inside a heart.

He wasn't hungry. He'd managed, despite a lack of appetite, to get some dinner at the hospital. He'd also already showered there after another bloody night at the ER. Still, nothing like the scene the night before as they treated the victims of the Interstate pile-up.

So much of that day was a blur starting from when he left Trey's side. Early into those first moments of noise and frenetic action, staunching blood-flow and flushing wounds, identifying broken bones and defibrillating hearts, it got even more unreal. Concentrated as he was on applying vigorous chest compressions, he barely heard the intercom calling a code down in the infusion clinic. Then, mere instants later, a gurney shot into the ER and past him to another, till-then-empty bay.

A quick glance gave him the image of Brian Callahan atop the orderly-propelled stretcher, mirroring Dan's own motions of forceful CPR while Vinny Orlander ran alongside, squeezing an ambu-bag. Little could be seen of the patient's pale face beneath the oxygen, but the close-cropped red hair was unmistakable.

As in a dream, Dan heard the voices swirling around him—not only everything that'd already been going on in his room, but, rising above that the excited, incredulous words that included the name "Trey Hartmann!"

Stunned, Dan had only a fraction of a second to consider this impossibility before putting all his attention back on the man whose chest he was pumping as he called for the medications and procedures necessary to save that man's life.

It was hours later, only after he and his colleagues had helped the patients they could and had dealt with distraught relatives and investigating police officers, before he could finally take a moment to search out the answer to the tiny, recurrent mental question: How can Trey be *dead*?

Nikki showed up on her way home after her nursing seminar. Of course, she'd heard the news. The DCH grapevine had crackled into action before Trey's gurney had left the infusion clinic. She joined Dan in his quest for information, gripping his hand with comforting strength. But they found few details. No one who'd come up from the clinic with Trey was still around to question. Nurse Mary Dahl, who'd been part of the ER code, shared everything she knew.

As soon as Brian had called the death, one considered unusual and unexpected, the body had been transported exactly as it was, directly into the custody of the medical examiner. Cardiac arrest in an athlete so young raised many questions, even without his celebrity status. It was left to the M.E. to remove and preserve all the tubing, lines and I.V. bags used, pending autopsy.

The sum-total of known facts was few. Nurse Nancy Eaton had found Trey going into cardiac arrest on the infusion recliner and had called a code. Brian, on rotation in the next-door oncology unit, was the first physician to arrive, finding Vinny already there. Together, they'd intubated Trey and worked on him all the way to the ER, but they never got him back. End of story. So far, at least.

Dan was on till midnight, so Nikki went on home . . . to the apartment where they'd all planned for Trey to have dinner and stay the night.

When Dan had finally dragged himself home, he found Nikki waiting up for him. He couldn't face even the chicken soup she had ready, but she insisted he drink one of her nutrition shakes before falling into bed.

She'd let him sleep nine hours, waking him to a hearty brunch. Then they'd walked to DCH together with time to nose around before his noon shift and the next segment of her seminar. They'd hoped to talk to Brian in person, but he wasn't on duty. No one seemed to know much of anything new. The autopsy had yet to be performed, pushed off till much later that day, due to the prior occupancy of the DCH morgue and the M.E.'s schedule.

Frustrated in their investigation, Dan reported to the ER, and Nikki went off to visit with some of her DCH staff friends, perhaps learning more, until it was time for her lecture to begin.

Now, just past two on Saturday morning, Dan moved quietly across the living room. In the doorway of the bedroom, ambient light revealed Nikki's sleeping form in their bed. Dan went to use the bathroom and change into his sleep sweats hung on the back of the door.

Nikki stirred and woke as he tried to slide into bed without disturbing her. She snuggled close in her comforting way and murmured, "How was the rest of today—uh, yesterday?"

He shrugged. "Not bad, ER-wise, till we got jammed toward the end of shift."

"Another accident?"

"No. Another wanta be gang shoot-out."

She grimaced and changed the subject: "Find out anything else?"

"Not much. Everyone's talking about it, but little's known. No one can really believe it. A buncha people know we were friends, so they've gone out of their way to sympathize with me and ask what *I* know, but they usually know everything I do. How was *your* sleuthing?"

"About the same. Any news on the autopsy?"

"Not much," Dan said again. "Kinda strange though. It got performed, but then everything went all hush-hush. No one would give a single detail about the results."

"DCH trying to control the media while they investigate?"

"Probably." Dan yawned. "I *did* get called to a Care Review Committee meet—"

"Really?" She'd rolled back, propping her head with one hand. "That was quick."

"There's a lotta pressure, I guess. The media's certainly all over the place."

"Yeah, I noticed that too. Well, how did it go?"

"It was no big deal. I went in, met five people I'd never heard of before . . . very courteous and pretty formal. I answered a dozen or so questions about why I was with Trey, why I was the one to start the I.V., why I left, whether I worked on him in the ER, if there was anything else I remembered, stuff like that. They took notes, thanked me for my time, and that was it."

"Whatta y'think they'll find?" Nikki asked.

Dan felt the sadness crowding into him. "The truth, I hope. I hear that DCH's Quality Assurance is pretty thorough." He took a shaky breath against his pain and frustration. "Every person who knew Trey, family, friends, everyone in baseball, the public, all of us deserve answers about how and why he died. Right?" The last word came out on an unexpected sob.

Instead of answering, Nikki pulled him close again. "I guess it was just his time, honey."

Startled, Dan pulled back to stare at her. "Cardiac arrest at 24? No way. Even with MS, he had a long *life* ahead of him."

She reached up to brush his hair away from his forehead. "I hate to see you so upset, sweetie. I remember how hard it was on you when Joe Bonfiglio died."

"Sure I was upset. He was barely older than me and with a great family and a new baby. That kind of 'unfair' is hard to watch. But even so, it really *was* Joe's time. We all knew it, and he made sure to go out on his own terms with a DNR. Completely different from Trey's situation."

Nikki glanced away, tugging at her sleepcap, and murmured, "At least they're both out of their misery now."

Dan hesitated. Was she thinking of her own cancer. Should he push? He chose the safer path. "Trey wasn't in misery. He wasn't sick like Joe."

"But he was miserable in his life. Talking about not having a future . . . about taking his own life."

Seeing the misery on *her* shadowed face, he gave her a little squeeze and lightened his tone. "Nikki, you're thinking like a woman. I think that was just Trey's 'guy' way of saying, 'I'm devastated. I'm scared. I don't think I can handle this.' I think I could've gotten him past all that. I was already planning how to get him support and counseling. Something I know I should have pushed Alex to sooner." The lightness slipped away from Dan, chased by lurking despair. "But Trey didn't even get a chance to start hoping again."

"Oh, Dante, it breaks my heart to see you so sad. You did everything you could and it's not your fault he's dead. You have to know that"

He rubbed a hand across his face. "Yeah, Joe was a sorrow, but Trey is the heartbreak. Most especially for those close to him. Poor Charlie Monroe."

"Charlie?" She seemed eager for a change of subject. "You talked to him?"

"Yeah, he called me to find out what more I knew about Trey's MS. Apparently he'd talked to Choi. I told him I was sorry that Trey had sworn me to secrecy, and maybe it was better for him to get all the medical details from Dr. Choi himself." Dan sighed. "He wasn't happy with me, especially how Trey and I had deceived him."

"How'd you leave it?"

"Well, it was awkward. We kept falling silent.

She gave him a tiny smile. "Yes, but there're definitely warmer kinds of comfort available." Nikki's voice had dropped low and inviting as she ran one hand down his ribs and hip to rest on his thigh.

He appreciated the offer of her body's comfort, but, patting her hand, he turned on his side, away from her. "Thanks, Nik, but I'm just dead . . . uh, tired." He punched his pillow into a better shape beneath his cheek, blotting his tears, hoping she couldn't hear them in his voice. "See ya in the morning."

Just as sleep took him, Dan thought he heard Nikki crying into her own pillow.

CHAPTER FIFTY-SEVEN

Dan awoke from a nightmare that it was still May and he was still assigned to the ER. He lay, sweating, alone in the bed, hearing the sounds of Nikki out in the kitchen, making breakfast. He inhaled deeply the perfume of brewing coffee, and when the scent of freshly chopped cilantro also delighted his nostrils, he remembered. She had promised huevos rancheros this morning.

Closing his eyes gratefully, he waited for the relief to help slow his heart rate. It was Saturday—the first one in June. Off today, he would go back to work on Sunday on a nice, safe medicine floor. Good to have a reprieve from the ER, though he had to admit the second two weeks of May hadn't been as bad as the first. Sure, there were tragedies. But nothing like that interstate pile-up or losing Trey.

There'd even been some lighter moments: the guy with a live moth in his ear and the "orange girl" who just didn't want to admit to her worried college roommates that she'd used way too much sunless tanning lotion. Dan'd enjoyed some satisfying successes, including a few interesting diagnoses. Then a long Memorial Day weekend of extreme sunburns; various food-borne illnesses; two cases of fireworks burns; and all the bites: bug bites, three dog bites, and even an incidence of "deer bite" at Candlebury Park. Nothing worse, thank the saints.

Finally, June and another rotation...his last! Then on to his second year of residency at DCH, welcoming July's crop of newbie interns.

"Hey, sleepyhead!" Nikki's voice pulled him from his reverie. He opened his eyes to see her smiling at him from the bedroom doorway, wiping her hands on a dishtowel. "Breakfast in ten." Turning back toward the kitchen, she called, "Y'might wanta rethink the whole 'shorts' thing. It's raining—for now at least."

Dan rolled out of bed, still thinking about the changes coming in July. By the middle of the month, Nikki could be back to work—at least part time. Norm Tischler and the whole peds Department were eager to have her back and were helping her get ready, including the group who met her in the gym several days a week to make sure she kept up with her exercise and weight-training. She was looking more fit and had more stamina. With only two remaining ABVD treatments, all her MUGA scans had shown her heart muscle was still fine after so many treatments. All indications pointed toward remission. In fact, everything was looking brighter for her future.

Pulling on jeans and a long-sleeve T-shirt, Dan wondered why he was still feeling so drained and blue. Of course, it *was* only three weeks and two days since Trey's death, and there were still so many questions unanswered about all that. The autopsy had shown an elevated potassium level, certainly enough to cause cardiac arrest. But Trey's bloodwork for Dr. Choi, only the day before, revealed a perfectly normal level. And it just got stranger from there. When the M.E. tested the I.V. bag and lines, he'd found traces of potassium; an anaesthetic, lidocaine; and the tranquilizer Ativan. What in the world were *those* doing in with the solu-medrol? The logical jump was that someone had purposely taken Trey out of this world.

Of course, all the DCH gossipers and paranoids were having a field day, saying someone must've injected Trey with potassium chloride, adding the anesthetic lidocaine to keep the chemical from burning too much and the Ativan to let him nod off. Otherwise, the patient would likely complain loud enough to raise an alarm. That, at least, makes sense, Dan thought as he tried, not for the first time, to think who could have wanted to kill his friend..

Everybody loved Trey. That was clear at his Pittsburgh memorial service, the one held before his parents took him back home to Nebraska for burial in the family plot. Dan'd found it really hard, meeting Trey's mom and dad . . . embarrassed to hear how well their son had spoken of him. It reminded him of the Alex situation—but without the redemptive ending.

The church was packed with members of the public and the press, with every single one of Trey's fellow Pirates and many of their families. All the team big-wigs showed up, including, of course, Charlie Monroe. Though the Pirates had played in town a whole week after Trey died, and had returned again after another week away for games in Cincinnati and Arizona, the memorial was the only time Dan'd had contact with Charlie. Having tried calling twice and leaving messages, but never getting a call back, Dan decided not to be pushy. At the service, they'd shaken hands and commiserated, but Charlie's demeanor was still very cool.

Nikki set a big plate of food in front of him—two sunny-side eggs resting on corn tortillas and generously topped by her homemade enchilada sauce sprinkled with the fragrant, dark-green cilantro. Grated cheddar melted invitingly on the accompanying portion of refried beans. Despite himself, Dan felt suddenly ravenous and reached for his fork with an *"Mmmmm!"* of appreciation and gratitude.

Nikki smiled as she sat with her own plate and remarked, "That was a pretty big sigh, cowboy." She let it trail off in a question, and he knew he'd have to tell her what was on his mind.

"I was thinking about Charlie," Dan admitted.

She nodded sympathetically as she swallowed her first bite. "Yeah, it's too bad he's still keeping you at a distance." She shrugged. "We've both seen this before. Some people need to have someone to blame."

Dan felt the need to defend the old man. "Well, he's pretty busy, y'know. I bet most of the team looks to him more than anyone else to be the 'glue' right now."

"Uh-huh. He's done pretty well, considering. Last night was a heartbreaker though: 0-7! And after whipping the Brewers in all four games this week."

Dan sipped his coffee slowly. And the Pirates had been worth talking about recently. In the last three weeks, though they'd lost four out of five away games, they'd won six out of eight at home in PNC. "Think they'll get rained out today?"

She shook her head. "Doubt it. Prediction is just drizzle for the afternoon."

"That's good for us too for the high school game."

Her face brightened. "Yeah. I'd hate for the team to have their big game called."

The Deerwood High baseball team was facing its biggest cross-town rival today, and its star player was a former patient of Nikki's. Dan had been with Nikki when they ran into the strapping lad Luke Mirren in the market. The boy's affection for his former nurse was clear, and he shyly told Dan, "She saved my life, you know. I was so sick, I'd sort of given up, but she made me fight and get better. Seemed every time I opened my eyes she'd be sitting there humming!"

"And look at you now!' Nikki beamed.

"So you have to come to my big game on June 3, okay? I'm getting the Most Improved Player Award afterwards."

"Wouldn't miss it," Nikki had promised.

Now, finishing breakfast, Nikki smiled wistfully and told Dan, "Wish all my patients could've recovered so well."

He drained the last of his coffee and glanced at his watch. "We'd better get a move on if we wanta get everything you want at the nursery and still be back in time for Luke's game."

She grinned at him. "Can't wait to have those new flowerboxes on the balcony! Nothing like some colorful petunias to brighten your day."

They both rose at the same time and started to clear the table. Dan leaned to kiss her temple. "Thanks for an awesome breakfast, Nik. Let me take care of the dishes."

As she went, smiling to get ready, he contemplated her recent fixation on improving their outdoor space, her endless dedication to making the world cheerier, prettier, more pleasant and comforting. He wondered whether that was a woman thing or a nurse thing. Probably both he decided.

By mid-afternoon, when Dan parked his blue Accord at Candlebury Park, the rain and drizzle had pulled back into a sky that was merely sulky and dank.

They were early for the game, so Dan easily found a street-side parking space quite near the baseball diamond's bleachers. Rolling up her passenger-side window to within an inch of the top, Nikki commented, "At least we don't have to worry about it being too hot for the plants. Sorry it took so long at the nursery but it was worth it, no?" She slid out of her seat and turned back to place Dan's medical bag in the space she'd just vacated. They'd had to move that black-leather gift from his parents, because the trunk was packed with bags of potting soil and plant food.

The back seat, covered by plastic sheeting, barely had room for the three redwood flowerboxes, each crowded full of bright-bloomed, still-potted plants individually chosen by Nikki for their colors and patterns.

He went around to her side of the car where she was shouldering a green-and-tan canvas tote. Emblazoned with the Deerwood High Bucks logo, it was serving today as her purse and, of more interest to Dan, a carrier for their snacks and bottled water. He'd noticed she was looking tired but when he offered to take the tote for her, she declined. "I'm okay, but thanks. Gotta start doing more for myself again."

He squeezed her arm gently. "You just say when you want help."

She stepped close to hug him, murmuring, "How'd I ever get so lucky?"

He leaned against the car, and, resting one cheek on top of her head, he held her for a long minute, feeling her fragility.

Then, with a smile, they walked across the street together, and toward the bleachers, each with one arm around the other.

Some of the Bucks were on the field, warming up. Nikki waved to Luke Mirren on the pitcher's mound, and he saluted her with a ball-touch to his cap. When the boy executed a sweet fastball, left-handed, Dan felt a twinge in his heart, remembering the joy Trey had found on the mound.

The lower parts of the stands were beginning to fill up. Dan guessed they were mostly friends and families of the players. A few parents were taking advantage of what Diane Werner had once disdained as "crowd childcare": allowing one's kids to run wild in public places and trusting "the village" to keep an eye on them. About four or five around the age of seven were now whooping it up, throwing popcorn at each other as they ran up and down the concrete stairways separating the rows of green-painted, wooden-bench seating.

Nikki winced at the noise but laughed wistfully. "If only someone could *bottle* that kind of energy!"

One of the kids had now fallen on the rough steps and was crying, which provoked a parent into shouting orders and admonishments that went largely ignored. "Hey, Nik?" Dan asked. "Wanta go up top where it'll be quieter?"

"Yes!" They started up the steep stairway. About halfway to the top, Dan slipped the tote's straps from Nikki's shoulder and onto his own. She didn't protest.

Finally they sat, two rows from the very top and some distance from any other spectators. Nikki was puffing a little, but they both pretended she was just sighing in relief at the comparative tranquility. The view was good from there and they settled in. Dan put his arm around her again, and she leaned heavily against him, closing her eyes as she let her breathing return to normal.

"Ni-kki!" bellowed a voice nearby. "Nikki Sax-on!" This time the emphasis was on the last name. Beside him, Dan felt Nikki tense and sit up, but she didn't try to leave the comfort of his encircling arm.

That voice pierced the air again: "Hey, *Missus* Saxon!"

Dan saw a tall, dark-haired man, disheveled and red-faced, charging up the stairway toward them. He had seen that face on a photo with Nikki's stuff...Matt Saxon.

As Dan wondered what Nikki was feeling, what exactly he should do or say, Nikki took a deep breath and patted his leg, as if to say, *"Don't worry. I've got this."*

When he reached their row, Matt approached with shoulders hunched high and fists balled. "I thought that was you." His words, slightly slurred, addressed Nikki as if she were alone. "No one fills out a T-shirt quite like my Nikki. Though you look a little thin, honey."

Dan's jaws clenched. Nikki stared up at her estranged husband and said coolly, "We're only s'posed to communicate through our lawyers."

Matt went on as if he hadn't heard. "I saw you an' your big-shot doctor gettin' all lovey-dovey right there on the street." With a too-wide sweep of his arm, he gestured back toward Deerwood Boulevard, almost unbalancing himself. He took a wobbly step to compensate. "Dish-gusting."

Though Dan's arm could feel the tension crackling through her, Nikki said nothing, just stared at Matt as if waiting for him to leave.

Now the intruder turned his attention to Dan, though his words still addressed Nikki. "So this is your hot-shit doctor, huh? Jesus, Nik. Up close, he looks like he's seventeen!" Matt guffawed at his own joke and glared at Dan. "You sure you're a *real* doctor, kid? Or you jus' like *playin'* doctor with another man's *wife!?*"

Nikki probably sensed Dan gathering his energy for a response. All this time, she'd left her hand resting on Dan's blue-jeaned thigh, and now she squeezed slightly, reminding him she still wanted to be in charge. But Dan could tell her patience had eroded; her tone was sharper. "Go home, Matt. Sleep it off. We're done; it's over."

"Like hell it is! We're done when I say we're done!" Moving more quickly than anyone would expect, Matt reached down and grabbed Nikki's wrist and started dragging her up from the bench, ignoring her gasp of surprise and pain. "You're coming home with me where you belong! You're still *married* to *me!*"

That was too much for Dan. He shot to his feet, stepping between Matt and Nikki, one hand outstretched toward the aggressor but not intending to touch him. "Let her go! You're hurting her. Don't you remember she's been sick?"

Matt'd been forced to release her, both by her struggle against him and Dan's block. But this tipped him off-balance again, and he staggered forward, brushing Dan's open hand. "Don't touch me!" Matt roared.

Dan knew he needed to dial this back, "Listen, man; let's just calm down—"

A noise like a beast in pain tore from Matt as he wheeled his arms wildly. "Don't you ever tell *me* what to do—you piss-ant, mother-fuckin' home-wrecker!"

He swung, a wild haymaker of a punch, but Dan had only to step back and let it go past without connecting. The momentum carried Matt, and, as he lurched in the tight space, his foot caught the back of the next-down row of seats. He pitched face-forward over that row and his chest smacked down with a sickening sound on the seat back of the row below that. He thrashed a moment, turning himself part way over, but then he lay still.

Wordless, Dan and Nikki both clambered over the intervening row of seats to crouch beside the unconscious man. In that moment, conflict forgotten, all relationships and history fell away. They were functioning entirely as doctor and nurse with a patient.

Dan observed that Matt was breathing but with shallow and labored breaths. Nikki, fingers pressed to the carotid artery in Matt's neck, reported his pulse: "He's at 30."

"Not good, I need access to his chest. Help me move him." He didn't have to tell her to support and stabilize Matt's head and neck. She did it instinctively as Dan gently shifted Saxon from collapsed across the wooden slats of the seatback to lying face-up on the narrow concrete walkway below the bench.

They knelt in the narrow space beside the man, who lay limp as discarded laundry, his eyes rolled back, his mouth sagging open. Dan saw some green splinters in a small laceration on Matt's brow, but it didn't look deep.

Pushing aside Matt's soiled T-shirt, Dan methodically palpated the neck and chest wall and felt a telltale sensation . . . like bubble wrap breaking under his fingertips. "We've got crepitus." He glanced up, met Nikki's gaze riveted on him. "Probable pneumo on the left." He saw the fear flare brighter in her eyes.

"Can we help?" a female voice asked. Dan turned his head and saw, in the minutes he'd been so concentrated on Matt, a group of spectators had gathered in a semi-circle around the drama. Most hung back, gawking, but a few stood forward, looking ready to assist, the closest a middle-aged couple in matching Hawaiian shirts.

"Yes," Dan told the woman. "Call 9-1-1. Tell them there's a severe chest injury, and there's a physician on site. Can you remember to say 'probable tension pneumothorax'?" Nodding, she moved away to a quieter spot as she jabbed the three numbers on her cell phone.

Dan looked next to the man who'd been standing with her. Lifting himself enough to fish his car keys from his pocket, Dan handed them over. "Please go down to the blue Honda Accord across the street. There's a medical bag on the front passenger seat—"

"Bring it?" the Hawaiian-shirt guy asked, already on the move. "Will do." He hustled off.

"Dan," Nikki called. "I can't tell if he's still breathing. . . . and I don't feel a pulse."

Immediately, he laced his fingers and brought the heel of the bottom hand over Matt's sternum, saying, "CPR, Nik."

It wasn't easy for either of them, kneeling on the concrete and squeezed as they were between the rows of benches, but there wasn't any option.

Then, as he applied himself to forceful chest compressions, and Nikki kept Matt's airway open and puffed breaths into him, Dan heard someone else in the crowd comment, "My, those are sure more forceful than I would think from TV."

Ignoring the inane comment, Dan defaulted to his inherently courteous nature, managing, even as he attended to the compressions, to explain, "He's not doing well. We hafta get his blood circulating."

The inquisitive guy had moved closer and was crouched on the next-higher walkway, where Dan and Nikki's feet had been before Matt arrived. "Oh, yeah," said the guy who watched TV. "I get that. Moving the oxygen to the brain and stuff. But aren't you worried about breaking his ribs?"

Dan's quick glance upward showed him a round face, peering owlishly, as if the guy had left his glasses at home.

Mercifully, before Dan could formulate a reply, the Hawaiian-shirt man returned, panting, with Dan's car keys and black doctor's bag.

Dan glanced at Nikki, and, without being asked, she took over the chest compressions, freeing his hands for other tasks. He thanked Hawaiian Man as he pocketed the keys and opened the bag. He rummaged quickly, making sure he had the components he'd need to fashion an emergency chest tube like the one he'd used to save, momentarily at least, the life of Rory Maguire back in March: Gelco syringe, Vacutainer, hemostat, tape— but no saline.

Meanwhile, the owlish guy had been nattering on: "I heard you say pneumothorax. That's a collapsed lung, isn't it?" And now, seeing Dan's actions, he pressed. "Am I right? Are you going to try to fix it—here?"

"Yes," Dan said. "Can you help me?" He pointed to Nikki's green-and-tan tote still leaning where she'd set it on their bench. "Can you get that bag for me, please."

It was only about ten feet away from Owl Guy, and he scrambled to grab it and hand it to Dan.

"Great," Dan acknowledged the retrieval, though his attention was on freeing the Gelco and the Vacutainer from their respective wrappers. "I need one of those water bottles."

Still bustling importantly, Owl Guy complied, then held out the bottle, asking, "Whatcha gonna do?"

Even as Dan took it, Nikki looked up and told the man with what politeness she could still muster, "No more questions now, please. Let the doctor work. And you can just set my bag down here. Thanks." She never interrupted the rhythm of her compressions despite her increasing exhaustion.

Dan noticed her fatigue but could do little to help as he removed the vacutainer's red glass cap and filled the tube—once destined to draw and transport a blood sample, now drafted to release the air trapped around a collapsed lung.

Dan stared for a long heartbeat at the needle now attached to the water-filled tube, fully aware of how critical his next actions would be. If his diagnosis was correct, and precise placement of the needle avoided nicking anything unintentionally, the pressure in Matt's pleural cavity would instantly rebalance, and the lung could reinflate itself. But what chilled him to the bone was the certitude that, since out here he couldn't get a confirming chest X-ray, if his diagnosis or technique was wrong, he could actually *cause* Matt's lung to collapse, endangering his life even more.

Either way, time and judgment were crucial and there were no sirens in the background signaling help was close. Glancing up, Dan saw his spectators had moved closer and formed a loose ring around the drama. The woman was back, cell phone still to her ear. When she saw she had Dan's attention, she called out to him. "There was a traffic snarl just outside the hospital, but they're on their way."

He nodded and turned back. Poised with the makeshift chest tube above Matt's inert form, Dan stared into Nikki's glistening green eyes. She knew as well as he did Matt would die if he waited too long. "What if it's *not* a pneumo?"

"Do it," she breathed without hesitation and stopped compressions. Dan quickly shoved back the T-shirt and felt for the intercostal space. Deftly, he pushed the needle deep and listened for the *whoosh!* that'd mean air was being released.

There was none. But he could hear sirens now in the distance.

He looked up into Nikki's stricken face. They both knew the score and glanced quickly to the Vacutainer, hoping to see air bubbling into the water. No bubbles.

"Fuck!" Dan whispered hoarsely. Matt had just lost his one chance at a quick fix...and there was a better chance now that he'd not pull through. Unable to bring himself to look at Nikki's face again, Dan kept staring at the useless chest tube as they restarted CPR. A litany of curses continued in his head, competing with the sound of sirens getting louder, coming closer . . . now that time had maybe run out.

CHAPTER FIFTY-EIGHT

In a far corner of the ER waiting lounge, Dan sat beside Nikki, holding her hand with their fingers entwined. The numerous occupants of the room showed the ER was busy, even for a Saturday. Of course, Matt'd been admitted right away, whisked in secured to the paramedics' gurney.

He wanted to forget the whole damn experience, but all he could do was to put his thoughts elsewhere for the time being. Nikki had become an island unto herself, gripping his hand but not inviting him into her own thoughts and emotions. He understood. No matter the current state of affairs, Nikki and Matt had lived together as a married couple for seven years, most of those happily, according to her, and they were still legally married. What a blow, to witness one's spouse involved in such a traumatic accident. Not to mention being part of unsuccessful efforts to help him.

It's up to the ER staff now. Paramedics did what they could, getting him here to the ER in a matter of minutes. And while

Upton was a social prick, as an ER doc his knowledge, skill and decisive calm in moments of crisis were well respected. Matt couldn't be in better hands.

He cast his gaze around the big room, upholstered for comfort and noise-absorption, and studied the faces and demeanors of the occupants. A few seemed rather unconcerned, even bored; a few chatted and laughed as if at a party. Perhaps the person they awaited, their "loved one", might have an urgent need for care but clearly nothing too dire. Like the toddler he had treated last week with a fat crayon shoved up one nostril—or perhaps they didn't fully understand the gravity of the situation . . . or were simply in denial. Then there were those looking shocked, terrified, maybe even guilty. Some of these might never see that loved one alive again. And in between were the others wearing various aspects: confused, apprehensive, impatient, hopeful, even prayerful.

All of them would probably agree on one thing: *this waiting is the pits!*

Mike Upton arrived, looking haggard in his blood-spattered scrubs inadequately covered by his wrinkled white coat. His bald head shone dully under the lighting; five-o'clock-shadow threatened the neatness of his well-trimmed goatee.

Upton acknowledged Dan with eye contact and a tiny nod but put all his attention on Nikki. He spoke quietly and slowly, pausing between the bits of information to make certain she was keeping up with him. "Nikki, we did a stat echo . . . it showed massive cardiac contusions and hemorrhaging into the pericardial sac . . . which led to tamponade."

Dan watched her as she gazed up at Mike, biting her lip as she gave a little nod to show she understood that the impact to Matt's chest had bruised his heart so much that the leaking blood filled the surrounding sac, making it nearly impossible for the heart to keep beating.

"There was also significant blood around his lung, a hemothorax," Mike continued. "We couldn't keep his blood pressure up. Nikki, I'm very sorry. We tried everything to resuscitate Matt, but we couldn't save him."

A kind of gasp escaped her. Not of surprise, probably. Knowing what they knew as medical professionals, Dan was sure she'd been, as he was, steeling herself to face this outcome. Nikki sat another long moment, staring past Mike and gripping Dan's hand so fiercely he began to lose circulation, but he didn't let go. He couldn't imagine what she was thinking . . . feeling . . . remembering . . . regretting.

Upton gave her that moment— Dan had never seen this side of Mike; who knew it was there?—and then asked in a kindly voice, "Is there anyone you'd like us to help you notify?"

She shook her head tiredly. "No. He was an orphan like me. Except for his lawyer, who can wait till Monday, I guess I'm it."

Upton nodded. "I confirmed everything's in order for the organ transplants."

"Thank you, we always felt strongly about being donors. You just never really expect that it will happen when you're so young."

He nodded again and asked gently, "The transplant team is on the way, do you want to see him first?"

"Yes," Nikki said softly. She pulled herself to her feet, giving Dan's hand a squeeze before releasing it.

"Want me to go with you, Nik?" Dan asked.

She shook her head. "No need. But thanks." She gestured toward her now-empty chair. "Take a load off, doc; I know it's been intense in there today. I can do this on my own."

"Thanks," Upton said with a grateful sigh, dropping into the chair beside Dan. "Matt's in Bay Three."

She turned to look at Dan, but before she could speak, he told her, "No sweat. I'll be right here whenever you're ready."

She nodded and started moving away. Upton called after her, "Just tell 'em to beep me if they need me back." She gave a little wave of her hand to show she'd heard.

A really big sigh gusted out of the ER doctor. "What a nightmare," he observed quietly. "Must be extra weird for you under the circumstances."

"Damn straight!" Dan agreed in a low voice that wouldn't carry to the families nearby. "Uh . . . about that hemothorax—" He shifted uncomfortably. Upton's gaze focused fully on him, waiting as Dan stumbled on: "We were in a public place with few tools . . . no equipment. I had to make a call."

Upton took the time to look directly at Dan. "Listen, the rest of his injuries, especially the tamponade would've done him in no matter what. It's a wonder he lasted as long as he did. And by the way, that was a nifty emergency test tube you rigged in the field. Would've worked if…"

"If I had gotten the diagnoses right in the first place. I should have thought tamponade with that crush injury. If I had…"

"Beep! Beep! Beep!"

Upton checked his pager unit and popped to his feet, saying, "No rest for the wicked." He took a quick moment to grasp Dan's shoulder in a sympathetic, encouraging grip. "Hey, you got to get used to the ones you lose somehow or you'll never be around for the ones you save. You and Nikki take care, okay?" Then he was on his way to face his next emergency.

Who *are* you, and what have you done with the real Mike Upton? Dan thought. But the humor felt hollow in his heart as he sat alone now in his corner, staring across the commotion of the waiting room.

Nurse Gail Sanduski had come to get family members for a patient now ready to see them; she was smiling. But even as that group hurried out, another trio of loved ones shuffled in to wait: a distraught man in his late thirties with a teen-aged girl trying to comfort him, even as she held the hand of a boy about five years old. In the next moment, that child looked directly into Dan's eyes and held his gaze. Dan could read it all there on that stricken, bewildered face: *What's going to happen now?*" Dan knew just how he felt.

CHAPTER FIFTY-NINE

Revelling in the pull of his muscles, the deep inhalations of breath swelling his lungs, the beads of sweat gathering momentum on his face and torso, the slap of his Nikes on the path paralleling the shore of Candlebury Lake, Dan ran.

Lack of physical exercise certainly hadn't helped lighten the heaviness of his mood over the last few weeks. And the last week, six days since Matt Saxon fell on those bleachers, had been especially hard. It would've been challenge enough coping with the loss of a patient where his efforts probably hastened the bad outcome; but, beyond that, his main support system, Nikki, was hard-pressed to console him when she, herself, was so devastated and needed *him* to comfort *her*.

He was glad to have work to look forward to after he took a few unexpected days off. DCH had been really understanding, allowing him to shuffle his schedule with Frank Ryan, Spence Austin and Patty Yates. This freed him up for Sunday, Monday and Tuesday so he could spend those days keeping Nikki company and helping her start with all the logistical and legal stuff that came from a spouse's sudden death.

They spent Sunday quietly with the phone turned to voicemail. It wasn't much of a day for gardening. Yesterday's drizzle had returned intermittently with distant curls of thunder, and the temperature never went much above sixty. But Nikki had insisted, citing forecasts for continued wet. Shrugging into her waterproof windbreaker and holding his out to him, she'd predicted, "This may be our best chance." Dan knew she wasn't talking just about the weather, but also about the uncertainty of what the next days would bring.

Together, and mostly in silence after Nikki turned on her favorite Fugee CD, they worked in concert, securing the redwood flowerboxes around the rim of the waist-high balcony railing. After filling them with the potting soil she mixed, they got all the individual plants settled into their new homes, each in just the placement she thought best maximized their visual impact.

When they'd finished, and were enjoying the colorful new panorama from the shelter of the living room, Dan found himself physically tired but somehow soothed, more peaceful. There was something relaxing about working with your hands in the dirt. Guess that's why they call it getting "grounded", he acknowledged to himself.

It had, indeed, been a strange experience, accompanying Nikki into the home she'd shared with her late husband. Dan knew she hadn't been to the site since the end of November when, while moving into his apartment, she'd taken several boxes from the Saxon storage unit and into his bedroom, covered by leaf-print sheeting.

Dan hadn't known what to expect of Lake Harbor Homes, the gated community on the wealthy side of Candlebury Lake, but found well-shaded four-plexes with textured exteriors in an unobtrusive sand color that seemed almost organic to the shoreline environment.

Inside the unit, he took in great views of the water, neutral walls and carpeting. The furnishings, décor and art all hinted at a hard-working young couple focused on creating a permanent home and building a future together.

Dan's overall impression of the condo's current condition could be summed up in the phrase "bachelor pad", and there was certainly ample evidence of Matt's drinking to excess. But beyond that, Dan couldn't shake the sense that things were even more disarrayed than customary, as if they'd been moved in a casual search . . . and not moved back to where they would naturally have come to rest. However, Nikki, who would certainly know what kind of mess Matt might leave, mentioned nothing, so Dan let go of the notion.

He watched her move through the place as if in a trance, touching a few pieces of furniture and decorative items, seeming to avoid others. Upstairs in the master bedroom, she averted her eyes from the unmade bed as she moved to a painting on the far wall. There she pressed a concealed button on the top of the frame, and the painted woodland glade swung away from the wall, revealing a safe.

Though Nikki didn't seem to care if Dan observed, he looked away as she punched in an elaborate code.

His gaze strayed back to the bed where Nikki used to sleep . . . make love . . . laugh, cry . . . share secrets and dreams—all with Matt Saxon. The stale bedclothes were only rumpled open on one side.

From behind him, he was vaguely aware of the sound made by the safe's tumblers reengaging, the framed painting clicking back into place.

He turned to Nikki, who gestured with a translucent green envelope full of retrieved papers. She kept her eyes on Dan's face instead of anything else in the room. "I think this's all I'll need for now. Could you do me a favor? Please check all the windows on this level . . . make sure they're locked and they haven't been leaking in this wet weather. And no plumbing problems in the bathroom?"

"Sure."

"Thanks. I'll do the same downstairs."

He found nothing amiss anywhere, including the sliding glass of the master bedroom's doors out onto a small balcony, which stood above the larger deck below at ground level. On both he saw redwood flowerboxes like those they'd just bought and installed, but these were empty of all but neglected soil. It gave Dan a little shiver as he went down to find Nikki.

In the little laundry room off the kitchen, mopping at the floor with a handful of paper towels, she reported, "He had everything buttoned up down here, but Matt always forgets to tighten this cranky spigot after he uses the washer. We fight about it all the time." She fell silent, hearing her own words, and stood staring at Dan. Before either of them could speak, the doorbell rang followed by rapping.

Nikki threw away the paper towels and went to answer the door. Dan followed her into the living room but hung back a bit, curious but feeling no need to hide.

Neighbors. He remembered her saying once she'd never really connected with anyone who lived at Lake Harbor. But now these four people were reaching out to Nikki, hugging her, professing condolences, asking what they could do to help.

All the while, they studied him curiously, so Nikki ended up gesturing them into the room, though she didn't invite them to sit, and introduced him as "Dr. Dante Marchetti from the hospital." Dan responded warmly but didn't offer any conversation. Almost immediately, he'd forgotten their names. Two well-nourished couples in their mid-thirties: blandly good-looking men with attractive wives, one with wavy, platinum blond hair, the other sporting a spiky hairdo in a color he could only call *maroon*.

"So it's true," Platinum demanded. "Poor Matt fell in the ballpark bleachers and smashed his chest and died at the hospital?"

"Yes," Nikki answered stoically.

"Well, what's all the mystery then?" asked Platinum's husband.

"Mystery?" Nikki echoed.

"Oh, yeah," Maroon chimed in. "The police were here. Searched your house yesterday."

Platinum turned a bold gaze on Dan. "They asked about *you*. By name." All the other eyes swung to him.

"Me?! Whatever for?"

"They wanted to know if we'd ever met you . . . seen you here." Maroon began to answer.

Platinum followed up. "Of course, we haven't, so. . . ."

Nikki gave a little laugh. A person who didn't know her well might think it sincere. "Hunh, that's very strange. Dante and I were at the ballgame . . . gave Matt emergency care till the ambulance arrived. If they need to talk to either of us, all they have to do is ask at DCH."

All four guests opened their mouths as if to say more, but Nikki grabbed up the green envelope she'd left on the coffee table and cut them short with a sad smile and a white lie. "Well, I'm afraid we'll have to be on our way. I have an appointment with my lawyer. Lots to straighten out, you know."

The group "Oh, of course"-d themselves out, and moments later, the condo was locked, and Nikki sat shaking beside Dan in his car. "Jackals," she said under her breath, and Dan agreed, though he thought the judgment a bit harsh. As they drove back to G,G&B in silence, Dan couldn't help revisiting unanswered questions: Police. Whatever for? What were they looking for?

After they'd dropped off the documents at G,G&B, without seeing Jenna since there was no actual appointment, Nikki seemed a little stronger again. She asked him to take her to the local moving van company where she could purchase packing boxes and tape so she could begin straightening up the condo. "Whether the place is mine or not—whether I sell it or keep it to rent, I'll have to get it cleaned up. Now rather than later. Especially since I'll be going back to my job soon."

And today, another day on a medicine floor promised more of the same; keeping track of several patients who'd been sick enough to need a hospital stay, but no one ready to crash and burn or even take a turn for the worse.

He had bypassed his usual scrubs for pressed khakis and a favorite light blue shirt given the lower risk of a body fluid spill while on the wards. Leaving his Nikes to air, he laced up his second-best sneakers, then slipped on the last fresh lab coat in his closet. He pinned on his DCH badge and pocketed his wallet and keys. On his way out, when he stopped to grab the apple, he took a moment to scrawl *C U 2nite!*

He was out the door and on his way, whistling until he took the first big bite of apple. The crisp, sweet flesh of the green-skinned pippin burst in his mouth and he munched happily all the way to DCH, determined to move forward and concentrate on just medicine as an intern for the little while remaining before July moved him up in both the pecking order and responsibility.

Inside the front doors, the security desk stood empty. Dropping his apple core in the trash there, Dan surveyed the area, hoping to see Greg Vandenbosk for a quick update on Ivy. But the guard was on the far side of the lobby, dealing with what appeared to be a druggie having hallucinations. Nothing dangerous-looking.

Dan glanced at his watch and decided to catch Greg later. He had just enough time to check on some lab results before rounding. Besides, Dave Levine, in his effort to cheer Dan, had promised to make a Starbucks run before shift.

Dan hurried off to the medicine floor, where he greeted his colleagues. Third-year resident Jackie Norris stood yawning and complaining about an all-nighter. Patty Yates was logged in at one of the computers. Nurse Cheryl Herrera, on loan this week from the CCU, waved as the phone began to ring and she picked it up

"Where's Dave?" Dan asked. "He's bringing Starbucks, right? He promised to treat me to an *espresso macchiato,* whatever that is."

Jackie yawned again, her eyelids threatening to drop the last fraction of an inch. "I just need *coffee*—hot and black."

Cheryl recradled the phone. "That was Dave. There's some kind of tie-up at Starbucks, but he'll be here soon."

They took a moment to speculate about what kind of emergency could tie up a Starbucks—a barista melt-down? Running out of stir sticks? A whipped cream riot? Dan slid into the seat in front of one of the other computer terminals, eager to check the lab results on his patient Clark Resko, who was battling an infection resulting from wound neglect. But yesterday's labs showed he was responding to the antibiotic coverage that took into account both his penicillin allergy and his compromised immune system thanks to his diabetes. Dan hoped to see evidence of more improvement now.

"Hey, Patty," Dan said after a minute. "You been having any trouble with your computer? My log-ins aren't working."

Patty shook her head, eyes still riveted on her own screen's information. "No trouble at all."

"Weird," Dan said, searching the countertop for a staff directory so he could find the help-desk extension.

His beeper went off, but on *Text,* so he had to look to read it. Surprised, but pleased, he told the others, "Hunh. I'm being called to Ballard's office. Be back when he's done with me."

Cheryl, rising to go answer a patient's blinking call button, twinkled up at Dan, "Oh, yeah, sure. Dr. Marchetti—in trouble again!"

The three women laughed as Jackie made a shooing motion at him. "Don't keep the Chairman of Medicine waiting. We'll soldier on without you."

As Dan hurried for the elevator, he heard Patty's response to Jackie: "Pretty soon you and I'll be rounding alone." She called after him, "Hey, Dan—you're remembering our trade? You've got my shift tomorrow?"

"You bet!" he called from inside the elevator as the doors were closing. Alone in the car, he tweaked at his clothing, though nothing had yet gotten out of place; the creases were still fresh in the khakis. He was glad he had dressed professionally today even if no tie. Watching the floors tick by, he speculated on the upcoming meeting. Dan'd rarely been called to the chairman's office, a spacious kingdom the staff joked was big enough for staff sleep-overs, and always for more formal circumstances. Possibly this was about next year's rotations?

Dan approached Dr. Ballard's office bathed in the glow of how much promise and potential these icons apparently saw in him; determined to do his best and not disappoint.

At the imposing desk outside a closed door, Dan stopped and grinned at the secretary stationed there. "Good morning, Peggy."

He'd expected her characteristic smile and greeting, but she seemed nervous and distracted today, her eyes averted above a mumbled, "Mornin'", as she set aside the papers she was shuffling and buzzed her boss. "Dr. Marchetti is here, sir." Listening for a response through her headset, Peggy picked up the papers to shuffle and then nodded at Dan. "Go in, please." All without eye contact.

Puzzled but realizing everyone could have a bad day, Dan moved to the door emblazoned with Ballard's name and title, pausing to knock politely just the same.

Hearing the chairman's deep, familiar voice, "Yes, come in", Dan opened the door and entered.

Dr. Hugh Ballard stood, impeccable as always, behind his desk at the far side of the room. Unsmiling. "Come in, Dr. Marchetti." Dan's heart began to pound. He had been 'Dan" to the Chair for quite awhile. Something was wrong. "Sit down."

Dan, his attention riveted on the bespeckled physician, let the door swing shut behind him and moved toward the chair the man had indicated. As he crossed about a mile of plush carpeting, Dan quickly went through his last couple of weeks. There must have been a patient complaint or maybe one from the nurses? Maybe Clark Resko? Even though he had been frustrated at the guy's lack of cooperation he thought he had stayed relatively courteous...only calling him a fuckin' idiot in his head.

When Dan got to his destination, he didn't sit right away. The Chairman of Medicine was still standing, looking taller and straighter than he ever had before. For a moment, Dan thought he'd seen Ballard's gaze dart past him, delivering an expression that seemed to say, *"Remember, I'm in charge here."*

But almost as quickly, the gaze came back to Dan, the expression softening. Folding himself into his own chair, Ballard gestured again with his open palm. "Sit, Dan."

Feeling more confused by the moment, Dan complied. Ballard's bright blue eyes pinned Dan where he sat, but not unkindly. "I'm sorry, but I need to ask you to hand over any and all hospital property in your possession, including your identification badge and keys, your pager and your employee parking access card."

What the hell? He twisted around to see where the Chairman had glanced earlier and was stunned to see two uniformed policemen standing at ease in a part of the office that'd been obscured by the door as he entered.

Dan froze, staring at the badges, the belt-clipped handcuffs . . . the holstered guns. Incredibly, he could still find his voice: "Dr. Ballard—what's going on?"

"Dan . . ." Hearing the Chairman speak his name, made Dan turn back to his mentor. Though the Chairman's tone was as professional as always, Dan could sense the reluctance and compassion underlying the rather formal words. "Under the circumstances, as Chairman of Medicine and Director of your Residency Program, I have no choice but to immediately suspend your employment at this hospital, pending resolution of this matter."

Dan felt his jaw drop open as the phrases skittered around in his brain: *the circumstances . . . suspend employment . . . pending resolution . . . this matter.*

What could he have said to Resko? "This matter?" he echoed aloud. "Dr. Ballard, I don't understand."

But the chairman, his usually affable face twisted by a pained expression, simply looked toward the officers as if to communicate to Dan, *"This part's out of my hands."* He came to his feet and told Dan gently, "I'll need those items now."

Somehow, Dan realized that he had to cooperate, do as he was told and let it all get sorted out later. He stood up too and began emptying his pockets onto Ballard's desk. He separated his two keyrings, then returned his own, and his wallet, to his pants pockets.

"Rest assured," Ballard was saying, "the department will make arrangements to deliver any personal items that may still be in your staff locker." Dan nodded as if he understood what was happening, and, as he reluctantly removed his I.D. badge from the front of his lab coat, Ballard spoke again. "I'll need your white coat as well."

Not that!, Dan thought. But after only a moment's hesitation, he slipped it off feeling strangely like a defrocked priest. Mechanically, he folded it, placed it on the desk beside the other items stripped from him. He felt all eyes in the room on him, and, though he stood still clad in his khakis and favorite blue shirt, he felt naked.

The policemen came up beside him. "I'm Officer Emmett," said the taller, balding one; "Officer Dransfield," supplied the other. "Deerwood Police Department."

"Officers, please," Dan implored. "What's this about?"

Neither answered the question right away. "Step this way, please." The one named Emmett indicated a path around Dan's chair and toward the office wall. "Turn and put your hands against the wall."

As soon as Dan complied, Dransfield began to pat him down. Though both men had behaved professionally and courteously, Dan could remember no experience quite this bizarre, humiliating or unsettling. His mind was suddenly numb.

He didn't bother trying to ask any questions aloud again. Like a robot, he submitted to all the instructions, which ended with, "Put your hands behind your back." Then he felt the cool metal click close around his wrists. Handcuffs.

"Dante Marchetti," intoned Officer Emmett, "We're placing you under arrest in connection with the deaths of Trey Hartmann and Matthew Saxon."

"What?" Dan exclaimed. "That's crazy! I'm a doctor—not a killer!"

"You have the right to remain silent," Emmett began. Dan listened numbly to the rest of his rights being read, responding, as prompted, that he understood.

As the officers nudged him toward the door, Dr. Ballard's authoritative voice made them pause a moment. "I'll remind you gentlemen that this is a functioning hospital . . . a community comprising hundreds of employees, patients and visitors. I respectfully request, for the well-being of all, including Dr. Marchetti, that you escort him from the premises with as little disruption as possible."

One or both of the policemen answered Ballard in a short, courteous exchange, but all Dan could think about was the prospect of being perp-walked through that DCH community of his friends, colleagues and superiors. Then the chairman's voice cut through the buzz in Dan's head, calling his name.

When Dan looked back at the white-haired man standing again behind his desk, Ballard said, "I wish you well." Dan got the impression the next words were not just for *his* benefit but meant to communicate to the other two men: "And I want you to know, this will be cleared up, I'm sure!"

Such a wave of gratitude swept through Dan that tears filled his eyes. He wanted desperately to thank the Chairman, but nothing could squeeze past the knot in his throat. All he could do was return that steady gaze of those clear blue eyes and give a little nod before he was maneuvered out through the office door.

He caught a glimpse of Peggy, her eyes big as saucers before she averted them, and then he was hustled down the hallway toward the main lobby.

The usual hubbub of the hospital seemed especially intense. Dan couldn't help feeling that he was the center of the tumult; all eyes staring at him, every whispered conversation about him. He heard more than one surprised voice call his name, but even if he'd been allowed, he was incapable of answering.

He managed not to focus on any of the startled faces that flowed around and past him, until he met the eyes of Greg Vandenbosk at the front door security desk. Not so much surprise there, he would've had a heads-up on an imminent arrest, but absolute disbelief . . . and grave concern.

The officers hurried him through the first set of glass doors that were sliding open. They crossed the vestibule, stepped through the outer doors into the sunlight and into another ring of Hell.

A noisy mob of people pressed toward him, forming a semicircle at the hospital entrance. Still-cameras clicked and whirred; shouldered video-cameras stared at him like baleful Cyclops; fists reached toward him, brandishing microphones. Someone demanded, "Is that him? Is that the suspect?" even as another voice gave the call letters of the local TV station, followed by "This is Carolyn Regis, reporting live from outside Deerwood Community Hospital—"

How in the world did so much media find out about this?, he wondered dispassionately as if this was a scene from a TV crime show and not, horribly, in his real life.

"That's gotta be him . . . Dante Marchietti." The speaker managed to mangle the pronunciation of both names.

"Sir," called the woman from WDWD, "just a brief statement, please. Did you kill Trey Hartmann and Matthew Saxon? Can you tell us why you killed them both? How are you related to the victims….."

All the while, the police officers were moving him into and through the crowd, making it near impossible for him to separate the shouted queries. A gaggle of voices all began shouting at once: "Why'd you do it, Marchetti?" "Hey Marchetti—over here! You trying to skunk the Pirates?" "Is it true Matthew Saxon was the husband of your lover?" "Marchetti—

Dan and his escorts had reached the waiting car. Emmett went around to the driver's side and Dransfield bent to open the back door. It gave Dan a moment to look over his shoulder and catch Dave, the tray of Starbuck's coffee occupying both hands.

"Leave him the fuck alone!" bellowed Dave, who'd leapt close to push the cameraman back. The tray tilted and Starbucks was splashing all over.

But Dan didn't see what happened next, because that's when Officer Dransfield admonished, "Watch your head," and firmly pushed him down and into the back seat of the patrol car.

CHAPTER SIXTY

Linda Ferrante sipped the hot, black coffee and grimaced, not at the taste, the Kona had been perfectly brewed in Scott Bradden's Jura, but at the spectacle she was being forced to witness. There, on the huge plasma screen in the D.A.'s home office, she watched Dr. Dante Marchetti being hustled out of DCH toward a waiting police vehicle amidst a frenzy of press attention. Another young doctor, trying to juggle a tray of Starbucks as he leapt to defend his colleague, was bungling both efforts.

She cringed as the situation escalated: dismayed shouts from reporters and camera crew suddenly spattered with hot coffee, whipped cream and sprinkles—countered by angry words and gestures of the now-drenched physician.

But Bradden actually guffawed, and Stacy Conover, lounging in the comfy chair near hers, chuckled around the toothpick clinging to his lip as he opined. "Always thought those fou-fou drinks should get stronger lids!"

Meanwhile, as most attention focused on the sidewalk scuffle, the patrol car slipped away from the curb, bearing the arrested Dr. Marchetti.

When the news segment ended in a series of broadcaster questions—among them: "Who *is* this Dr. Dante Marchetti? . . . Can it be one of Deerwood's newest and most talented physicians is a murderer? . . . What links has the D.A.'s office found to several other suspicious patient deaths at DCH?"—a viewer might easily be left with a solid impression that the intern was guilty of at least two murders and that the D.A. had an airtight case, which was far from the truth, despite whatever that D.A. might hope.

"Nice!" Bradden crowed. Leaning back in his executive desk chair, he used a remote to click off the TV and activate a sliding panel that hid the set from view behind an antique map of Pennsylvania's counties. "Very nice indeed!"

Conover lifted his coffee mug, saluting his employer. "Great collar."

"You're awfully quiet, Linda."

Her eyes snapped to her boss. Vaguely conscious of how the two men had been congratulating themselves on their investigation, she pointed out, "This could've been done more discreetly . . . just in case the man's innocent." Bradden and Conover both snorted at the word *innocent,* and she felt the stubbornness flowing up through her, straightening her spine. "Well, the case is pretty thin—"

Big snort from the detective. "Marchetti's been on my list from the beginning—at least for the deaths recorded since he started working here. Remember, I'm not convinced there's only one culprit. That Orlander's been at DCH a long time. Maybe *he* brought the new doctor into the mercy business till Marchetti branched out on his own."

"If we squeeze Marchetti—" Bradden started to say.

"Maybe he'll squeal on an accomplice?" Conover finished.

Linda could tell her boss didn't like being interrupted by the detective, but he donned his politician's smile. "Precisely. And lucky for us, the Hartmann murder is high-profile enough to draw the notice this case needs . . . uh, deserves."

She leaned back in her chair, hiding behind the huge coffee mug she'd been given. It was difficult to stand how delighted Bradden was at the thought of trying and winning this case. A case that would serve to propel him to Harrisburg. As she sorted her own thoughts, she stayed peripherally aware of the men's conversation. She heard nothing new in their listing of facts: many came from Conover's interviews and investigation, some came from her own research and Bradden had heard them all from her in their weekly meetings.

Certainly, they all knew by now that Trey Hartmann had been murdered. The introduction of potassium chloride to his drug infusion had clearly been intentional, especially since the I.V. rate was changed from what'd been entered on the chart. And, no questions here, Marchetti's fingerprints were on that I.V. equipment, the closest thing they had to solid evidence. Though he had reaily admitted to the DCH committee that he had started the infusion. And, both Bradden and Conover, separately, had dismissed the report that some slight smears *could* have been made by overlying contact from gloved fingers. The bag had been transported with the ballplayer to the ER so it was likely there were many hands involved. But those considerations were secondary to the scenario they were shaping

True, Marchetti had been alone with Hartmann when he started the infusion and a while before being called to the ER for the car crash patients. So he'd been present in the ER when the young pitcher's death was officially called, but, according to several sources questioned, Marchetti wasn't ever close to Hartmann in the ER. Whatever he did had happened alone in the infusion room.

On the other hand, that Vincent Orlander had been there in the infusion clinic when the code was called. And he offered up nothing as to why except that he was curious to see the celebrity. And he'd gone all the way to the ER with the kid, supposedly oxygenating him until the final pronouncement.

Savoring the last of her coffee in tiny sips, she tried to make the case for Marchetti: opportunity, means and motive. Without question, as a doctor and a DCH employee, he'd had means and opportunity to commit murder, both at the hospital and at the ballpark. Didn't he even have everything he needed for an emergency chest tube ready in his car? Though it was hard to imagine how he might've planned such an encounter. Still, with the right motive, he might have just used the opportunity fate had given him.

When Linda set her empty mug on the little table beside her, it made such a resounding *thunk!* that the two men paused in their spate of self-congratulation and looked at her. "What about motive?" she asked in the momentary silence. "I thought this investigation was about finding a mercy killer."

"Yes," Bradden said, "and all that still stands. According to our psych consultant, it happens that sometimes serial killers change their focus or modus operandi to fit the situa—"

On a bark of laughter, Conover interrupted Bradden yet again. "Like I said, our boy is branching out." Taking the toothpick from his mouth, he used it to emphasize his points. "See, I think *these* two murders have to do with sex."

"What?!" Linda couldn't have been more startled.

"Think about it: the second vic, Matthew Saxon, is still married to the woman who co-habits with Marchetti, Nikole Smith Saxon—a nurse from the hospital. Witnesses at the ballpark said the two men were fighting about her relationship with our young doctor. After all, it *was* adulterous."

Linda didn't feel the need to share her former relationship with Nikki and what she knew, from Nikki, of Matt and Dante. "Well, how does Hartmann fit into that?"

Bradden leaned forward on the desk blotter, his eyes avid as he asked Conover, "You have some new information?"

Finishing his coffee, the detective grinned. "Scuttlebutt around the hospital. Just gathered the last few days." He set his empty mug next to Linda's on the little table. "Apparently, Marchetti got really friendly with some of the Pirates team, especially this Trey Hartmann kid. Marchetti and Ms. Saxon attended a game back in May and Hartmann took them out to dinner afterwards and ended up coming home with them, staying overnight. Who knows what the three of them got up to?"

Linda's breath sucked in as a little gasp of surprise. "Nik—Ms. Saxon has cancer! She's in treatment and has been in poor health."

Conover gave Bradden a broad wink. "She looks plenty good to *me.* A mighty attractive woman, but a little thin and pale. Guess that explains it."

She slowed her breath, willed relaxation into her face and body. "Is that all?"

Conover gave her a lazy grin. "According to the nurse who set up the infusion, Hartmann was s'posed to stay over again that night of the day he died. Maybe Marchetti thought the kid was moving in on *his* woman." The detective twirled the toothpick with his tongue. "In fact, two of our witnesses, a pair of physical therapy girls, heard Marchetti arguing with Hartmann in a hospital courtyard just before that fatal infusion."

"Arguing about what?" Linda wanted to know.

"Well, they couldn't hear the actual words. But the tone was unmistakable."

Frowning, she shook her head. "I don't buy it. I don't like this a bit."

Bradden's palm slapped down on his blotter. "Too bad. Because it's still *your* case and you'll be seconding me at trial. I'm sure you can find a way to introduce the idea he's been under suspicion for unexplained deaths at the hospital, even if we can't yet find anything to link him directly. Y'don't think the case is strong enough? Make it that way. I want you to put this Marchetti away—or better, put him on death row. We can't have our doctors running around killing their patients . . . sports celebrities . . . or even jealous husbands, can we?"

Linda, hearing the makings of a stump speech in his words, opened her mouth for rebuttal, but Bradden came to his feet, obviously signaling an end to the meeting. As his guests rose too, he came around his desk to pump Conover's hand and thank him for all his efforts. "Keep up the good work. I'll see you back at the office, Linda." He checked his Rolex. "Don't dawdle. There's a lot of work to do."

Drawing, not for the first time in this job, on her training as an actress, she portrayed a pleasant and compliant demeanor.

With a cheerful nod toward the men, she shouldered her purse and headed for the door.

Out in her Prius, she squeezed the life out of her steering wheel and tried to unclench her jaws. Clearly Bradden planned for her to do all the dirty work, *eviscerating* that young intern, and taking the credit if she managed to pull it off.

Not that she wanted to. Somehow, she just couldn't believe that man could be a killer. She shuddered at the thought of prosecuting Dante Marchetti and how that would affect Nikki Saxon, who now would be drawn into the whole mess, have her love life and divorce torn open in the public eye. With the Trey Hartmann connection, there were sure to be tabloids salivating even more.

Linda's eyes moistened as she started her motor.

CHAPTER SIXTY-ONE

Vinny Orlander arrived early for the four p.m. meeting. That way he could hide himself in a shadowed corner of the spacious room, where a quirk of the architecture formed a little alcove beyond the draperies. He couldn't suppress a tiny smile of pride. No one knew all the nooks and crannies for hiding at DCH better than he. Because, of course, he hadn't been invited to *this* meeting. His smile slid into a scowl. This one was for the elite—the *doctors*—and would be led by the Chairman of Medicine, Dr. Hugh Ballard. Vinny's meeting, called for even later in the afternoon and in a much larger conference room, was for all the rest of the staff and would be chaired by some lesser mortal, probably the head of Human Resources.

As usual, Vinny found satisfaction and amusement in how a person as big as a Viking could "disappear" in plain sight if he held still long enough, allowing him to stand only partially obscured but able to observe everything in the room.

From his vantage point, he could see the place beginning to fill up fast. The arrivals weren't limited to the invited physicians who happened to be on the schedule. The email memo for the house staff had attracted even those who were off-duty: nearly all the interns had showed up and most of the residents and more attendings than you'd expect. But then, everyone cared about Dan Marchetti . . . what exactly had happened to him . . . what was *going* to happen to him. Even those who did not know him directly, found it a bit exciting to be in the middle of their very own Law and Order episode.

An agitated buzz crowded the room, the voices of people eager for solid information and anxious about what they might learn. But the moment Chairman Ballard entered, all conversation ceased, everyone not sitting, sat.

Ballard, rubber soles whispering across the carpet in the silence, walked to the lecturers' desk at the front of the room but didn't sit behind it. Instead of putting that furniture between himself and his audience, he went to stand in front of it, leaning back against it and folding his arms across his chest. Vinny thought he looked tired. Especially those blue eyes peering over the wire-rim spectacles at everyone gathered.

"Well," Ballard said into the expectant hush, "this has been one helluvva month, hasn't it?"

Laughter rippled through the room, easing the tension, and the Chairman, too, grinned. Vinny had seen that smile many times while working at DCH, though it was never aimed at a mere respiratory therapist, and he'd seen it beaming like a little sun on the accomplishments and challenges as year after year of neophyte doctors needed that man's compassionate reassurance and steadfast encouragement.

"It's good to see all of you here," Ballard was saying. "I'm sure our Dr. Marchetti will be pleased to know he has so many people concerned about him."

Unfolding his arms, the Chairman moved into a more relaxed position, hefting one haunch up onto the edge of the desk, leaning forward to rest his arms on the upbent leg. "Dan Marchetti is one of us and his arrest, I know, has been a tremendous shock to us all." Murmurs of assent escaped a few of his listeners.

"As for the charges," he continued, "I'm sure they're completely without merit. In my judgment, Dan Marchetti is not only an exemplary physician, but also a fine human being. I believe in his innocence, and I stand behind him 100 percent."

The audience responded with some applause and cheers. When that'd quieted down, but before Ballard could say more, Willow Blackstone was moved to interrupt with a passionate, "But does anyone know what's going on? Can he get a good lawyer?"

Dave Levine raised his hand, and Ballard nodded to him.

"I called Nikki just an hour ago," Dave told the gathering. "She's been in touch with Dan's brother, who said the family would cover any costs. Nikki has connections with the Glickman firm, and she says she's got their best defense attorney."

When expressions of relief had swelled and subsided around him, Dave answered a question from Diane Werner. "Nikki said Dan was arraigned within a few hours of his arrest, but no bail was allowed because of his being charged with capital crimes. However, the lawyer says he can petition for bail at Dan's preliminary hearing set for Tuesday morning—"

"That's three more days—four nights in jail?!" exclaimed Theo Epplewhite.

After the groans and expressions of outrage and worry subsided, Dave picked up the thread, saying, "According to Nikki, the lawyer says chances for bail are better if there's a show of support from people who know Dan."

"We can sure make that happen!" Diane proclaimed and other voices agreed. "Should we call Nik to find out the best way to proceed?"

Dave shook his head. "She's asking we not call her for now. She has a lot to deal with and also needs to rest. She'll post email updates. We can take it from there."

Seeming satisfied with this, the house staff turned its attention back to the Chairman. Vinny made a note to himself to find out the exact time of the arraignment.

"Thanks, Dave," Ballard said. "I'm glad someone has current info." He paused a moment to survey the faces focused on him. "Now we need to talk about the craziness that's probably coming our way. I know many of you were questioned by the police, the Care Review Committee, or both, last month, after Trey Hartmann's death. Law enforcement personnel will undoubtedly be questioning you very soon about Dan, the daily routines here at DCH, and so forth. Just be truthful and stick to the facts. It's possible they'll ask you about other employees here who might be capable of euthanizing patients. Do not, I repeat, do not, offer up theories, conjectures and the like. Are we clear?"

Everyone in the room nodded, and many voices offered an emphatic "Yes."

In his corner, Vinny also nodded but with a smirk knowing that the theories and conjectures were already flying fast and furious up and down the DCH grapevine. The Chairman could mandate all he liked but nothing would stop a good scandal from rocketing through the floors.

Ballard sighed. "We can only guess the level of media and tabloid scrutiny about to descend on us. Should you be approached by reporters for your comments, refer all of them to our public media team. If you see any strangers in the patient areas without a visitor tag, tell them to return to the lobby and call security if you need to. Don't let yourself get into a bad situation. We've instructed the guards to do more frequent rounding and you all know the code for security if needed."

Vinny chuckled. The media had already found the gathering spots outside the hospital grounds and there was jockeying among many of the staff for face time or being the designated 'confidential source' they could brag to their friends about. He expected even some of the docs to get involved once a few more days had passed.

Dave Levine ducked his head, avoiding the chairman's gaze, remembering that he was already notorious for the Starbucks escapade which had run on newsfeed throughout the day.

"Understandably," Ballard continued, "emotions are running high just now, but, no matter how we may be tempted to react, we must remember our responsibility to this place and our colleagues. Likewise, it serves no one, you, the hospital or Dan himself, for us to, in effect, try his case in the public eye. Let's allow the judicial system to do its job. I have every confidence Dr. Marchetti will prevail."

Ballard stood up from his perch on the desk edge. The movement was slow, hinting at the toll of a very long and stressful day. But then he straightened to his full height, and some of the weariness dropped away. "We'll get through this," he assured them all. "If you need someone to talk to, my door is always open, as are those of the counselors here at Deerwood. Talking helps. In fact, is there anything anyone wants to say now?"

"The whole thing just makes me feel really vulnerable," blurted Brian Callahan. "That you can be as good a doc as Dan and get accused of such horrible stuff."

"Yeah," Frank Ryan chimed in. "And no matter how it turns out, it could tarnish your reputation and career, put your life in the crapper."

As Vinny waited for the meeting to be over and the room empty so he could leave, the house staff talked on for a time, airing anxieties and attempting to reassure themselves and each other. Vinny watched with interest, realizing the more experienced docs had hung back, even though those senior residents and attendings must have trepidations of their own, allowing the interns to open up first, then doing their best to console and guide.

It's actually sort of a beautiful thing, Vinny had to admit, seeing how the seniority system could work at times to protect the more vulnerable.

Having stood very still for quite a long time, he flexed and relaxed some of his muscles, a tactic he'd perfected through years of covert action, and felt extremely grateful he'd clocked out before coming to this meeting.

After a bit, some of the house staff began to excuse themselves, especially those who were on duty for the day. A few, including Dr. Ballard, were summoned by their beepers. The young doctors moved toward the door, talking about "Poor Dan" and what a terrible year it'd been for him, Nikki's illness, Alex's meltdown, losing Trey Hartmann, and now *this!*

They left the room, some with arms around each other, all vowing to be there for Dan and for one another.

At last Vinny was able to make his escape and head for his own staff meeting. Reflecting, with a twinge of envy, on the interns'camaraderie, he prepared for the larger meeting where he was sure most of the questions would be directed at job security and overtime pay if this arrest began to impact the hospital operations. He felt like he was leaving the mountaintop to return to the valley dwellers...again.

CHAPTER SIXTY-TWO

Nikki Saxon sat motionless in the bleakly lit courtroom, trying desperately to make it all seem real. There, beyond the railing, a few feet ahead of her and to the left, sat Dan, impossibly garbed in the dark-green-and-tan-striped jumpsuit issued by the county jail. From this angle, she could see part of his face, but he never turned to look at her. He'd also kept his eyes down as he was escorted into the courtroom. She hoped he'd been able to note how many DCH staff had joined her and his family in unfettered support. According to Diane Werner, who was compiling a supporters' list for her daily 'Dan is innocent' email, there were also a number of former patients of Dan's on the hard benches facing the judge.

Earlier, arriving with the Marchettis, Nikki was surprised to see Charlie Monroe parking his motorized chair in the courthouse hallway. He'd stopped her long enough to assure her, as mad as he'd been about the Trey situation, he'd "Never for a moment believed Dan killed him. Please make sure he knows that."

As Nikki reassured *him,* she noted how exhausted he looked, how labored his breathing. Automatically switching into nurse mode, she asked, "Are you doing okay? Getting enough sleep?"

Charlie grimaced. "Wanted to be here." He pulled out an inhaler and used it before finishing, "Flew red-eye from San Francisco right after our win last night."

She nodded, realizing the rest of the Pirates would be flying in for tonight's game against the Cards at PNC. After thanking him for the effort and admonishing him to take care of himself, she quickly introduced the Marchettis, and Sal remarked solemnly, "Thank you for your support of my son, Dante."

As if that name reminded them all of why they'd convened, they said their good-byes and went in to find seats.

Sitting now between Gloria, with Sal on the other side of her, and the steadfast Jerry, Nikki felt in the bosom of Dan's family. Nikki wasn't surprised to see how quickly they had dropped everything to focus on helping their son and brother, but she was awed by how concerned they were for her welfare. They seemed almost as determined to make sure she was OK as they were concerned about getting Dan the best lawyer. She hadn't been allowed to cook or clean since they got there and had barely let her give them the apartment while she moved her stuff to the Cleary house.

Nikki gave a little shiver now, remembering that one pre-arraignment phone call allowed from the police station. She'd never before heard that voice from Dan: stunned, mortified, scared. It made her immediately set aside any notion that a call to say he'd been arrested for murder was some kind of lame-ass practical joke. It took her breath away for a moment, even there in the spot where she felt safest: Shadymead on the Cleary property.

"And I have to keep this short," he'd told her. "I'm so very sorry to put this on you, Nik, but I can't think of any other way. I said I wanted a lawyer, but I haven't a clue–"

"Don't worry, honey. I'll call GG&B. What about bail?"

"Not for these charges. Don't know how I'd pay it anyway, much less the lawyer. Look, I need you to call my brother and tell him what's going on. I hate to stick *him* with telling our folks, but that's gotta be blood family."

"I understand," she said, hiding her relief.

"I'm getting the signal to hang up. Listen, I have to write the names of people, other than the lawyer, I'm willing to have visit. I'm only gonna put you and Jer on that list. I don't want anyone else to see me like this, especially not mom and pop. Bad enough for the two of you. . . ."

The call ended on the break in his voice. Thankfully, she had Jerome Marchetti's number in her cell. Still in shock but with a surprisingly strong voice, she hit the key.

His delighted surprise at hearing from her turned immediately to disbelief and grave concern when she told him what'd happened to his brother. "God, Nikki, I can't process this. Dan once mentioned in passing that he'd have to be prepared for the possibility of fighting a malpractice suit, that came with being a doctor. But *murder?!* Y'say you know the best local law firm? Good! You get the ball rolling. Don't worry about the money; we'll pull that together. Let me take care of all that, and telling the folks."

"Thanks, Jerry. I'll get back to you when I know more about the lawyer. And you let me know anything you need at this end."

"Well, I'm sure we'll be driving down as soon as we've taken care of everything at this end. Can you book lodging for us, starting tomorrow? Nothing fancy."—a hollow chuckle came across the line—"We'll be economizing."

Nikki was brought out of her reverie. "The Commonwealth of Pennsylvania," a voice boomed now in the courtroom, "versus Dante Michael Marchetti." With Gloria's hand crushing her own in its grip, Nikki watched as Dan, prompted by his attorney's elbow-touch, came to his feet. On the other side of Nikki, Jer squeezed her left hand gently, gave it a little pat.

Dante looked like a zombie, she thought as she watched him rise as if the weight of the world was pushing him down. She was grateful, once again, for the presence of Eric Müeller.

Back on Friday—as soon as she'd ended her call with Jerry and while she still sat in the sanctuary of Shadymead, Nikki'd dialed the GG&B law office and spilled her predicament to Jenna Hudson, who put her through to Samuel Glickman himself. That man, ever-grateful for Nikki's role in his daughter's recovery, had declared, "Don't you worry now. Your Dr. Marchetti will have Eric Müeller. He's our best, the best in three counties. And tell the family not to worry about the finances right now; we'll work something out."

On such short notice, and with his packed schedule, Müeller was unable to participate in Dan's arraignment, but met with him at the jail late Friday for an intensive interview. In the end, Nikki learned, Müeller had expressed confidence he could actually get Dan out on bail after all, by requesting bail reduction at the preliminary hearing when the defendant actually entered his pleas.

"Not guilty on all counts, Your Honor," Dan was saying now to the robed judge with the red bowtie. Nikki became aware she was holding her breath when she heard Gloria crying softly beside her. She gently squeezed Gloria's left hand, even as Sal put a comforting arm around his wife.

The injustice of what was happening, that fine young doctor being humiliated, his family traumatized, suddenly overwhelmed Nikki. She sat woodenly, trying to listen, as the rest of the hearing unfolded.

She *did* hear Müeller begin working to secure bail. Even after his speech about all the character support Dan'd been offered, reinforced by spontaneous utterances from the audience, quickly silenced by the gavel meeting the desk with loud whacks, and the assertion the defendant posed neither a danger nor a flight risk, the bombastic D.A. objected until there was an agreement Dante's passport would be surrendered. Then negotiation began over the amount, which was finally lowered to fifty thousand with Dan submitting to house arrest, wearing an ankle bracelet. It would be a kind of freedom, at least.

Then Müeller went on, moving for a speedy trial. That, too, was part of the game plan. When Nikki had gotten, to visit Dan at the jail on Saturday morning —one of those horrible scenes, just like TV with glass between them, talking on phones—he'd filled her in on his meeting with Eric Müeller. Beyond all the information about his innocence, beyond possibilities for differing levels of freedom if bail was granted, Dan had emphasized his wish to have this over as quickly as possible so he could get back to his life before his budding career was irreversibly damaged.

Dan'd stared into her eyes through the smudged glass partition as he related the conversation to her. "I told Eric this can't be too hard a case to try. I'm completely innocent, so there can't be any *evidence* of anything. Just get the truth out there as quickly as possible. He said if we're granted the speedy trial, it will have to start within 180 days."

"Six months!" Nikki said. "That's early December."

His face washed with pain. "God, I know."

She spoke quickly then to counter the negativity she'd introduced. "But that's nothing when you consider how long regular cases can take, years sometimes. And if you can get out on bail, we'll cope, honey. You're innocent, so it'll all be okay."

Now she stared at Dan's striped back as Eric Müeller, a stout, blond man nearing forty, well-dressed, well-groomed, well-spoken, wrapped up his pitch for a speedy trial. The swaggering D.A. wasted a lot of words saying he had no objections. He seemed as eager as the defendant to bring the case to trial, though, of course, not for the same reasons.

At last, it ended. Müeller'd secured both the financially manageable bail and the speedy trial, vowing to do his best to get that trial started much sooner than December. But Dan couldn't be released yet, not until the bail paperwork was actually processed. An officer came to escort him back to his cell.

There were a few brief moments at the railing where he was allowed contact with his family: Gloria and Sal hugging him together, Jerry gripping his arm as if he'd refuse to let go. Nikki hung back, letting the family have this moment. She, at least, had been able to see and talk to, if not touch, him. Jerry, too, had had the privilege of a glass-partitioned visit in the jail. At first, the parents had been miffed they weren't authorized, but after Nikki and Jerry explained how painfully embarrassing it would be for Dan, and how much he wanted to protect *them* from the experience, they resigned themselves to their son's decision and the too-short, emotional phone calls he was able to make.

As her eyes met his now, over the tops of his parents' heads, Nikki could tell Dan was coming back to himself. She saw not only relief in those brown depths, but also gratitude, and he managed a little smile.

Then he was on his escorted way back to jail. In the next moment, a weeping Gloria was embracing her, then the other two Marchetti men.

The courtroom was clearing for the next case, and they turned to leave. Nikki's gaze fell on someone sitting at the prosecution's table. Nikki'd seen her there earlier, not recognizing her from behind. In retrospect, it seemed the woman had made a point of not being noticed . . . of, perhaps, not wanting to be there at all.

But she was no longer invisible, and seeing her face, making eye contact, was like getting punched in the gut for Nikki. *Linda Ferrante!* After a quick flurry of confused mental questions, Nikki reminded herself that Linda had left GG&B to work for the DA. Not surprising that she'd be present for such a high-profile murder case. Linda appeared slightly sheepish, as if she wanted to look away but made herself hold Nikki's gaze.

Meanwhile, the Marchettis were on the move, shepherding her toward, and then along, the courthouse hallway. Nikki started seeing friends and colleagues, and faces unknown to her, looking to her, wanting to make sure she saw *them*, recognized their support. And though most waved or nodded, smiled or gave a thumbs-up, thankfully, none of them came over to insert themselves into the Marchetti family dynamic. She acknowledged the well-wishers with her own smiles and nods, and then, eventually, they were out of the building and headed for the parking lot.

Jerry drove his parents' old yellow Impala with Sal on the passenger side. In the backseat, Nikki and Gloria clung together, each trying to comfort the other. The men traded a few impressions of how the hearing had gone; how good Eric Müeller was;

how lucky they were to have him; how relieved they were at the amount of bail which trailed into the logistics of getting Dan's bond processed and getting him out of jail.

"Now, are you sure you really want to do this today, honey?" Gloria's brow knit in a motherly frown, continuing the discussion about Nikki's next chemo session that had begun at the apartment this morning. "You look awfully tired. I'm sure they'd reschedule you."

Nikki patted the woman's soft hand. "It's already been rescheduled," she reminded her again. "They could barely squeeze me in so I don't get off-schedule. Only two more ABVD treatments, and I'm through with chemo. I want my life back, our life back. Dante needs me, and I have to do everything I can to get him through what's coming next until he's exonerated."

"He's so lucky to have you," Gloria was saying as tears continued to silently track down her cheeks. "While you're gone, we'll make a good, healthy meal . . . but gentle on the tummy. A nice minestrone, some good bread, a little salad. . . .And I am sure Dante will be home before you get done." She said the last bravely before a sudden sob sent her back into Nikki's arms.

Now as they pulled up at the Outpatient Infusion Clinic entrance. Jerry looked back over the seat at her as she slid to open her door. "You just call the apartment when you're done, and I'll come get you."

"Thanks so much!" She closed the heavy yellow door, waved and hurried up the sidewalk wondering what it was like to have such a nurturing family. As Jerry'd predicted in that first phone call, the family was quick to make arrangements at home—other-relatives notifications, financial preparations, schedule modifications—and were on the road very early Saturday morning, arriving in Deerwood mid-afternoon, with only a brief pit-stop at Aunt Carmella's in Allentown. Fortunately, Sal wasn't working summer school, and his community-team coaching was easily passed to one of the capable assistant coaches among the parents. Gloria got substitutes for her volunteer duties and neighbors to look after her garden. Jerry left his business in Misty's hands, trusting her to reschedule his meetings and field his phone calls.

They were here in Deerwood for the duration; whatever it took to get Dan out of jail. They had already had a quick phone call with Donna, the owner of the Six Bucks Motel, and had confirmed that two connecting rooms with efficiencies would be available whenever they needed it. For now, the Marchettis were drawn like magnets to Dan's apartment where they had last laughed and hugged and eaten together over the holidays.

Thankfully, Nikki'd foreseen the possibility she'd lose her usual privacy with Dan's family in town. In the time between her calls on Friday and their arrival on Saturday, she'd not only made certain the whole apartment was spotlessly tidy and the kitchen stocked with healthful snacks and beverages, but also, despite the fact that they now knew she and Dan lived together, that anything she wanted kept private was locked in the trunk of her Camry.

She wished she could write in her journal right now as the clinic doors whispered closed behind her. There was so much to say about today: the legal proceedings, seeing Dan like that, feeling so grateful for GG&B's getting us Eric Müeller, watching that asshole D.A., seeing Linda Ferrante in the enemy camp.

Walking down the cool, quiet corridor that looked out on the Terrace, Nikki shook herself. She needed to focus on the positive. But she knew what was coming. How harrowing it will be to have their personal relationship, their friendship with Trey, her stormy separation from Matt, all dragged into the headlines and TV sound bites? But the scariest was the thought she tried to bury as deeply as possible...what if Dan never really came home again as a free man?

Now, lying back on the infusion lounge, Nikki squeezed her eyes shut to blot out the room around her. She was settled into 3A, where Trey had breathed his last breath. Rescheduling her every-other-Tuesday chemo appointment in order to attend Dan's hearing had pushed her out of the familiar community room and into one of the spaces meant for the privacy of wealthier patients—though with no extra charge to her.

While relieved to have a bit of seclusion, she also understood the interest and good will of her friends. She'd anticipated her

DCH family would be eager for updates on Dan's plight and to express their support and concern for her own well-being, but she'd been unprepared for the overwhelming waves of emotion from others and from within herself. Profoundly grateful as she was for their compassion, still it was good to escape all that to a private place.

But why did it have to be this particular room? The last time she'd been here, the last moment she'd spent here, was as Trey was drifting off, never to wake again…no more pain, no talk of guns and with a thank you for Dan's friendship. Could that have really been only weeks ago?

She thought of how it would have been for Trey at the end. By now everyone at DCH knew how he had died. Potassium chloride was a good choice for euthanasia; often used in lethal injection of criminals and in putting animals "to sleep". It was the drug-of-choice when Dr. Kevorkian performed his famous on-film assisted suicide that landed *him* in prison. But straight potassium was quite painful. So Ativan and lidocaine for comfort, then potassium to stop the heart. He wouldn't have suffered.

How easy for any staffer to mix up a cocktail. Anyone with keys or access to keys carelessly left on a counter. Easy. And now the one person she wanted to always protect, the one person she had swore to comfort, was in a jail cell. What did it matter that he was innocent when he had been stripped of all that mattered to him and had to face his family across a wooden bar. Against the darkness of her closed eyelids, she pictured a tightly bolted door. She didn't want to look at, or even think about, what was stuffed behind that barrier. But a crack of light pushed out around its edges as the thought came: *It was Trey's fault! He should have been stronger and not pulled Dante into his illness when he was still reeling from Alex! If Dante had not felt like he needed to sit with him and to start Trey's treatment, he wouldn't be the one sitting alone and scared in a jail cell. I hate him, I hate him!* The light, the energy, behind the door intensified, pushing against the barrier of darkness, bulging it around the bolt. *How could I have let this happen?* The intensity of her feelings frightened her and she felt the same thumping of her heart in her chest and moving to up to her throat and temples. It felt like she was out of control, that Tony was coming back and her mom was still in danger.

Through all the hellish challenges and indignities of chemotherapy, she'd taken pride in feeling she'd never suffered the cognitive disturbances commonly called "chemo brain." Some cancer patients noted worrisome side effects: memory loss, confusion, anxiety, poor judgment, erratic behavior. Had she, after all, succumbing to chemo brain?

Am I wrong *about Trey Hartmann?* That bolted door burst open, and out flooded all the thoughts and questions she'd stashed there so she wouldn't have to consider them while she was coping with Dan's incarceration and court appearance. In surviving her childhood, Nikki'd learned to box up and store experiences she couldn't confront in the moment. Sometimes she could open those boxes later and sort things out, come to resolution about what she'd done or what others had done to her. *Trey was the victim, a patient. He wasn't the cause of Dante's pain. Only the killer....the killer was responsible for Dante's pain.* Nikki's knew that pain. She was twelve when she first saw what life and death could mean to those who relied on her.

Walking home from school, Nikki didn't hurry her steps. She wasn't eager to be inside that dingy apartment, even if she could *wake Mom from her usual afternoon stupor.*

Nikki loved being out in the fresh air along this well-shaded street where she didn't have to worry about getting too much sun. There were birds to listen to and squirrels to watch and neighborhood cats to pet, pretending they were her own.

In the thicket of bushes bordering the sidewalk, she caught the unmistakable flash of orange and white as her favorite feral cat angled toward her. "Hey, Ginger!" she called in greeting. She didn't know the big, striped tom's real name, but what else would you call a cat that color?

Pulling a plastic baggie from her pocket, she fished out the single cheese stick she'd saved from her lunch. Ginger slipped out of the greenery and trotted to her with his own gift in his mouth: a captured bird. He dropped it at her feet and gazed up proudly, waiting for praise. No! Nikki didn't blame Ginger. But knowing that this was what cats do couldn't keep her heart from ripping just a bit as she looked at the broken creature.

Careful not to litter, she returned the plastic to her pocket, then broke the cheese stick into pieces and flung them away from her into the bushes. Ginger was quick to go after them.

Squatting down, Nikki studied the speckled-brown sparrow and realized, it's not dead after all! With one unblinking eye, it stared up at her, obviously terrified but unable to move, wings pressed close against the crushed body leaking blood; the beak gaped open, gasping.

Nikki sat then and took the bird gently into her hands. As soon as she felt it in her cupped palms, she knew the truth…it's dying. It's suffering . . . helpless . . . scared. Nikki knew what those things felt like. Suffering such helplessness and fear she'd sometimes wished she *could die. And when she'd been feeling this—she flashed to that night on the floor of her closet-bedroom, trying to breathe beneath the door while Tony raged on the other side—she'd wanted nothing more than to be released from that misery . . . for someone to set her free.*

Who knew how long the bird would have to suffer before it could die? Death, Nikki could handle, birds died all the time, but not the suffering. What can I do? What should I do?

With great certainty, she knew the right thing was to ease the fear, stop the pain, end the suffering. That's what a veterinarian would do.

"I'll help you," she whispered. "You're going to be okay."

Nikki pulled the little plastic bag back out of her pocket and carefully slid the sparrow inside with its beak pointed down into one corner. Smoothing the plastic as closely as possible around the wounded body, she made sure her pressure was gentle but firm, reassuring, as she made comforting sounds. "I'll just sit here and keep you company till you're ready to go."

She began crooning a little wordless song so the sparrow could be sure it was not alone. As it breathed the last of the trapped oxygen, the bird struggled, but only just a little, and Nikki said, "It's okay. You can let go now."

She sat cradling her charge, long time past any struggle, past even the point where she was certain she could sense the tiny spirit lift from the body and depart. Half a heartbeat later, from somewhere in the leaves above her came a sudden burst of joyous birdsong.

She felt a deep sadness for what she'd had to do, but she also felt the enormous rightness of it in her body, in her mind, in her soul.

Stirring now on the infusion recliner, Nikki recalled it was years later before she felt that sensation again, and by that time she was a nurse at St. Mary's. That was where she'd learned she had a special ability to tell who would live and who would not survive. Repeatedly, she saw her intuition borne out, and she grew tired of watching patients have to suffer to their inevitable ends, often leaving their families financially, as well as emotionally, devastated.

It's so frustrating! she would think._We euthanize our pets because we care about them. Don't humans deserve the same loving respect?

Nikki knew that someone had to do the right thing. As a nurse, it was her job and her calling to soothe fear, ease pain, alleviate suffering. At first, it was only within her own realm of pediatrics, and, of course, the death of any child was especially sad. But, she told herself, it put an end to some of that suffering and allowed parents to go on, especially in families with other children who almost inevitably were pushed to the sidelines by a sibling's terrible illness.

Certainly, she took extreme care in deciding who she needed to help, spending a great deal of time assessing her intuition coupled with all the medical findings. Some of the right ones even came to her imploringly in dreams; a few said, "Please. . . ."

And there weren't many. Perhaps three a year at St. Mary's. But she hadn't considered as many aspects as she should've: they were all patients under her care and while she was on duty That made it easier as she went into rooms and stood besides cribs and beds to readjust equipment or modify respiratory or medication levels. Rarely did she have to intervene more actively than that.

But by the time Matt got the job offer at Anchor Security in Pennsylvania, Nikki was sensing her hospital was beginning to suspect her actions. When she learned there was an opening at DCH, she'd been thrilled. A hospital that good in a town called Deerwood! What better place to live and work? She saw it as a sign. A new beginning.

She hadn't hurried to heed her calling again too soon at her new hospital home. She needed to learn the complete dynamic of the place, its politics and values, its staffing strengths and its security weaknesses, its equipment, supplies, routines and floor plans, before she could know how to be invisible there.

Her first couple of cases had come, quite naturally, in her home base of peds, but she didn't make the same mistake of limiting herself there and perhaps raising suspicions. As her genuine friendships grew with coworkers, especially her fellow nurses, she heard of other patients, most in the critical-care units, who worried their caregivers, weighing them with the heartsickness of those forced to watch helplessly as patients died slowly, sometimes by inches.

As before, Nikki employed her special sense of knowing who would live or not . Patients like Abby Glickman—who would survive, despite all indications and common wisdom. She and others just needed someone to believe.

She'd worried about Steve Bailey, the meningitis patient, who'd been sent out of the ER and to the regular ICU before she was sure he would make it. But then, in visiting Dan there, she'd learned the boy was doing well. No need to intervene with him, and a real success for Dan.

But two other patients of Dan's *had* been right ones. Roscoe Delmar, the dissecting aortic aneurysm in the pressure pants, and Jane Salter, who lay dying in a coma while her husband screwed the wife of another expiring patient—right there in the waiting room. No question she'd helped those two escape their pain, fear and last days of suffering. And saved Jane from any possibility of returning to the care of that conceited, philandering husband who didn't deserve her.

There were few things in life Nikki was more certain of than the rightness of her mission. So how did everything go so wrong? When did everything start to change? That, at least, she could pinpoint: the death of Myra Cleary. No question she was a right one. Existing in Ondine's was a living hell. *Everybody* but Julia knew it and was relieved when Myra passed away. Nikki had loved that woman like a mom, and couldn't stand to see her continue suffering just because Julia wasn't ready. And, yes, Nikki had to admit another perhaps selfish motive: she wanted her friends to be happy, and Myra had become a hindrance to the development of Julia's relationship with Alex. With her out of the way, the young couple could spend more time together, move in together if they wanted, and see if they were really meant for each other.

But that wasn't what happened. Julia freaked out, blamed Alex, accused him of murder, rejected him completely. Then she ran away to her family and got sucked in; now she may never escape from Ohio. Meanwhile, Alex imploded. Losing Julia, losing his professional confidence must've made him feel he couldn't go on. Thank God Dan blocked his suicide attempt. Otherwise she would have to feel responsible for his death too.

It occurred to Nikki that she'd never had to contemplate the concept of responsibility before. She'd never been around to see the results of her actions. Perhaps there'd been collateral damage in those lives too: consequences of her choosing when a person died instead of leaving that to God or Nature or to loved ones who were finally ready to let someone go.

Unbidden, another word threaded back into her thoughts, m*urder*. She mulled it, and decided she had not murdered Myra Cleary, or any of the other right ones before her, any more than I murdered that wounded sparrow. Maybe she'd *killed* them, but she preferred to see her actions as releasing them from misery when they were trapped in a dying body.

Trey Hartmann. She'd tried to keep that name again at bay, but now it flared across the darkness of her thoughts with insistent inquiry. It'd all been so easy—except for the nerve-wracking wait to have Trey alone with enough time before her seminar. As soon as she'd heard the argument on the Terrace, witnessed Trey's continued resistance to treatment and anguished decision toward suicide coupled with Dan's growing apprehension and sense of helplessness, Nikki'd clearly perceived her mission: serve both men by releasing Trey from his agony.

Moving through the hospital dressed in scrubs and wearing her I.D. badge, a familiar face there even though on leave for several months, she'd felt invisible With the short staff, she found it easy to slip unnoticed in the med closet. It wasn't hard to fool the trusting Trey about her presence or her intentions. It'd also been easy to dispose of the wiped-clean syringe and gloves, in two separate HazMat containers, before she slipped in among the nurses at the seminar.

She drew a shaky breath. *I guess I have to face the fact that he wasn't a right one. I s'pose I misread his misery and inclination toward suicide. Apparently, Dante believes all that was temporary and could've been worked through. I was blinded by my own selfishness: focusing on protecting Dante from another suicide drama and* our *life together. And the result of that? I made it worse for Dante! He's lost another friend . . barred from the hospital he loved, lost his job, his income and his good name. Beyond all that, he'd lost his freedom and could even lose his life. But at least that won't happen, there's no way he can be convicted of a murder he didn't commit. That's not how justice worked!*

Because, she had to admit to herself now, Trey's death *was* murder. Yes, it was release from suffering, but the situation wasn't life-threatening. He was not about to die. *I killed him,* she admitted. *I* murdered *Trey Hartmann!* And as her anguished defenses fell away, all recollections of that sweet, charming, talented young man, of what he might've done with his life despite MS came rushing in along with more truths of the pain and hardship she may have caused others. Beyond the shaken Charlie Monroe and the whole Pirates organization, beyond Trey's devastated parents, beyond the administrative and PR nightmare at the hospital or the anxious worry of colleagues, there was the agony of Dan's family to face.

Weeping silently now, Nikki pictured those dear people, Gloria, Sal, and Jerry who'd so embraced her. The financial drain, the stress and disruption of their three lives . . . *All my fault. And I can't help them out of this hell. I can't even help financially which will only become a bigger burden as this nightmare drags on.* House arrest meant Dan had to stay in Deerwood and pay rent and utilities with no income, supported only by his family. *Even returning to work next month, between my medical bills and other expenses, it'll be a long time till I can help in any real way.*

And *there* was the irony! Only yesterday, Nikki'd heard an update from Jenna Hudson. Matt had never made changes to his will, and, since they were still married at the time of his death,

Nikki was his sole heir. So, instead of having to split all their property and assets in a divorce, she would inherit everything left after attorney fees, including a life insurance policy and his separate savings account, as well as title to his SUV and the condo. But, according to Jenna, it could take months to sort it all out. Months...even though the will and her inheritance met no obstacles despite the second murder charge against Dan. The D.A. was unwilling to implicate a popular local nurse who was battling cancer. At least that's what his remarks had implied today in Dan's preliminary hearing; that she was innocent in events where her lover eliminated a jealous husband.

How absurd it all was! Dan would never have harmed Matt. And the D.A. would have a tough time making that case. Not only was Dan innocent of wrong-doing, but there had *been* no murder and plenty of witnesses who saw him try to save Matt.

Trey, though, was a different story. She had no idea anyone had been investigating deaths at DCH, much less that Dan was high on a list of suspects, since he was closely involved with Roscoe, Jane and Myra.

Nikki could feel the panic rising in her as she considered the jeopardy Dan faced because of her. But panic would not serve any of them; she had to remain calm so she could be clear-thinking, *no more chemo brain allowed,* and make things right. She used deep breathing to relax herself and searched for reassurance in what she knew to be true: Dan had committed no murders, so there simply could be no evidence of wrong-doing.

As she felt her tensed muscles loosening, her breath coming easier, a new thought slipped in: she'd soon be back on duty at DCH. If she happened to find a right one or two, especially outside her own department, it would deflect some of the suspicion from Dan. She'd have to be much more careful . . . make sure her thinking was accurate and unselfish .

But that was in the future. For now, she just had to get through this with Dan and his family. That's all she *could* do; trust in his innocence and in the wisdom and righteousness of the judicial system.

CHAPTER SIXTY-THREE

Dan tried to sit motionless in the uncomfortable wooden chair, but the thin spindles of wood that were to support his back had been worn down from years of use, and he couldn't help shifting his position every minute or so. He gazed around the poorly lit courtroom where the jury was being chosen and where his sole job was to look sincere, young and professional. It reminded him of the only other courtrooms he was familiar with: the one in *Inherit the Wind,* where Spencer Tracy stood behind a large mahogany desk, and the one in *To Kill a Mockingbird,* where Gregory Peck addressed the black citizens of his town sitting in the second-tier balcony.

The four months since his arrest had been one long, continuous nightmare. He would never forget those first few days in jail. Or the first time he talked to his brother after Nikki had contacted him . "Jesus, Dan, how…?" his brother blurted in shock. Dan, who had been able to keep his composure on the front lines of hundreds of bizarre and terrifying medical emergencies, lost it and pleaded, "Jer, get me out of here, man. Please. Get me out of here."

At that, Jerry's voice had also broken. They had been raised to be strong, proud Marchetti men, but now both betrayed one of the greatest fears of their lives, that they could lose each other. "Hang tight, bro. I will." Dan shuddered as he remembered hanging up the receiver and being quickly ushered into a holding cell in an adjoining building, where he would remain until Jerry kept his promise… if he could. It was a narrow, drafty, noisy cell with a cement floor, utilitarian steel sink and toilet, hard cot, no window. Dan's belongings had been taken, and he had been issued standard jail garb slightly too big for him and hardly any warmer then the tailored shirt and pants he had ironed so proudly that morning. The police had tried to question him earlier, but he had remembered that he shouldn't talk until he had a lawyer, whenever that might be. For one of the rare times in Dan's twenty eight years, he felt, and was, utterly powerless. By nature, Dan was not a selfish person, but as the hours of pacing, staring and worrying had worn on, he could no longer think about his parents, about Jerry, Nikki, his colleagues or the patients he was leaving in the lurch. He was, plain and simple, terrified for himself, for his promising medical career forestalled for now, and perhaps permanently. His very life in the balance for crimes he knew he had not committed.

Of course, Jerry had come through, and so had his mom and pop and distant relatives whose names he had forgotten. By early in the day following Dan's arrest, his lawyer was secured and he would never forget that day when the judge set bond and he was freed on money scraped together from every aunt and uncle and cousin who saw the travesty as a personal attack on the whole family. Later, when Dan had asked, Jerry had cut him off with, "Don't worry about it. We Marchetti's do what we gotta do for our own." Guiltily, Dan imagined his family urgently telephoning various relatives in order to raise the money. He wouldn't put it past one of his Marchetti aunts to broadcast his need and take up a collection in his boyhood church, an idea he found profoundly embarrassing. Perhaps, he speculated, that's why Jerry wouldn't tell him. In any case, he had gotten out of jail and home for the months before the trial.

So here he sat, accused of two murders.

It was incredible. Dan had spent days with Eric Müeller going over hundreds of details, dealing with every possible fact that might undercut what his loyal friends saw as Bradden's political gambit. The D.A.'s contentions were based on circumstantial evidence and conclusions derived from a fertile imagination and what seemed to be a pathologic craving for publicity. The case was blatantly contrived, yet it had gone forward and now Dan had to convince the jury of the flimsiness of both cases.

And then there was Nikki. Her behavior had been bizarre these last weeks. Throughout the period of fact-gathering and grand jury testimony, she had been in a perpetual state of bewilderment. Depression and worry seemed natural since Trey's and Matt's deaths, but she had also become alarmingly disengaged. Dan had needed her corroboration on numerous facts, his whereabouts and opinions, but her memories of events during the months leading up to the alleged crimes were foggy and she seemed incapable of corroborating his version of precisely what had transpired. Often at home, when he would confide his fears to her, she would reply quickly with something like, "You'll get through it. I'm sure you'll be okay." That was the polite response, Dan recognized, of casual acquaintances who meant well but didn't know what else to say. It was not at all what he expected or wanted from a girlfriend with whom he'd been living for months. In his blacker moments, he sometimes wondered if, in her mind, she really did blame him for Matt's death or maybe questioned why Trey had died so quickly after Dan left his side. But when he tried to discuss anything related to the trial or the future, she would change the subject, often finding an errand she suddenly needed to do outside the apartment. He knew this was hell for her, and on top of everything else, she was juggling her return to work, finishing the mounds of paperwork associated with Matt's estate and still waiting for a final word from Klonter on her end-of-chemo blood and scan results. Even so, he felt like he was living with a human robot who says all the right things and does all the right things, even sex, but can't connect. If it wasn't for Jerry calling every night and letting him pour out his fears, he wouldn't have survived house arrest without wondering whether Alex had the right idea. That last thought shocked even Dan who had managed to get through the long restless days and nights by re-reading text books and devouring medical journals as if to constantly remind himself that he was a doctor. He returned his focus to the judge who was dismissing the gathered until 10 am the next morning.

Dan and his lawyer exited through the aged mahogany doors of the courtroom and then through the underground parking facility that allowed them to bypass the media that swarmed the courthouse hoping to get a glance at the *Intern Killer* as he had been termed by the tabloids. In them, he was a sex-starved sociopath who had gotten rid of the two men who he feared would steal his woman.

Reaching their cars, angled near each other in the dimly lit space, they shook hands and parted ways for the day. "Things are progressing as expected, Dan. Get some rest and we should have the jury set soon." Dan headed home, just wanting to sit quietly and forget this chaotic life for a few hours.

Back at the apartment, Dan changed out of his formal court clothes, took a quick shower and shared a simple meal of soup and sandwiches with Nikki. There were many messages on their answering machine and in Dan's email; concerned inquiries from friends and relatives all over the world who wanted updates on how things were going. Dan was touched by all of the support, but couldn't muster the energy to repeat the same non-news over and over again, leaving almost all of the messages for later. In his accumulated postal mail, he saw a blue greeting card envelope with a familiar postmark and handwriting that had gotten just a bit shakier over the decades. This one he had to read.

Carefully, he extracted it from the pile, opened the envelope and withdrew a card with "Thinking of You" on the front. Inside, his godmother had written: *Danny, I know in my heart who the real Dante Michael Sebastian Marchetti is. Stand tall and proud before the world, humble before God. You will prevail. Love, Aunt Carmela.*

These few simple sentences were enough to move Dan to tears. They came from a woman he had known all his life, who had loved him as an aunt and godmother should in the best of worlds. Her story was one of the ones that Dan had told Trey to give the ball-player hope, one that he recalled every time he was tempted to regard a patient as just a body, a diagnosis or a case number. She had taught him that. Her influence, he was sure, had made him a better doctor, and it was a factor in his absolute revulsion to the idea that anyone could believe he would murder Trey, let alone Matt. In one moment of weakness in the jail cell, he had wondered whether his godmother would think he had actually done it, and if that would change her relationship with him. But of course, she didn't, and knowing that gave him a new wave of strength to do what he needed and what she expected him to do.

As with many young Catholics, Dan had drifted away from many of the rituals and beliefs he had been taught in childhood, much to the dismay of his mom. But Aunt Carmela was always there, gently encouraging him to do the right thing and assuring him that the Church was waiting when he was ready. While godparents were often family or friends whom new parents wanted to honor with no real responsibility, Aunt Carmela, always devout, had taken the traditional role of overseeing Dan's spiritual development very seriously. It had not escaped his notice that in writing out his name, she had included his Confirmation name, which, as was customary, he had chosen himself at the time as unofficial second middle name: "Sebastian" for the patron saint of athletes. Fourteen year old Dan had pronounced that utterly cool, engendering the envy of his brother and several of their male peers who hadn't thought of it first. Later, as a pre-med undergraduate, Dan had amused to discover that his namesake was also the patron saint of plague sufferers. But that, he was sure, was not Aunt Carmela's point. She was reminding him to conduct himself well through this literal and figurative trial in his life, and to hold onto the faith that he would survive whatever was meant to be. Though Dan still wasn't sure what "the man upstairs" was getting at, at this point, if trusting God would help the situation, he was more than willing to try. Difficult as it was, he would fight the good fight for as long as it took.

CHAPTER SIXTY-FOUR

"Now, Mr. Quinton, you were present at the Deerwood High School baseball diamond on the morning of Saturday, May 21, of this year. Is that correct?" Scott Bradden's voice reverberated in the courtroom. It was the third day of testimony in Dan's trial, and one of the three bystanders at the ball field on the day Matt died was now on the witness stand testifying for the prosecution. It was the person who made the inane comment about the CPR looking different then it did on TV. Just recently, Dan had learned that the man's name was Cecil Quinton, and while Dan was hardly a disinterested observer, in his opinion, Quinton's demeanor didn't exactly inspire confidence.

"Yes" the witness replied.

"Why were you in the stands that day, Mr. Quinton?"

"I was watching my nephew and his friends. The kid needed a ride to and from the field, and y'know, it was a little inconvenient to drop him off, leave and then come back so soon. So I stayed."

"I see," Bradden said. "So you saw the defendant and Nikole Saxon at the field that day and witnessed the incident with Matthew Saxon in its entirety?"

"I did, sir," Quinton affirmed.

"Thank you, Mr. Quinton. Now, can you tell us where you were sitting?"

"On the bleachers near home plate."

"And where were the defendant and Mrs. Saxon?"

"Near the top, fifteen or twenty feet to the side of me."

"Which side, please, Mr. Quinton?"

"Right,"

"You could see and hear from that distance, Mr. Quinton?"

"Of course. I have excellent sight and hearing. And after the other man showed up, they were all rather loud, y'know."

At the defense table, Dan scribbled two words in pencil on Eric Mueller's legal pad and showed them to the attorney: *Ophthalmology? Audiology?*

When he saw them, Müeller smiled. *Good question,* he wrote back as a teacher would to a bright student. *Ok. Will follow up.*

"When you say 'After the other man showed up,' are you referring to the arrival of Matthew Saxon?" Bradden inquired.

"Of course," the witness said.

"Now, this is a photograph of the deceased, Matthew Saxon. Take a good look at it please. Is this the man you saw in the alleged altercation with Dr. Marchetti?"

"Yes, absolutely," Quinton testified.

"Fine. Could you tell us in your own words what occurred, Mr. Quinton, starting with the arrival of Mr. Saxon?"

"He came up into the bleachers on the left side of me and cut across their row. I noticed because he was causing a lot of commotion, trying to get past other people. Also, he was yelling."

"What was he yelling, Mr. Quinton?" Bradden asked.

"NIKKI, NIKKI!"

"I see. Go on, please."

"Saxon went over to the two of them. The woman asked him. 'What do you want?' He said, 'Just want to say hello to my wife; is there anything wrong with that?' Then he said, 'So this is lover boy. He looks like he's a kid. Are you sure he's a real doctor, or does he just like playing one?' The wife told him to shut up. The two of them had words, going back and forth for a while. His speech was slurred like he'd been drinking and he looked like he was going to grab her, so Marchetti told him to stay clear. Saxon said, 'Oh, you object, lover boy? We must all follow doctor's orders? I don't think so.' That's when Marchetti stood up, got between them, put his hands and pushed Saxon off the bleachers."

"Could you repeat that last part, Mr. Quinton?" Bradden prompted. "What did you see Dr. Marchetti do?"

"Push Saxon off the bleachers," Quinton reiterated to the prosecutor's approving nod. "Saxon fell backwards, flipped in the air a couple of times and slammed down on the lower bleachers."

"How did Dr. Marchetti and Mrs. Saxon react?"

Dan noticed ruefully how often Bradden got the 'Mrs. Saxon" into the questions. While Nikki did use Matt's last name, probably because her original one seemed to be charged with negative emotions, he had never heard anyone refer to Nikki, nor did she refer to herself as *Mrs.* Saxon. Bradden evidently wanted Dan portrayed as the aggressor breaking up a happy couple by picking on a poor, defenseless man who'd had one shot of liquor too many, when the truth was that from the start, Nikki was the one who had pursued Dan.

"The wife reacted first," Quinton reported. "She called out Saxon's name and ran down to where he'd landed. Marchetti followed her. A bunch of us who'd seen the whole thing happen went up to see if we could help or anything. Somebody called the paramedics and I think Marchetti sent somebody else to his car for his doctor's bag. I was there with Marchetti and the wife for a while, just keeping an eye on things while they did their thing with Saxon."

Dan grimaced. He was tempted to retort aloud that this joker wouldn't know proper CPR if he saw it, but knew that would be contempt of court. Müeller must have seen Dan's face, as the attorney made a discreet calming gesture.

"What were they doing, Mr. Quinton?" Bradden asked.

"Pounding on Saxon's chest," Quinton replied. "CPR, I guess, but it looked pretty violent to me. Marchetti was practically on top of the man for a while."

"I see," Bradden continued. "Did Dr. Marchetti appear to know what he was doing?"

"Objection!" Eric Müeller's dignified but firm voice interjected from next to his client. "The witness is not a medical professional. Such speculation is inappropriate."

"Sustained," the judge ruled. "Rephrase the question or withdraw it."

"Yes, your honor," Bradden acquiesced politely. "Mr. Quinton, please describe Dr. Marchetti's demeanor at the time he and Mrs. Saxon were working on Mr. Saxon?"

"Pretty confident," Quinton testified. "Kind of abrupt too. I mentioned how hard he was pounding, and Marchetti just brushed off my concerns. He sent me for water."

"What was the water for?"

"I don't really know. Something to do with a crazy MacGyver needle thing he rigged up to stick in Saxon's chest. He seemed to be a little unsure then because he asked the wife about it, and she said to do it. Next thing I knew, it seems like something had gone wrong because Marchetti was, excuse me, cursing with words not fit for polite company."

Dan wanted to put his head in his hands. Better yet, he wanted to crawl under a rock; this guy's testimony was so bad, but with the eyes of the world on him, he knew he couldn't do that. He managed to sit through several minutes before Quinton finished his initial testimony and the judge called a brief recess.

In the hallway, Dan exchanged hurried greetings with his family and Nikki, who had been sitting through the entire proceedings as spectators. He was glad to have them there. Since Nikki was also testifying, he had thought that she might be sequestered from the other witnesses, but nether side had filed such a motion, so she had heard everything, including Quinton's distortions.

After a moment of two, Dan and Müeller headed off to a quiet corner to confer. Dan told his lawyer, "This Quinton guy is off, Eric. Plain and simple, just wrong!"

"Are you suggesting he perjured himself?" Müeller inquired.

"No, but he's got a selective memory and no clue at what he was looking at when we were trying to save Matt," Dan explained. "Most of the details are right, but there's a lot of context missing!"

"I noticed that," Müeller acknowledged. "I'll get him on some of that in the cross-exam." He paused thoughtfully. "Dan, I don't think you have anything to worry about as far as the collapsed lung is concerned. We'll have testimony of two of the ER docs and the autopsy report that it wasn't a factor in Matt's death. But the alleged pushing is another issue."

"Eric, I didn't do it. Nikki was there. I didn't touch Matt then. I just stood between them. He fell!" Dan insisted.

"I believe you," Müeller assured him. "But it's a question of how it looks. If the jury finds Quinton and the other witness credible..."

"Nikki will corroborate the truth," Dan said.

"Yes, but as the estranged spouse, she's not necessarily seen as an objective party," Müeller reminded him gently.

"What are you saying, Eric?" Dan asked.

"At this point, we may need a change of strategy and you might want to reconsider a plea bargain."

"No," Dan said without hesitation. "I am not guilty and I am not consenting to anything that will say I am."

"You want your life back, don't you?" Müeller asked as Nikki, on her way back from the restroom, approached. "Dan, you're potentially facing lethal injection or life without parole for Trey's death and twenty or thirty years for Matt's. If you plead guilty to involuntary manslaughter, which is basically what the alleged pushing charge is, the usual sentence is five years, and I've almost never seen anyone actually serve that long."

"Are you saying you can't win my case, Eric?" Dan challenged him as his voice became tight and angry.

"No, I'm not down yet," Mueller said, putting his hand soothingly on Dan's shoulder. "But I would be remiss as your attorney if I didn't advise you of all the possibilities in the big picture."

"What makes you think Bradden would go for it if I did want to plea bargain?" Dan asked curiously as his voice recovered..

"He probably wouldn't," Müeller acknowledged. "But Linda Ferrante just might." He nodded in the direction of the assistant prosecutor as she passed them.

"I can't do it, Eric," Dan reiterated. "Anything but not guilty would be simply untrue, an abomination. This is already breaking my family's hearts. You do anything legal you need to do to win this, all right? I intend to fight all the way."

"All right, Dan," Müeller said.

CHAPTER SIXTY-FIVE

Saturday came. Court was not in session so Dan had bit of a break. After breakfast, Nikki said that she had to go to the condo to do more sorting of Matt's belongings and take care of related business. Dan said he would miss her as he lightly kissed her goodbye.

Dan was just being polite. What he really wanted to do, after months of exhaustion and tension, was just be alone for a while and not to have to think at all. Thus, he retreated to the bedroom, flopped on the bed, and turned on the TV which they had never bothered to move back into the living room even as Nikki recovered her strength. Flipping back and forth among cable channels as the mood struck him, he watched several sitcom reruns, a game show he'd never seen before, a bit of a French cooking demonstration and, finally, an adventure movie. He stopped only periodically to use the bathroom or to raid the refrigerator for quick cold leftovers. After several hours, he was definitely relaxed enough to almost forget where he was. He hadn't had this much alone time it seemed for weeks. Funny how seldom he let house arrest dictate his day as he kept it filled with studying and using the weights and second hand treadmill Jerry had got for him so he could 'keep up the Marchetti hard body'! True leisure time, like today, was rare.

As the sun began to set, the apartment turned colder, so Dan got up to adjust the thermostat and turn on some lights. He was logging on to his laptop to check the day's scores when he heard a key in the front door. He was glad Nikki was home. By now, he could use some company again.

He walked out into the main room and took note of her bulging tote bag, no doubt filled with various items for the condo, on one of the end tables. He found Nikki out on the little balcony. She didn't turn when he approached. He wrapped his arms around her from behind, kissing her cheek. Just being here with her still made it better. Maybe this was all he really needed.

He followed her gaze to the clear sky and took in the early autumn crispness of the air. The odor of faintly burning charcoal mixed with the scents of grilling meat and some condiment or other food that Dan couldn't identify. One of the neighbors must be squeezing in one last barbeque before the weather turned cold again.

"It's a beautiful evening," Dan said.

Nikki just nodded, her left hand finding his own.

"You know, I'm thinking seriously of leaving medicine. Getting up one day and just packing it in."

Her soft body suddenly stiffened. She turned to face him.

"Are you serious? I mean, there's no telling how successful you can become. A great fellowship, a lucrative practice…"

Dan's face flushed with anger. "Damn it, I'm not interested in living up to some phony image. I just want to be happy." The words seemed to filter through his clenched teeth.

Nikki stiffened, taken aback.

"I'm sorry, Nik," he softened. "I didn't mean to take it out on you. It's just…all of this misery, this death. Hell, I feel like a gatekeeper collecting tokens to heaven and hell." He bit his lip. "Dante's Inferno!"

"I understand."

Dan looked at her in surprise. "You do?"

"It's like me. I'm not going to make it. You and I both know it." Tears began to appear on her smooth, pale cheeks.

"Oh, Jesus, Nik, that's not what I meant."

"But it's true. It's not worth fighting it anymore. It's why I wrote this."

He noticed the envelope in her hands for the first time. "What is that?"

"The thing is, for me to simply leave isn't enough."

"Leave?" The air suddenly seemed to get very still.

She pressed the envelope into his hand. "You can read it if you want. It won't make any difference soon, anyway. I know what I have to do." She kissed him softly and left his side, going into the bedroom.

Dan slowly opened the envelope, his hands trembling. Tears rushed down his face as he devoured each word. The prose was beautiful, her unquestioned love for Dan ringing through each word. Suddenly, he moved his hand to his mouth, his sanity ready to implode. He read on, each moment increasing the madness.

"Oh, my God!" he whispered as he finished reading her suicide letter. "Oh, my God!"

He turned to call out to her just in time to see her waiting in the living room behind him, a handgun pointed at her chest.

Nikki's long, thin fingers, tipped with red nail polish, looked strange gripping the 9 millimeter Glock as she flipped off the safety. Her eyes were riveted on Dan's as she continued to point the gun at herself.

"Nikki? What are you doing?" His voice felt wobbly but he managed to maintain eye contact with her.

"I never wanted to cause you this much pain, Dante, I'm sorry."

"You haven't. You've done nothing but love me."

"It wasn't enough. Your life is in shambles now, and it's my fault. I hate seeing you suffer like this." She calmly approached him, moving the gun to her temple.

He shook his head, incredulous. "I'm not suffering."

She grinned reassuringly as tears welled in her eyes. "You don't have to fight it anymore. It'll all be over soon."

Dan felt sick. This couldn't be happening. The shocking realization of what she intended to do was sending nausea throughout his system as if he were overcome by a flu-like illness. If he couldn't talk her out of this, then he would get only one chance to disarm her, only one well- timed leap. "This isn't what I want, Nik, I want you to stay with me. I need you. Please, give me the gun."

Slowly, he reached a hand toward her. She stiffened to attention, and as she gripped it more tightly, the shiny black gun, which must have been Matt's, began to shake slightly in her right hand.

"Okay, how about you just put it down. We'll go for a walk and talk this out," said Dan, trying to keep his voice calm. Hoping to distract her, he stepped softly to the front door and began to undo the locks and crack open the door.

Nikki's eyes widened but she didn't lower her weapon. "NO!" She screamed so violently that her entire body seemed to quake in the word's aftermath. "I want this to be over! Now! I can't take all the hurt anymore. All I've done to you."

Dan left go of the door and held up a hand. "Okay, okay. We can talk here." He paused and took a deep breath. "What is this all about?" The feminine features Dan had always thought so beautiful were now contorted, unrecognizable.

"I called Linda," Nikki said. "I told her to come over here."

"Linda, what Linda?" Dan felt he had fallen once again into a nightmare where nothing made sense. But he had no time to make sense out of the scene in front of him. He needed to get her to put the gun down.

"The lawyer from the DA's office. I'm the one who caused all your problems, so I'm going to fix everything now."

"Nik, what are you talking about?" Dan asked, genuinely perplexed.

"You know what he would have become. He couldn't take life as a cripple and you couldn't just stand by. He would have pulled you into his hell" she replied. "I helped him leave all that pain and misery behind." The memory and her words unnerved her and she began to shiver, causing the gun to wobble.

The realization hit him. *Trey.* "Oh, God." Then a moment later, "Nikki! How could you!" he demanded as his vision blurred with the hot tears of betrayal. Who was this woman in front of him? What had he missed? It took all his will to push his emotions back and concentrate again that there was a human being on the brink of shooting herself in front of him.

Suddenly out of his peripheral vision, he could see Linda Ferrante standing in the half-open doorway a few yards from him.

Nikki saw Linda too and let out an odd, strangled little laugh. She reached for an object from her handbag on the end table, and tossed it vaguely in Linda and Dan's direction. "It's all there. Every single last one of them." She made that last statement almost profoundly. "Every one of them was the right thing to do. They needed me and I wasn't afraid. I'm not sorry." Her face seemed to close in. "Except for Trey. I'd take that back if I could."

The faded white vinyl book with a lock and a faded side strap, like a young girl's diary, lay on the carpet where it had been tossed. Dan and Linda both looked down at it, then at each other, then finally back at Nikki, both unsure what to do. Finally, Linda stepped forward and gingerly picked up the book. Though the lock was open, Linda still fumbled as she undid the frayed strap. A thin ribbon attached to the book marked the last used page. Linda opened to it and glanced at the page. She drew her breath in sharply, grimaced and quickly flipped back through the many previous pages meticulously logging years of names, dates, diagnoses, manners of death...Linda didn't even want to think how many. "Mother of God!" she exclaimed.

Nikki looked at Linda impassively and did not reply. "Anyway, it's time. Dante, I love you. I'm sorry." The gun seemed to steady.

"Oh, Jesus." Dan leapt forward, the momentum causing them both to go crashing to the floor. A crisp, deafening roar rent the air of the small room.

The pain was sudden and sharp. As Dan grabbed his side, a warm, sticky substance flowed onto his hand. The initial awareness of pain was replaced by a surreal sensation, as if Dan's head were no longer attached to his body. He fought the feeling, not wanting to black out before getting the gun away from Nikki. Then, as he still clutched his side, the lancing pain returned with a vengeance. He was losing blood rapidly now. He looked up to see tears streaming down Nikki's face.

She gasped, slumping down on the carpet next to him.

"My God, what have I done?" She wiped away tears with the back of her hand.

Linda, shocked into action by the gunshot and Dan's incapacity, had quickly dropped the book and pulled out her cell phone, dialing 911 with unsteady fingers as she slowly moved towards the fallen two. She softly pleaded, "Honey give me the gun now! Dante's hurt, we need to help him"

The command startled Nikki, who rose and whirled around to face Linda. A curious smile appeared on Nikki's face, she looked back at Dan, and without further hesitation, she turned her gun on herself and said "Goodbye."

"No!" Dan screamed, as she fired.

Nikki lay motionless. The gun had slipped from her fingers. Dan tried to crawl toward her to check if she was still breathing, but the pain seared into him, and he sank back down. He closed his eyes. He couldn't bear to see any more. As he felt himself slipping away, he thought he would be joining her soon anyways.

Linda ran over to him, and gently but firmly slapped his face with her fingertips. "Dan! Dan! Keep awake, keep awake." After quickly moving the gun away from the still unmoving Nikki just in case there was more to come, Linda yelled the address into the phone while trying to apply pressure to Dan's bleeding side with her wadded up suit jacket." Stay with me, now," she ordered.

"Shit!" Linda checked to make sure he was still breathing. Throwing aside her jacket she pressed hard with both hands and thought she saw the stream of blood lessen. She quickly snatched a tampon from her purse, unwrapped it and quickly shoved it into the hole made by the bullet. The EMTs finally arrived, sirens screaming, after five minutes, three hundred seconds that seemed like an eternity. Two male and one female police officer arrived shortly thereafter. Clearly, the dispatcher had heard the gunshots and relayed the need for plenty of backup.

"Faint pulse. Let's get the airway protected," one of the paramedics working on Dan called out.

"This one's expired, head's pretty much gone" another voice, Linda couldn't tell whose, added with professional distance.

Dazed, Linda sat on the carpet and leaned her head on the stereo unit while the team worked feverishly on their patient. Before long, they had placed IVs, attached EKG wires, and started oxygen as they hustled Dan on a stretcher out the door and into the ambulance.

"Are you okay?" asked a gravelly-voiced policeman with a shaved scalp, gray moustache and pock-marked face. Linda just looked up. She couldn't answer.

"You want to tell me what happened?" he asked rhetorically.

She tried to summon a sense of professional detachment about the pools of blood on the light-colored rug and the pieces of scalp strewn about, as well as Nikki's covered body yet to be removed from the scene. She grabbed a nearby wastebasket and threw up.

"Oh." Her reddened face revealed acute embarrassment. "Give me a few minutes, please," she said, and upon his nod, walked out onto the balcony. She breathed fresh air, contemplating the mosaic of twisted threads of reality that had been woven in the mind of this woman. She rubbed her eyes. Then she took out her blackberry and made a note to remind herself to look into pediatric deaths at St. Mary's Hospital in Grand Rapids, Michigan. Returning it to her shoulder bag, she saw the white logbook and remembered that she needed to give it to the police as evidence. The thought immediately made her want a cigarette. She reached for one, thinking of those children, all those people. And then another incredulous thought, Conover was right. He just gave up too quickly once Bradden got his 'Intern Killer'.

Linda took a deep drag and allowed the smoke to slowly filter through her nostrils. Then leaning over the balcony, she vomited again.

EPILOGUE

Beep, beep. "Dr. Marchetti, stat call 7100, 7100..."

There would be no slow testing of the waters here; Dan had gone right back into the belly of the beast. He dialed the numbers for the emergency room.

"Dr. Marchetti, a twenty year old respiratory arrest," a voice filled him in.

"Be right down." Dan hurried down the three flights of stairs, his heart pumping madly. His mind was working fast en route, thinking of all the possibilities: drug overdose, status epilepticus, motor vehicle trauma, status asthmaticus...

Once inside the crash room, Dan saw a blue-tinged young man, with baggy jeans, a tattoo of a snake on his torso and two circular earrings in the middle of his right ear. He was having his chest pounded on repeatedly by an EMT while the respiratory therapist, not Vinny who had been fired when he was awaiting a court date, alternately squeezed the ambu bag and allowed it to fill for the best breath. Vinny's fate had been sealed when he had removed his lab coat to attend to a slight stain on his scub shirt and a doctor had mistakenly put it on as his own. Finding the ampules of paralytic drugs in the inner pockets had lead to an internal investigation and then a theft charge and pending loss of his license. In a way, Vinny was lucky Nikki had meticulously documented her killings or Vinny's story of using the drugs only on animals would not have been believed.

A nurse Dan didn't recognize began informing him of the patient's vitals. "BP sixty systolic, pulse forty and thready, IV in, normal saline wide open," she said. "Was partying, probably alcohol, narcs and maybe coke."

"Endotracheal tube," Dan replied, making his way to the head of the stretcher, all the while keeping his eyes on the monitor. "One amp atropine, one amp Narcan. How's the I.V. running?"

"We'll need a central line," the EMT replied.

"Okay, after I tube him." Dan was handed a laryngoscope and endotracheal tube. Taking the patient's head in his hands, Dan extended the neck and, with the blade of the scope, pinned the tongue back to expose the vocal chords. He inserted the long tube through the opening in the chords, moving quickly, every moment precious. "Got it!" He pulled out the metal rod within the tube, which functioned to keep the tube rigid during placement. Attaching the ambu bag to the end of the tube, he felt a momentary sense of relief as he watched the chest expand in concert with his squeezing of the bag.

The nurse took her stethoscope and listened for breath sounds. "You're in," she stated emphatically. The patient's color was now pink, thanks to the new supply of oxygen. "BP 100/60, pulse 120 and regular."

"Sinus tach. We may not need the central line after all," he said to the EMT. "A foley catheter, please."

The EMT nodded.

"Once you're in, let's send some urine for drug screen. What blood work has been sent?" he continued.

"CBC, SMAC 19, ABG," the young nurse replied quickly.

"Perfect." At that moment, the patient began to thrash in response to the sight of strange people hovering over him, the tube in his throat intensifying his madness.

"Good stuff, that Narcan," Dan quipped, the ironic humor about the drug overdose antidote a welcome break in the tension. "I'll be out talking to the family. Let me know when the lab work is back or if there's a change. I'll get an ICU bed ready."

Only then did he realize that his hands were shaking uncontrollably. He quickly hid them in the pockets of his white coat. Once his injury was stabilized and healed, he had been reinstated at the hospital, though he was more than five months behind his original cohort and had to make up the rotations, watching as his friends rapidly moved towards their final year of residency. Although in a perfect world, Dan would have preferred to keep up with them, above all he knew he was very lucky that this was the only concrete impact of his ordeal on his employment, and that his future career trajectory seemed to have survived essentially intact. Dan would always be grateful for the intervention and steadfast support of Dr. Ballard who held open Dan's residency slot long enough for him to return. He had offered the same for Alex but Alex had decided to take the year off and help his parents close up their business before he made any future career moves. But last time they had talked, Dan had a sense that Alex would be back sooner rather than later.

Personally, he was glad he'd been able to get back to work quickly instead of sitting at home with too much time to think. Ironically, the bullet's entrance through his anterior chest wall had collapsed his left lung, but a promptly-placed chest tube had treated that, and after a week in the hospital he was back home. Not that he'd wanted to go back there. He'd quickly made arrangements to move into a different building.

While he recovered, Linda Ferrante had filled him in on what she had discovered as she worked through the legal channels to present the evidence from Nikki's journal. The goal was obviously to have Dan's indictments dropped quickly. While Trey's death was quickly moved to 'closed', it took awhile before the DA would officially drop the charges on the Saxon case. It took a high powered public relations consultant to finally convince Bradden that prosecuting a young capable doctor for what was clearly an accident made little political sense. Just this morning,

Linda had called to inform him that it was official, he was free and clear. She also asked to meet him for lunch.

At one pm, Dan headed for the lobby to meet Linda. He spotted her in an armchair reading a magazine. It struck him that she looked different, not at all like the lawyer he had dreaded during the court proceedings. In her jeans and sandals, she looked younger and less imposing.

Linda looked up and caught sight of him approaching. She, too, was struck by Dan's appearance, distinctly different from their previous encounters. His face, once drawn, with deep, dark circle obscuring his brown eyes, now seemed to have awoken from a long sleep. His eyes sparkled and seemed to radiate a reborn zest for life.

"Hey," she greeted him as he reached her. "How are you holding up?"

"It's tough," he said, "but I'm happy to be alive and free. What about you? Got any cool legitimate cases at the D.A.'s?" he asked with a bit of a grin.

"I'm no longer working for the D.A.'s office, actually. I am officially 'resigned' as of the end of next week."

Dan raised an eyebrow. "Why?"

"Let's just say that I disagreed in principle with the ethical proclivities of the department," she quipped, a twinkle of amusement in her eyes. "Or in English, Bradden's an asshole. He wants to be the next Attorney General, nothing less, and he'll go to any length to do it. You just happened to be one of the pawns in his political chess game.

"Anyway, I decided I was more interested in defense law," she added. "I've got my resume out on the hunt."

They went down to the cafeteria for sandwiches and sodas and, spotting a free table, they claimed it and sat down.

"Must be good to be back," Linda said, sipping her soda.

Dan picked up his sandwich, a strange half smile appearing on his face. "You know, for a little while there I didn't think that I could ever trust myself to take care of sick patients again. I really didn't."

"Why not? You didn't do anything wrong. Those were fabricated charges. A sham. You're no more responsible for anyone's death than I am."

Dan arched his face toward his lunch-time companion.

"Listen, before their deaths, I felt myself sinking deeper and deeper into this pit..."

Linda tilted her head slightly. "How do you mean?"

Dan continued, "We see a lot of bad shit. It's a motherlode to take in." He ran his fingers through his thick hair.

Linda began, "I guess you have to..." but he interrupted her in mid sentence.

"I know, detach ourselves from their problems. I am so tired of hearing that meaningless crap."

Linda found herself taken aback by this response but quickly regrouped, asking,

"What option do you have?"

Dan struggled for the right words. "They don't teach that kind of 'reality' in medical school. Instead you simply learn diseases and how to treat them. I used to think I had all the right answers or at least knew where to find them.." He laughed, embarrassed. "I guess you could have called me arrogant."

"How do you mean?" Linda asked.

"All of this disease, it is all pretty heartbreaking stuff...and just when I thought it couldn't get any worse, bam!" he punched the air with his fist.

Linda sat back in the booth and smiled.

"I'm reminded of that Willie Nelson song where he says, 'I keep looking for that light at the end of the tunnel'...

Dan finished the thought, "only to see the headlights of the onrushing train."

They both laughed. He paused, his voice suddenly cracking with emotion, and said, "But what Nik did was pretty twisted. I mean, look at Christopher Reeve or the Kittle boy with neurofibromatosis. They found meaning in going on."

Linda nodded in agreement.

Dan took a deep breath. "Dr. Ballard, the old guy, tells us on rounds, 'when you are dead, you are dead for a long time.' It's been kind of devastating. I had such a decent, kind image of Nikki and now it's been relegated to that of a pathetic, misguided vigilante. I mean to go up to the peds floor like you're happy to see your co-workers, go into the med room, swipe meds and go back downstairs to kill a man you called your friend."

"No," Linda said quietly, trying to reassure him. "I spoke with several people who knew her in Michigan. A former staff member at the group home where she lived after her mother died, teachers and classmates from high school and college, coworkers at St. Mary's Hospital. We had long talks, and people were surprisingly candid. One word that kept coming up in their descriptions of her was "intense."

Dan nodded ruefully at the familiar adjective.

"Even as far back as her teens, people appear to have seen a young woman with a very strong sense of her own mind," Linda continued. "Given what we learned about her childhood, I'd guess that's how she learned to survive, but that same personality trait may not have served her well in other ways. It seems Nikki also experienced great difficulty adjusting to, well…things. Her mother's death, for one, was an enormously traumatic transition and she didn't get nearly enough counseling as she probably should have. There was still a great sense of neediness underneath the bravado, and while many of the people I spoke to believe Nikki genuinely meant well, her natural compassion ultimately channeled itself into seriously misguided directions, sociopathic ones."

Dan began to feel tears forming as he realized the truth of that assessment in his own experience. "Why didn't anyone get help for her?"

"Some of them tried, but like many people, some never understood how deep the problems ran, because she seemed to be doing fine for the most part. There were others who needed their help more obviously than Nikki, and well, to the end, I think she probably let all of us see what she wanted us to see, and not much more. Once she was an independent adult, outsiders could reach out, but there wasn't much they could do to force the issue." Linda said.

"This year…all of these images flashing across my mind… sometimes" Dan stopped to take a deep breath while shaking his head in disbelief. "I'm still surprised people so ill could get that far without someone noticing. Nikki—Alex Cole—"

"The health care professions may not do a particularly good job of policing themselves," Linda observed quietly.

Dan winced, his tired eyes groping for answers.

"Maybe God allows people to suffer so they can appreciate each good moment so much more..." He paused. "I don't know," he continued.

Linda listened intently. "Honestly, I don't even believe there is a God, Dan."

"Yeah, a lot of people don't. You are definitely not alone. I'm still open to the possibility of a loving God but whether that is just wishful thinking..." He stared straight ahead. "You know, most of the patients I took care of this year taught me something...each life I touched was special." He looked directly into her eyes now. "You like poetry?"

Linda nodded. "Some. Not much." She tilted her head, her face registering confusion.

His voice was now just a whisper. Dan just shook his head. "William Blake, *Auguries of Innocence.* It's about the small moments in one's life that are truly significant, good or bad. Each person's story, their struggle..." He paused, his face reddened with embarrassment. "Jeez, listen to me, citing poems," his voice trailed off.

Linda shook her head. "I like that." Suddenly, she wished she could get to know him better.

"Guess what I did yesterday?" Linda inquired, her impish smile suddenly appearing, prompted by a random thought that suddenly danced into her head.

"What?" Dan inquired. He couldn't help noting how child-like, yet womanly, this fine lawyer could be.

"I decided to go on-line and check out what courses I would need to take to apply to vet school."

"You want to be a vet?"

"I think I might. I much prefer critters....they are always loving, non-judgmental, no real agendas, and of yeah, when they look in a mirror, they don't feel the need to run marathons."

They both laughed.

"Good point. Go for it! It's very competitive, you know. Harder than getting into med school I think."

"I'm sure. But Dan, I am coming to realize that if I were to fast-forward my life to, let's say, one week before I die, what would I like to conclude from my days on this earth? How many people I outsmarted, or how much suffering I alleviated?"

Dan just shook his head. He motioned for the waitress. "Check please."

Turning towards Linda he said, "I got it. After all, a veterinary student has to watch her spending.

"Excuse me, aren't you Dr. Marchetti?" said another voice.

Dan looked up at the woman who had just spoken. "Yes, I am. We've met before?"

"Yes. I'm Brendan McCarthy's mother, Kathryn."

Dan recognized the name and her face immediately now, the vision of her son's mangled body quickly coming to mind. The last memories of Brendan were tragic ones, his ravaged body lying in a near vegetative state while Dan lay prone on the ICU floor, courtesy of Brendan's brother's errant fist.

"I…I never got to apologize to you for what my son did…"

Dan held his hand up "Not necessary." He winced at the reminder of the incident; the physical pain had been considerable, and he'd rather not think about it. "It wasn't a total waste," he said to Mrs. McCarthy. "I learned how much I loved a good steak, after going a few weeks on jello and yogurt."

Dan cringed at his thoughtless remark, as Kathryn McCarthy shifted her feet nervously.

"I'm sorry. I was trying to be funny."

After Dan was attacked, McCarthy had been transferred to the care of another intern and Dan hadn't been involved in Brendan's inevitable demise.

"You must really miss him."

"Miss him? Doctor, Brendan lived! Thank the good Lord! And you were one of the reasons he did!" the petite woman said fervently in her unmistakable Irish brogue.

"I didn't know. How is he doing?" Dante asked incredulously.

"Actually that's why I'm here. Had to pick up some old records before I go over to see Brendan at the rehab hospital where he still gets therapy daily."

Dan's mouth fell open. There must be some misunderstanding, he thought. The same Brendan McCarthy was still alive, months later? It couldn't be...

Mrs. McCarthy continued, her eyes moist and glassy, "He's a survivor, and I just can't thank you doctors enough for all the good you did him. Having Brendan alive is still better than the alternative...In fact, he's starting to build cabinets and other pieces of furniture. His dad and half of the men in the neighborhood built this beautiful workshop in the basement, wheelchair accessible and all." She shrugged and sighed.

"He had been so depressed, didn't want to live...Then he just stopped feelin' sorry and I guess stopped asking why this all happened, and now works hard to..." Her voice cracked. "Listen to me babble on, God bless ya darling." She gave Dante a gentle kiss on his cheek, some of her tears transferred to his face.

Dan watched her walk away, then turned back to Linda.

"He's alive. McCarthy's still alive. I'm amazed."

"It wasn't his time." Linda remarked. She smiled knowingly. "To see the world in a grain of sand..."

Dan continued the poem in a whisper, "...and heaven in a wild flower. Hold infinity in the palm of your hand and eternity in an hour..."

THE END